PEBBLE AND WREN

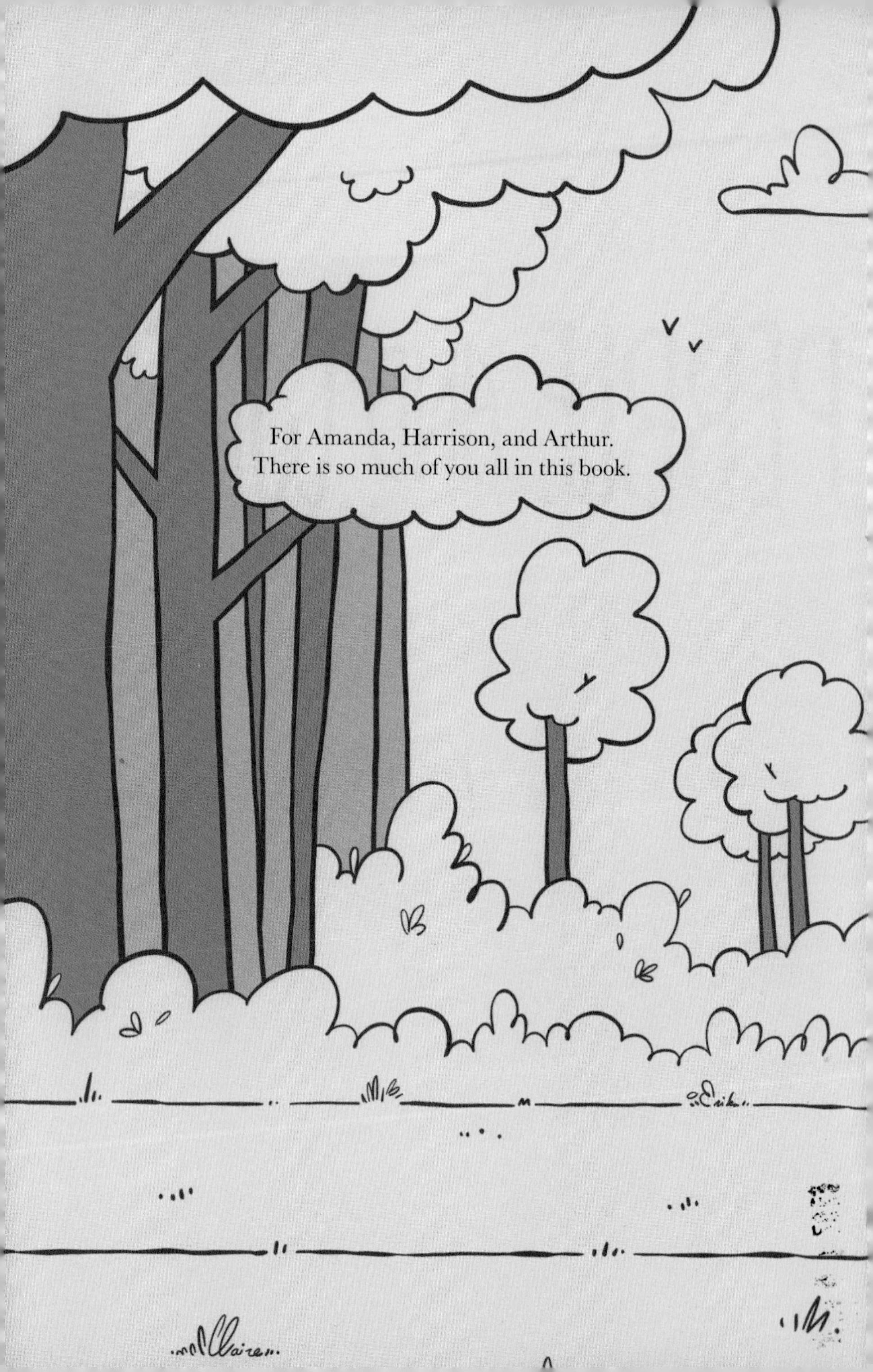

For Amanda, Harrison, and Arthur.
There is so much of you all in this book.

PEBBLE AND WREN

Created by Chris Hallbeck

Clarion Books
Imprints of HarperCollinsPublishers

HARPER
alley

CHAPTER ONE

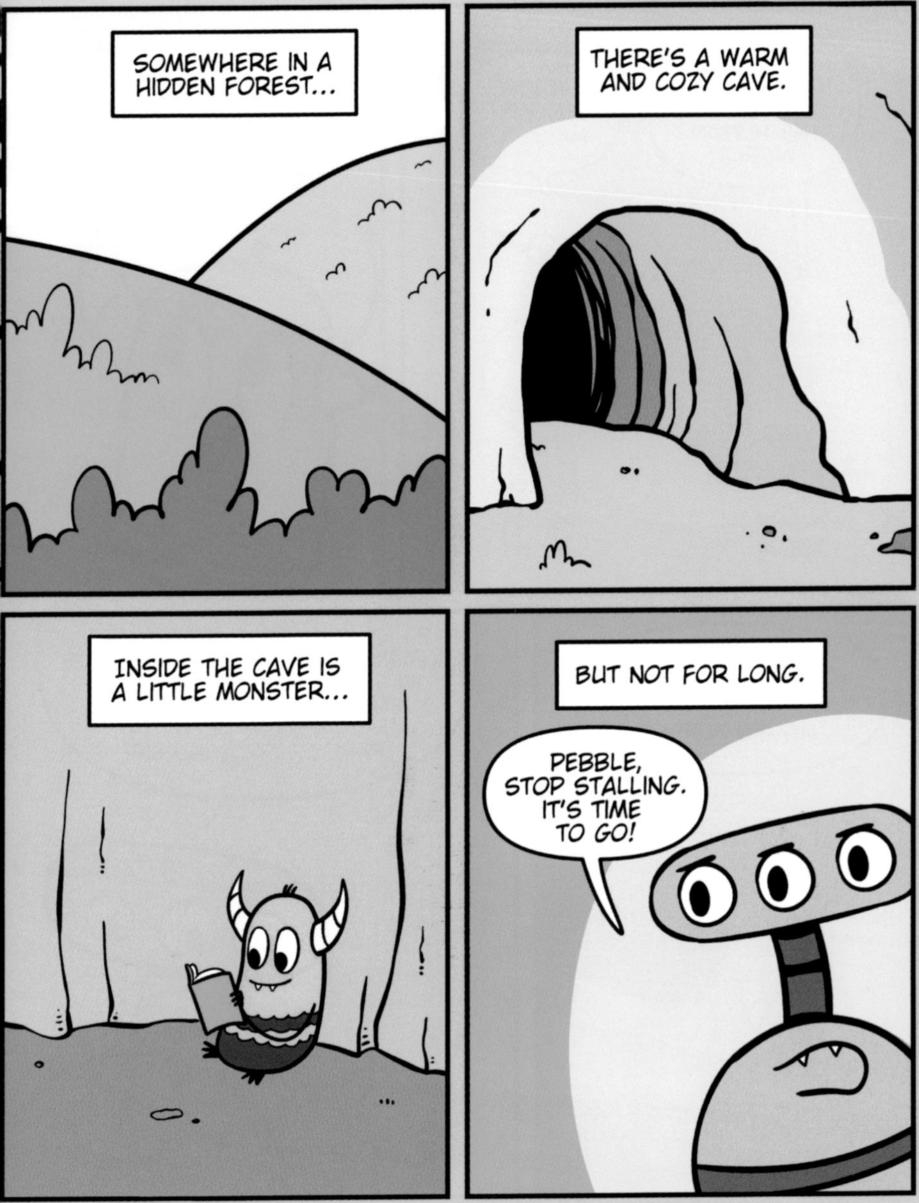
SOMEWHERE IN A HIDDEN FOREST...
THERE'S A WARM AND COZY CAVE.
INSIDE THE CAVE IS A LITTLE MONSTER...
BUT NOT FOR LONG.
PEBBLE, STOP STALLING. IT'S TIME TO GO!

MOM, I DON'T WANT TO GO TO THE HUMAN WORLD!

I KNOW, BUT YOU HAVE TO.

BUT WHY?

TO UNLOCK YOUR SKILLS.

AS YOU GROW UP, YOU ARE PROTECTED BY THE MAGIC OF OUR HIDDEN FOREST.

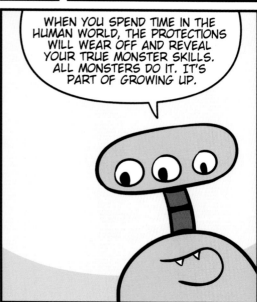

WHEN YOU SPEND TIME IN THE HUMAN WORLD, THE PROTECTIONS WILL WEAR OFF AND REVEAL YOUR TRUE MONSTER SKILLS. ALL MONSTERS DO IT. IT'S PART OF GROWING UP.

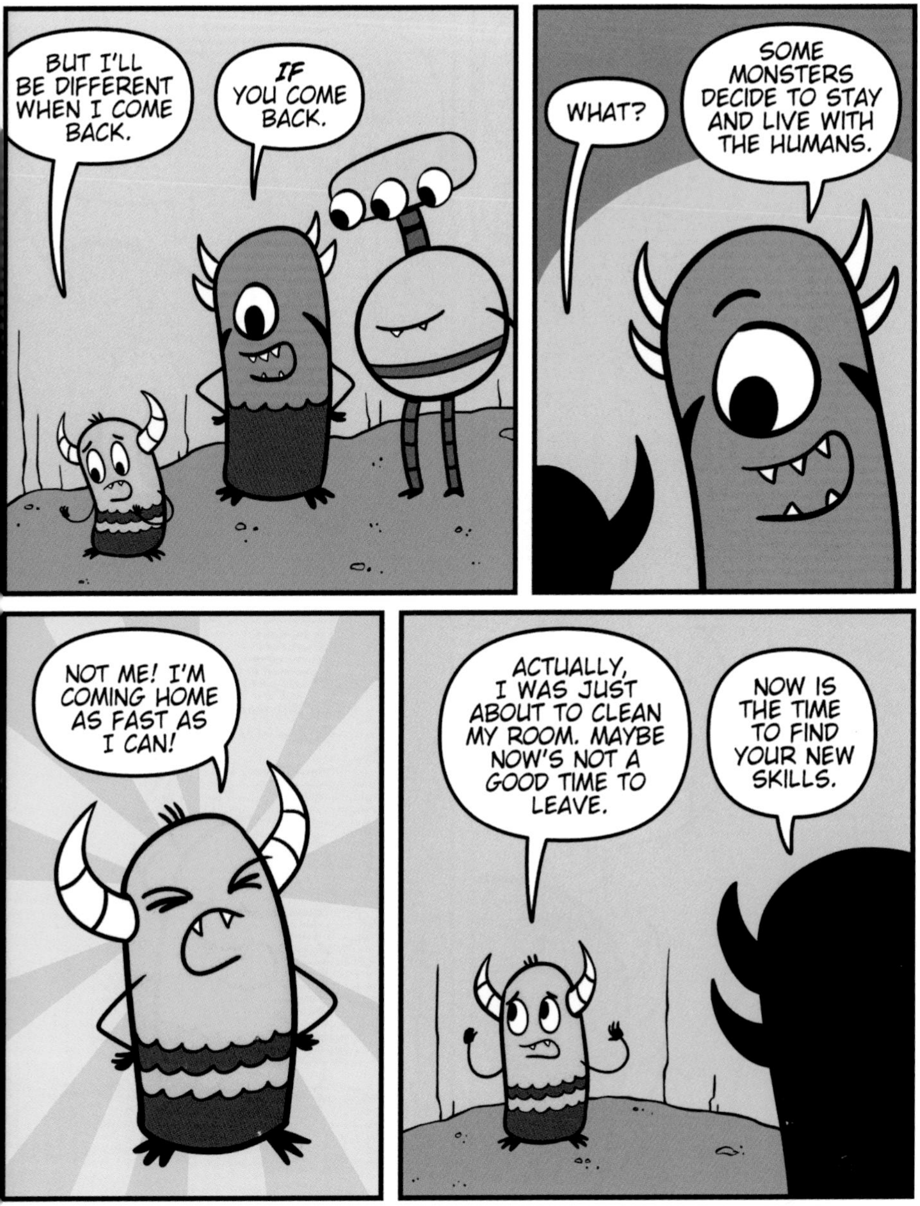
BUT I'LL BE DIFFERENT WHEN I COME BACK.
IF YOU COME BACK.
WHAT?
SOME MONSTERS DECIDE TO STAY AND LIVE WITH THE HUMANS.
NOT ME! I'M COMING HOME AS FAST AS I CAN!
ACTUALLY, I WAS JUST ABOUT TO CLEAN MY ROOM. MAYBE NOW'S NOT A GOOD TIME TO LEAVE.
NOW IS THE TIME TO FIND YOUR NEW SKILLS.

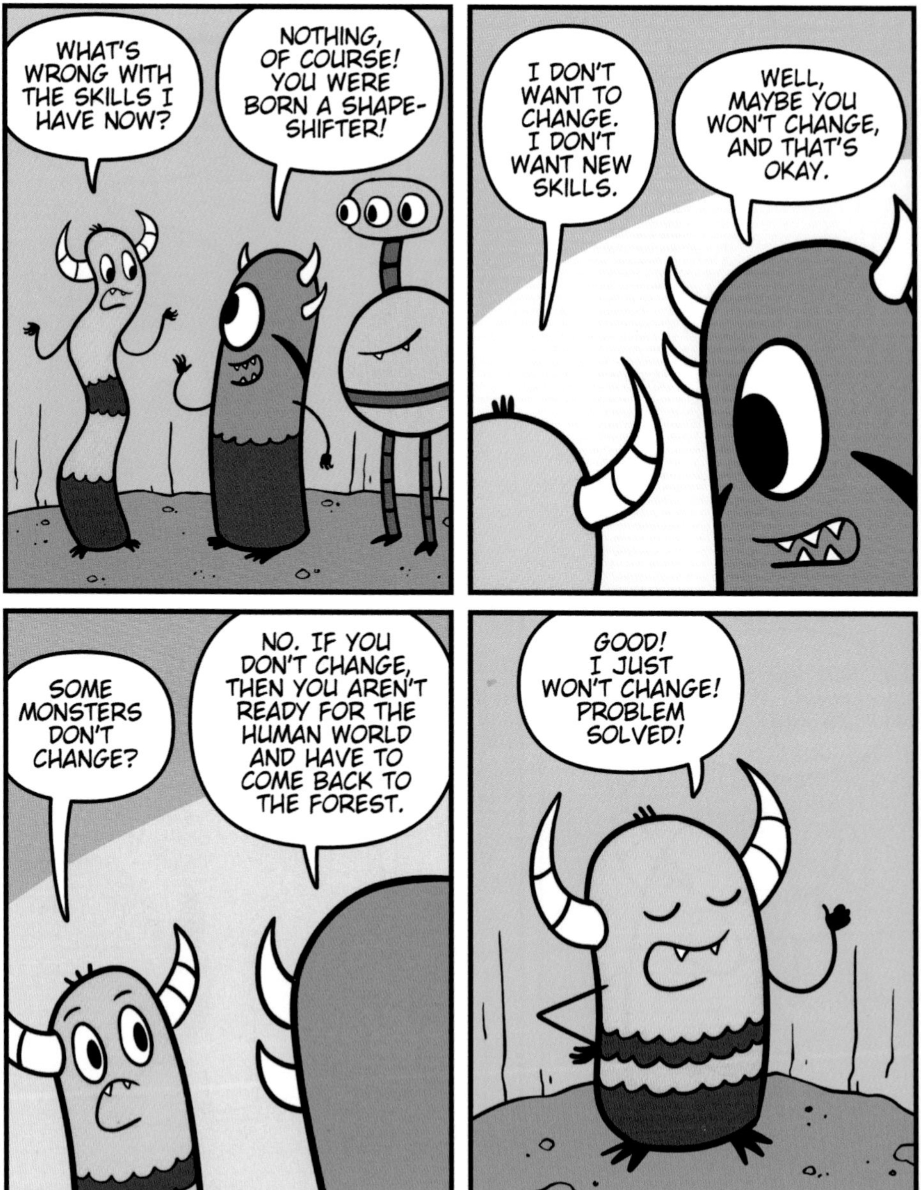
WHAT'S WRONG WITH THE SKILLS I HAVE NOW?
NOTHING, OF COURSE! YOU WERE BORN A SHAPE-SHIFTER!
I DON'T WANT TO CHANGE. I DON'T WANT NEW SKILLS.
WELL, MAYBE YOU WON'T CHANGE, AND THAT'S OKAY.
SOME MONSTERS DON'T CHANGE?
NO. IF YOU DON'T CHANGE, THEN YOU AREN'T READY FOR THE HUMAN WORLD AND HAVE TO COME BACK TO THE FOREST.
GOOD! I JUST WON'T CHANGE! PROBLEM SOLVED!

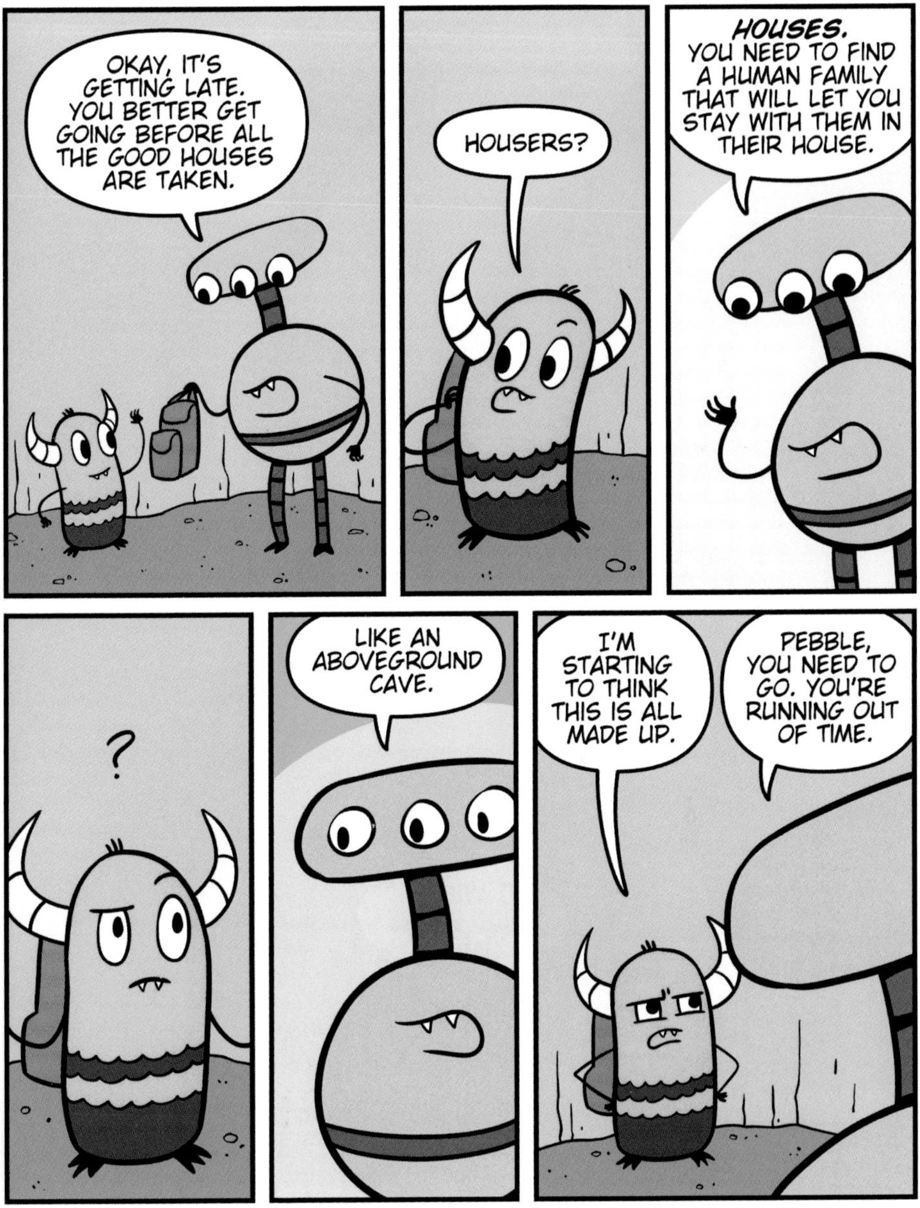
OKAY, IT'S GETTING LATE. YOU BETTER GET GOING BEFORE ALL THE GOOD HOUSES ARE TAKEN.
HOUSERS?
HOUSES. YOU NEED TO FIND A HUMAN FAMILY THAT WILL LET YOU STAY WITH THEM IN THEIR HOUSE.
?
LIKE AN ABOVEGROUND CAVE.
I'M STARTING TO THINK THIS IS ALL MADE UP.
PEBBLE, YOU NEED TO GO. YOU'RE RUNNING OUT OF TIME.

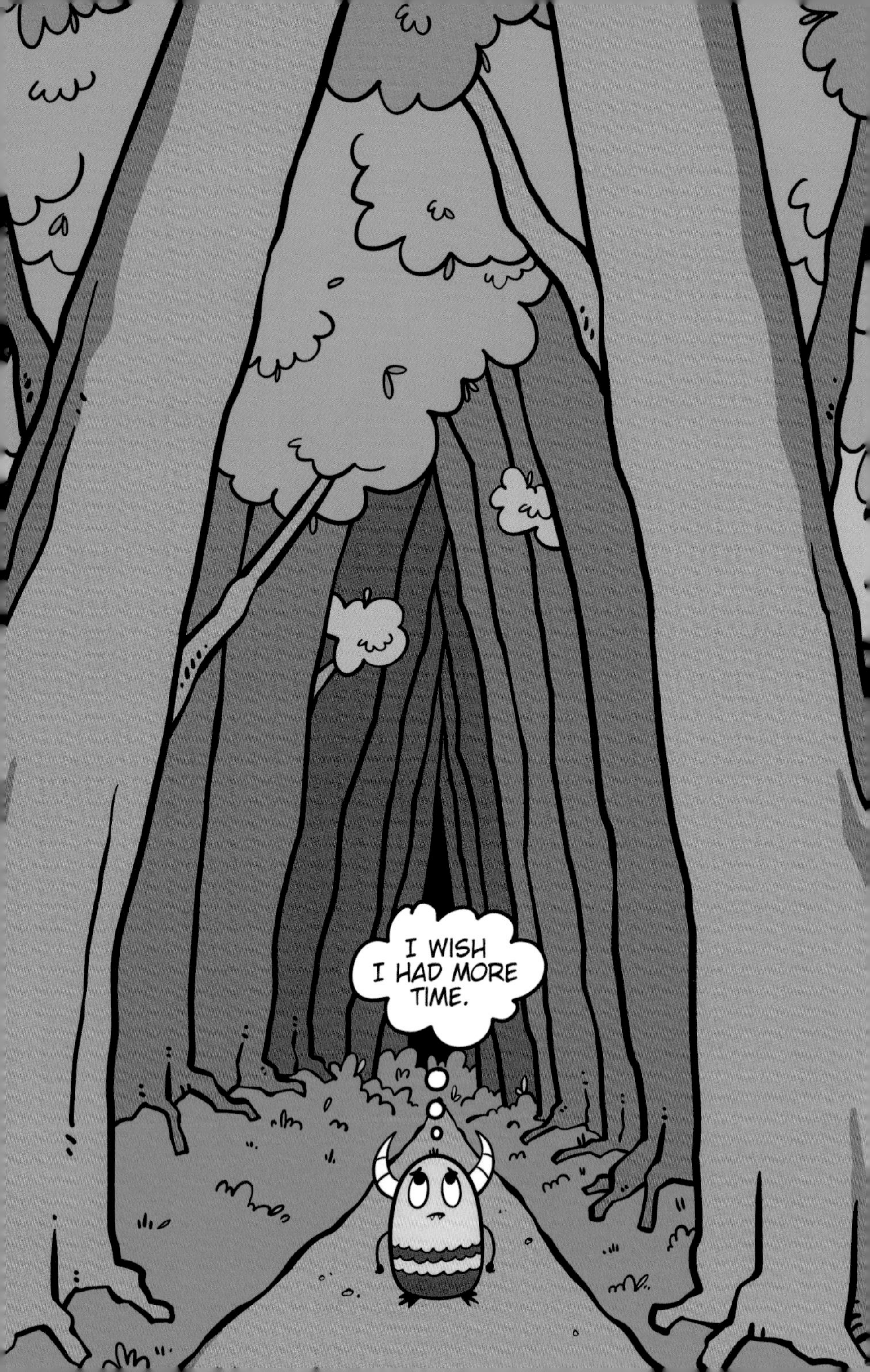
I WISH I HAD MORE TIME.

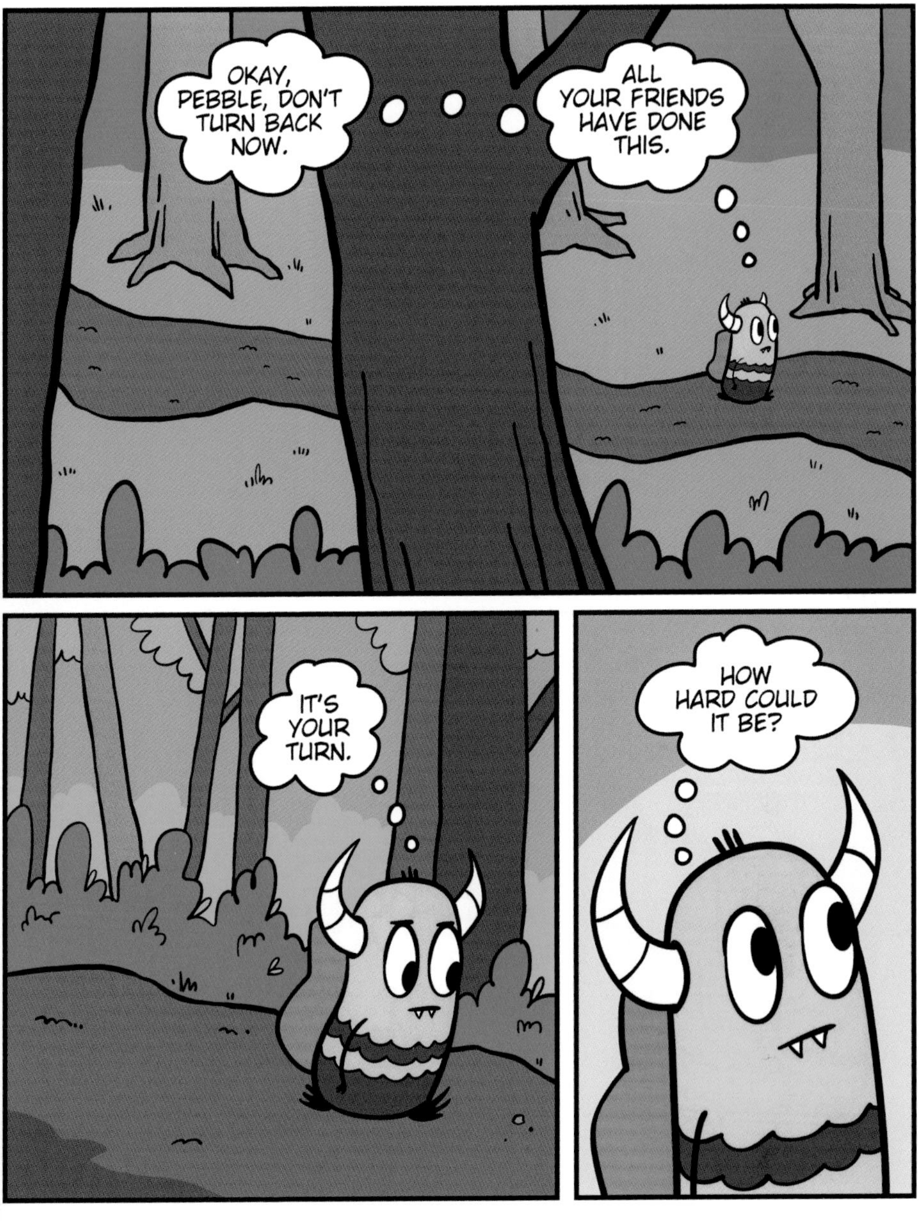
OKAY, PEBBLE, DON'T TURN BACK NOW.
ALL YOUR FRIENDS HAVE DONE THIS.
IT'S YOUR TURN.
HOW HARD COULD IT BE?

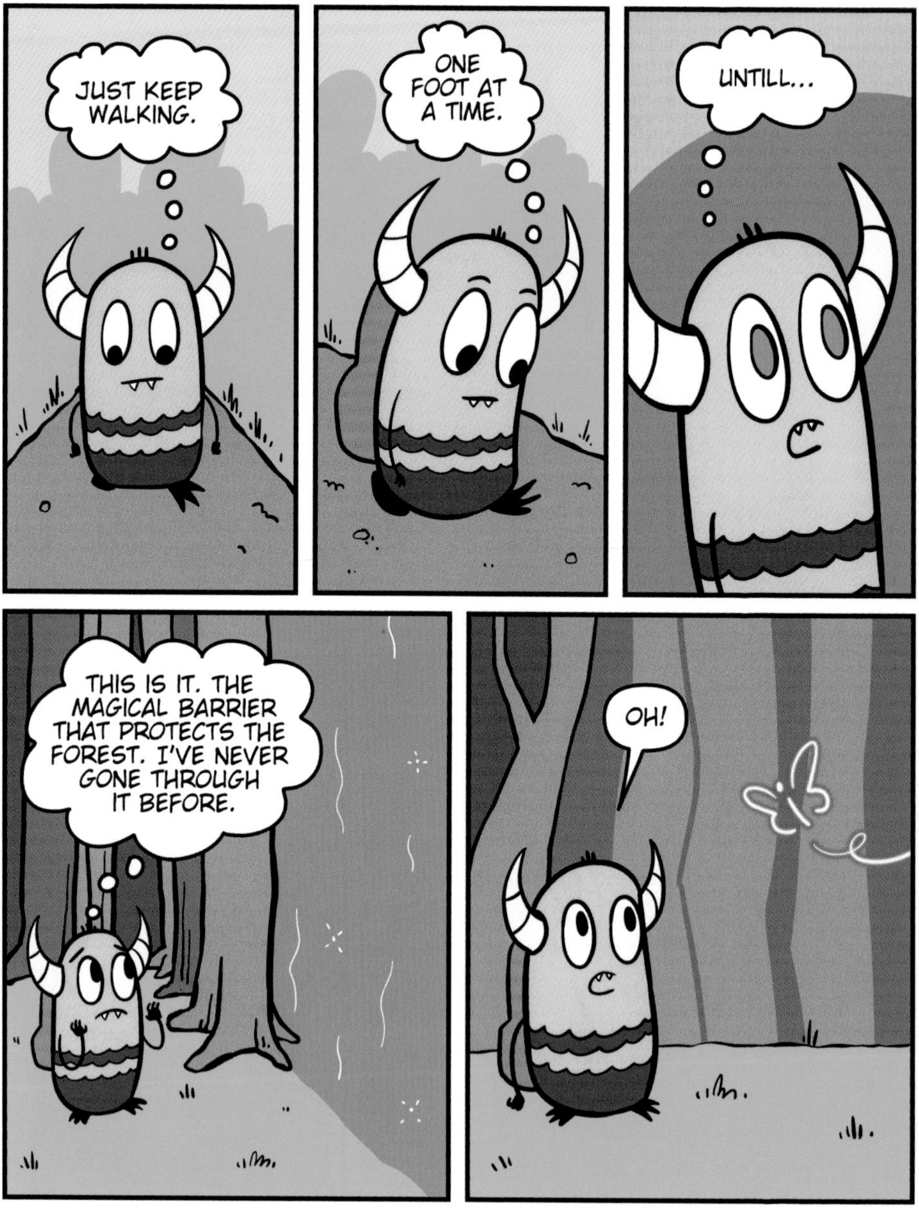
JUST KEEP WALKING.
ONE FOOT AT A TIME.
UNTILL...
THIS IS IT. THE MAGICAL BARRIER THAT PROTECTS THE FOREST. I'VE NEVER GONE THROUGH IT BEFORE.
OH!

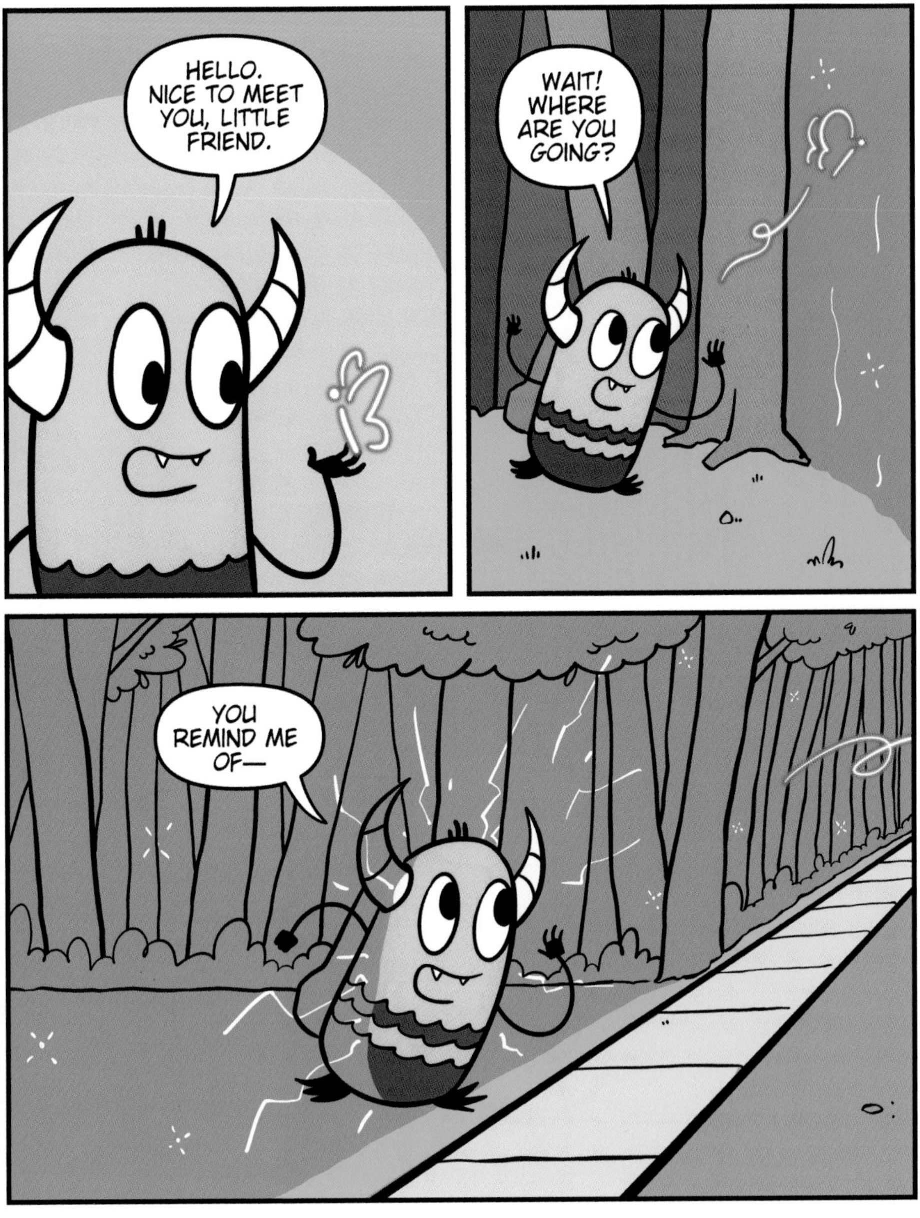
HELLO. NICE TO MEET YOU, LITTLE FRIEND.
WAIT! WHERE ARE YOU GOING?
YOU REMIND ME OF—

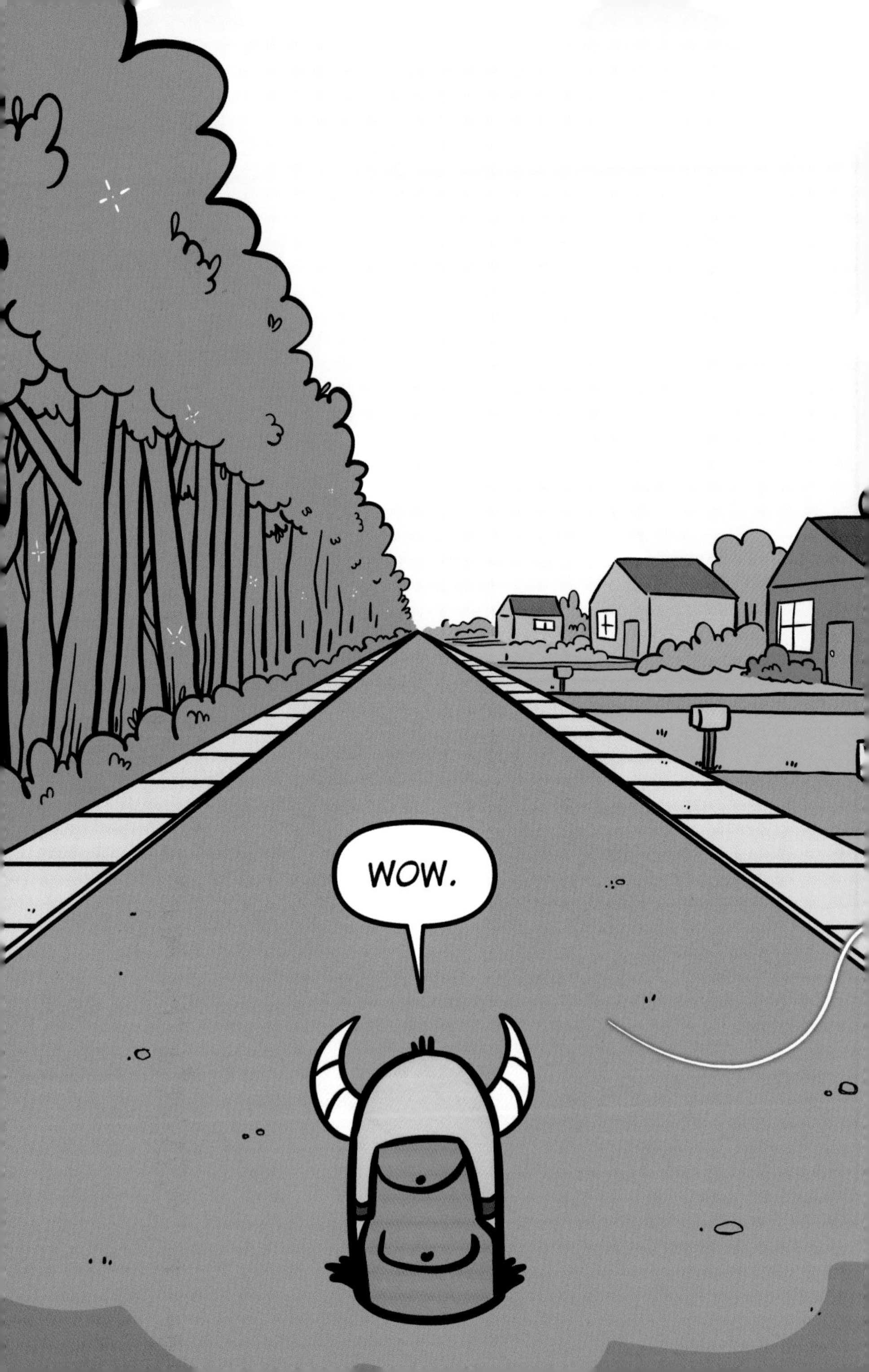
WOW.

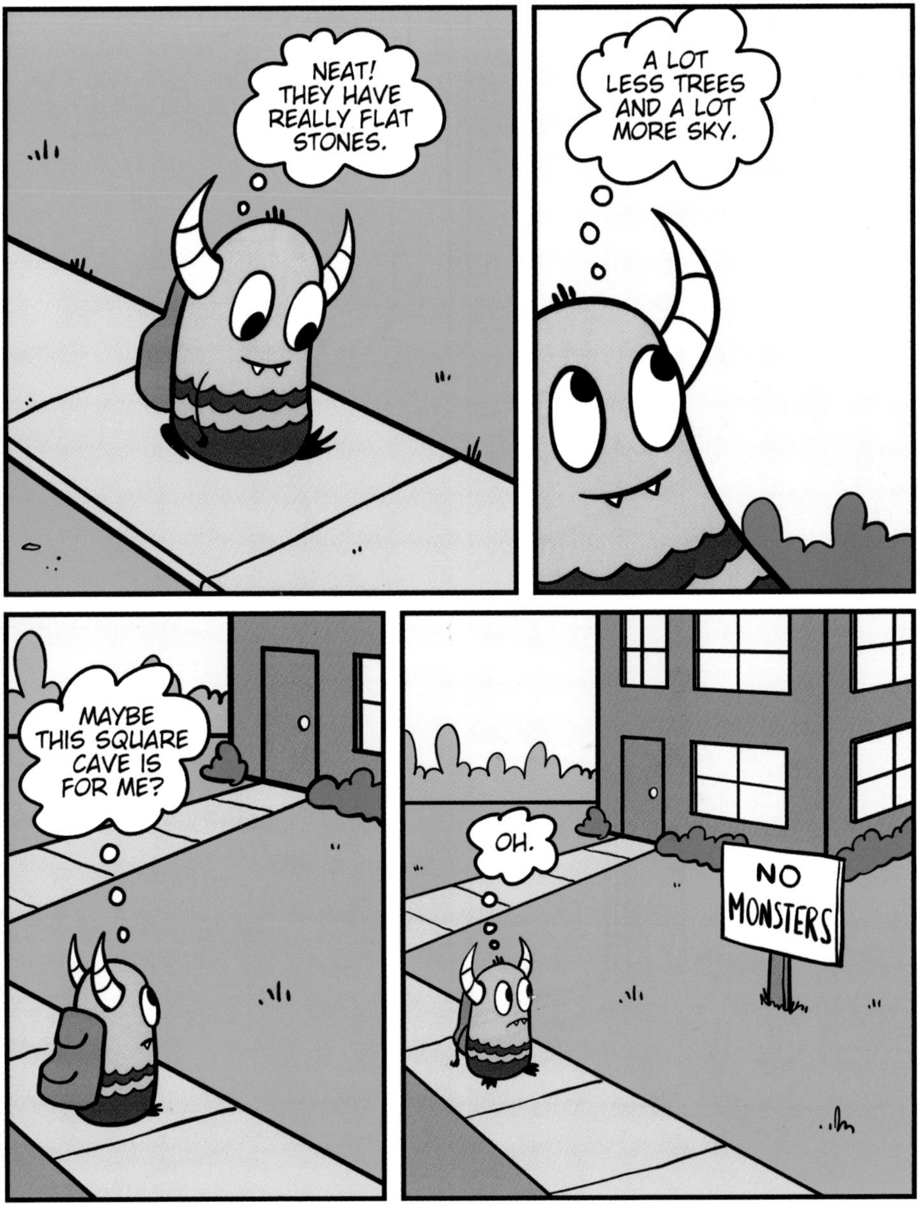
NEAT! THEY HAVE REALLY FLAT STONES.
A LOT LESS TREES AND A LOT MORE SKY.
MAYBE THIS SQUARE CAVE IS FOR ME?
OH.
NO MONSTERS

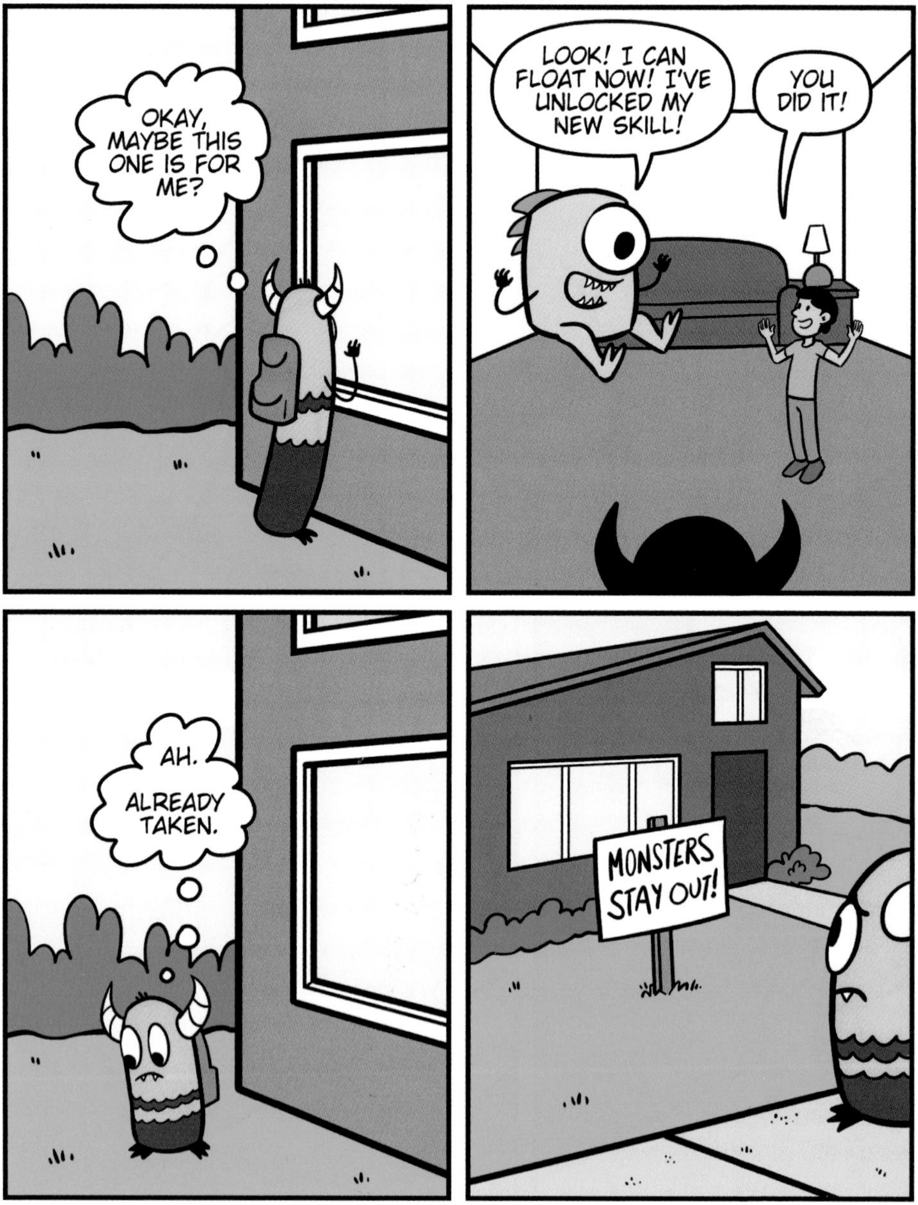
OKAY, MAYBE THIS ONE IS FOR ME?
LOOK! I CAN FLOAT NOW! I'VE UNLOCKED MY NEW SKILL!
YOU DID IT!
AH.
ALREADY TAKEN.
MONSTERS STAY OUT!

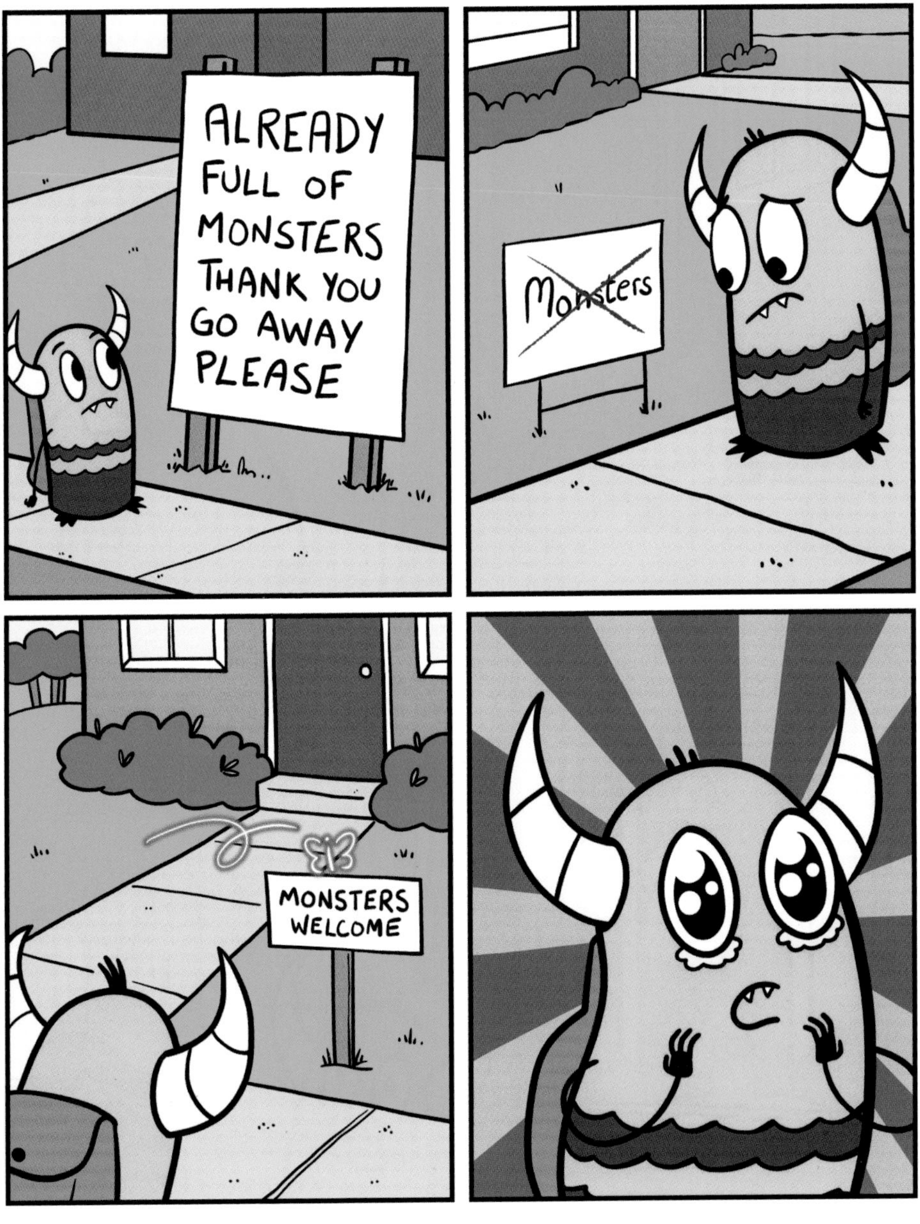
ALREADY FULL OF MONSTERS THANK YOU GO AWAY PLEASE
Monsters
MONSTERS WELCOME

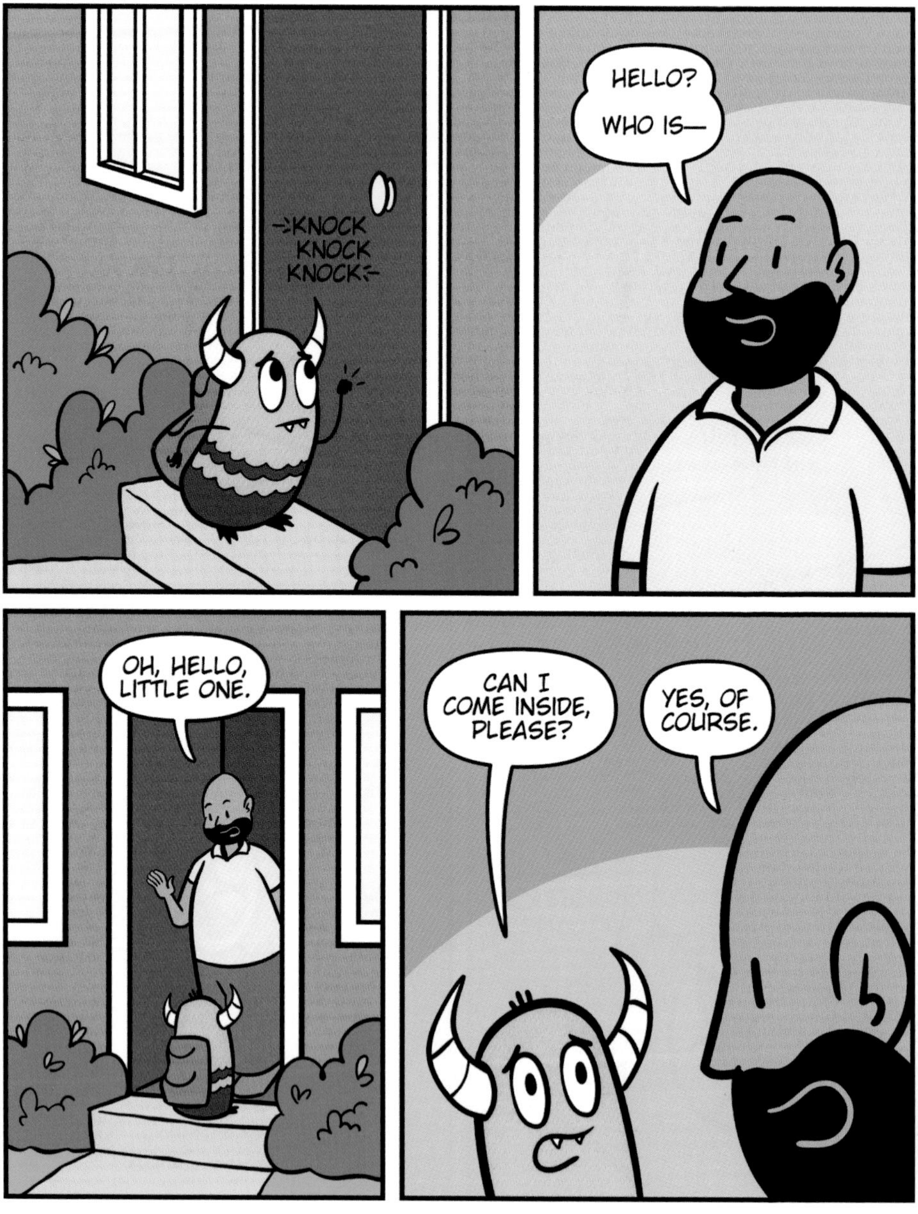
KNOCK
KNOCK
KNOCK
HELLO?
WHO IS—
OH, HELLO, LITTLE ONE.
CAN I COME INSIDE, PLEASE?
YES, OF COURSE.

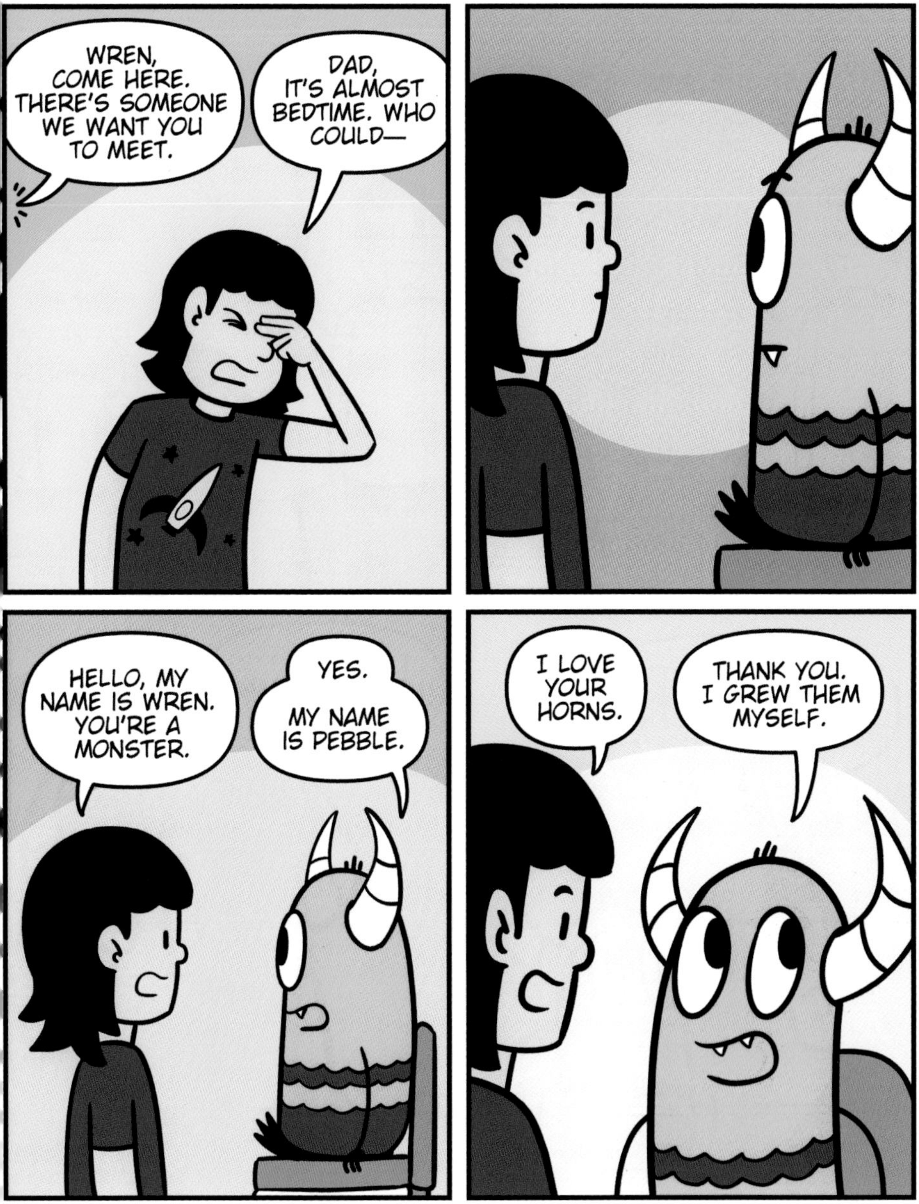
WREN, COME HERE. THERE'S SOMEONE WE WANT YOU TO MEET.
DAD, IT'S ALMOST BEDTIME. WHO COULD—
HELLO, MY NAME IS WREN. YOU'RE A MONSTER.
YES.
MY NAME IS PEBBLE.
I LOVE YOUR HORNS.
THANK YOU. I GREW THEM MYSELF.

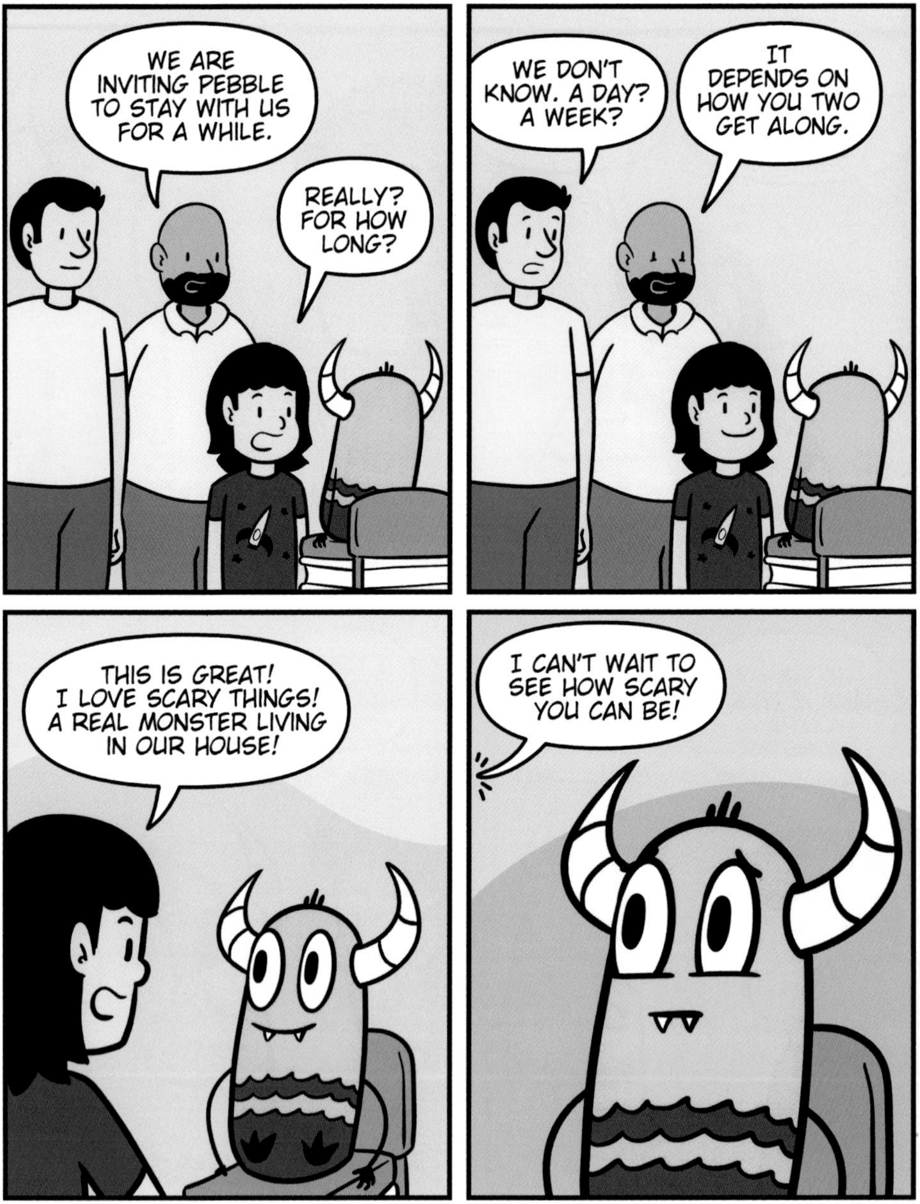
WE ARE INVITING PEBBLE TO STAY WITH US FOR A WHILE.
REALLY? FOR HOW LONG?
WE DON'T KNOW. A DAY? A WEEK?
IT DEPENDS ON HOW YOU TWO GET ALONG.
THIS IS GREAT! I LOVE SCARY THINGS! A REAL MONSTER LIVING IN OUR HOUSE!
I CAN'T WAIT TO SEE HOW SCARY YOU CAN BE!

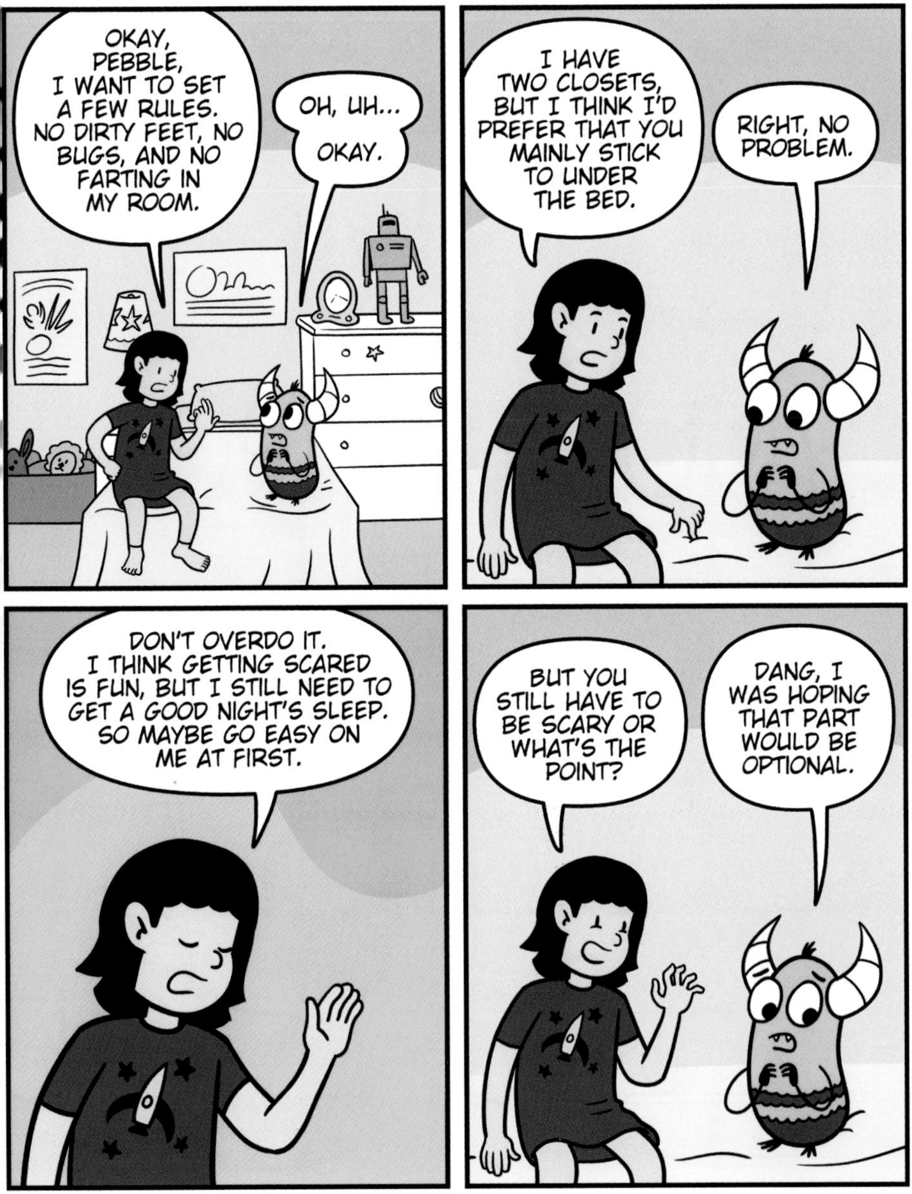
OKAY, PEBBLE, I WANT TO SET A FEW RULES. NO DIRTY FEET, NO BUGS, AND NO FARTING IN MY ROOM.
OH, UH... OKAY.
I HAVE TWO CLOSETS, BUT I THINK I'D PREFER THAT YOU MAINLY STICK TO UNDER THE BED.
RIGHT, NO PROBLEM.
DON'T OVERDO IT. I THINK GETTING SCARED IS FUN, BUT I STILL NEED TO GET A GOOD NIGHT'S SLEEP. SO MAYBE GO EASY ON ME AT FIRST.
BUT YOU STILL HAVE TO BE SCARY OR WHAT'S THE POINT?
DANG, I WAS HOPING THAT PART WOULD BE OPTIONAL.

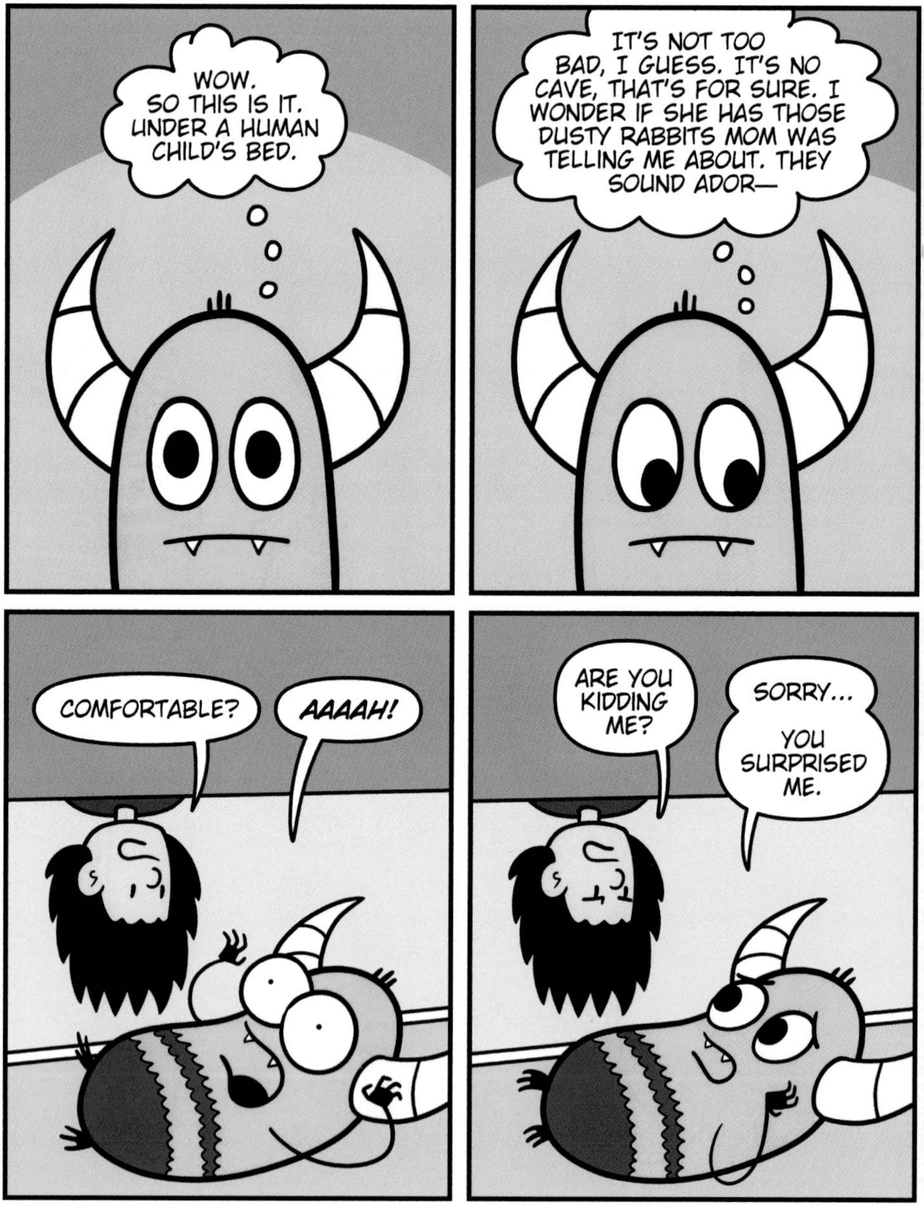
WOW. SO THIS IS IT. UNDER A HUMAN CHILD'S BED.
IT'S NOT TOO BAD, I GUESS. IT'S NO CAVE, THAT'S FOR SURE. I WONDER IF SHE HAS THOSE DUSTY RABBITS MOM WAS TELLING ME ABOUT. THEY SOUND ADOR—
COMFORTABLE?
AAAAH!
ARE YOU KIDDING ME?
SORRY...
YOU SURPRISED ME.

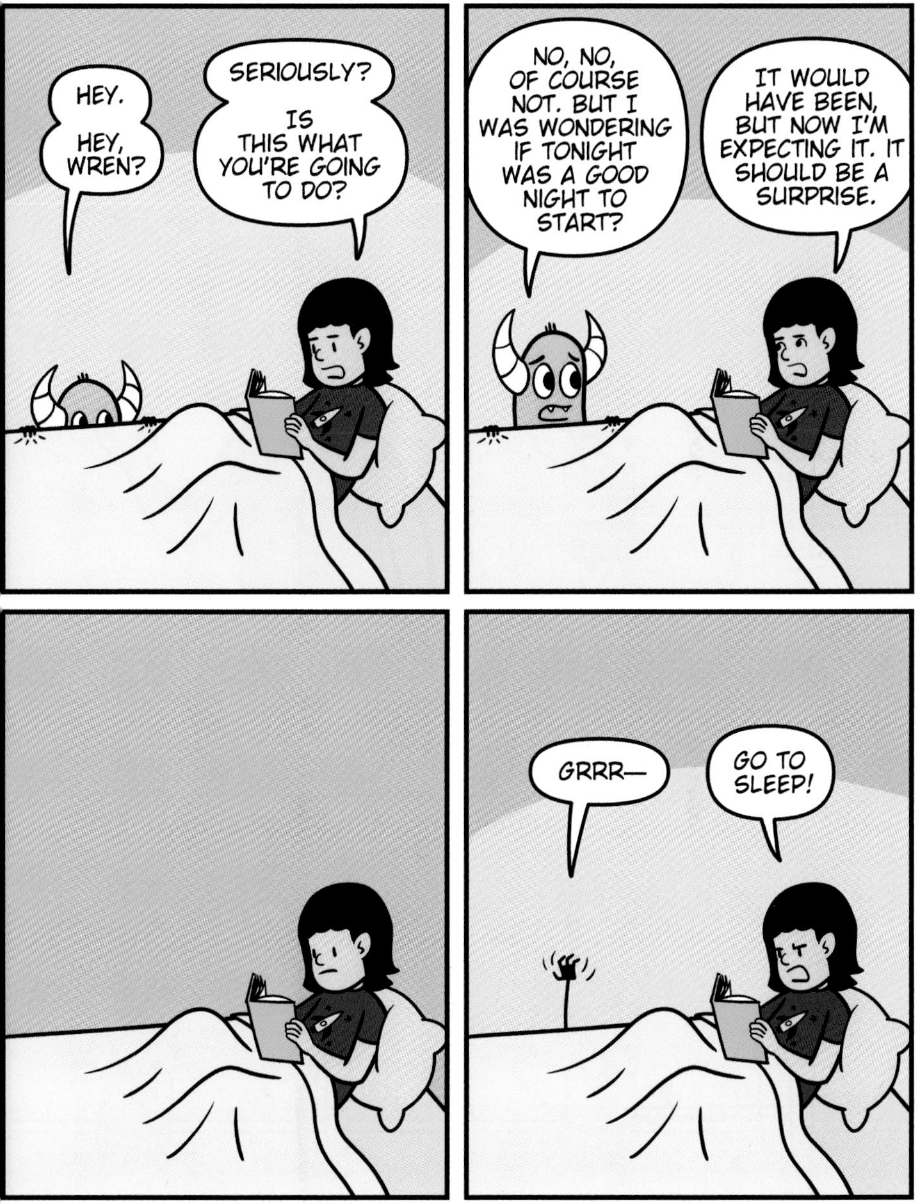
HEY.
HEY, WREN?
SERIOUSLY?
IS THIS WHAT YOU'RE GOING TO DO?
NO, NO, OF COURSE NOT. BUT I WAS WONDERING IF TONIGHT WAS A GOOD NIGHT TO START?
IT WOULD HAVE BEEN, BUT NOW I'M EXPECTING IT. IT SHOULD BE A SURPRISE.
GRRR—
GO TO SLEEP!

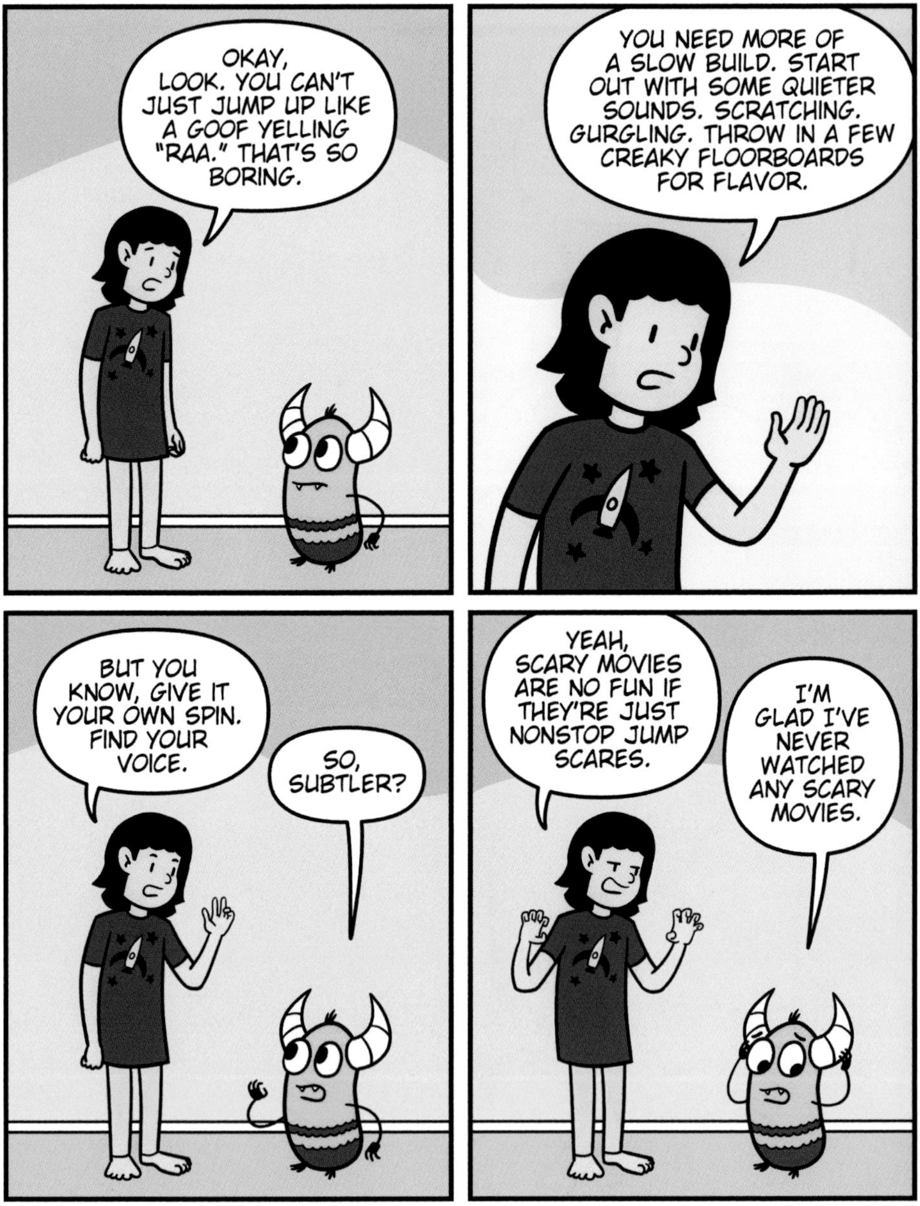
OKAY, LOOK. YOU CAN'T JUST JUMP UP LIKE A GOOF YELLING "RAA." THAT'S SO BORING.
YOU NEED MORE OF A SLOW BUILD. START OUT WITH SOME QUIETER SOUNDS. SCRATCHING. GURGLING. THROW IN A FEW CREAKY FLOORBOARDS FOR FLAVOR.
BUT YOU KNOW, GIVE IT YOUR OWN SPIN. FIND YOUR VOICE.
SO, SUBTLER?
YEAH, SCARY MOVIES ARE NO FUN IF THEY'RE JUST NONSTOP JUMP SCARES.
I'M GLAD I'VE NEVER WATCHED ANY SCARY MOVIES.

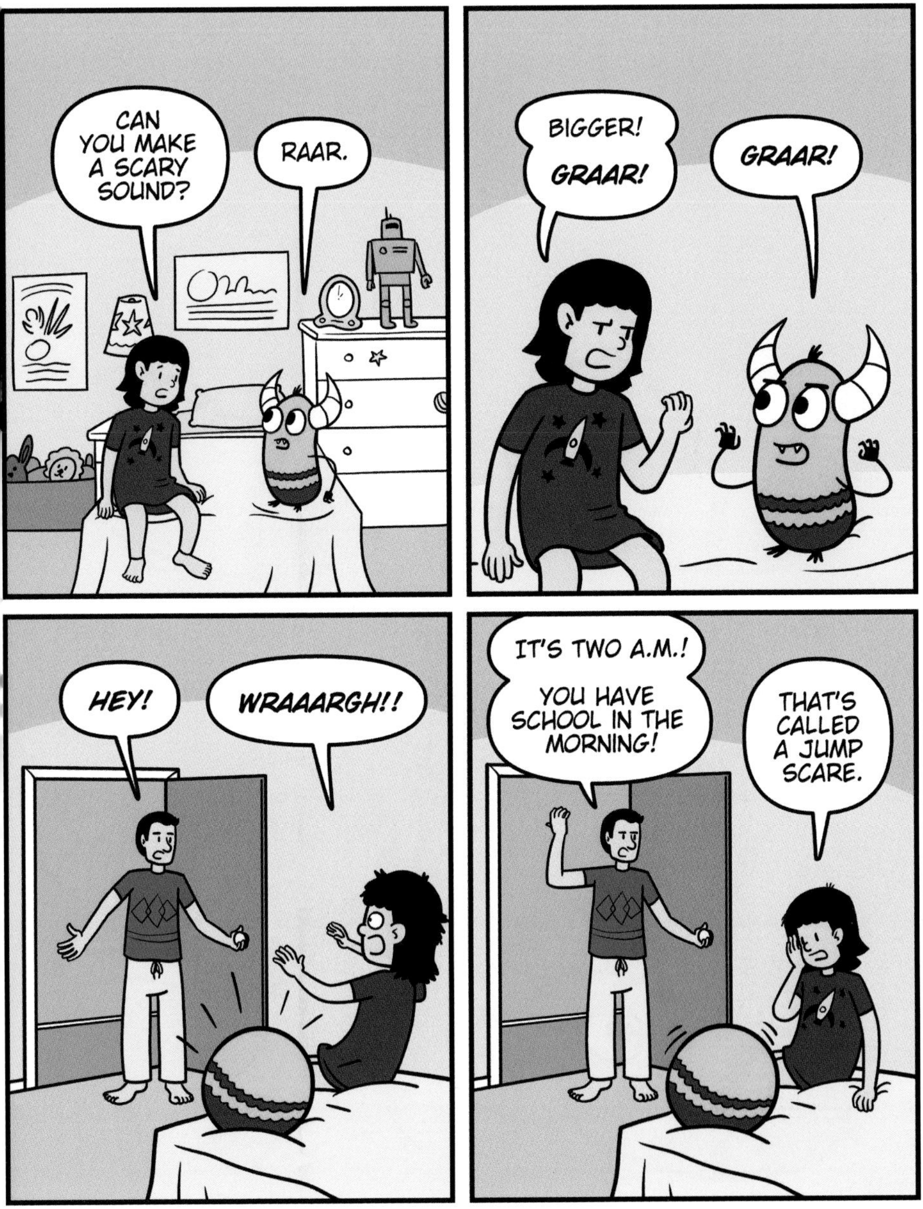
CAN YOU MAKE A SCARY SOUND?
RAAR.
BIGGER!
GRAAR!
GRAAR!
HEY!
WRAAARGH!!
IT'S TWO A.M.!
YOU HAVE SCHOOL IN THE MORNING!
THAT'S CALLED A JUMP SCARE.

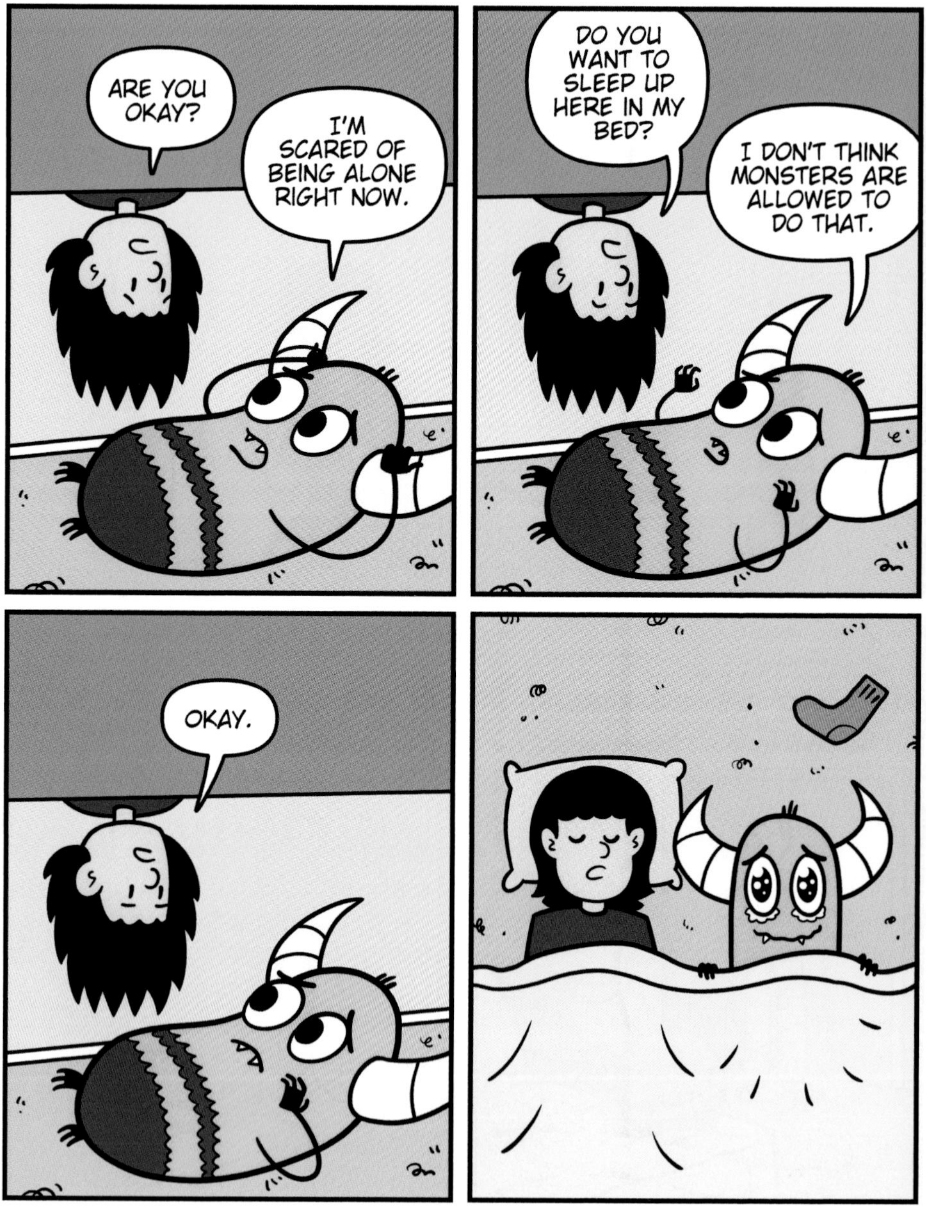
ARE YOU OKAY?
I'M SCARED OF BEING ALONE RIGHT NOW.
DO YOU WANT TO SLEEP UP HERE IN MY BED?
I DON'T THINK MONSTERS ARE ALLOWED TO DO THAT.
OKAY.

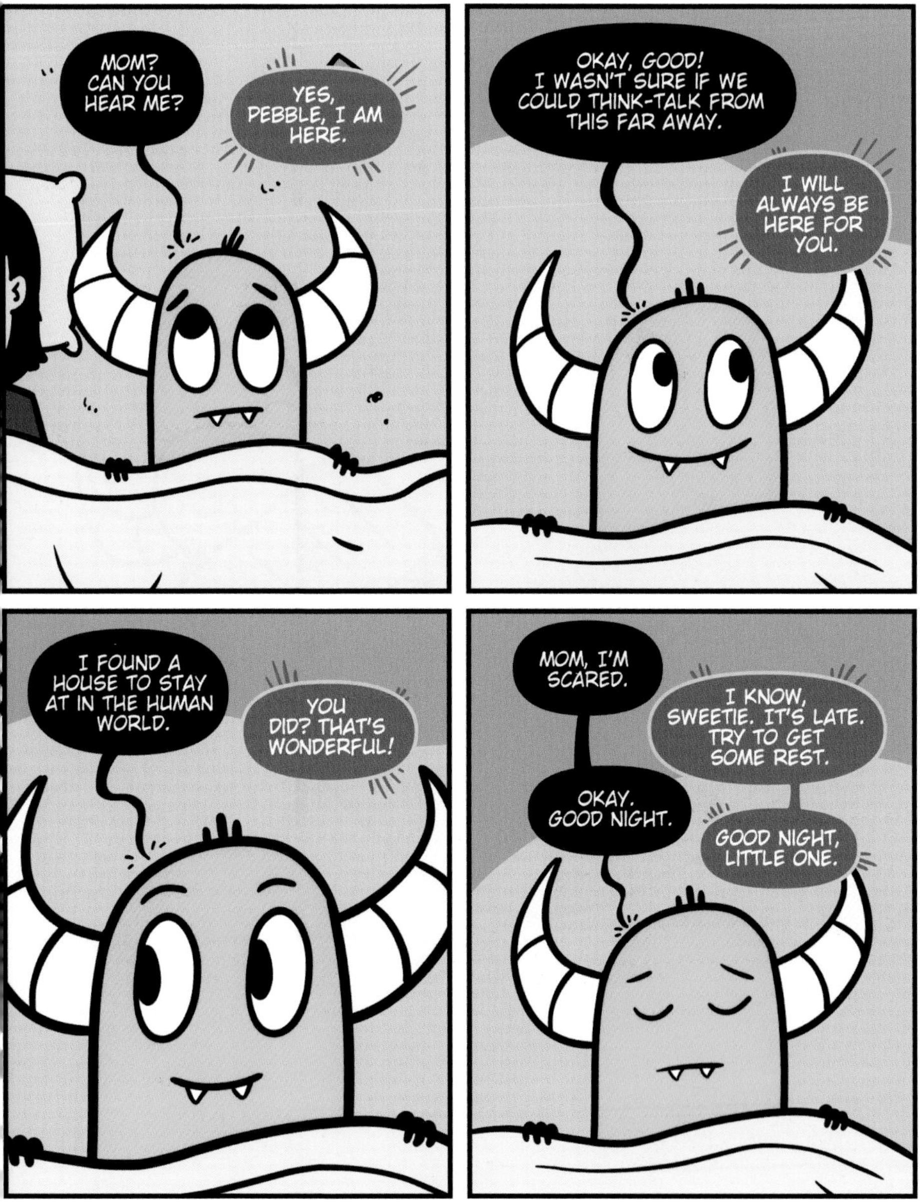
MOM? CAN YOU HEAR ME?
YES, PEBBLE, I AM HERE.
OKAY, GOOD! I WASN'T SURE IF WE COULD THINK-TALK FROM THIS FAR AWAY.
I WILL ALWAYS BE HERE FOR YOU.
I FOUND A HOUSE TO STAY AT IN THE HUMAN WORLD.
YOU DID? THAT'S WONDERFUL!
MOM, I'M SCARED.
I KNOW, SWEETIE. IT'S LATE. TRY TO GET SOME REST.
OKAY. GOOD NIGHT.
GOOD NIGHT, LITTLE ONE.

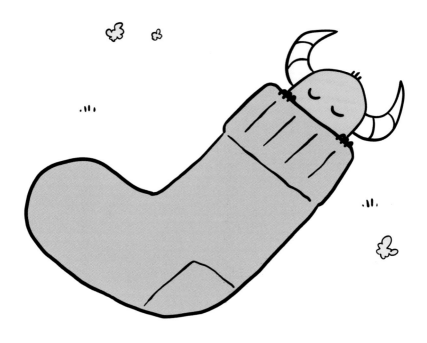

CHAPTER TWO

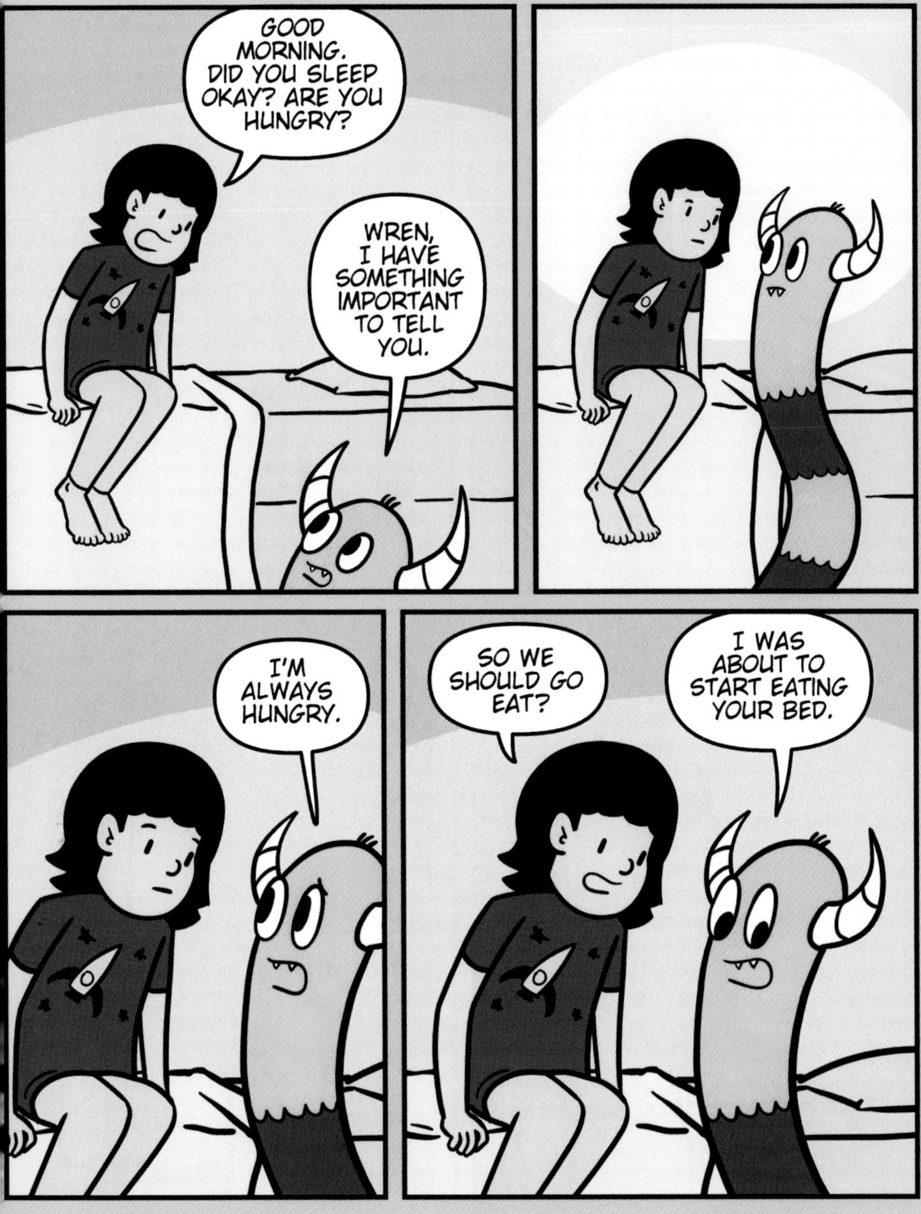

GOOD MORNING. DID YOU SLEEP OKAY? ARE YOU HUNGRY?
WREN, I HAVE SOMETHING IMPORTANT TO TELL YOU.
I'M ALWAYS HUNGRY.
SO WE SHOULD GO EAT?
I WAS ABOUT TO START EATING YOUR BED.

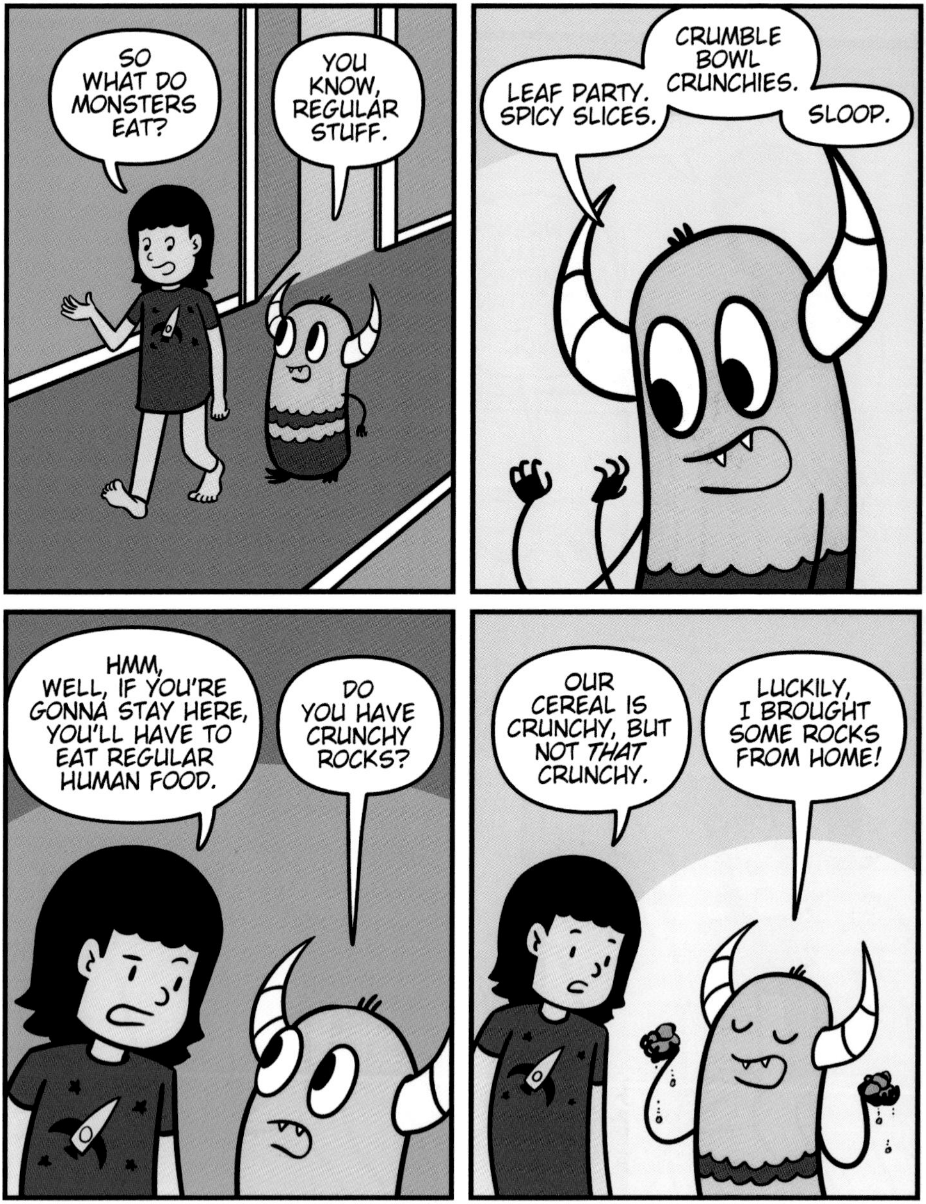
SO WHAT DO MONSTERS EAT?
YOU KNOW, REGULAR STUFF.
LEAF PARTY. SPICY SLICES.
CRUMBLE BOWL CRUNCHIES.
SLOOP.
HMM, WELL, IF YOU'RE GONNA STAY HERE, YOU'LL HAVE TO EAT REGULAR HUMAN FOOD.
DO YOU HAVE CRUNCHY ROCKS?
OUR CEREAL IS CRUNCHY, BUT NOT *THAT* CRUNCHY.
LUCKILY, I BROUGHT SOME ROCKS FROM HOME!

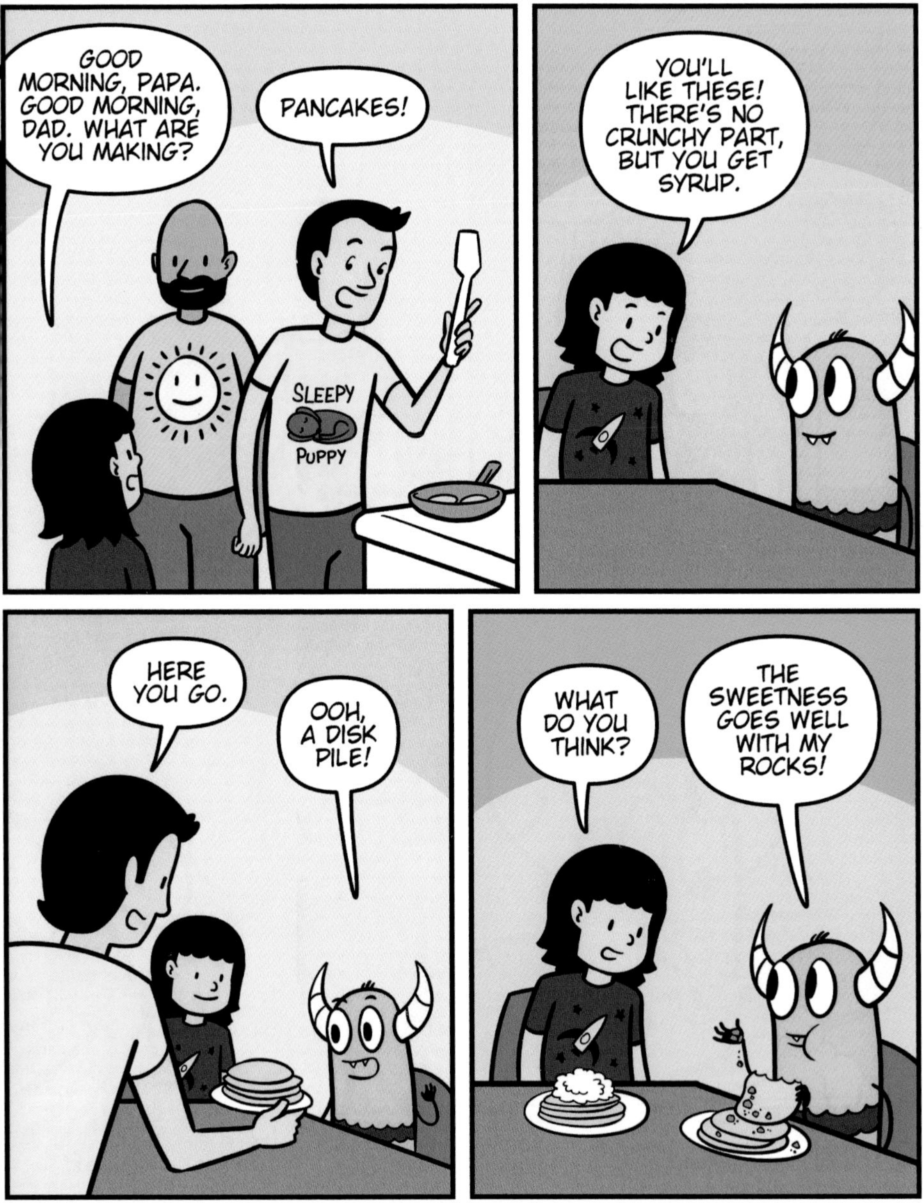
GOOD MORNING, PAPA. GOOD MORNING, DAD. WHAT ARE YOU MAKING?
PANCAKES!
SLEEPY PUPPY
YOU'LL LIKE THESE! THERE'S NO CRUNCHY PART, BUT YOU GET SYRUP.
HERE YOU GO.
OOH, A DISK PILE!
WHAT DO YOU THINK?
THE SWEETNESS GOES WELL WITH MY ROCKS!

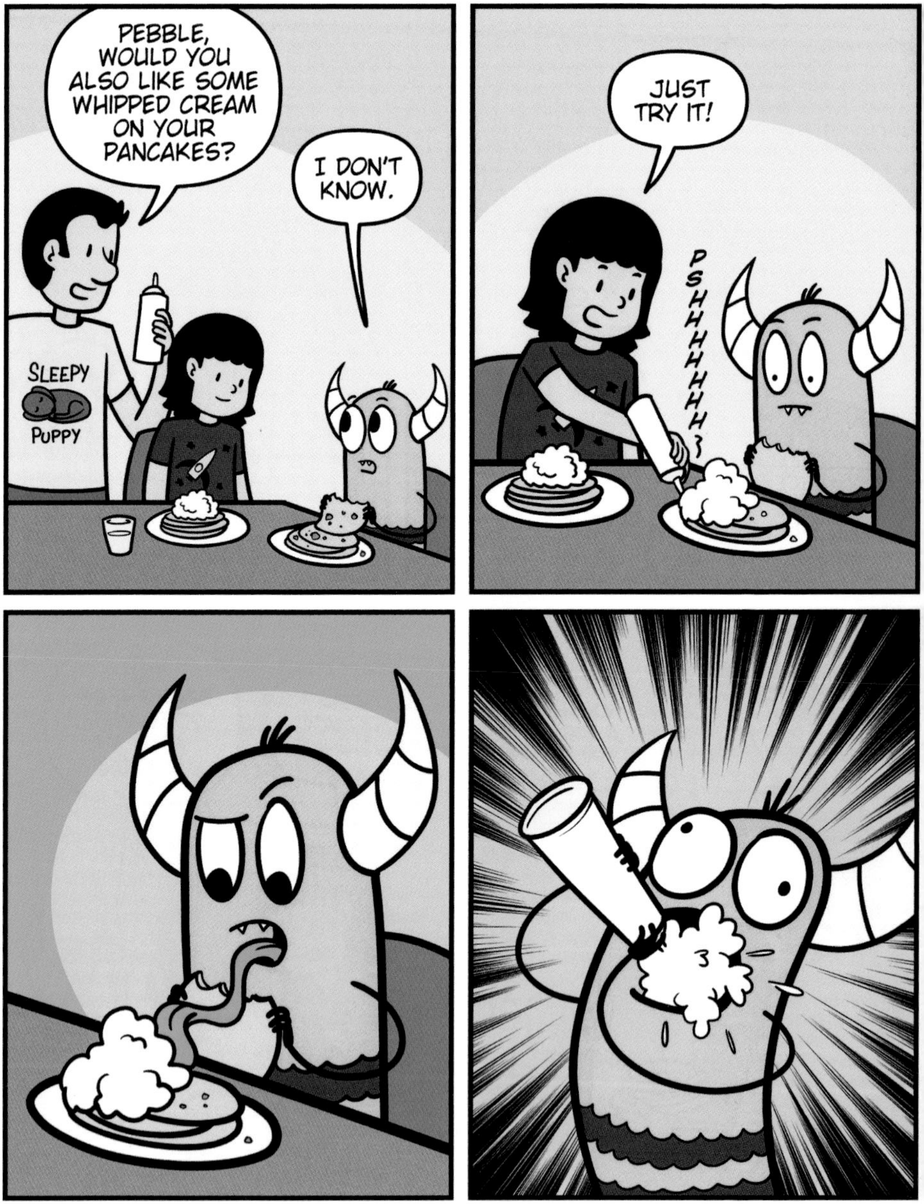
PEBBLE, WOULD YOU ALSO LIKE SOME WHIPPED CREAM ON YOUR PANCAKES?
I DON'T KNOW.
SLEEPY PUPPY
JUST TRY IT!
PSHHHHHHH

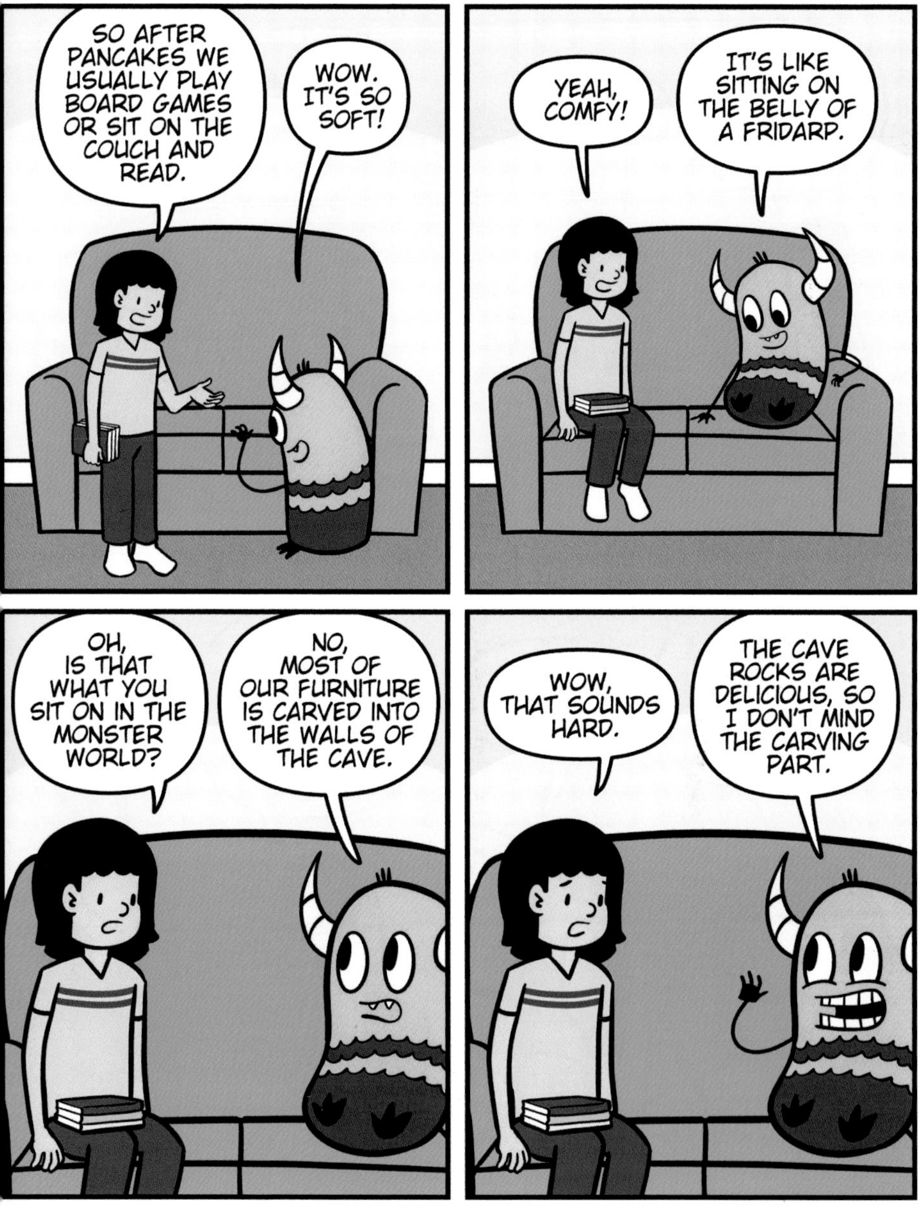
SO AFTER PANCAKES WE USUALLY PLAY BOARD GAMES OR SIT ON THE COUCH AND READ.
WOW. IT'S SO SOFT!
YEAH, COMFY!
IT'S LIKE SITTING ON THE BELLY OF A FRIDARP.
OH, IS THAT WHAT YOU SIT ON IN THE MONSTER WORLD?
NO, MOST OF OUR FURNITURE IS CARVED INTO THE WALLS OF THE CAVE.
WOW, THAT SOUNDS HARD.
THE CAVE ROCKS ARE DELICIOUS, SO I DON'T MIND THE CARVING PART.

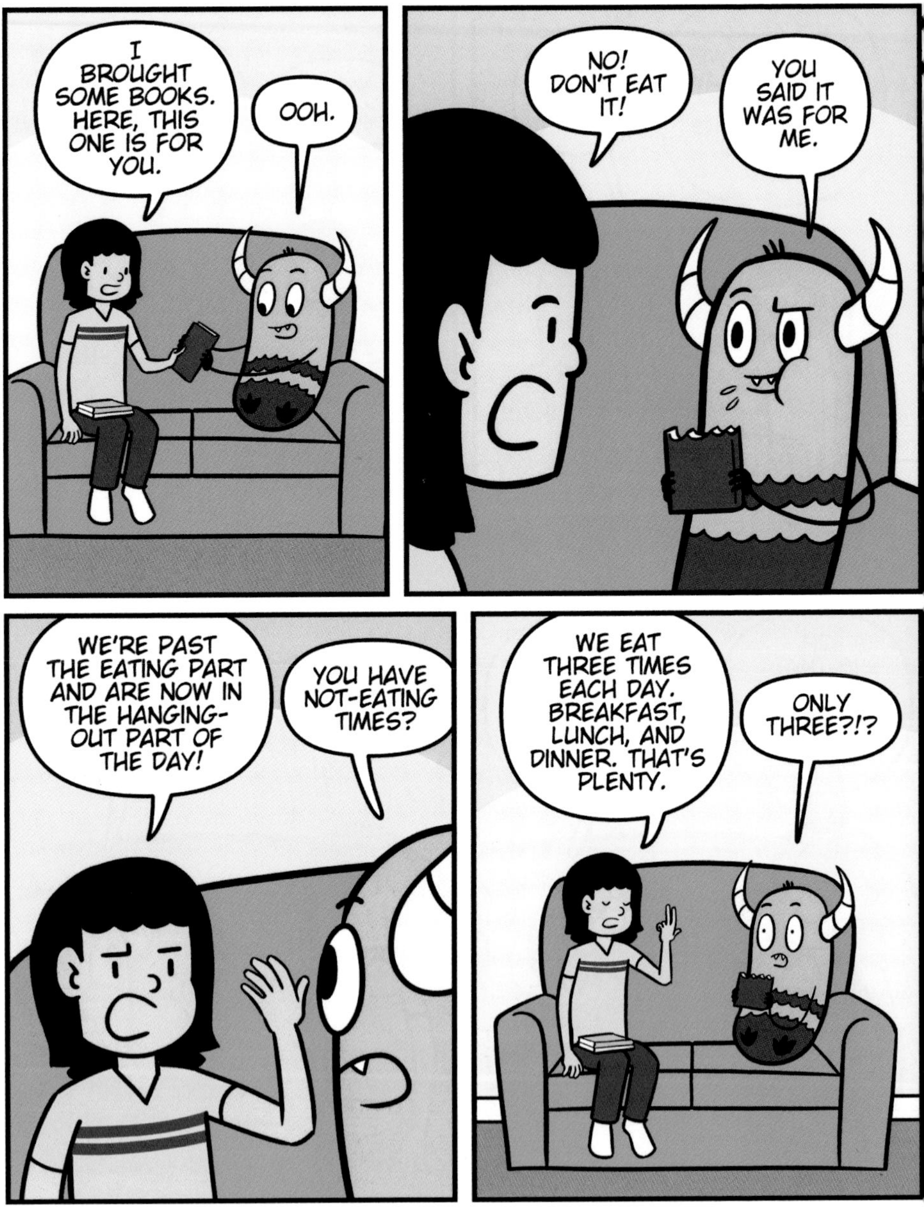
I BROUGHT SOME BOOKS. HERE, THIS ONE IS FOR YOU.
OOH.
NO! DON'T EAT IT!
YOU SAID IT WAS FOR ME.
WE'RE PAST THE EATING PART AND ARE NOW IN THE HANGING-OUT PART OF THE DAY!
YOU HAVE NOT-EATING TIMES?
WE EAT THREE TIMES EACH DAY. BREAKFAST, LUNCH, AND DINNER. THAT'S PLENTY.
ONLY THREE?!?

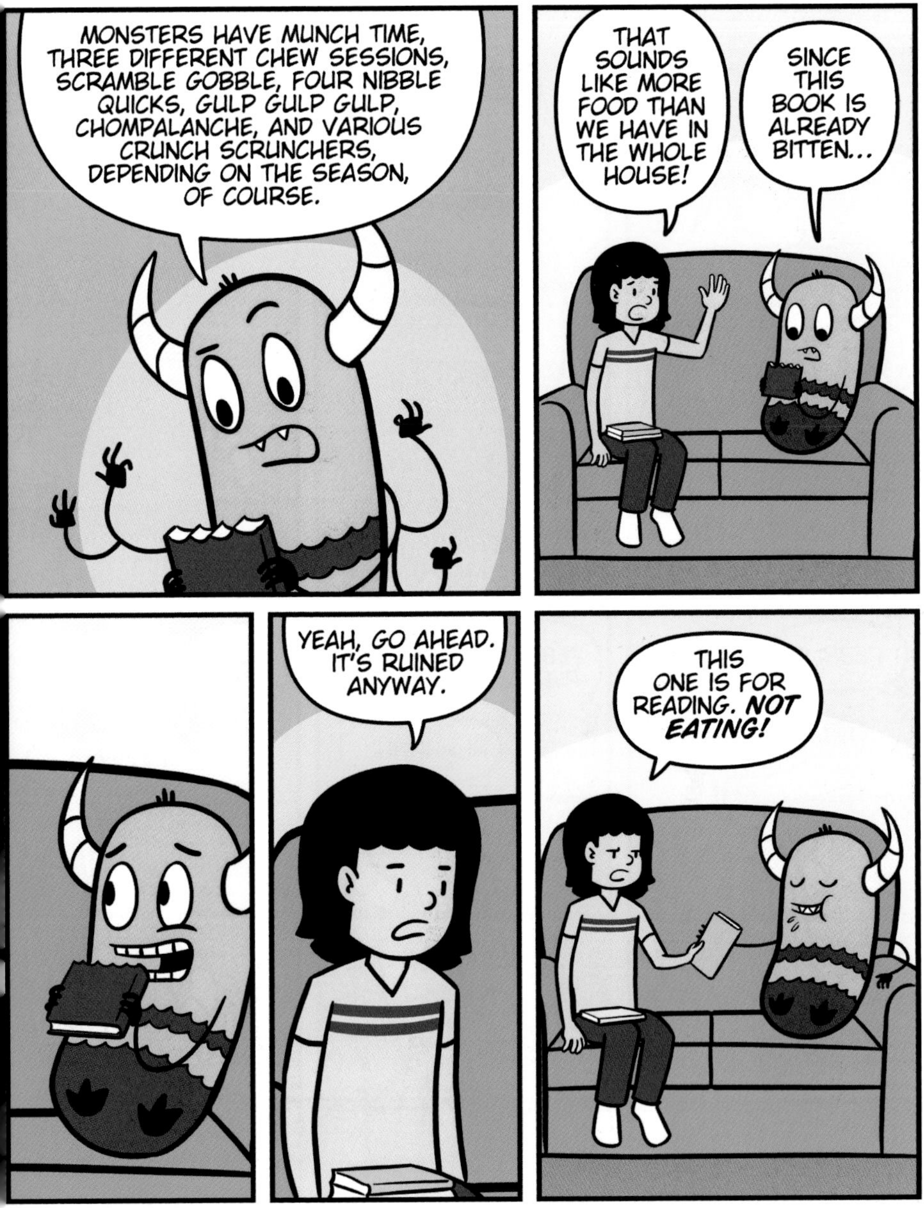
MONSTERS HAVE MUNCH TIME, THREE DIFFERENT CHEW SESSIONS, SCRAMBLE GOBBLE, FOUR NIBBLE QUICKS, GULP GULP GULP, CHOMPALANCHE, AND VARIOUS CRUNCH SCRUNCHERS, DEPENDING ON THE SEASON, OF COURSE.
THAT SOUNDS LIKE MORE FOOD THAN WE HAVE IN THE WHOLE HOUSE!
SINCE THIS BOOK IS ALREADY BITTEN...
YEAH, GO AHEAD. IT'S RUINED ANYWAY.
THIS ONE IS FOR READING. ***NOT EATING!***

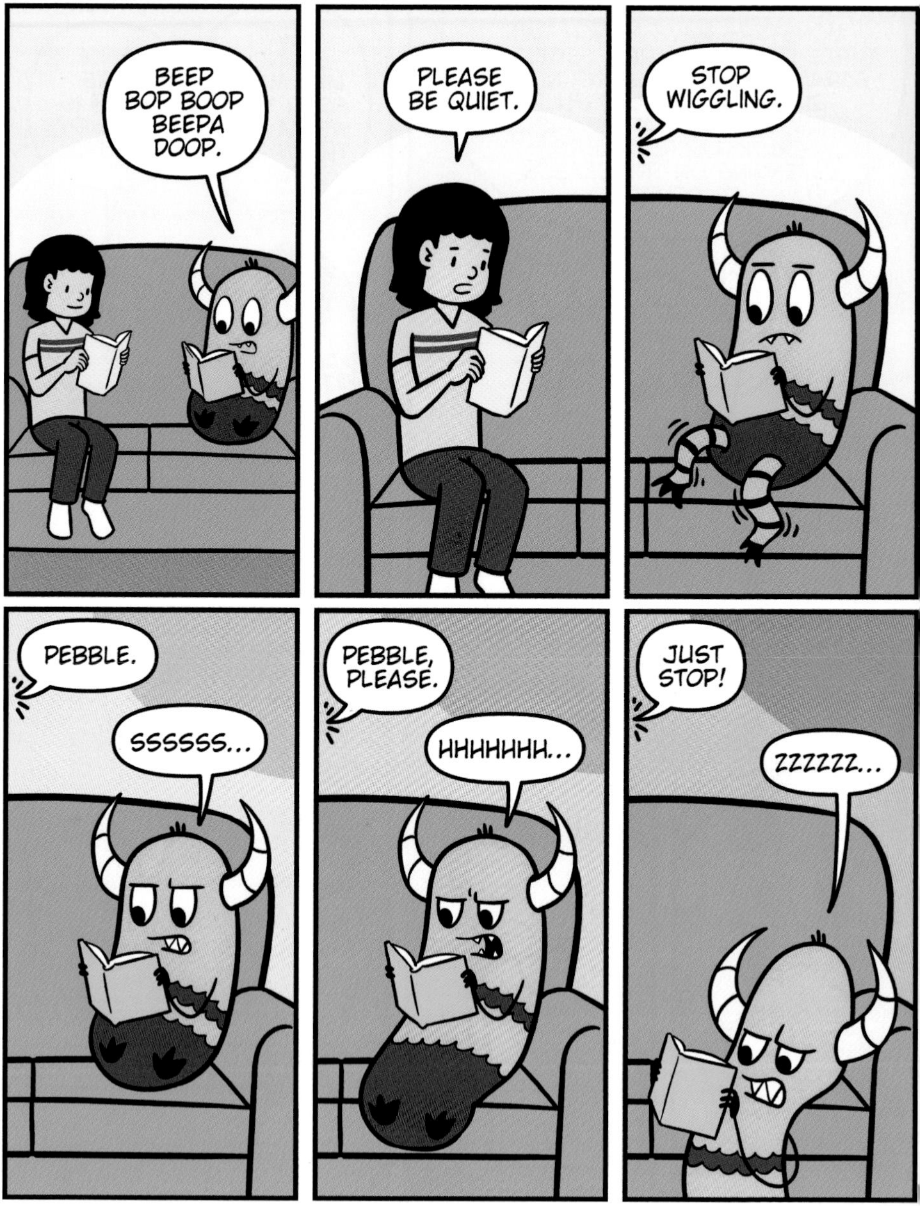
BEEP BOP BOOP BEEPA DOOP.
PLEASE BE QUIET.
STOP WIGGLING.
PEBBLE.
SSSSSS...
PEBBLE, PLEASE.
HHHHHHH...
JUST STOP!
ZZZZZZ...

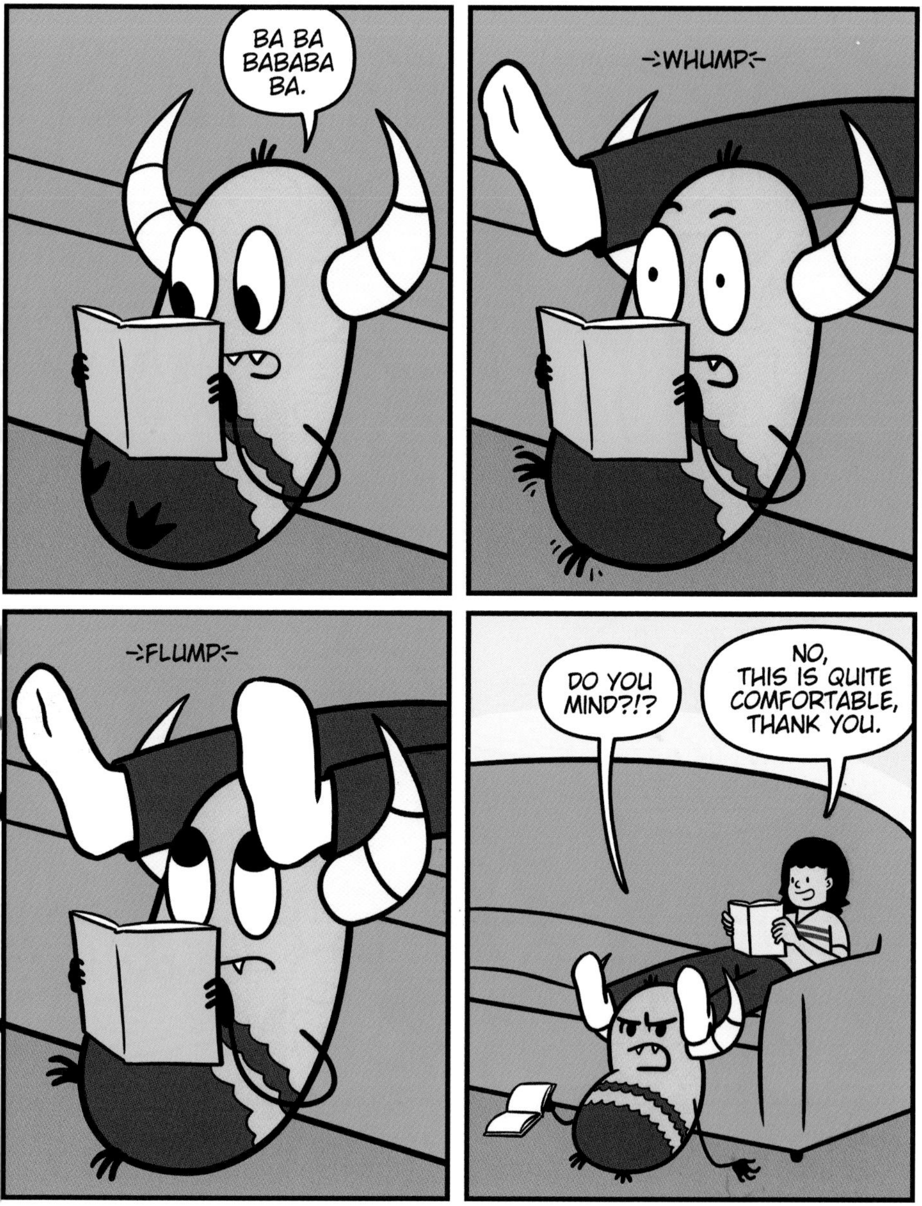
BA BA BABABA BA.
WHUMP
FLUMP
DO YOU MIND?!?
NO, THIS IS QUITE COMFORTABLE, THANK YOU.

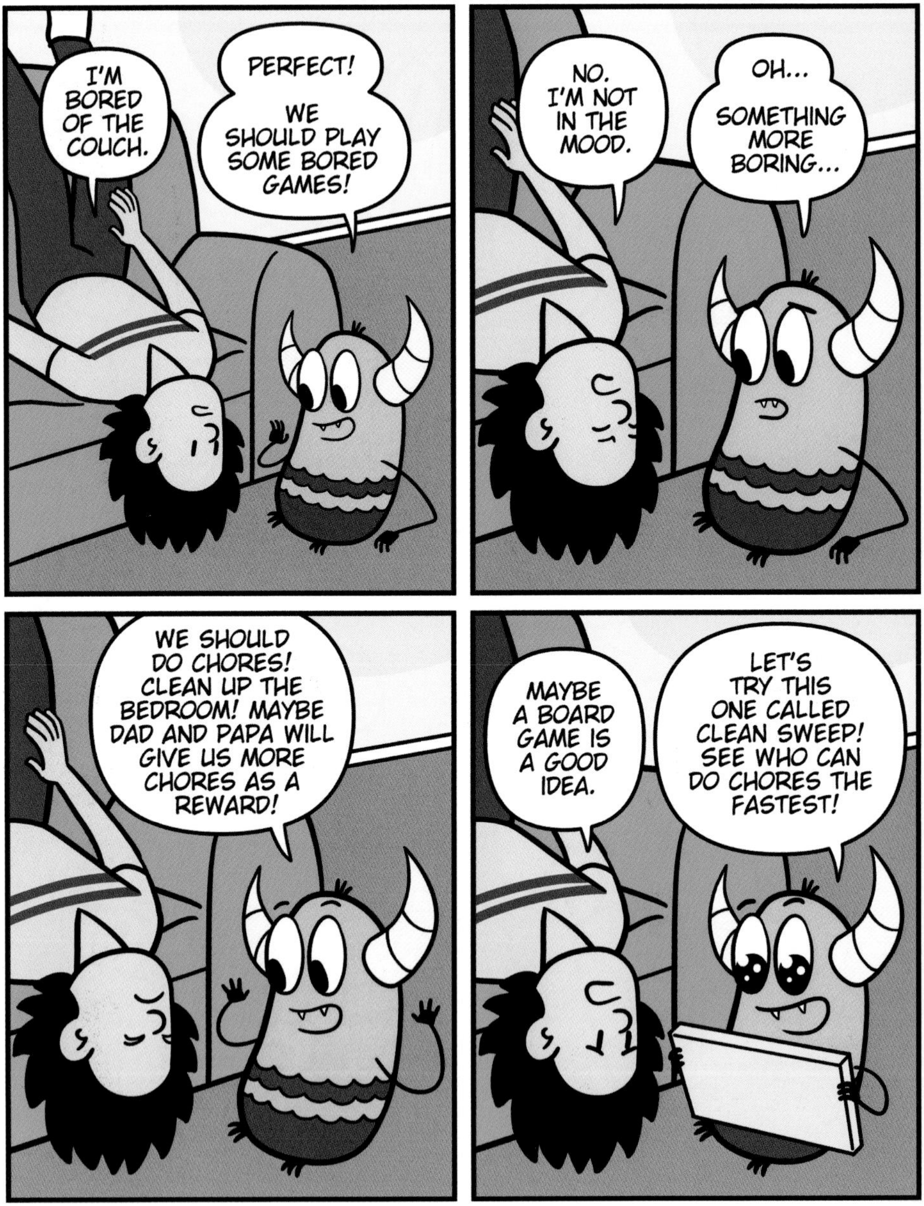
I'M BORED OF THE COUCH.
PERFECT!
WE SHOULD PLAY SOME BORED GAMES!
NO. I'M NOT IN THE MOOD.
OH...
SOMETHING MORE BORING...
WE SHOULD DO CHORES! CLEAN UP THE BEDROOM! MAYBE DAD AND PAPA WILL GIVE US MORE CHORES AS A REWARD!
MAYBE A BOARD GAME IS A GOOD IDEA.
LET'S TRY THIS ONE CALLED CLEAN SWEEP! SEE WHO CAN DO CHORES THE FASTEST!

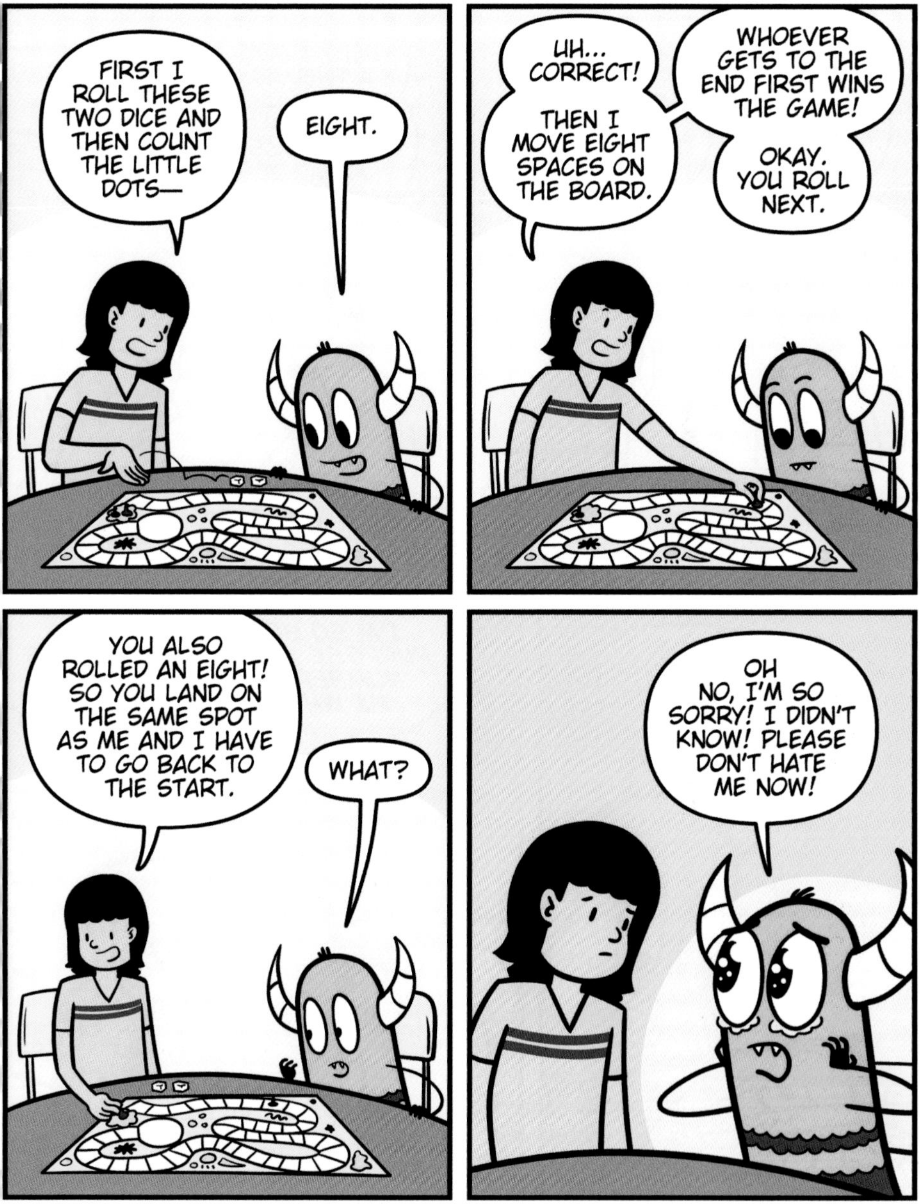
FIRST I ROLL THESE TWO DICE AND THEN COUNT THE LITTLE DOTS—
EIGHT.
UH... CORRECT!
THEN I MOVE EIGHT SPACES ON THE BOARD.
WHOEVER GETS TO THE END FIRST WINS THE GAME!
OKAY. YOU ROLL NEXT.
YOU ALSO ROLLED AN EIGHT! SO YOU LAND ON THE SAME SPOT AS ME AND I HAVE TO GO BACK TO THE START.
WHAT?
OH NO, I'M SO SORRY! I DIDN'T KNOW! PLEASE DON'T HATE ME NOW!

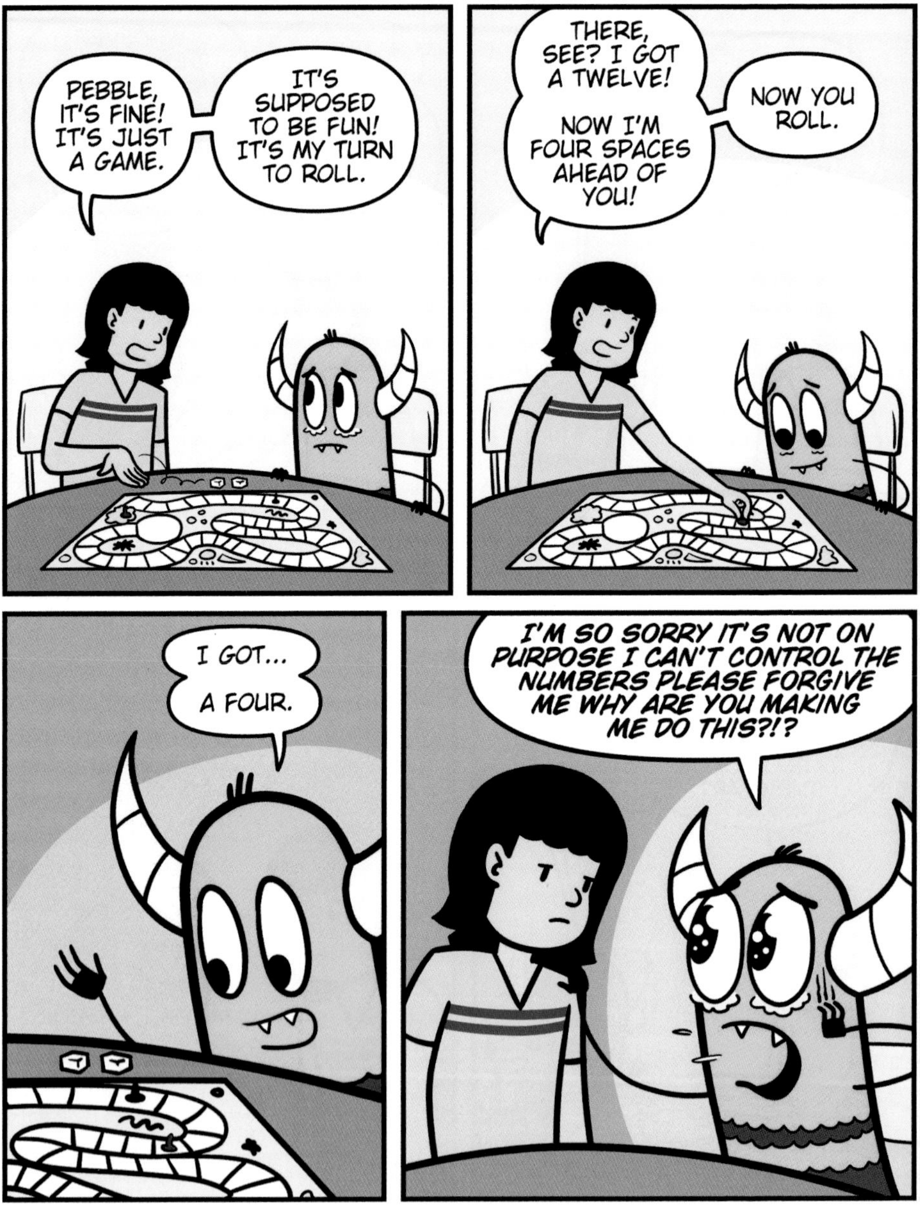
PEBBLE, IT'S FINE! IT'S JUST A GAME.
IT'S SUPPOSED TO BE FUN! IT'S MY TURN TO ROLL.
THERE, SEE? I GOT A TWELVE!
NOW I'M FOUR SPACES AHEAD OF YOU!
NOW YOU ROLL.
I GOT...
A FOUR.
I'M SO SORRY IT'S NOT ON PURPOSE I CAN'T CONTROL THE NUMBERS PLEASE FORGIVE ME WHY ARE YOU MAKING ME DO THIS?!?

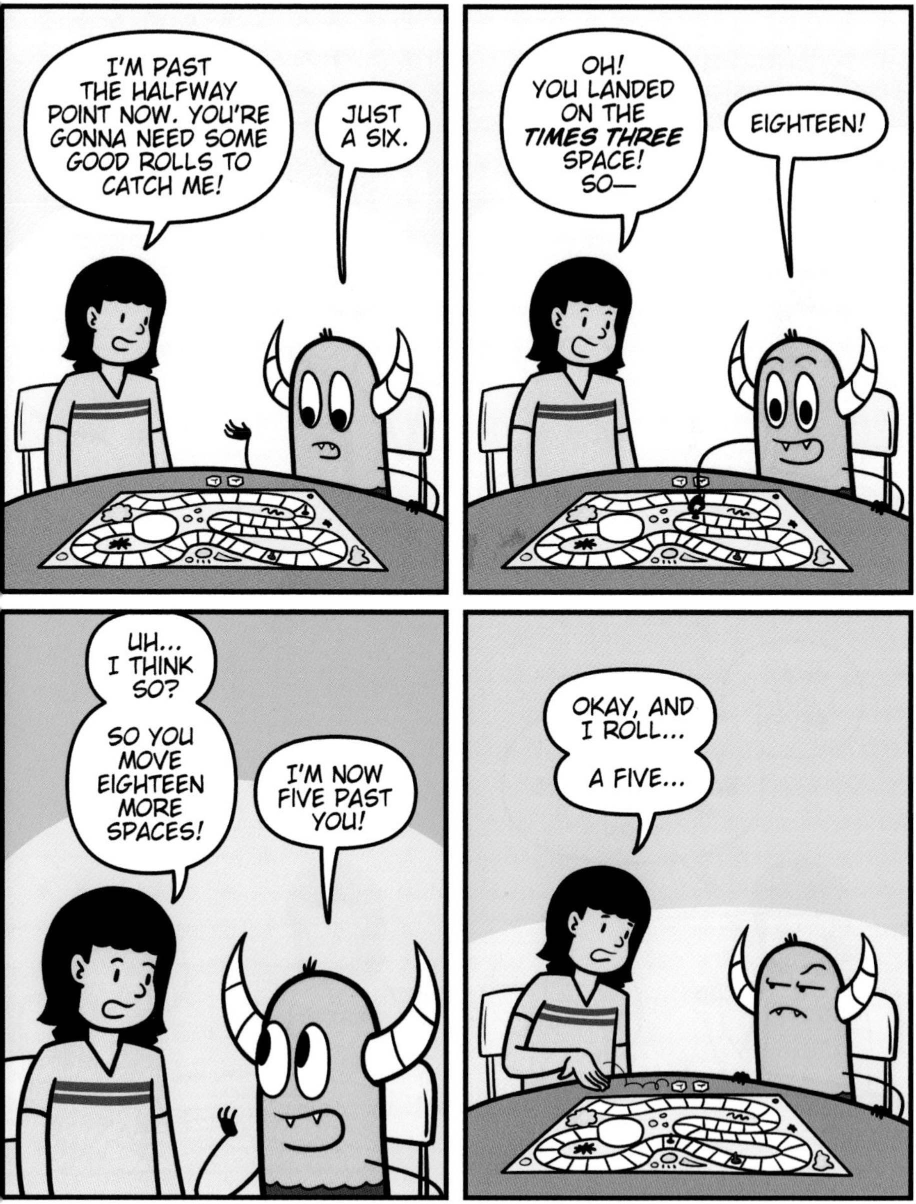
I'M PAST THE HALFWAY POINT NOW. YOU'RE GONNA NEED SOME GOOD ROLLS TO CATCH ME!
JUST A SIX.
OH! YOU LANDED ON THE *TIMES THREE* SPACE! SO—
EIGHTEEN!
UH... I THINK SO?
SO YOU MOVE EIGHTEEN MORE SPACES!
I'M NOW FIVE PAST YOU!
OKAY, AND I ROLL...
A FIVE...

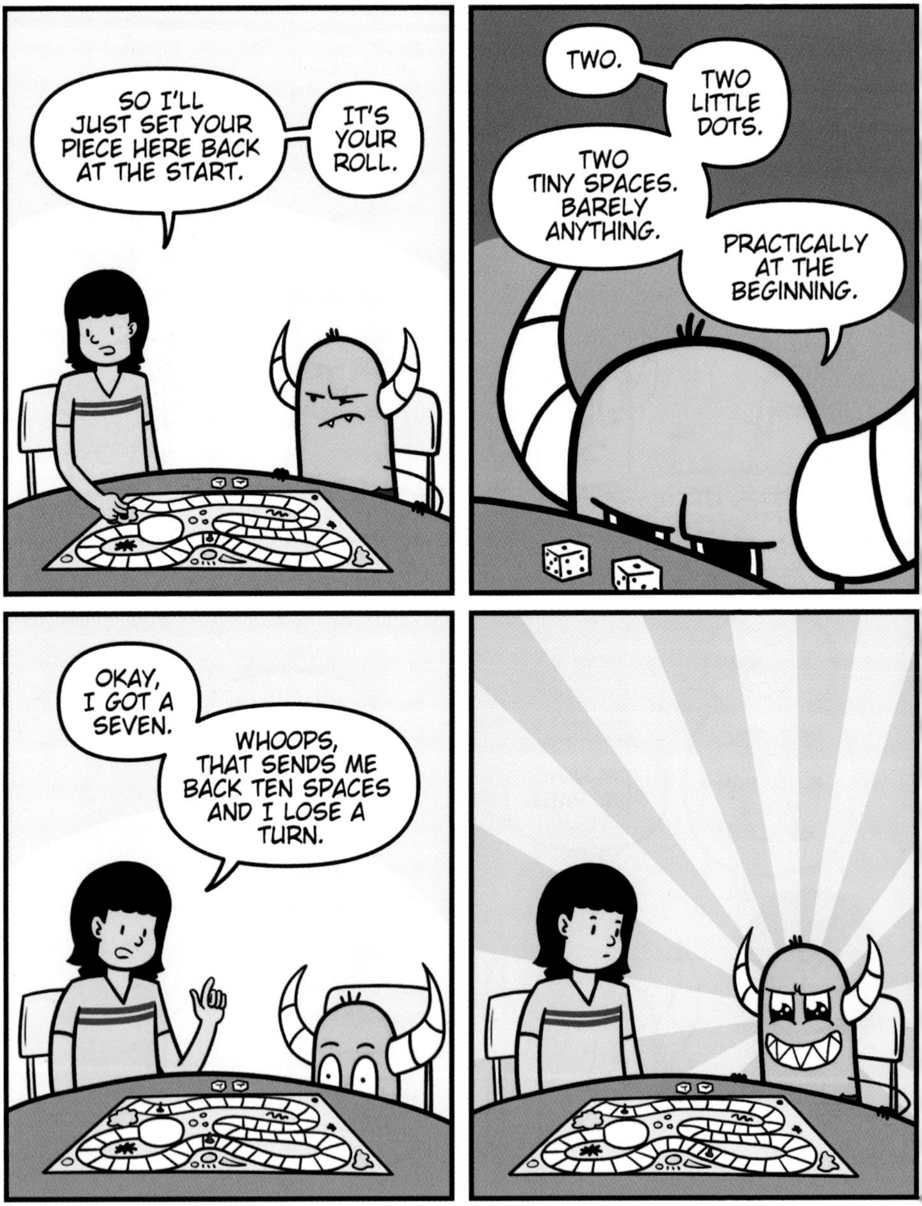
SO I'LL JUST SET YOUR PIECE HERE BACK AT THE START.
IT'S YOUR ROLL.
TWO.
TWO LITTLE DOTS.
TWO TINY SPACES. BARELY ANYTHING.
PRACTICALLY AT THE BEGINNING.
OKAY, I GOT A SEVEN.
WHOOPS, THAT SENDS ME BACK TEN SPACES AND I LOSE A TURN.

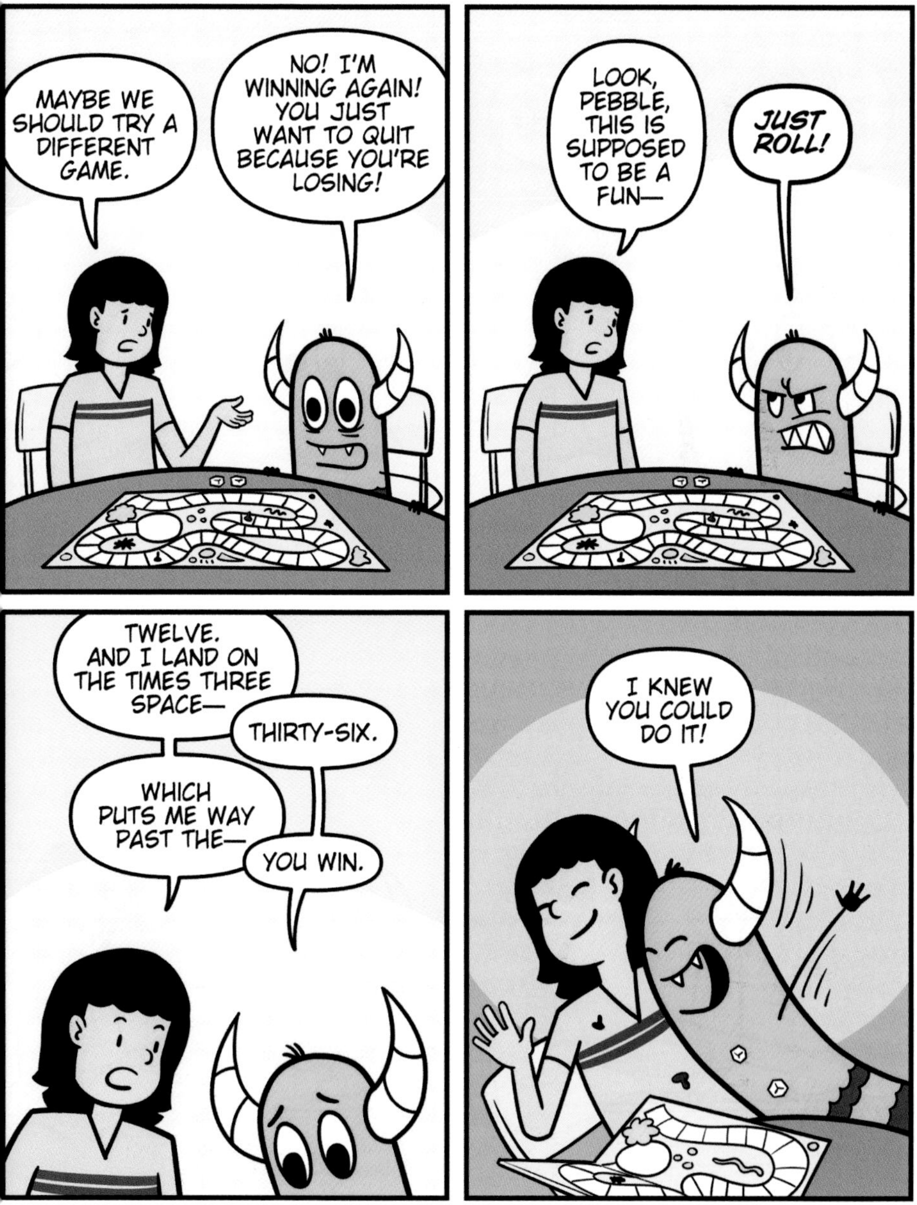
MAYBE WE SHOULD TRY A DIFFERENT GAME.
NO! I'M WINNING AGAIN! YOU JUST WANT TO QUIT BECAUSE YOU'RE LOSING!
LOOK, PEBBLE, THIS IS SUPPOSED TO BE A FUN—
JUST ROLL!
TWELVE. AND I LAND ON THE TIMES THREE SPACE—
THIRTY-SIX.
WHICH PUTS ME WAY PAST THE—
YOU WIN.
I KNEW YOU COULD DO IT!

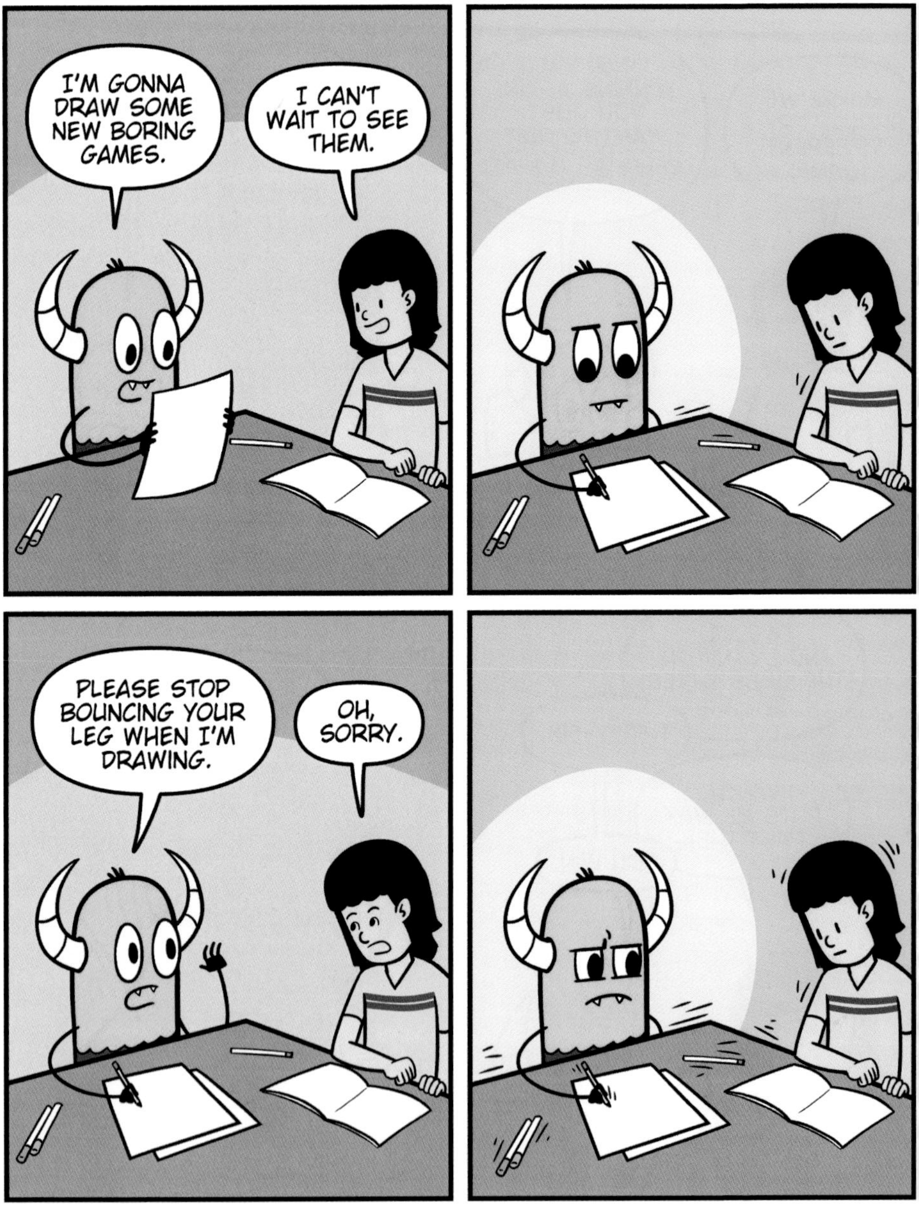
I'M GONNA DRAW SOME NEW BORING GAMES.
I CAN'T WAIT TO SEE THEM.
PLEASE STOP BOUNCING YOUR LEG WHEN I'M DRAWING.
OH, SORRY.

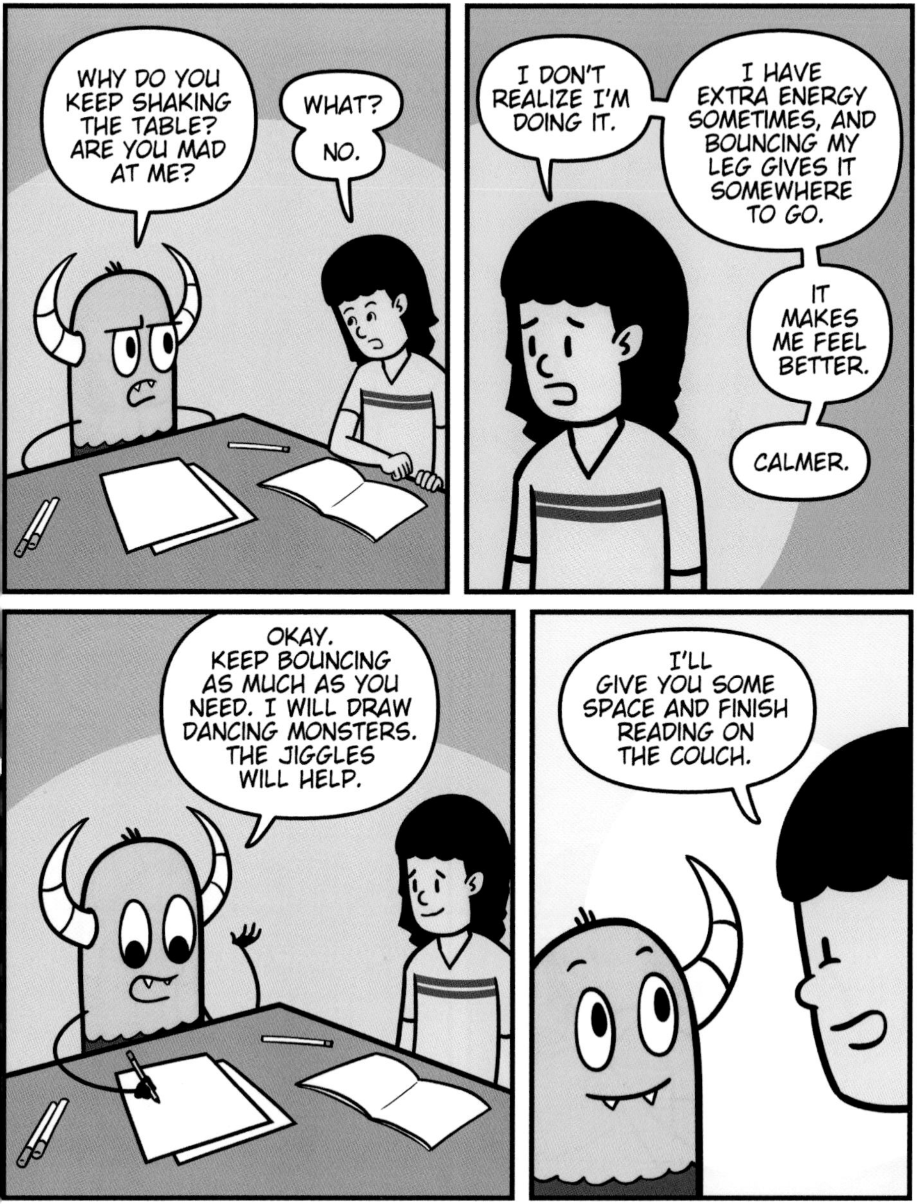
WHY DO YOU KEEP SHAKING THE TABLE? ARE YOU MAD AT ME?
WHAT?
NO.
I DON'T REALIZE I'M DOING IT.
I HAVE EXTRA ENERGY SOMETIMES, AND BOUNCING MY LEG GIVES IT SOMEWHERE TO GO.
IT MAKES ME FEEL BETTER.
CALMER.
OKAY. KEEP BOUNCING AS MUCH AS YOU NEED. I WILL DRAW DANCING MONSTERS. THE JIGGLES WILL HELP.
I'LL GIVE YOU SOME SPACE AND FINISH READING ON THE COUCH.

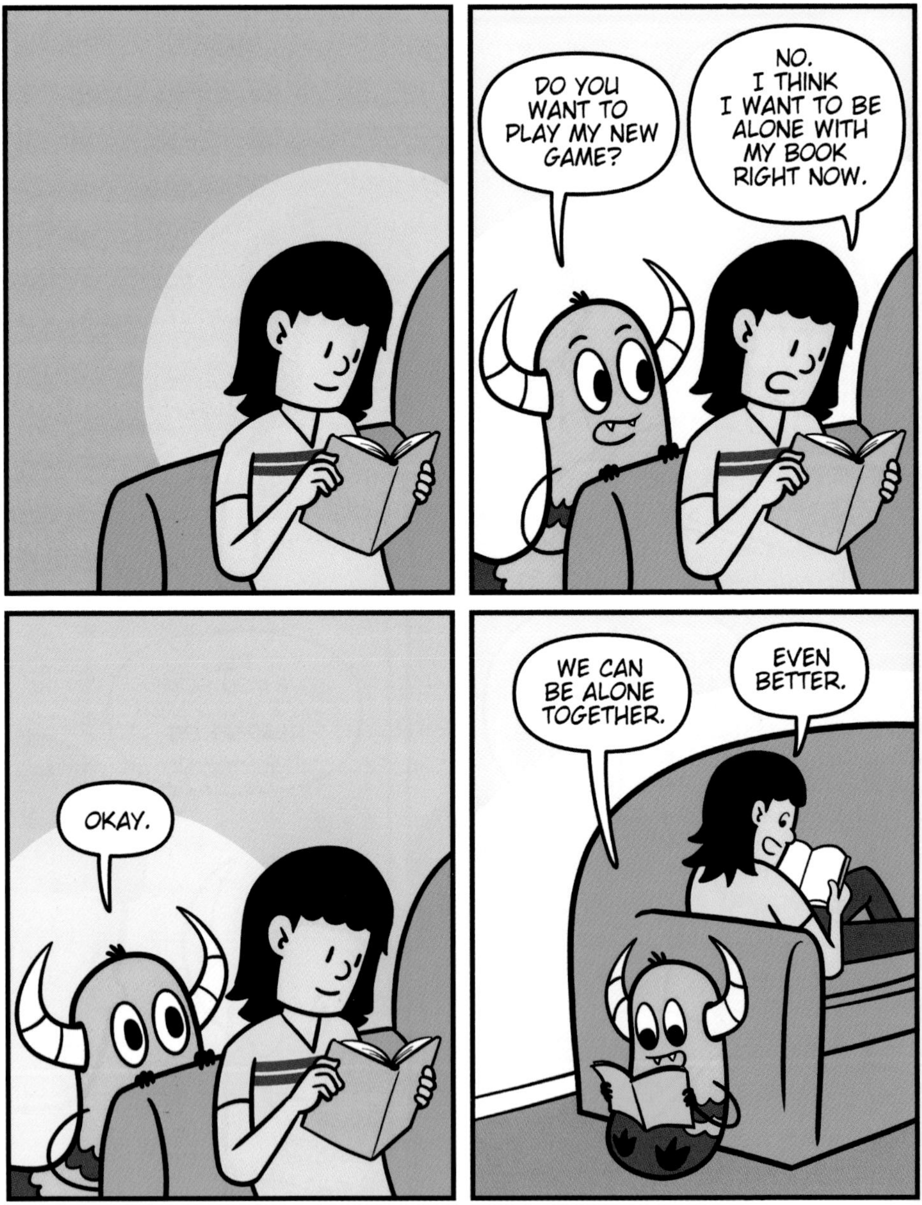
DO YOU WANT TO PLAY MY NEW GAME?
NO. I THINK I WANT TO BE ALONE WITH MY BOOK RIGHT NOW.
OKAY.
WE CAN BE ALONE TOGETHER.
EVEN BETTER.

CHAPTER THREE

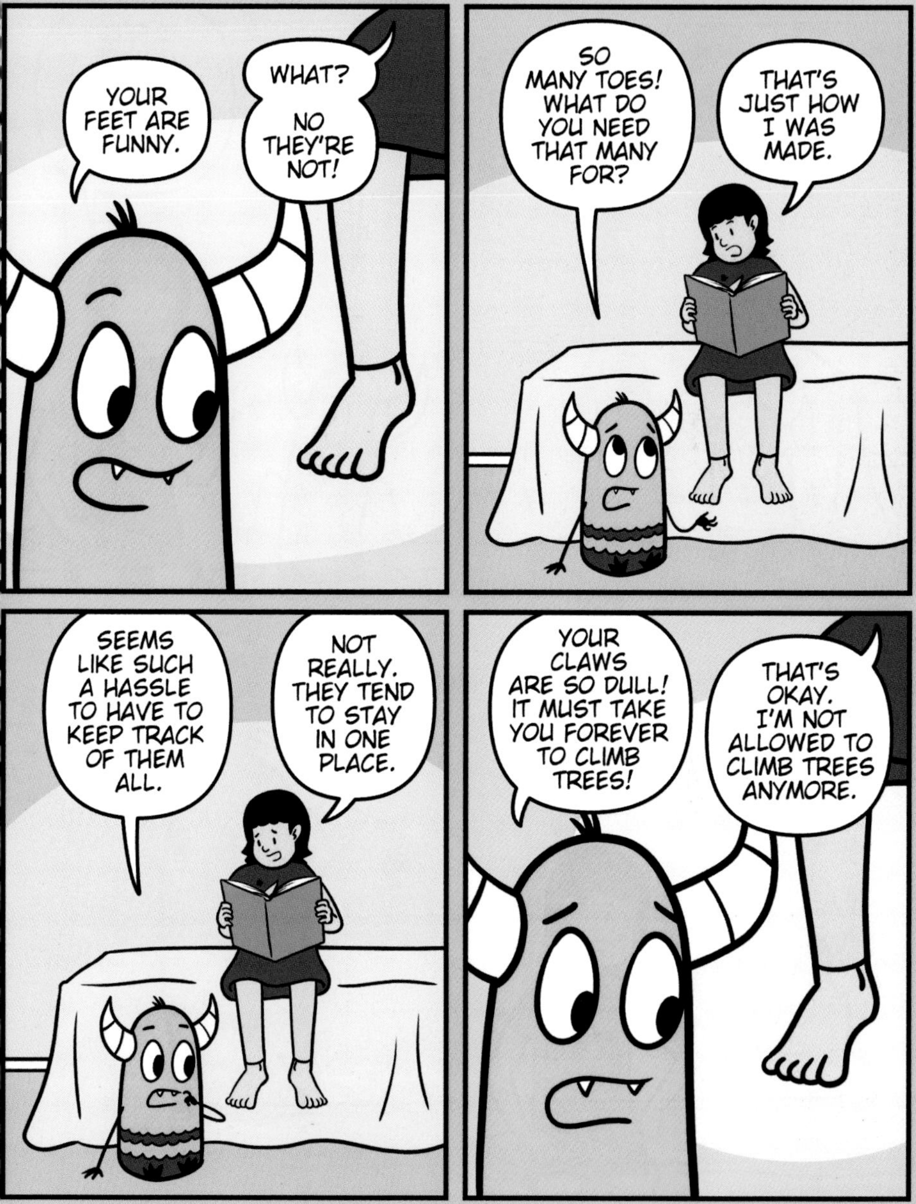

YOUR FEET ARE FUNNY.
WHAT? NO THEY'RE NOT!
SO MANY TOES! WHAT DO YOU NEED THAT MANY FOR?
THAT'S JUST HOW I WAS MADE.
SEEMS LIKE SUCH A HASSLE TO HAVE TO KEEP TRACK OF THEM ALL.
NOT REALLY. THEY TEND TO STAY IN ONE PLACE.
YOUR CLAWS ARE SO DULL! IT MUST TAKE YOU FOREVER TO CLIMB TREES!
THAT'S OKAY. I'M NOT ALLOWED TO CLIMB TREES ANYMORE.

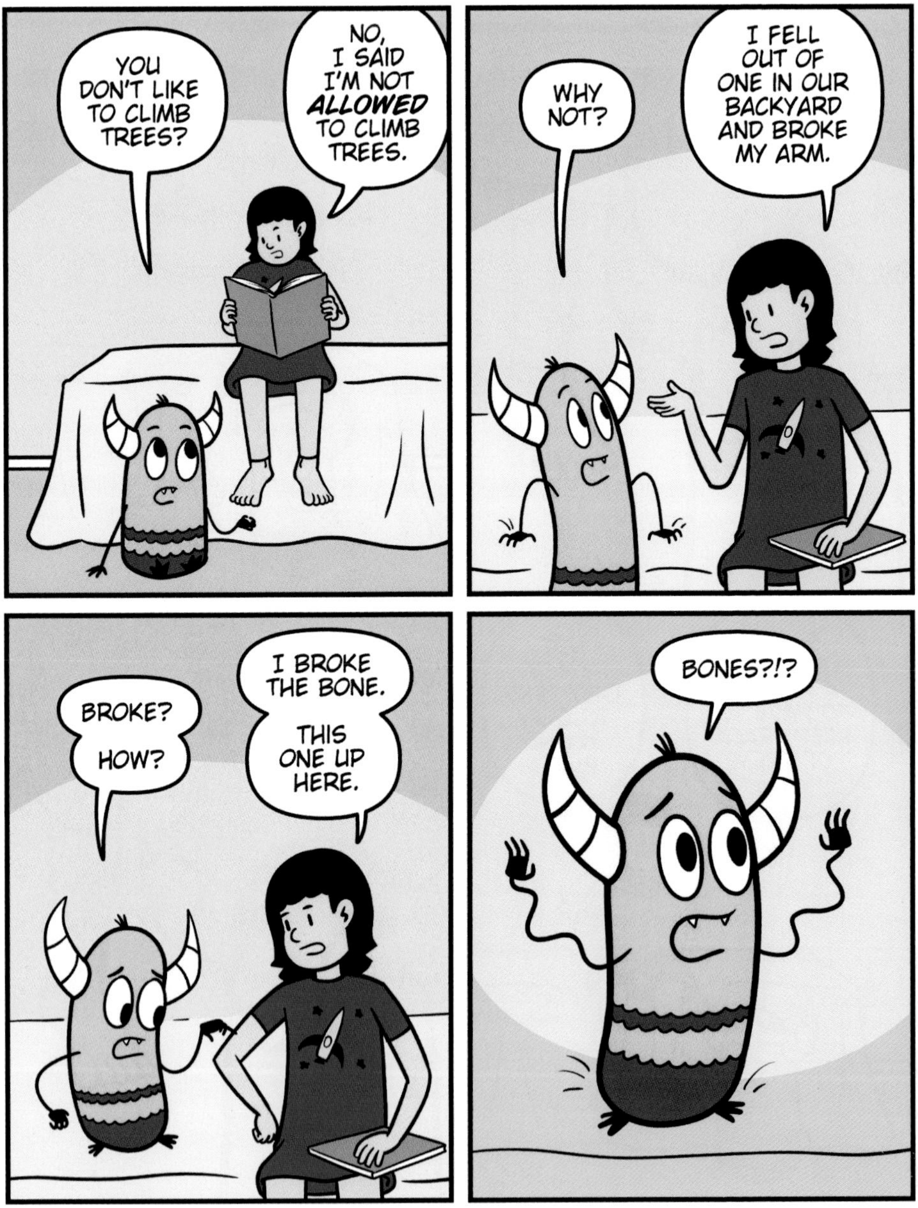
YOU DON'T LIKE TO CLIMB TREES?
NO, I SAID I'M NOT ***ALLOWED*** TO CLIMB TREES.
WHY NOT?
I FELL OUT OF ONE IN OUR BACKYARD AND BROKE MY ARM.
BROKE?
HOW?
I BROKE THE BONE.
THIS ONE UP HERE.
BONES?!?

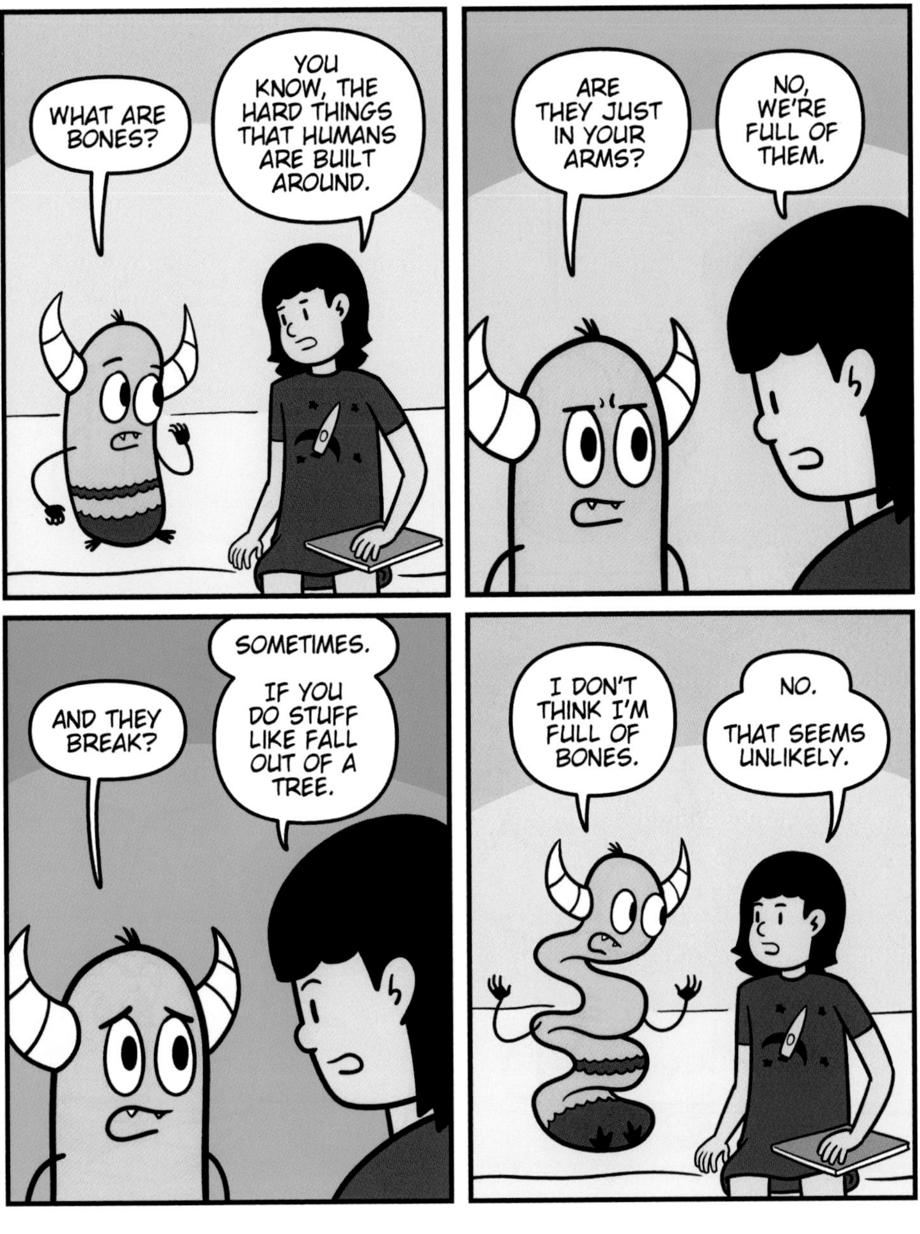
WHAT ARE BONES?
YOU KNOW, THE HARD THINGS THAT HUMANS ARE BUILT AROUND.
ARE THEY JUST IN YOUR ARMS?
NO, WE'RE FULL OF THEM.
AND THEY BREAK?
SOMETIMES.
IF YOU DO STUFF LIKE FALL OUT OF A TREE.
I DON'T THINK I'M FULL OF BONES.
NO.
THAT SEEMS UNLIKELY.

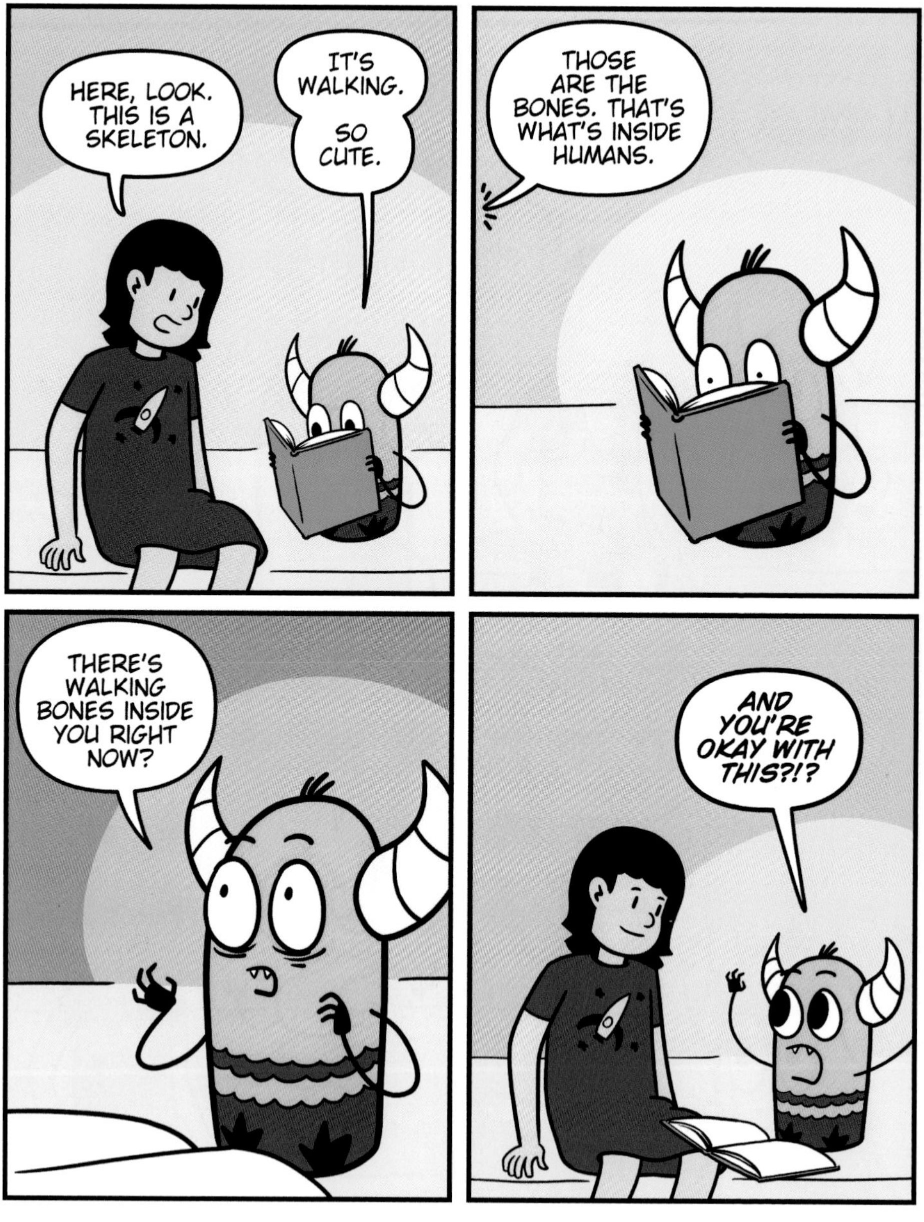
HERE, LOOK. THIS IS A SKELETON.
IT'S WALKING.
SO CUTE.
THOSE ARE THE BONES. THAT'S WHAT'S INSIDE HUMANS.
THERE'S WALKING BONES INSIDE YOU RIGHT NOW?
AND YOU'RE OKAY WITH THIS?!?

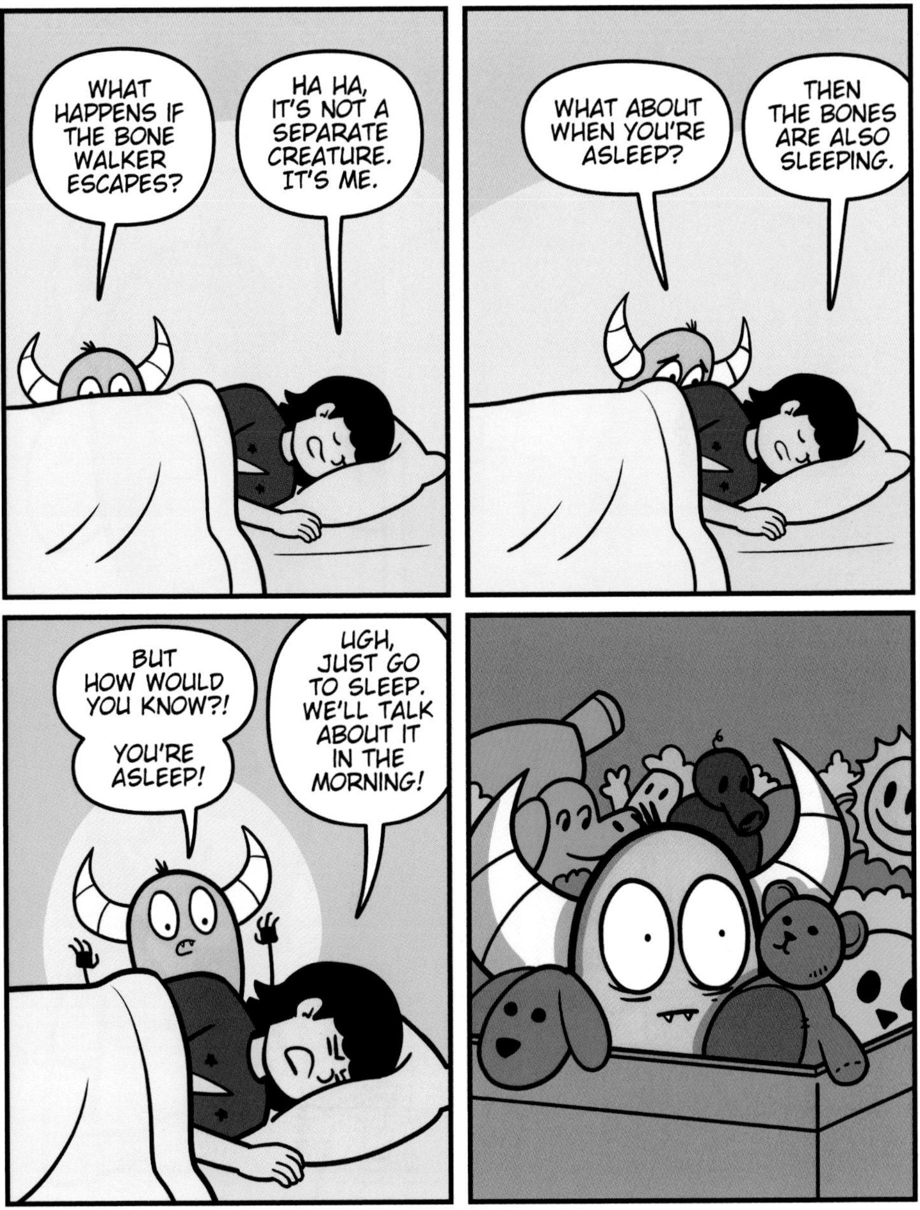
WHAT HAPPENS IF THE BONE WALKER ESCAPES?
HA HA, IT'S NOT A SEPARATE CREATURE. IT'S ME.
WHAT ABOUT WHEN YOU'RE ASLEEP?
THEN THE BONES ARE ALSO SLEEPING.
BUT HOW WOULD YOU KNOW?!
YOU'RE ASLEEP!
UGH, JUST GO TO SLEEP. WE'LL TALK ABOUT IT IN THE MORNING!

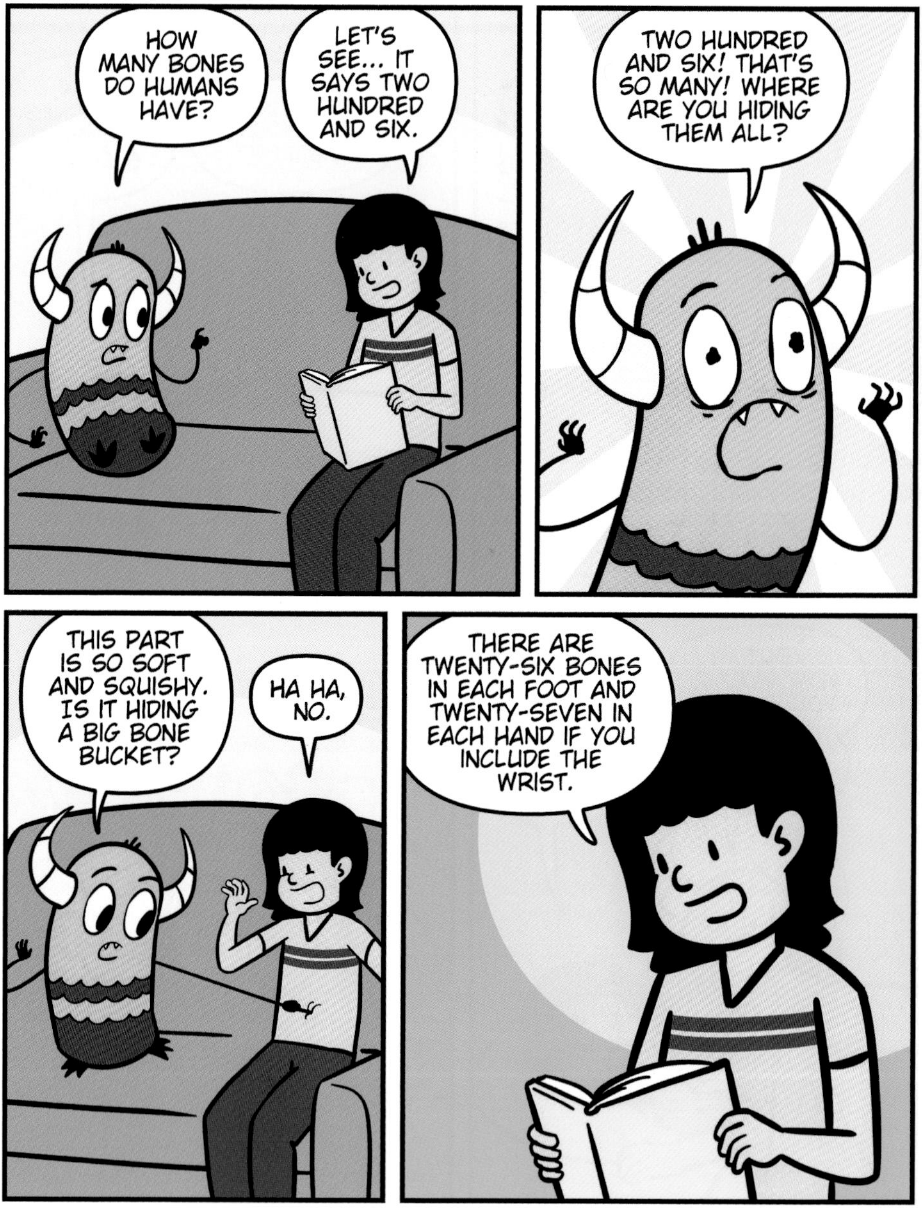
HOW MANY BONES DO HUMANS HAVE?
LET'S SEE... IT SAYS TWO HUNDRED AND SIX.
TWO HUNDRED AND SIX! THAT'S SO MANY! WHERE ARE YOU HIDING THEM ALL?
THIS PART IS SO SOFT AND SQUISHY. IS IT HIDING A BIG BONE BUCKET?
HA HA, NO.
THERE ARE TWENTY-SIX BONES IN EACH FOOT AND TWENTY-SEVEN IN EACH HAND IF YOU INCLUDE THE WRIST.

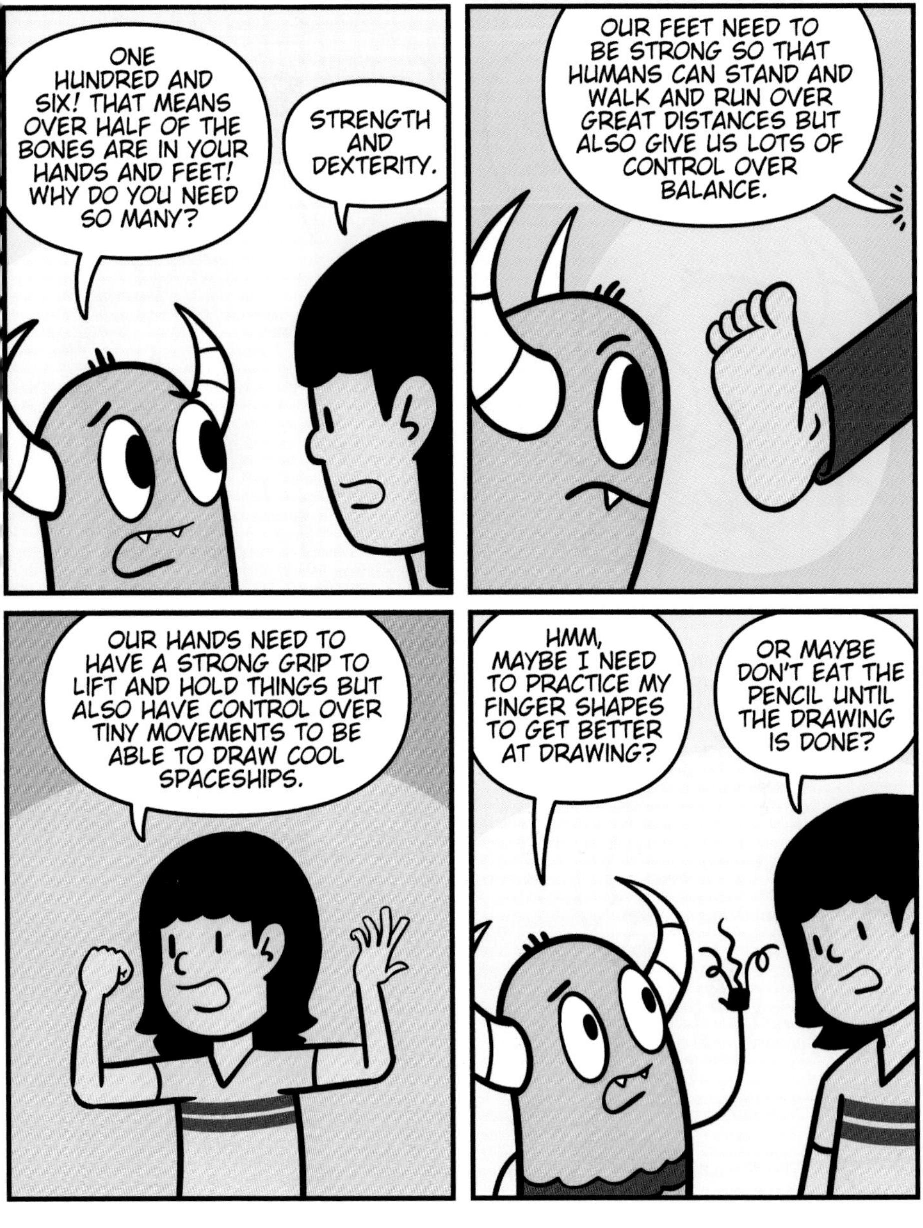
ONE HUNDRED AND SIX! THAT MEANS OVER HALF OF THE BONES ARE IN YOUR HANDS AND FEET! WHY DO YOU NEED SO MANY?
STRENGTH AND DEXTERITY.
OUR FEET NEED TO BE STRONG SO THAT HUMANS CAN STAND AND WALK AND RUN OVER GREAT DISTANCES BUT ALSO GIVE US LOTS OF CONTROL OVER BALANCE.
OUR HANDS NEED TO HAVE A STRONG GRIP TO LIFT AND HOLD THINGS BUT ALSO HAVE CONTROL OVER TINY MOVEMENTS TO BE ABLE TO DRAW COOL SPACESHIPS.
HMM, MAYBE I NEED TO PRACTICE MY FINGER SHAPES TO GET BETTER AT DRAWING?
OR MAYBE DON'T EAT THE PENCIL UNTIL THE DRAWING IS DONE?

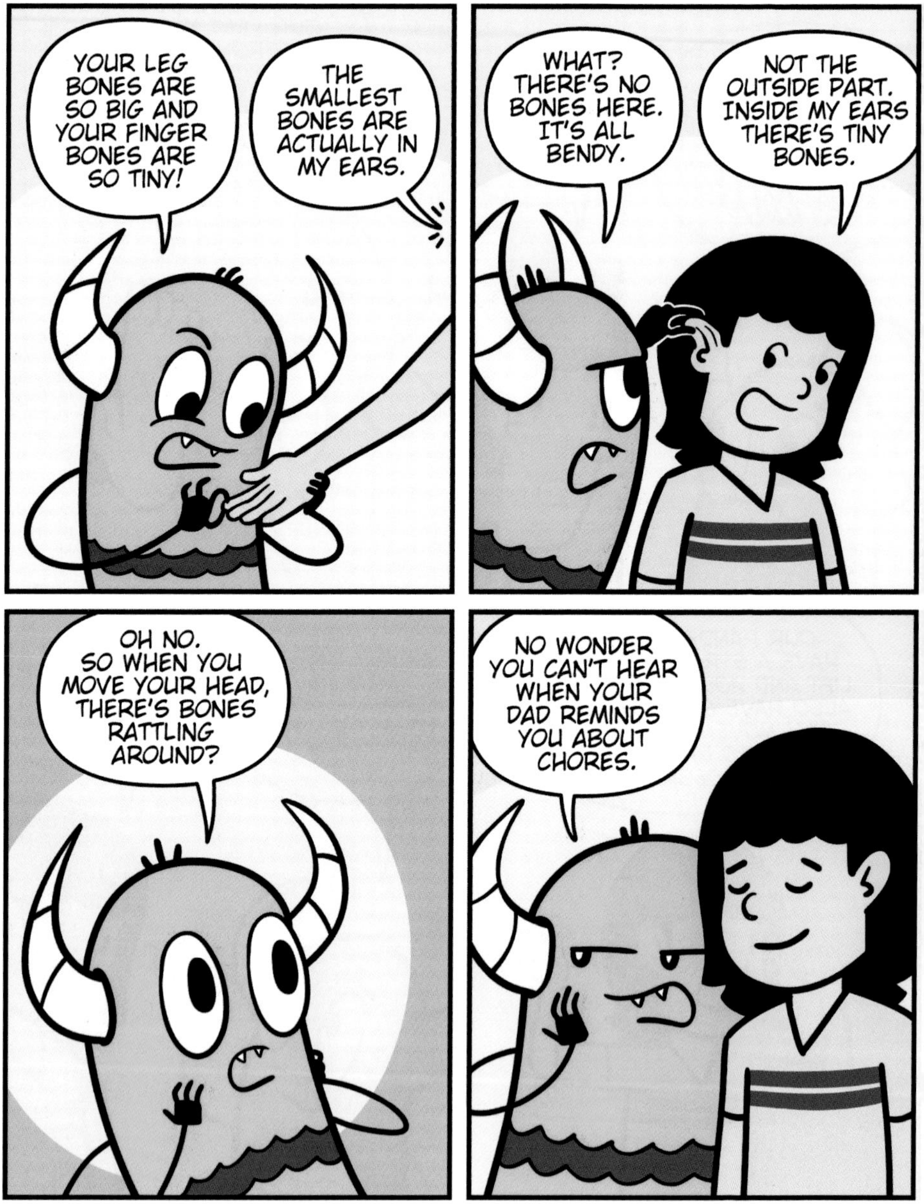
YOUR LEG BONES ARE SO BIG AND YOUR FINGER BONES ARE SO TINY!
THE SMALLEST BONES ARE ACTUALLY IN MY EARS.
WHAT? THERE'S NO BONES HERE. IT'S ALL BENDY.
NOT THE OUTSIDE PART. INSIDE MY EARS THERE'S TINY BONES.
OH NO. SO WHEN YOU MOVE YOUR HEAD, THERE'S BONES RATTLING AROUND?
NO WONDER YOU CAN'T HEAR WHEN YOUR DAD REMINDS YOU ABOUT CHORES.

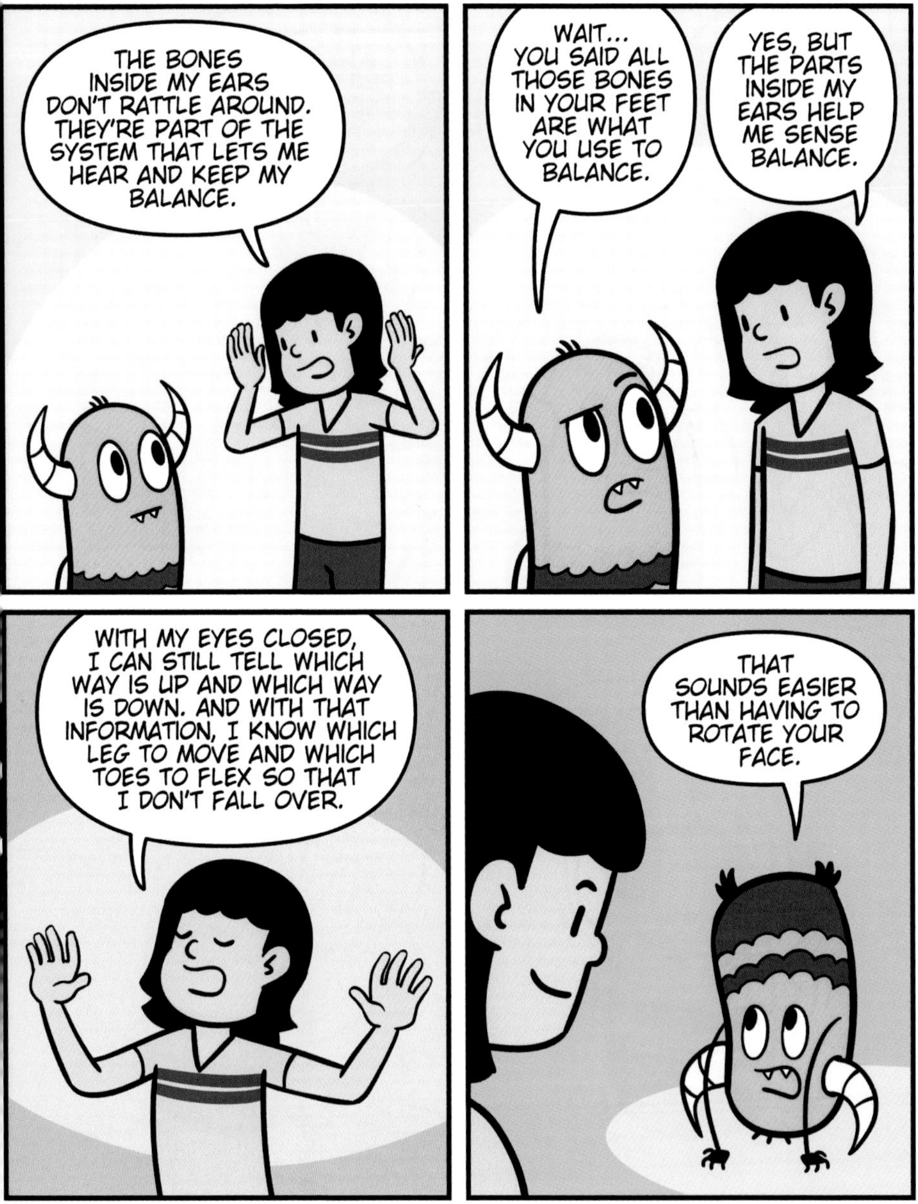
THE BONES INSIDE MY EARS DON'T RATTLE AROUND. THEY'RE PART OF THE SYSTEM THAT LETS ME HEAR AND KEEP MY BALANCE.
WAIT... YOU SAID ALL THOSE BONES IN YOUR FEET ARE WHAT YOU USE TO BALANCE.
YES, BUT THE PARTS INSIDE MY EARS HELP ME SENSE BALANCE.
WITH MY EYES CLOSED, I CAN STILL TELL WHICH WAY IS UP AND WHICH WAY IS DOWN. AND WITH THAT INFORMATION, I KNOW WHICH LEG TO MOVE AND WHICH TOES TO FLEX SO THAT I DON'T FALL OVER.
THAT SOUNDS EASIER THAN HAVING TO ROTATE YOUR FACE.

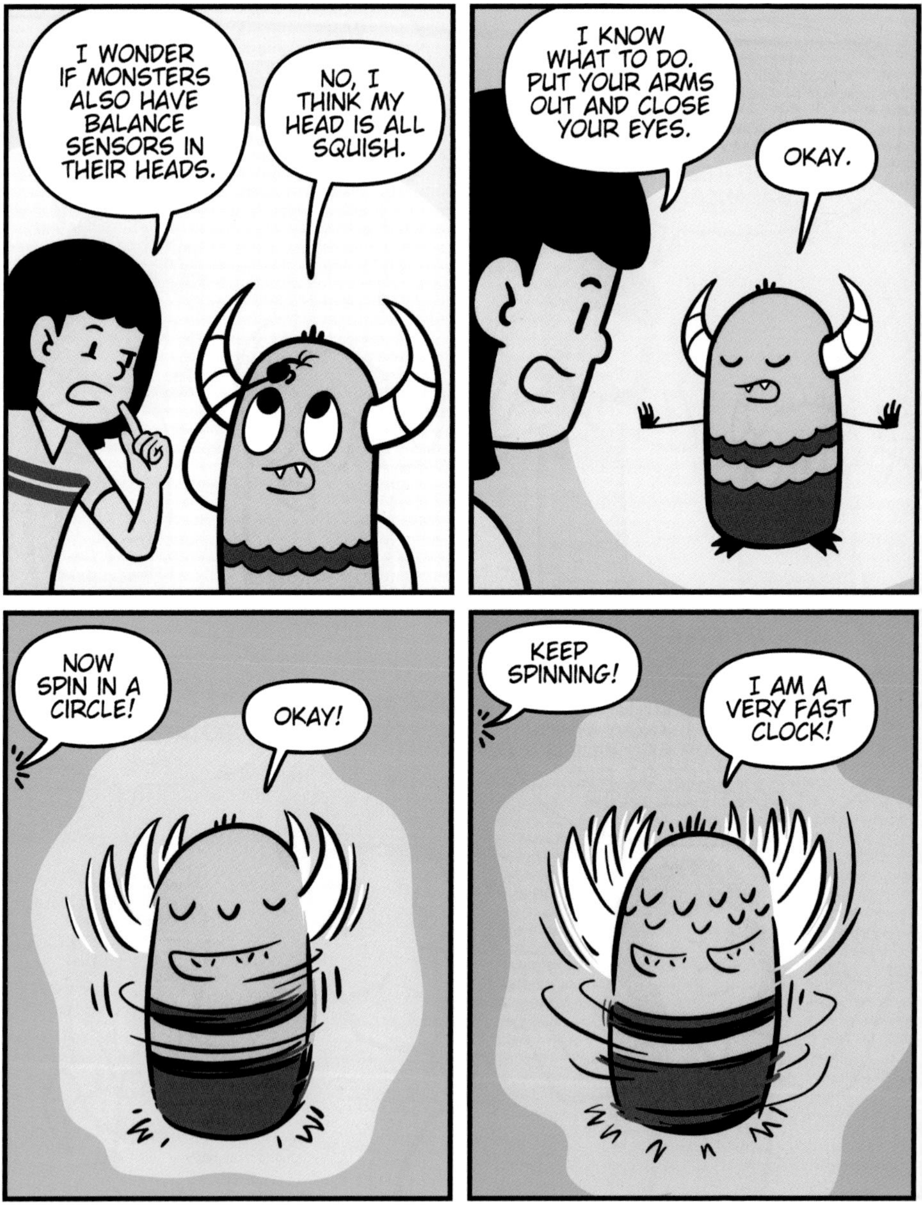
I WONDER IF MONSTERS ALSO HAVE BALANCE SENSORS IN THEIR HEADS.
NO, I THINK MY HEAD IS ALL SQUISH.
I KNOW WHAT TO DO. PUT YOUR ARMS OUT AND CLOSE YOUR EYES.
OKAY.
NOW SPIN IN A CIRCLE!
OKAY!
KEEP SPINNING!
I AM A VERY FAST CLOCK!

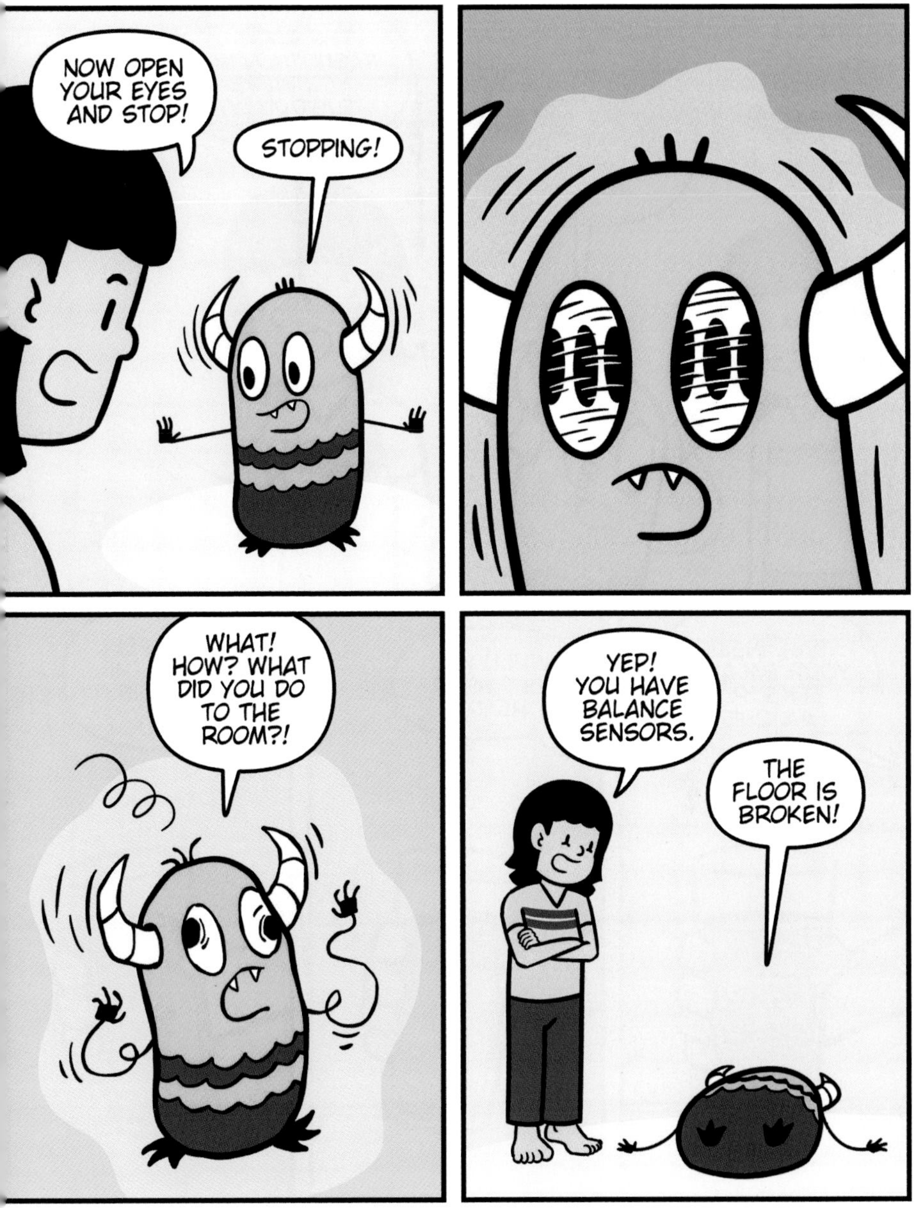
NOW OPEN YOUR EYES AND STOP!
STOPPING!
WHAT! HOW? WHAT DID YOU DO TO THE ROOM?!
YEP! YOU HAVE BALANCE SENSORS.
THE FLOOR IS BROKEN!

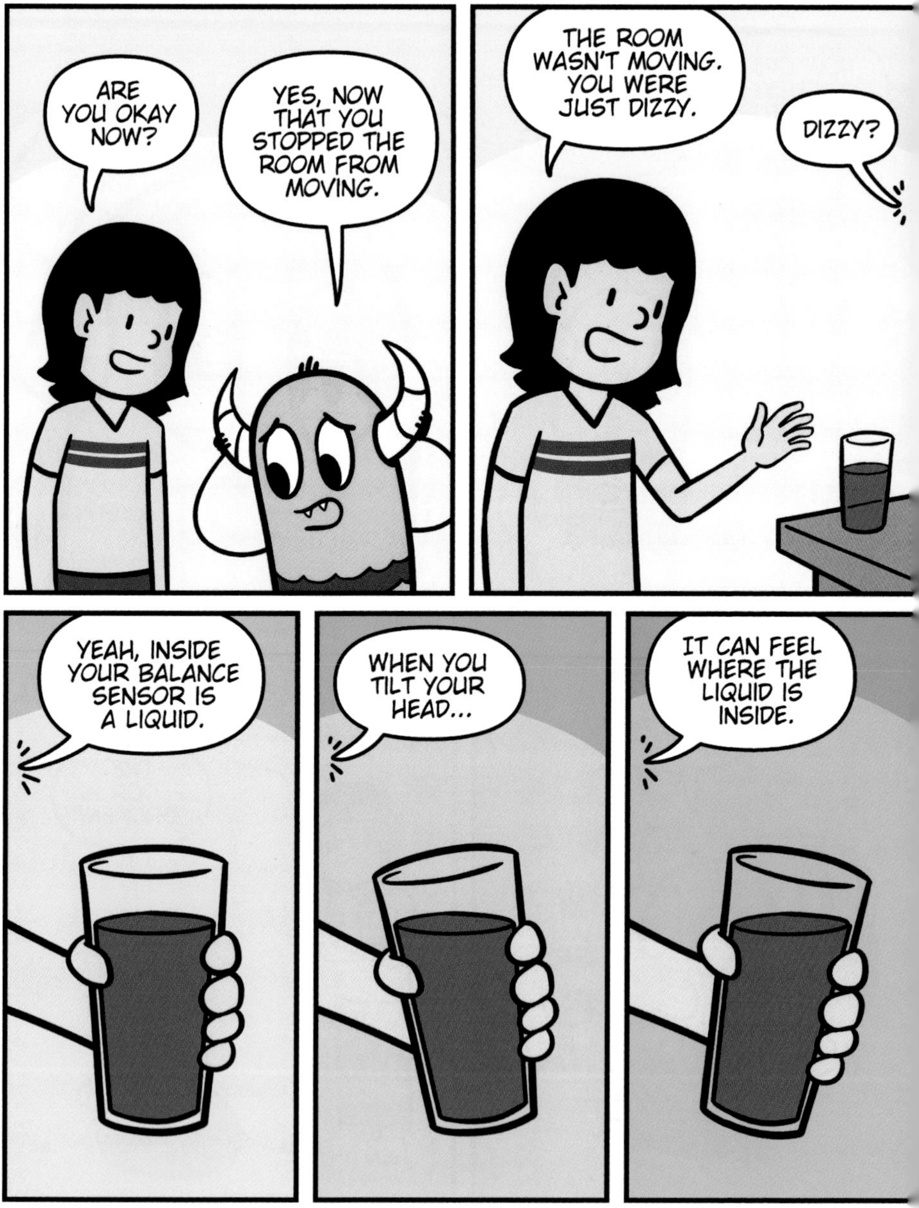
ARE YOU OKAY NOW?
YES, NOW THAT YOU STOPPED THE ROOM FROM MOVING.
THE ROOM WASN'T MOVING. YOU WERE JUST DIZZY.
DIZZY?
YEAH, INSIDE YOUR BALANCE SENSOR IS A LIQUID.
WHEN YOU TILT YOUR HEAD...
IT CAN FEEL WHERE THE LIQUID IS INSIDE.

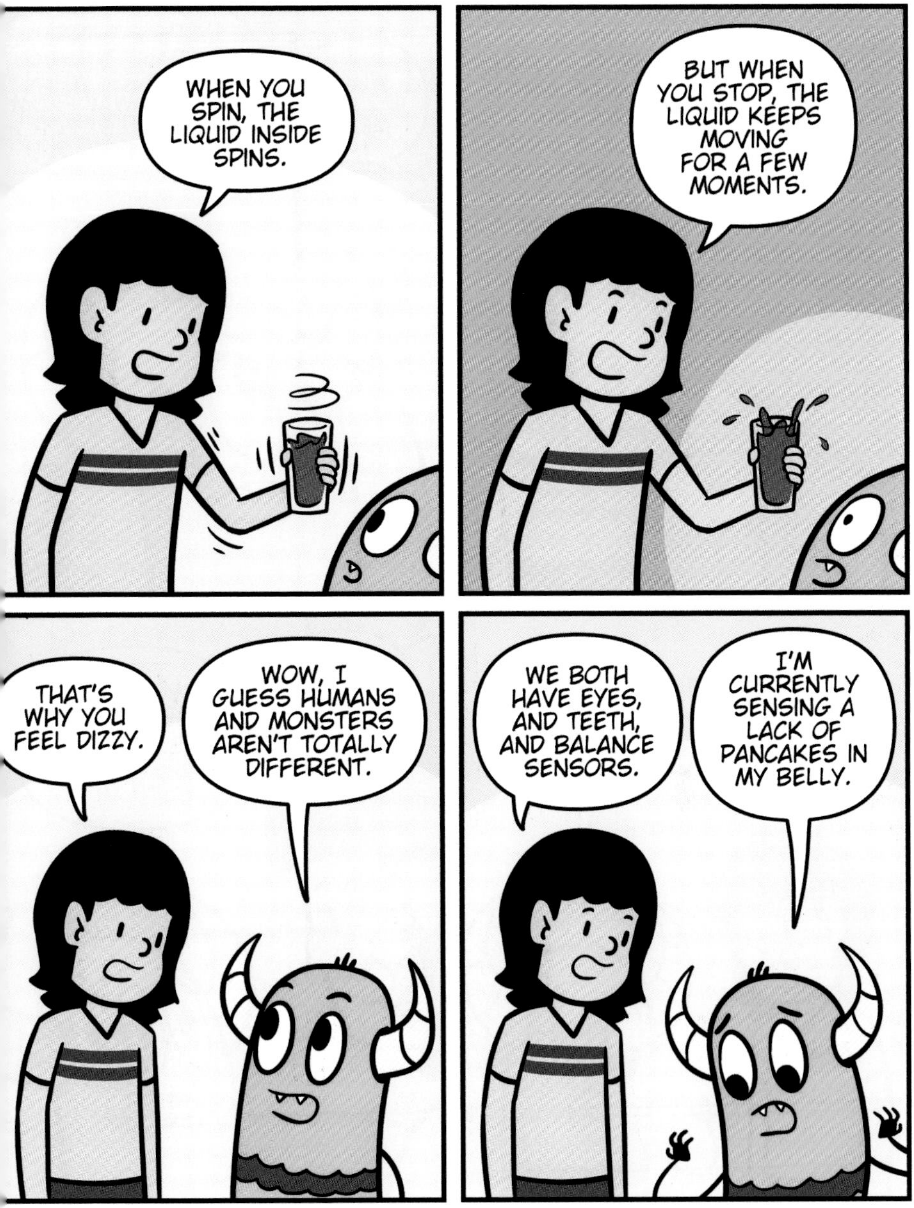
WHEN YOU SPIN, THE LIQUID INSIDE SPINS.
BUT WHEN YOU STOP, THE LIQUID KEEPS MOVING FOR A FEW MOMENTS.
THAT'S WHY YOU FEEL DIZZY.
WOW, I GUESS HUMANS AND MONSTERS AREN'T TOTALLY DIFFERENT.
WE BOTH HAVE EYES, AND TEETH, AND BALANCE SENSORS.
I'M CURRENTLY SENSING A LACK OF PANCAKES IN MY BELLY.

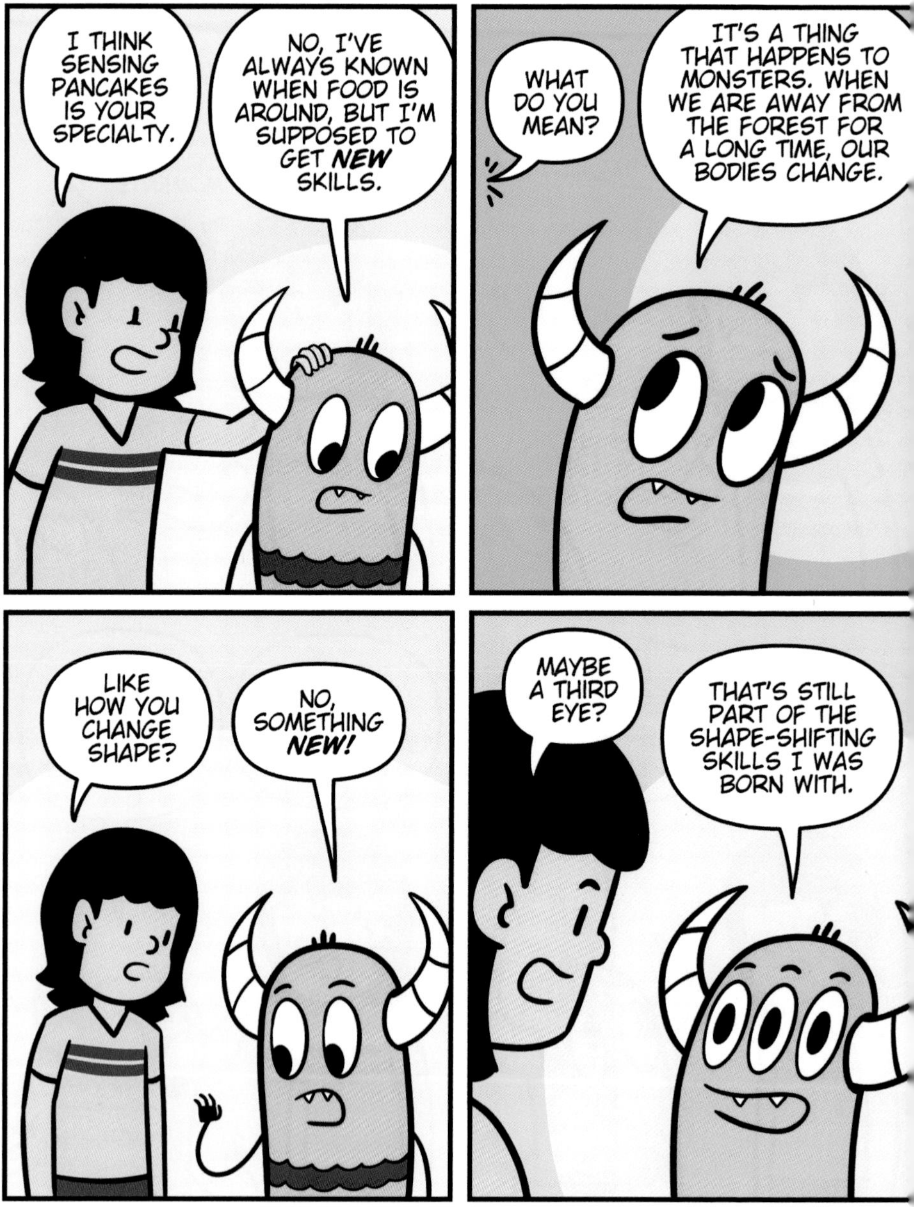
I THINK SENSING PANCAKES IS YOUR SPECIALTY.
NO, I'VE ALWAYS KNOWN WHEN FOOD IS AROUND, BUT I'M SUPPOSED TO GET **NEW** SKILLS.
WHAT DO YOU MEAN?
IT'S A THING THAT HAPPENS TO MONSTERS. WHEN WE ARE AWAY FROM THE FOREST FOR A LONG TIME, OUR BODIES CHANGE.
LIKE HOW YOU CHANGE SHAPE?
NO, SOMETHING **NEW!**
MAYBE A THIRD EYE?
THAT'S STILL PART OF THE SHAPE-SHIFTING SKILLS I WAS BORN WITH.

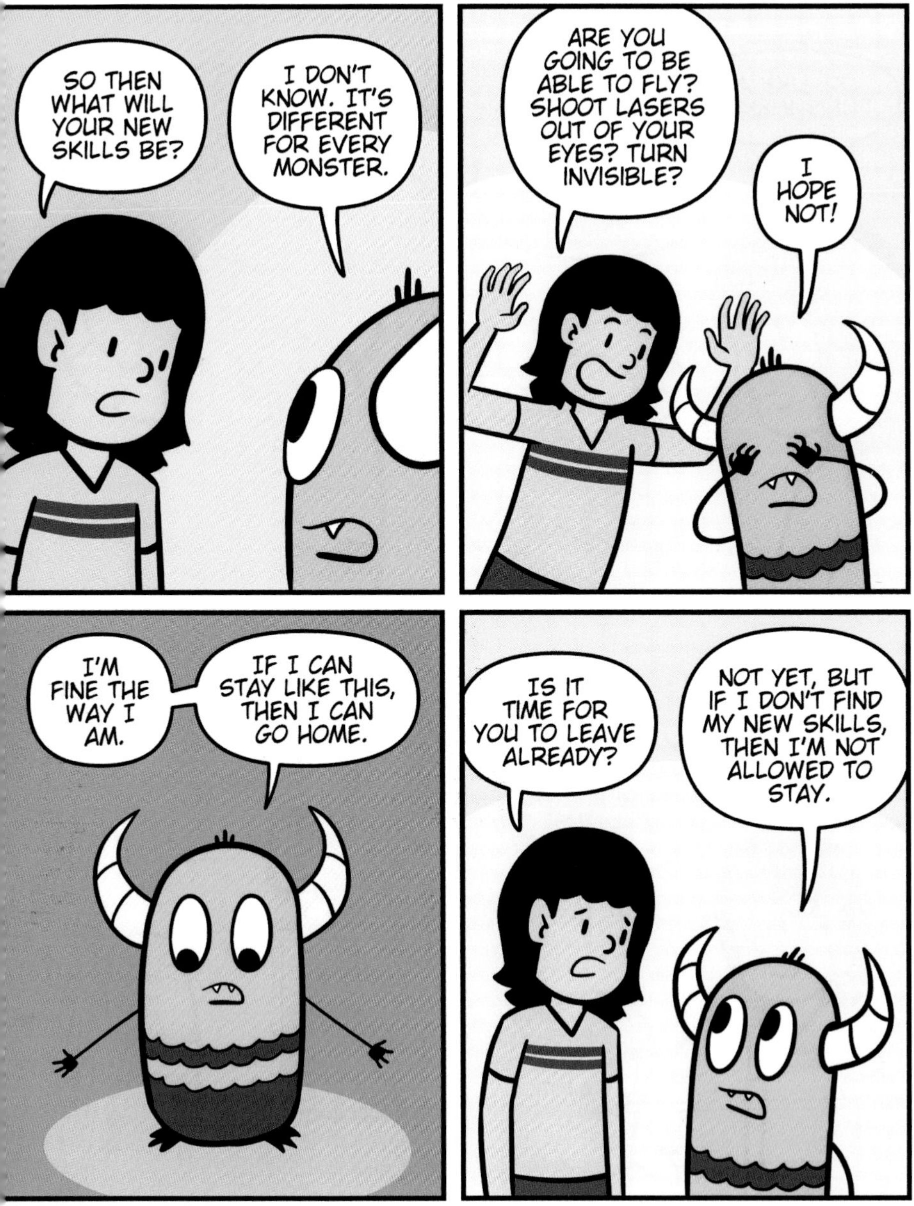
SO THEN WHAT WILL YOUR NEW SKILLS BE?
I DON'T KNOW. IT'S DIFFERENT FOR EVERY MONSTER.
ARE YOU GOING TO BE ABLE TO FLY? SHOOT LASERS OUT OF YOUR EYES? TURN INVISIBLE?
I HOPE NOT!
I'M FINE THE WAY I AM.
IF I CAN STAY LIKE THIS, THEN I CAN GO HOME.
IS IT TIME FOR YOU TO LEAVE ALREADY?
NOT YET, BUT IF I DON'T FIND MY NEW SKILLS, THEN I'M NOT ALLOWED TO STAY.

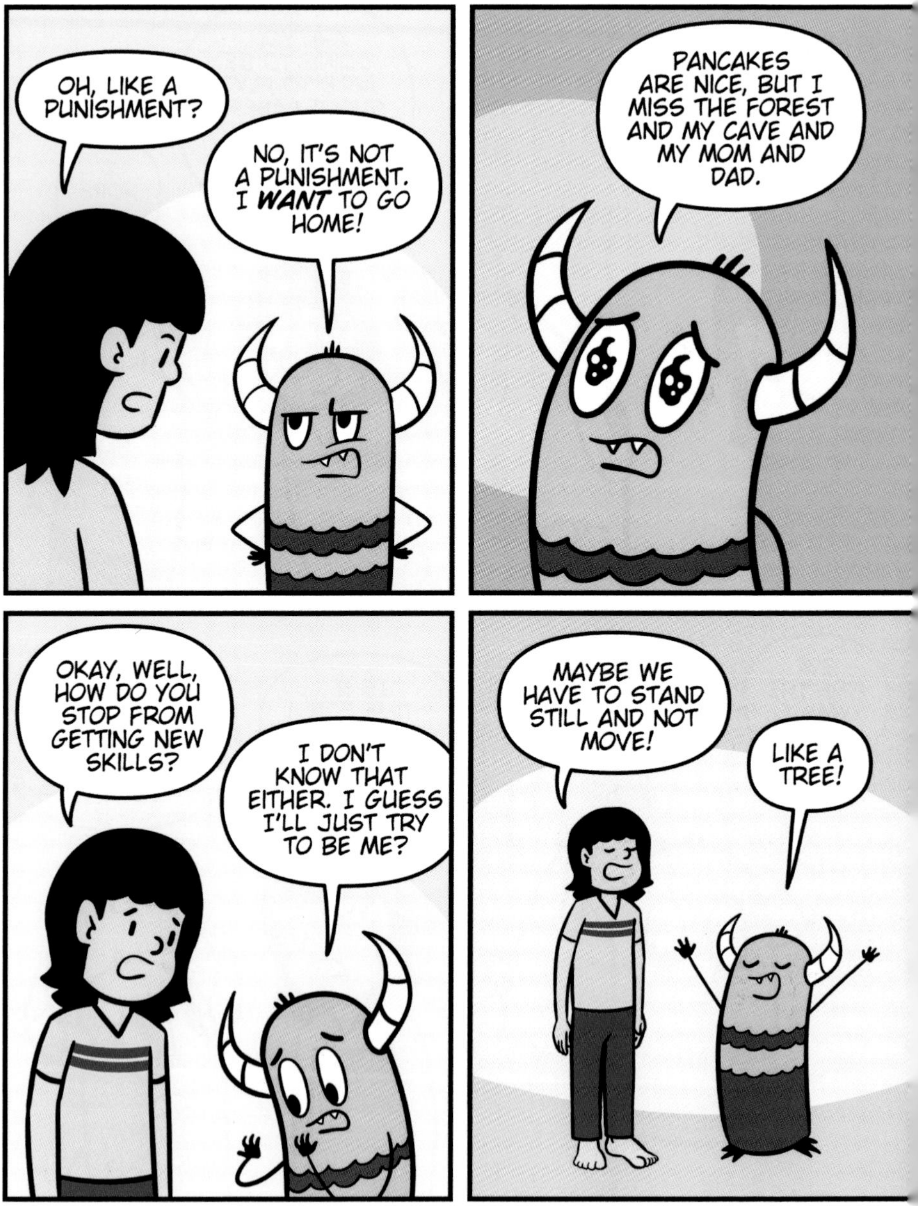
OH, LIKE A PUNISHMENT?
NO, IT'S NOT A PUNISHMENT. I *WANT* TO GO HOME!
PANCAKES ARE NICE, BUT I MISS THE FOREST AND MY CAVE AND MY MOM AND DAD.
OKAY, WELL, HOW DO YOU STOP FROM GETTING NEW SKILLS?
I DON'T KNOW THAT EITHER. I GUESS I'LL JUST TRY TO BE ME?
MAYBE WE HAVE TO STAND STILL AND NOT MOVE!
LIKE A TREE!

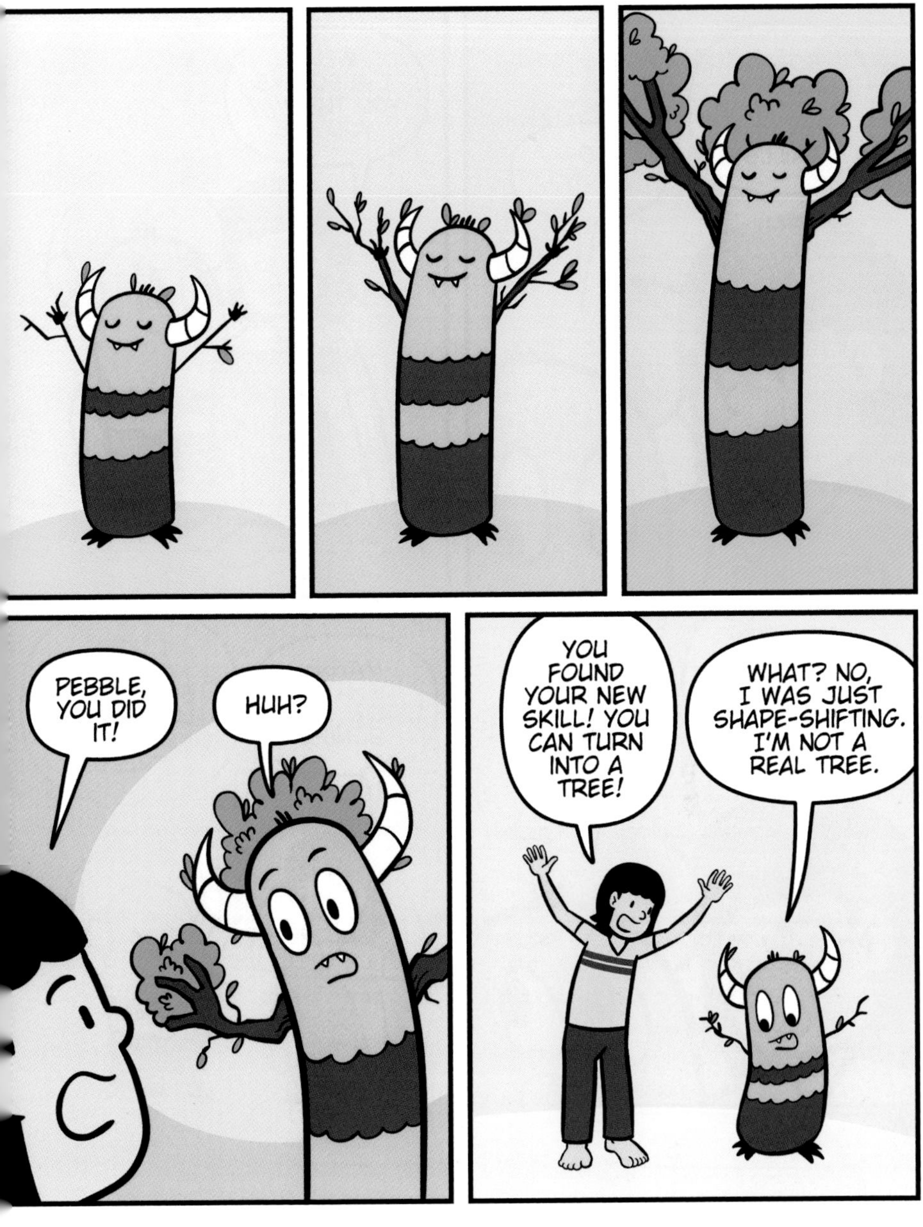
PEBBLE, YOU DID IT!
HUH?
YOU FOUND YOUR NEW SKILL! YOU CAN TURN INTO A TREE!
WHAT? NO, I WAS JUST SHAPE-SHIFTING. I'M NOT A REAL TREE.

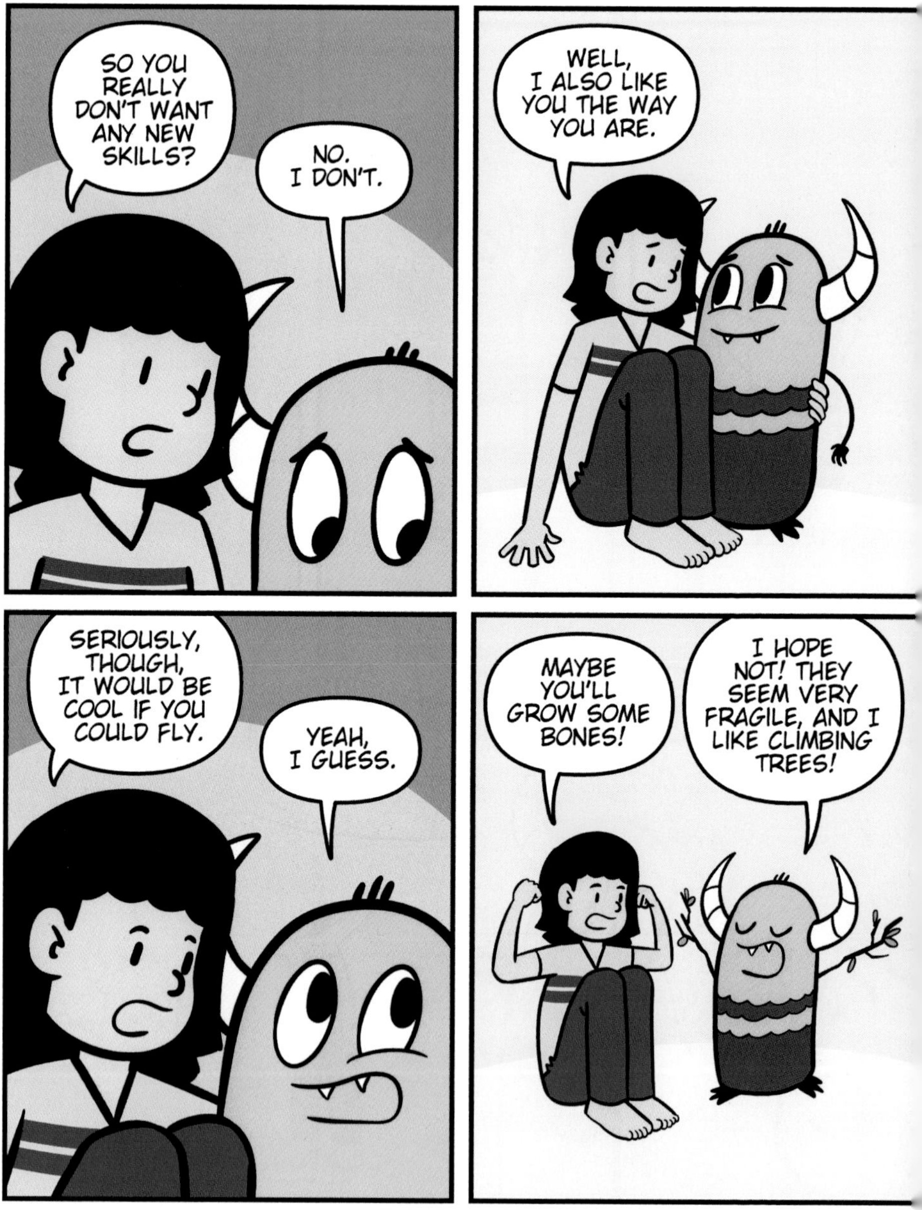
SO YOU REALLY DON'T WANT ANY NEW SKILLS?
NO. I DON'T.
WELL, I ALSO LIKE YOU THE WAY YOU ARE.
SERIOUSLY, THOUGH, IT WOULD BE COOL IF YOU COULD FLY.
YEAH, I GUESS.
MAYBE YOU'LL GROW SOME BONES!
I HOPE NOT! THEY SEEM VERY FRAGILE, AND I LIKE CLIMBING TREES!

CHAPTER FOUR

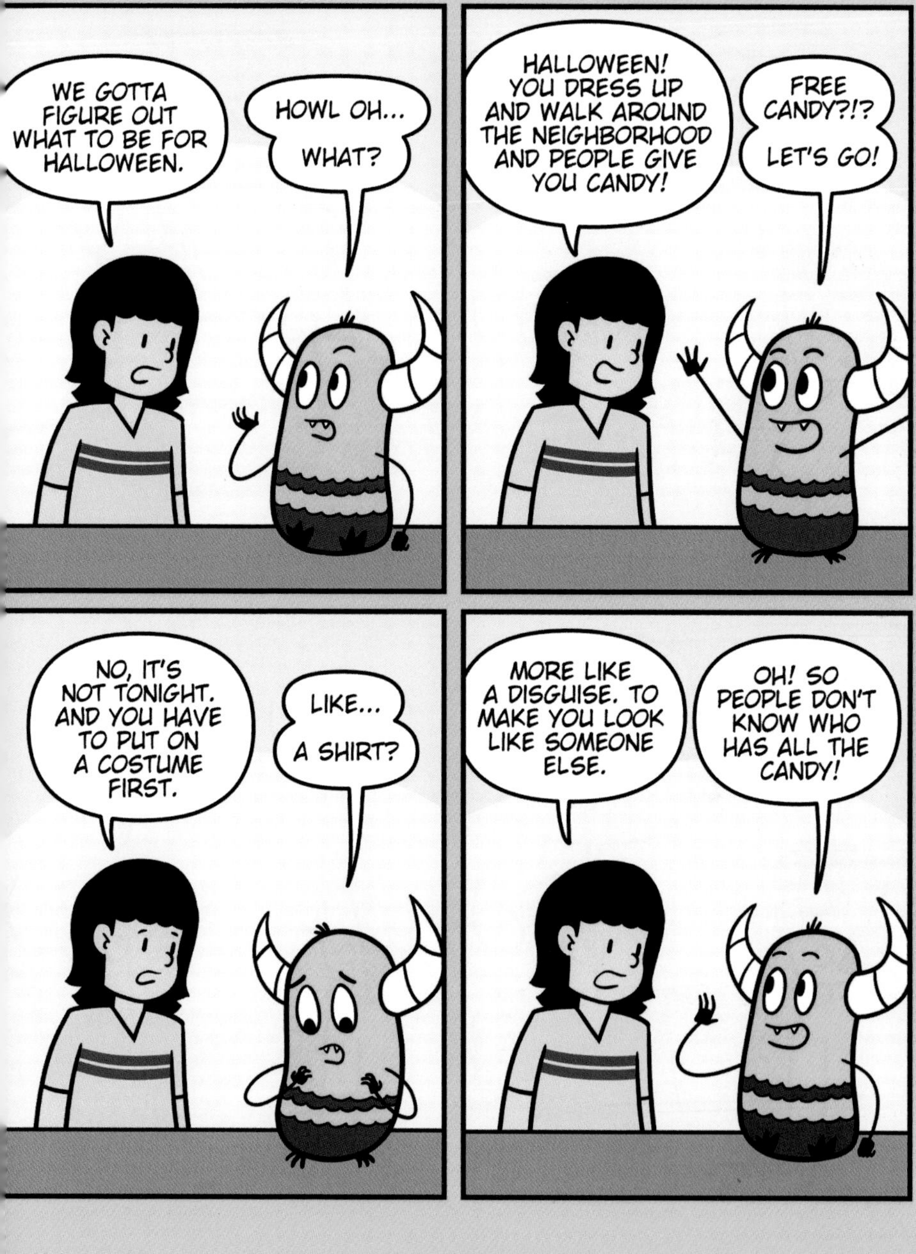
WE GOTTA FIGURE OUT WHAT TO BE FOR HALLOWEEN.
HOWL OH...
WHAT?
HALLOWEEN! YOU DRESS UP AND WALK AROUND THE NEIGHBORHOOD AND PEOPLE GIVE YOU CANDY!
FREE CANDY?!?
LET'S GO!
NO, IT'S NOT TONIGHT. AND YOU HAVE TO PUT ON A COSTUME FIRST.
LIKE...
A SHIRT?
MORE LIKE A DISGUISE. TO MAKE YOU LOOK LIKE SOMEONE ELSE.
OH! SO PEOPLE DON'T KNOW WHO HAS ALL THE CANDY!

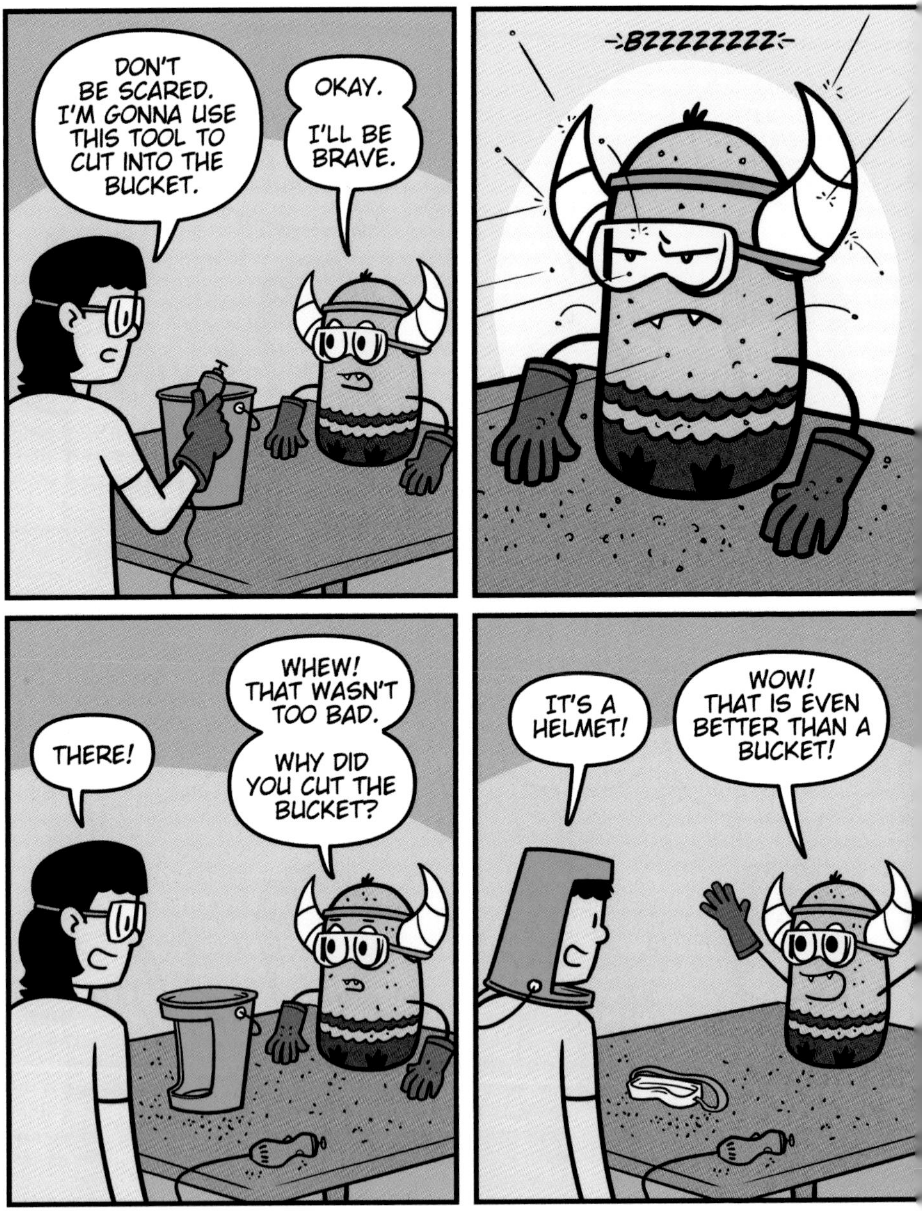
DON'T BE SCARED. I'M GONNA USE THIS TOOL TO CUT INTO THE BUCKET.
OKAY.
I'LL BE BRAVE.
-BZZZZZZZZ-
THERE!
WHEW! THAT WASN'T TOO BAD.
WHY DID YOU CUT THE BUCKET?
IT'S A HELMET!
WOW! THAT IS EVEN BETTER THAN A BUCKET!

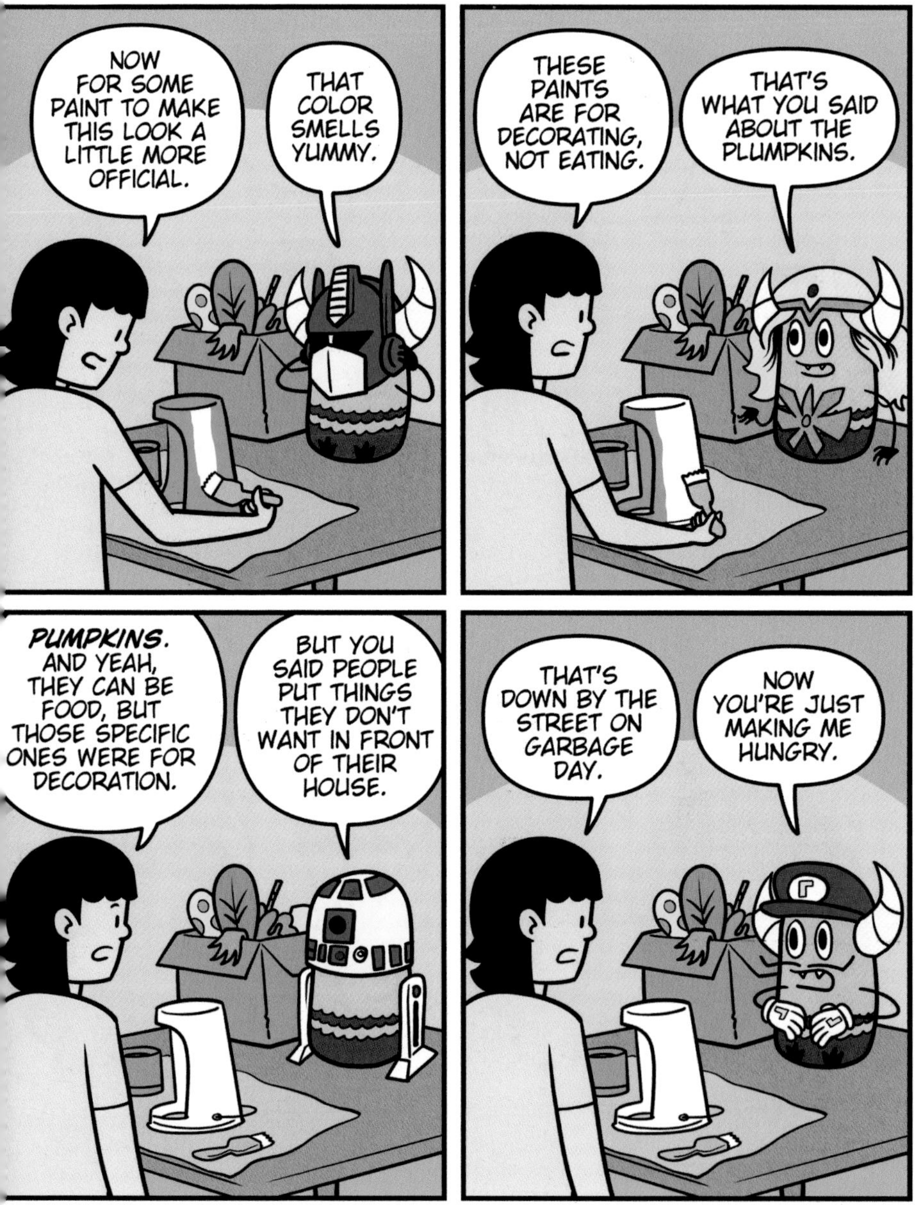
NOW FOR SOME PAINT TO MAKE THIS LOOK A LITTLE MORE OFFICIAL.
THAT COLOR SMELLS YUMMY.
THESE PAINTS ARE FOR DECORATING, NOT EATING.
THAT'S WHAT YOU SAID ABOUT THE PLUMPKINS.
PUMPKINS. AND YEAH, THEY CAN BE FOOD, BUT THOSE SPECIFIC ONES WERE FOR DECORATION.
BUT YOU SAID PEOPLE PUT THINGS THEY DON'T WANT IN FRONT OF THEIR HOUSE.
THAT'S DOWN BY THE STREET ON GARBAGE DAY.
NOW YOU'RE JUST MAKING ME HUNGRY.

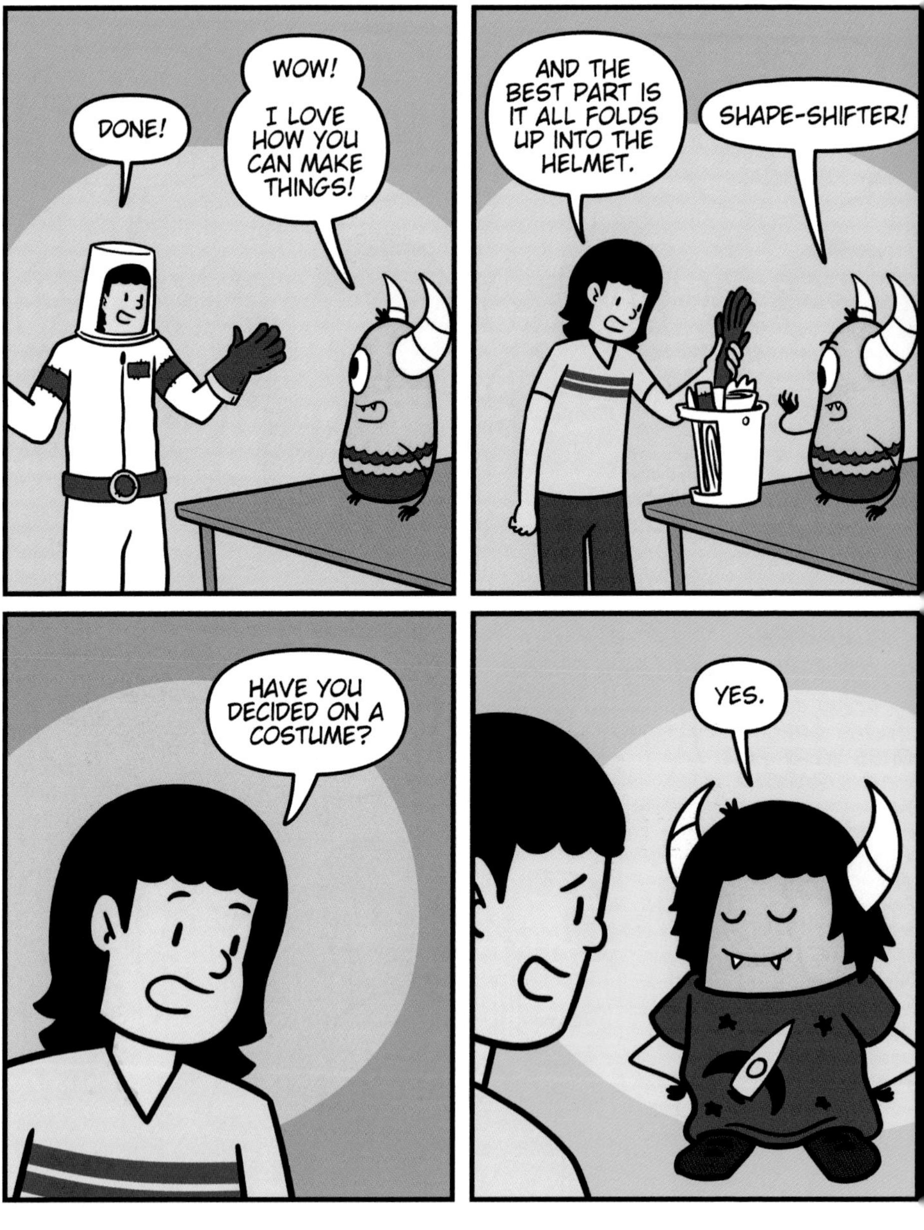
DONE!
WOW!
I LOVE HOW YOU CAN MAKE THINGS!
AND THE BEST PART IS IT ALL FOLDS UP INTO THE HELMET.
SHAPE-SHIFTER!
HAVE YOU DECIDED ON A COSTUME?
YES.

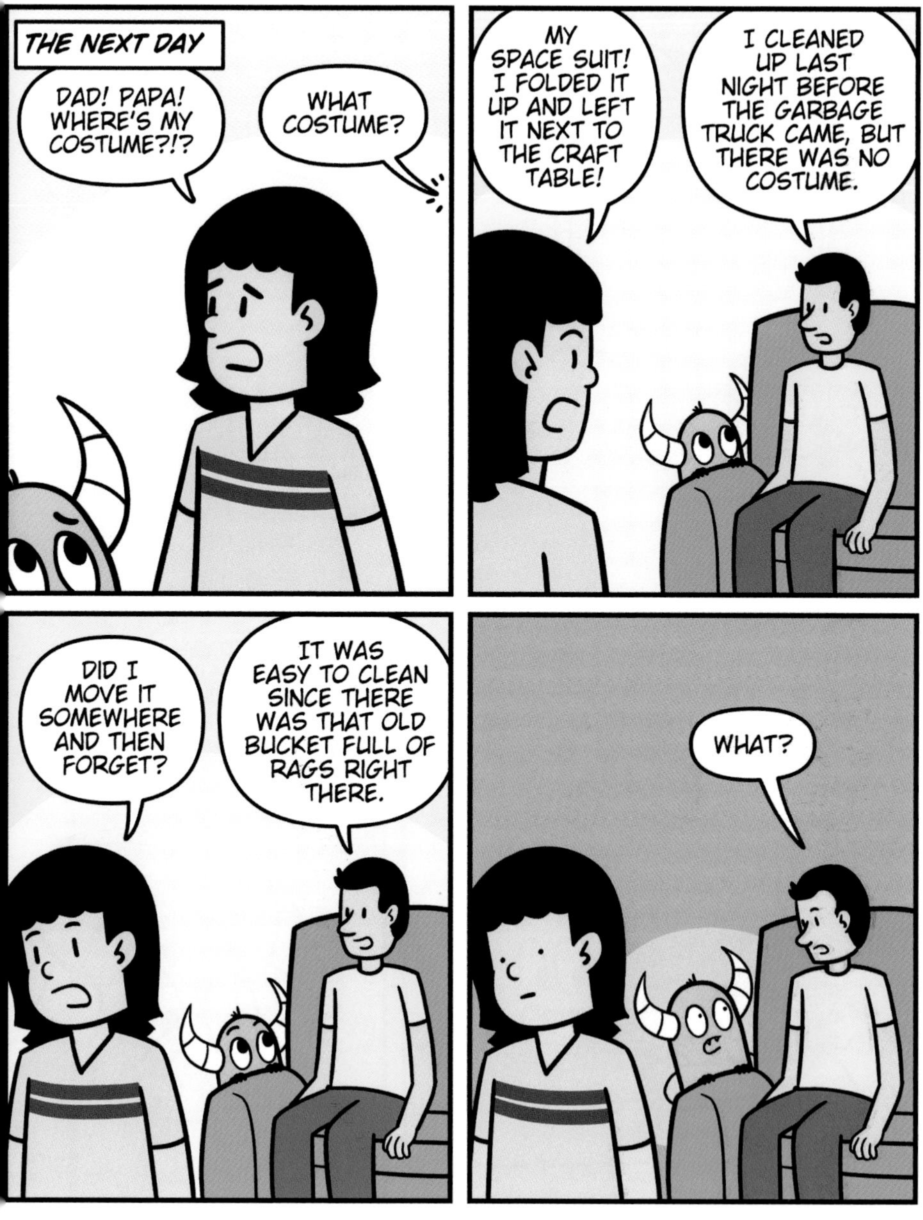
THE NEXT DAY
DAD! PAPA! WHERE'S MY COSTUME?!?
WHAT COSTUME?
MY SPACE SUIT! I FOLDED IT UP AND LEFT IT NEXT TO THE CRAFT TABLE!
I CLEANED UP LAST NIGHT BEFORE THE GARBAGE TRUCK CAME, BUT THERE WAS NO COSTUME.
DID I MOVE IT SOMEWHERE AND THEN FORGET?
IT WAS EASY TO CLEAN SINCE THERE WAS THAT OLD BUCKET FULL OF RAGS RIGHT THERE.
WHAT?

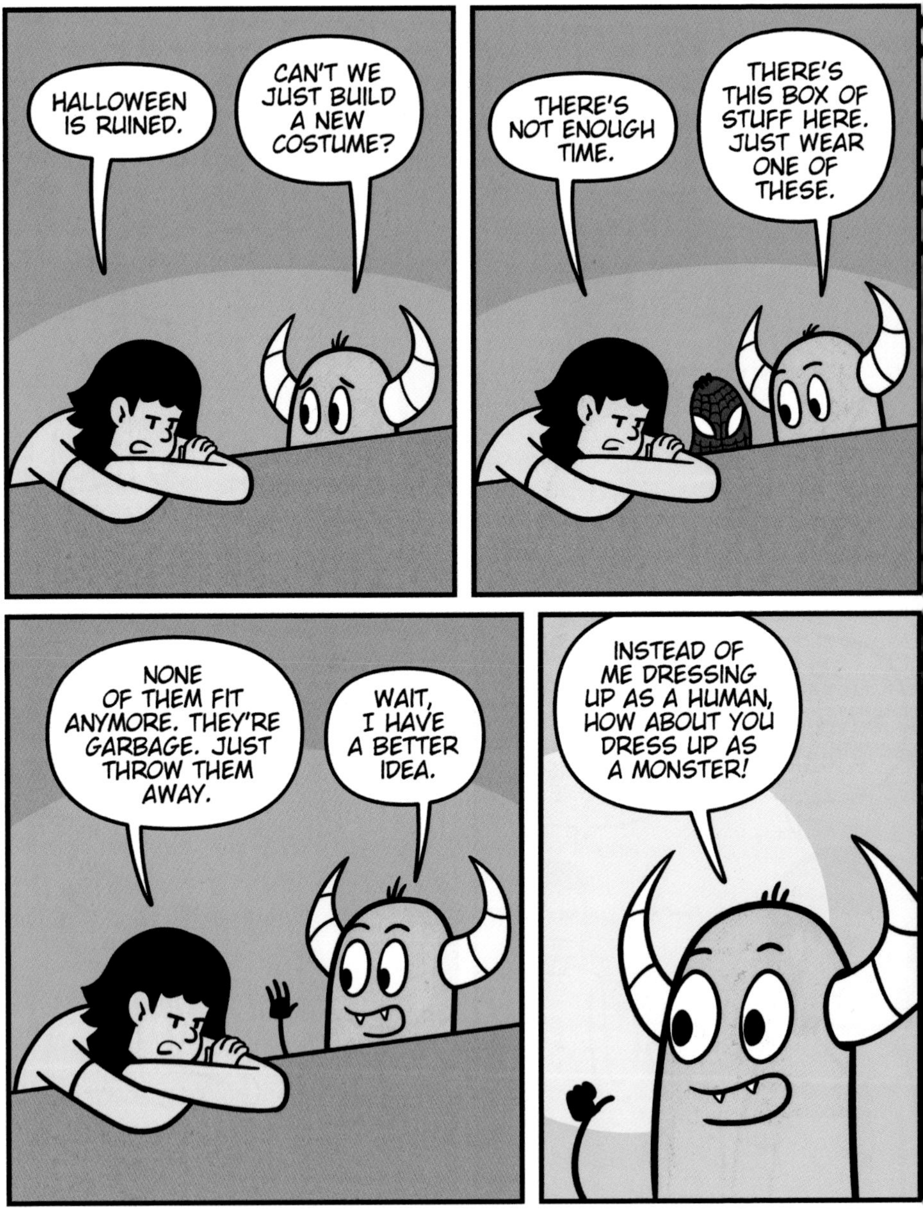
HALLOWEEN IS RUINED.
CAN'T WE JUST BUILD A NEW COSTUME?
THERE'S NOT ENOUGH TIME.
THERE'S THIS BOX OF STUFF HERE. JUST WEAR ONE OF THESE.
NONE OF THEM FIT ANYMORE. THEY'RE GARBAGE. JUST THROW THEM AWAY.
WAIT, I HAVE A BETTER IDEA.
INSTEAD OF ME DRESSING UP AS A HUMAN, HOW ABOUT YOU DRESS UP AS A MONSTER!

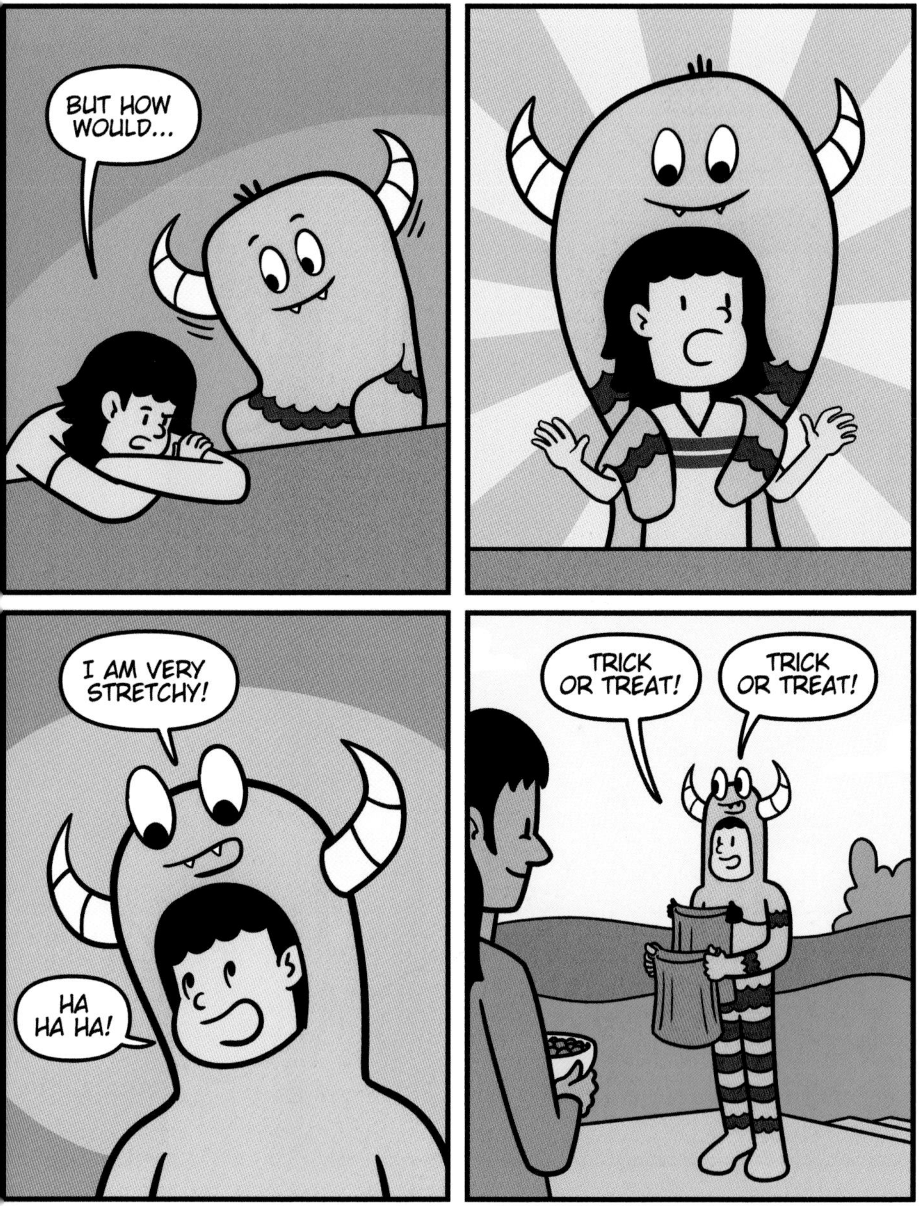
BUT HOW WOULD...
I AM VERY STRETCHY!
HA HA HA!
TRICK OR TREAT!
TRICK OR TREAT!

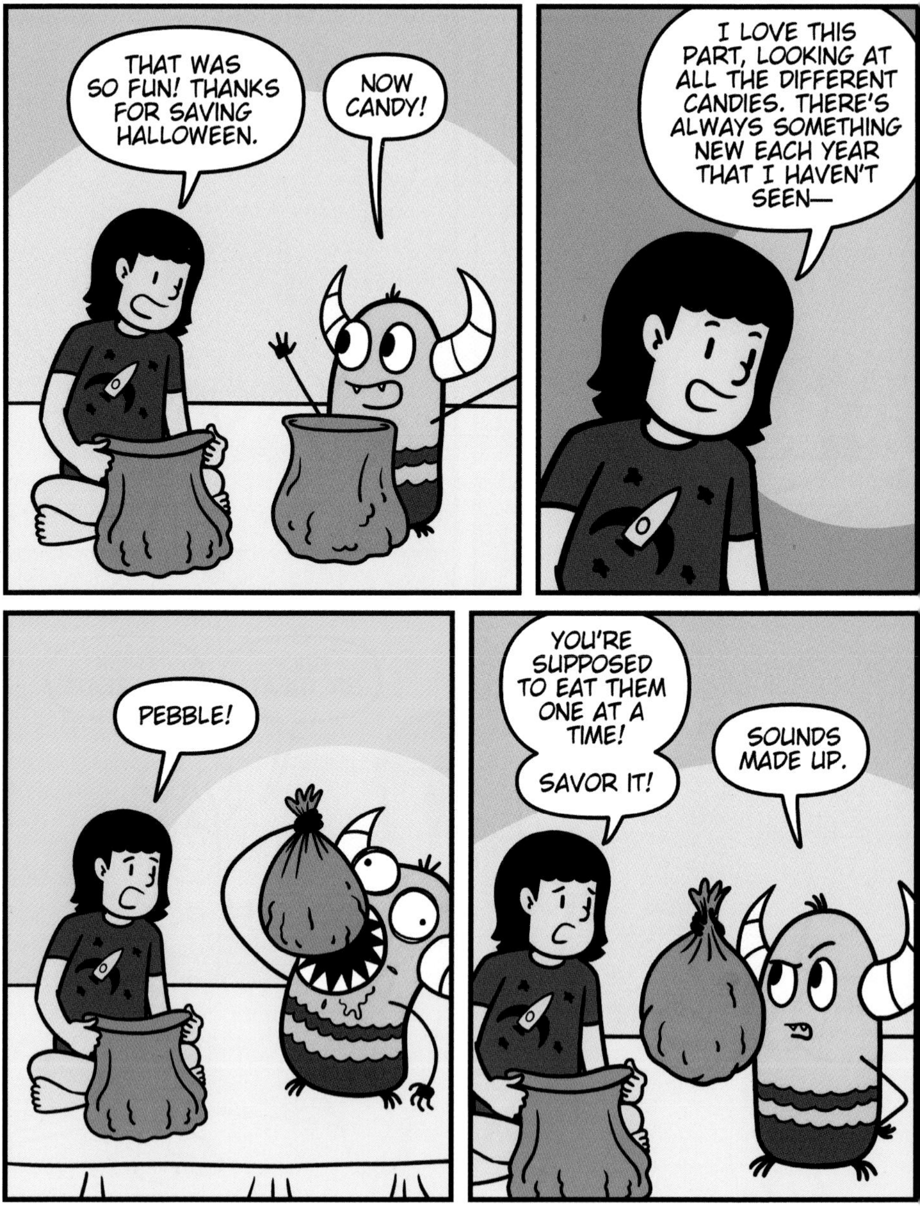
THAT WAS SO FUN! THANKS FOR SAVING HALLOWEEN.
NOW CANDY!
I LOVE THIS PART, LOOKING AT ALL THE DIFFERENT CANDIES. THERE'S ALWAYS SOMETHING NEW EACH YEAR THAT I HAVEN'T SEEN—
PEBBLE!
YOU'RE SUPPOSED TO EAT THEM ONE AT A TIME!
SAVOR IT!
SOUNDS MADE UP.

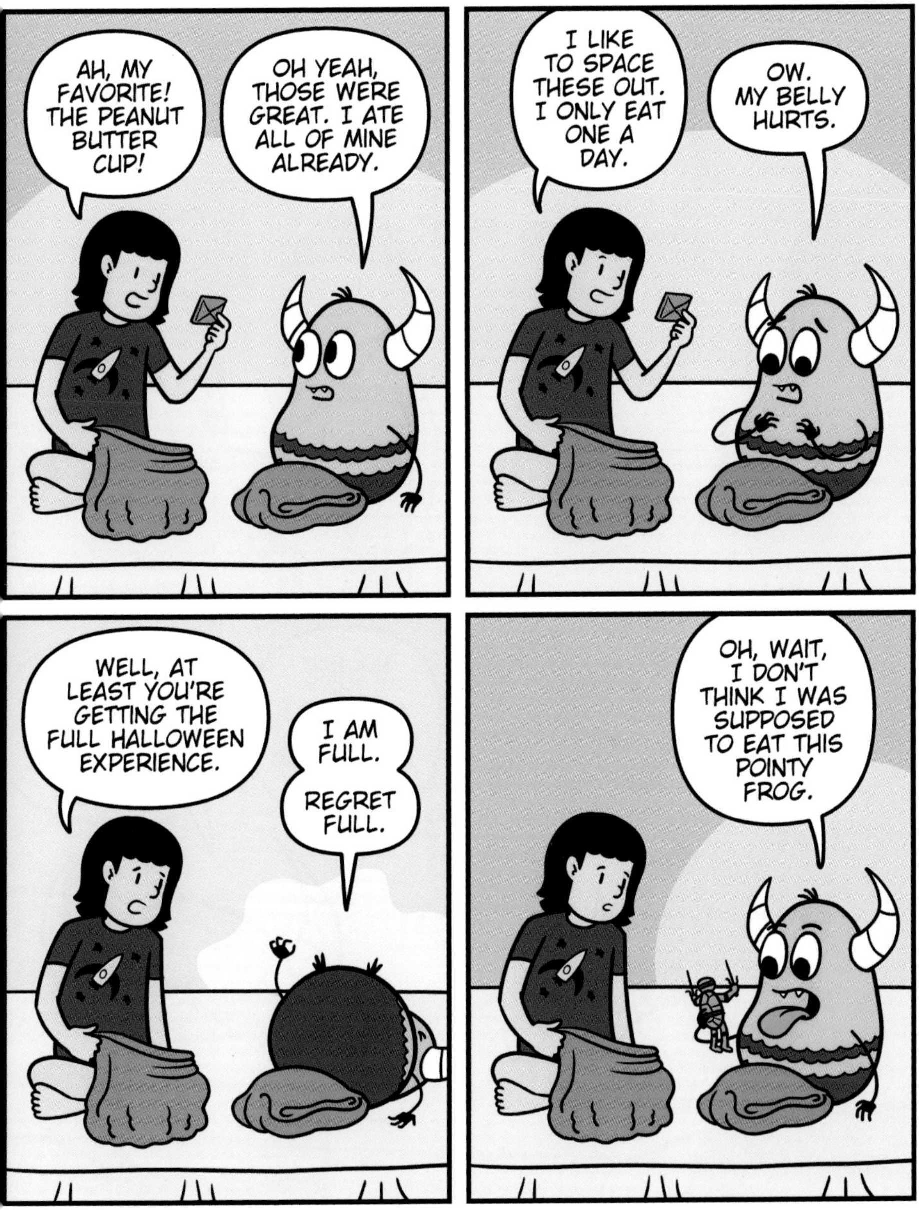
AH, MY FAVORITE! THE PEANUT BUTTER CUP!
OH YEAH, THOSE WERE GREAT. I ATE ALL OF MINE ALREADY.
I LIKE TO SPACE THESE OUT. I ONLY EAT ONE A DAY.
OW. MY BELLY HURTS.
WELL, AT LEAST YOU'RE GETTING THE FULL HALLOWEEN EXPERIENCE.
I AM FULL.
REGRET FULL.
OH, WAIT, I DON'T THINK I WAS SUPPOSED TO EAT THIS POINTY FROG.

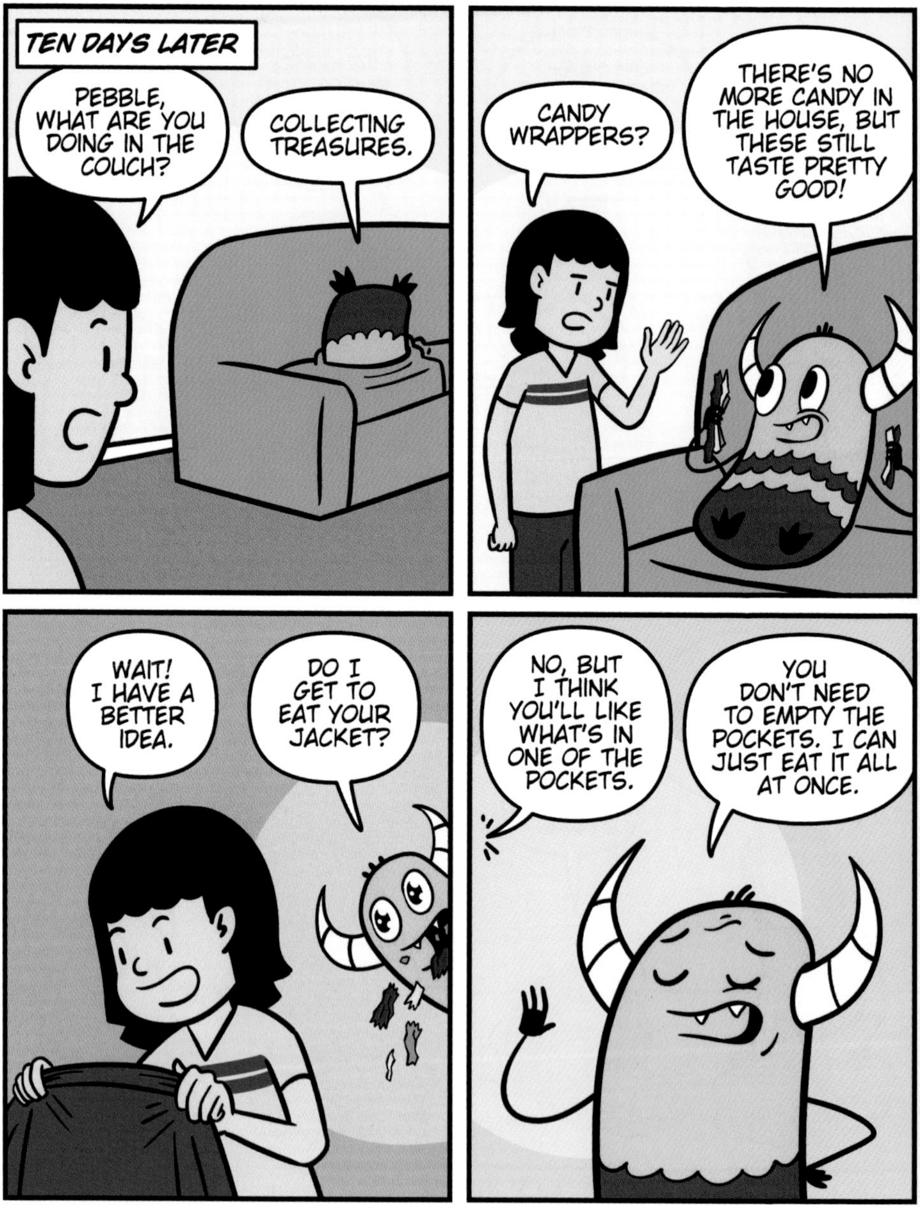

TEN DAYS LATER
PEBBLE, WHAT ARE YOU DOING IN THE COUCH?
COLLECTING TREASURES.
CANDY WRAPPERS?
THERE'S NO MORE CANDY IN THE HOUSE, BUT THESE STILL TASTE PRETTY GOOD!
WAIT! I HAVE A BETTER IDEA.
DO I GET TO EAT YOUR JACKET?
NO, BUT I THINK YOU'LL LIKE WHAT'S IN ONE OF THE POCKETS.
YOU DON'T NEED TO EMPTY THE POCKETS. I CAN JUST EAT IT ALL AT ONCE.

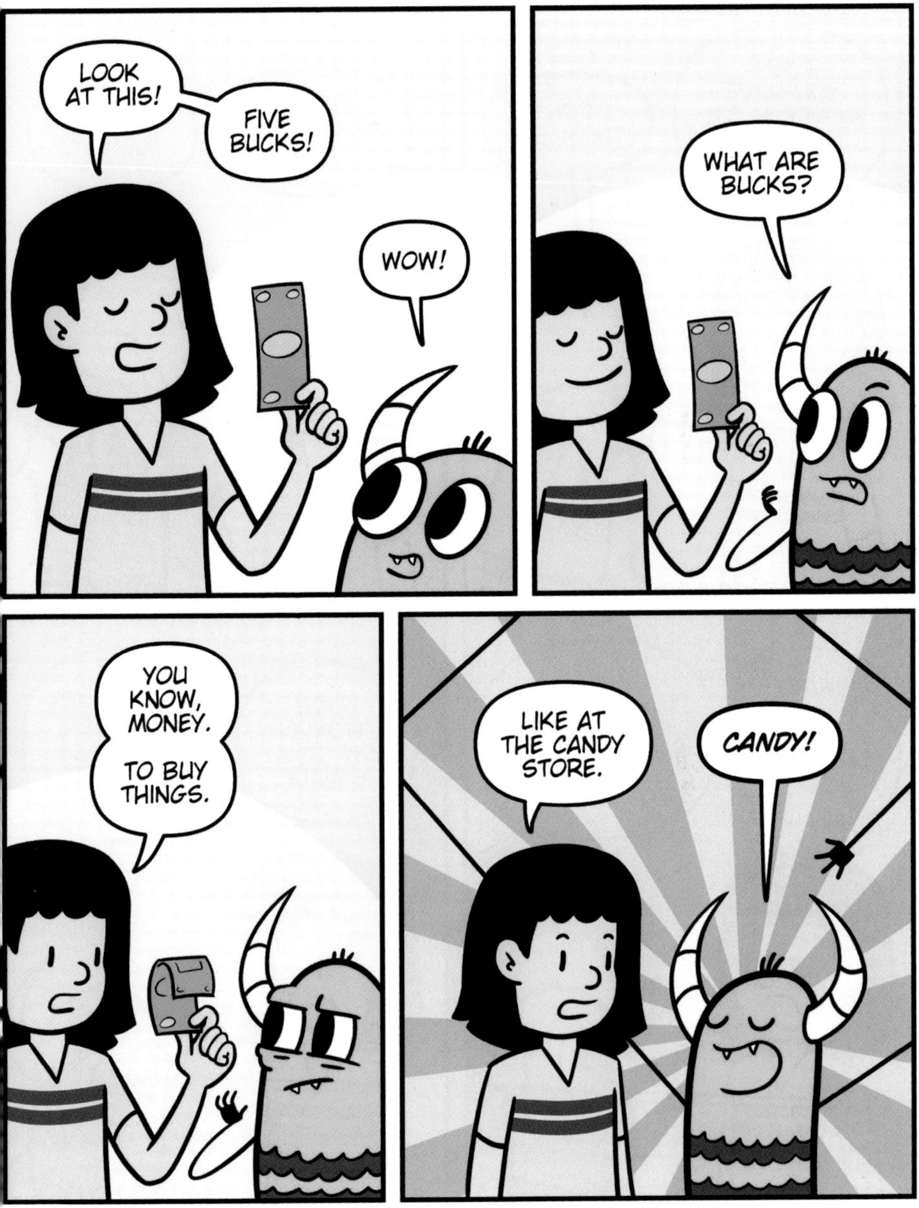
LOOK AT THIS!
FIVE BUCKS!
WOW!
WHAT ARE BUCKS?
YOU KNOW, MONEY.
TO BUY THINGS.
LIKE AT THE CANDY STORE.
CANDY!

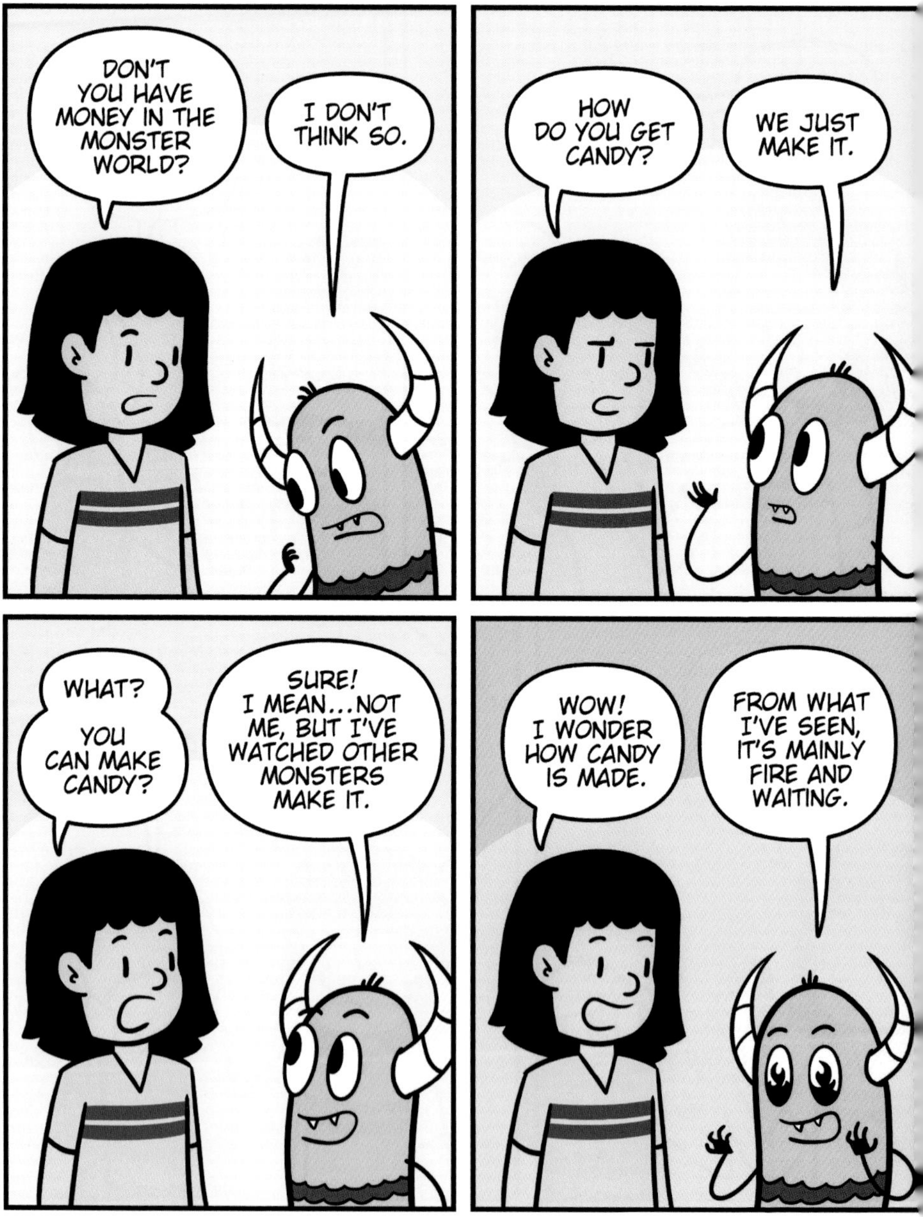
DON'T YOU HAVE MONEY IN THE MONSTER WORLD?
I DON'T THINK SO.
HOW DO YOU GET CANDY?
WE JUST MAKE IT.
WHAT?
YOU CAN MAKE CANDY?
SURE! I MEAN...NOT ME, BUT I'VE WATCHED OTHER MONSTERS MAKE IT.
WOW! I WONDER HOW CANDY IS MADE.
FROM WHAT I'VE SEEN, IT'S MAINLY FIRE AND WAITING.

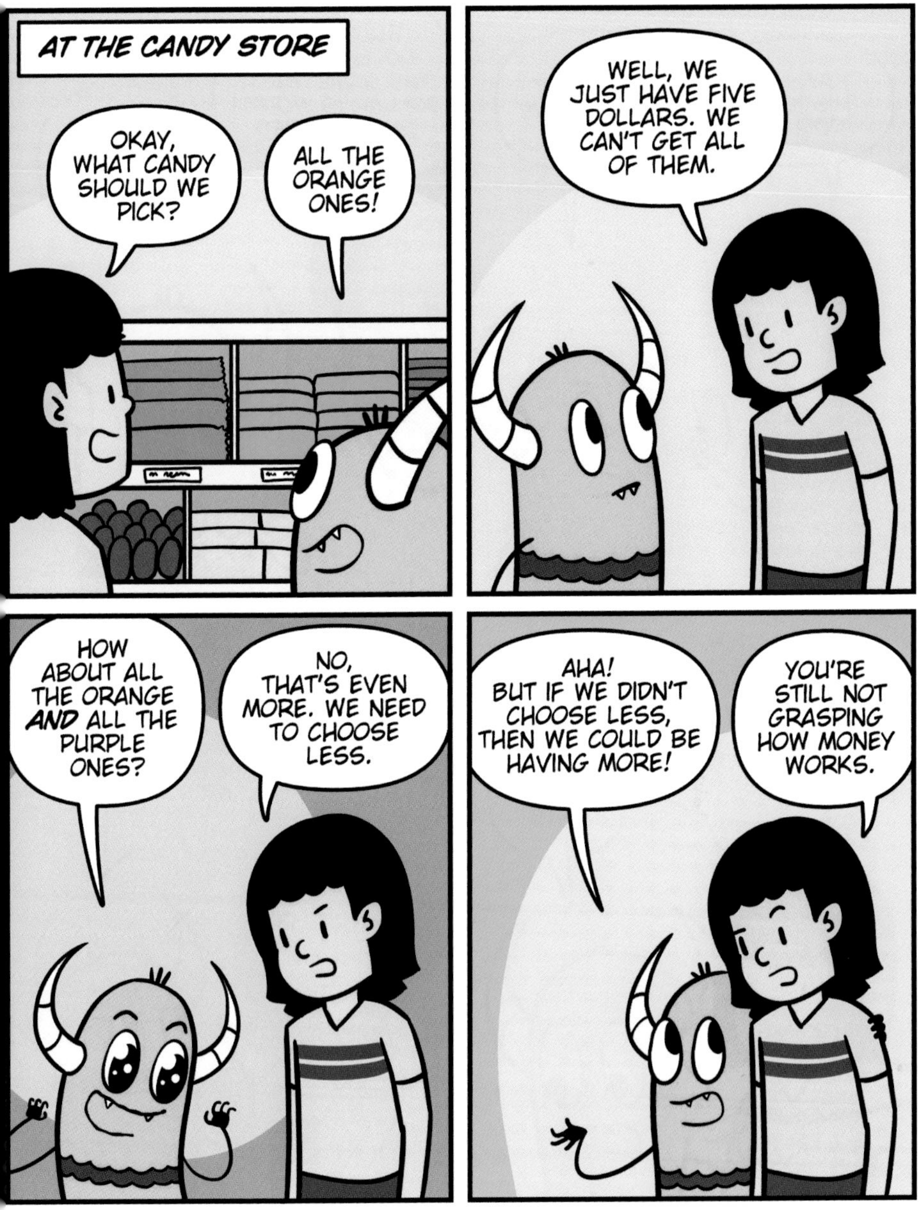
AT THE CANDY STORE
OKAY, WHAT CANDY SHOULD WE PICK?
ALL THE ORANGE ONES!
WELL, WE JUST HAVE FIVE DOLLARS. WE CAN'T GET ALL OF THEM.
HOW ABOUT ALL THE ORANGE AND ALL THE PURPLE ONES?
NO, THAT'S EVEN MORE. WE NEED TO CHOOSE LESS.
AHA! BUT IF WE DIDN'T CHOOSE LESS, THEN WE COULD BE HAVING MORE!
YOU'RE STILL NOT GRASPING HOW MONEY WORKS.

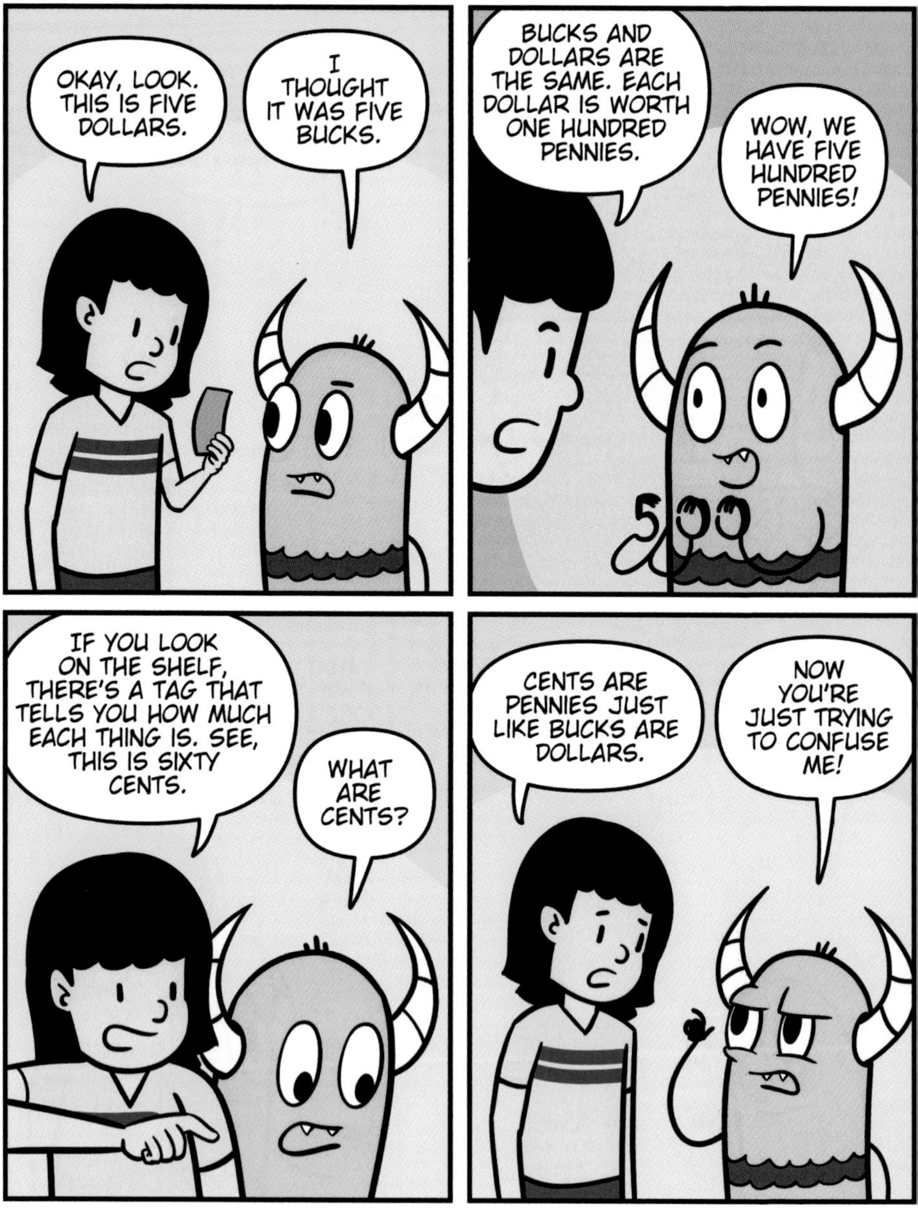
OKAY, LOOK. THIS IS FIVE DOLLARS.
I THOUGHT IT WAS FIVE BUCKS.
BUCKS AND DOLLARS ARE THE SAME. EACH DOLLAR IS WORTH ONE HUNDRED PENNIES.
WOW, WE HAVE FIVE HUNDRED PENNIES!
500
IF YOU LOOK ON THE SHELF, THERE'S A TAG THAT TELLS YOU HOW MUCH EACH THING IS. SEE, THIS IS SIXTY CENTS.
WHAT ARE CENTS?
CENTS ARE PENNIES JUST LIKE BUCKS ARE DOLLARS.
NOW YOU'RE JUST TRYING TO CONFUSE ME!

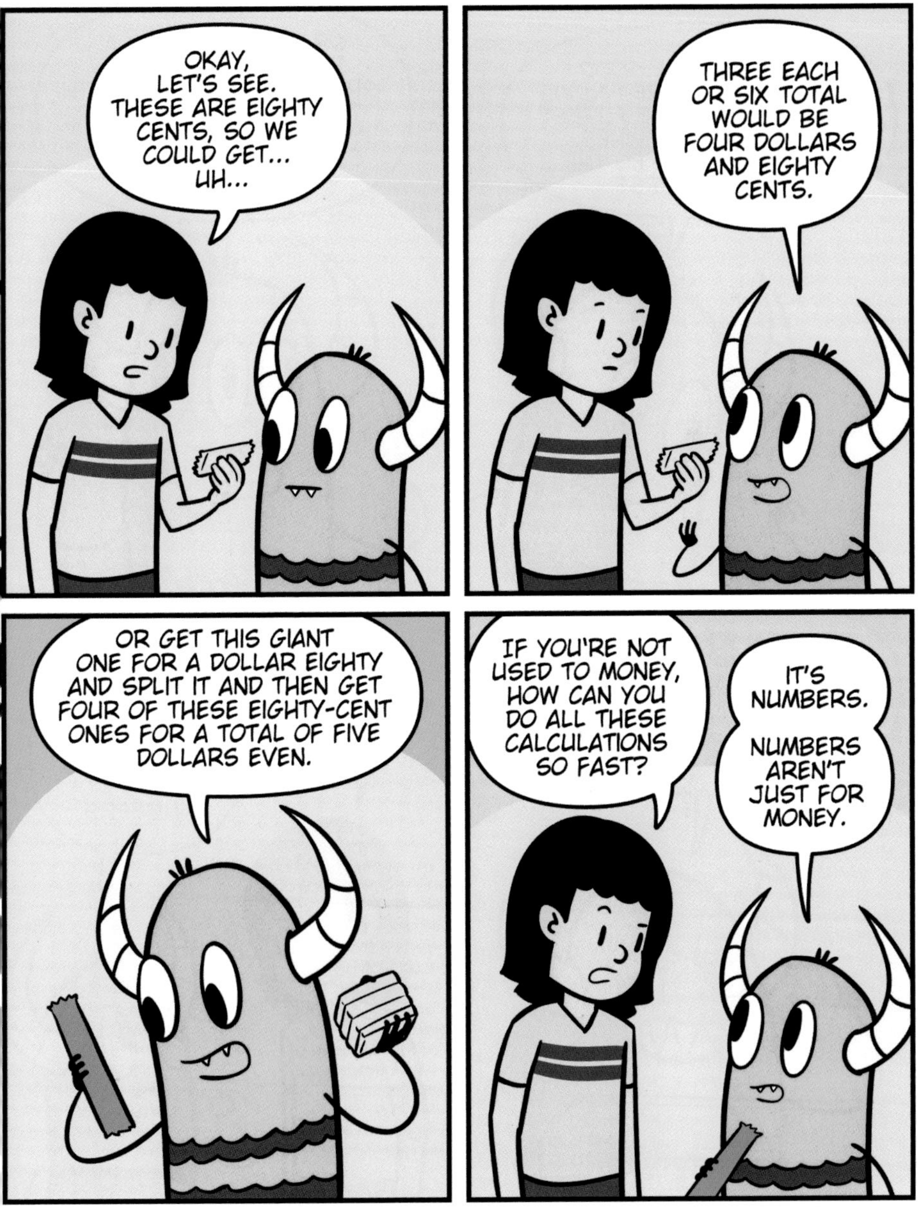
OKAY, LET'S SEE. THESE ARE EIGHTY CENTS, SO WE COULD GET... UH...
THREE EACH OR SIX TOTAL WOULD BE FOUR DOLLARS AND EIGHTY CENTS.
OR GET THIS GIANT ONE FOR A DOLLAR EIGHTY AND SPLIT IT AND THEN GET FOUR OF THESE EIGHTY-CENT ONES FOR A TOTAL OF FIVE DOLLARS EVEN.
IF YOU'RE NOT USED TO MONEY, HOW CAN YOU DO ALL THESE CALCULATIONS SO FAST?
IT'S NUMBERS.
NUMBERS AREN'T JUST FOR MONEY.

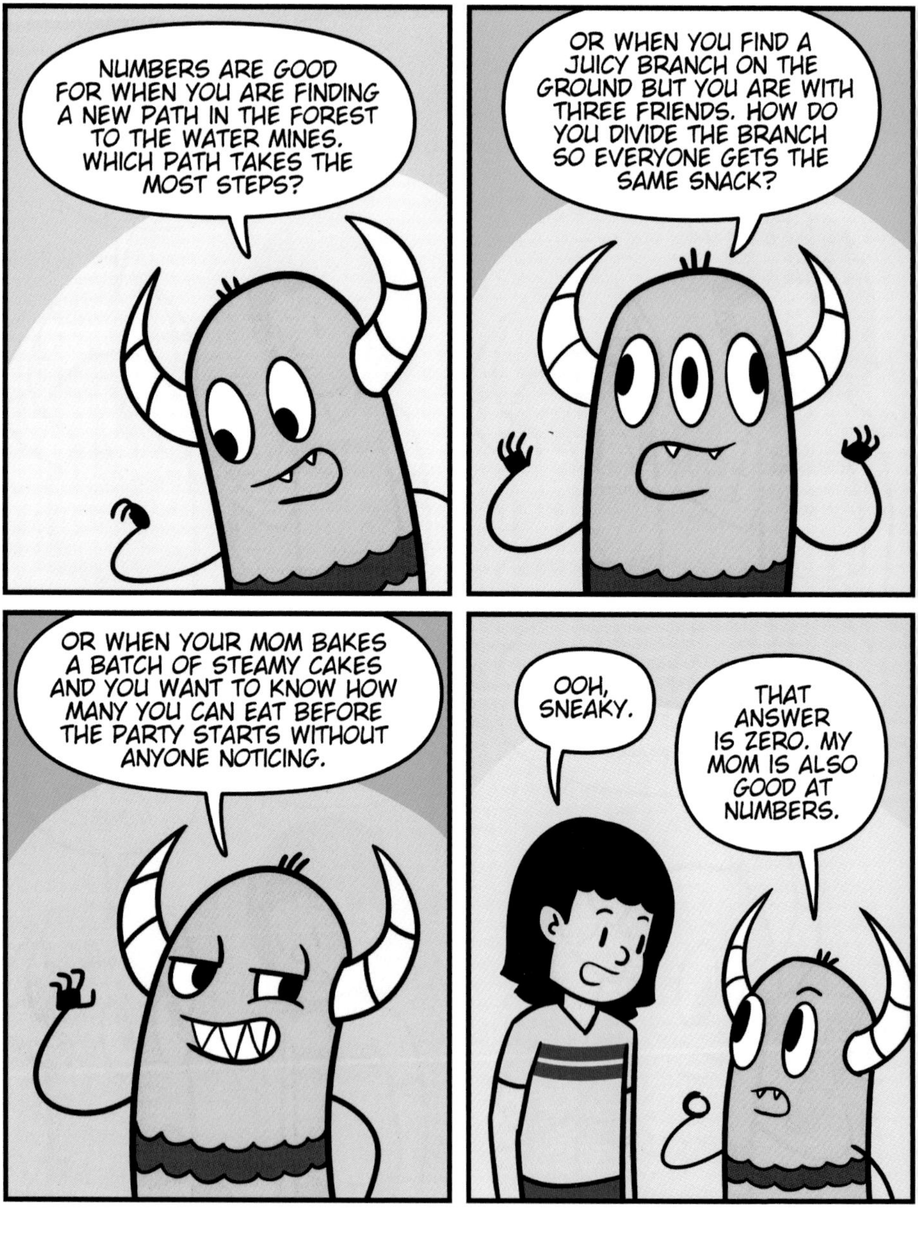
NUMBERS ARE GOOD FOR WHEN YOU ARE FINDING A NEW PATH IN THE FOREST TO THE WATER MINES. WHICH PATH TAKES THE MOST STEPS?
OR WHEN YOU FIND A JUICY BRANCH ON THE GROUND BUT YOU ARE WITH THREE FRIENDS. HOW DO YOU DIVIDE THE BRANCH SO EVERYONE GETS THE SAME SNACK?
OR WHEN YOUR MOM BAKES A BATCH OF STEAMY CAKES AND YOU WANT TO KNOW HOW MANY YOU CAN EAT BEFORE THE PARTY STARTS WITHOUT ANYONE NOTICING.
OOH, SNEAKY.
THAT ANSWER IS ZERO. MY MOM IS ALSO GOOD AT NUMBERS.

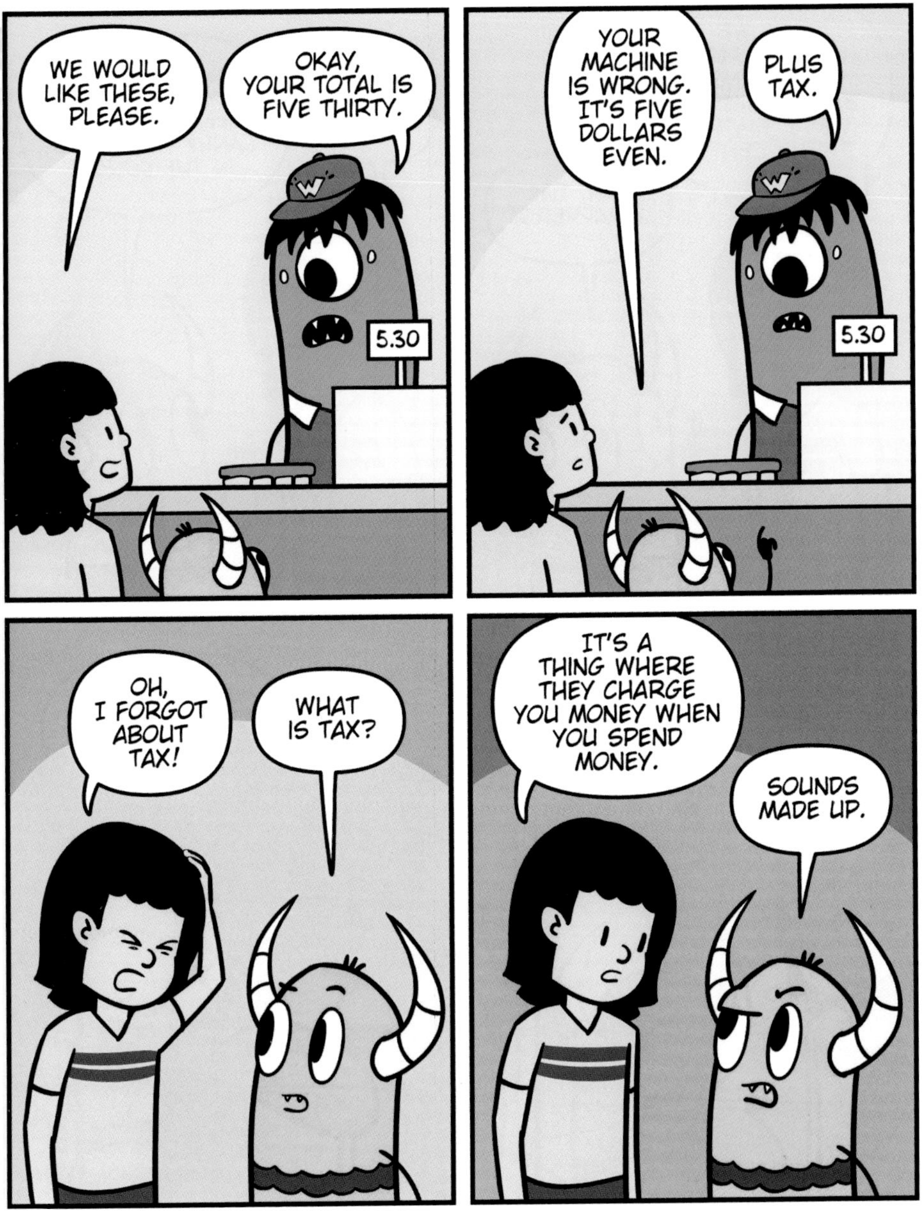
WE WOULD LIKE THESE, PLEASE.
OKAY, YOUR TOTAL IS FIVE THIRTY.
5.30
YOUR MACHINE IS WRONG. IT'S FIVE DOLLARS EVEN.
PLUS TAX.
5.30
OH, I FORGOT ABOUT TAX!
WHAT IS TAX?
IT'S A THING WHERE THEY CHARGE YOU MONEY WHEN YOU SPEND MONEY.
SOUNDS MADE UP.

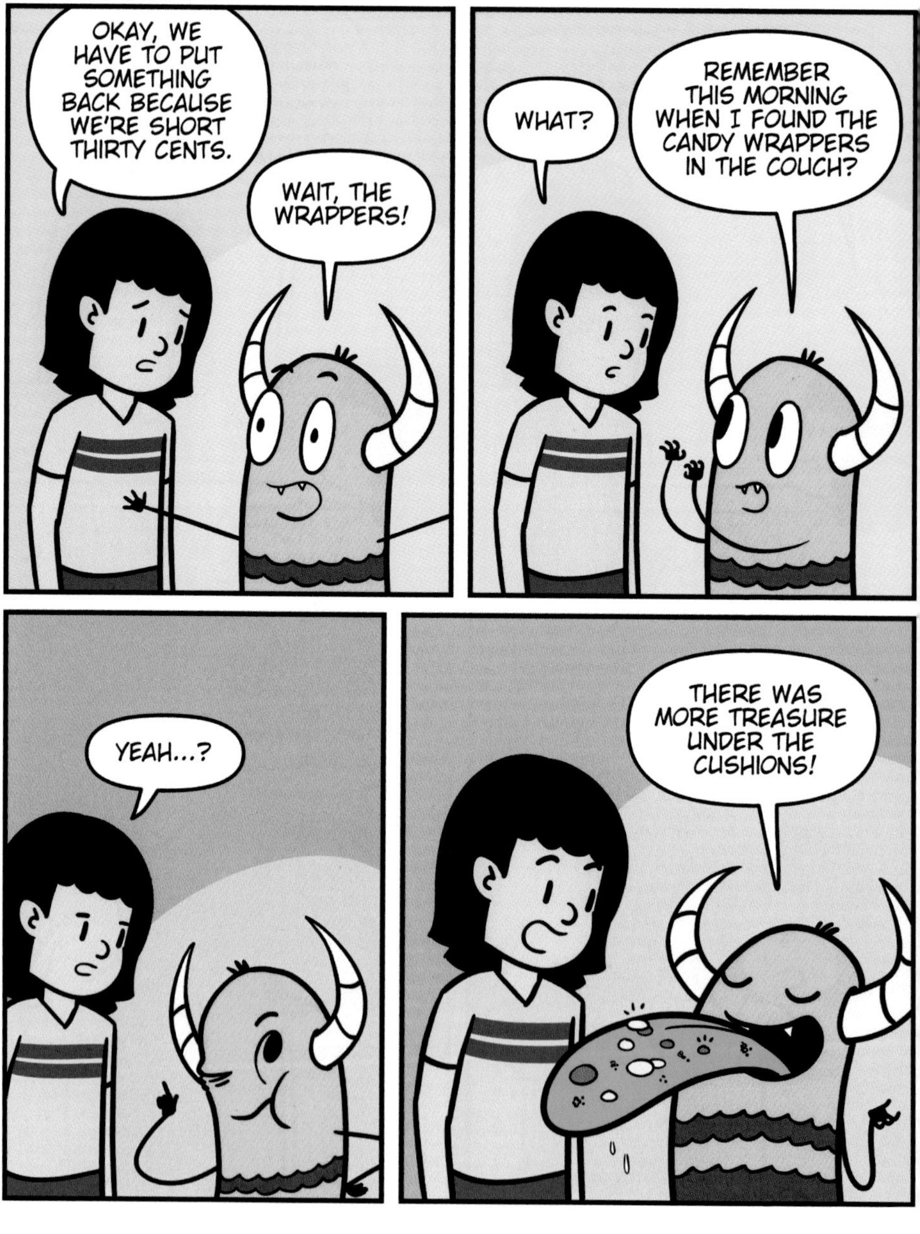
OKAY, WE HAVE TO PUT SOMETHING BACK BECAUSE WE'RE SHORT THIRTY CENTS.
WAIT, THE WRAPPERS!
WHAT?
REMEMBER THIS MORNING WHEN I FOUND THE CANDY WRAPPERS IN THE COUCH?
YEAH...?
THERE WAS MORE TREASURE UNDER THE CUSHIONS!

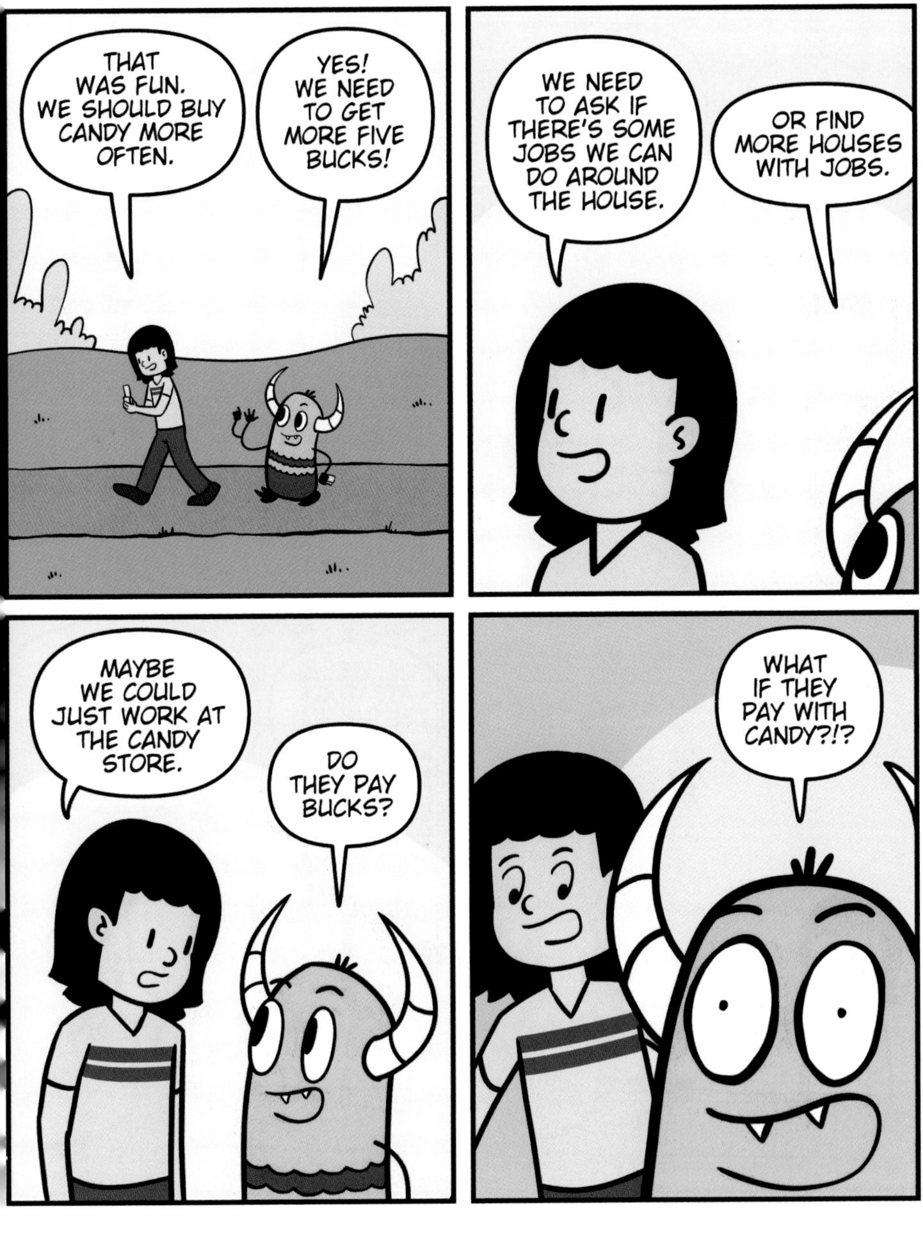
THAT WAS FUN. WE SHOULD BUY CANDY MORE OFTEN.
YES! WE NEED TO GET MORE FIVE BUCKS!
WE NEED TO ASK IF THERE'S SOME JOBS WE CAN DO AROUND THE HOUSE.
OR FIND MORE HOUSES WITH JOBS.
MAYBE WE COULD JUST WORK AT THE CANDY STORE.
DO THEY PAY BUCKS?
WHAT IF THEY PAY WITH CANDY?!?

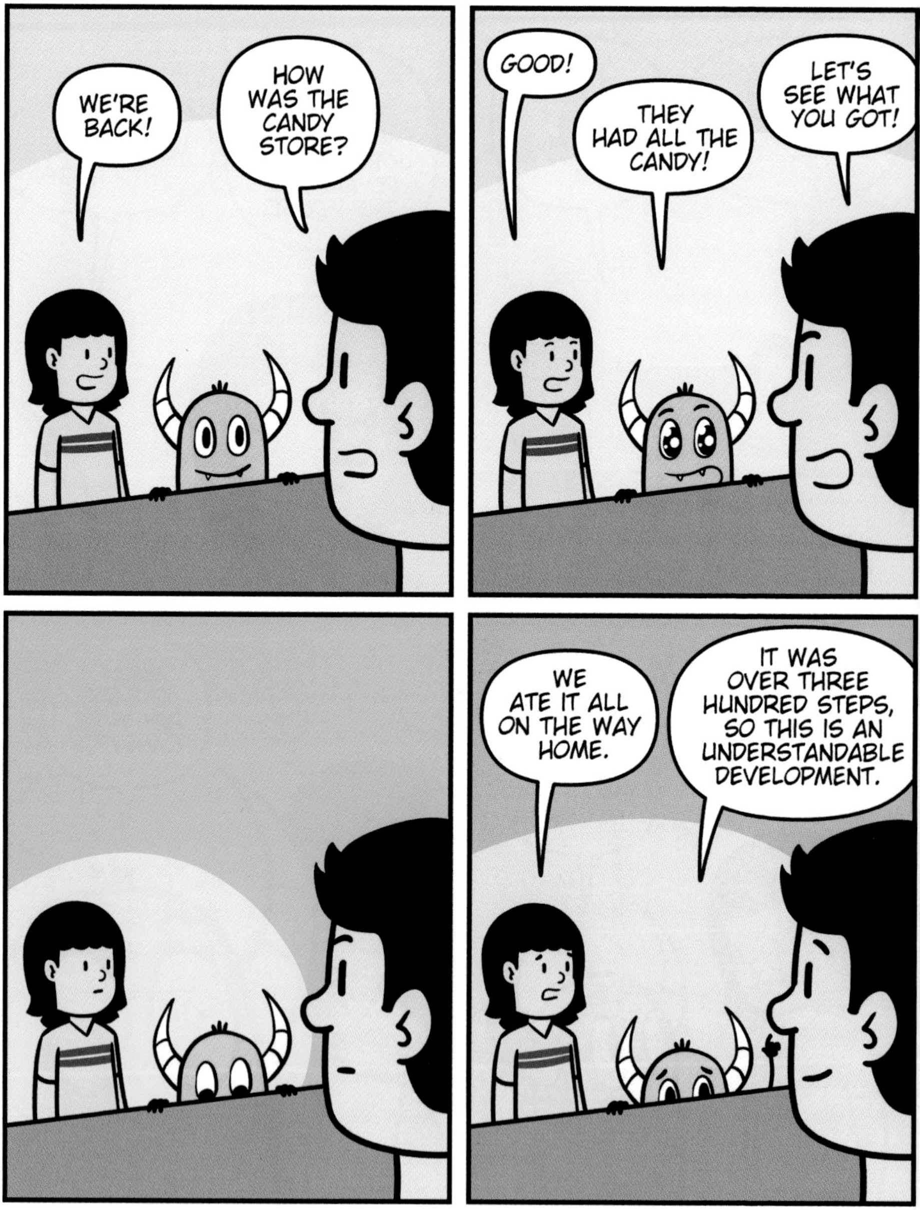
WE'RE BACK!
HOW WAS THE CANDY STORE?
GOOD!
THEY HAD ALL THE CANDY!
LET'S SEE WHAT YOU GOT!
WE ATE IT ALL ON THE WAY HOME.
IT WAS OVER THREE HUNDRED STEPS, SO THIS IS AN UNDERSTANDABLE DEVELOPMENT.

CHAPTER FIVE

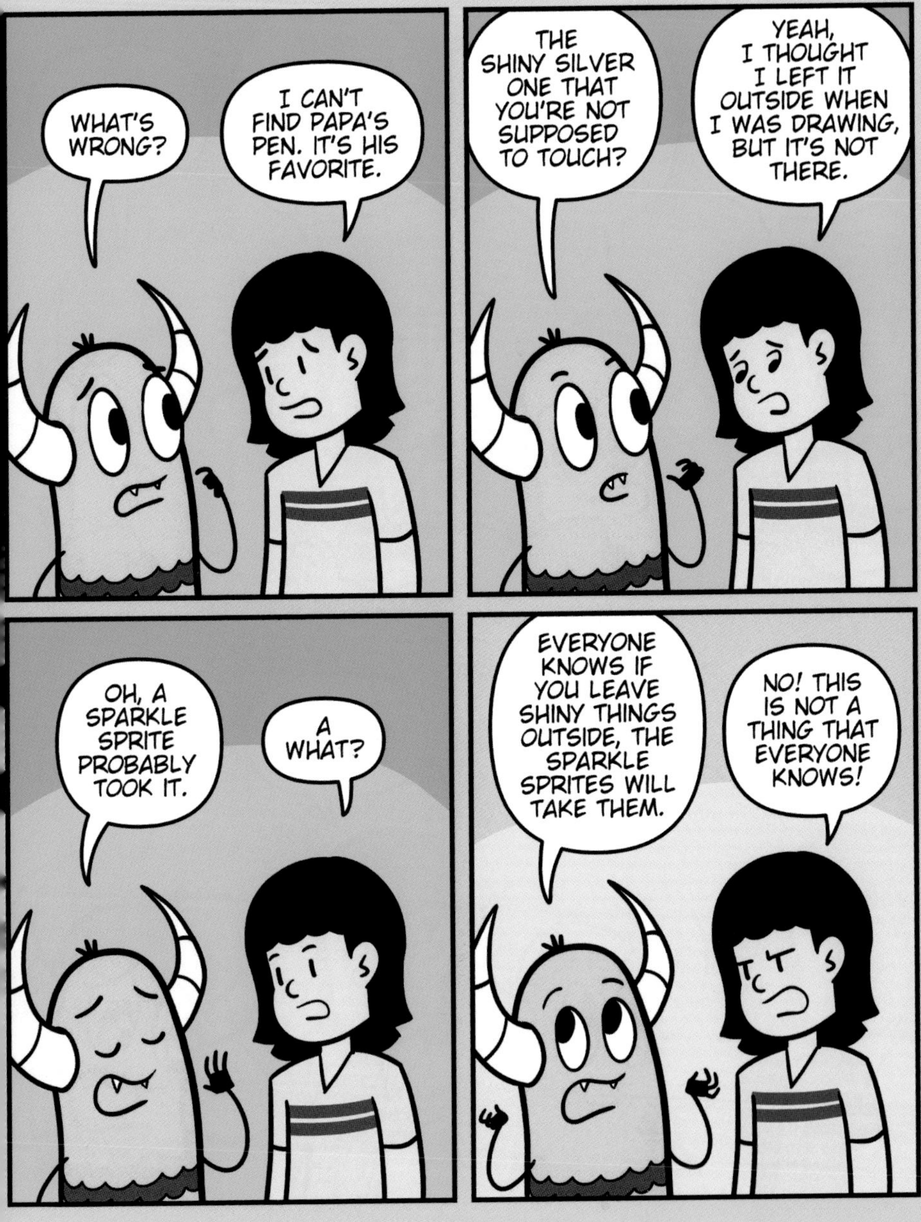
WHAT'S WRONG?
I CAN'T FIND PAPA'S PEN. IT'S HIS FAVORITE.
THE SHINY SILVER ONE THAT YOU'RE NOT SUPPOSED TO TOUCH?
YEAH, I THOUGHT I LEFT IT OUTSIDE WHEN I WAS DRAWING, BUT IT'S NOT THERE.
OH, A SPARKLE SPRITE PROBABLY TOOK IT.
A WHAT?
EVERYONE KNOWS IF YOU LEAVE SHINY THINGS OUTSIDE, THE SPARKLE SPRITES WILL TAKE THEM.
NO! THIS IS NOT A THING THAT EVERYONE KNOWS!

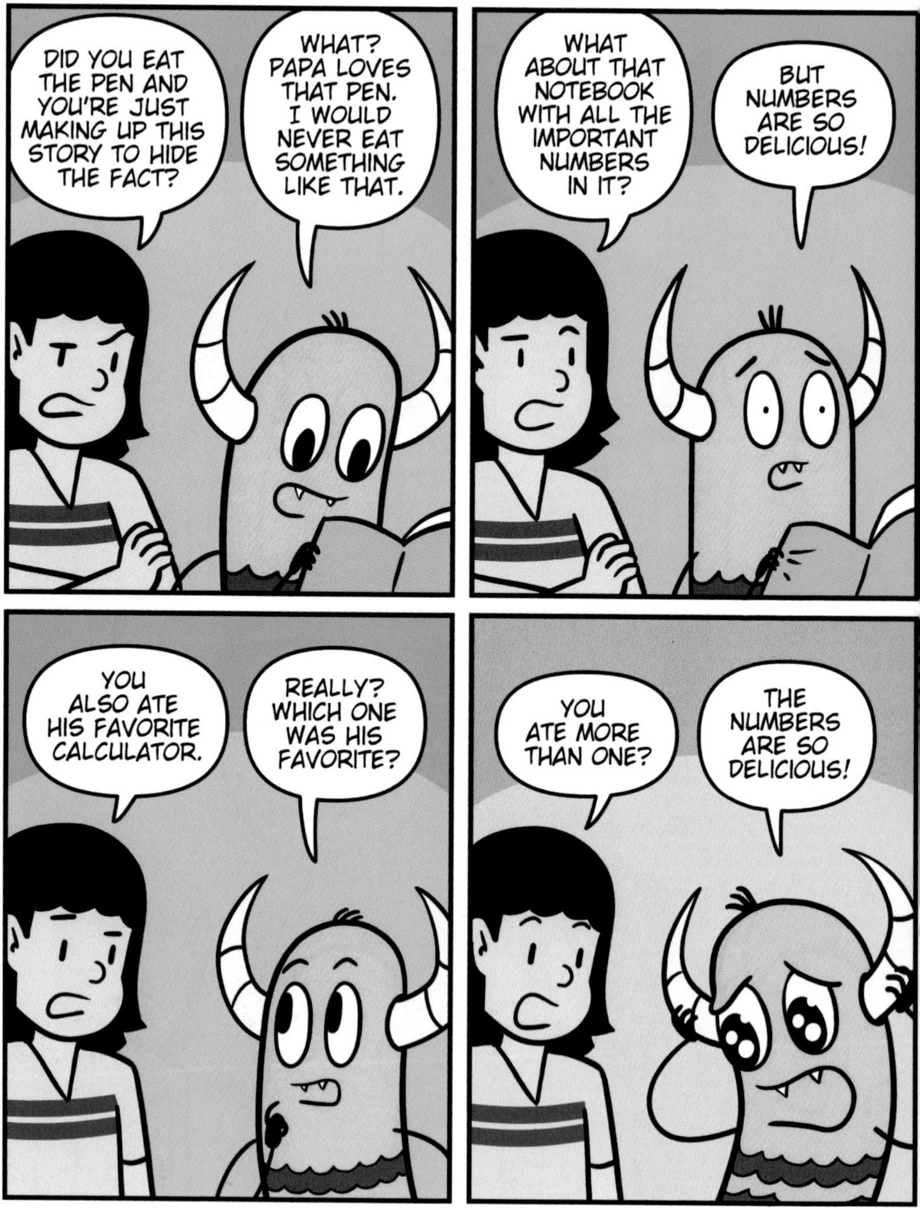
DID YOU EAT THE PEN AND YOU'RE JUST MAKING UP THIS STORY TO HIDE THE FACT?
WHAT? PAPA LOVES THAT PEN. I WOULD NEVER EAT SOMETHING LIKE THAT.
WHAT ABOUT THAT NOTEBOOK WITH ALL THE IMPORTANT NUMBERS IN IT?
BUT NUMBERS ARE SO DELICIOUS!
YOU ALSO ATE HIS FAVORITE CALCULATOR.
REALLY? WHICH ONE WAS HIS FAVORITE?
YOU ATE MORE THAN ONE?
THE NUMBERS ARE SO DELICIOUS!

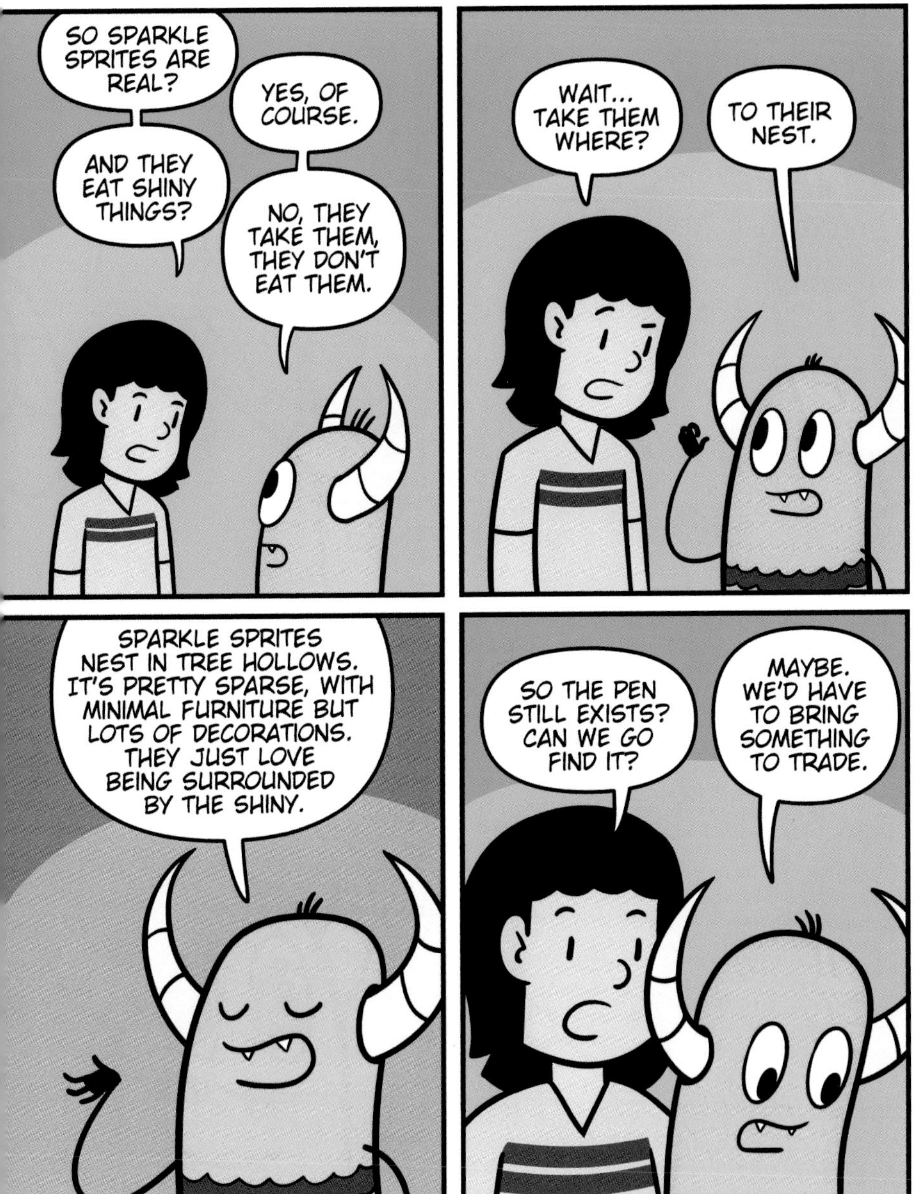
SO SPARKLE SPRITES ARE REAL?
YES, OF COURSE.
AND THEY EAT SHINY THINGS?
NO, THEY TAKE THEM, THEY DON'T EAT THEM.
WAIT... TAKE THEM WHERE?
TO THEIR NEST.
SPARKLE SPRITES NEST IN TREE HOLLOWS. IT'S PRETTY SPARSE, WITH MINIMAL FURNITURE BUT LOTS OF DECORATIONS. THEY JUST LOVE BEING SURROUNDED BY THE SHINY.
SO THE PEN STILL EXISTS? CAN WE GO FIND IT?
MAYBE. WE'D HAVE TO BRING SOMETHING TO TRADE.

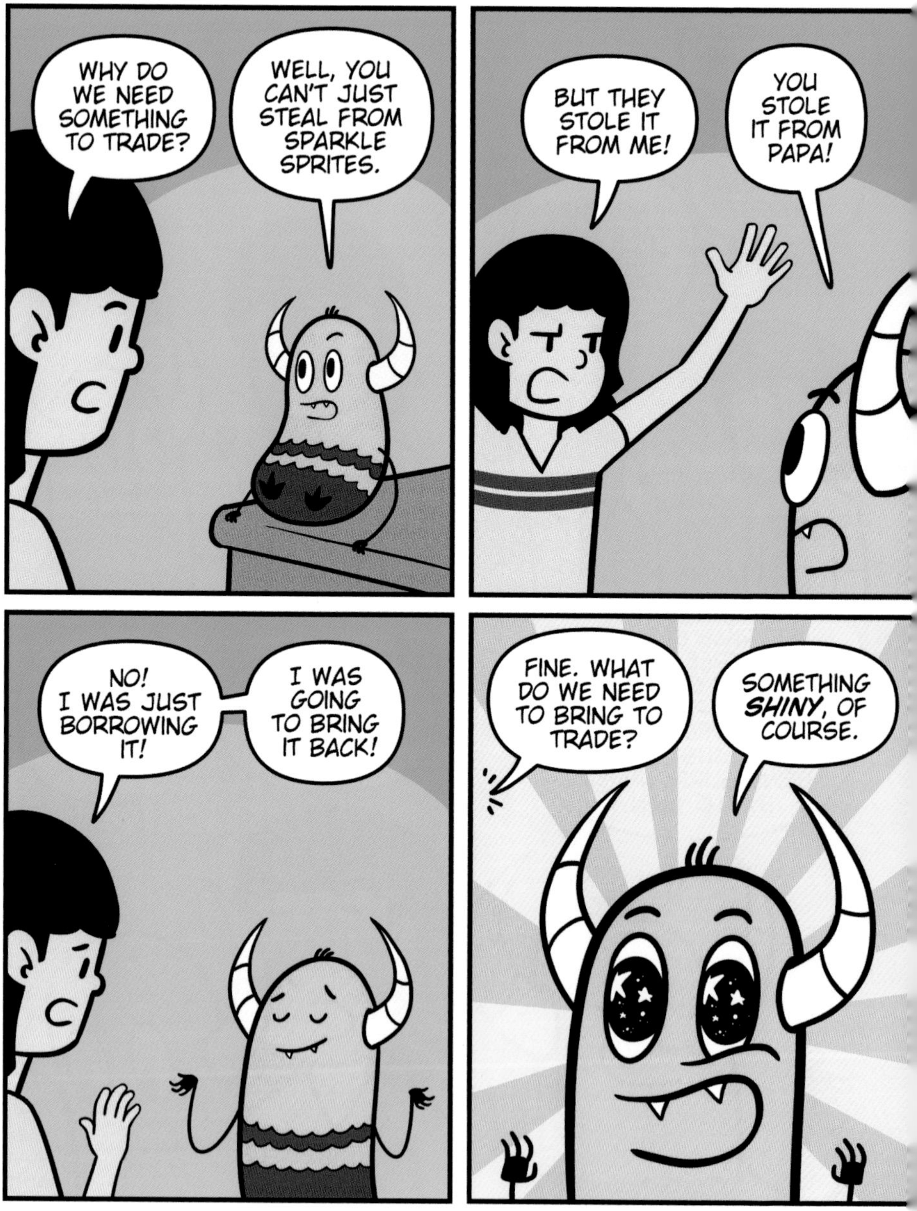
WHY DO WE NEED SOMETHING TO TRADE?
WELL, YOU CAN'T JUST STEAL FROM SPARKLE SPRITES.
BUT THEY STOLE IT FROM ME!
YOU STOLE IT FROM PAPA!
NO! I WAS JUST BORROWING IT!
I WAS GOING TO BRING IT BACK!
FINE. WHAT DO WE NEED TO BRING TO TRADE?
SOMETHING *SHINY*, OF COURSE.

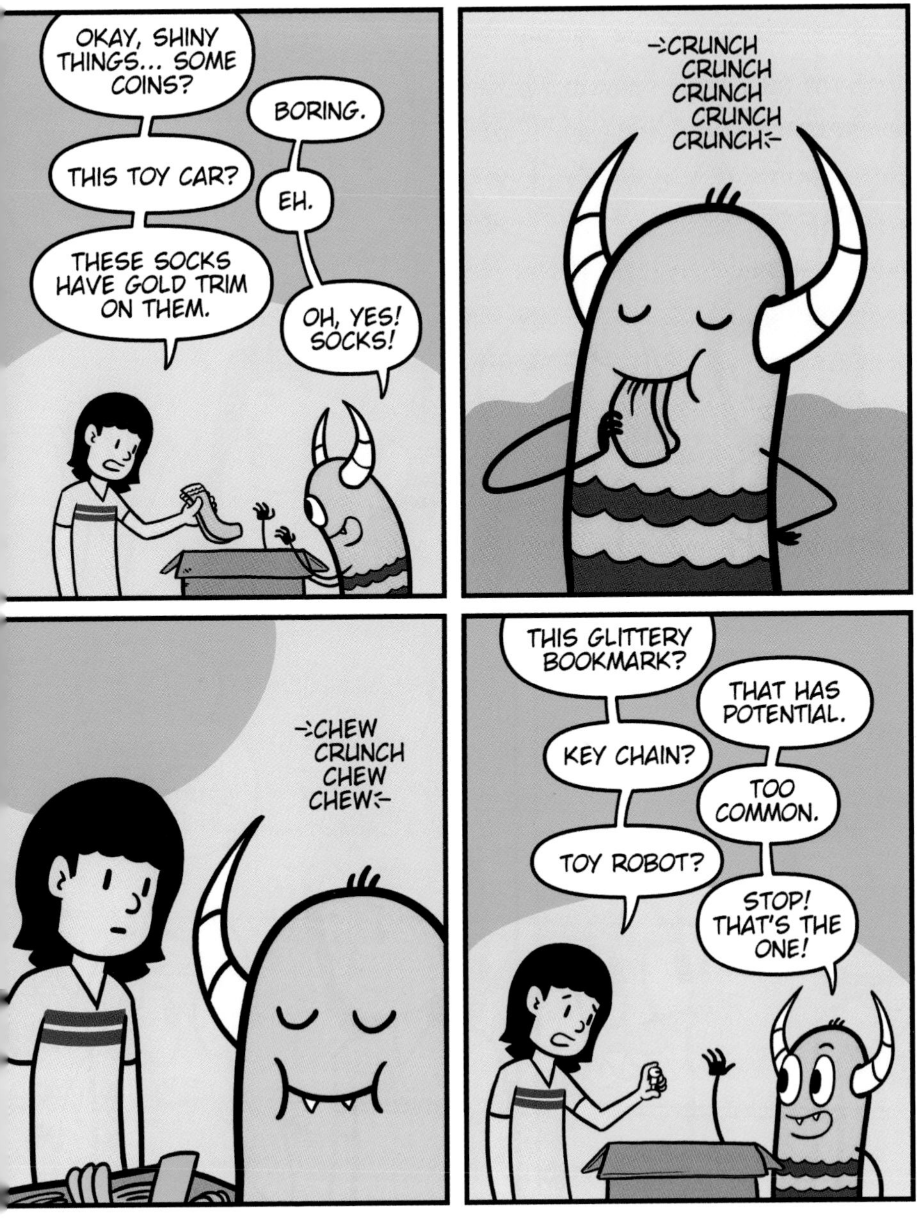
OKAY, SHINY THINGS... SOME COINS?
BORING.
THIS TOY CAR?
EH.
THESE SOCKS HAVE GOLD TRIM ON THEM.
OH, YES! SOCKS!
CRUNCH CRUNCH CRUNCH CRUNCH CRUNCH
CHEW CRUNCH CHEW CHEW
THIS GLITTERY BOOKMARK?
THAT HAS POTENTIAL.
KEY CHAIN?
TOO COMMON.
TOY ROBOT?
STOP! THAT'S THE ONE!

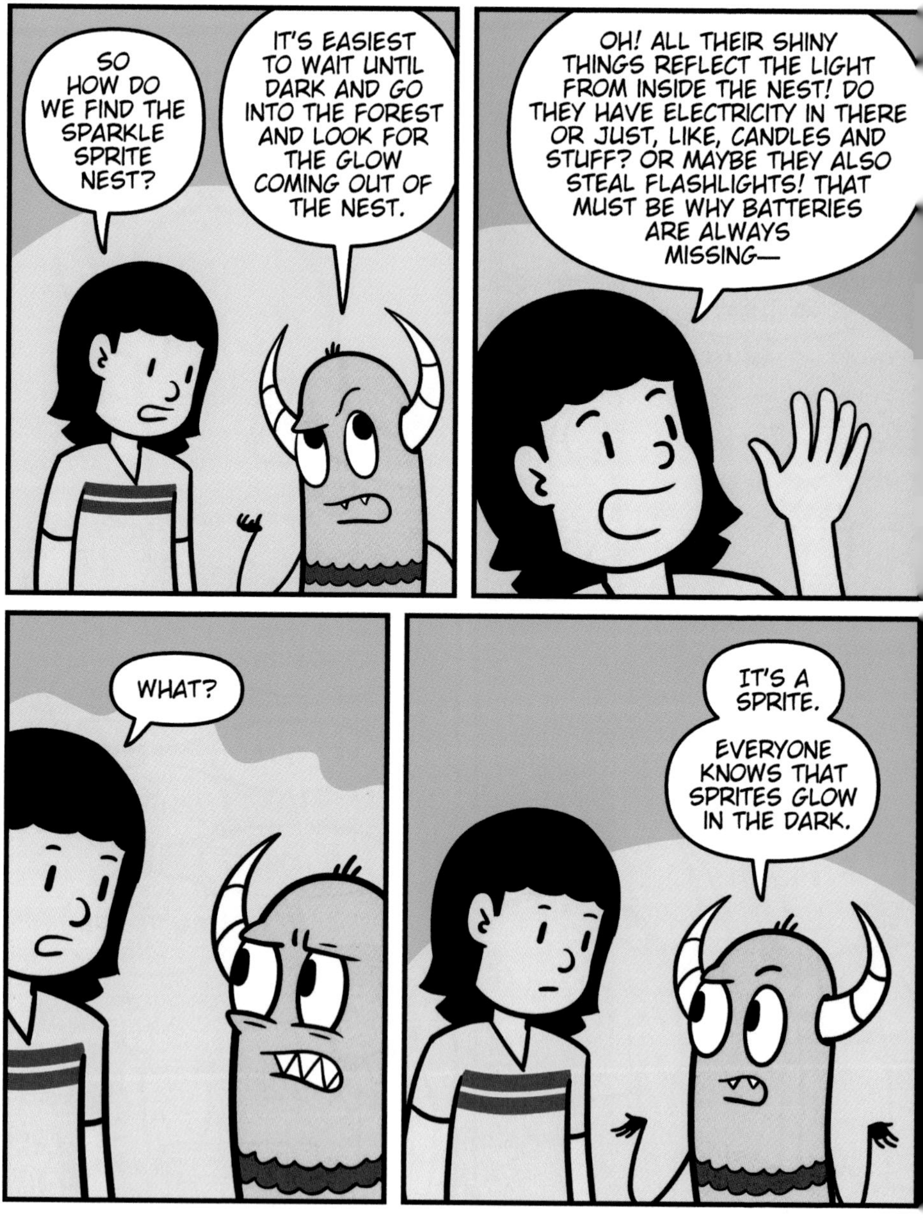
SO HOW DO WE FIND THE SPARKLE SPRITE NEST?
IT'S EASIEST TO WAIT UNTIL DARK AND GO INTO THE FOREST AND LOOK FOR THE GLOW COMING OUT OF THE NEST.
OH! ALL THEIR SHINY THINGS REFLECT THE LIGHT FROM INSIDE THE NEST! DO THEY HAVE ELECTRICITY IN THERE OR JUST, LIKE, CANDLES AND STUFF? OR MAYBE THEY ALSO STEAL FLASHLIGHTS! THAT MUST BE WHY BATTERIES ARE ALWAYS MISSING—
WHAT?
IT'S A SPRITE.
EVERYONE KNOWS THAT SPRITES GLOW IN THE DARK.

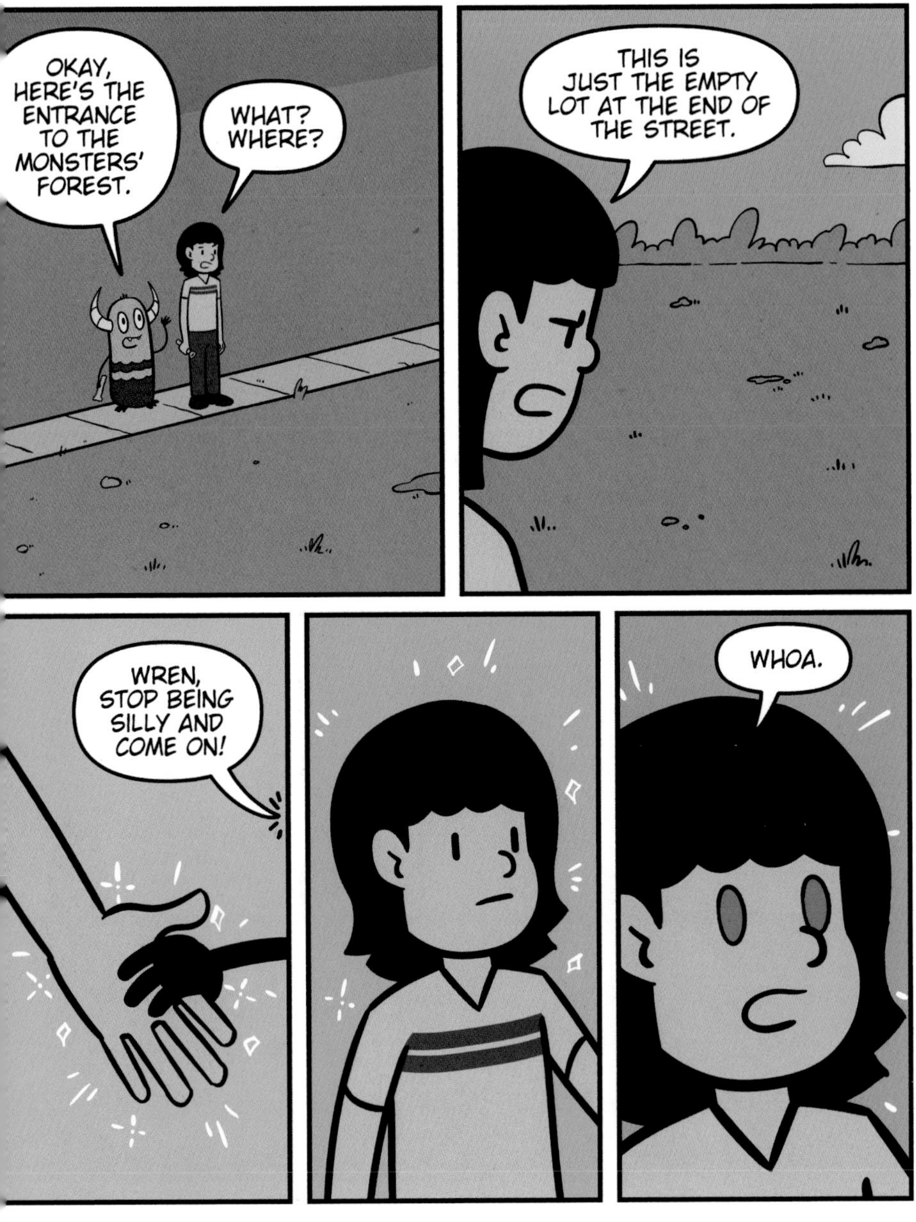
OKAY, HERE'S THE ENTRANCE TO THE MONSTERS' FOREST.
WHAT? WHERE?
THIS IS JUST THE EMPTY LOT AT THE END OF THE STREET.
WREN, STOP BEING SILLY AND COME ON!
WHOA.

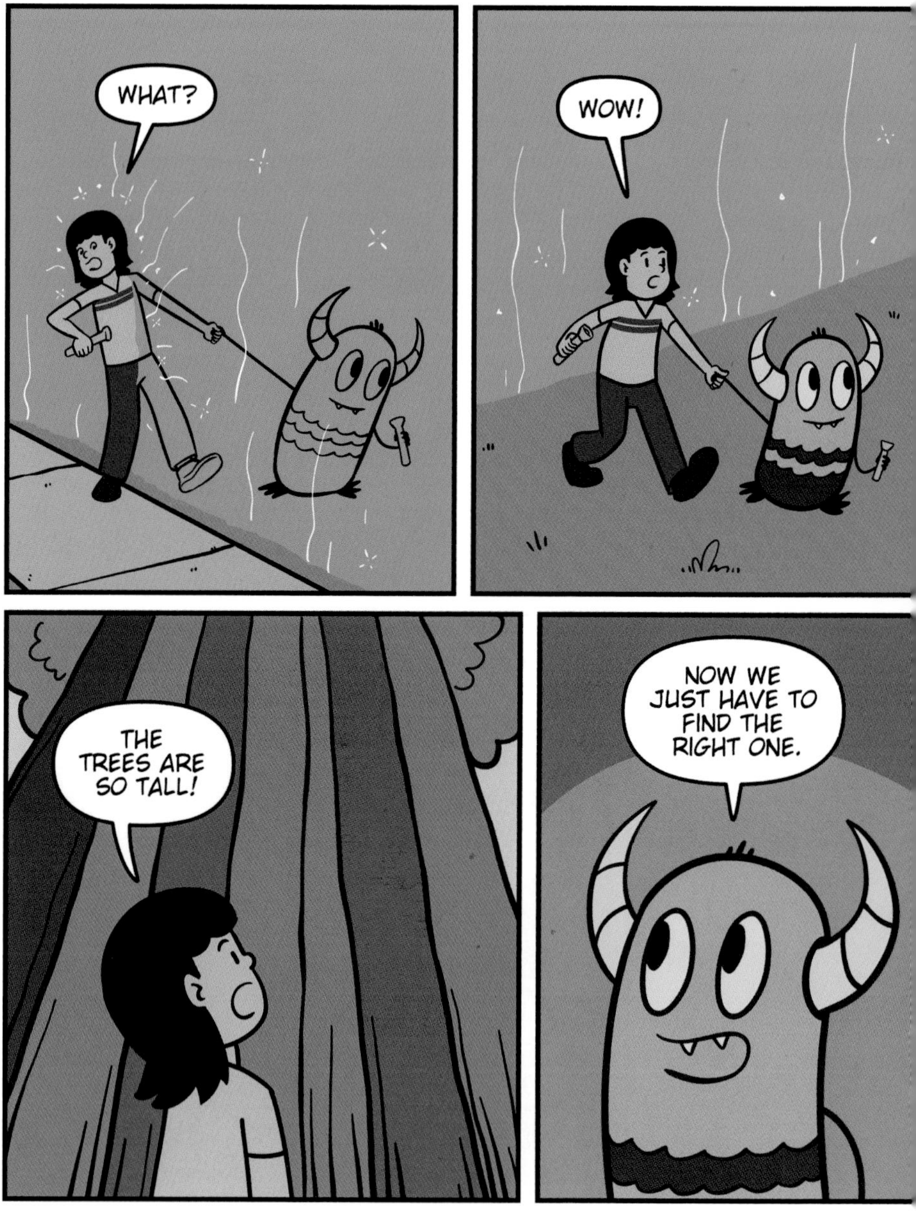
WHAT?
WOW!
THE TREES ARE SO TALL!
NOW WE JUST HAVE TO FIND THE RIGHT ONE.

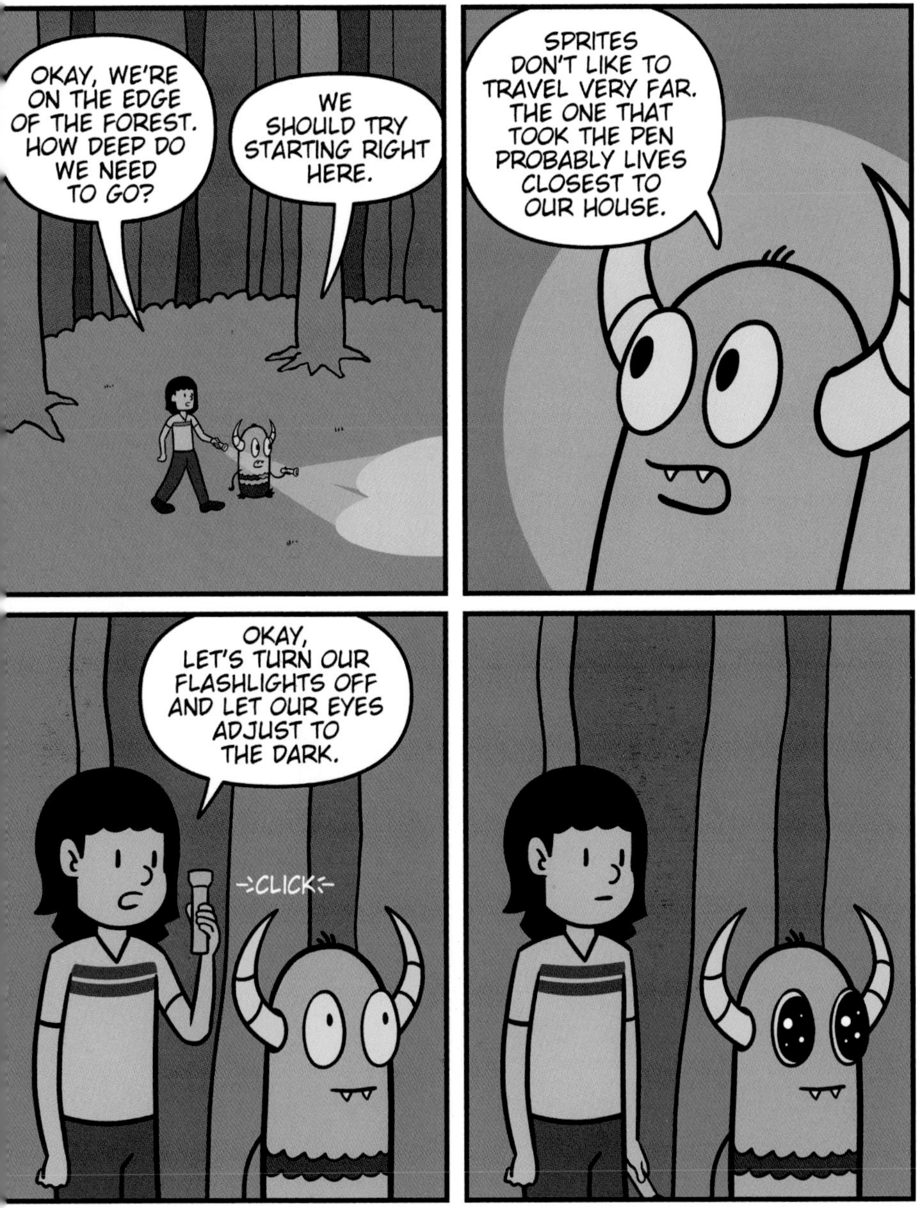
OKAY, WE'RE ON THE EDGE OF THE FOREST. HOW DEEP DO WE NEED TO GO?
WE SHOULD TRY STARTING RIGHT HERE.
SPRITES DON'T LIKE TO TRAVEL VERY FAR. THE ONE THAT TOOK THE PEN PROBABLY LIVES CLOSEST TO OUR HOUSE.
OKAY, LET'S TURN OUR FLASHLIGHTS OFF AND LET OUR EYES ADJUST TO THE DARK.
CLICK

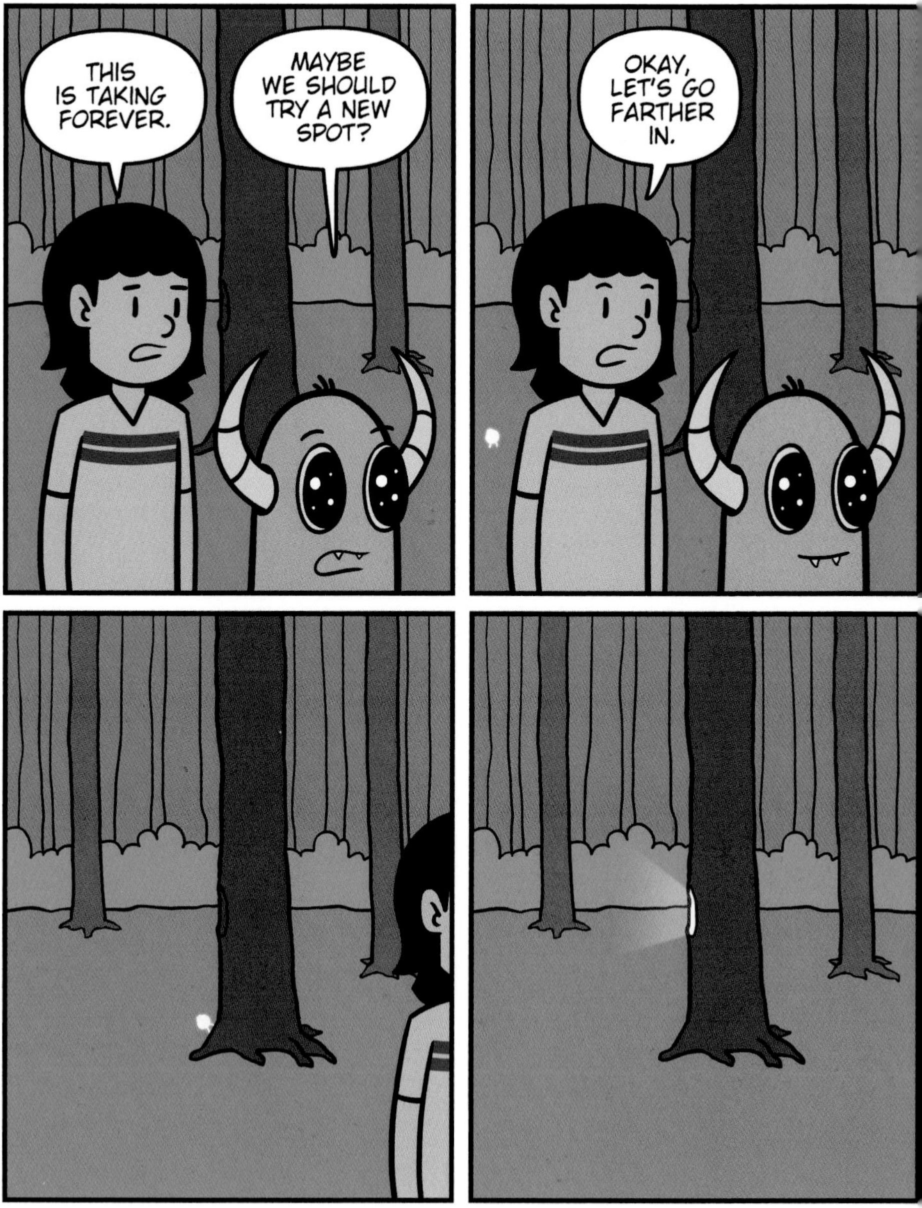
THIS IS TAKING FOREVER.
MAYBE WE SHOULD TRY A NEW SPOT?
OKAY, LET'S GO FARTHER IN.

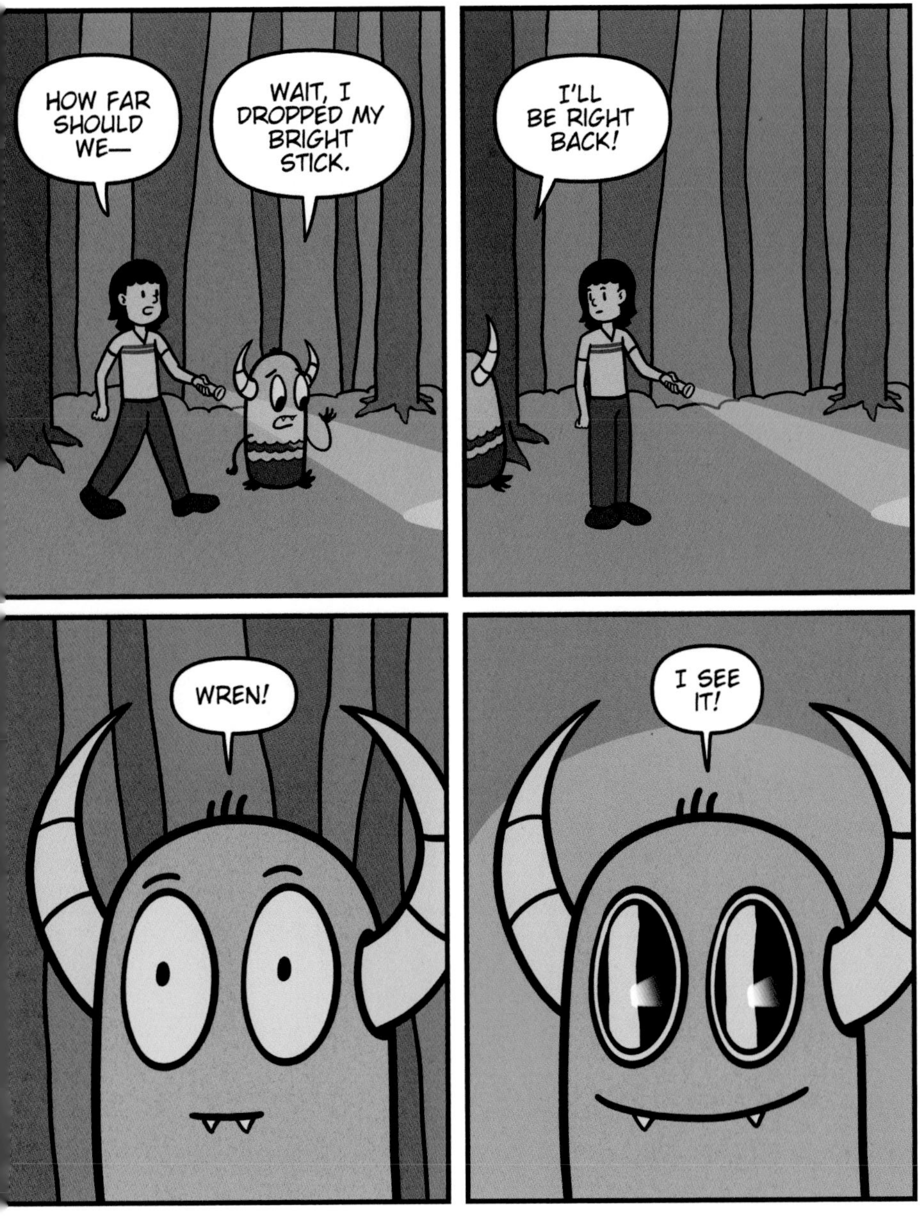
HOW FAR SHOULD WE—
WAIT, I DROPPED MY BRIGHT STICK.
I'LL BE RIGHT BACK!
WREN!
I SEE IT!

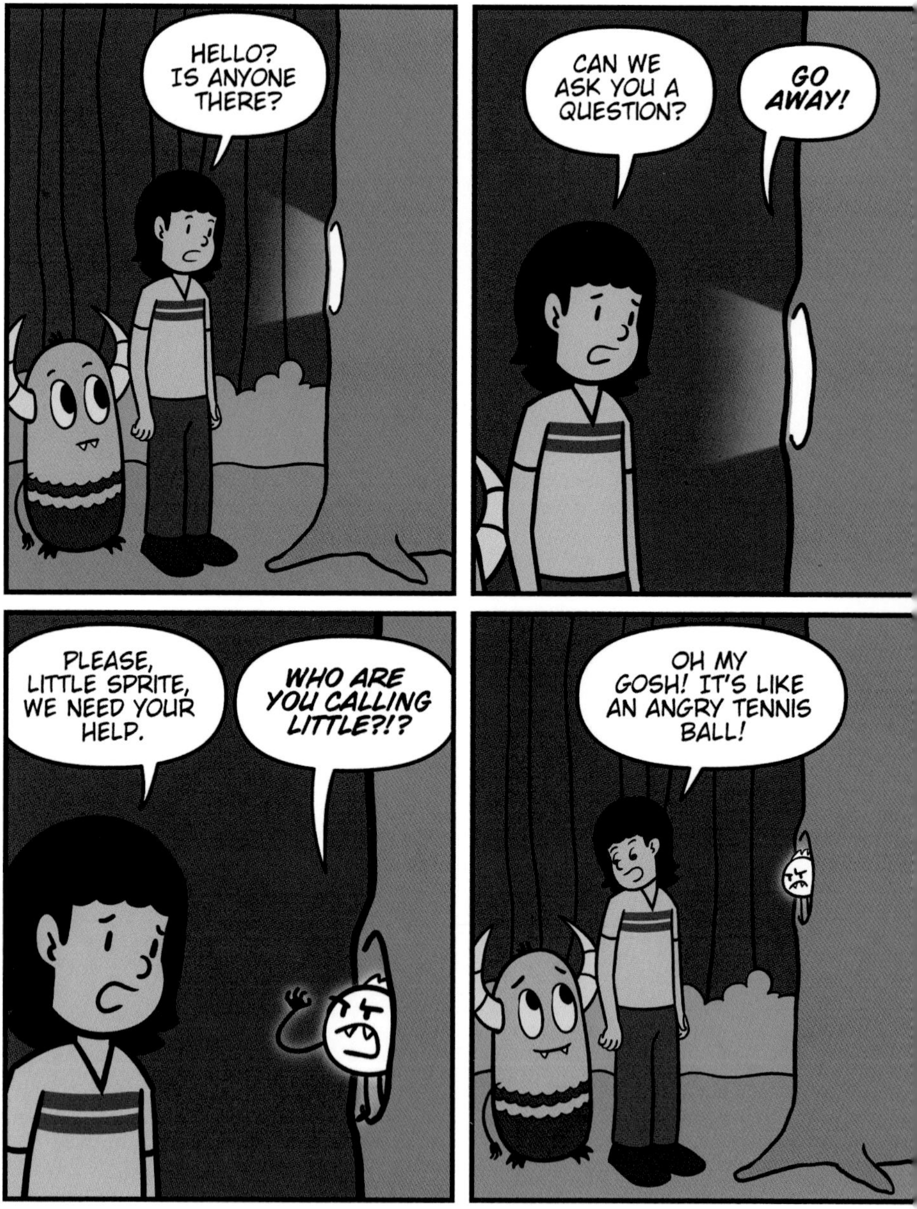
HELLO? IS ANYONE THERE?
CAN WE ASK YOU A QUESTION?
GO AWAY!
PLEASE, LITTLE SPRITE, WE NEED YOUR HELP.
WHO ARE YOU CALLING LITTLE?!?
OH MY GOSH! IT'S LIKE AN ANGRY TENNIS BALL!

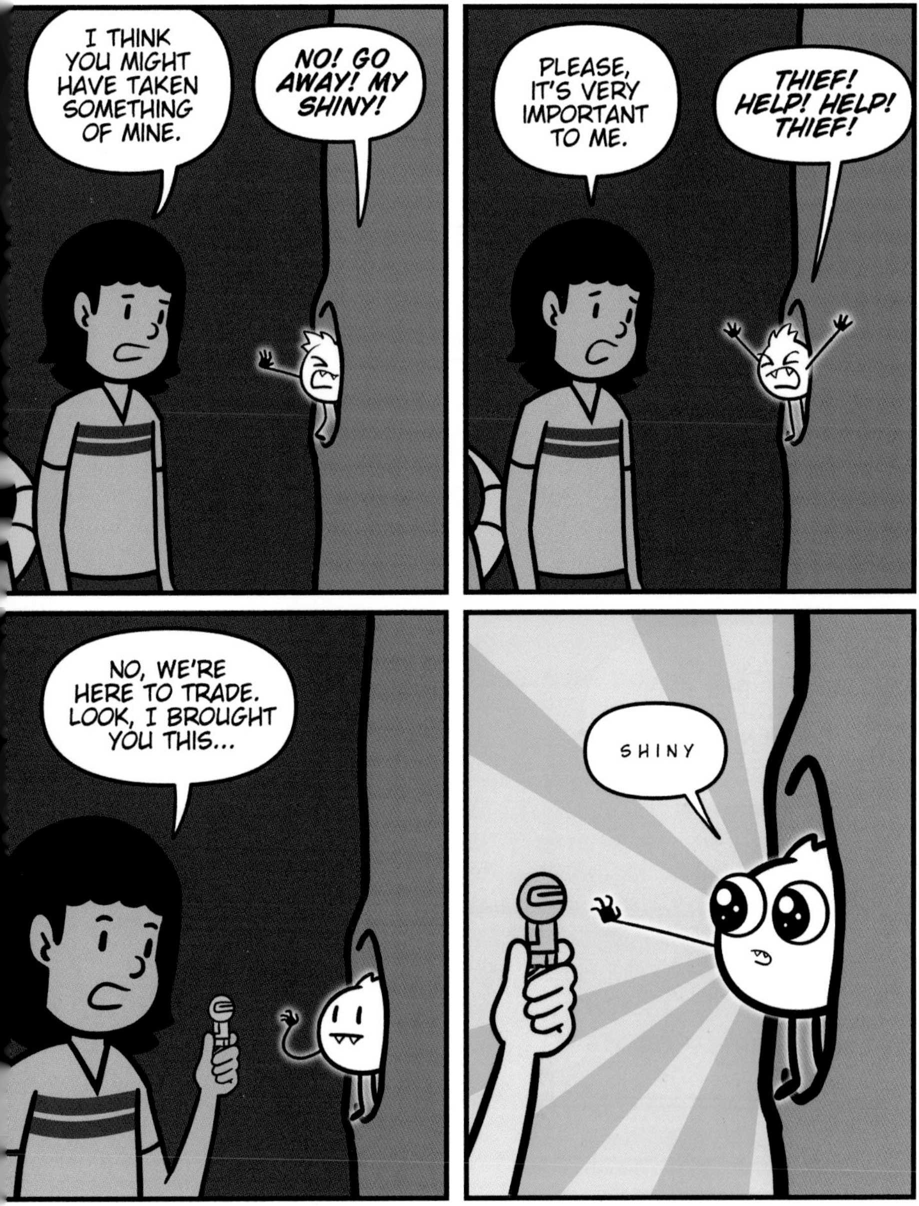
I THINK YOU MIGHT HAVE TAKEN SOMETHING OF MINE.
NO! GO AWAY! MY SHINY!
PLEASE, IT'S VERY IMPORTANT TO ME.
THIEF! HELP! HELP! THIEF!
NO, WE'RE HERE TO TRADE. LOOK, I BROUGHT YOU THIS...
SHINY

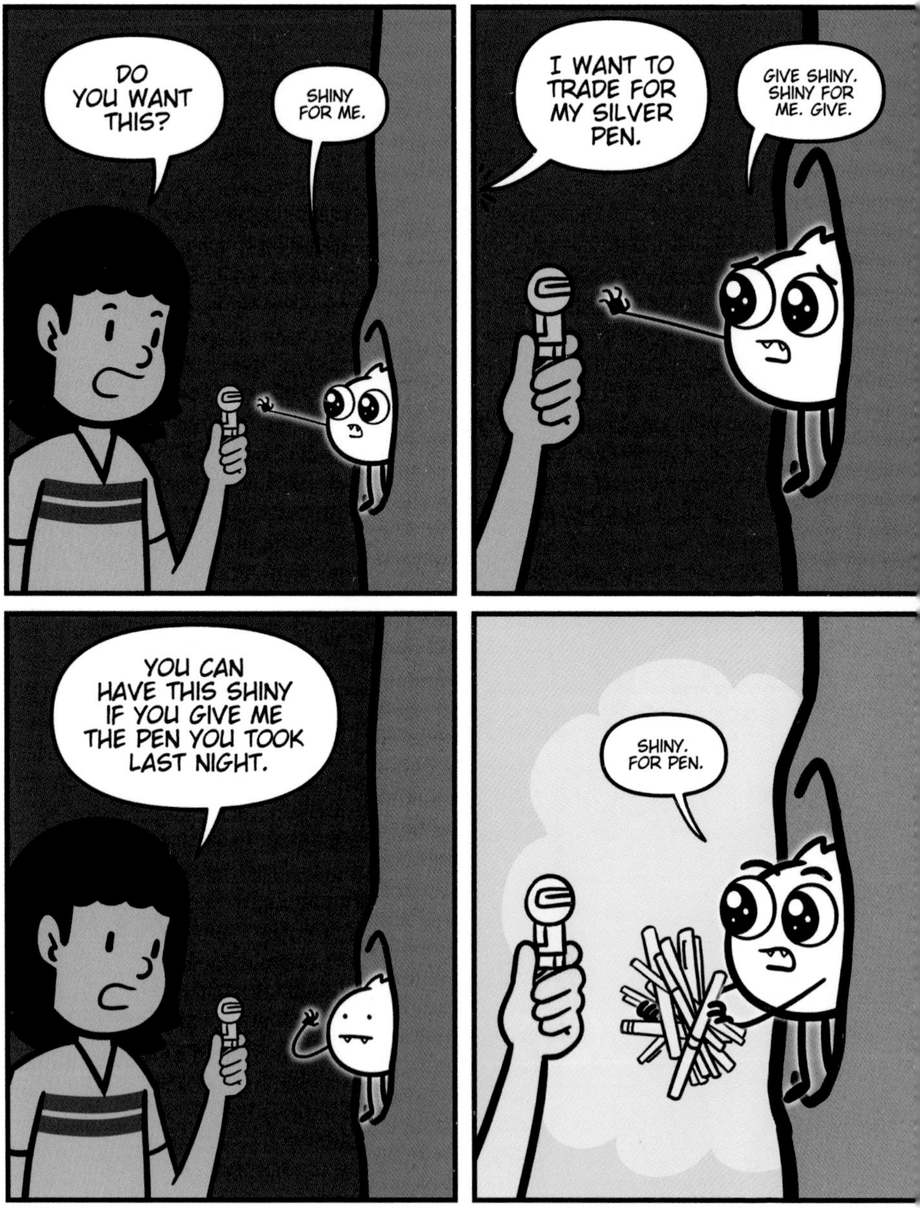
DO YOU WANT THIS?
SHINY FOR ME.
I WANT TO TRADE FOR MY SILVER PEN.
GIVE SHINY. SHINY FOR ME. GIVE.
YOU CAN HAVE THIS SHINY IF YOU GIVE ME THE PEN YOU TOOK LAST NIGHT.
SHINY. FOR PEN.

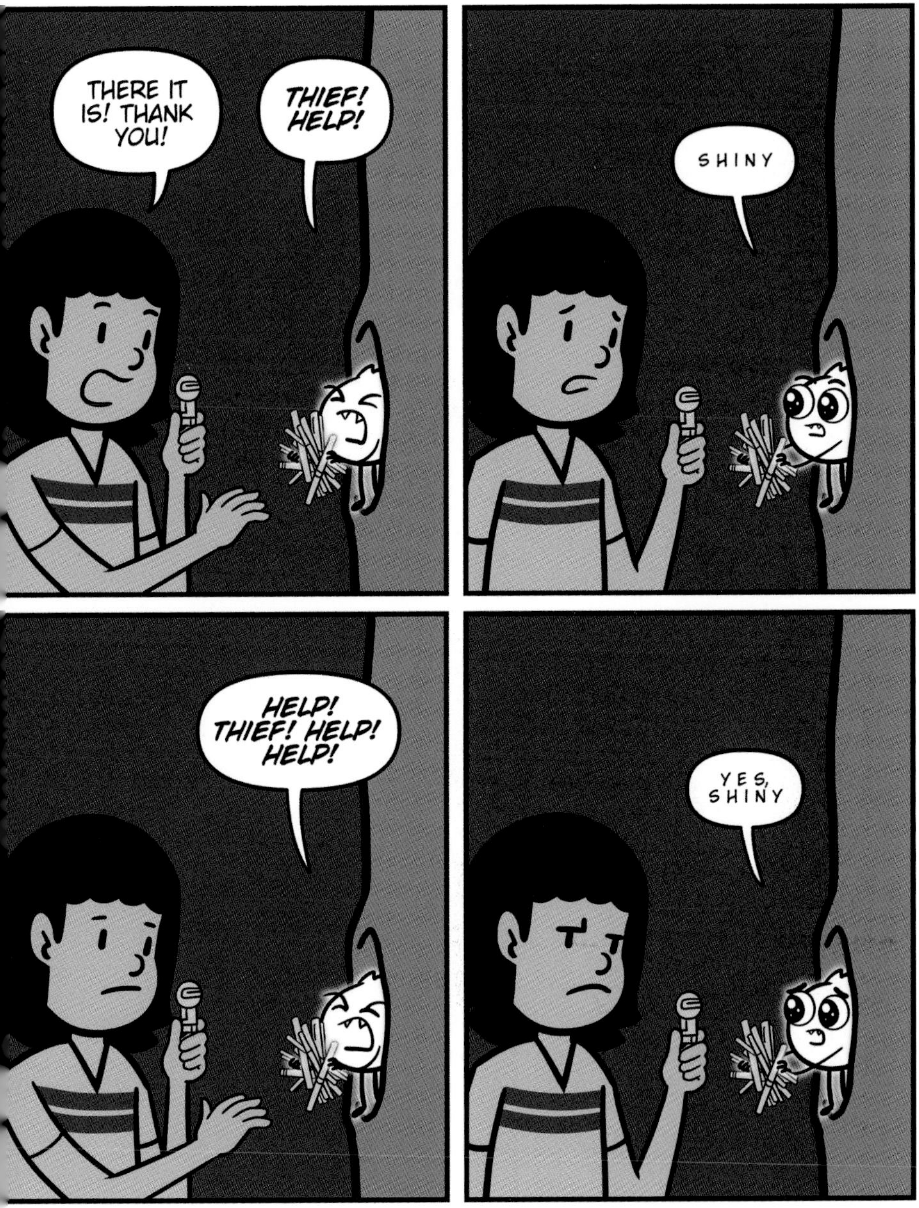
THERE IT IS! THANK YOU!
THIEF! HELP!
SHINY
HELP! THIEF! HELP! HELP!
YES, SHINY

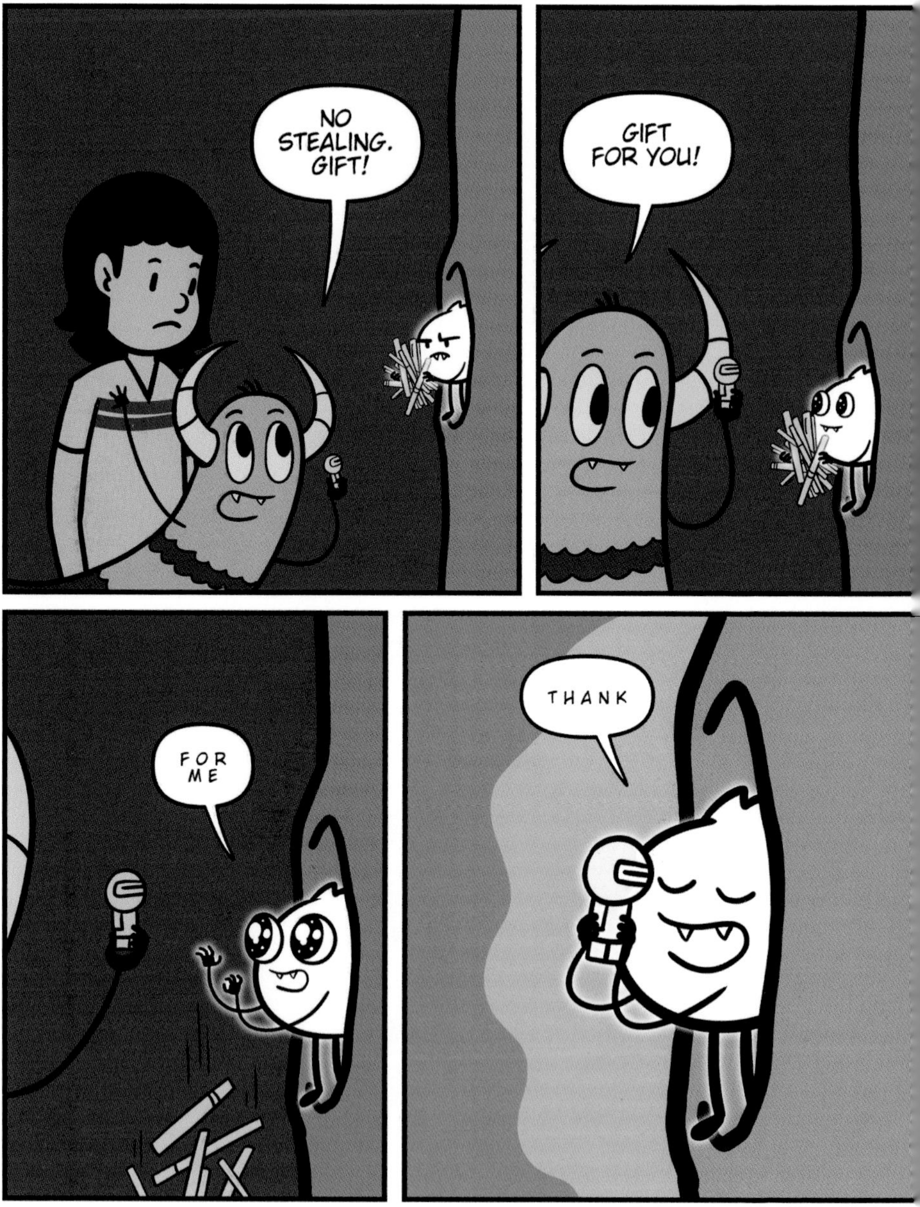
NO STEALING. GIFT!
GIFT FOR YOU!
FOR ME
THANK

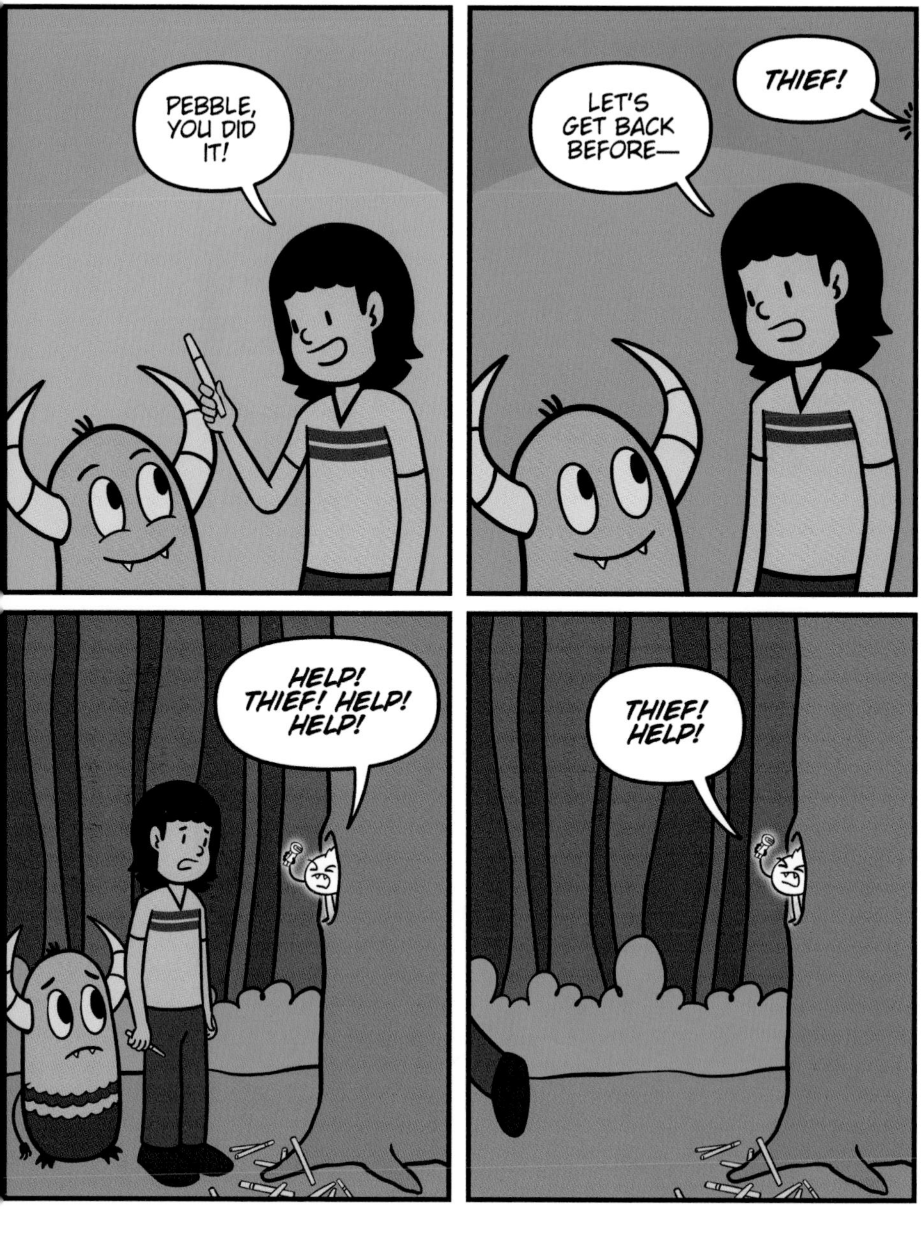
PEBBLE, YOU DID IT!
LET'S GET BACK BEFORE—
THIEF!
HELP! THIEF! HELP! HELP!
THIEF! HELP!

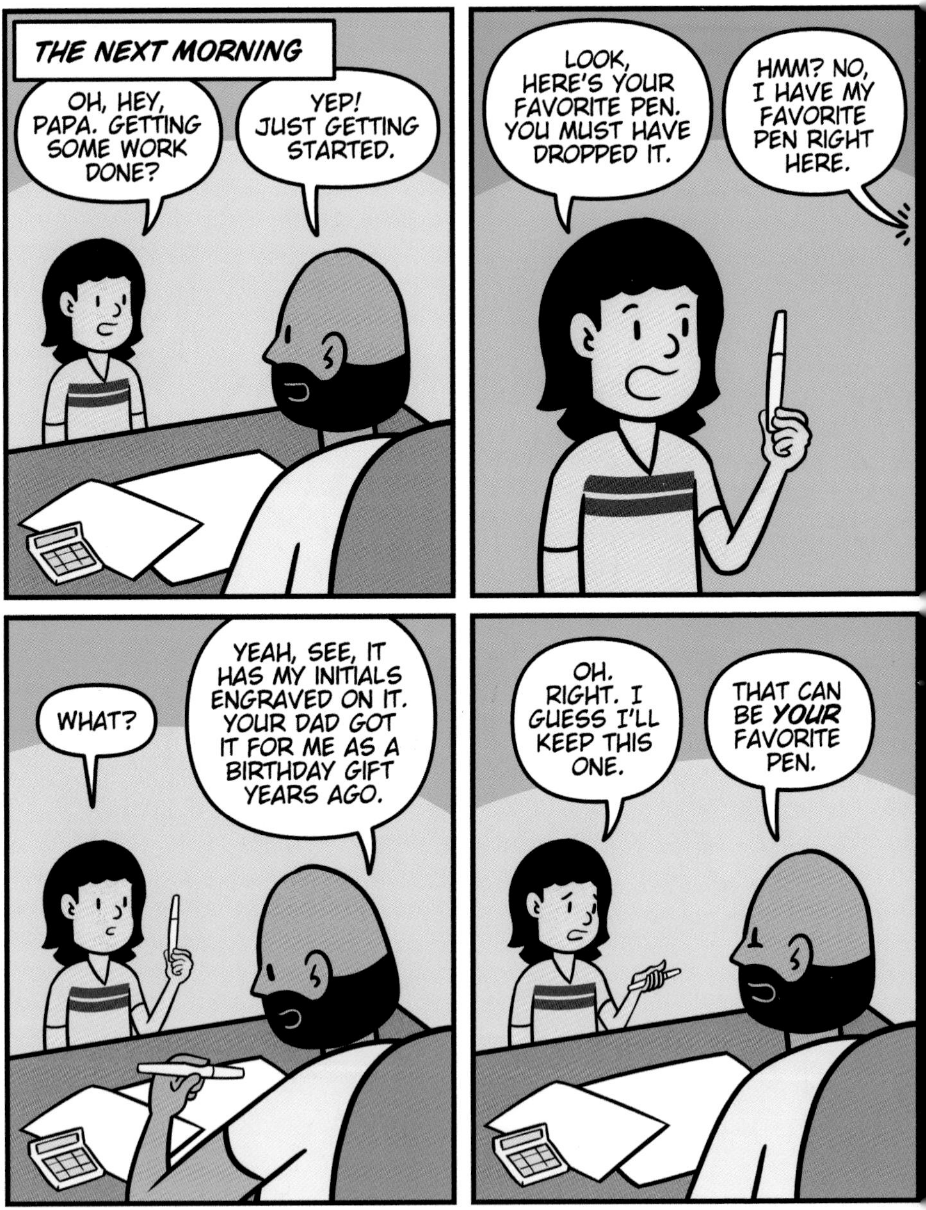
THE NEXT MORNING
OH, HEY, PAPA. GETTING SOME WORK DONE?
YEP! JUST GETTING STARTED.
LOOK, HERE'S YOUR FAVORITE PEN. YOU MUST HAVE DROPPED IT.
HMM? NO, I HAVE MY FAVORITE PEN RIGHT HERE.
WHAT?
YEAH, SEE, IT HAS MY INITIALS ENGRAVED ON IT. YOUR DAD GOT IT FOR ME AS A BIRTHDAY GIFT YEARS AGO.
OH. RIGHT. I GUESS I'LL KEEP THIS ONE.
THAT CAN BE *YOUR* FAVORITE PEN.

CHAPTER SIX

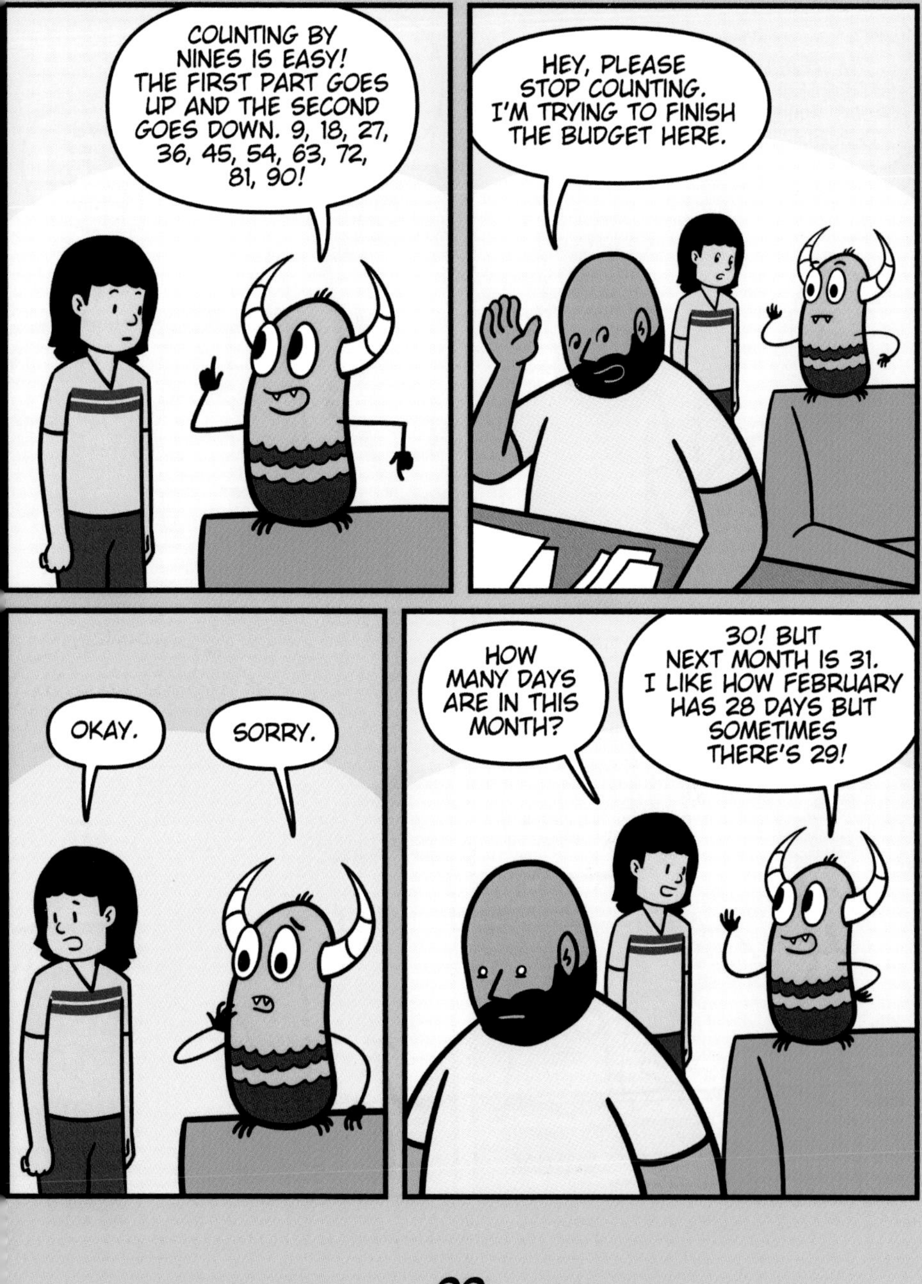
COUNTING BY NINES IS EASY! THE FIRST PART GOES UP AND THE SECOND GOES DOWN. 9, 18, 27, 36, 45, 54, 63, 72, 81, 90!
HEY, PLEASE STOP COUNTING. I'M TRYING TO FINISH THE BUDGET HERE.
OKAY.
SORRY.
HOW MANY DAYS ARE IN THIS MONTH?
30! BUT NEXT MONTH IS 31. I LIKE HOW FEBRUARY HAS 28 DAYS BUT SOMETIMES THERE'S 29!

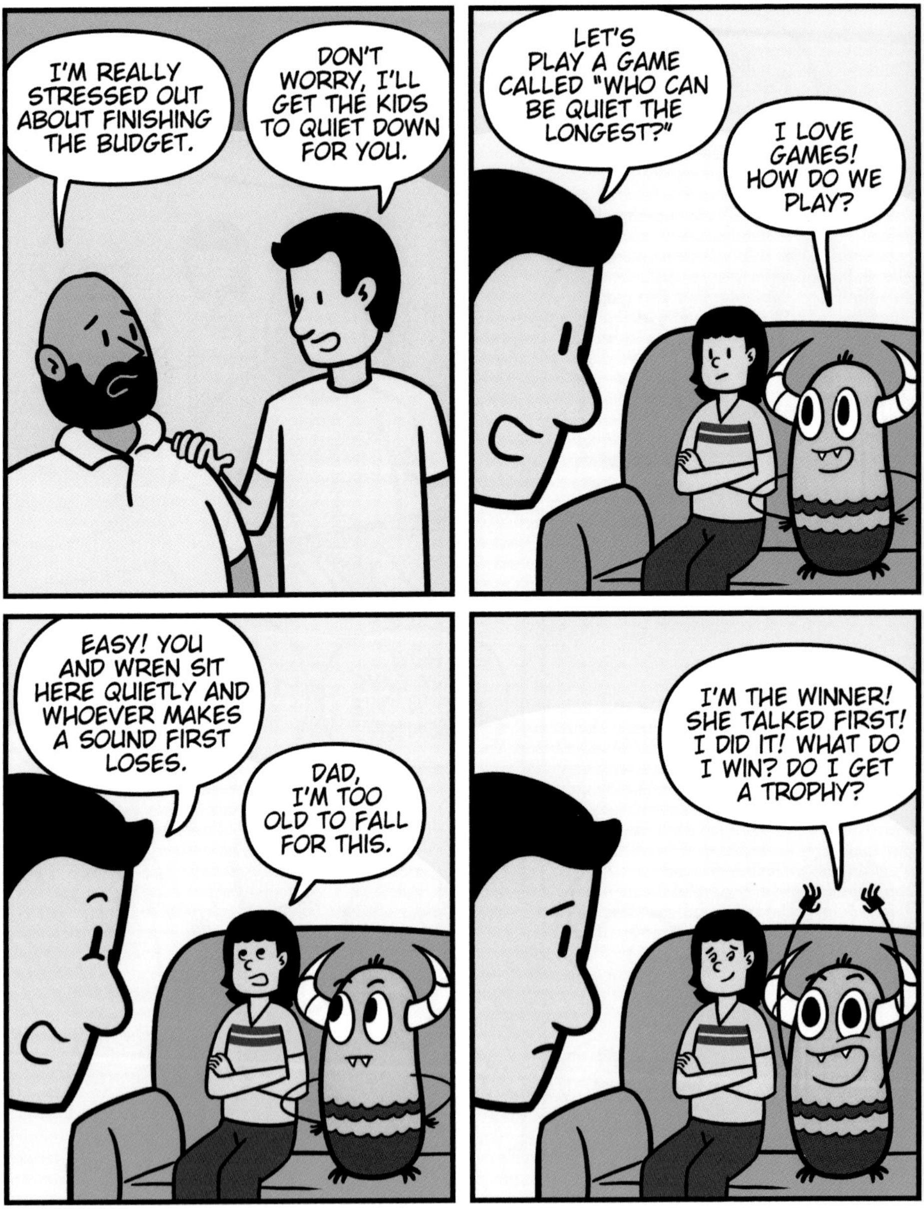
I'M REALLY STRESSED OUT ABOUT FINISHING THE BUDGET.
DON'T WORRY, I'LL GET THE KIDS TO QUIET DOWN FOR YOU.
LET'S PLAY A GAME CALLED "WHO CAN BE QUIET THE LONGEST?"
I LOVE GAMES! HOW DO WE PLAY?
EASY! YOU AND WREN SIT HERE QUIETLY AND WHOEVER MAKES A SOUND FIRST LOSES.
DAD, I'M TOO OLD TO FALL FOR THIS.
I'M THE WINNER! SHE TALKED FIRST! I DID IT! WHAT DO I WIN? DO I GET A TROPHY?

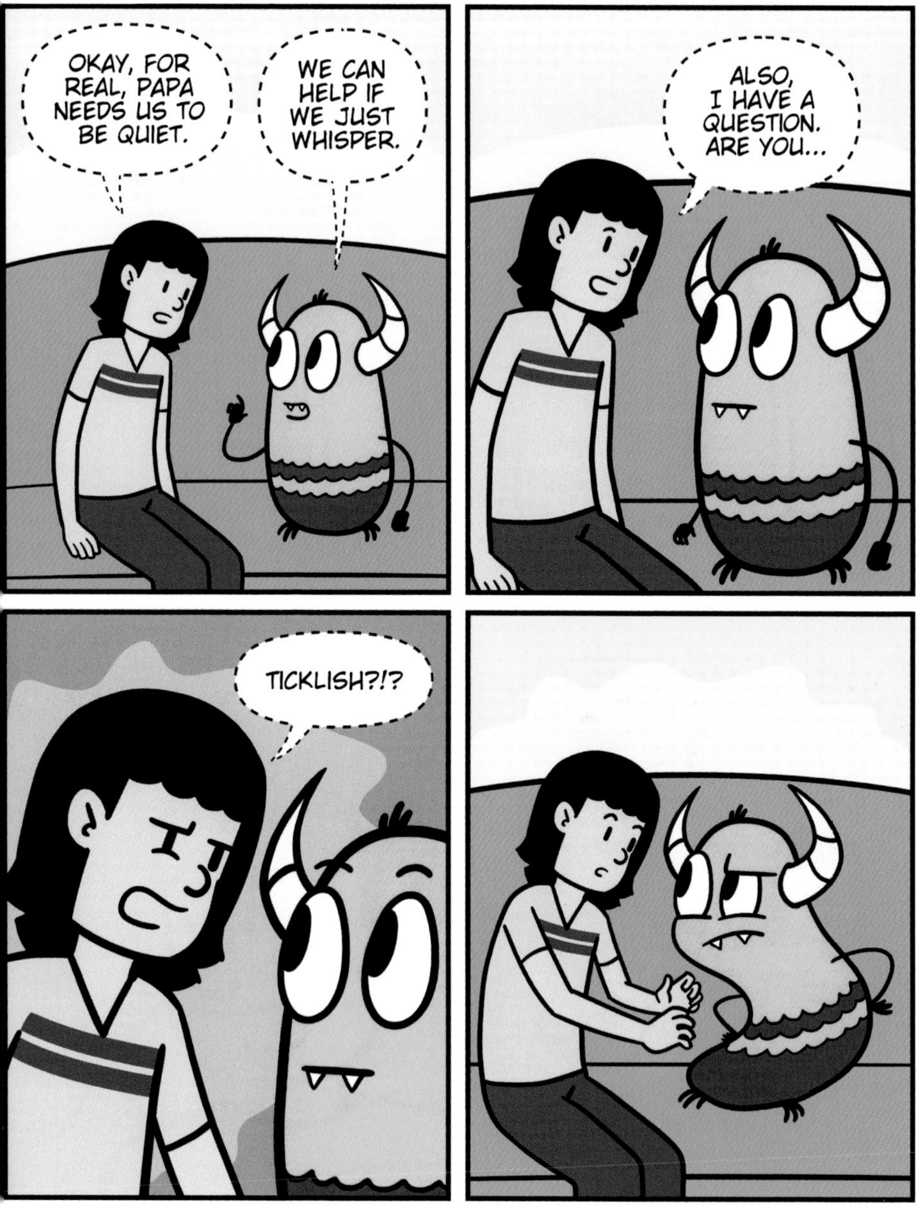
OKAY, FOR REAL, PAPA NEEDS US TO BE QUIET.
WE CAN HELP IF WE JUST WHISPER.
ALSO, I HAVE A QUESTION. ARE YOU...
TICKLISH?!?

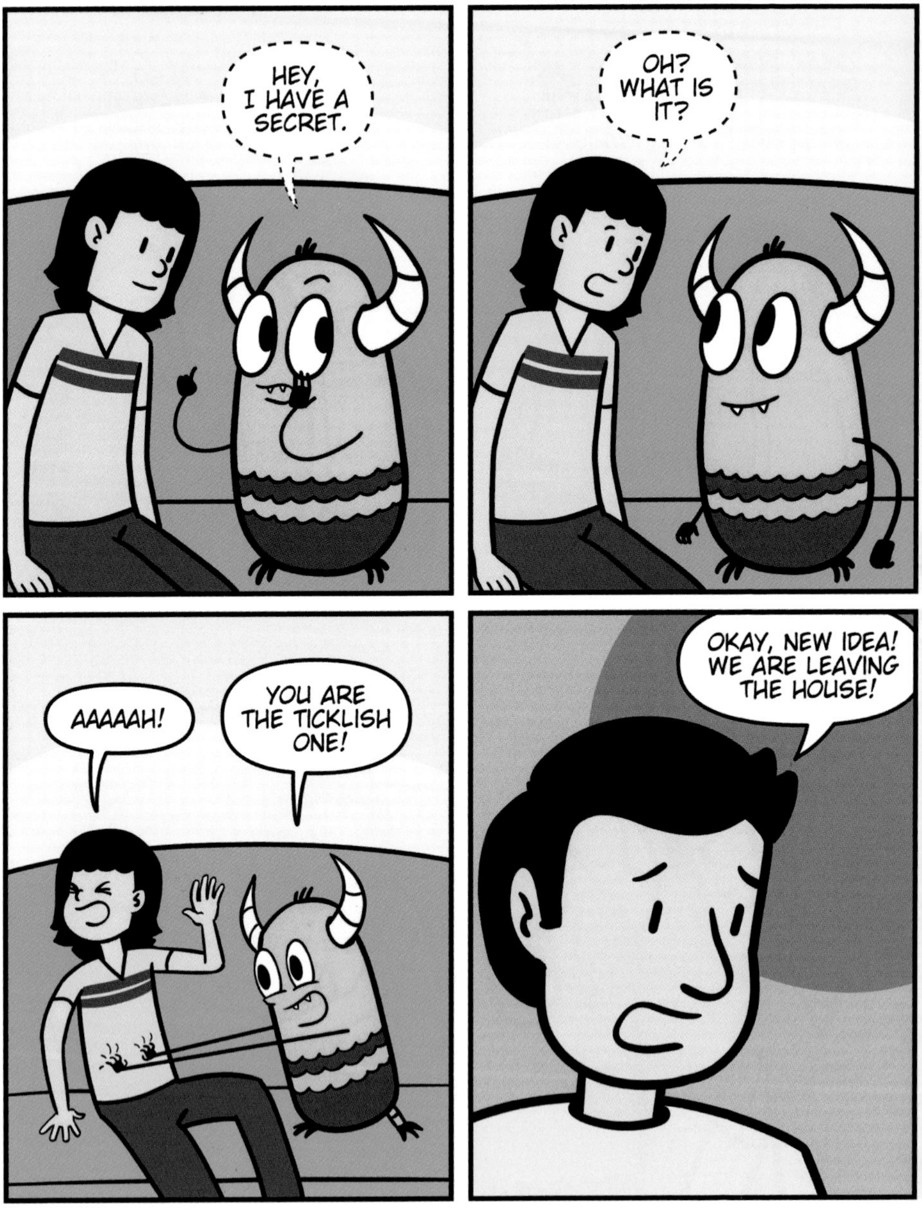
HEY, I HAVE A SECRET.
OH? WHAT IS IT?
AAAAAH!
YOU ARE THE TICKLISH ONE!
OKAY, NEW IDEA! WE ARE LEAVING THE HOUSE!

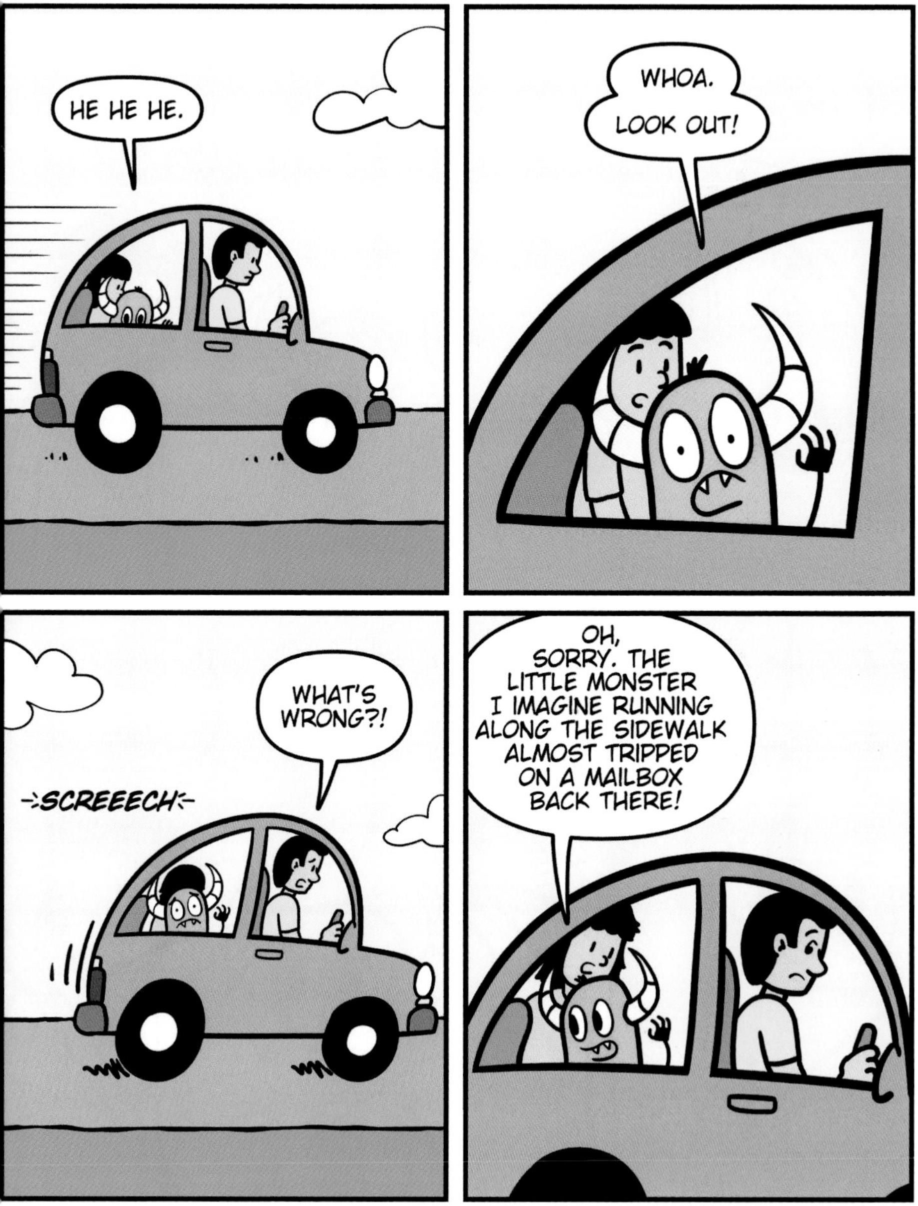
HE HE HE.
WHOA.
LOOK OUT!
WHAT'S WRONG?!
SCREEECH
OH, SORRY. THE LITTLE MONSTER I IMAGINE RUNNING ALONG THE SIDEWALK ALMOST TRIPPED ON A MAILBOX BACK THERE!

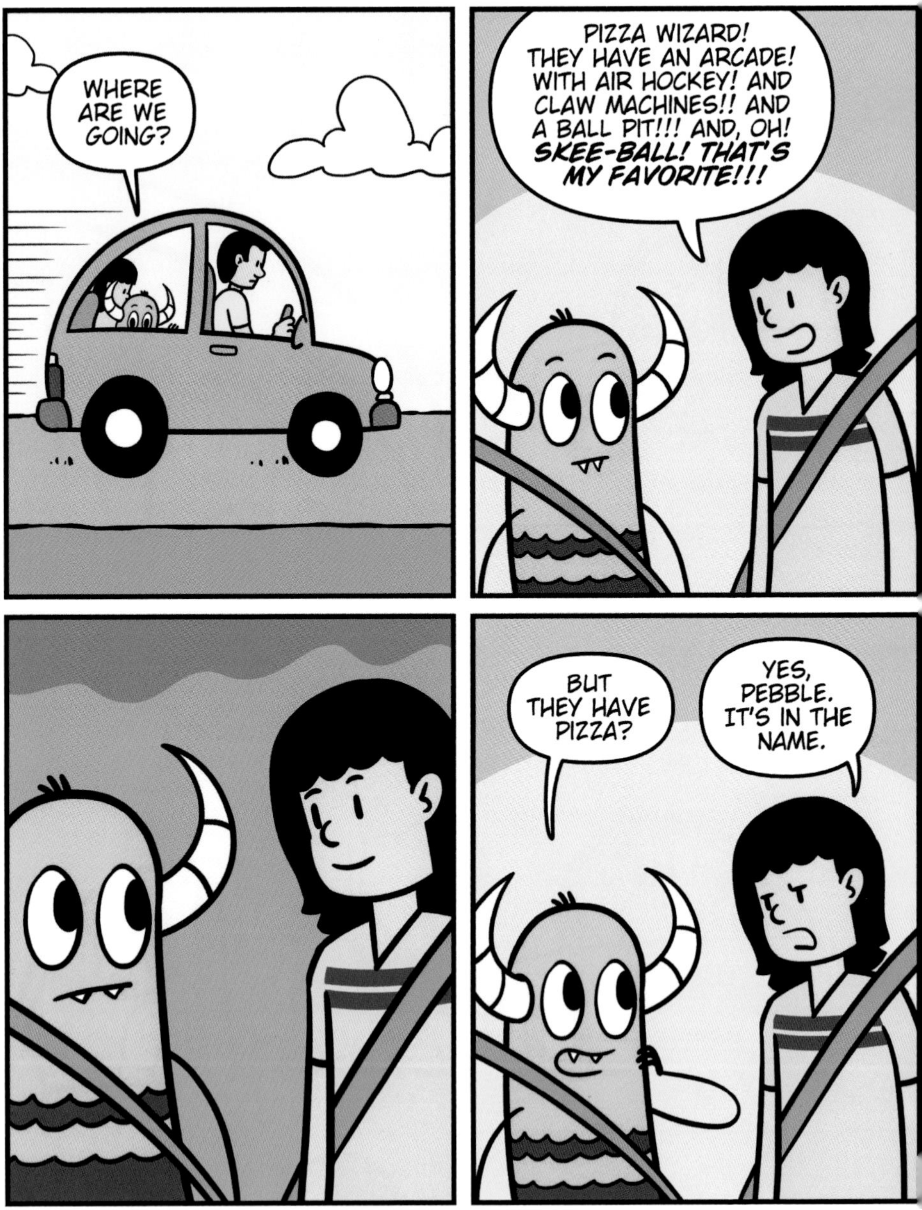
WHERE ARE WE GOING?
PIZZA WIZARD! THEY HAVE AN ARCADE! WITH AIR HOCKEY! AND CLAW MACHINES!! AND A BALL PIT!!! AND, OH! ***SKEE-BALL! THAT'S MY FAVORITE!!!***
BUT THEY HAVE PIZZA?
YES, PEBBLE. IT'S IN THE NAME.

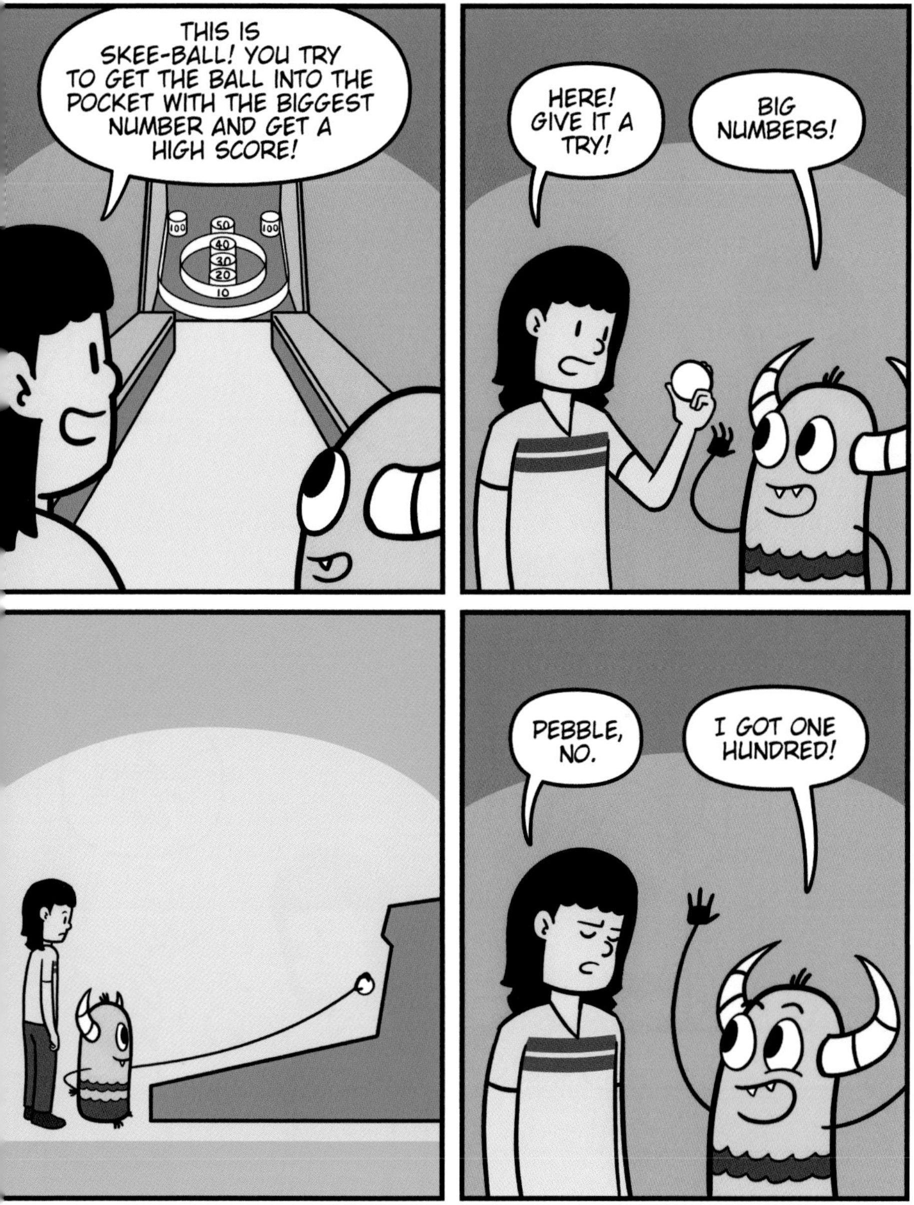
THIS IS SKEE-BALL! YOU TRY TO GET THE BALL INTO THE POCKET WITH THE BIGGEST NUMBER AND GET A HIGH SCORE!
100
50
100
40
30
20
10
HERE! GIVE IT A TRY!
BIG NUMBERS!
PEBBLE, NO.
I GOT ONE HUNDRED!

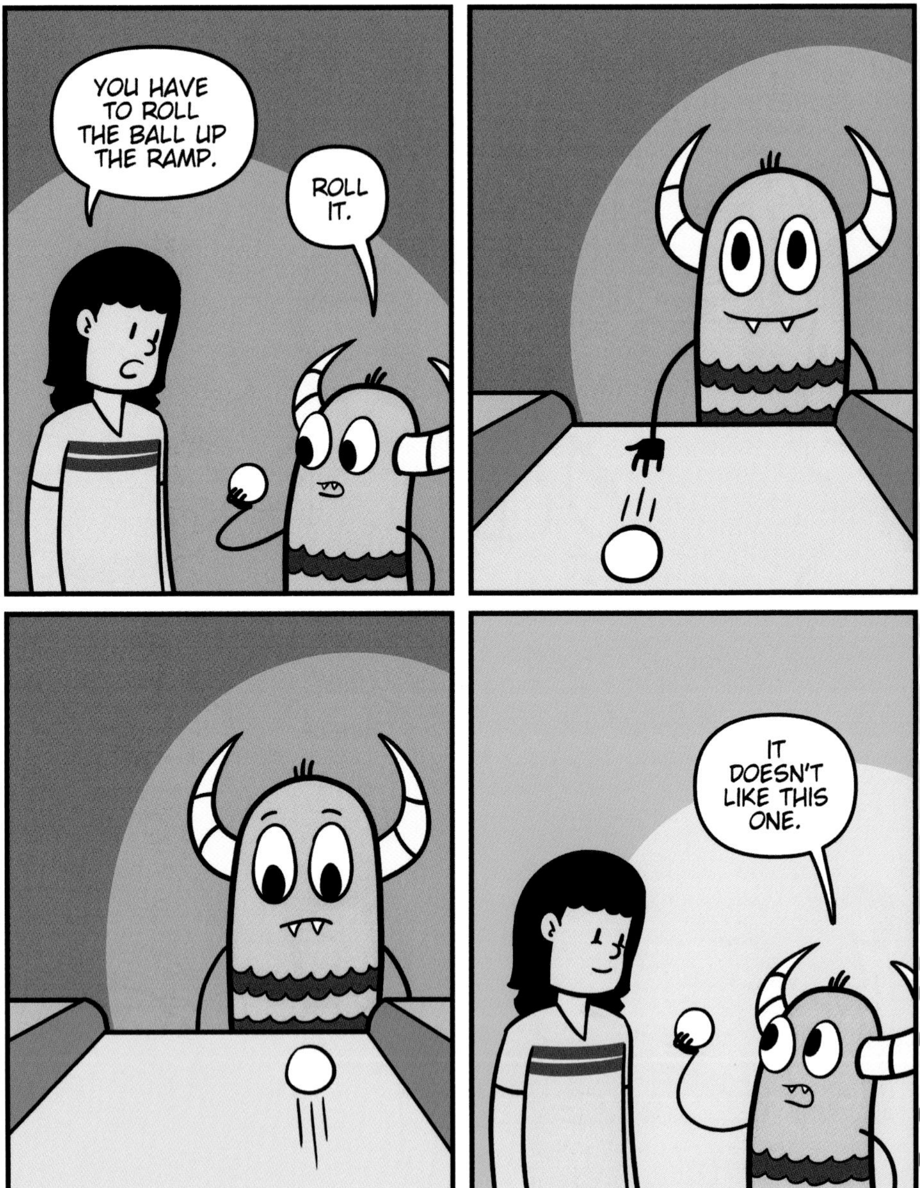
YOU HAVE TO ROLL THE BALL UP THE RAMP.
ROLL IT.
IT DOESN'T LIKE THIS ONE.

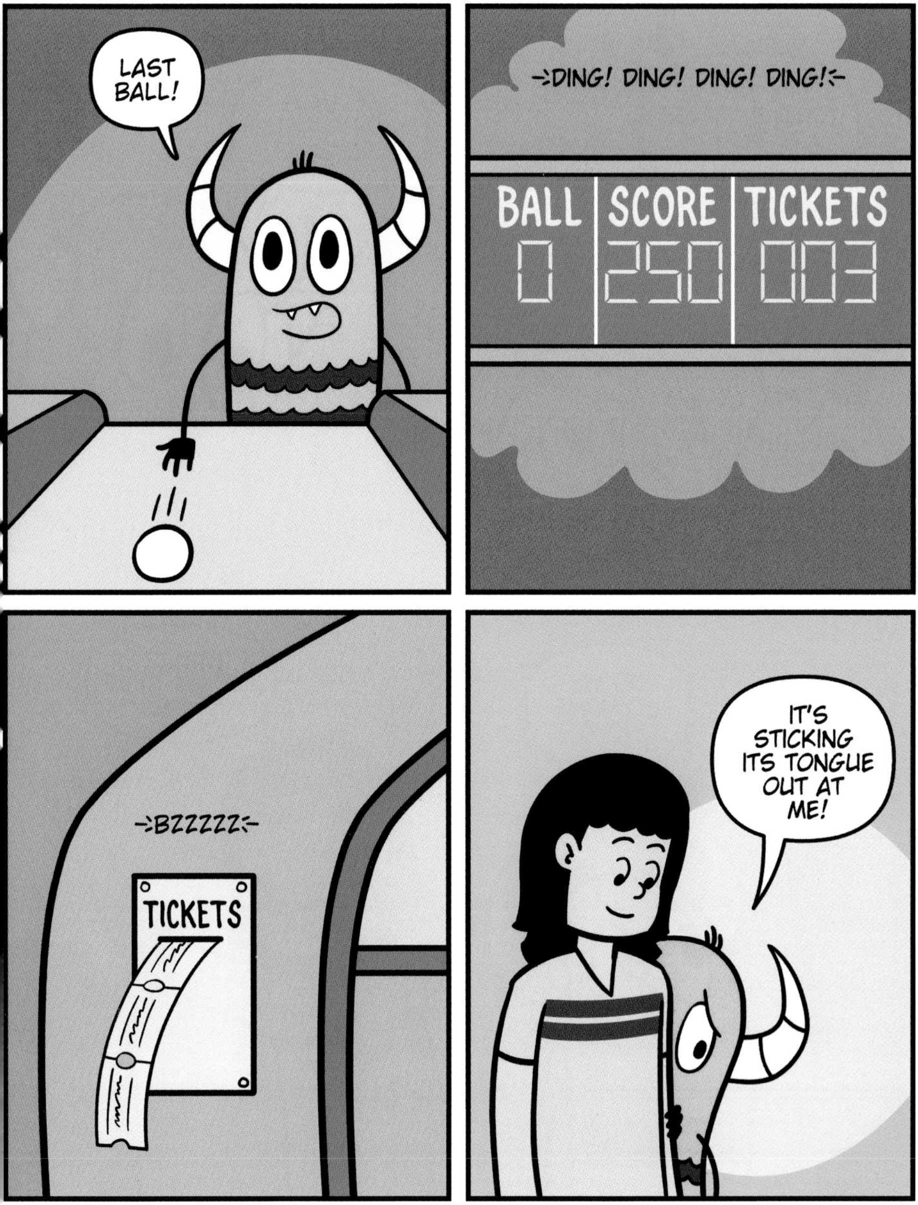
LAST BALL!
DING! DING! DING! DING!
BALL SCORE TICKETS
0 250 003
BZZZZZ
TICKETS
IT'S STICKING ITS TONGUE OUT AT ME!

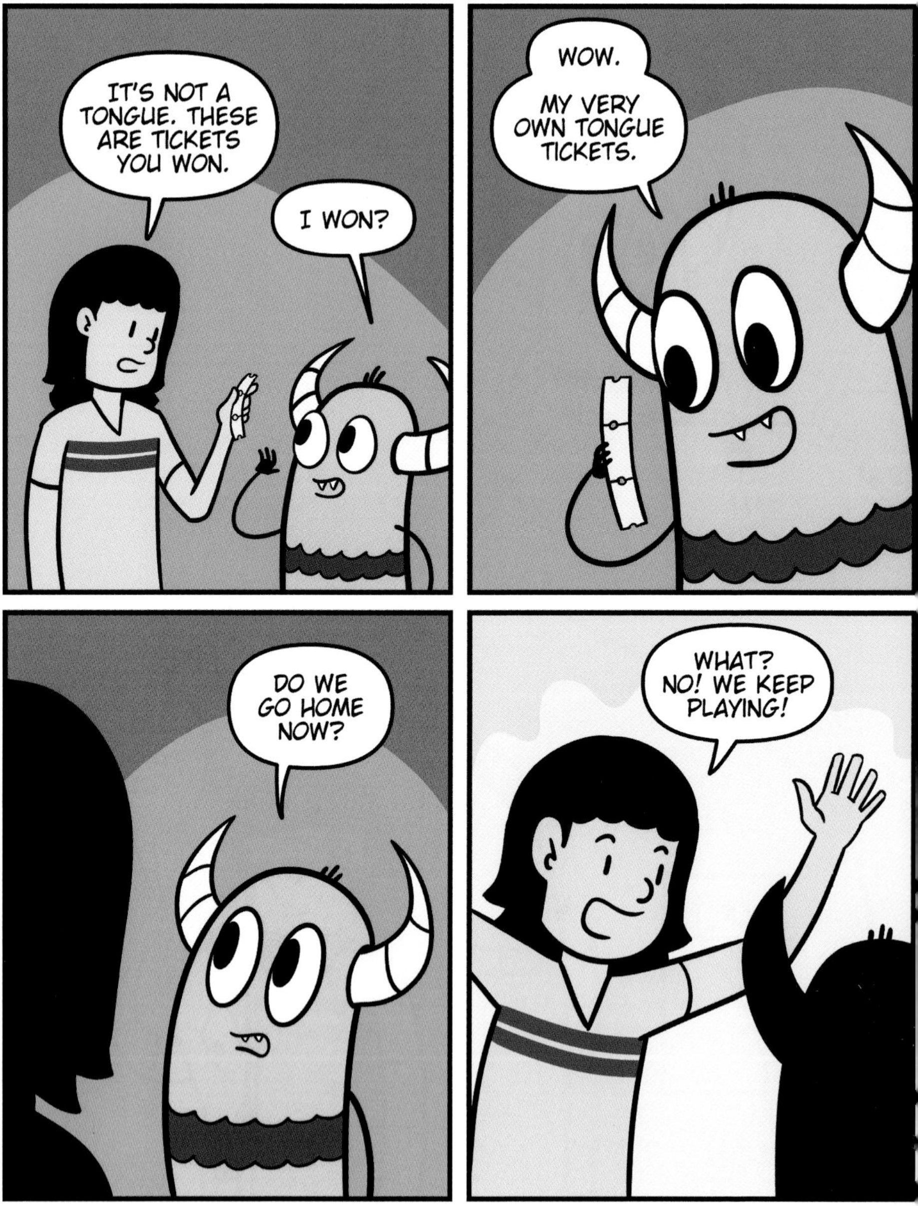
IT'S NOT A TONGUE. THESE ARE TICKETS YOU WON.
I WON?
WOW.
MY VERY OWN TONGUE TICKETS.
DO WE GO HOME NOW?
WHAT? NO! WE KEEP PLAYING!

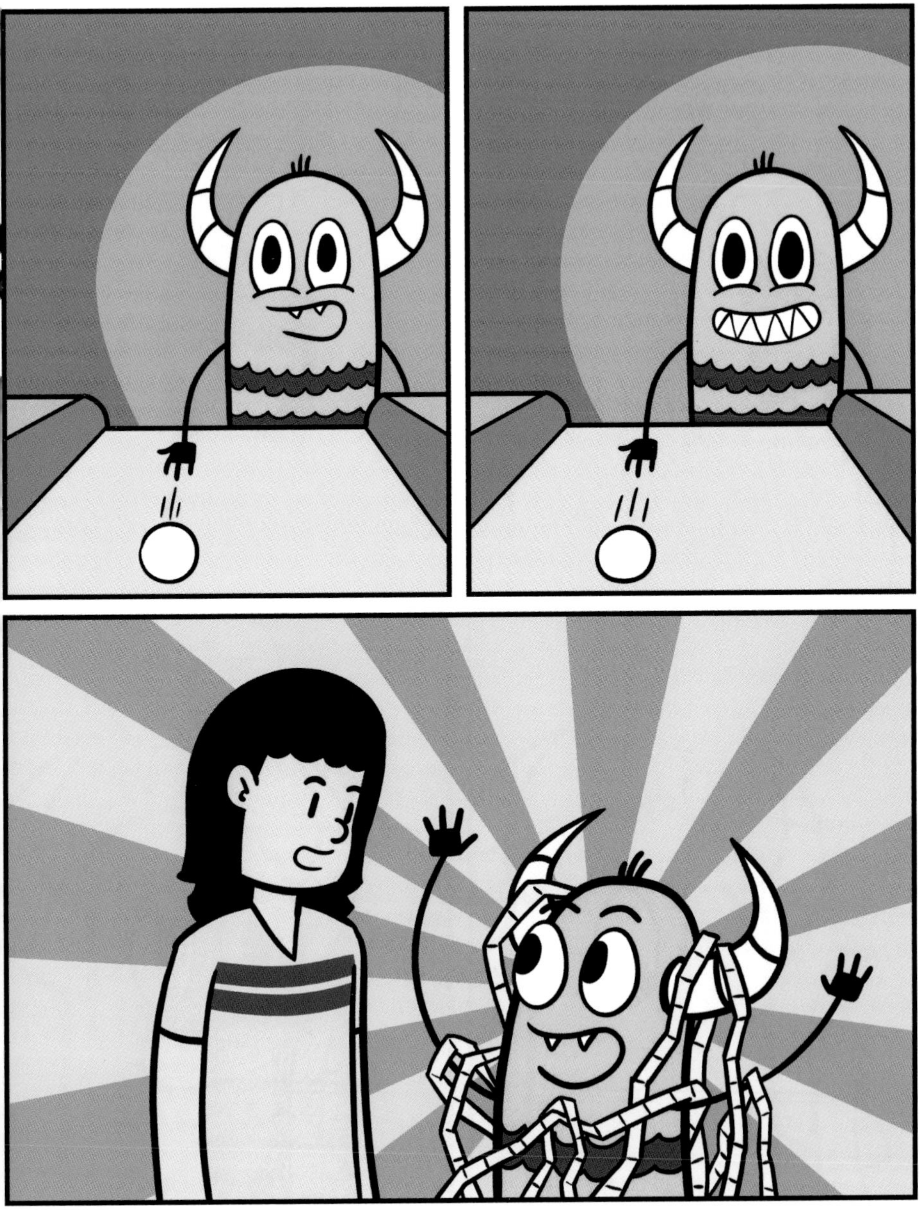

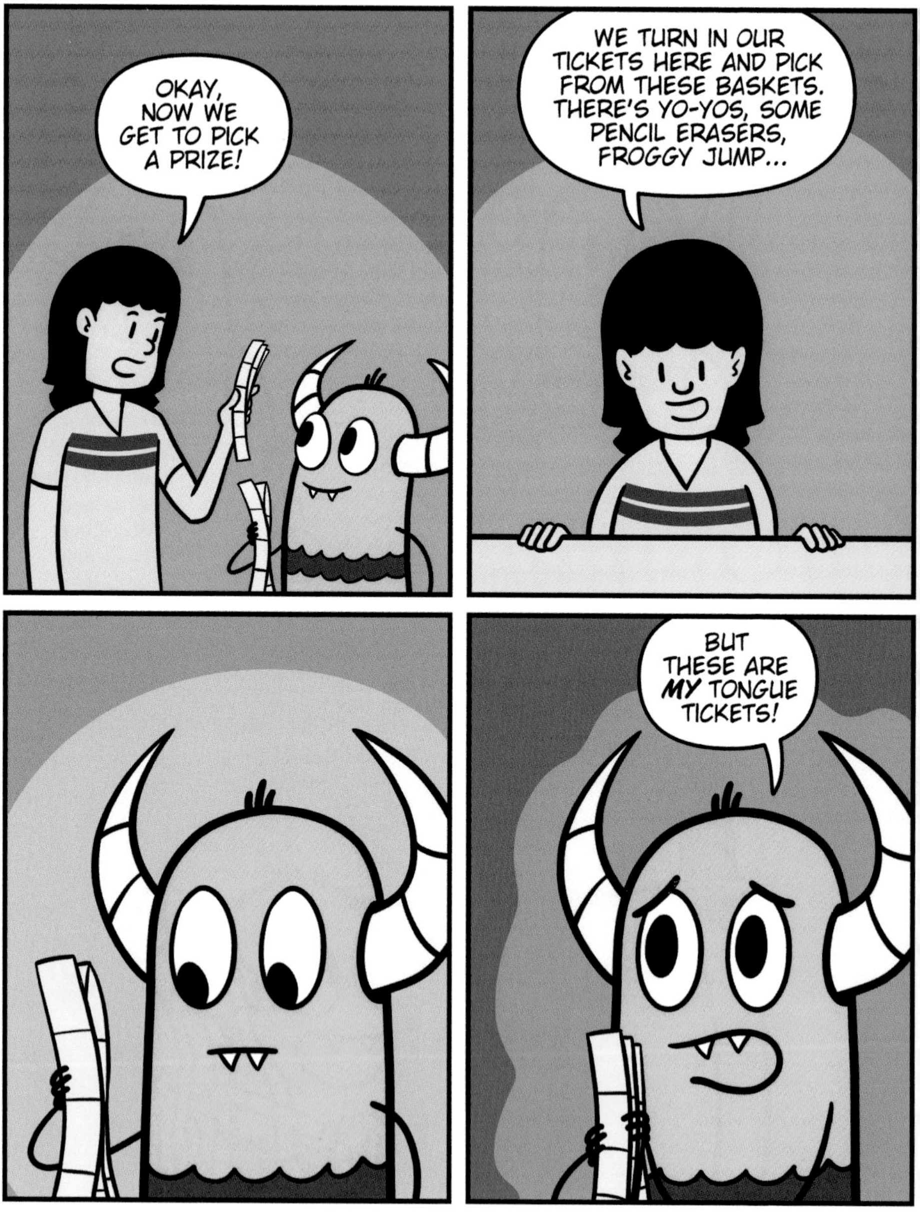
OKAY, NOW WE GET TO PICK A PRIZE!
WE TURN IN OUR TICKETS HERE AND PICK FROM THESE BASKETS. THERE'S YO-YOS, SOME PENCIL ERASERS, FROGGY JUMP...
BUT THESE ARE *MY* TONGUE TICKETS!

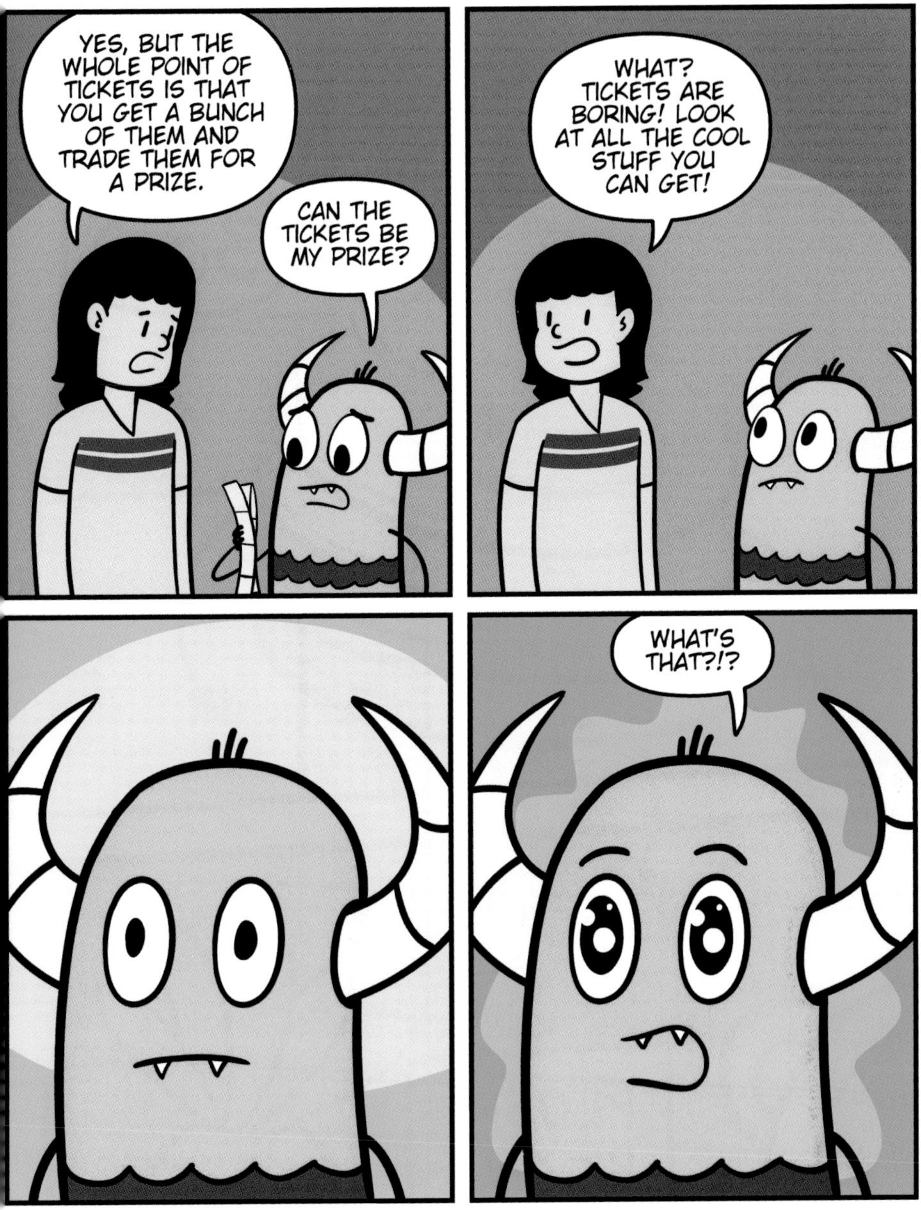
YES, BUT THE WHOLE POINT OF TICKETS IS THAT YOU GET A BUNCH OF THEM AND TRADE THEM FOR A PRIZE.
CAN THE TICKETS BE MY PRIZE?
WHAT? TICKETS ARE BORING! LOOK AT ALL THE COOL STUFF YOU CAN GET!
WHAT'S THAT?!?

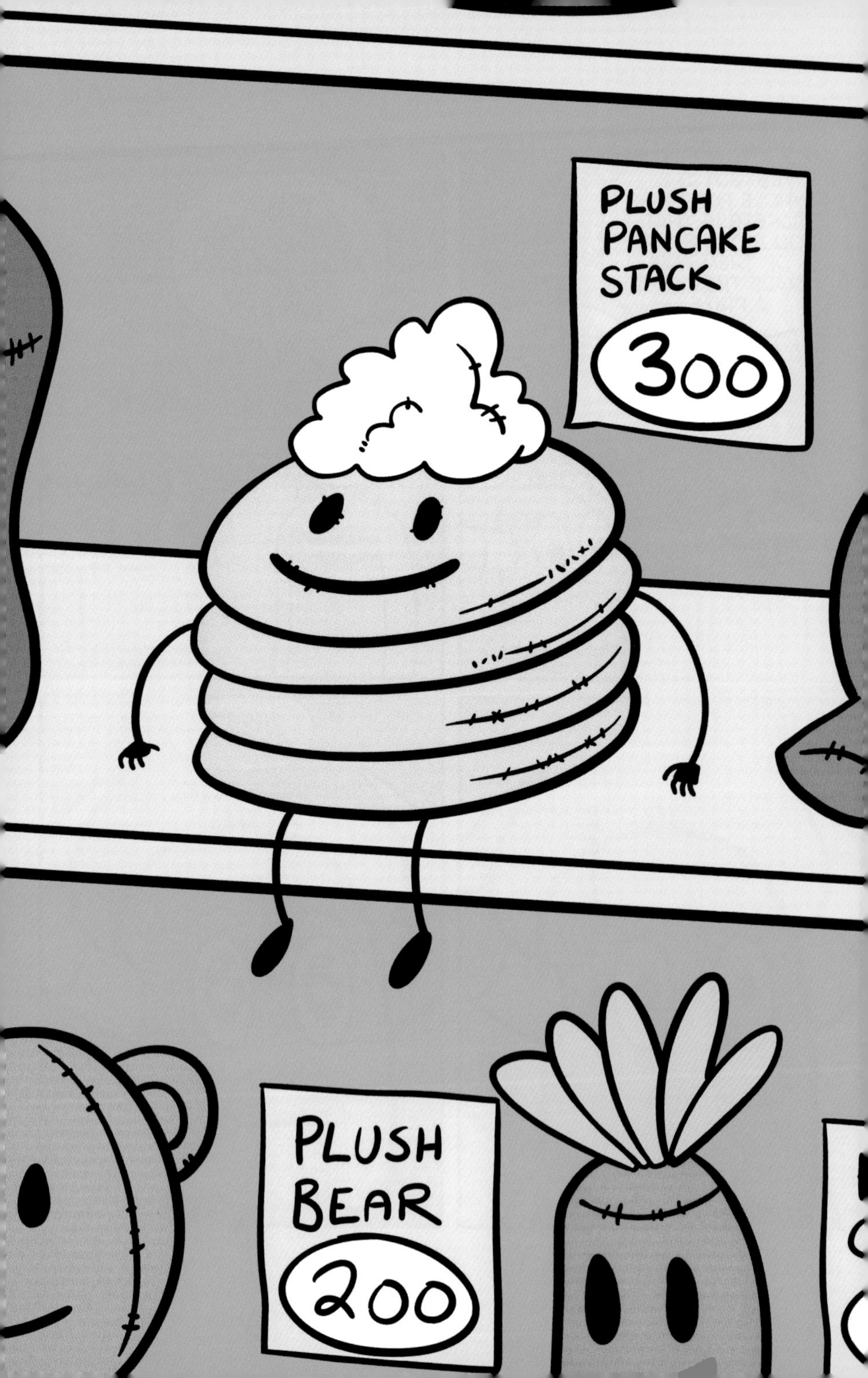
PLUSH PANCAKE STACK
300
PLUSH BEAR
200

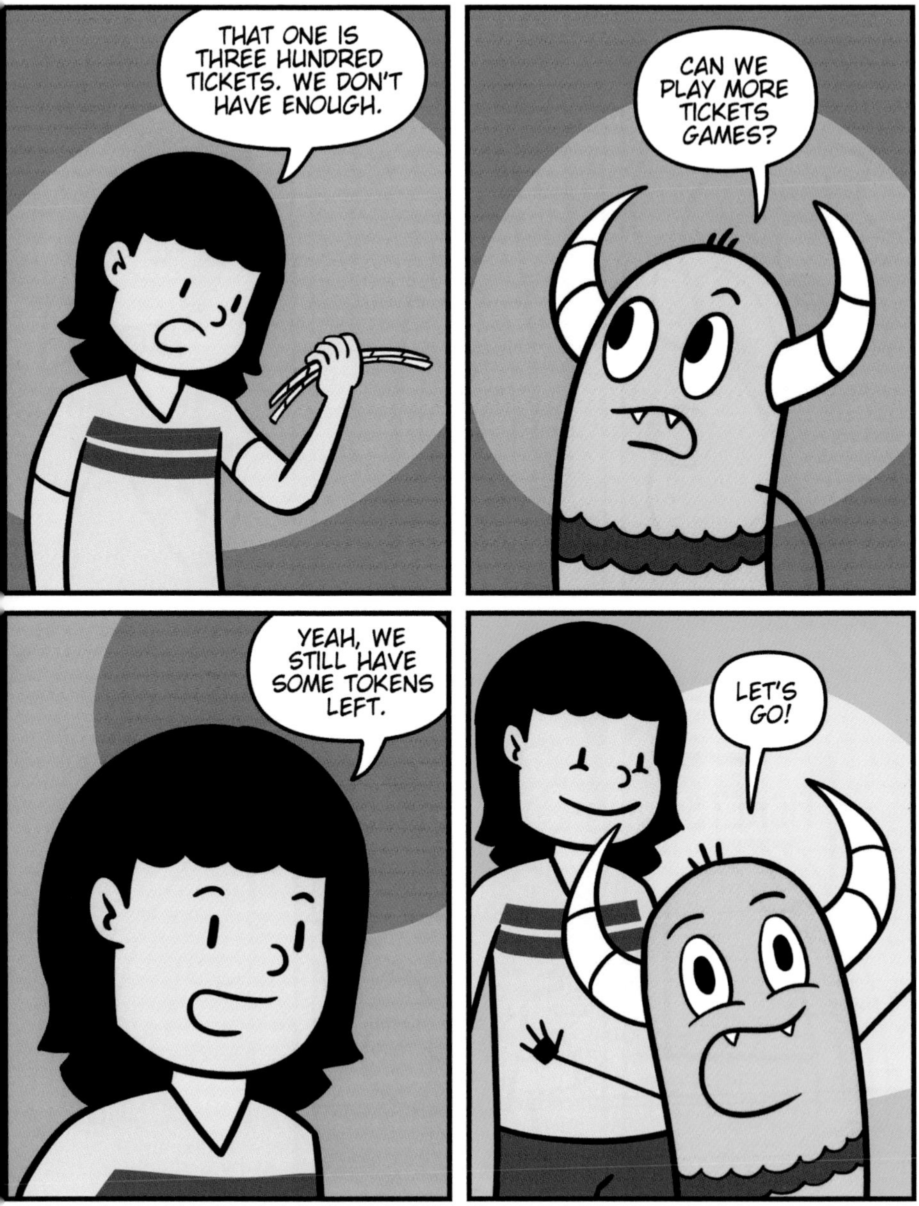
THAT ONE IS THREE HUNDRED TICKETS. WE DON'T HAVE ENOUGH.
CAN WE PLAY MORE TICKETS GAMES?
YEAH, WE STILL HAVE SOME TOKENS LEFT.
LET'S GO!

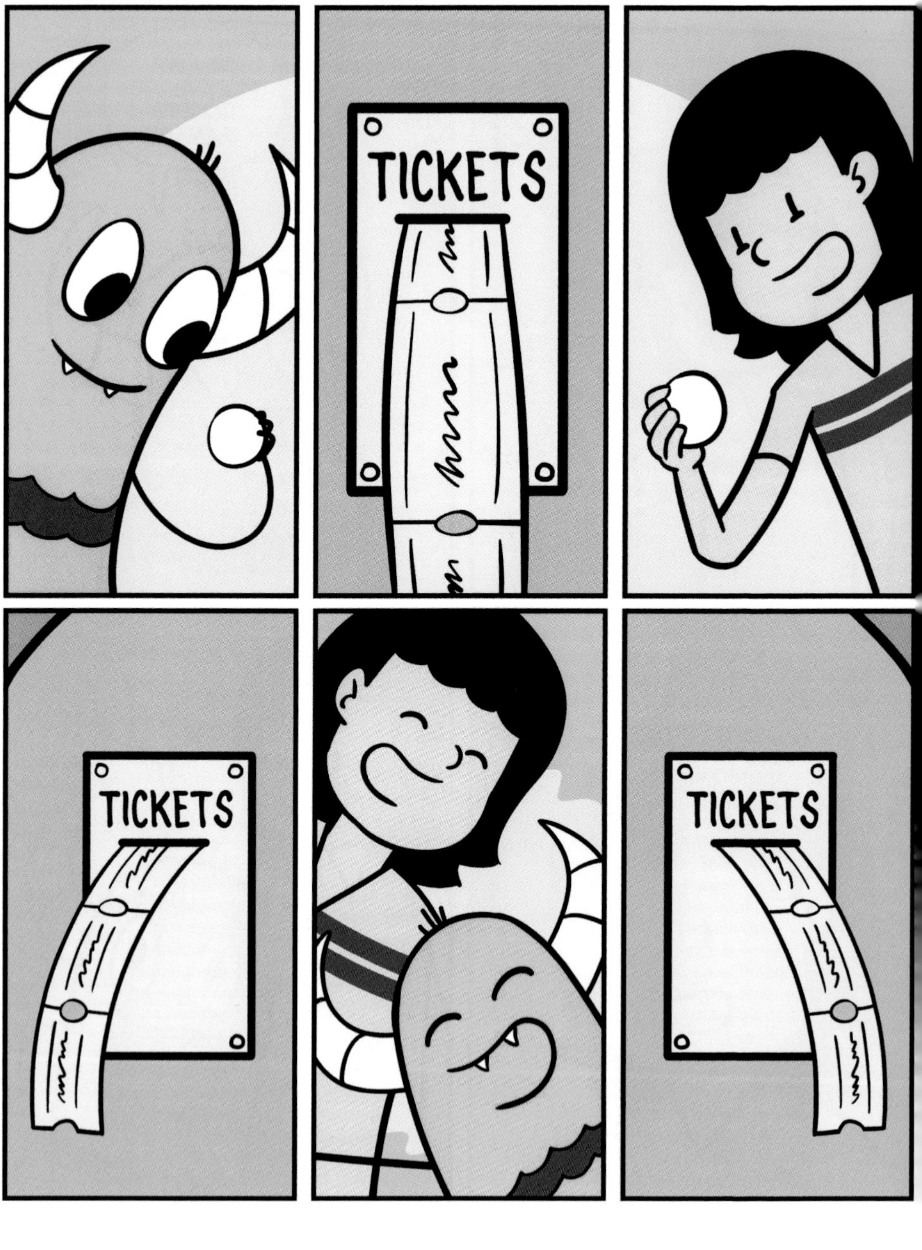
TICKETS
TICKETS
TICKETS

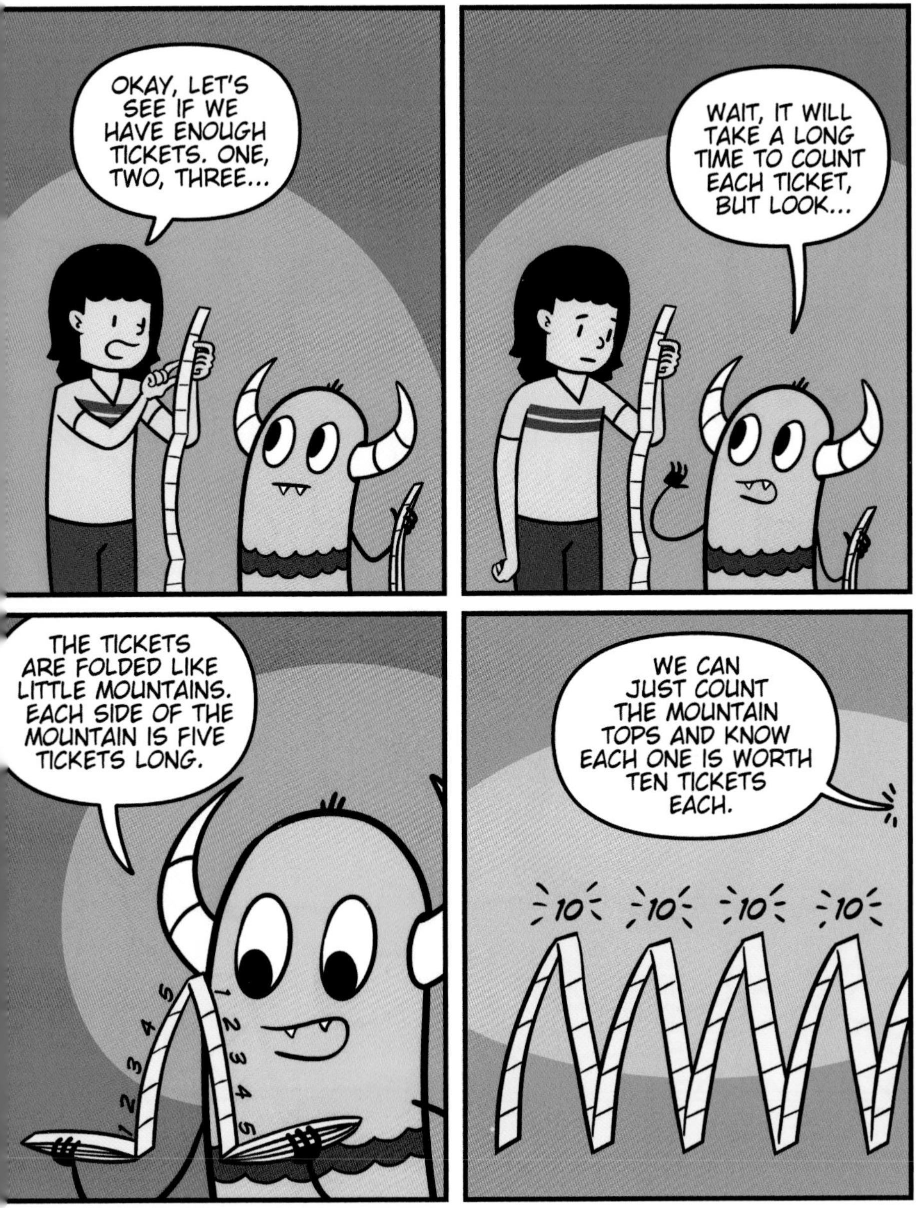
OKAY, LET'S SEE IF WE HAVE ENOUGH TICKETS. ONE, TWO, THREE...
WAIT, IT WILL TAKE A LONG TIME TO COUNT EACH TICKET, BUT LOOK...
THE TICKETS ARE FOLDED LIKE LITTLE MOUNTAINS. EACH SIDE OF THE MOUNTAIN IS FIVE TICKETS LONG.
1 2 3 4 5
1 2 3 4 5
WE CAN JUST COUNT THE MOUNTAIN TOPS AND KNOW EACH ONE IS WORTH TEN TICKETS EACH.
10 10 10 10

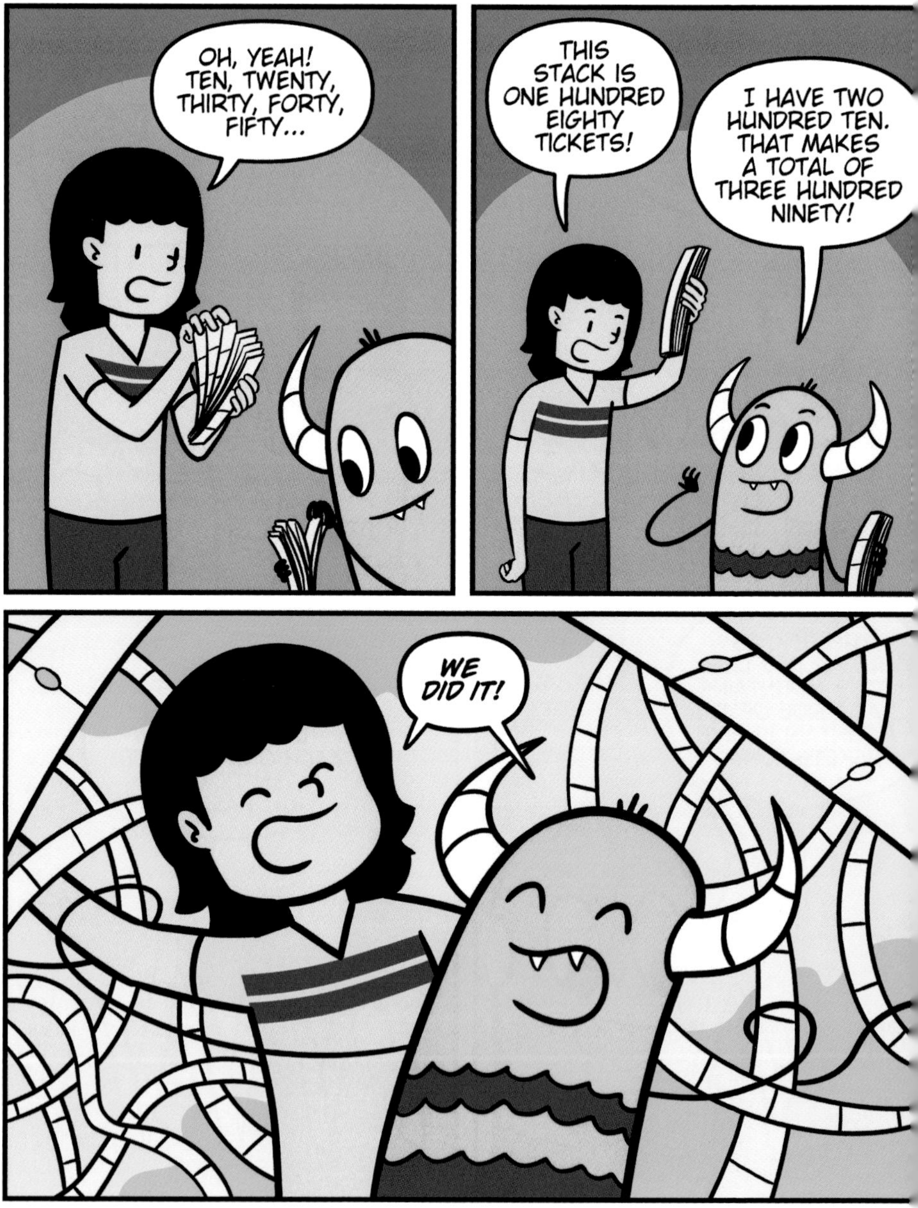
OH, YEAH! TEN, TWENTY, THIRTY, FORTY, FIFTY...
THIS STACK IS ONE HUNDRED EIGHTY TICKETS!
I HAVE TWO HUNDRED TEN. THAT MAKES A TOTAL OF THREE HUNDRED NINETY!
WE DID IT!

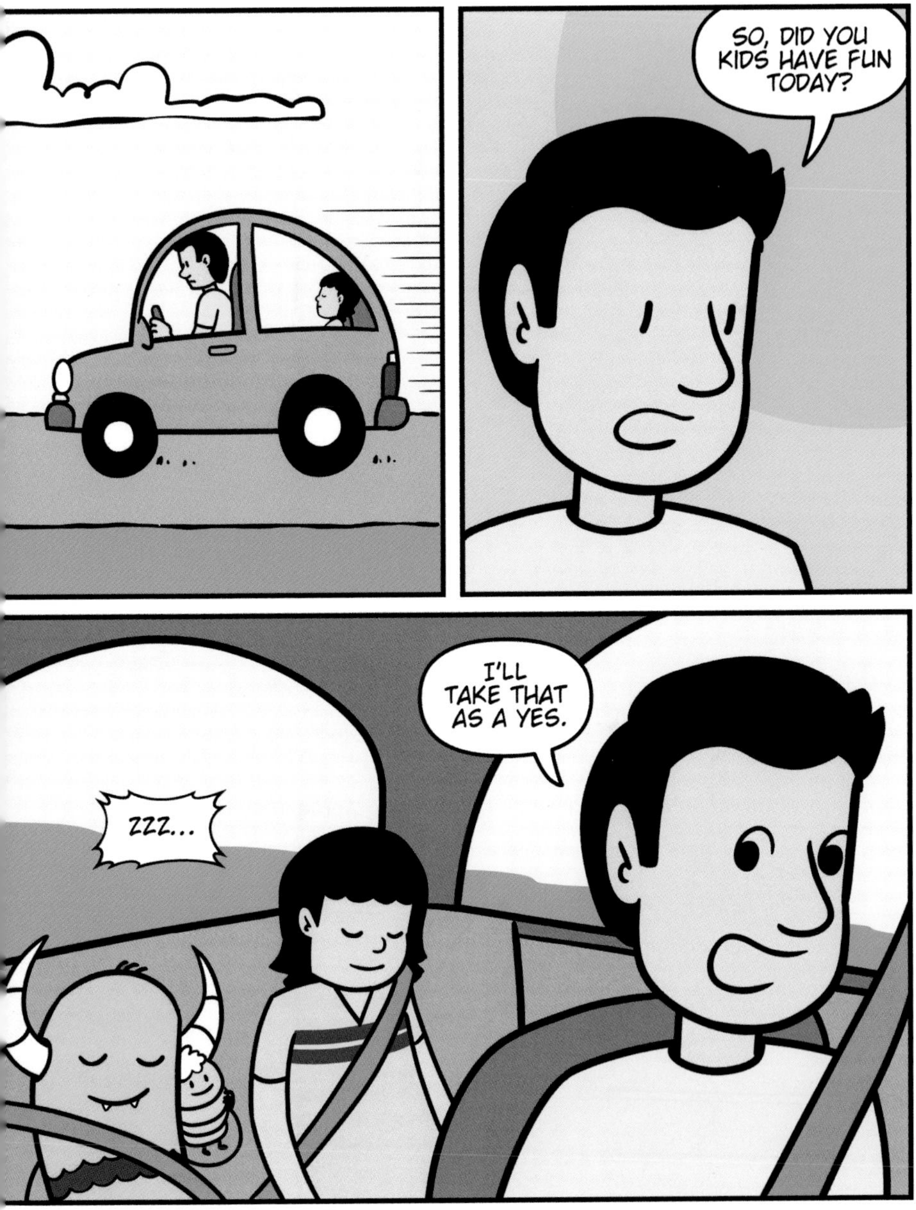
SO, DID YOU KIDS HAVE FUN TODAY?
I'LL TAKE THAT AS A YES.
ZZZ...

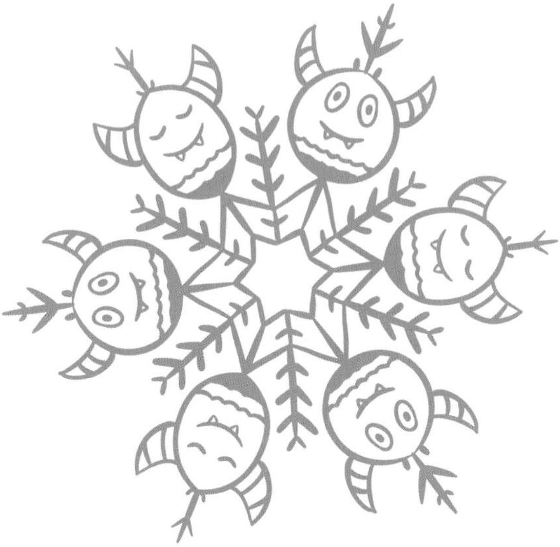

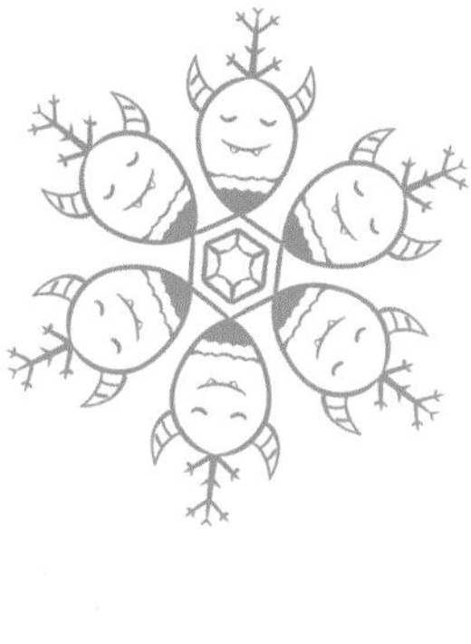

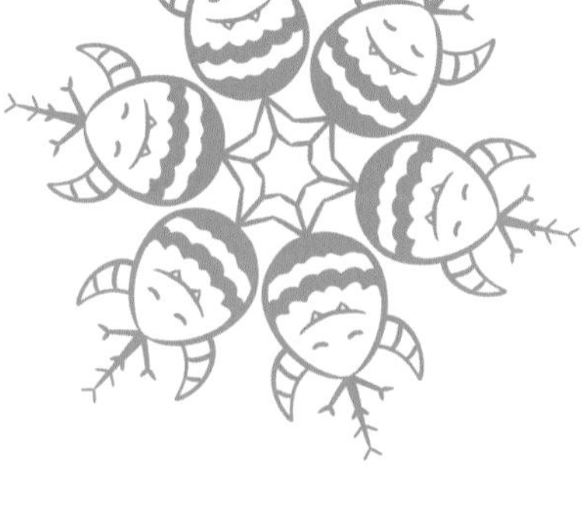

CHAPTER SEVEN

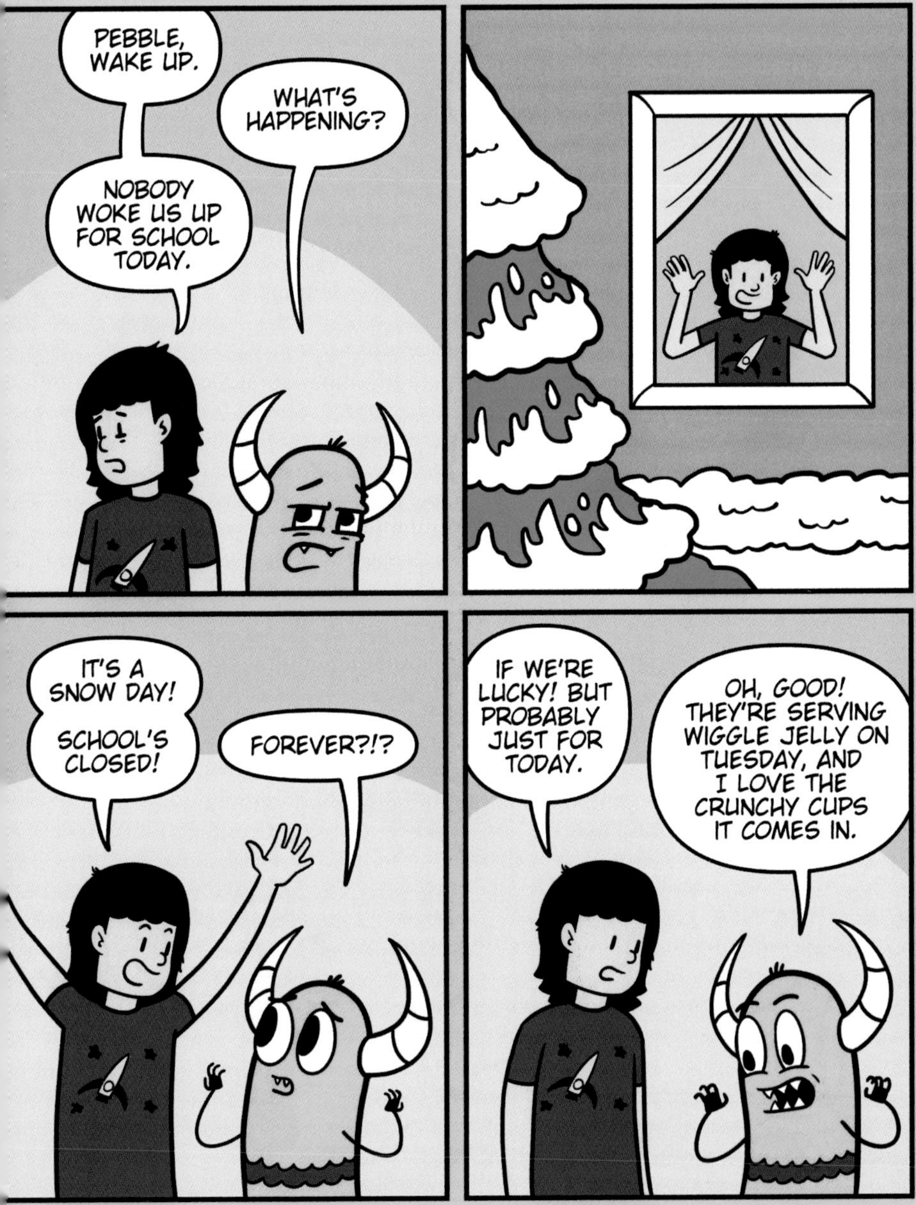
PEBBLE, WAKE UP.
NOBODY WOKE US UP FOR SCHOOL TODAY.
WHAT'S HAPPENING?
IT'S A SNOW DAY!
SCHOOL'S CLOSED!
FOREVER?!?
IF WE'RE LUCKY! BUT PROBABLY JUST FOR TODAY.
OH, GOOD! THEY'RE SERVING WIGGLE JELLY ON TUESDAY, AND I LOVE THE CRUNCHY CUPS IT COMES IN.

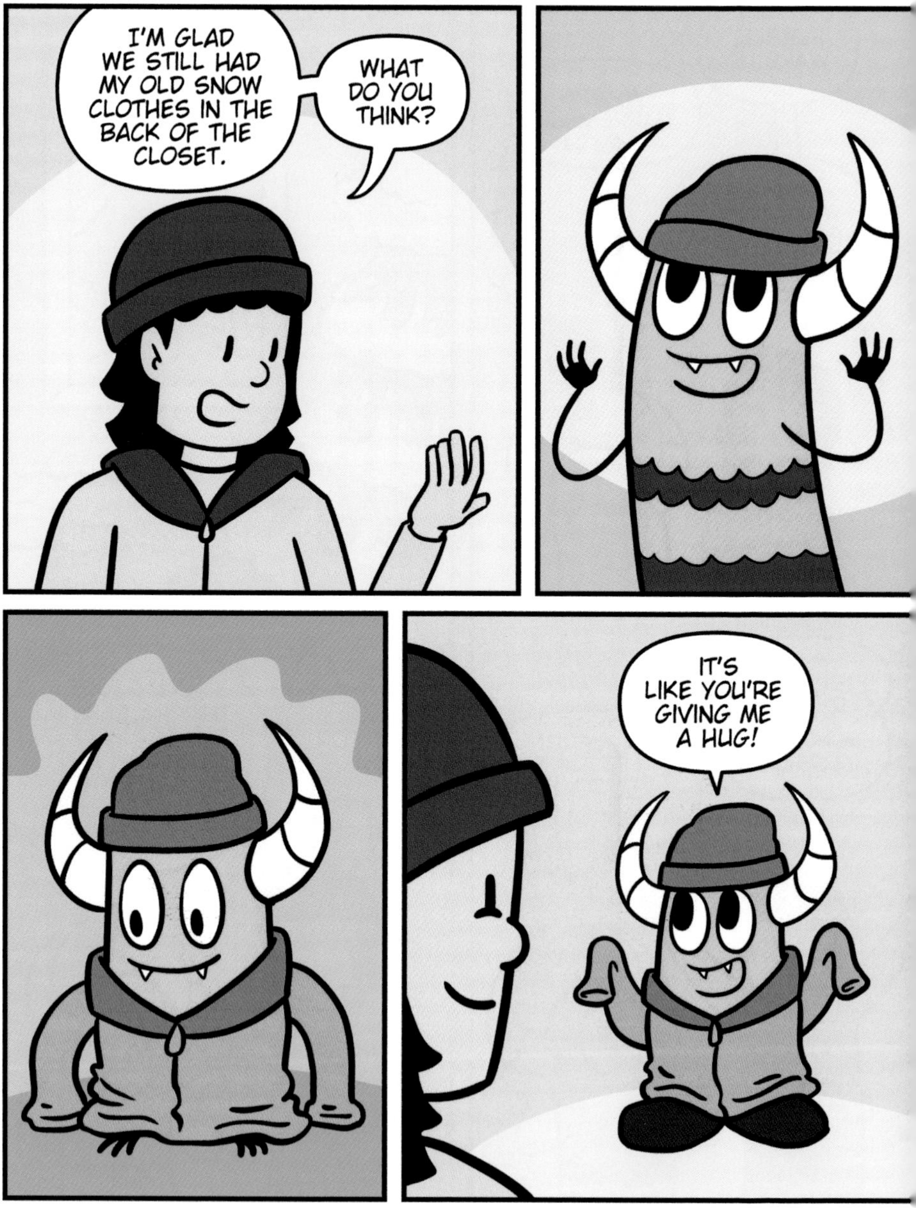
I'M GLAD WE STILL HAD MY OLD SNOW CLOTHES IN THE BACK OF THE CLOSET.
WHAT DO YOU THINK?
IT'S LIKE YOU'RE GIVING ME A HUG!

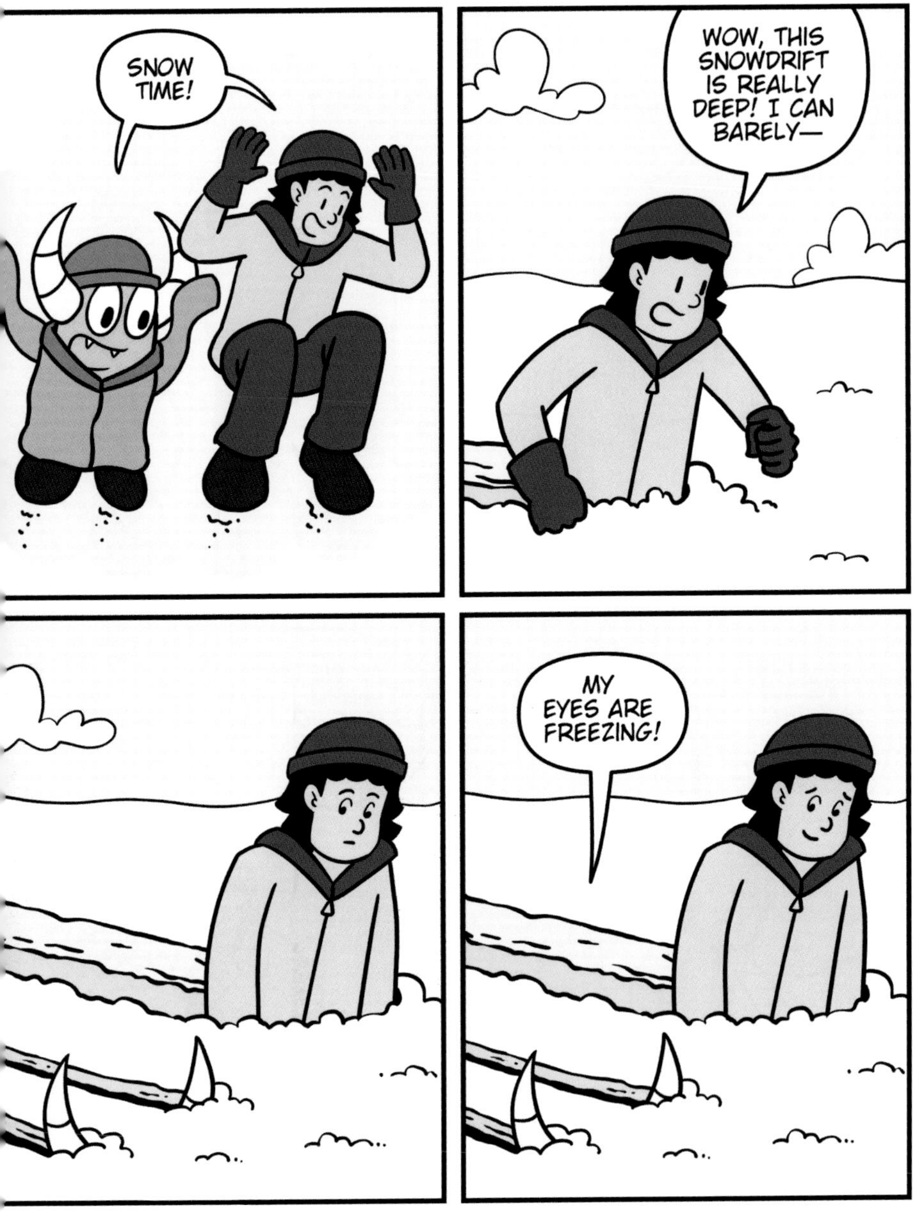
SNOW TIME!
WOW, THIS SNOWDRIFT IS REALLY DEEP! I CAN BARELY—
MY EYES ARE FREEZING!

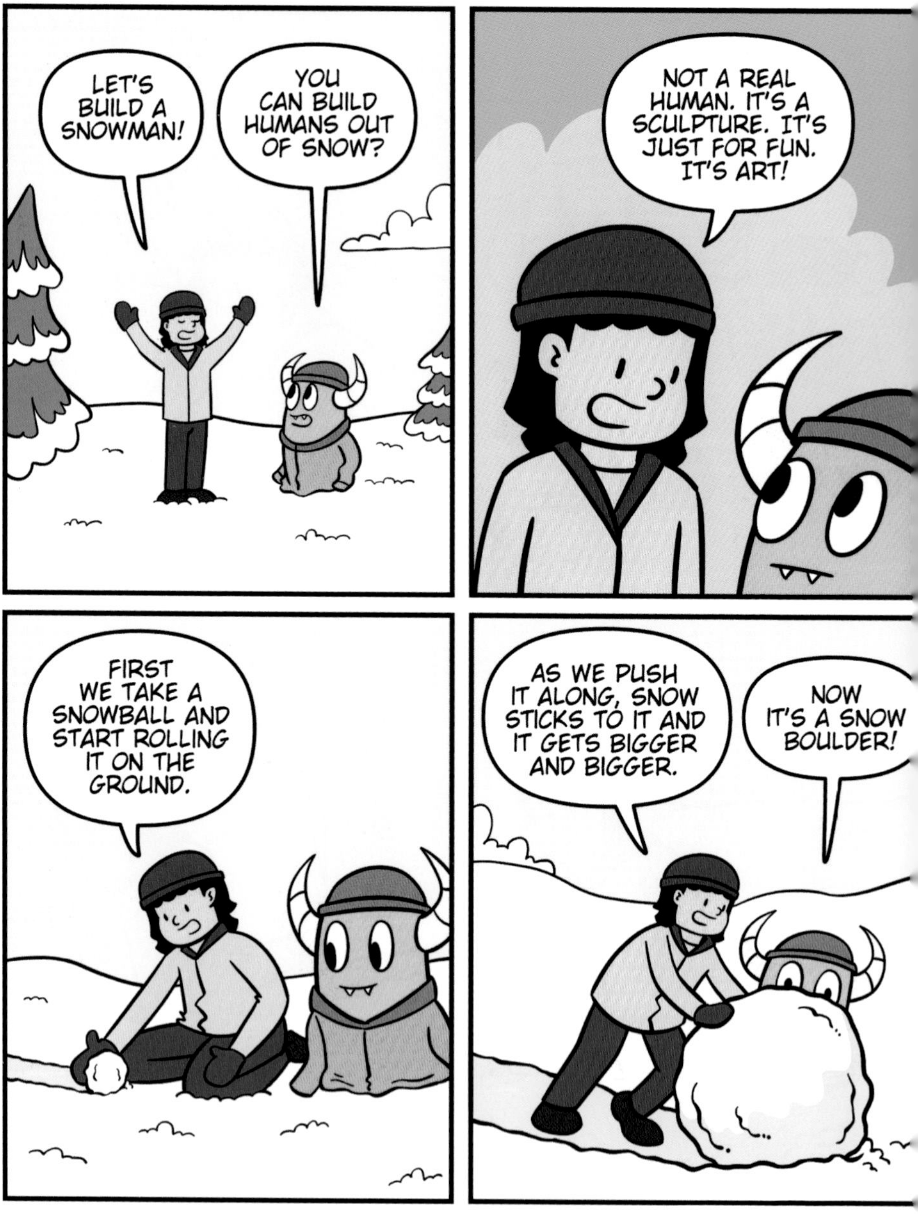
LET'S BUILD A SNOWMAN!
YOU CAN BUILD HUMANS OUT OF SNOW?
NOT A REAL HUMAN. IT'S A SCULPTURE. IT'S JUST FOR FUN. IT'S ART!
FIRST WE TAKE A SNOWBALL AND START ROLLING IT ON THE GROUND.
AS WE PUSH IT ALONG, SNOW STICKS TO IT AND IT GETS BIGGER AND BIGGER.
NOW IT'S A SNOW BOULDER!

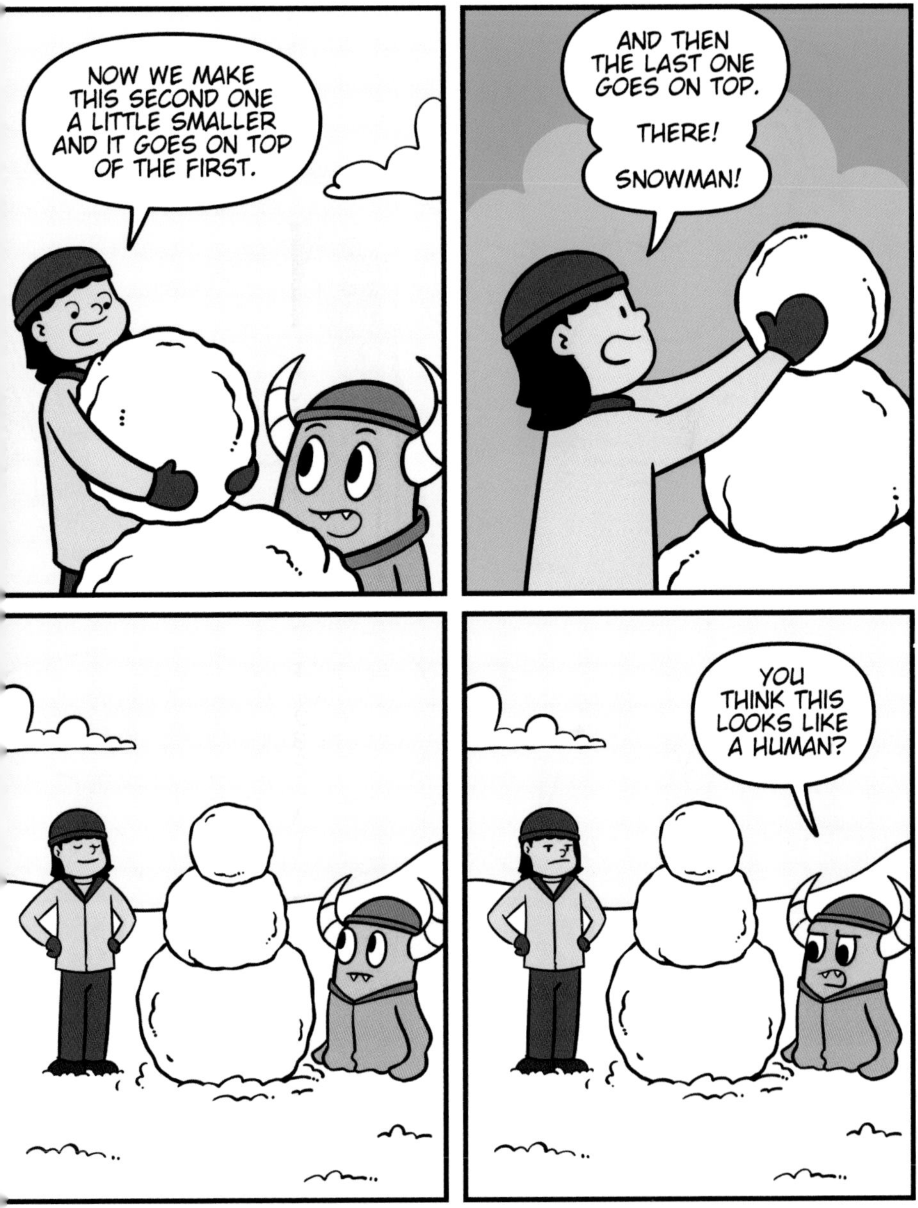
NOW WE MAKE THIS SECOND ONE A LITTLE SMALLER AND IT GOES ON TOP OF THE FIRST.
AND THEN THE LAST ONE GOES ON TOP.
THERE!
SNOWMAN!
YOU THINK THIS LOOKS LIKE A HUMAN?

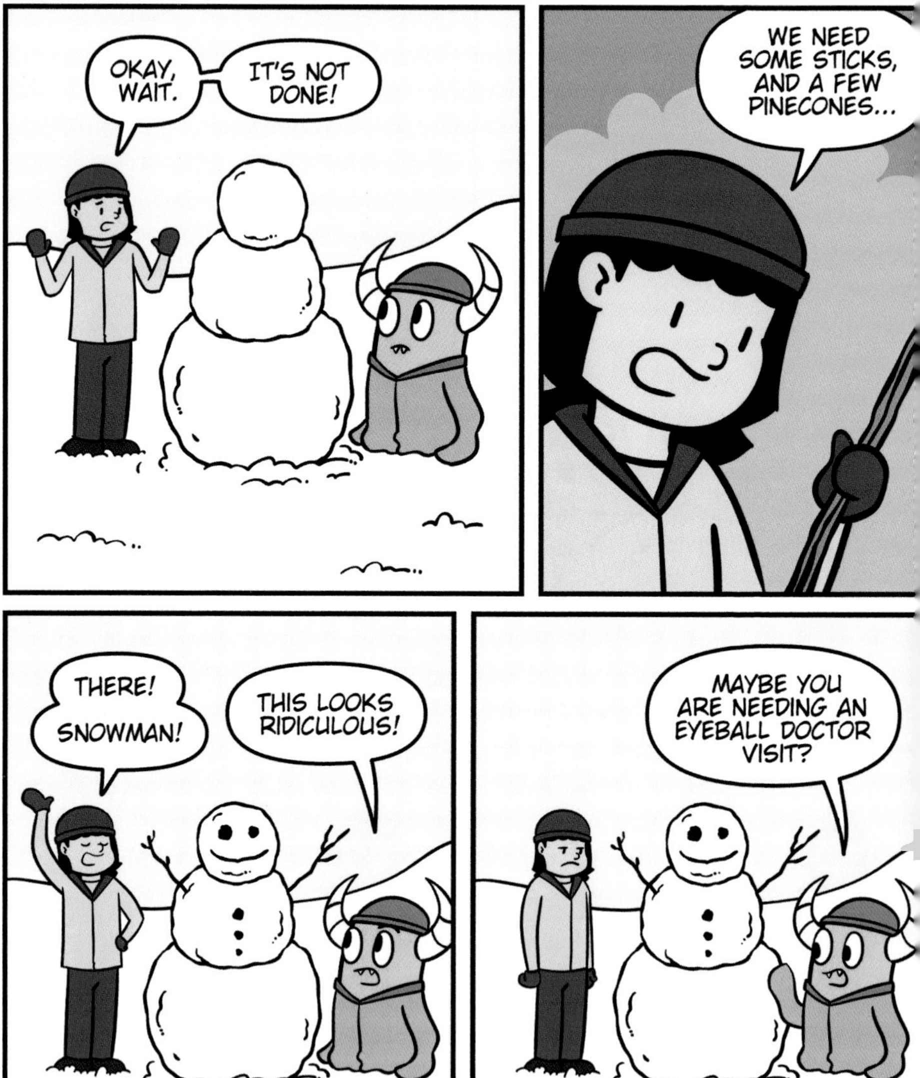
OKAY, WAIT.
IT'S NOT DONE!
WE NEED SOME STICKS, AND A FEW PINECONES...
THERE! SNOWMAN!
THIS LOOKS RIDICULOUS!
MAYBE YOU ARE NEEDING AN EYEBALL DOCTOR VISIT?

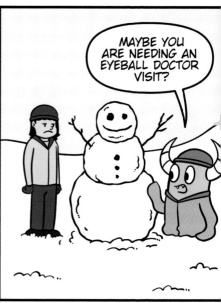

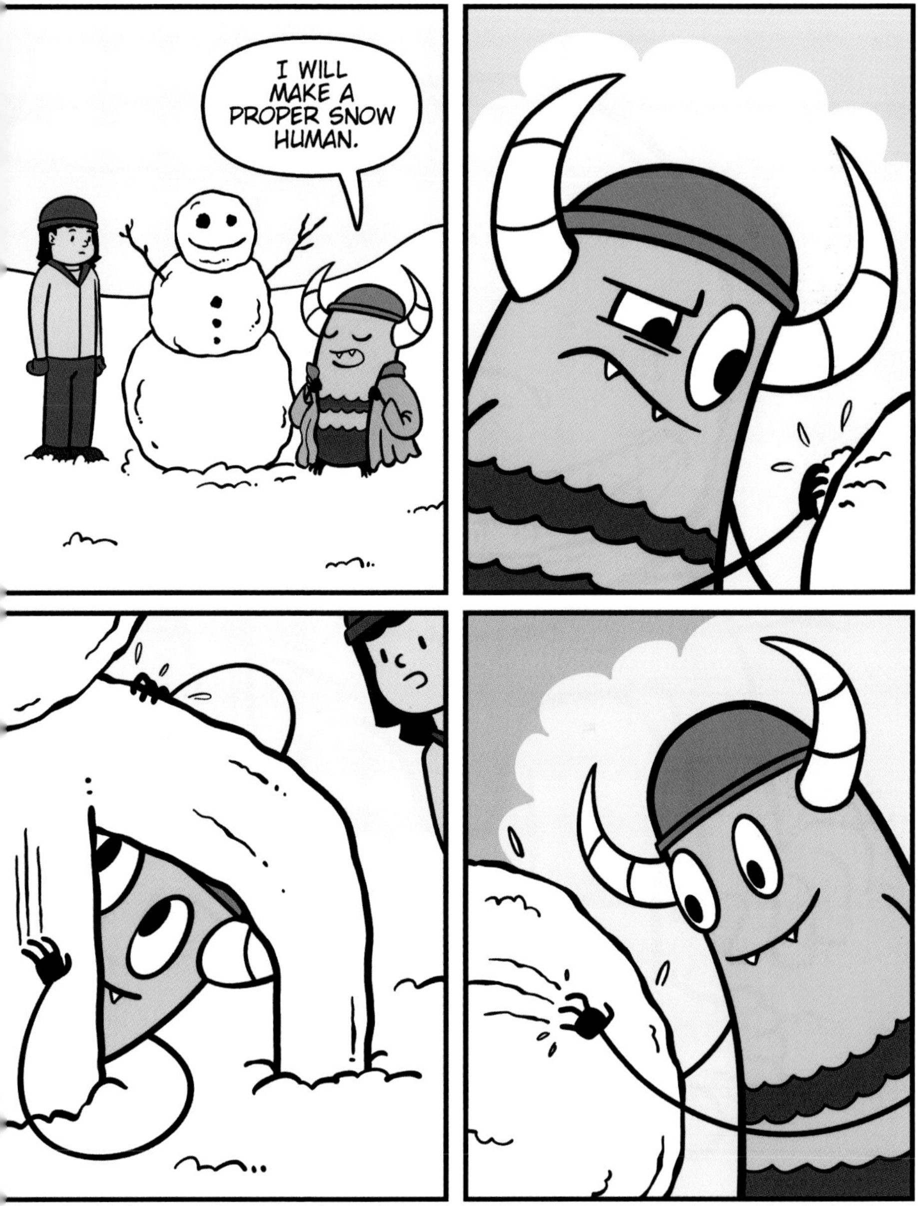
I WILL MAKE A PROPER SNOW HUMAN.

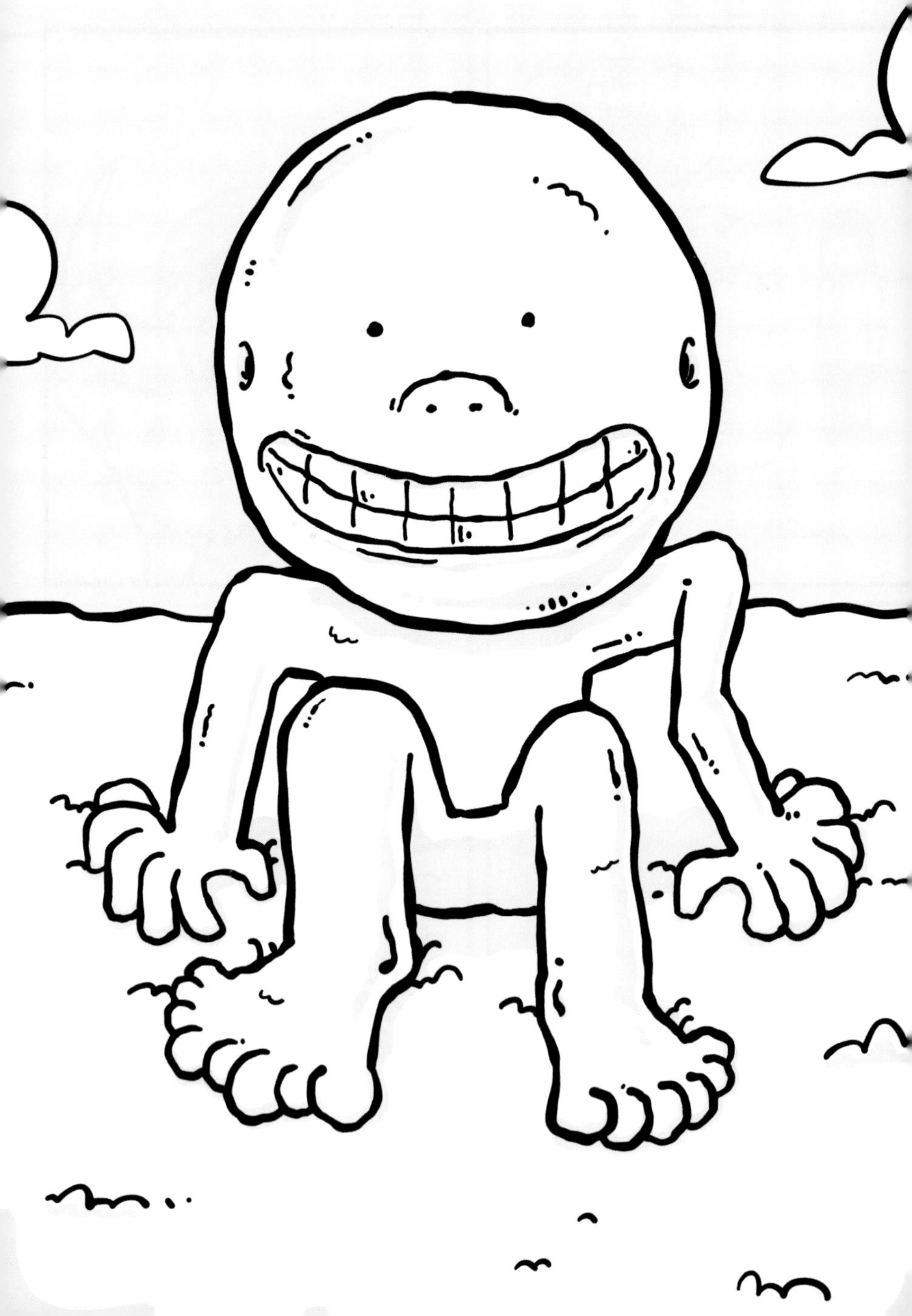

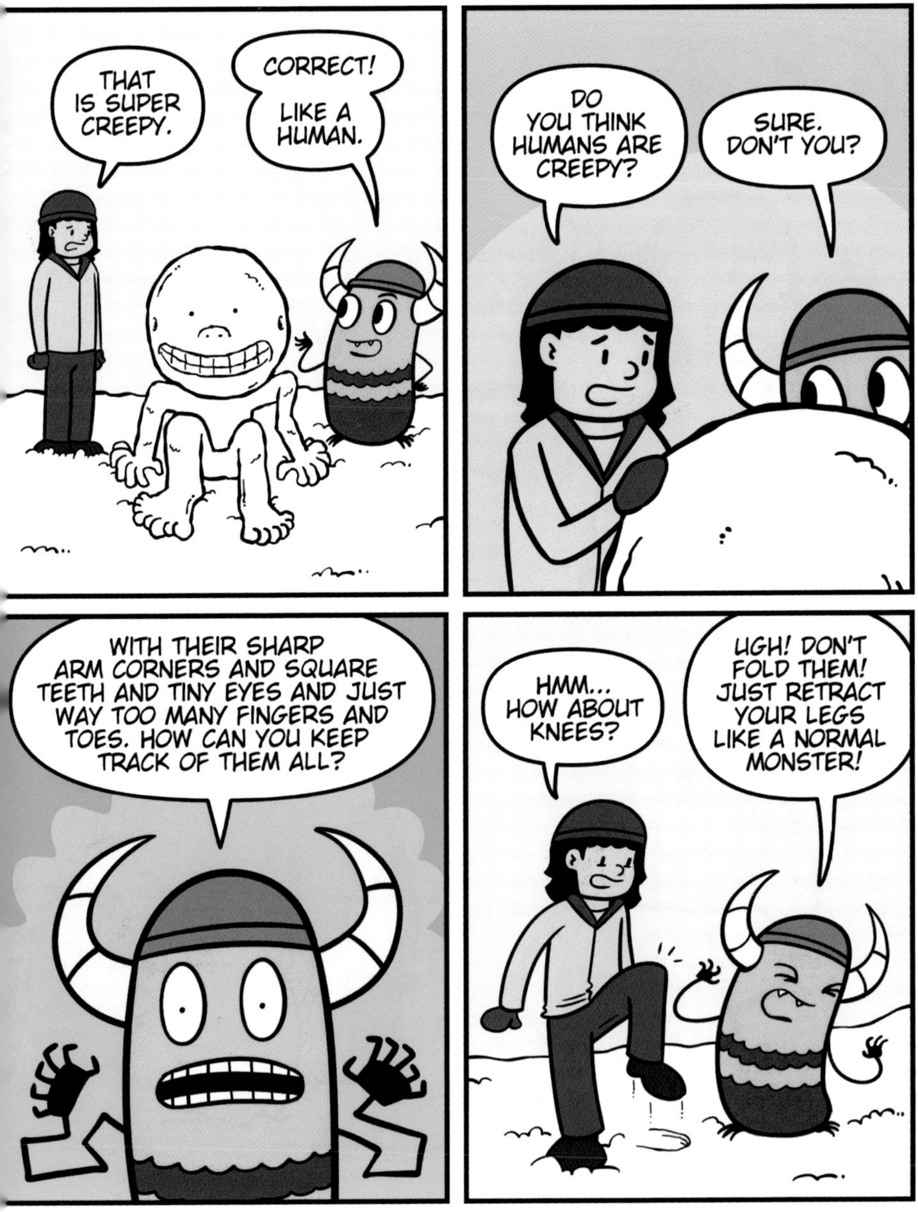
THAT IS SUPER CREEPY.
CORRECT! LIKE A HUMAN.
DO YOU THINK HUMANS ARE CREEPY?
SURE. DON'T YOU?
WITH THEIR SHARP ARM CORNERS AND SQUARE TEETH AND TINY EYES AND JUST WAY TOO MANY FINGERS AND TOES. HOW CAN YOU KEEP TRACK OF THEM ALL?
HMM... HOW ABOUT KNEES?
UGH! DON'T FOLD THEM! JUST RETRACT YOUR LEGS LIKE A NORMAL MONSTER!

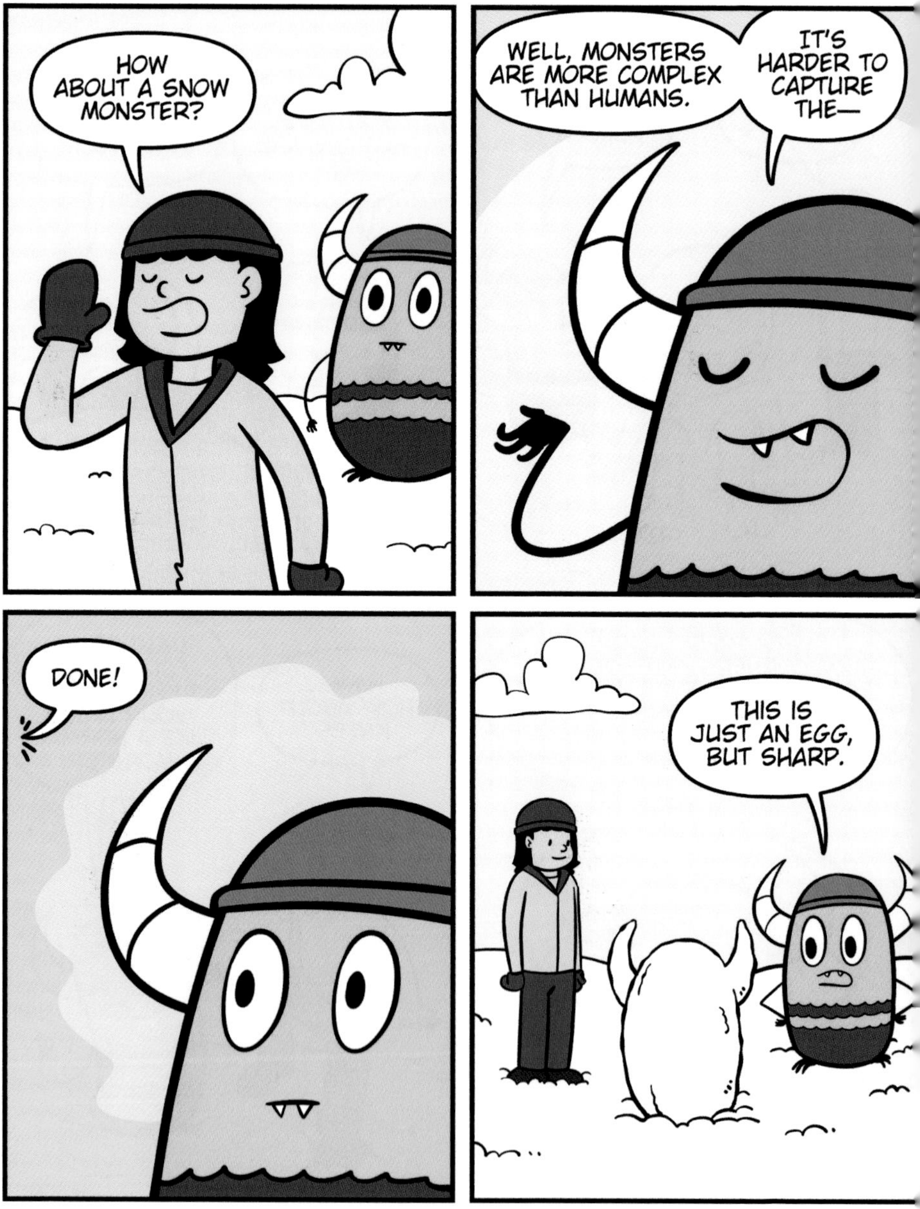
HOW ABOUT A SNOW MONSTER?
WELL, MONSTERS ARE MORE COMPLEX THAN HUMANS.
IT'S HARDER TO CAPTURE THE—
DONE!
THIS IS JUST AN EGG, BUT SHARP.

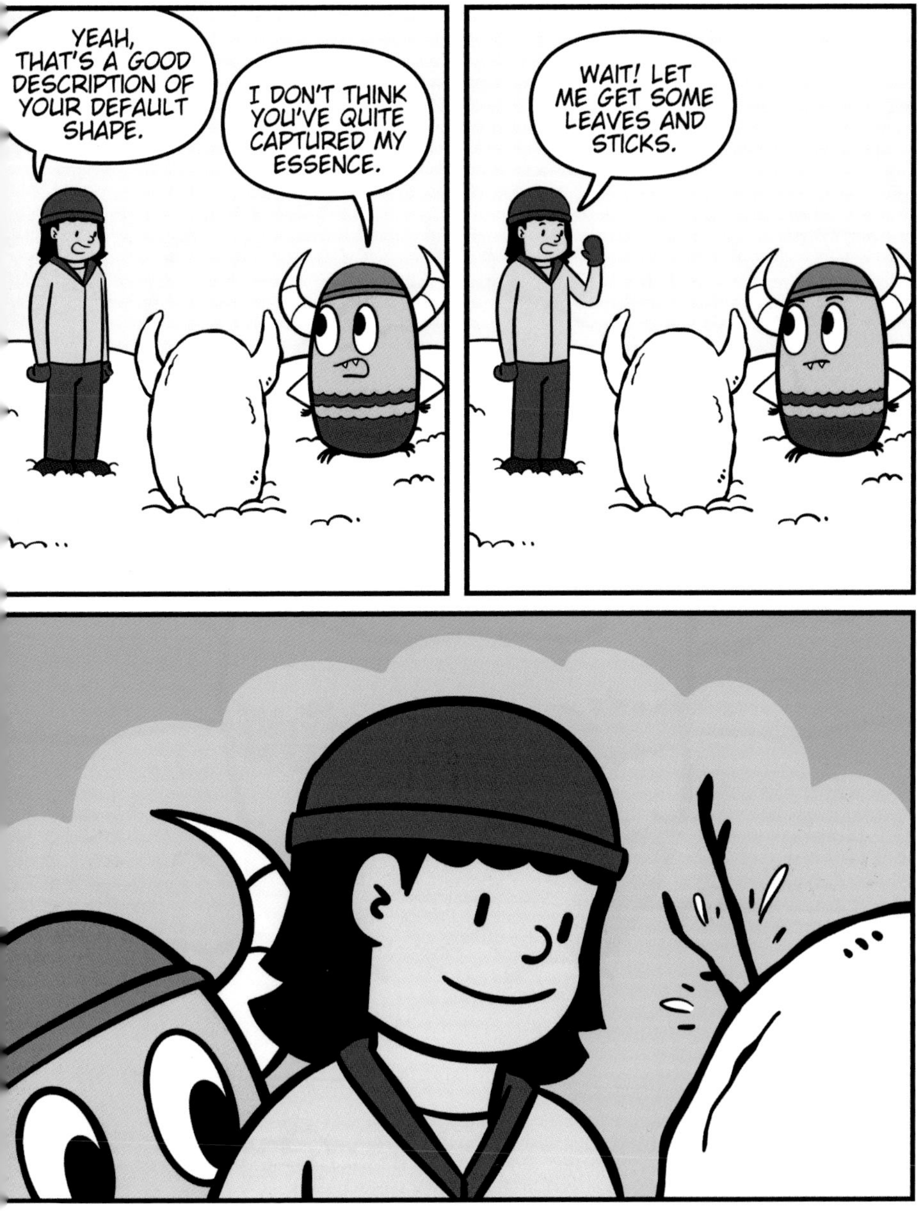
YEAH, THAT'S A GOOD DESCRIPTION OF YOUR DEFAULT SHAPE.
I DON'T THINK YOU'VE QUITE CAPTURED MY ESSENCE.
WAIT! LET ME GET SOME LEAVES AND STICKS.

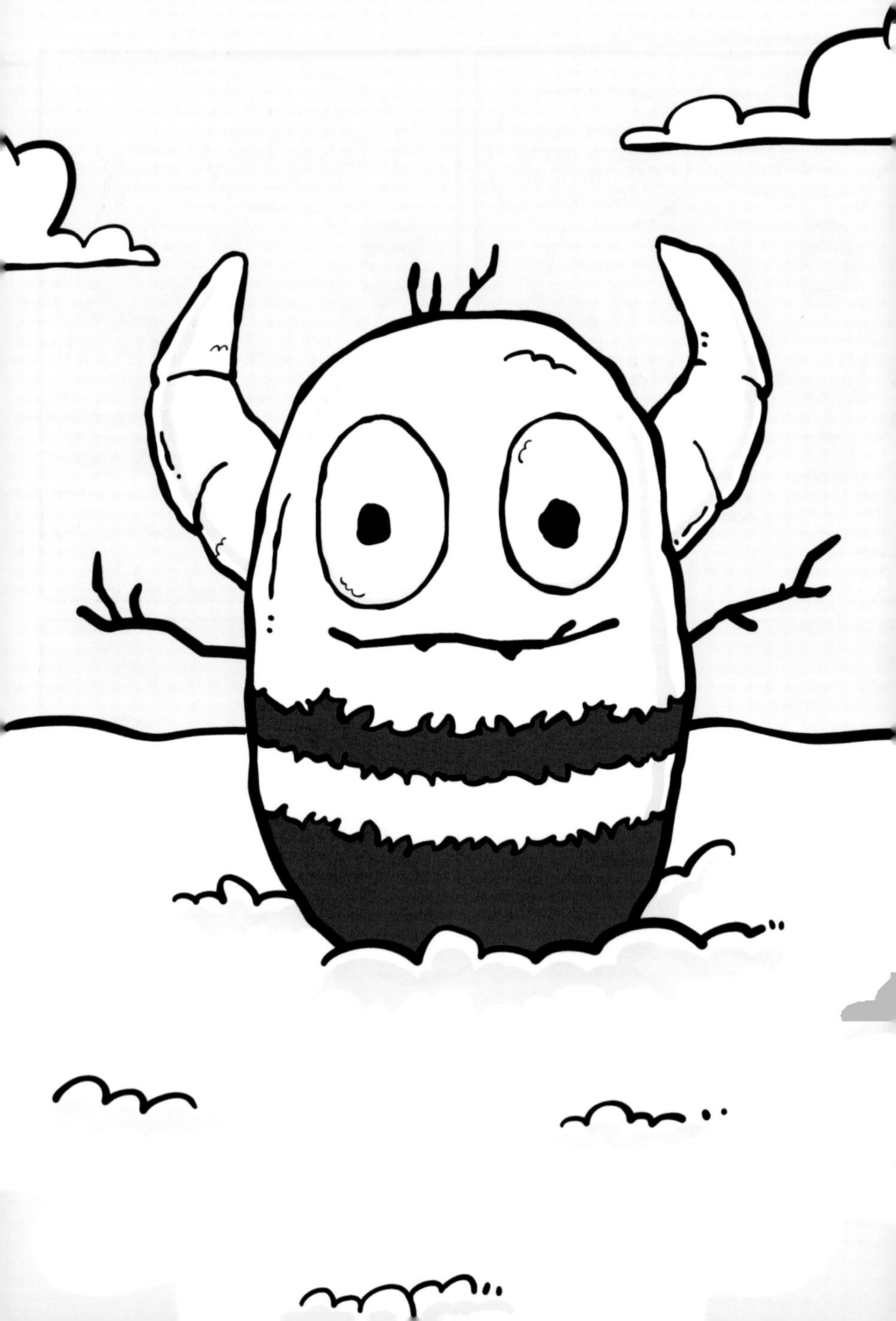

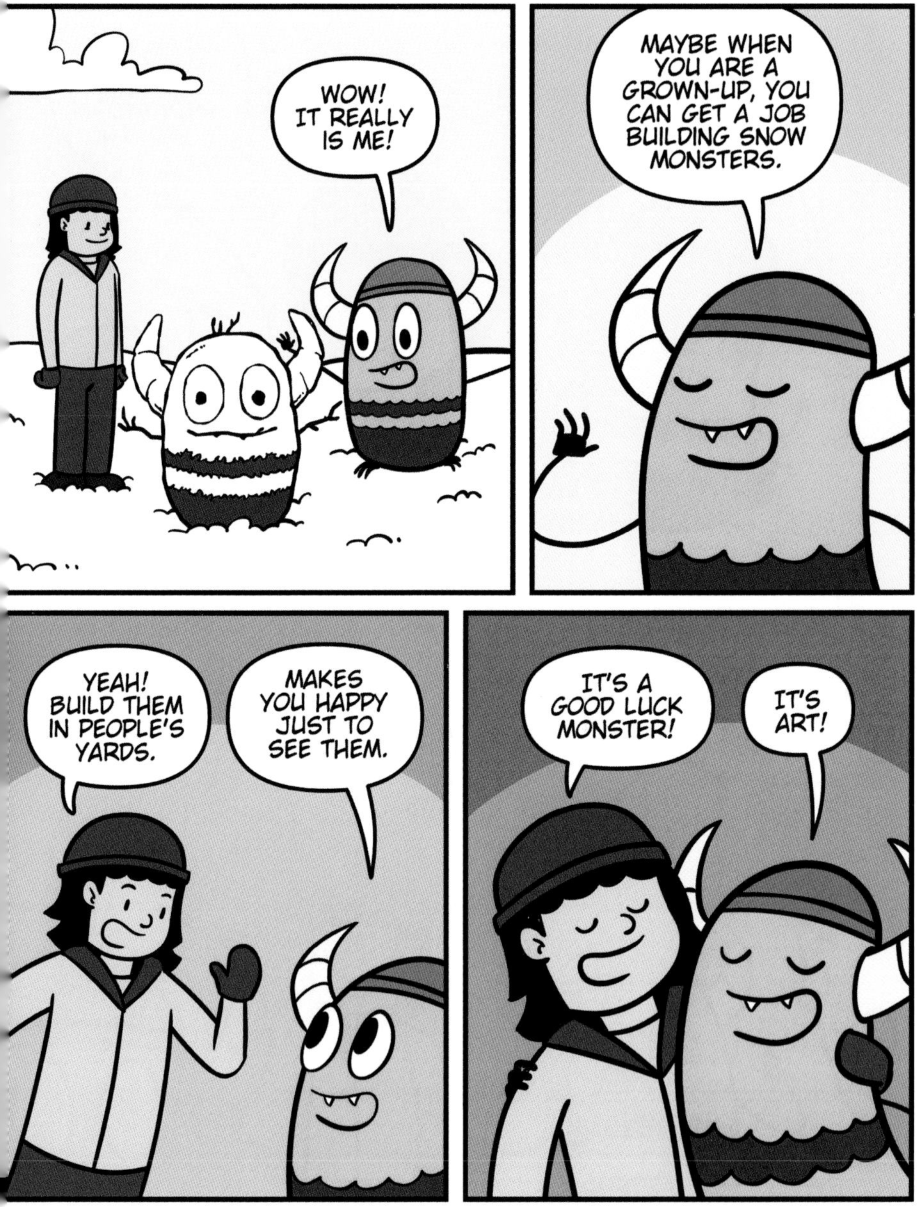
WOW! IT REALLY IS ME!
MAYBE WHEN YOU ARE A GROWN-UP, YOU CAN GET A JOB BUILDING SNOW MONSTERS.
YEAH! BUILD THEM IN PEOPLE'S YARDS.
MAKES YOU HAPPY JUST TO SEE THEM.
IT'S A GOOD LUCK MONSTER!
IT'S ART!

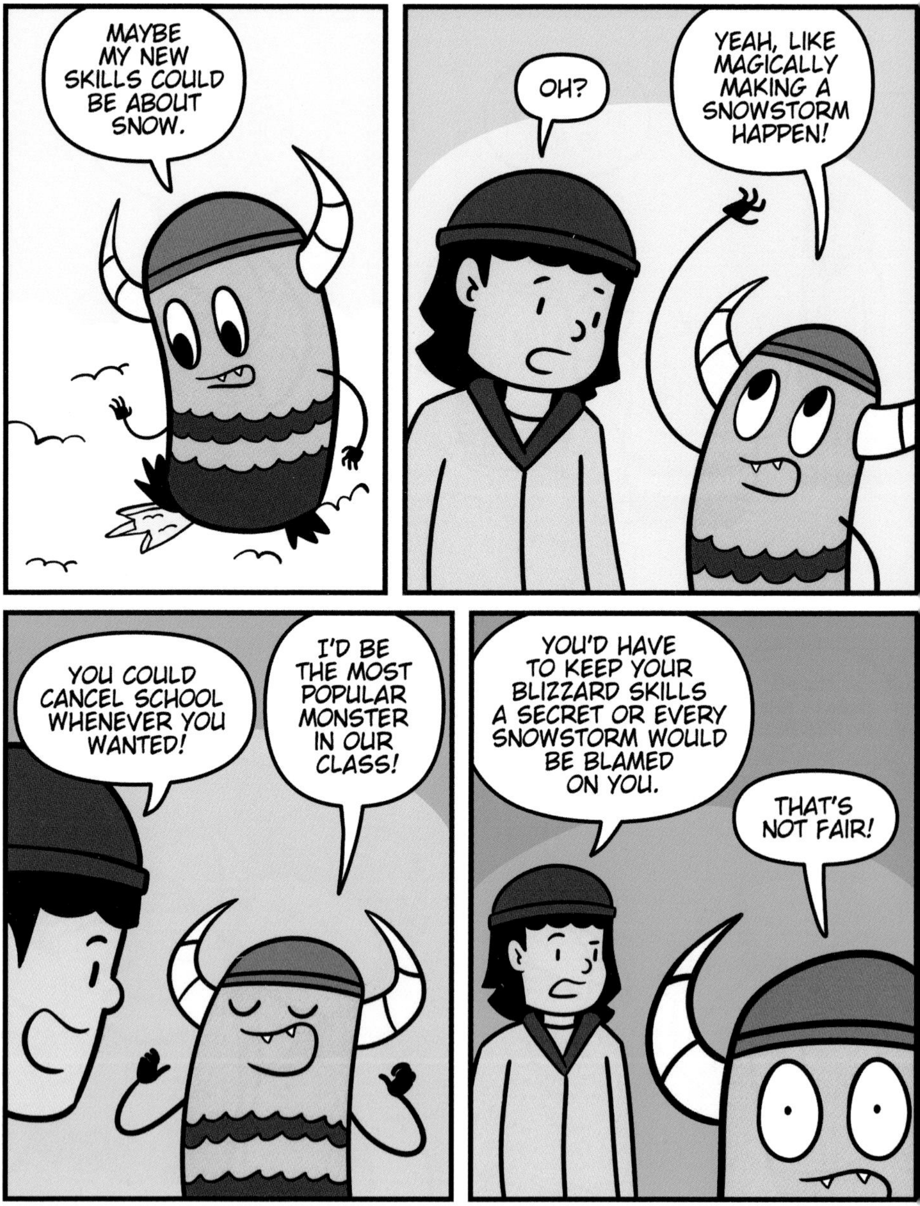
MAYBE MY NEW SKILLS COULD BE ABOUT SNOW.
OH?
YEAH, LIKE MAGICALLY MAKING A SNOWSTORM HAPPEN!
YOU COULD CANCEL SCHOOL WHENEVER YOU WANTED!
I'D BE THE MOST POPULAR MONSTER IN OUR CLASS!
YOU'D HAVE TO KEEP YOUR BLIZZARD SKILLS A SECRET OR EVERY SNOWSTORM WOULD BE BLAMED ON YOU.
THAT'S NOT FAIR!

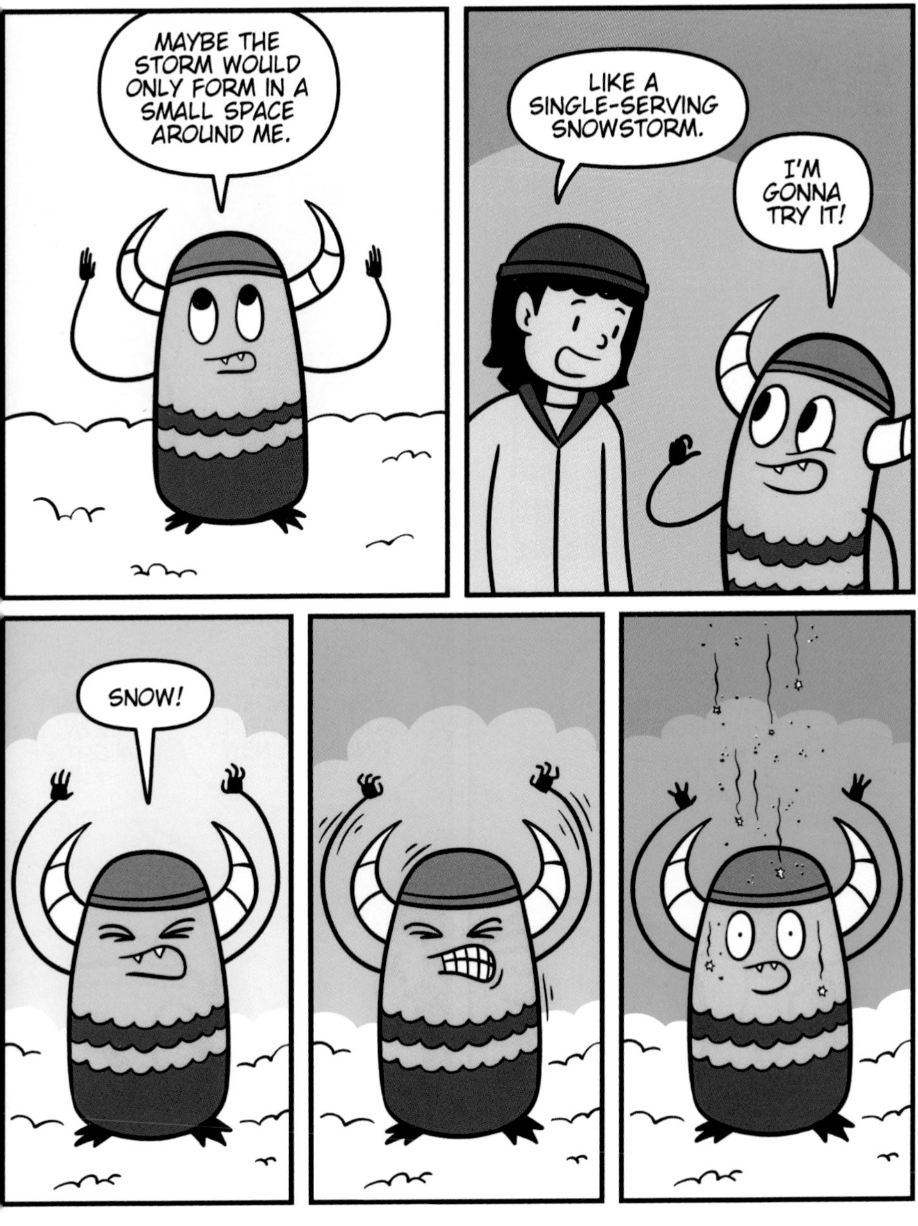
MAYBE THE STORM WOULD ONLY FORM IN A SMALL SPACE AROUND ME.
LIKE A SINGLE-SERVING SNOWSTORM.
I'M GONNA TRY IT!
SNOW!

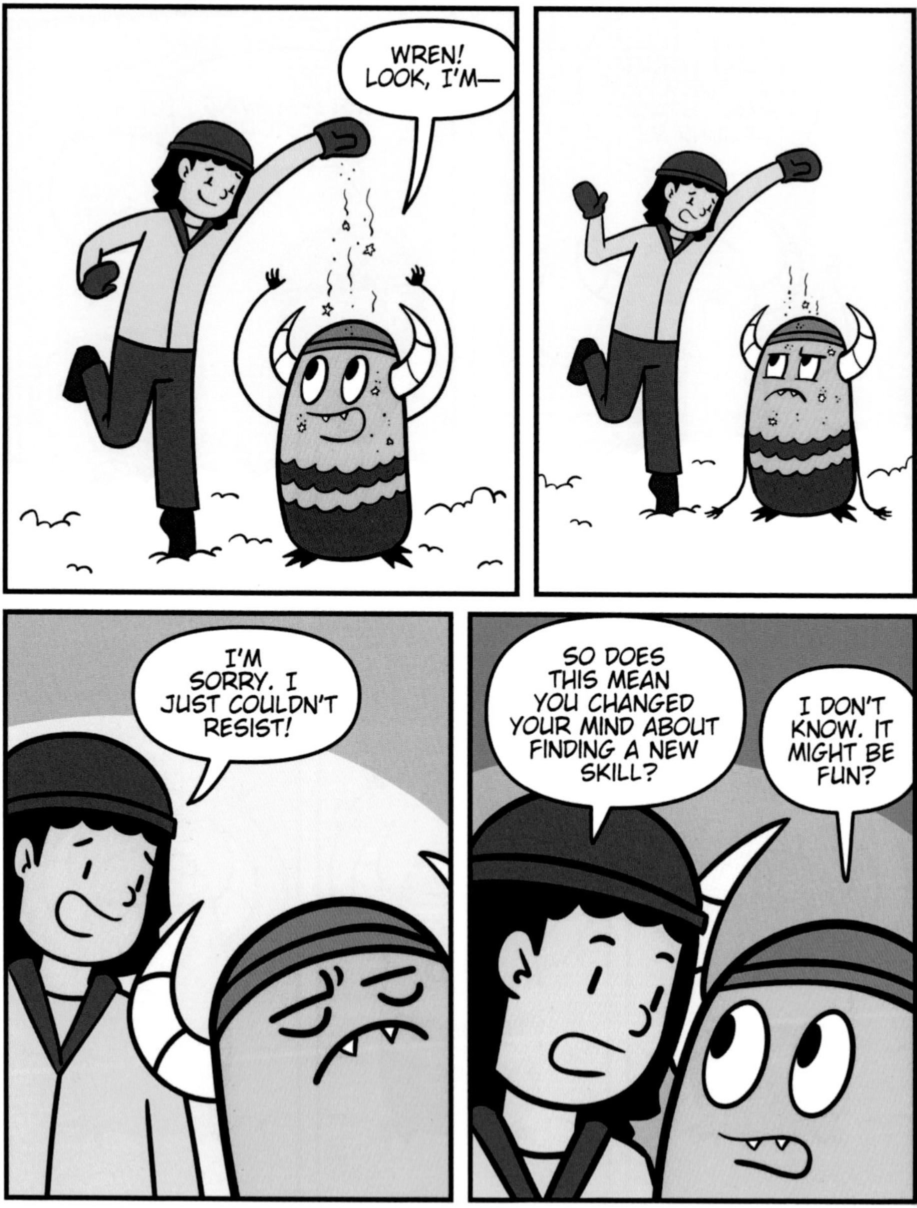
WREN! LOOK, I'M—
I'M SORRY. I JUST COULDN'T RESIST!
SO DOES THIS MEAN YOU CHANGED YOUR MIND ABOUT FINDING A NEW SKILL?
I DON'T KNOW. IT MIGHT BE FUN?

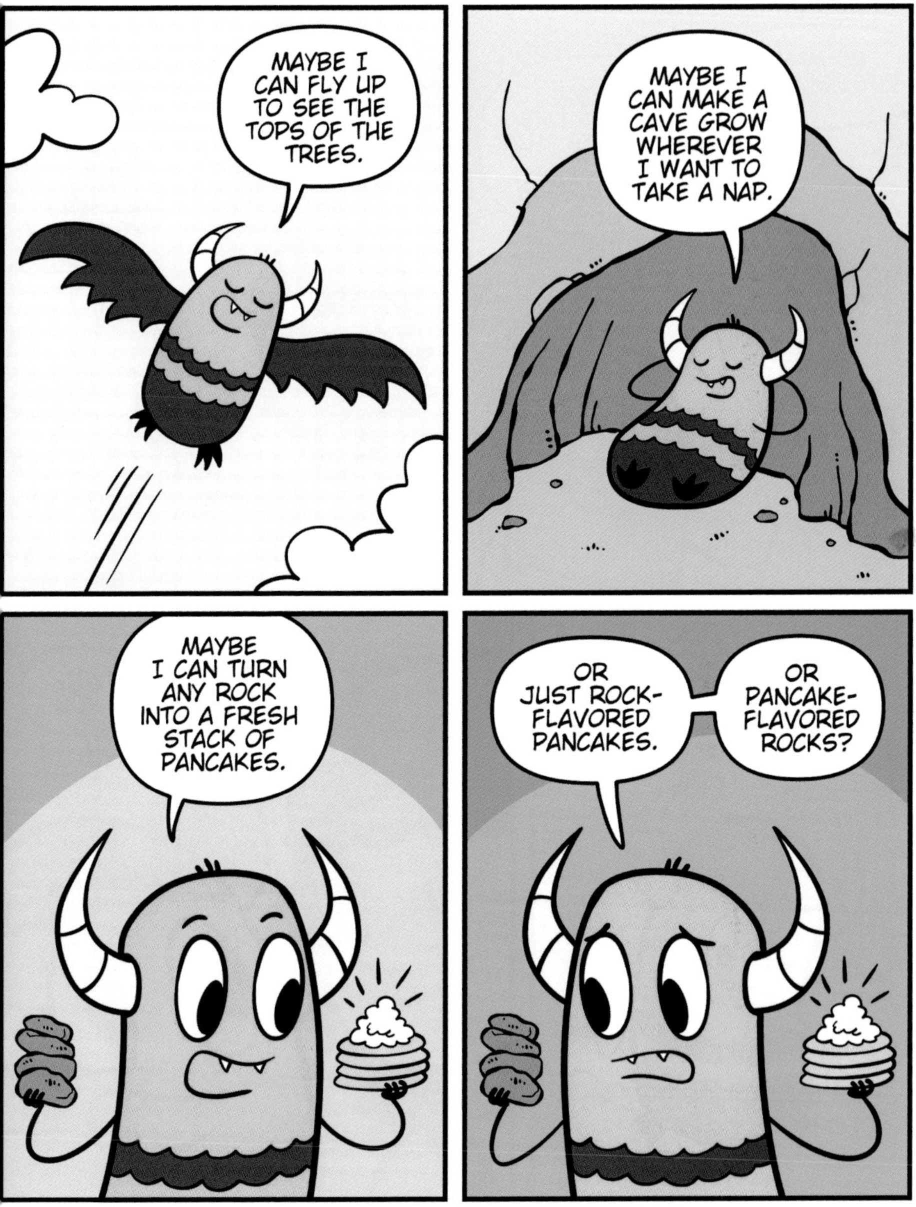
MAYBE I CAN FLY UP TO SEE THE TOPS OF THE TREES.
MAYBE I CAN MAKE A CAVE GROW WHEREVER I WANT TO TAKE A NAP.
MAYBE I CAN TURN ANY ROCK INTO A FRESH STACK OF PANCAKES.
OR JUST ROCK-FLAVORED PANCAKES.
OR PANCAKE-FLAVORED ROCKS?

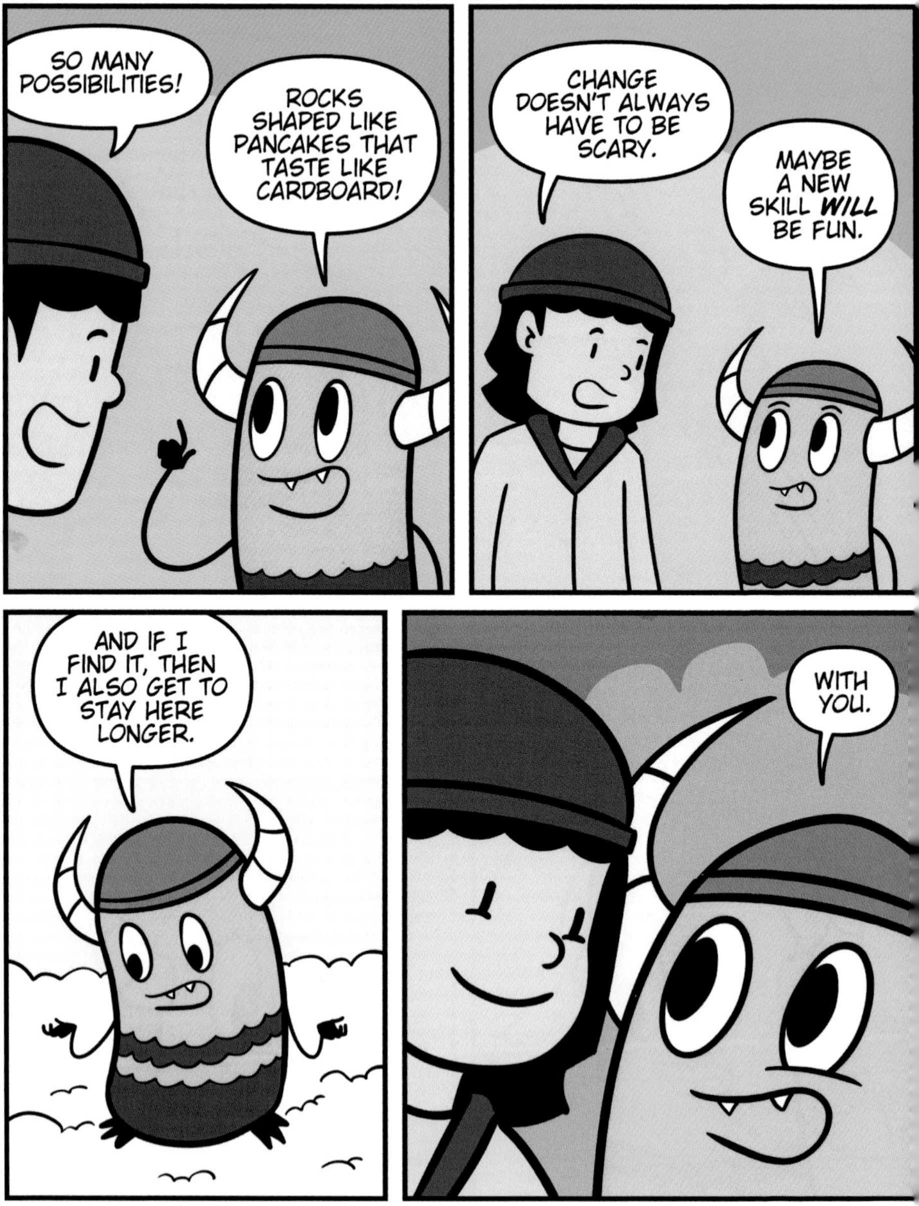
SO MANY POSSIBILITIES!
ROCKS SHAPED LIKE PANCAKES THAT TASTE LIKE CARDBOARD!
CHANGE DOESN'T ALWAYS HAVE TO BE SCARY.
MAYBE A NEW SKILL *WILL* BE FUN.
AND IF I FIND IT, THEN I ALSO GET TO STAY HERE LONGER.
WITH YOU.

CHAPTER EIGHT

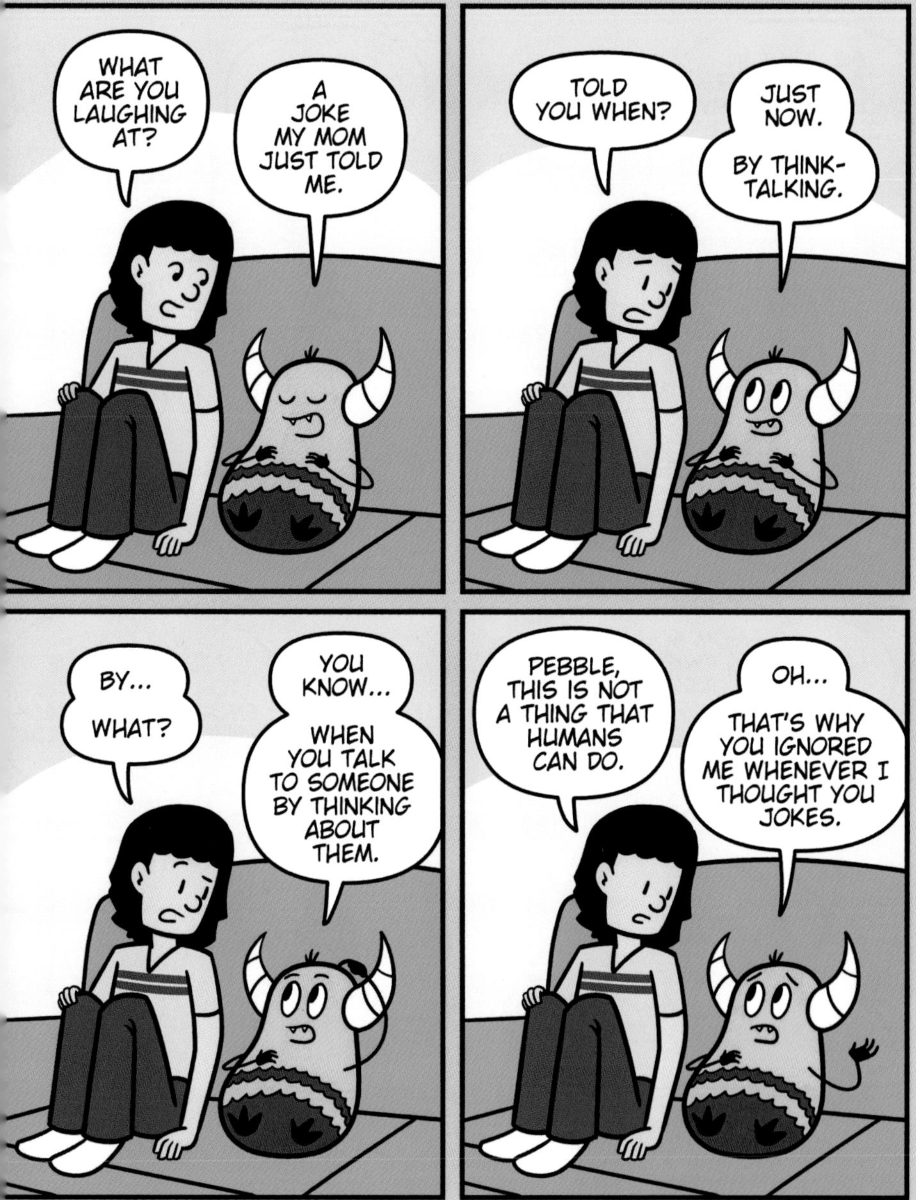
WHAT ARE YOU LAUGHING AT?
A JOKE MY MOM JUST TOLD ME.
TOLD YOU WHEN?
JUST NOW.

BY THINK-TALKING.
BY...

WHAT?
YOU KNOW...

WHEN YOU TALK TO SOMEONE BY THINKING ABOUT THEM.
PEBBLE, THIS IS NOT A THING THAT HUMANS CAN DO.
OH...

THAT'S WHY YOU IGNORED ME WHENEVER I THOUGHT YOU JOKES.

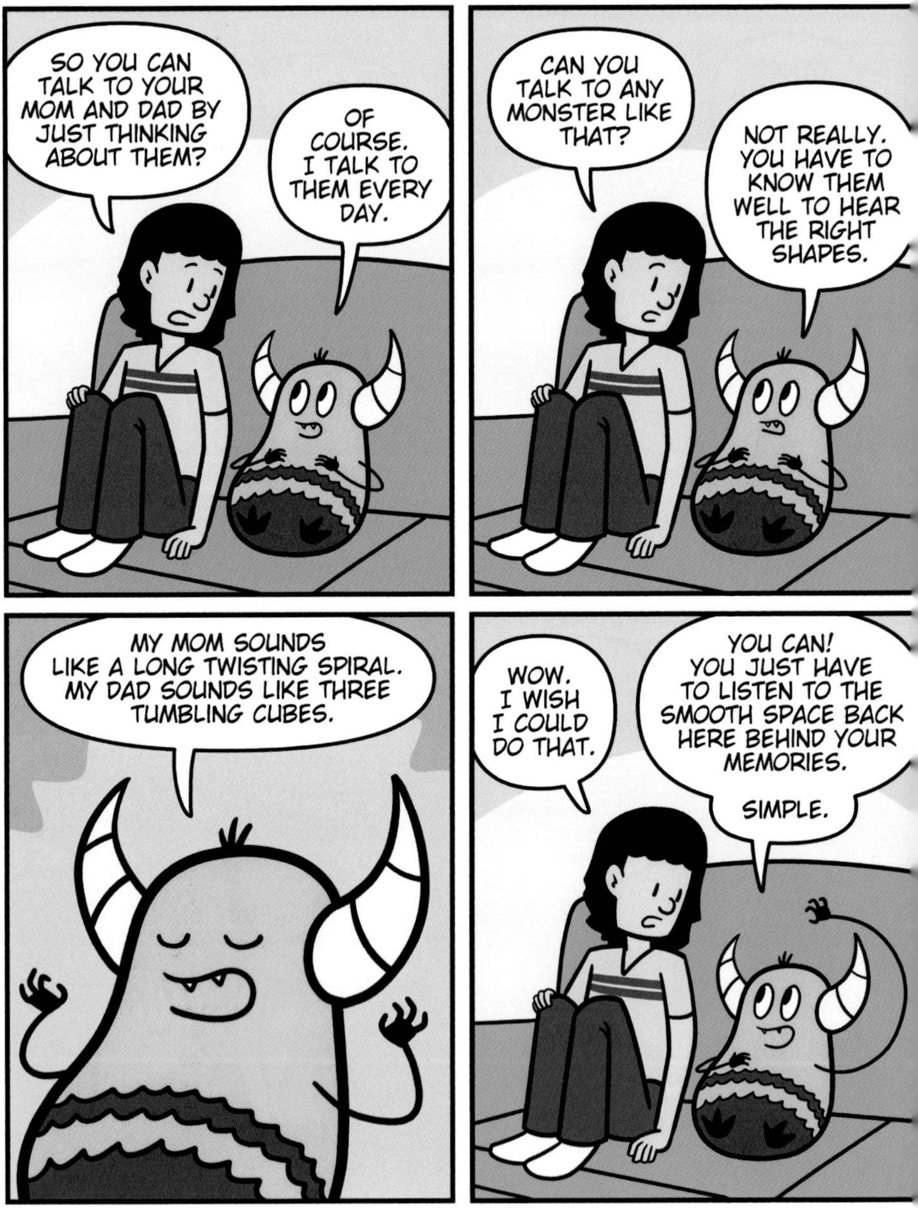
SO YOU CAN TALK TO YOUR MOM AND DAD BY JUST THINKING ABOUT THEM?
OF COURSE. I TALK TO THEM EVERY DAY.
CAN YOU TALK TO ANY MONSTER LIKE THAT?
NOT REALLY. YOU HAVE TO KNOW THEM WELL TO HEAR THE RIGHT SHAPES.
MY MOM SOUNDS LIKE A LONG TWISTING SPIRAL. MY DAD SOUNDS LIKE THREE TUMBLING CUBES.
WOW. I WISH I COULD DO THAT.
YOU CAN! YOU JUST HAVE TO LISTEN TO THE SMOOTH SPACE BACK HERE BEHIND YOUR MEMORIES.
SIMPLE.

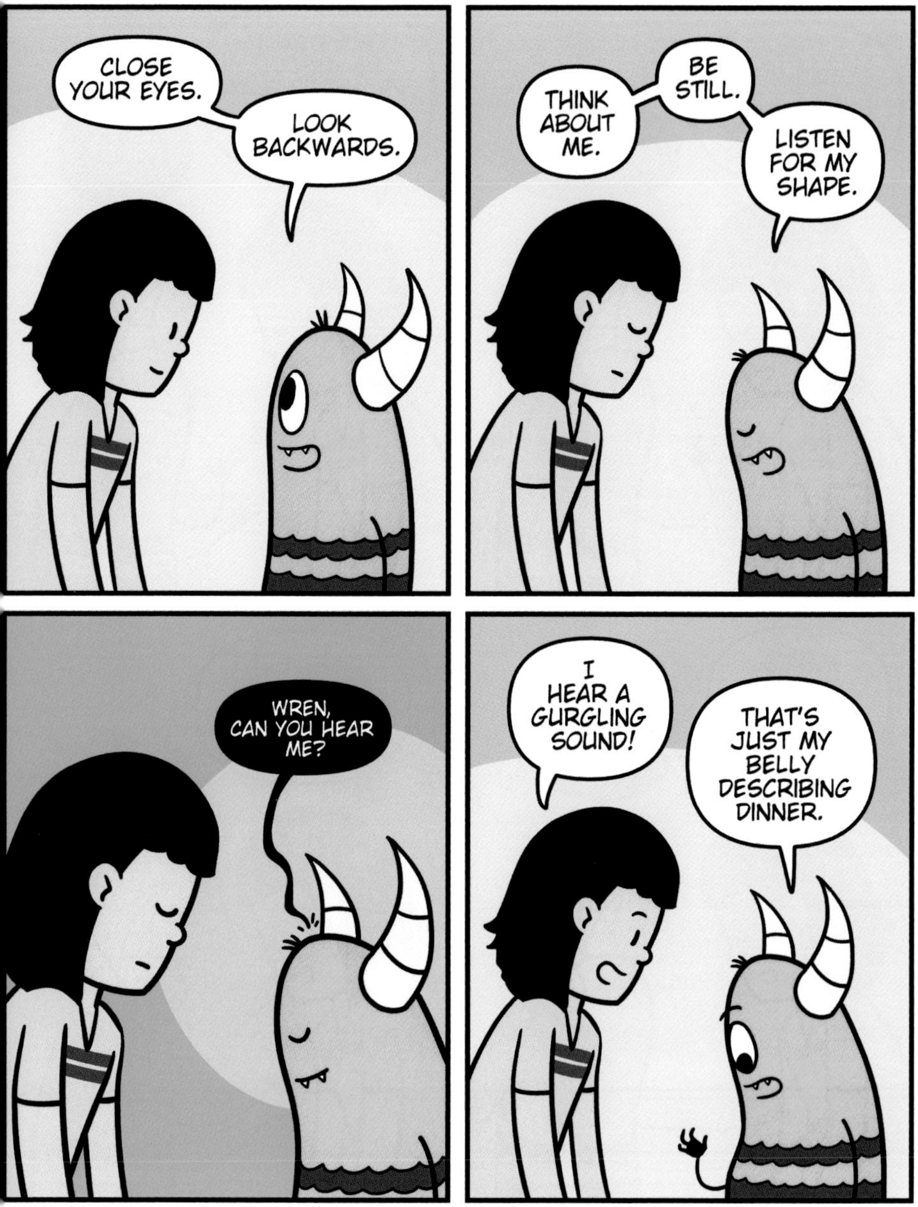
CLOSE YOUR EYES.
LOOK BACKWARDS.
THINK ABOUT ME.
BE STILL.
LISTEN FOR MY SHAPE.
WREN, CAN YOU HEAR ME?
I HEAR A GURGLING SOUND!
THAT'S JUST MY BELLY DESCRIBING DINNER.

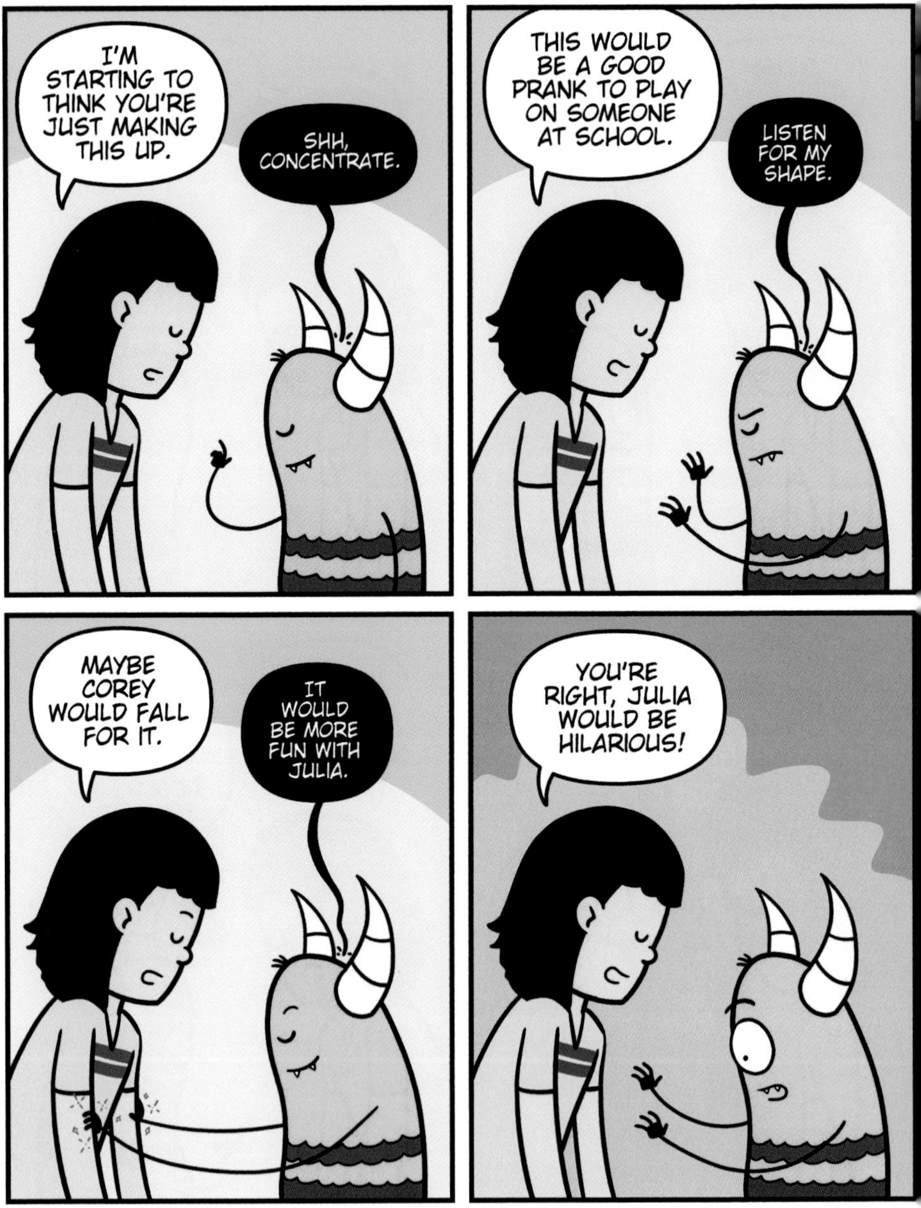
I'M STARTING TO THINK YOU'RE JUST MAKING THIS UP.
SHH, CONCENTRATE.
THIS WOULD BE A GOOD PRANK TO PLAY ON SOMEONE AT SCHOOL.
LISTEN FOR MY SHAPE.
MAYBE COREY WOULD FALL FOR IT.
IT WOULD BE MORE FUN WITH JULIA.
YOU'RE RIGHT, JULIA WOULD BE HILARIOUS!

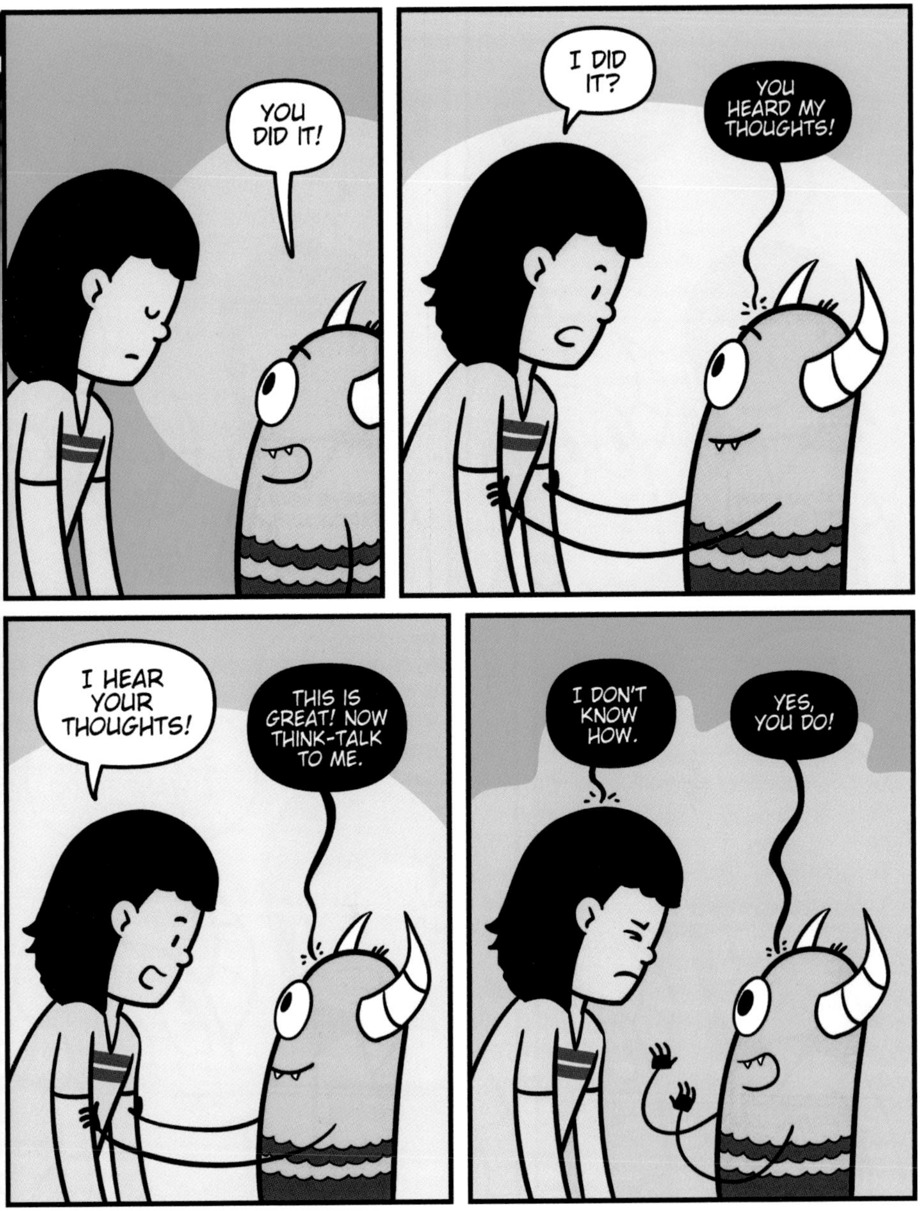
YOU DID IT!
I DID IT?
YOU HEARD MY THOUGHTS!
I HEAR YOUR THOUGHTS!
THIS IS GREAT! NOW THINK-TALK TO ME.
I DON'T KNOW HOW.
YES, YOU DO!

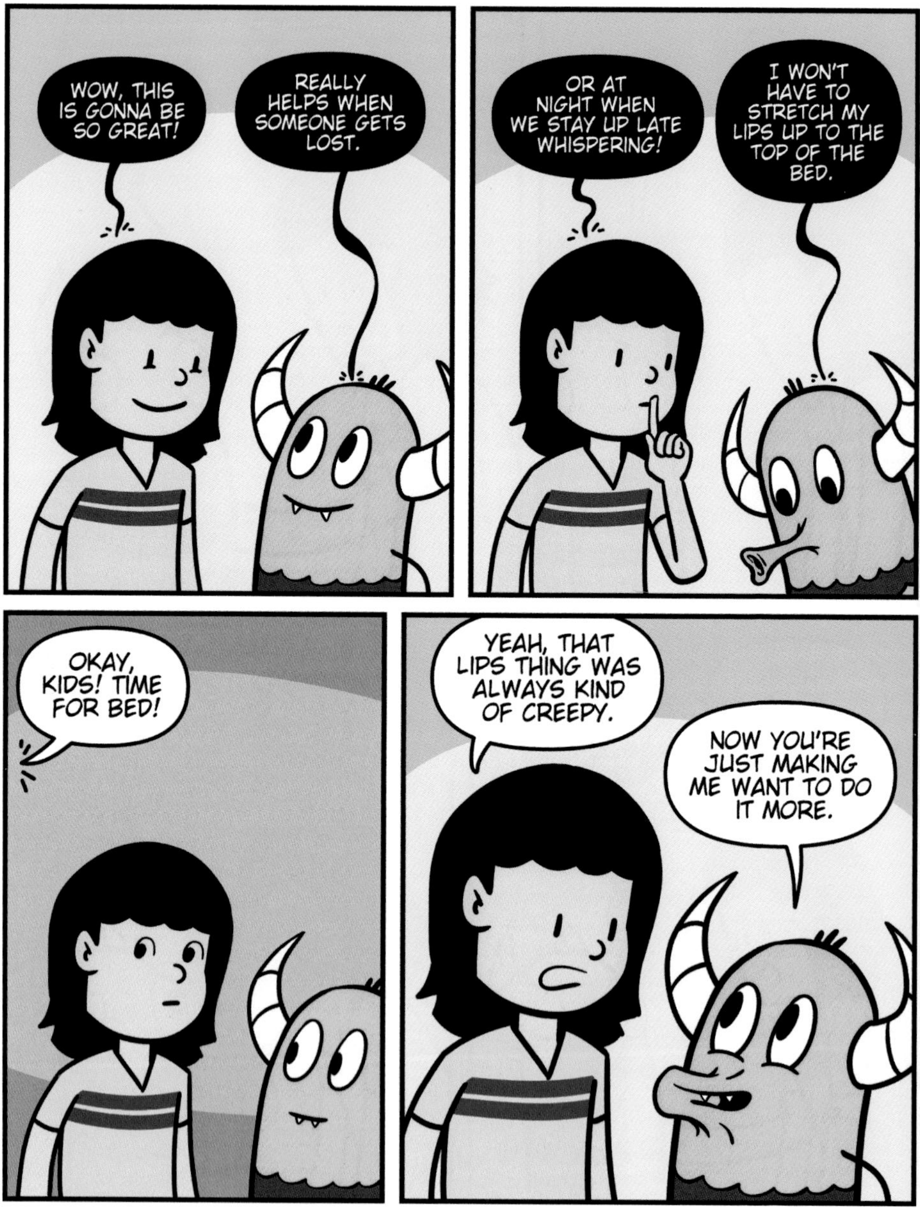
WOW, THIS IS GONNA BE SO GREAT!
REALLY HELPS WHEN SOMEONE GETS LOST.
OR AT NIGHT WHEN WE STAY UP LATE WHISPERING!
I WON'T HAVE TO STRETCH MY LIPS UP TO THE TOP OF THE BED.
OKAY, KIDS! TIME FOR BED!
YEAH, THAT LIPS THING WAS ALWAYS KIND OF CREEPY.
NOW YOU'RE JUST MAKING ME WANT TO DO IT MORE.

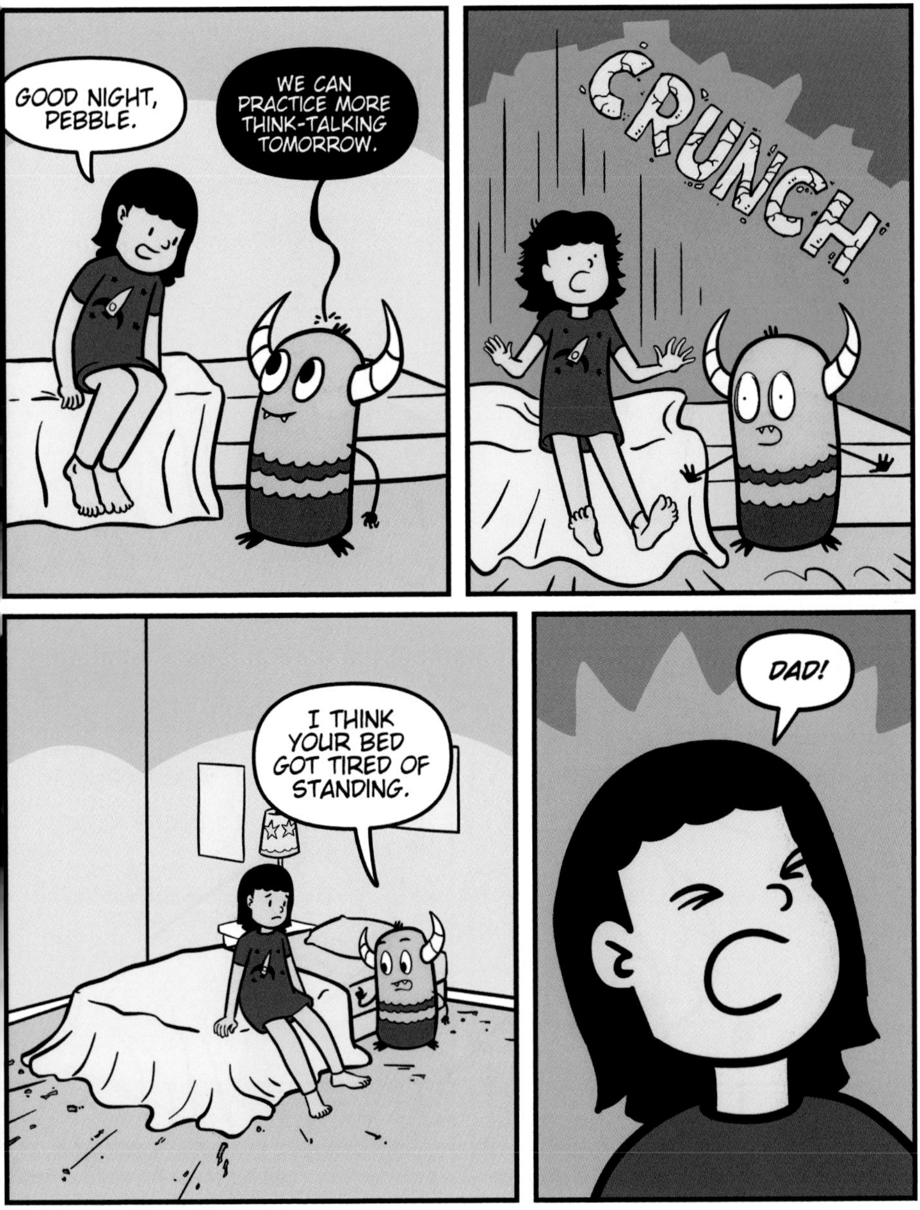
GOOD NIGHT, PEBBLE.
WE CAN PRACTICE MORE THINK-TALKING TOMORROW.
CRUNCH
I THINK YOUR BED GOT TIRED OF STANDING.
DAD!

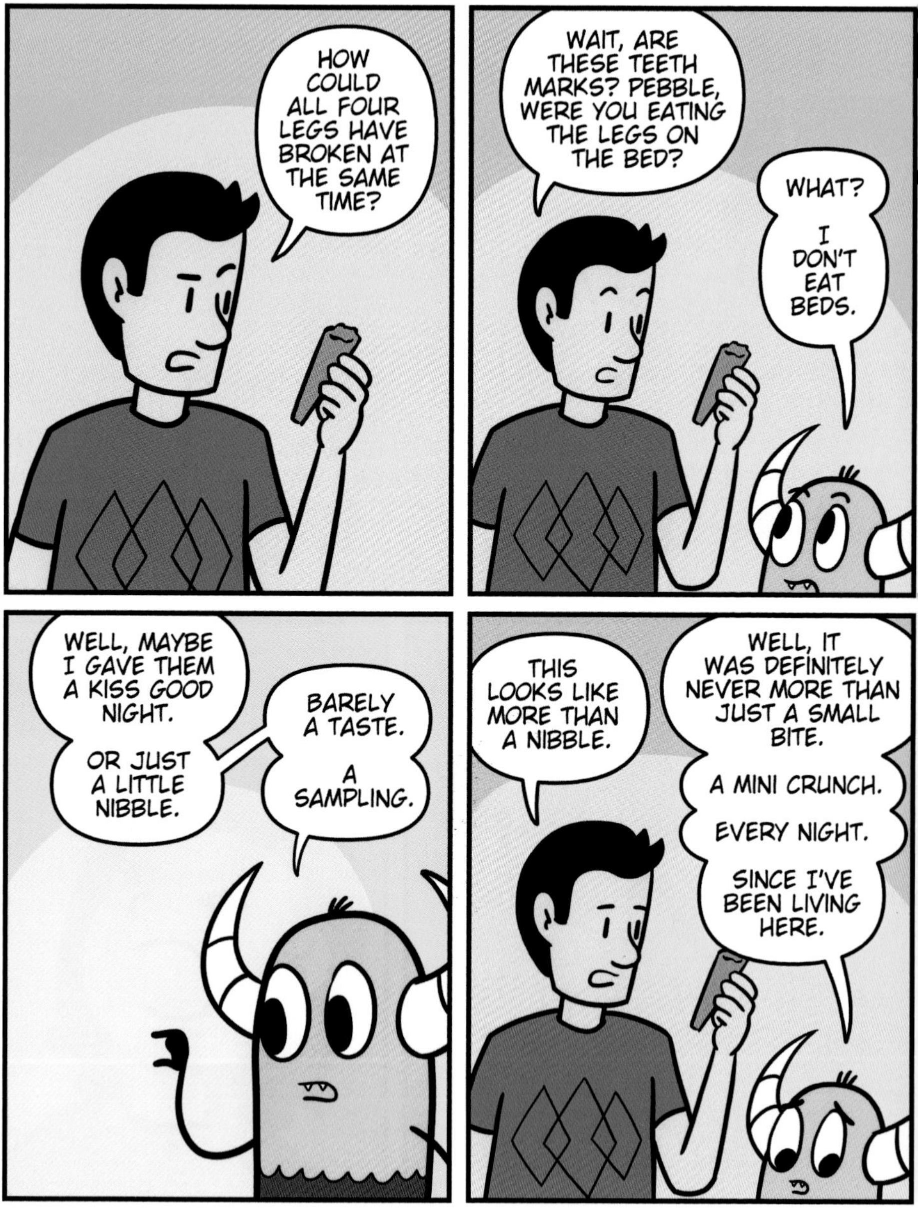
HOW COULD ALL FOUR LEGS HAVE BROKEN AT THE SAME TIME?
WAIT, ARE THESE TEETH MARKS? PEBBLE, WERE YOU EATING THE LEGS ON THE BED?
WHAT?
I DON'T EAT BEDS.
WELL, MAYBE I GAVE THEM A KISS GOOD NIGHT.
OR JUST A LITTLE NIBBLE.
BARELY A TASTE.
A SAMPLING.
THIS LOOKS LIKE MORE THAN A NIBBLE.
WELL, IT WAS DEFINITELY NEVER MORE THAN JUST A SMALL BITE.
A MINI CRUNCH.
EVERY NIGHT.
SINCE I'VE BEEN LIVING HERE.

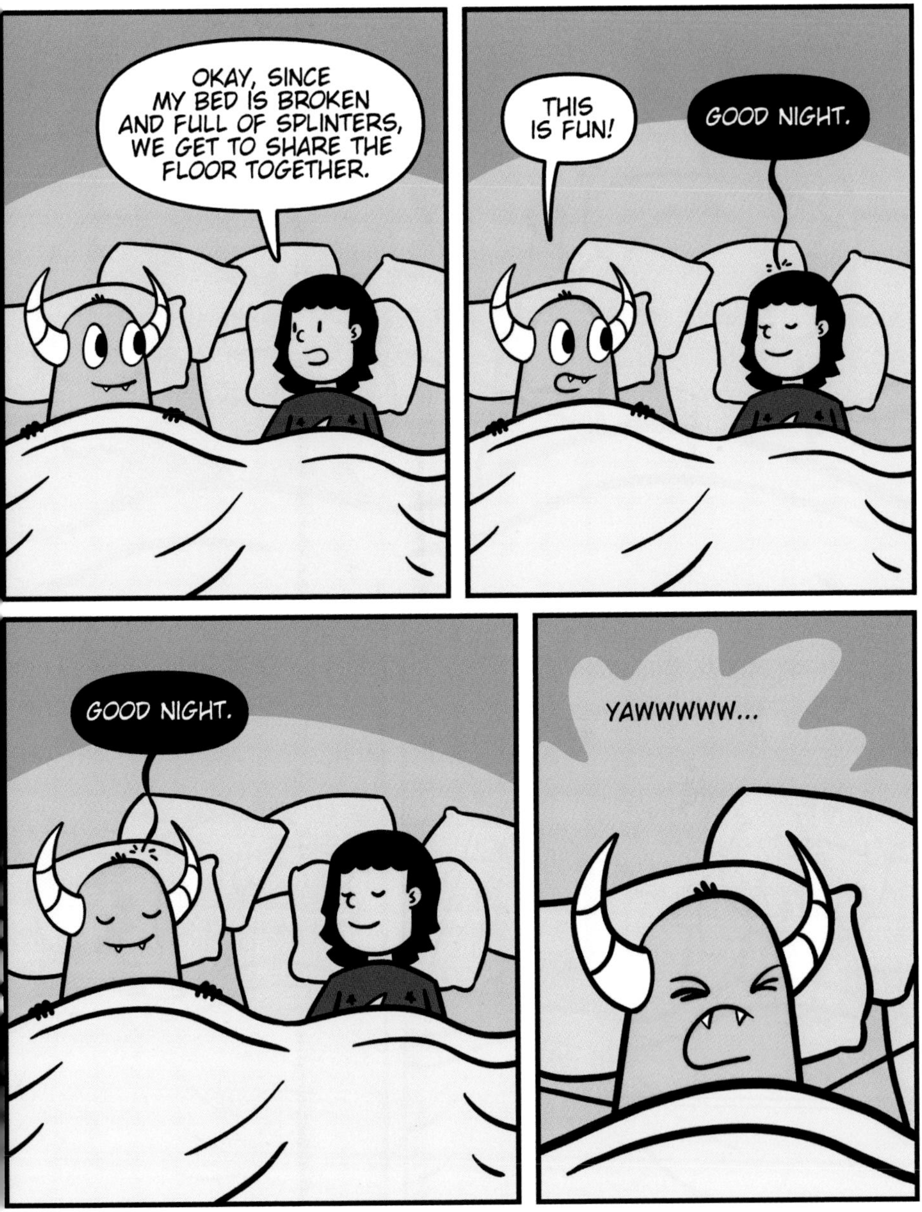
OKAY, SINCE MY BED IS BROKEN AND FULL OF SPLINTERS, WE GET TO SHARE THE FLOOR TOGETHER.
THIS IS FUN!
GOOD NIGHT.
GOOD NIGHT.
YAWWWWW...

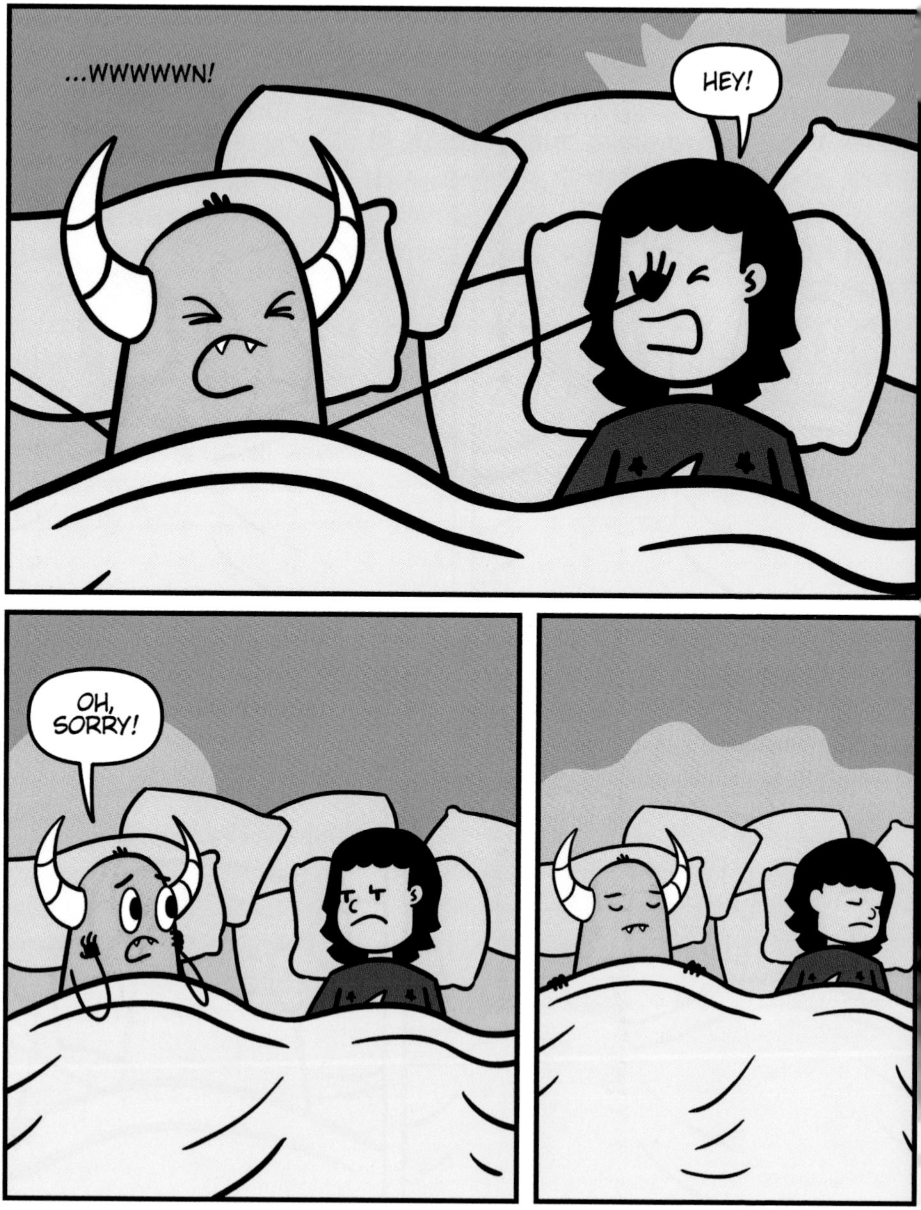
...WWWWWN!
HEY!
OH, SORRY!

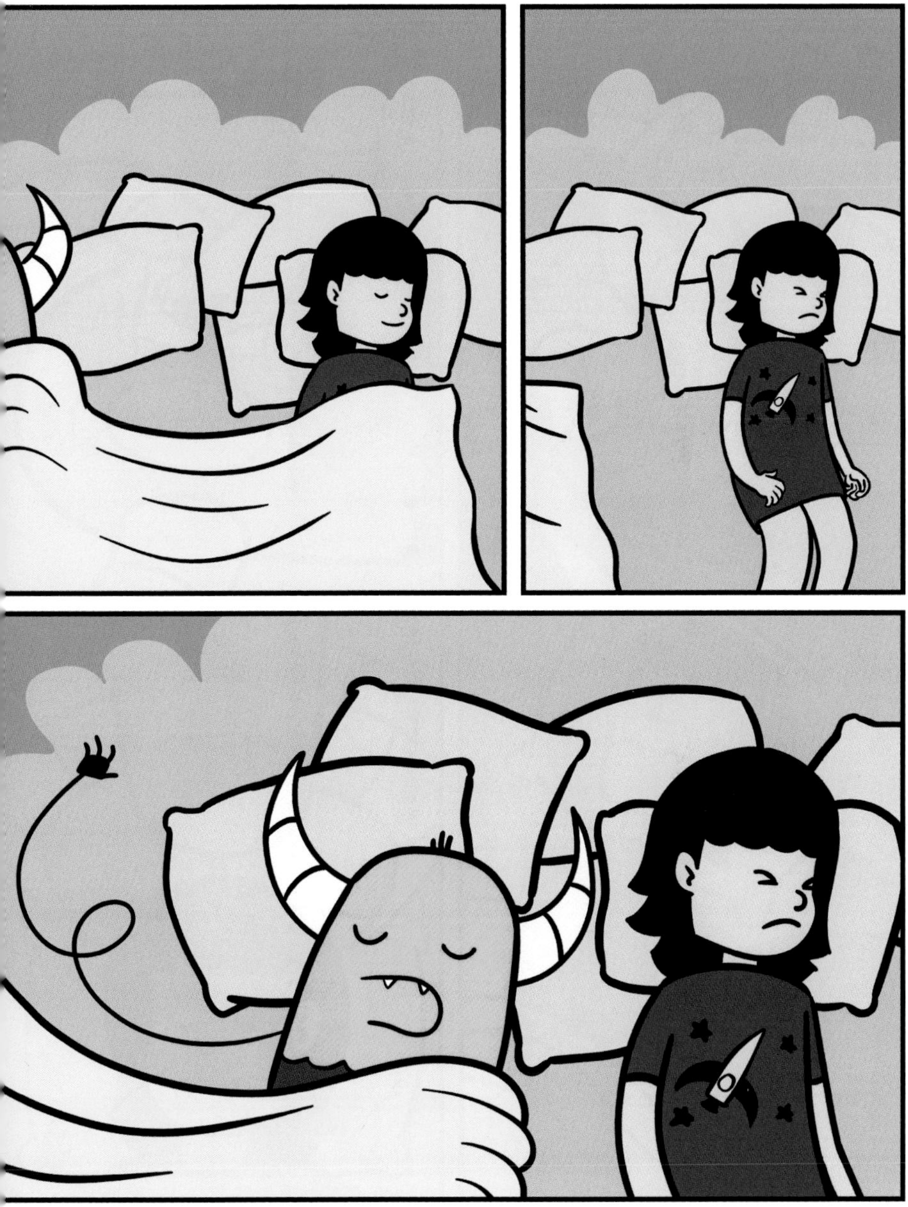

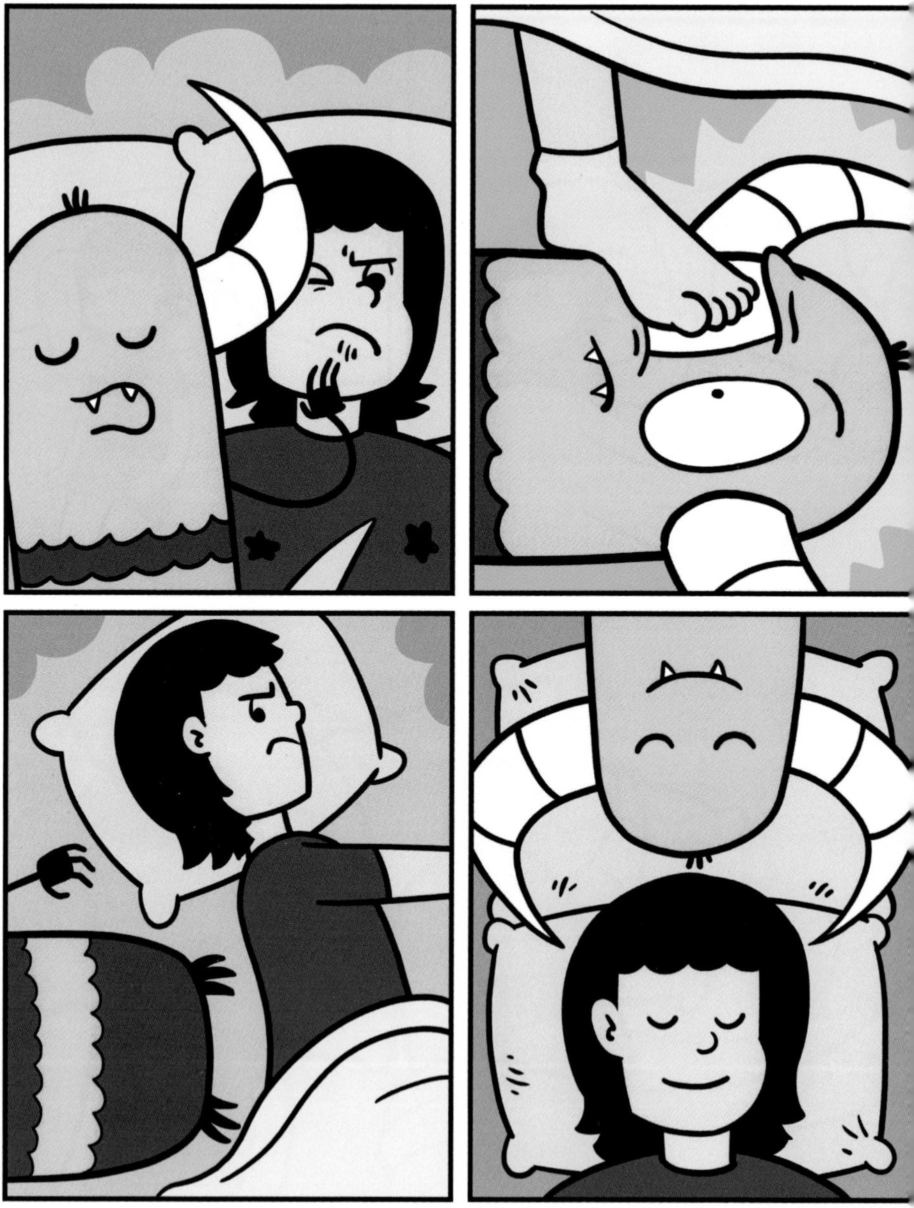

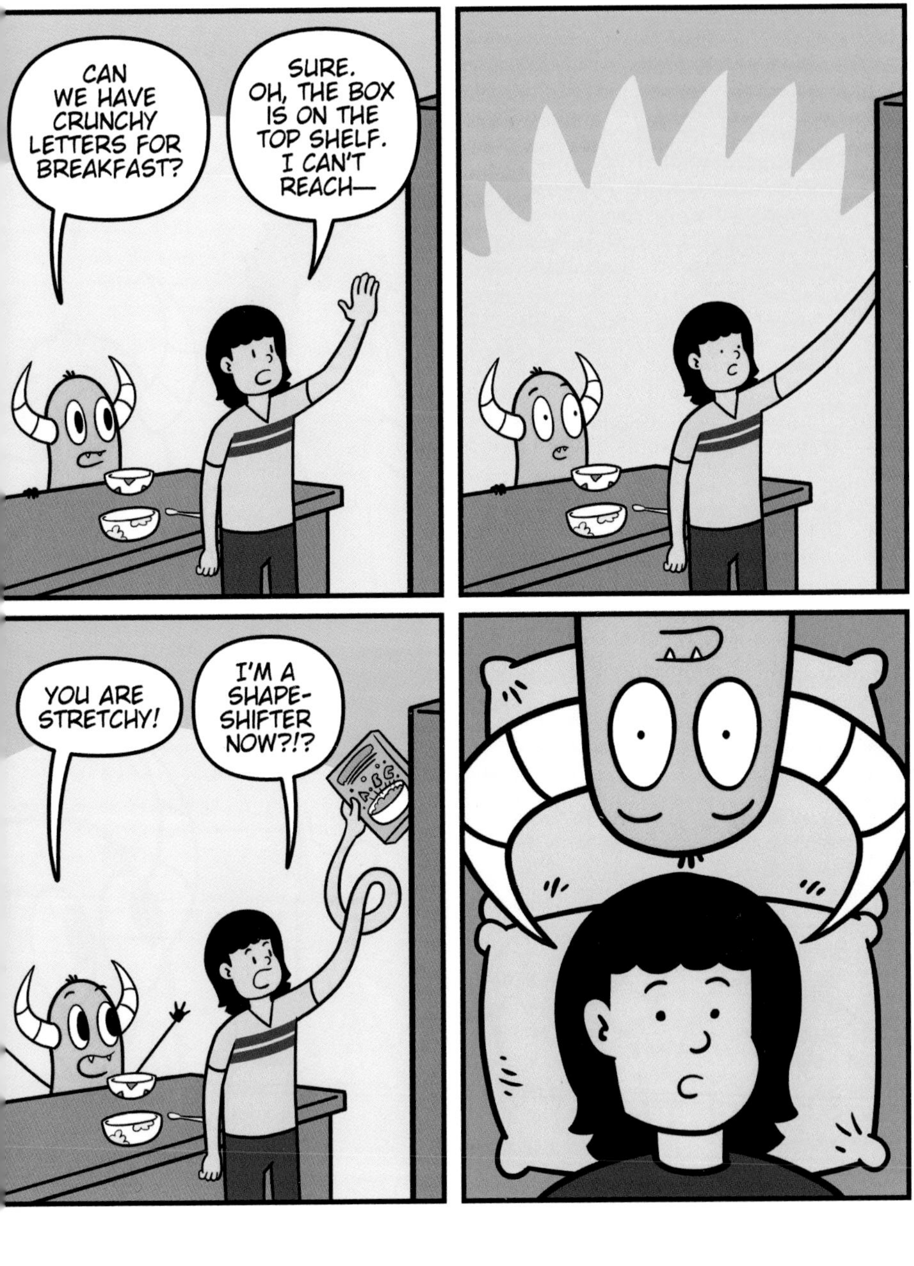
CAN WE HAVE CRUNCHY LETTERS FOR BREAKFAST?
SURE. OH, THE BOX IS ON THE TOP SHELF. I CAN'T REACH—
YOU ARE STRETCHY!
I'M A SHAPE-SHIFTER NOW?!?

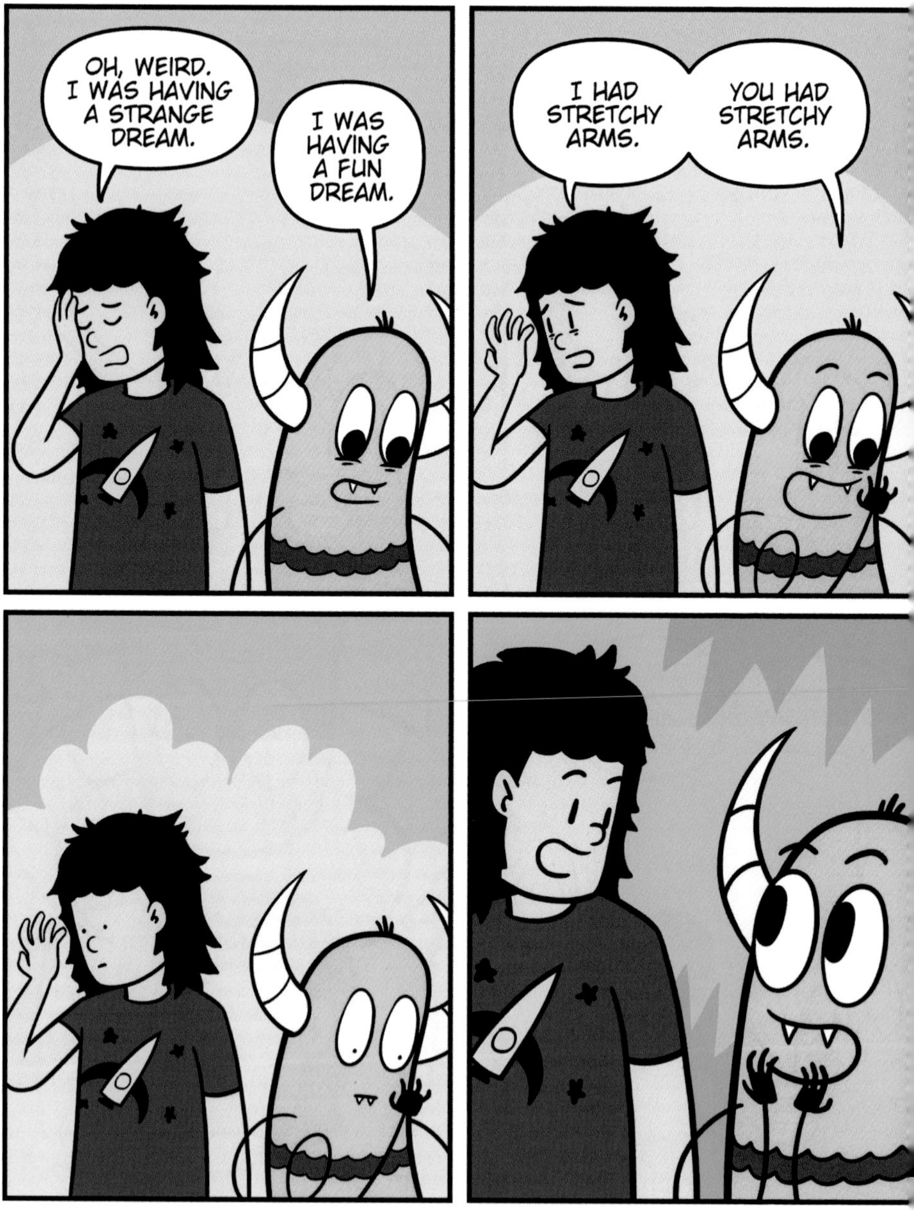
OH, WEIRD. I WAS HAVING A STRANGE DREAM.
I WAS HAVING A FUN DREAM.
I HAD STRETCHY ARMS.
YOU HAD STRETCHY ARMS.

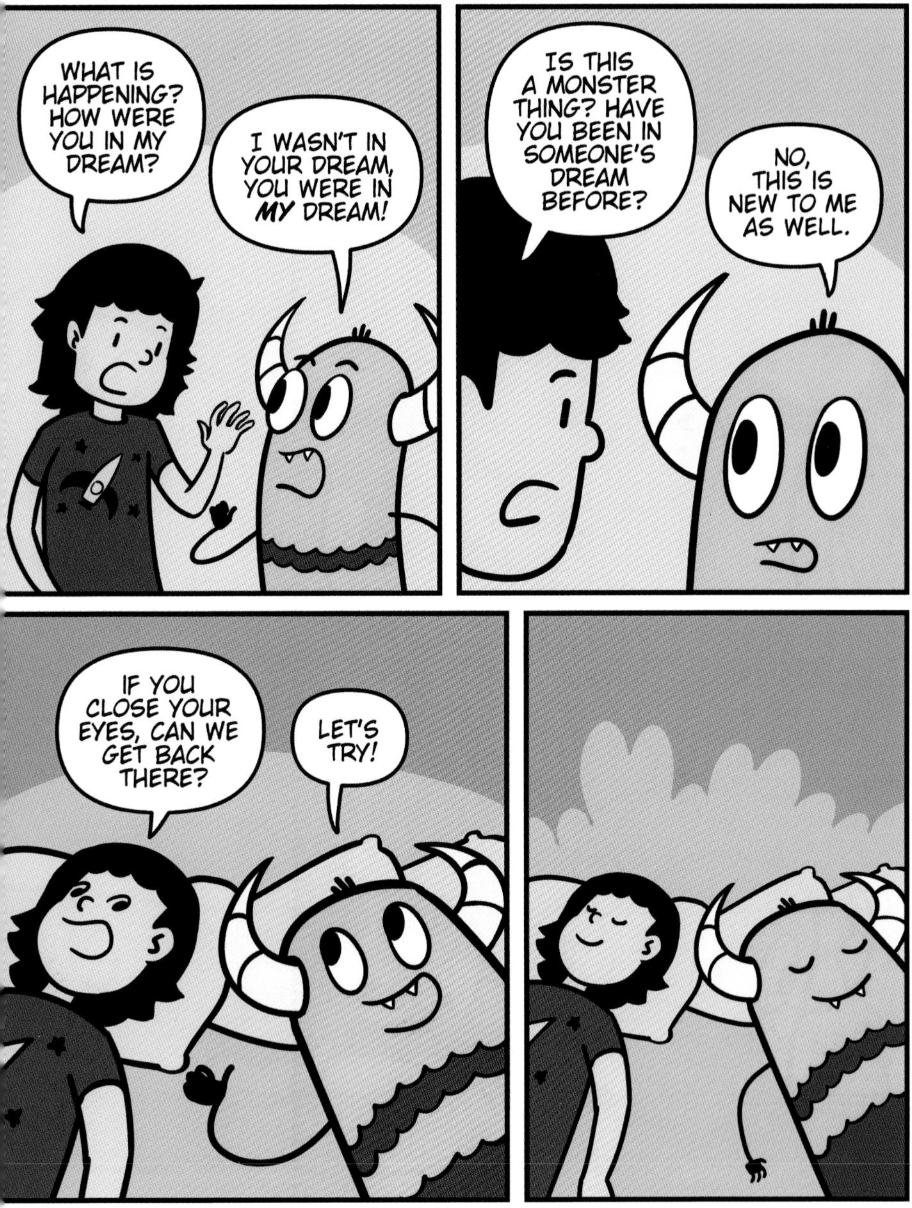
WHAT IS HAPPENING? HOW WERE YOU IN MY DREAM?
I WASN'T IN YOUR DREAM, YOU WERE IN *MY* DREAM!
IS THIS A MONSTER THING? HAVE YOU BEEN IN SOMEONE'S DREAM BEFORE?
NO, THIS IS NEW TO ME AS WELL.
IF YOU CLOSE YOUR EYES, CAN WE GET BACK THERE?
LET'S TRY!

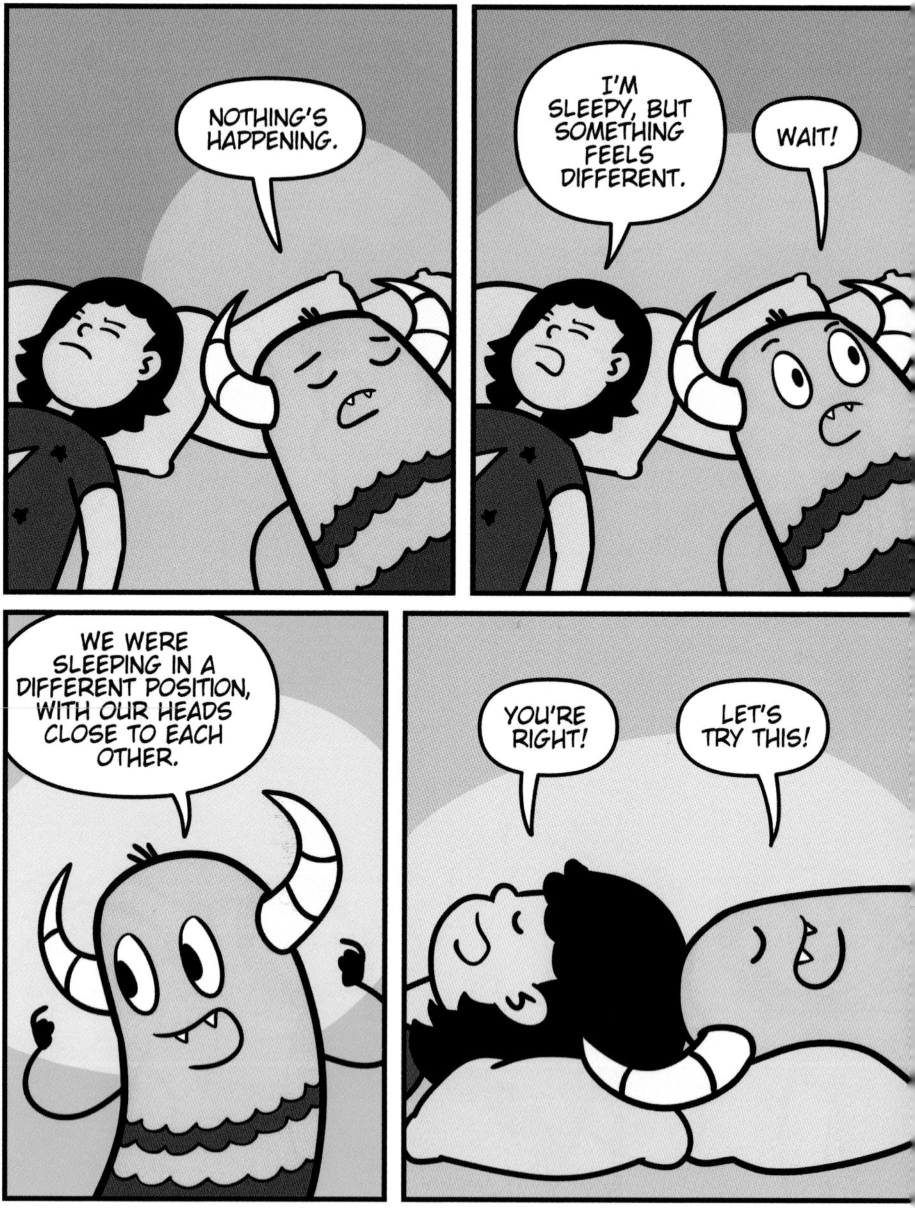
NOTHING'S HAPPENING.
I'M SLEEPY, BUT SOMETHING FEELS DIFFERENT.
WAIT!
WE WERE SLEEPING IN A DIFFERENT POSITION, WITH OUR HEADS CLOSE TO EACH OTHER.
YOU'RE RIGHT!
LET'S TRY THIS!

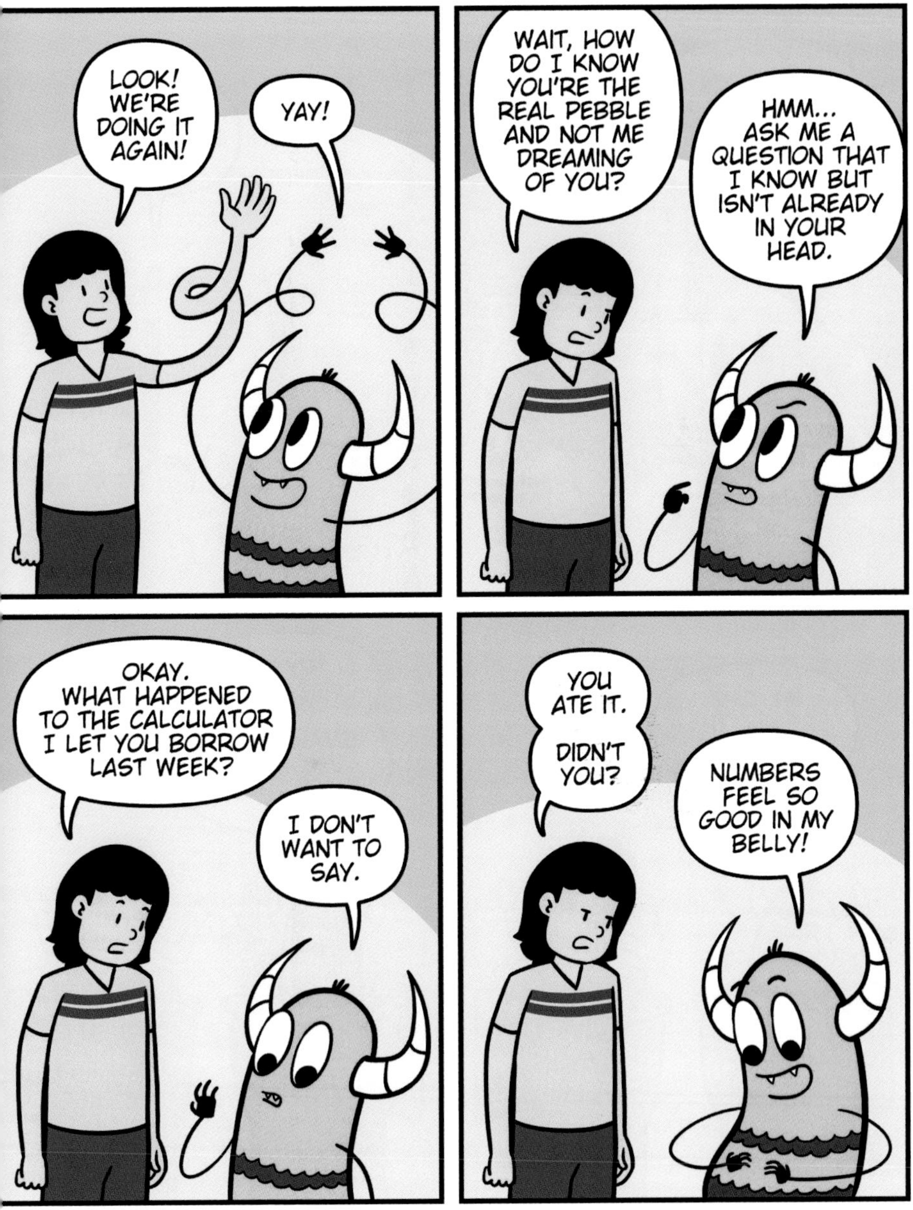
LOOK! WE'RE DOING IT AGAIN!
YAY!
WAIT, HOW DO I KNOW YOU'RE THE REAL PEBBLE AND NOT ME DREAMING OF YOU?
HMM... ASK ME A QUESTION THAT I KNOW BUT ISN'T ALREADY IN YOUR HEAD.
OKAY. WHAT HAPPENED TO THE CALCULATOR I LET YOU BORROW LAST WEEK?
I DON'T WANT TO SAY.
YOU ATE IT.
DIDN'T YOU?
NUMBERS FEEL SO GOOD IN MY BELLY!

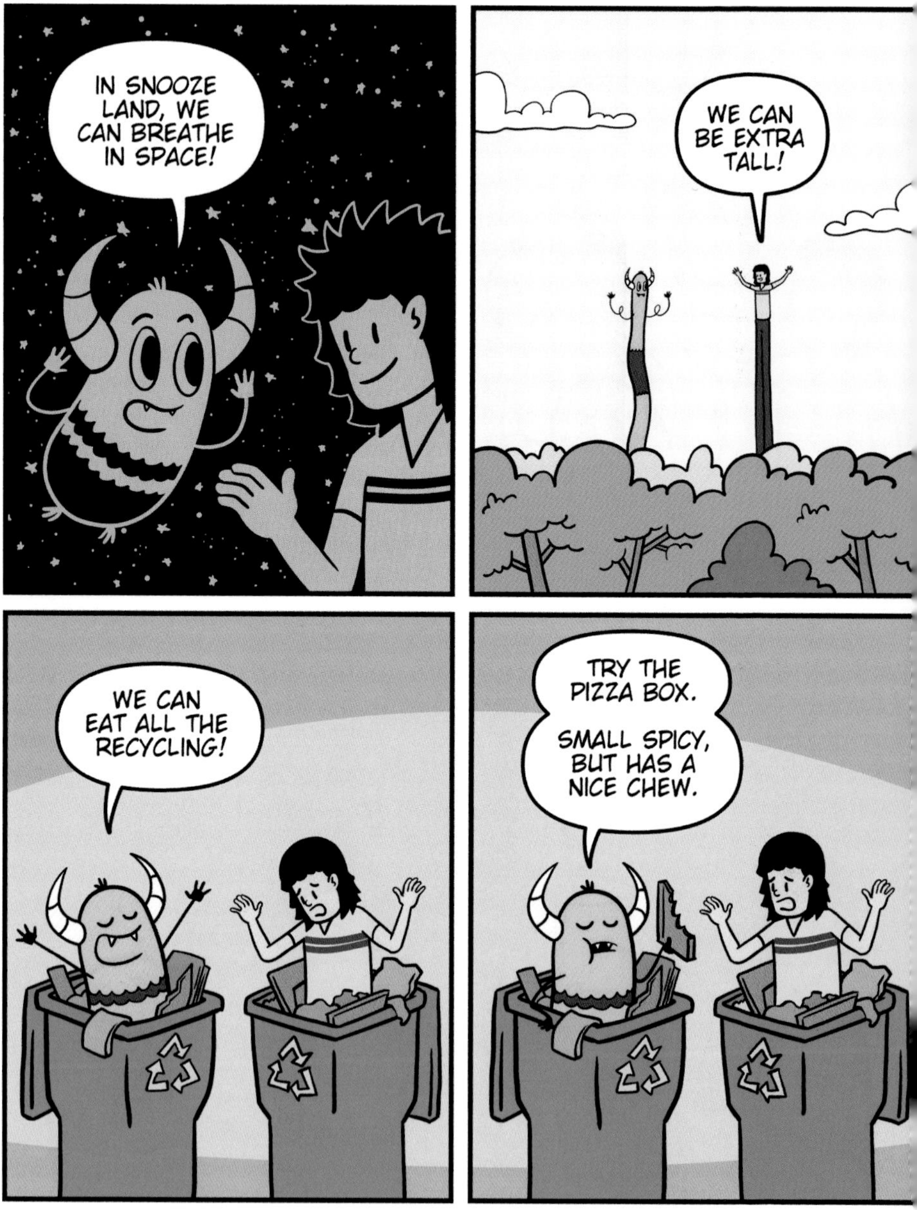
IN SNOOZE LAND, WE CAN BREATHE IN SPACE!
WE CAN BE EXTRA TALL!
WE CAN EAT ALL THE RECYCLING!
TRY THE PIZZA BOX.
SMALL SPICY, BUT HAS A NICE CHEW.

CHAPTER NINE

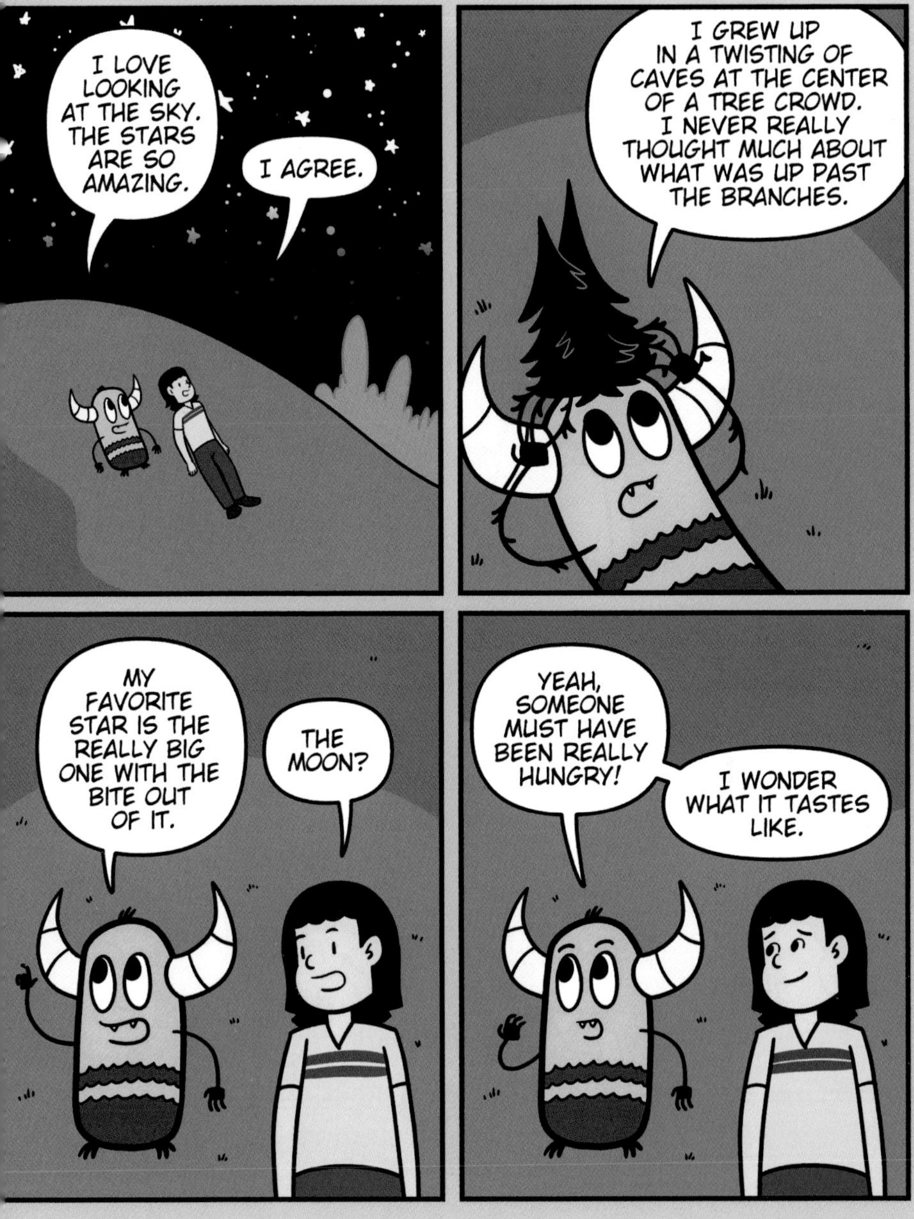
I LOVE LOOKING AT THE SKY. THE STARS ARE SO AMAZING.
I AGREE.
I GREW UP IN A TWISTING OF CAVES AT THE CENTER OF A TREE CROWD. I NEVER REALLY THOUGHT MUCH ABOUT WHAT WAS UP PAST THE BRANCHES.
MY FAVORITE STAR IS THE REALLY BIG ONE WITH THE BITE OUT OF IT.
THE MOON?
YEAH, SOMEONE MUST HAVE BEEN REALLY HUNGRY!
I WONDER WHAT IT TASTES LIKE.

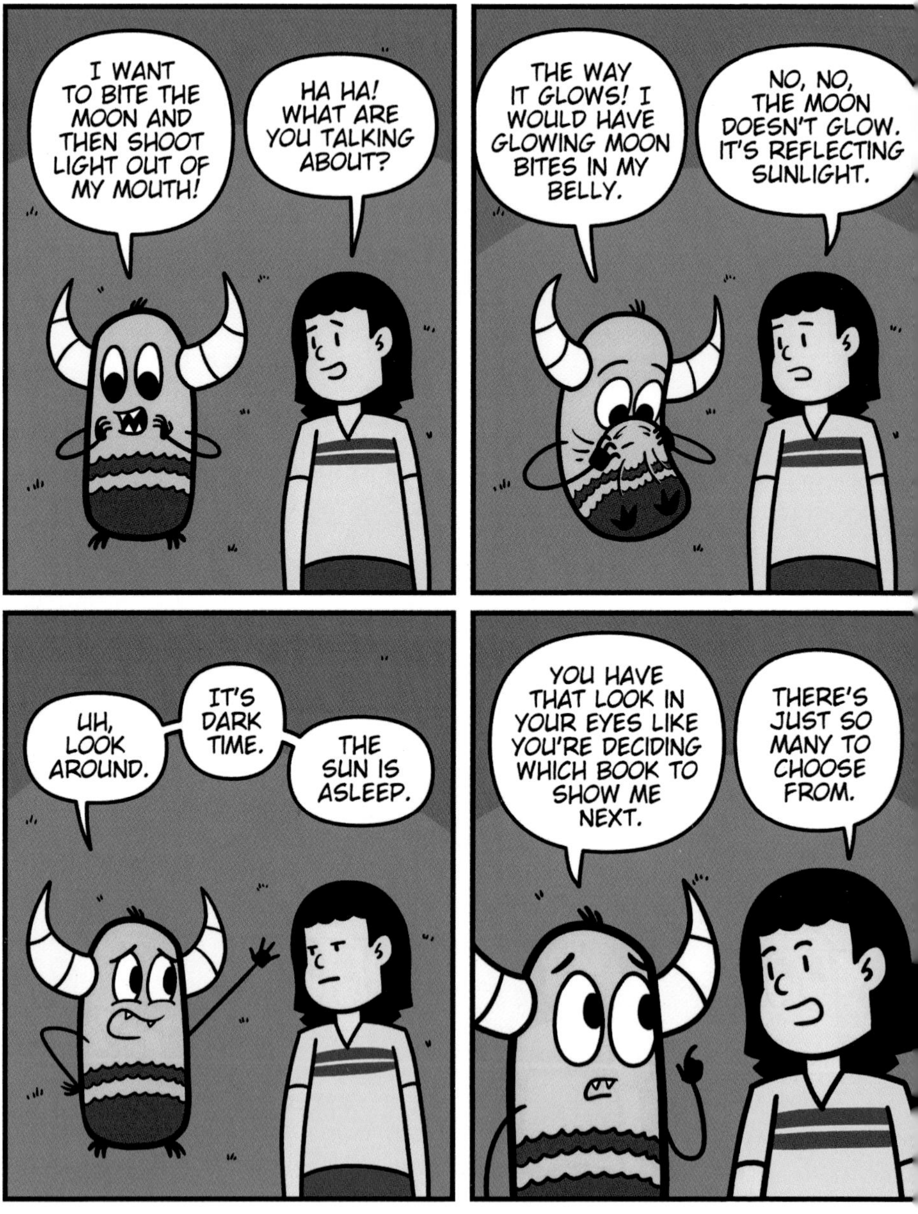
I WANT TO BITE THE MOON AND THEN SHOOT LIGHT OUT OF MY MOUTH!
HA HA! WHAT ARE YOU TALKING ABOUT?
THE WAY IT GLOWS! I WOULD HAVE GLOWING MOON BITES IN MY BELLY.
NO, NO, THE MOON DOESN'T GLOW. IT'S REFLECTING SUNLIGHT.
UH, LOOK AROUND.
IT'S DARK TIME.
THE SUN IS ASLEEP.
YOU HAVE THAT LOOK IN YOUR EYES LIKE YOU'RE DECIDING WHICH BOOK TO SHOW ME NEXT.
THERE'S JUST SO MANY TO CHOOSE FROM.

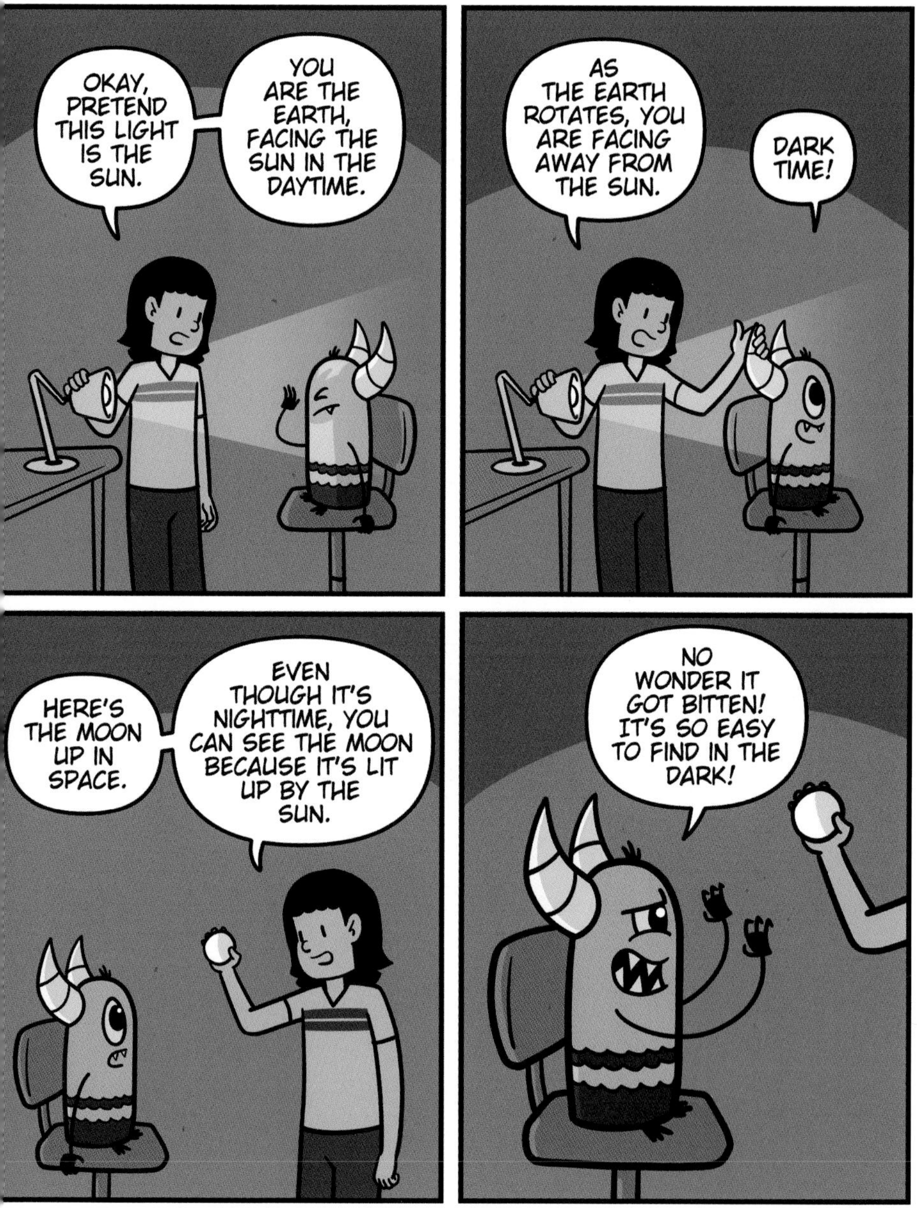
OKAY, PRETEND THIS LIGHT IS THE SUN.
YOU ARE THE EARTH, FACING THE SUN IN THE DAYTIME.
AS THE EARTH ROTATES, YOU ARE FACING AWAY FROM THE SUN.
DARK TIME!
HERE'S THE MOON UP IN SPACE.
EVEN THOUGH IT'S NIGHTTIME, YOU CAN SEE THE MOON BECAUSE IT'S LIT UP BY THE SUN.
NO WONDER IT GOT BITTEN! IT'S SO EASY TO FIND IN THE DARK!

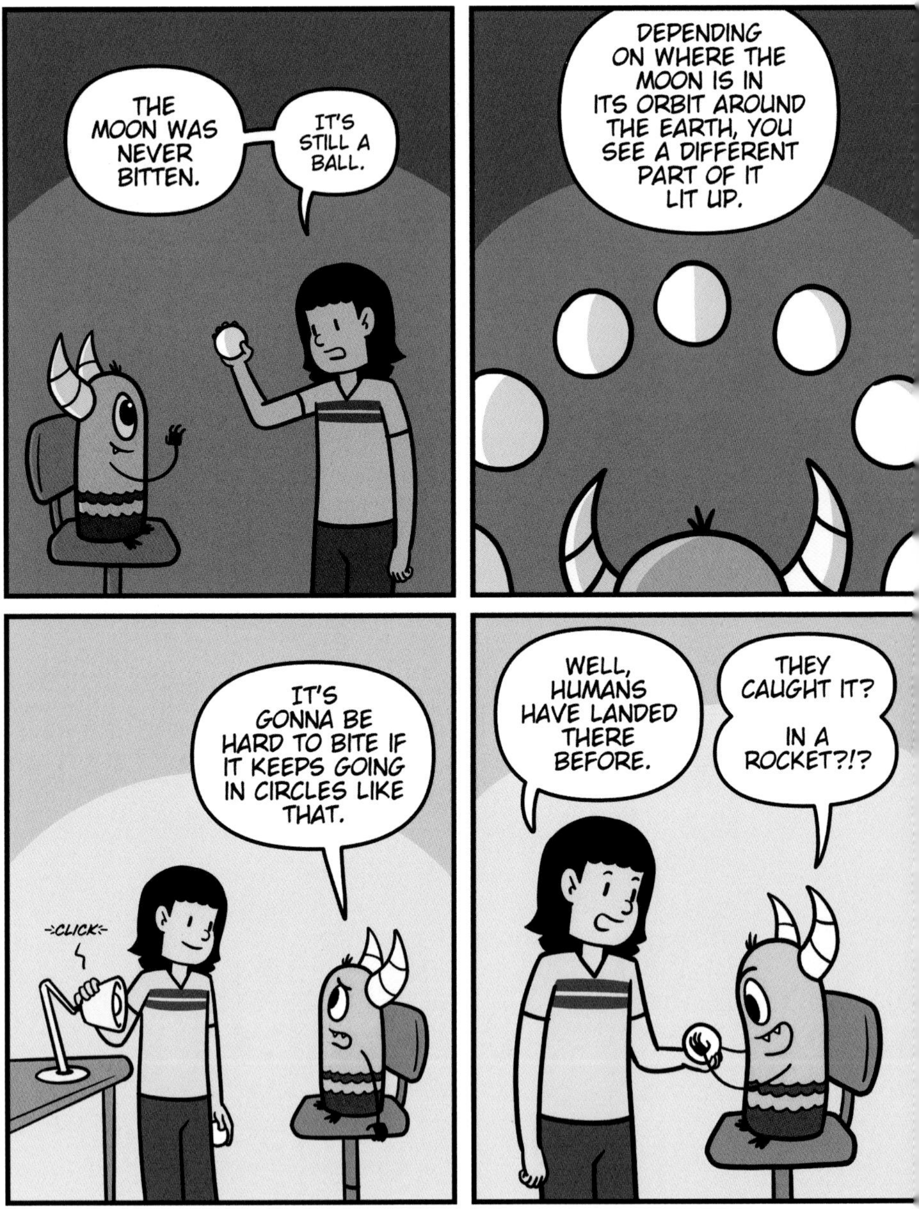
THE MOON WAS NEVER BITTEN.
IT'S STILL A BALL.
DEPENDING ON WHERE THE MOON IS IN ITS ORBIT AROUND THE EARTH, YOU SEE A DIFFERENT PART OF IT LIT UP.
IT'S GONNA BE HARD TO BITE IF IT KEEPS GOING IN CIRCLES LIKE THAT.
CLICK
WELL, HUMANS HAVE LANDED THERE BEFORE.
THEY CAUGHT IT?
IN A ROCKET?!?

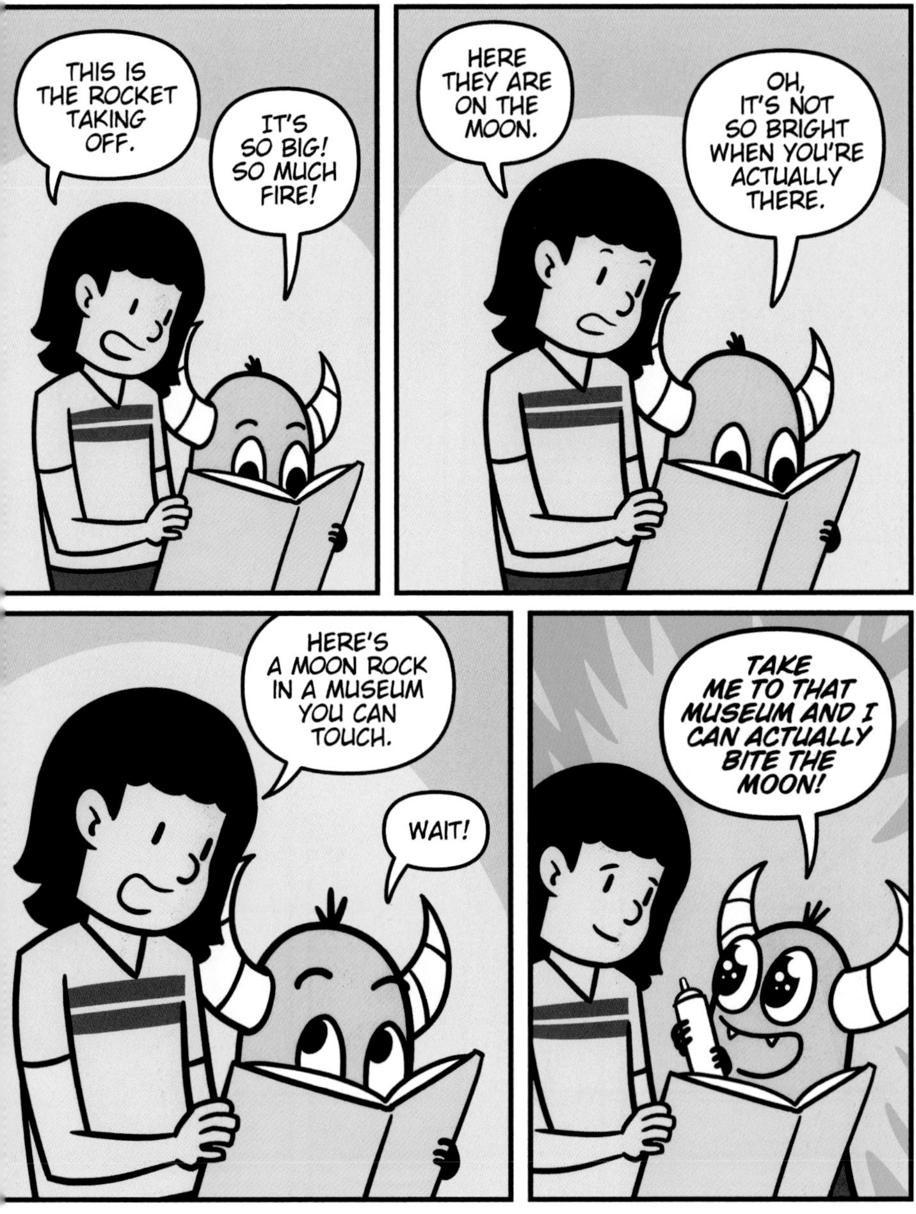
THIS IS THE ROCKET TAKING OFF.
IT'S SO BIG! SO MUCH FIRE!
HERE THEY ARE ON THE MOON.
OH, IT'S NOT SO BRIGHT WHEN YOU'RE ACTUALLY THERE.
HERE'S A MOON ROCK IN A MUSEUM YOU CAN TOUCH.
WAIT!
TAKE ME TO THAT MUSEUM AND I CAN ACTUALLY BITE THE MOON!

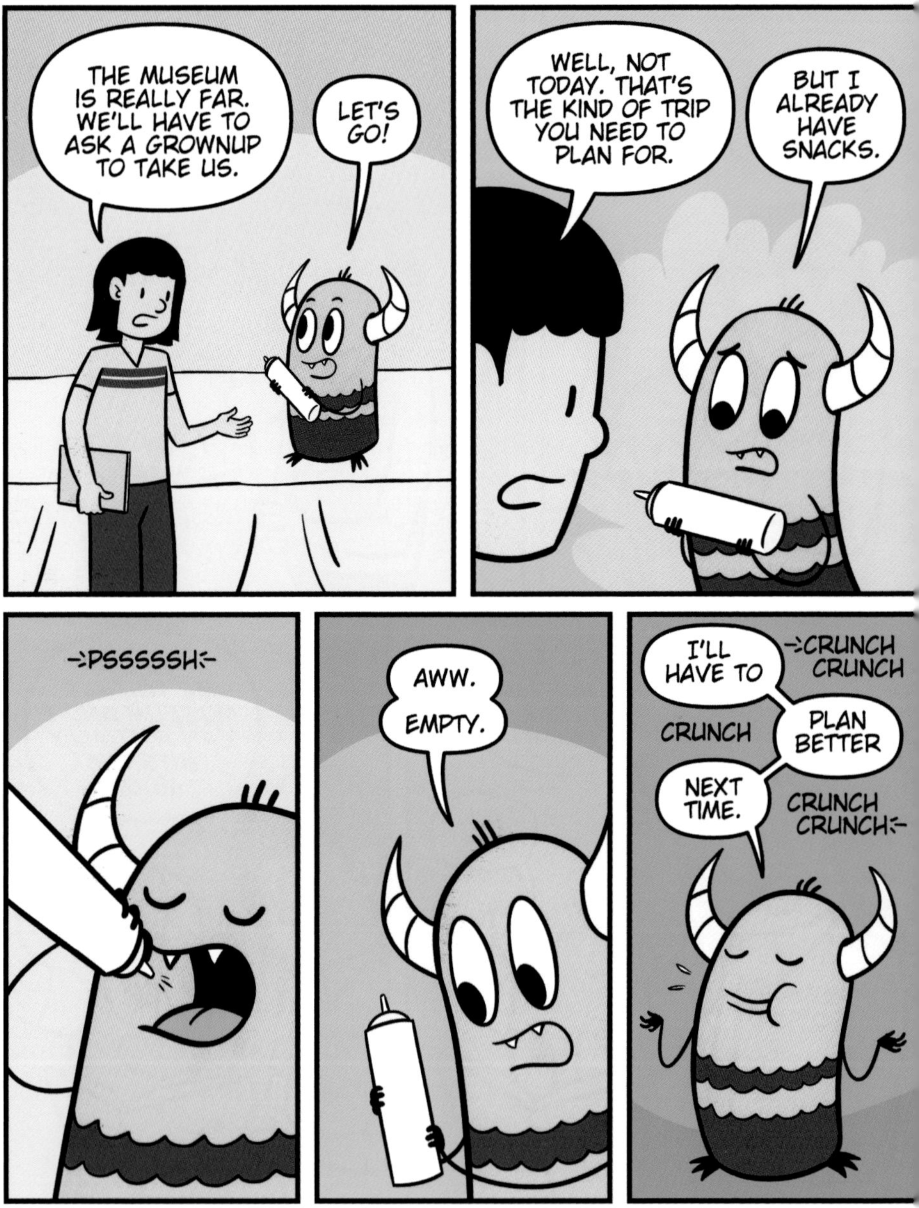
THE MUSEUM IS REALLY FAR. WE'LL HAVE TO ASK A GROWNUP TO TAKE US.
LET'S GO!
WELL, NOT TODAY. THAT'S THE KIND OF TRIP YOU NEED TO PLAN FOR.
BUT I ALREADY HAVE SNACKS.
PSSSSSH
AWW.
EMPTY.
I'LL HAVE TO
CRUNCH CRUNCH
CRUNCH
PLAN BETTER
NEXT TIME.
CRUNCH CRUNCH

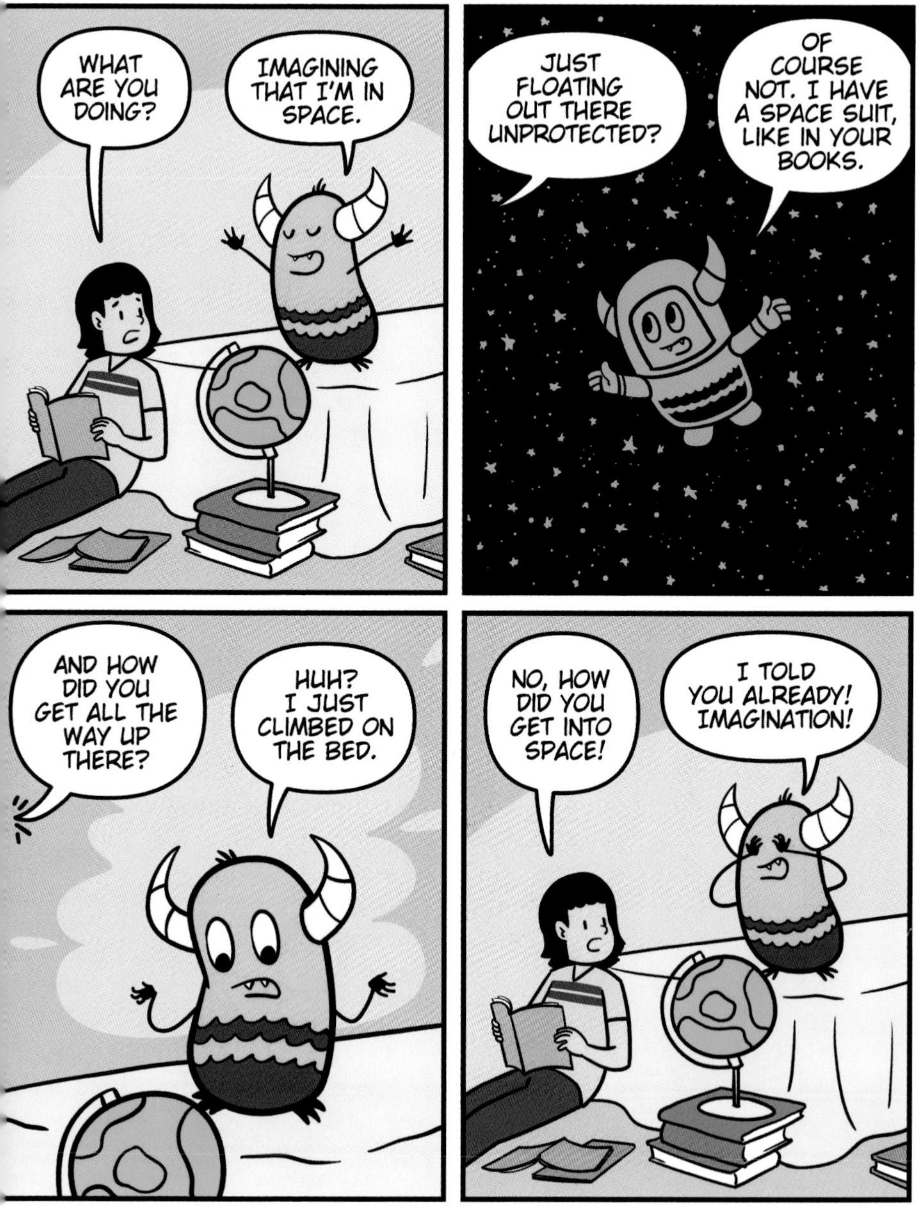
WHAT ARE YOU DOING?
IMAGINING THAT I'M IN SPACE.
JUST FLOATING OUT THERE UNPROTECTED?
OF COURSE NOT. I HAVE A SPACE SUIT, LIKE IN YOUR BOOKS.
AND HOW DID YOU GET ALL THE WAY UP THERE?
HUH? I JUST CLIMBED ON THE BED.
NO, HOW DID YOU GET INTO SPACE!
I TOLD YOU ALREADY! IMAGINATION!

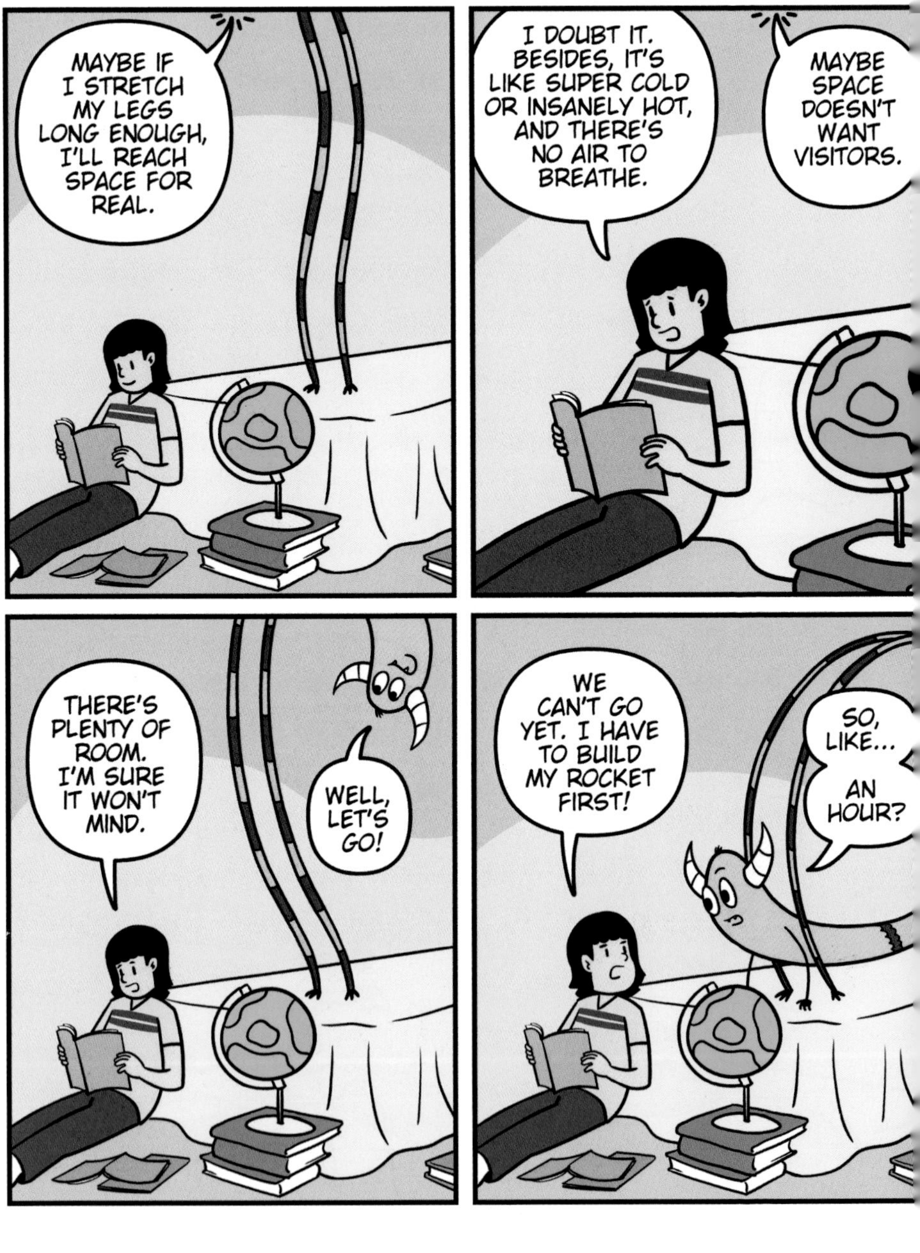
MAYBE IF I STRETCH MY LEGS LONG ENOUGH, I'LL REACH SPACE FOR REAL.
I DOUBT IT. BESIDES, IT'S LIKE SUPER COLD OR INSANELY HOT, AND THERE'S NO AIR TO BREATHE.
MAYBE SPACE DOESN'T WANT VISITORS.
THERE'S PLENTY OF ROOM. I'M SURE IT WON'T MIND.
WELL, LET'S GO!
WE CAN'T GO YET. I HAVE TO BUILD MY ROCKET FIRST!
SO, LIKE...
AN HOUR?

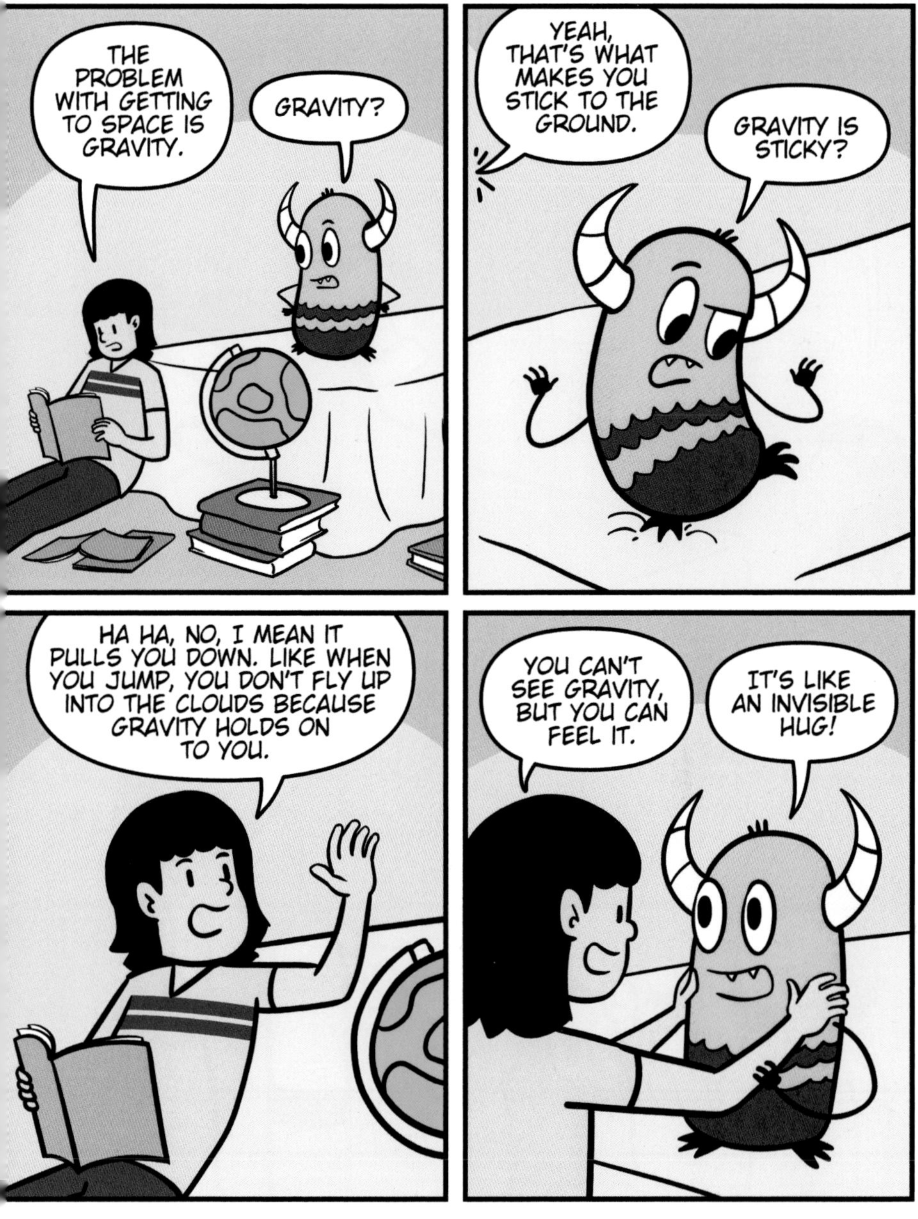
THE PROBLEM WITH GETTING TO SPACE IS GRAVITY.
GRAVITY?
YEAH, THAT'S WHAT MAKES YOU STICK TO THE GROUND.
GRAVITY IS STICKY?
HA HA, NO, I MEAN IT PULLS YOU DOWN. LIKE WHEN YOU JUMP, YOU DON'T FLY UP INTO THE CLOUDS BECAUSE GRAVITY HOLDS ON TO YOU.
YOU CAN'T SEE GRAVITY, BUT YOU CAN FEEL IT.
IT'S LIKE AN INVISIBLE HUG!

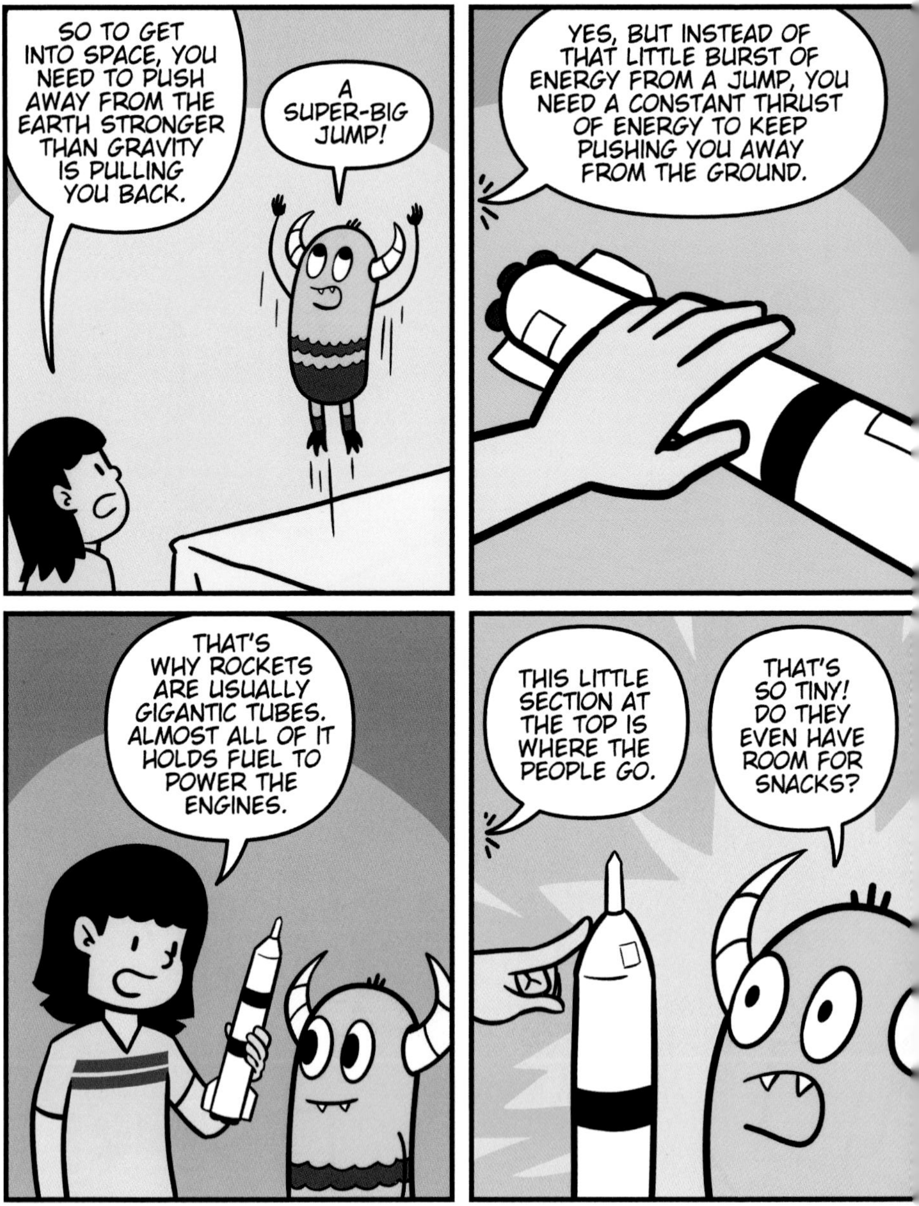
SO TO GET INTO SPACE, YOU NEED TO PUSH AWAY FROM THE EARTH STRONGER THAN GRAVITY IS PULLING YOU BACK.
A SUPER-BIG JUMP!
YES, BUT INSTEAD OF THAT LITTLE BURST OF ENERGY FROM A JUMP, YOU NEED A CONSTANT THRUST OF ENERGY TO KEEP PUSHING YOU AWAY FROM THE GROUND.
THAT'S WHY ROCKETS ARE USUALLY GIGANTIC TUBES. ALMOST ALL OF IT HOLDS FUEL TO POWER THE ENGINES.
THIS LITTLE SECTION AT THE TOP IS WHERE THE PEOPLE GO.
THAT'S SO TINY! DO THEY EVEN HAVE ROOM FOR SNACKS?

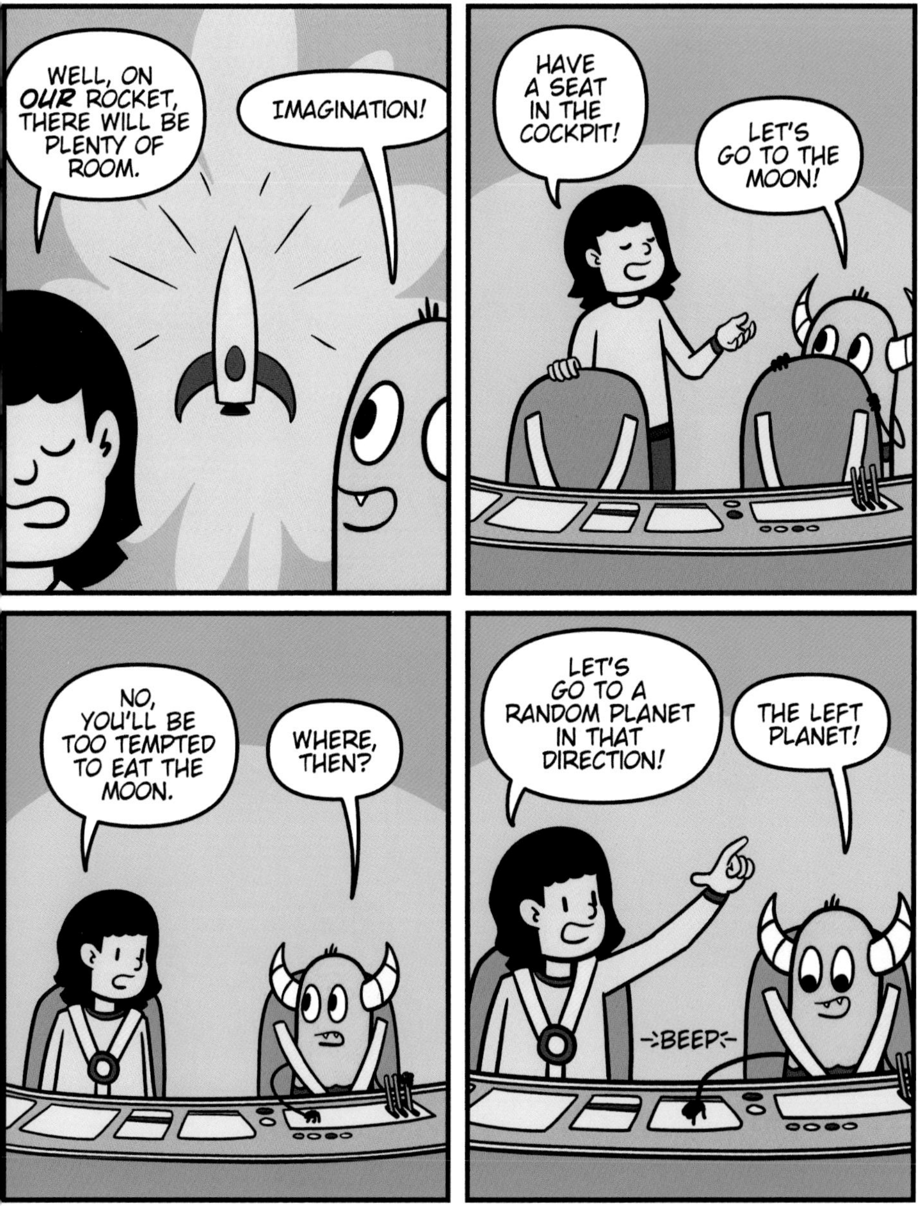
WELL, ON OUR ROCKET, THERE WILL BE PLENTY OF ROOM.
IMAGINATION!
HAVE A SEAT IN THE COCKPIT!
LET'S GO TO THE MOON!
NO, YOU'LL BE TOO TEMPTED TO EAT THE MOON.
WHERE, THEN?
LET'S GO TO A RANDOM PLANET IN THAT DIRECTION!
THE LEFT PLANET!
BEEP

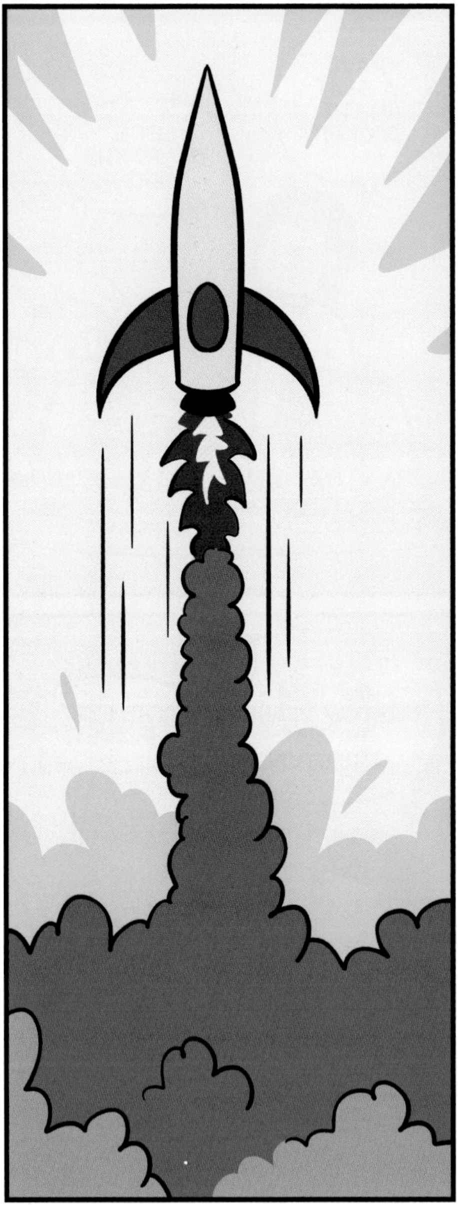

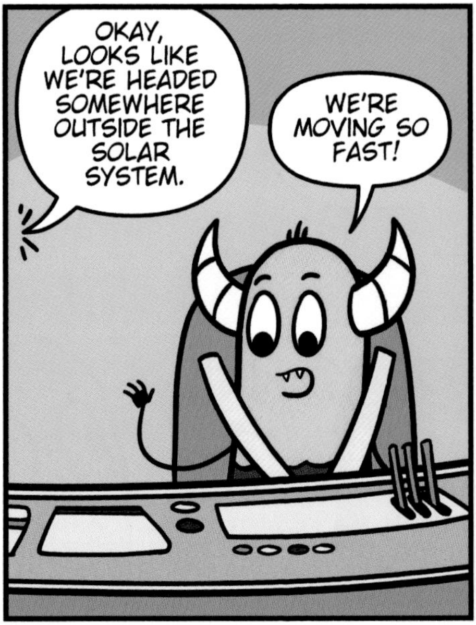
OKAY, LOOKS LIKE WE'RE HEADED SOMEWHERE OUTSIDE THE SOLAR SYSTEM.
WE'RE MOVING SO FAST!

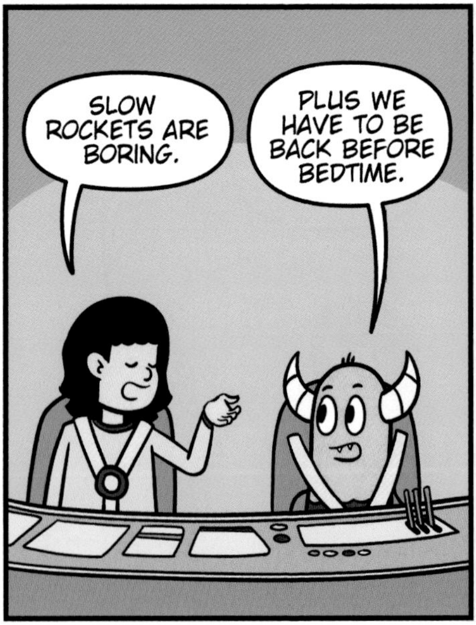
SLOW ROCKETS ARE BORING.
PLUS WE HAVE TO BE BACK BEFORE BEDTIME.

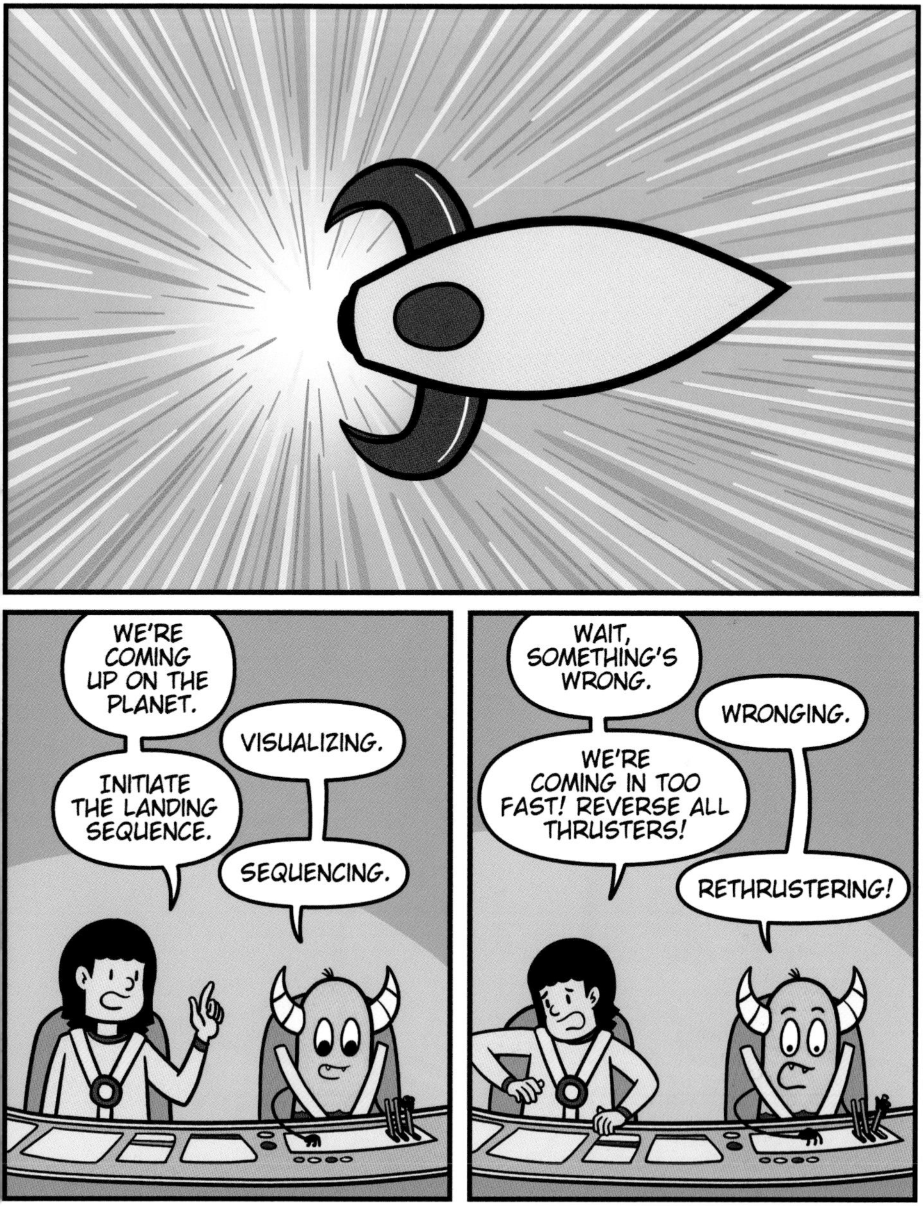
WE'RE COMING UP ON THE PLANET.
INITIATE THE LANDING SEQUENCE.
VISUALIZING.
SEQUENCING.
WAIT, SOMETHING'S WRONG.
WE'RE COMING IN TOO FAST! REVERSE ALL THRUSTERS!
WRONGING.
RETHRUSTERING!

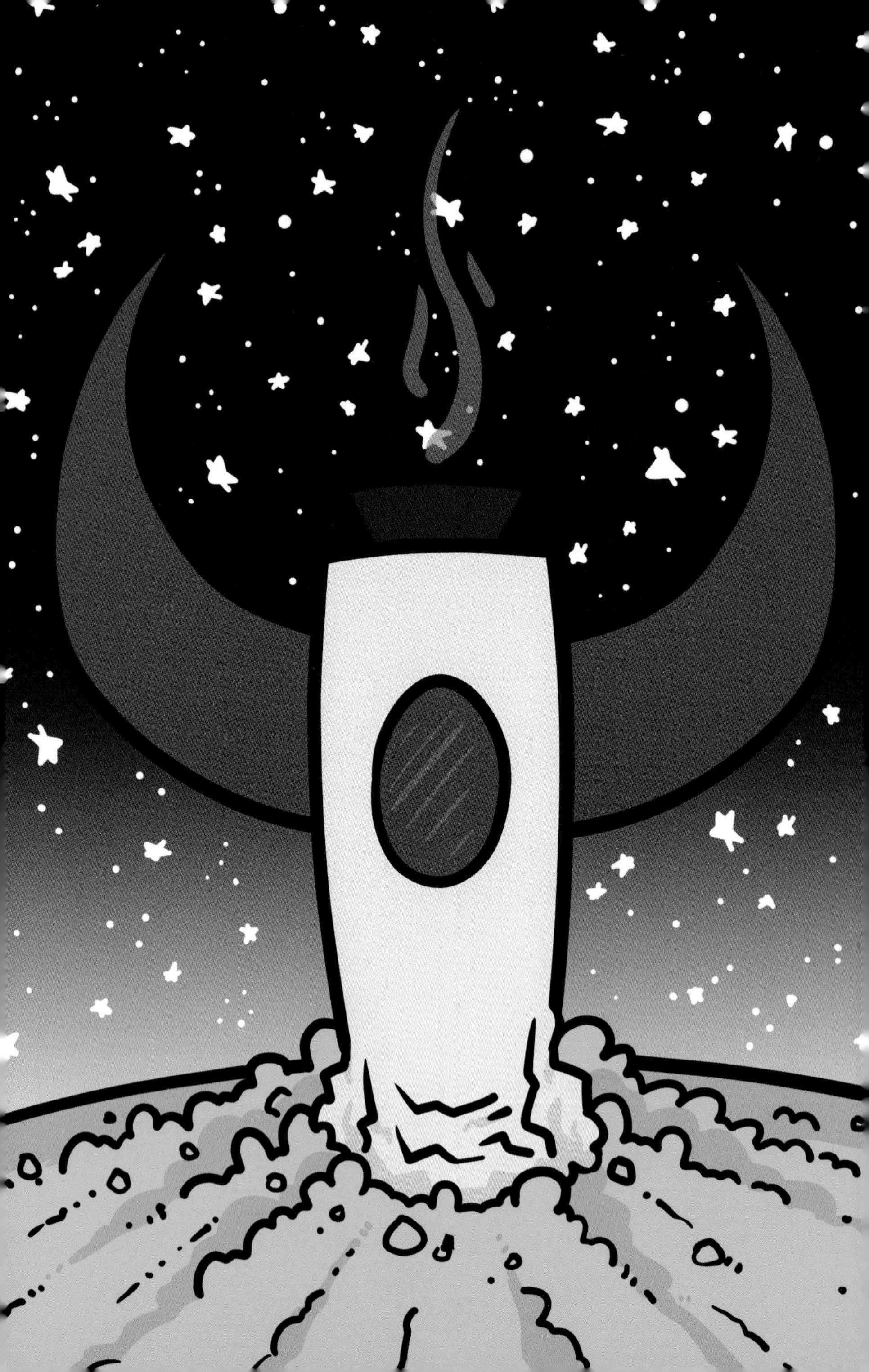

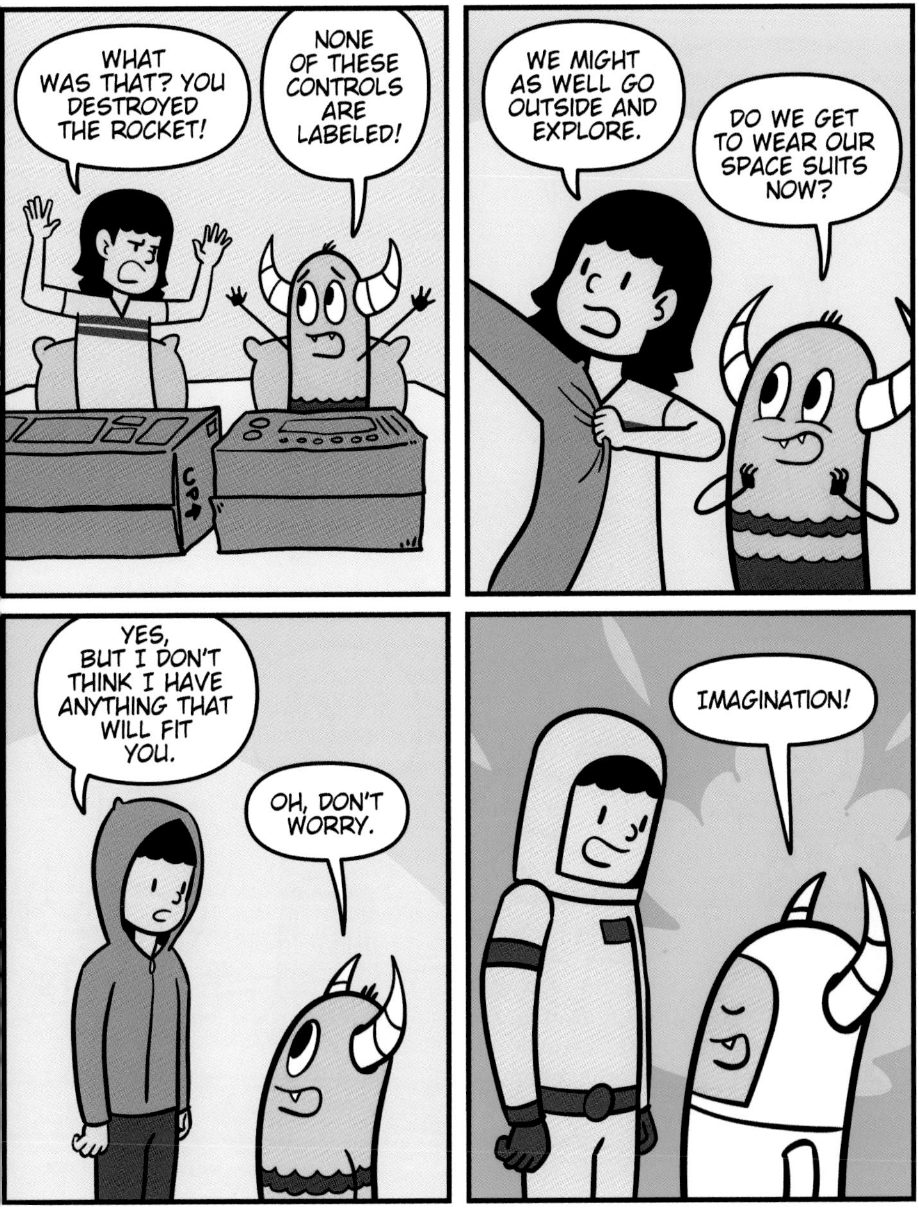
WHAT WAS THAT? YOU DESTROYED THE ROCKET!
NONE OF THESE CONTROLS ARE LABELED!
UP
WE MIGHT AS WELL GO OUTSIDE AND EXPLORE.
DO WE GET TO WEAR OUR SPACE SUITS NOW?
YES, BUT I DON'T THINK I HAVE ANYTHING THAT WILL FIT YOU.
OH, DON'T WORRY.
IMAGINATION!

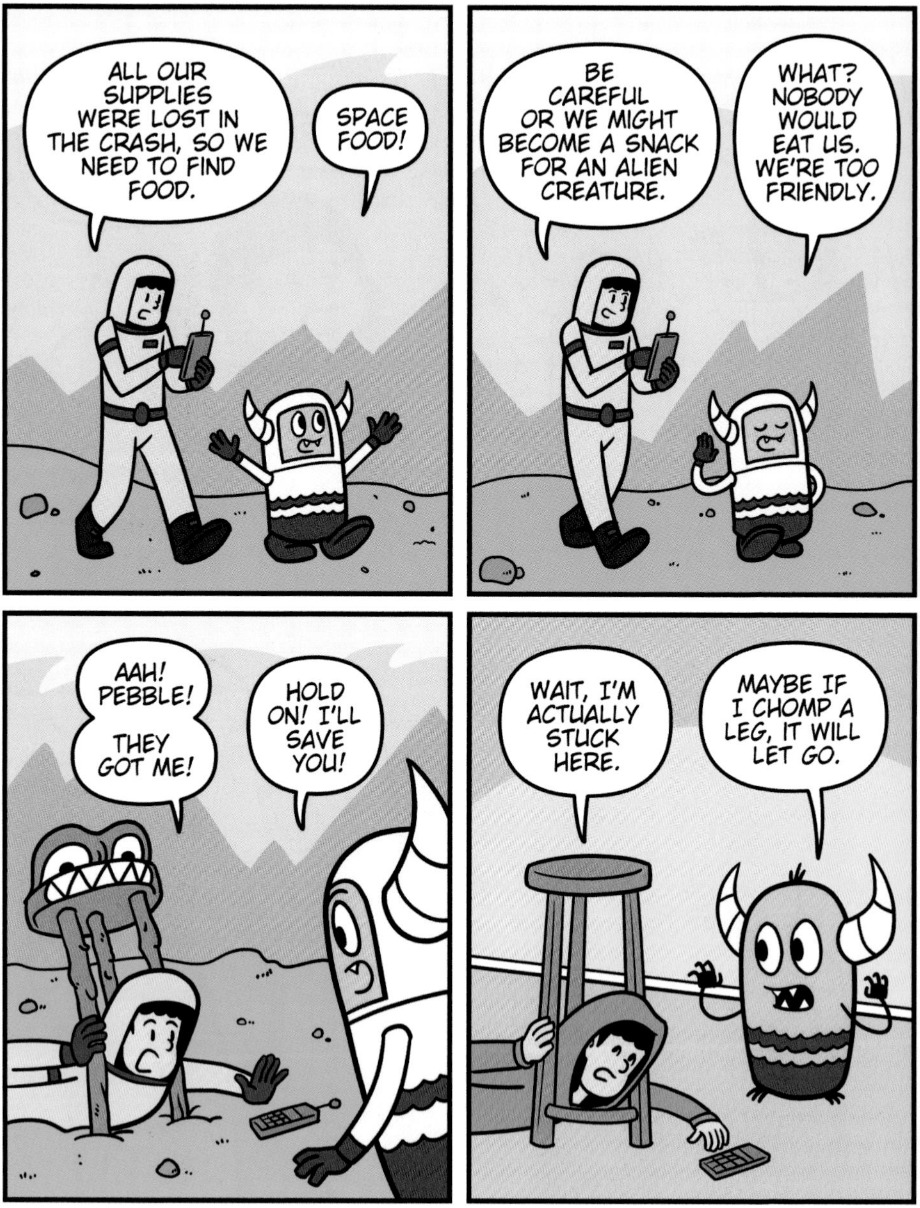
ALL OUR SUPPLIES WERE LOST IN THE CRASH, SO WE NEED TO FIND FOOD.
SPACE FOOD!
BE CAREFUL OR WE MIGHT BECOME A SNACK FOR AN ALIEN CREATURE.
WHAT? NOBODY WOULD EAT US. WE'RE TOO FRIENDLY.
AAH! PEBBLE!
THEY GOT ME!
HOLD ON! I'LL SAVE YOU!
WAIT, I'M ACTUALLY STUCK HERE.
MAYBE IF I CHOMP A LEG, IT WILL LET GO.

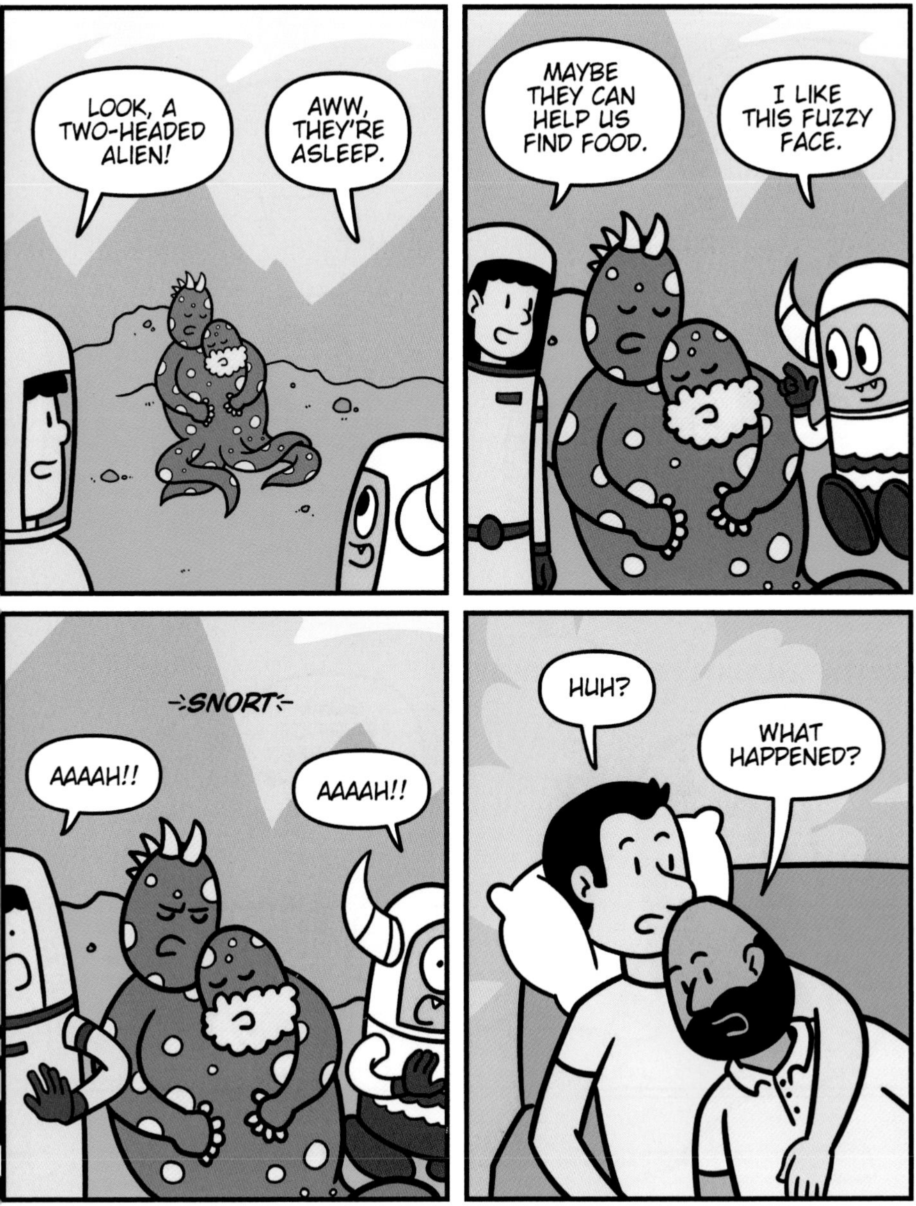
LOOK, A TWO-HEADED ALIEN!
AWW, THEY'RE ASLEEP.
MAYBE THEY CAN HELP US FIND FOOD.
I LIKE THIS FUZZY FACE.
SNORT
AAAAH!!
AAAAH!!
HUH?
WHAT HAPPENED?

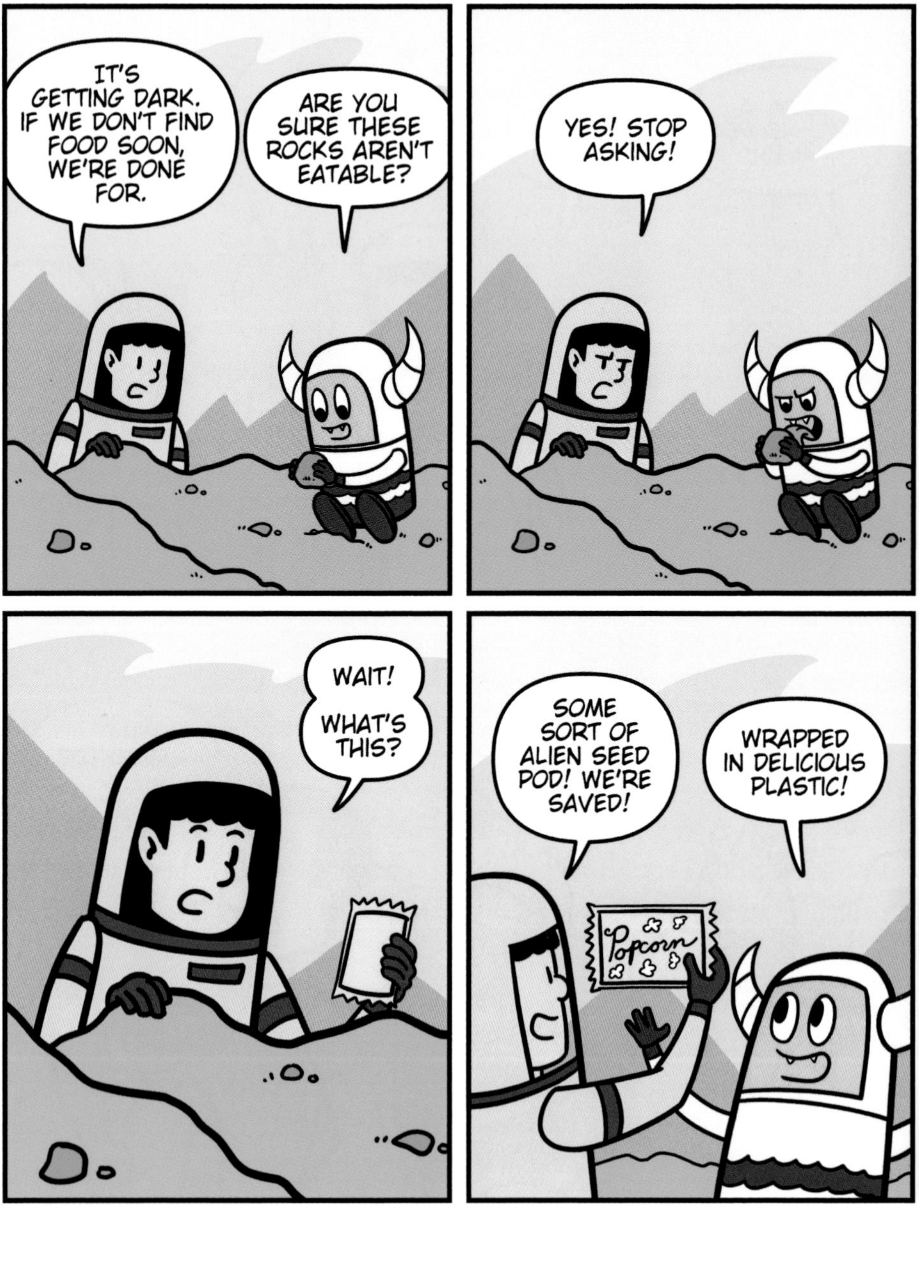
IT'S GETTING DARK. IF WE DON'T FIND FOOD SOON, WE'RE DONE FOR.
ARE YOU SURE THESE ROCKS AREN'T EATABLE?
YES! STOP ASKING!
WAIT!
WHAT'S THIS?
SOME SORT OF ALIEN SEED POD! WE'RE SAVED!
WRAPPED IN DELICIOUS PLASTIC!
Popcorn

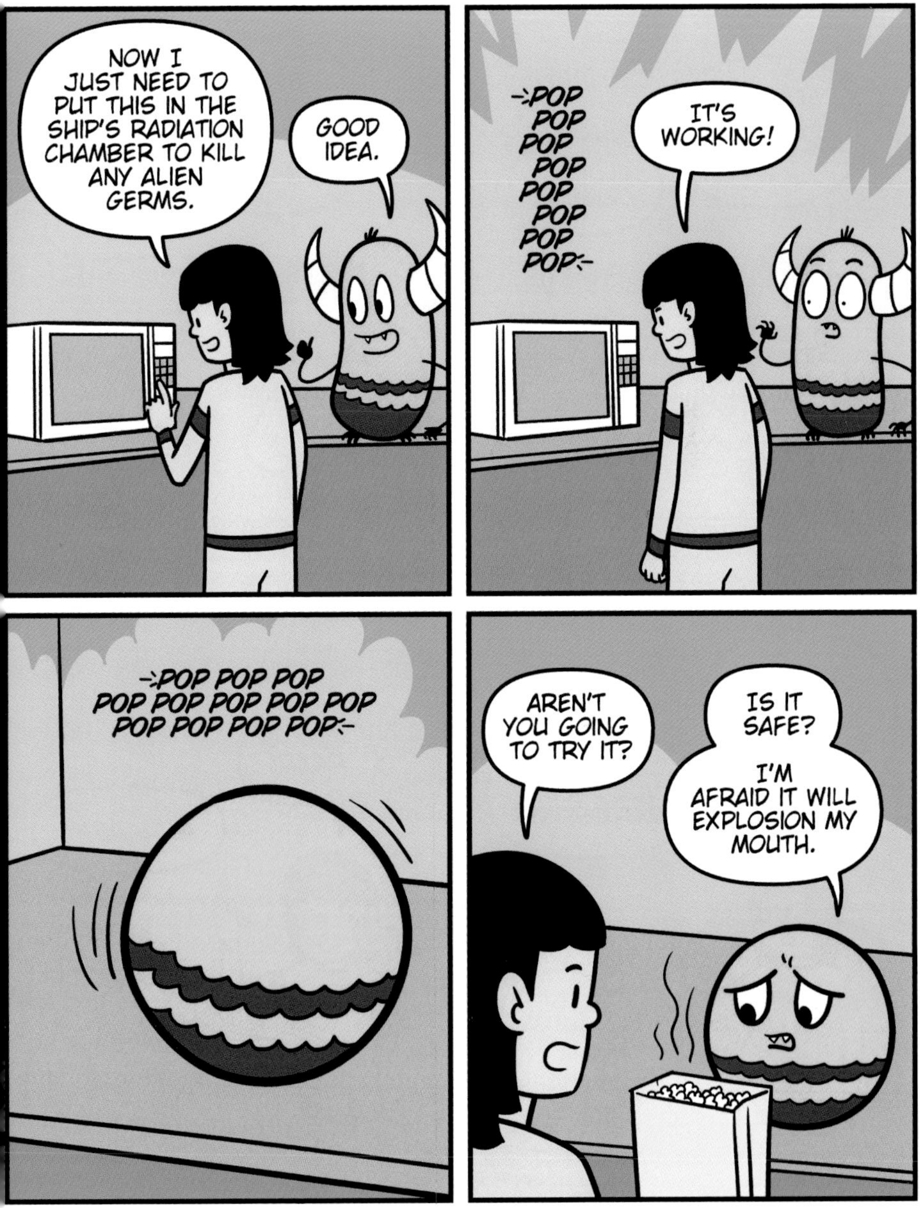
NOW I JUST NEED TO PUT THIS IN THE SHIP'S RADIATION CHAMBER TO KILL ANY ALIEN GERMS.
GOOD IDEA.
POP POP POP POP POP POP POP POP
IT'S WORKING!
POP POP POP POP POP POP POP POP POP POP POP POP
AREN'T YOU GOING TO TRY IT?
IS IT SAFE?
I'M AFRAID IT WILL EXPLOSION MY MOUTH.

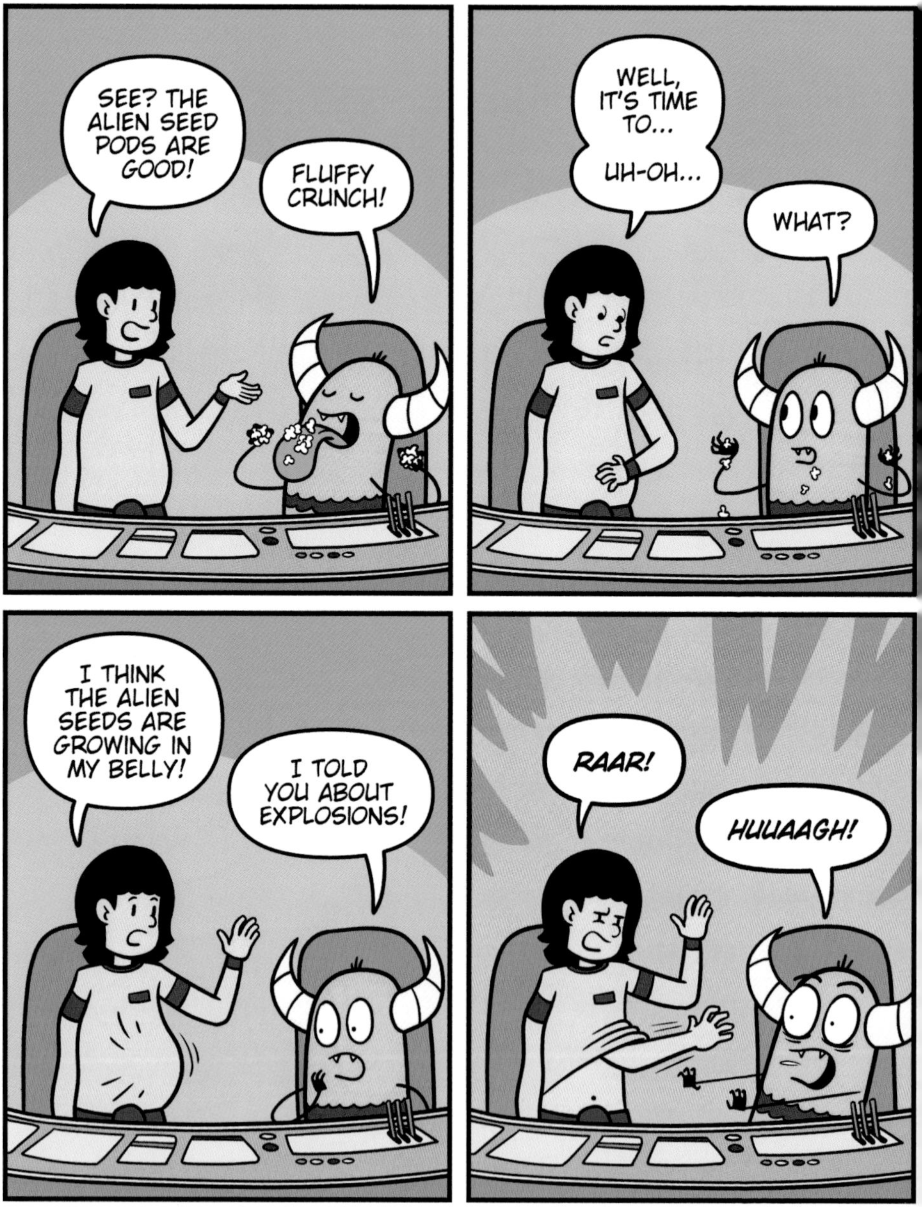
SEE? THE ALIEN SEED PODS ARE GOOD!
FLUFFY CRUNCH!
WELL, IT'S TIME TO...
UH-OH...
WHAT?
I THINK THE ALIEN SEEDS ARE GROWING IN MY BELLY!
I TOLD YOU ABOUT EXPLOSIONS!
RAAR!
HUUAAGH!

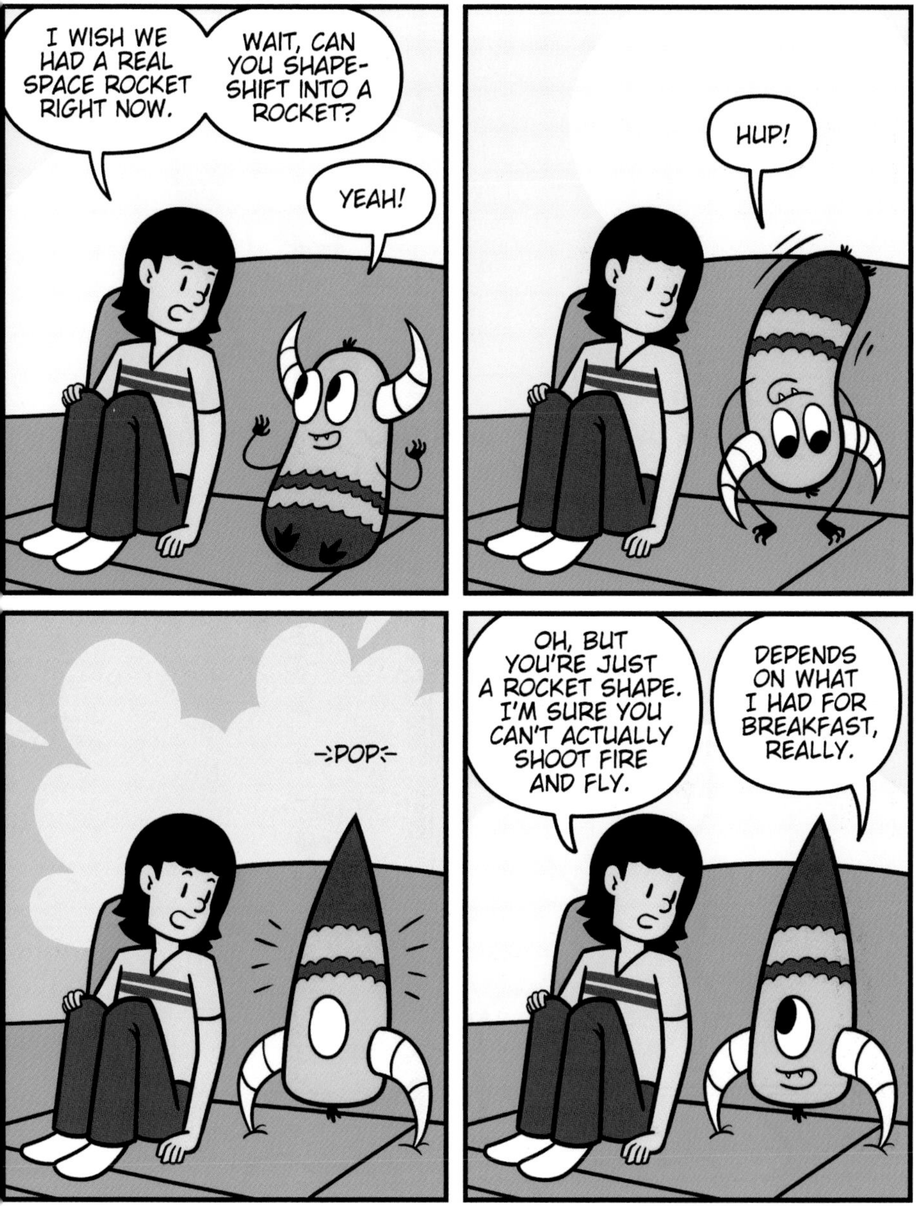
I WISH WE HAD A REAL SPACE ROCKET RIGHT NOW.
WAIT, CAN YOU SHAPE-SHIFT INTO A ROCKET?
YEAH!
HUP!
-POP-
OH, BUT YOU'RE JUST A ROCKET SHAPE. I'M SURE YOU CAN'T ACTUALLY SHOOT FIRE AND FLY.
DEPENDS ON WHAT I HAD FOR BREAKFAST, REALLY.

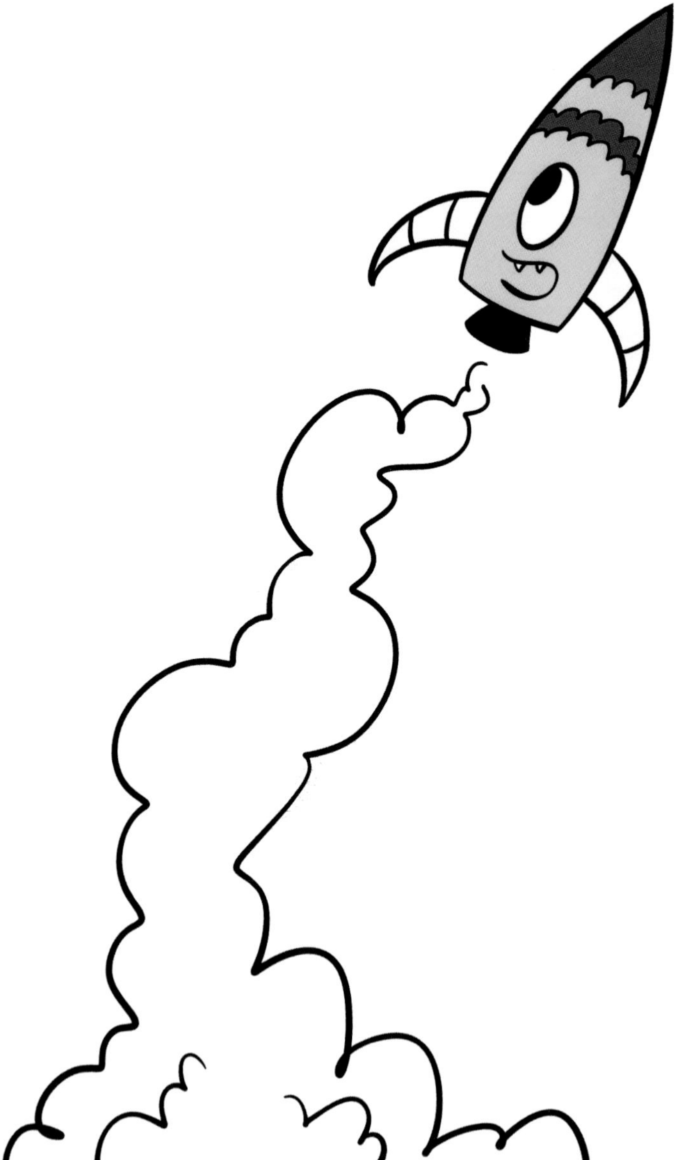

CHAPTER TEN

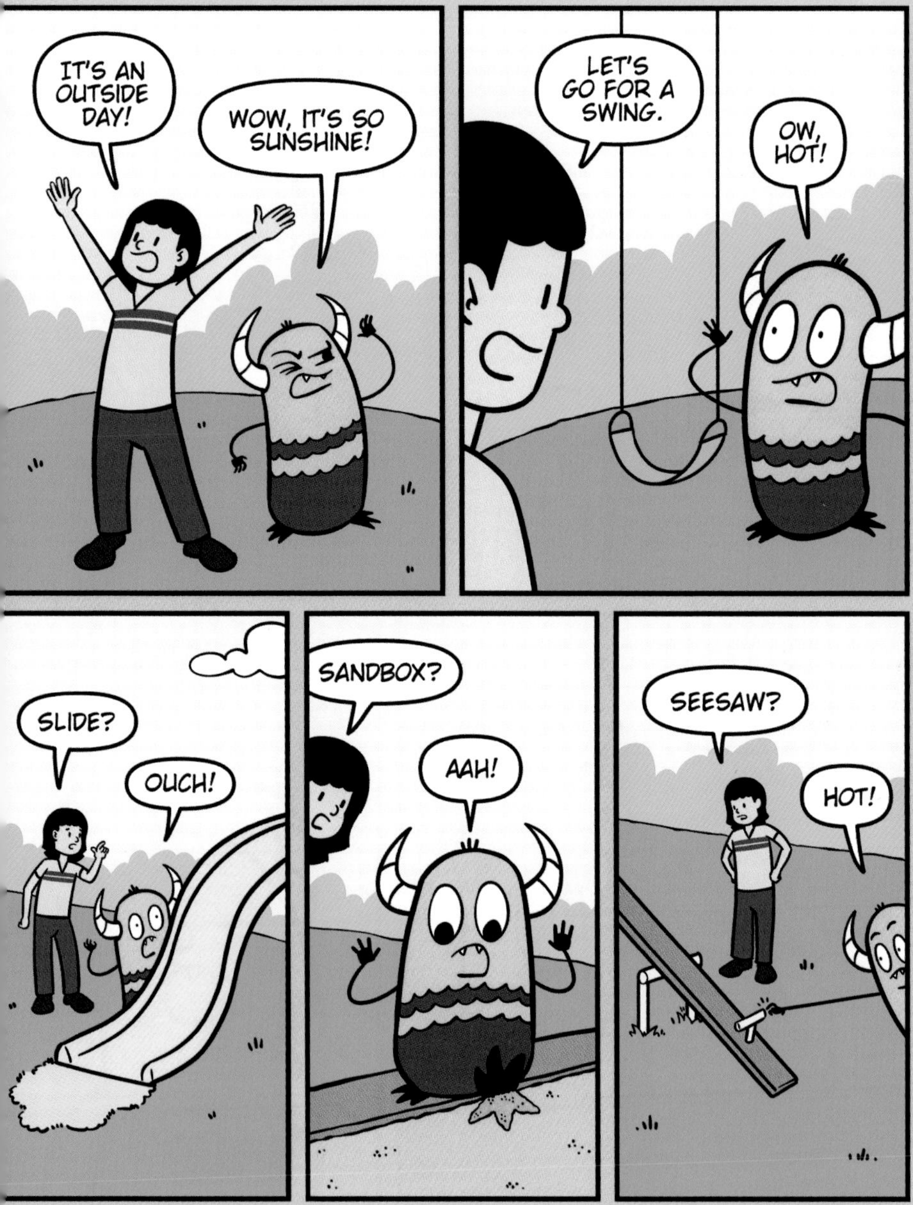
IT'S AN OUTSIDE DAY!
WOW, IT'S SO SUNSHINE!
LET'S GO FOR A SWING.
OW, HOT!
SLIDE?
OUCH!
SANDBOX?
AAH!
SEESAW?
HOT!

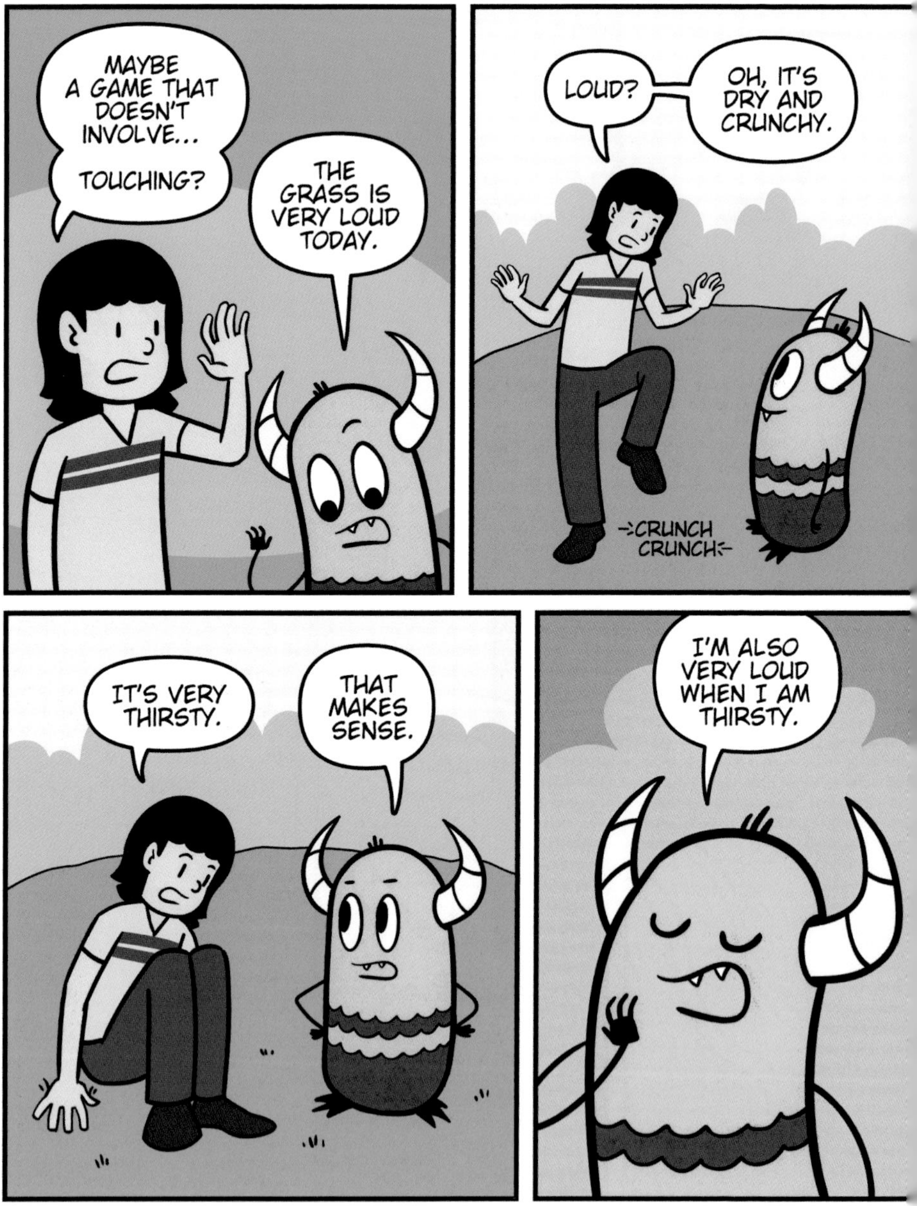
MAYBE A GAME THAT DOESN'T INVOLVE...
TOUCHING?
THE GRASS IS VERY LOUD TODAY.
LOUD?
OH, IT'S DRY AND CRUNCHY.
CRUNCH CRUNCH
IT'S VERY THIRSTY.
THAT MAKES SENSE.
I'M ALSO VERY LOUD WHEN I AM THIRSTY.

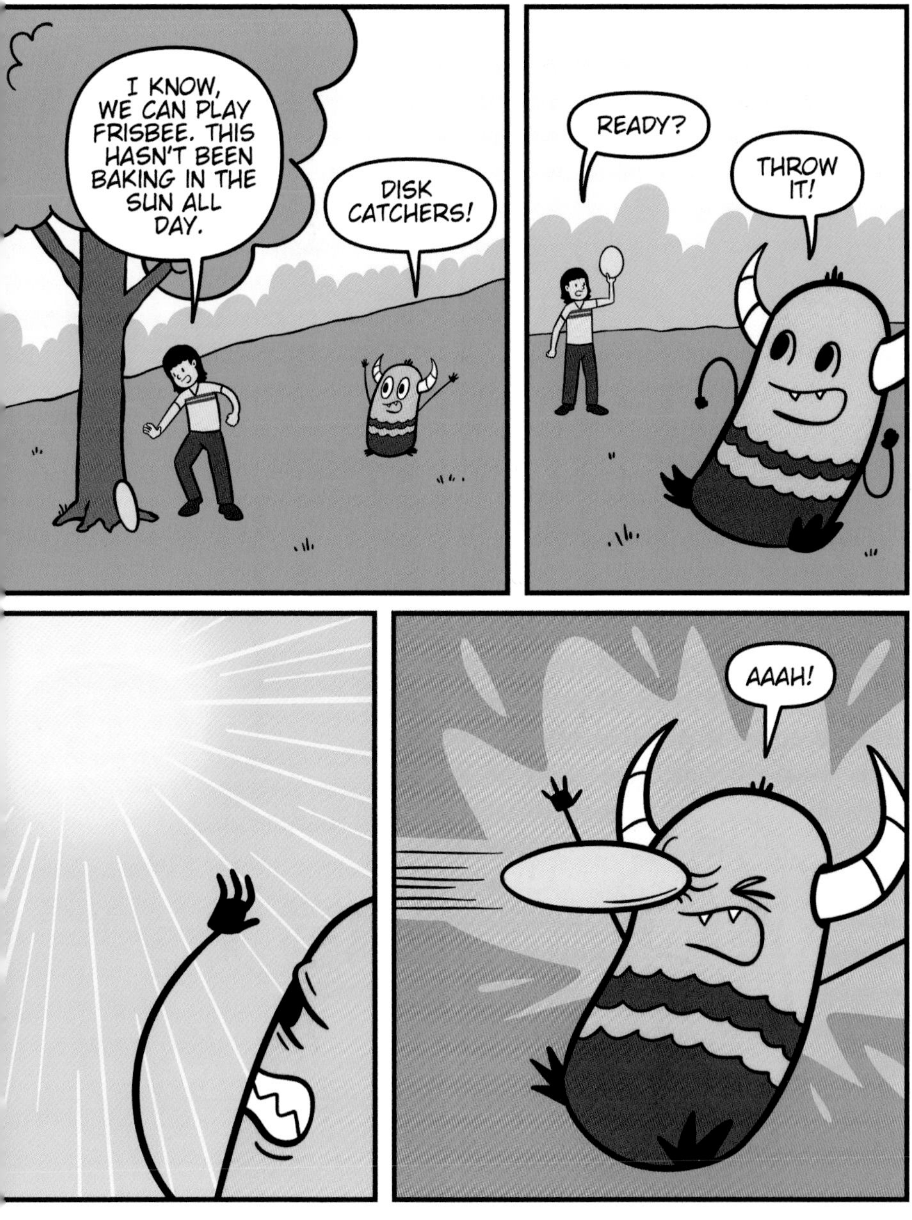
I KNOW, WE CAN PLAY FRISBEE. THIS HASN'T BEEN BAKING IN THE SUN ALL DAY.
DISK CATCHERS!
READY?
THROW IT!
AAAH!

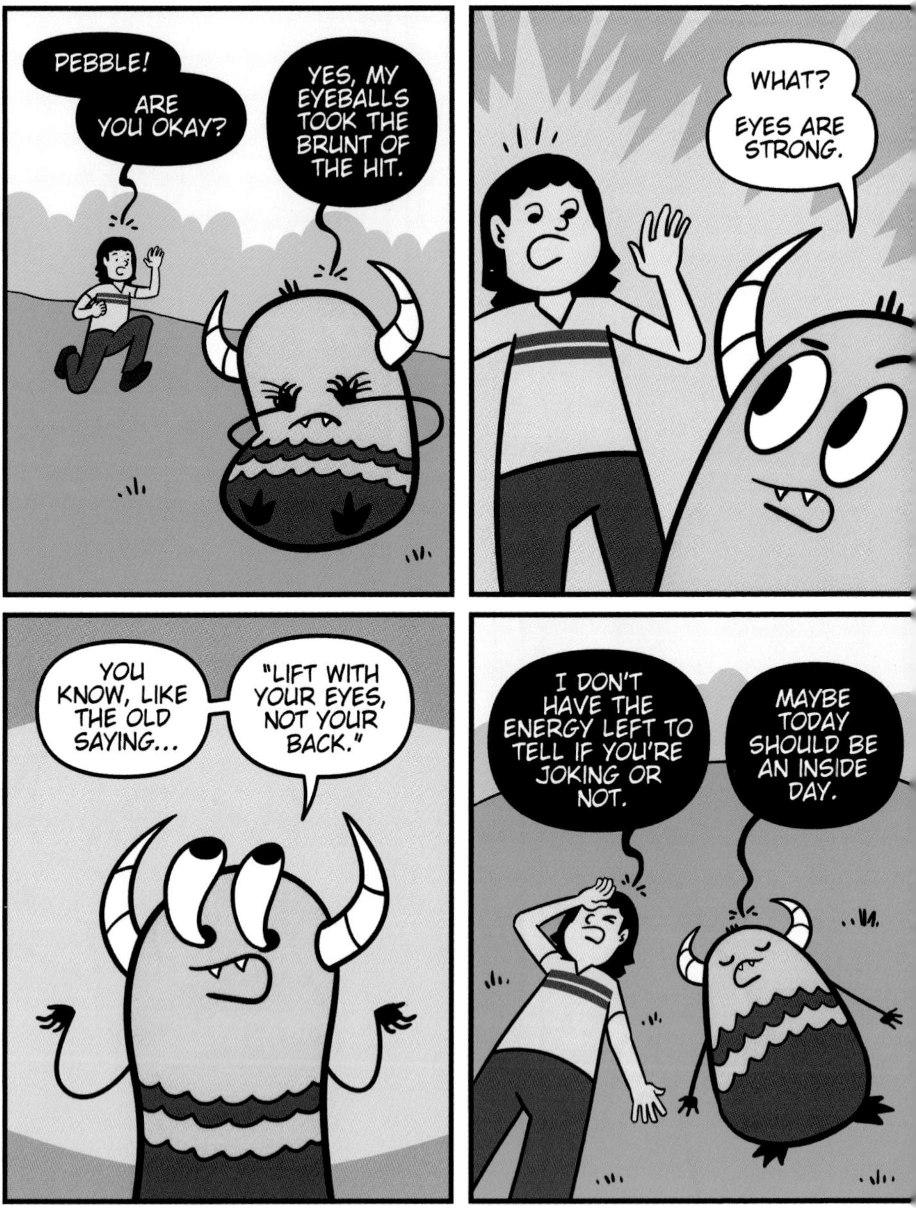
PEBBLE!
ARE YOU OKAY?
YES, MY EYEBALLS TOOK THE BRUNT OF THE HIT.
WHAT?
EYES ARE STRONG.
YOU KNOW, LIKE THE OLD SAYING...
"LIFT WITH YOUR EYES, NOT YOUR BACK."
I DON'T HAVE THE ENERGY LEFT TO TELL IF YOU'RE JOKING OR NOT.
MAYBE TODAY SHOULD BE AN INSIDE DAY.

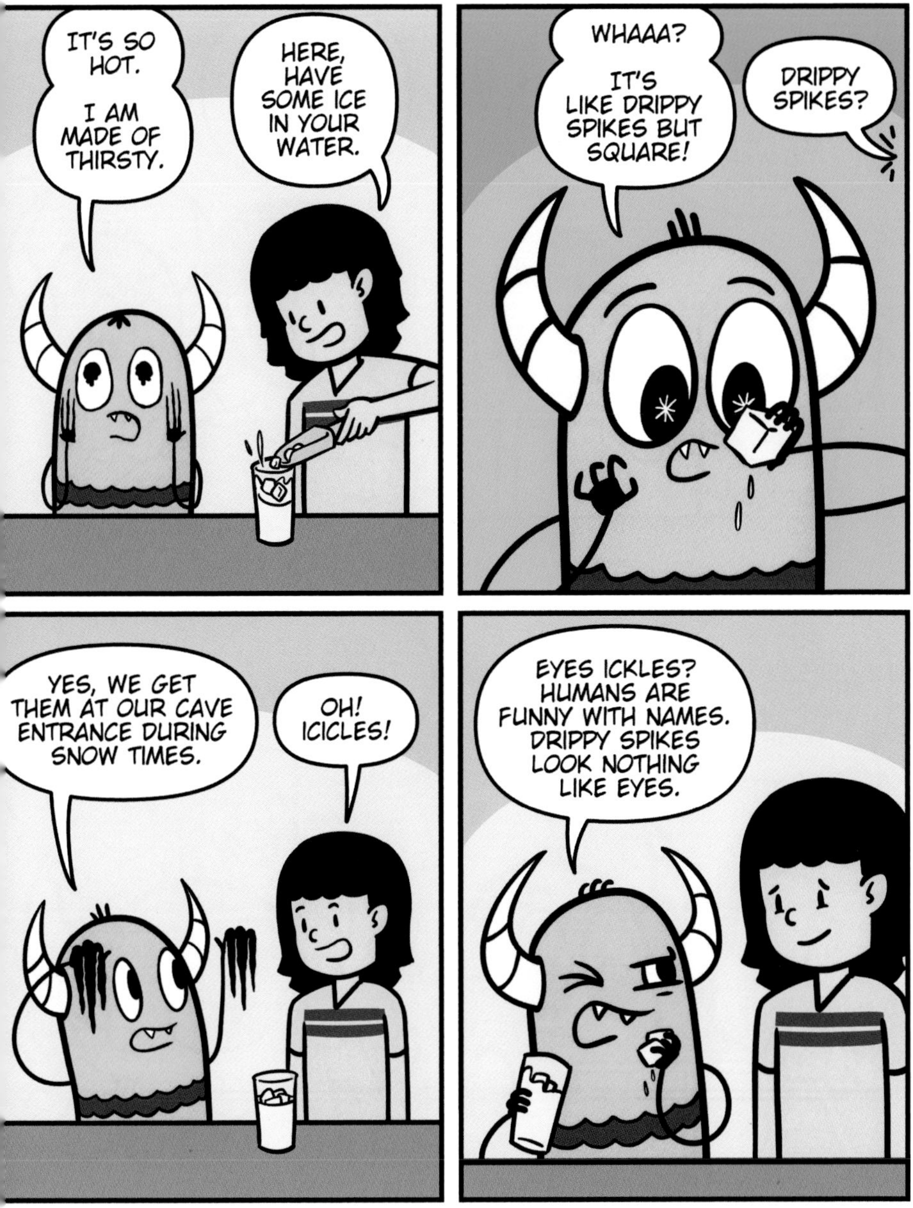
IT'S SO HOT.
I AM MADE OF THIRSTY.
HERE, HAVE SOME ICE IN YOUR WATER.
WHAAA?
IT'S LIKE DRIPPY SPIKES BUT SQUARE!
DRIPPY SPIKES?
YES, WE GET THEM AT OUR CAVE ENTRANCE DURING SNOW TIMES.
OH! ICICLES!
EYES ICKLES? HUMANS ARE FUNNY WITH NAMES. DRIPPY SPIKES LOOK NOTHING LIKE EYES.

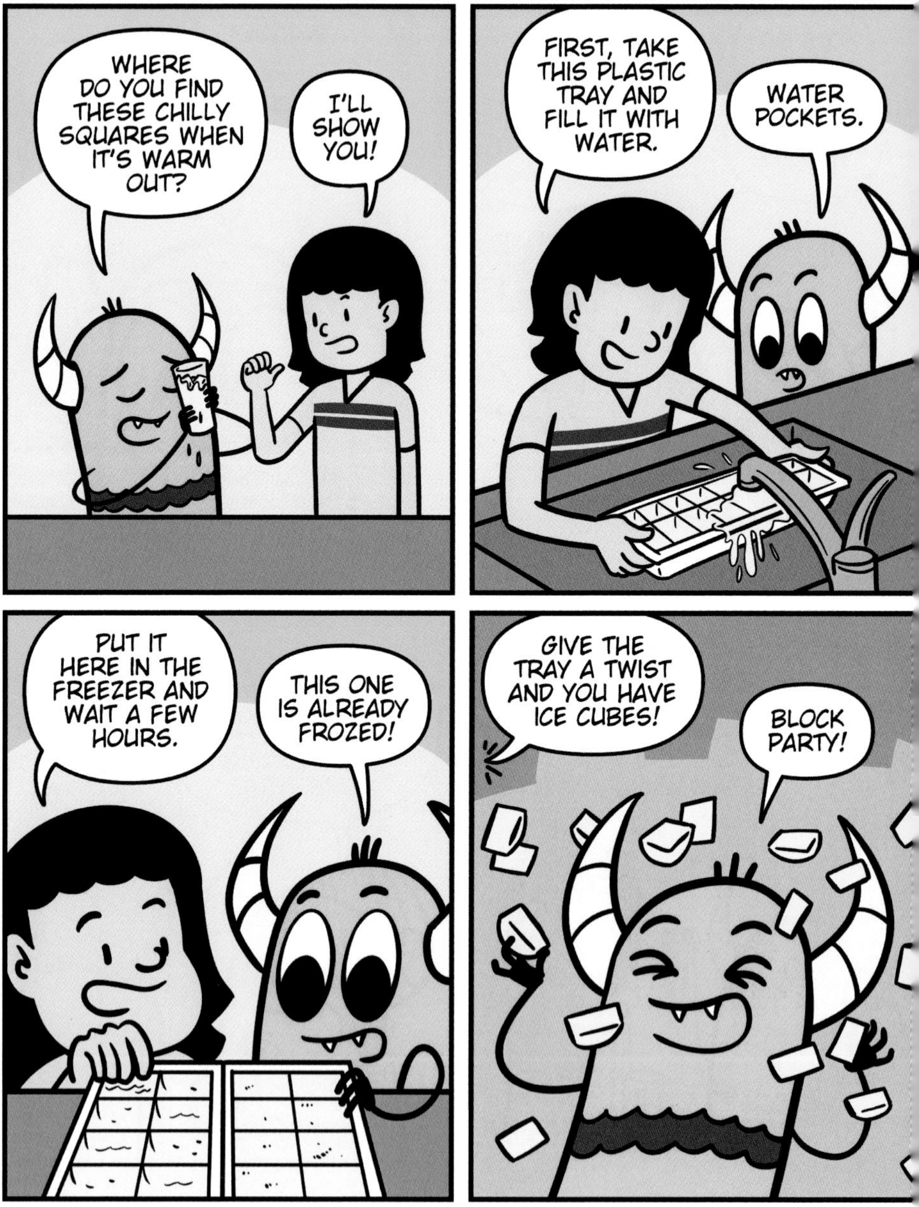
WHERE DO YOU FIND THESE CHILLY SQUARES WHEN IT'S WARM OUT?
I'LL SHOW YOU!
FIRST, TAKE THIS PLASTIC TRAY AND FILL IT WITH WATER.
WATER POCKETS.
PUT IT HERE IN THE FREEZER AND WAIT A FEW HOURS.
THIS ONE IS ALREADY FROZED!
GIVE THE TRAY A TWIST AND YOU HAVE ICE CUBES!
BLOCK PARTY!

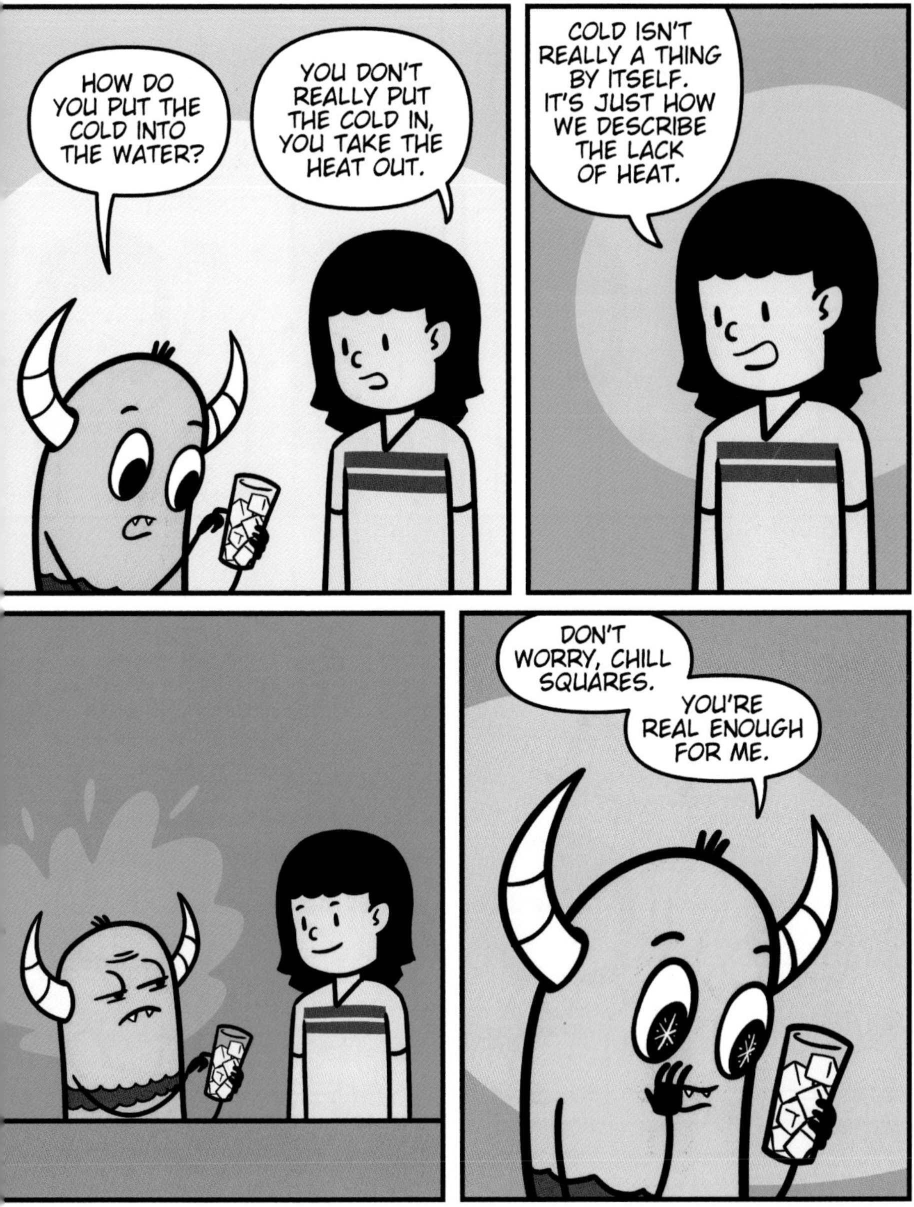
HOW DO YOU PUT THE COLD INTO THE WATER?
YOU DON'T REALLY PUT THE COLD IN, YOU TAKE THE HEAT OUT.
COLD ISN'T REALLY A THING BY ITSELF. IT'S JUST HOW WE DESCRIBE THE LACK OF HEAT.
DON'T WORRY, CHILL SQUARES.
YOU'RE REAL ENOUGH FOR ME.

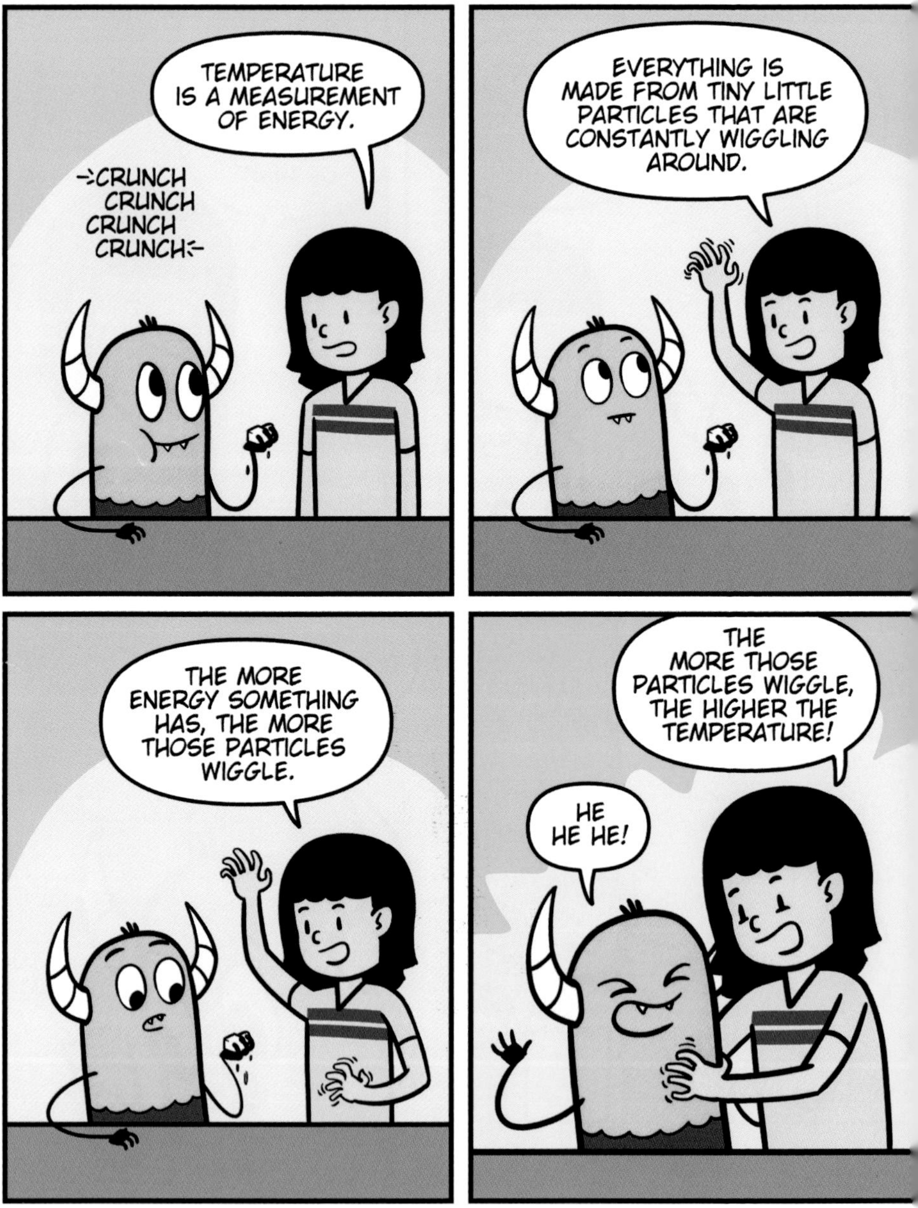
TEMPERATURE IS A MEASUREMENT OF ENERGY.
CRUNCH CRUNCH CRUNCH CRUNCH
EVERYTHING IS MADE FROM TINY LITTLE PARTICLES THAT ARE CONSTANTLY WIGGLING AROUND.
THE MORE ENERGY SOMETHING HAS, THE MORE THOSE PARTICLES WIGGLE.
THE MORE THOSE PARTICLES WIGGLE, THE HIGHER THE TEMPERATURE!
HE HE HE!

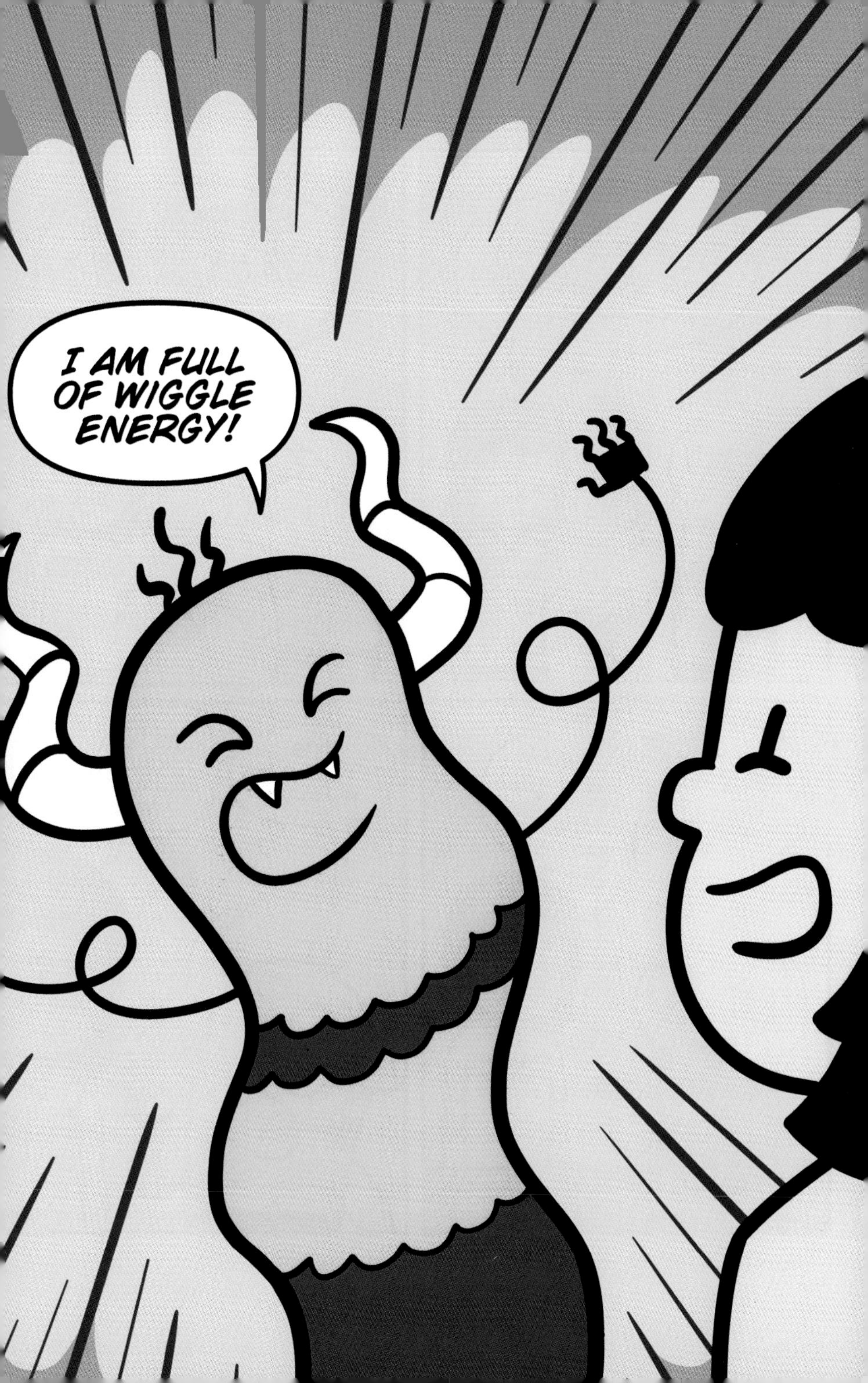
I AM FULL OF WIGGLE ENERGY!

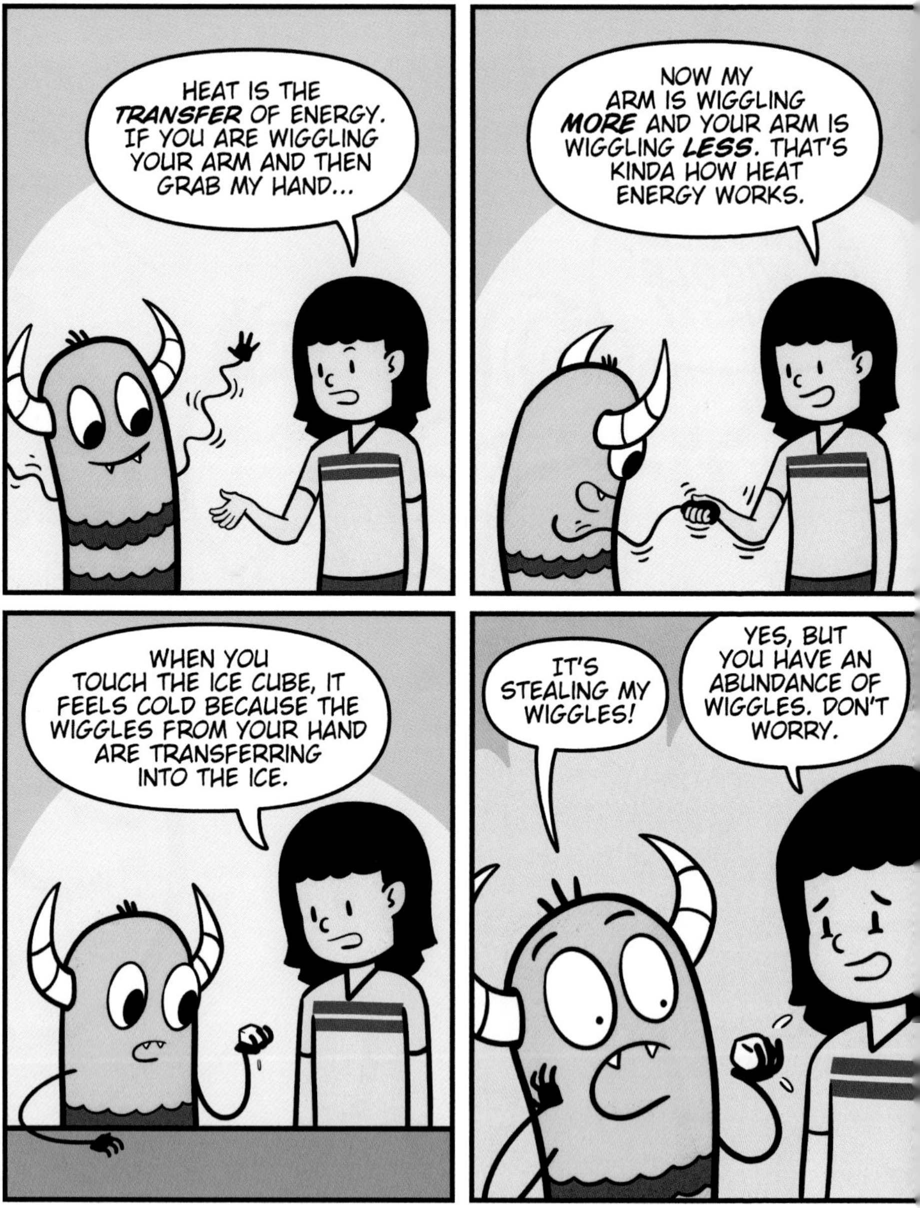
HEAT IS THE **TRANSFER** OF ENERGY. IF YOU ARE WIGGLING YOUR ARM AND THEN GRAB MY HAND...
NOW MY ARM IS WIGGLING **MORE** AND YOUR ARM IS WIGGLING **LESS**. THAT'S KINDA HOW HEAT ENERGY WORKS.
WHEN YOU TOUCH THE ICE CUBE, IT FEELS COLD BECAUSE THE WIGGLES FROM YOUR HAND ARE TRANSFERRING INTO THE ICE.
IT'S STEALING MY WIGGLES!
YES, BUT YOU HAVE AN ABUNDANCE OF WIGGLES. DON'T WORRY.

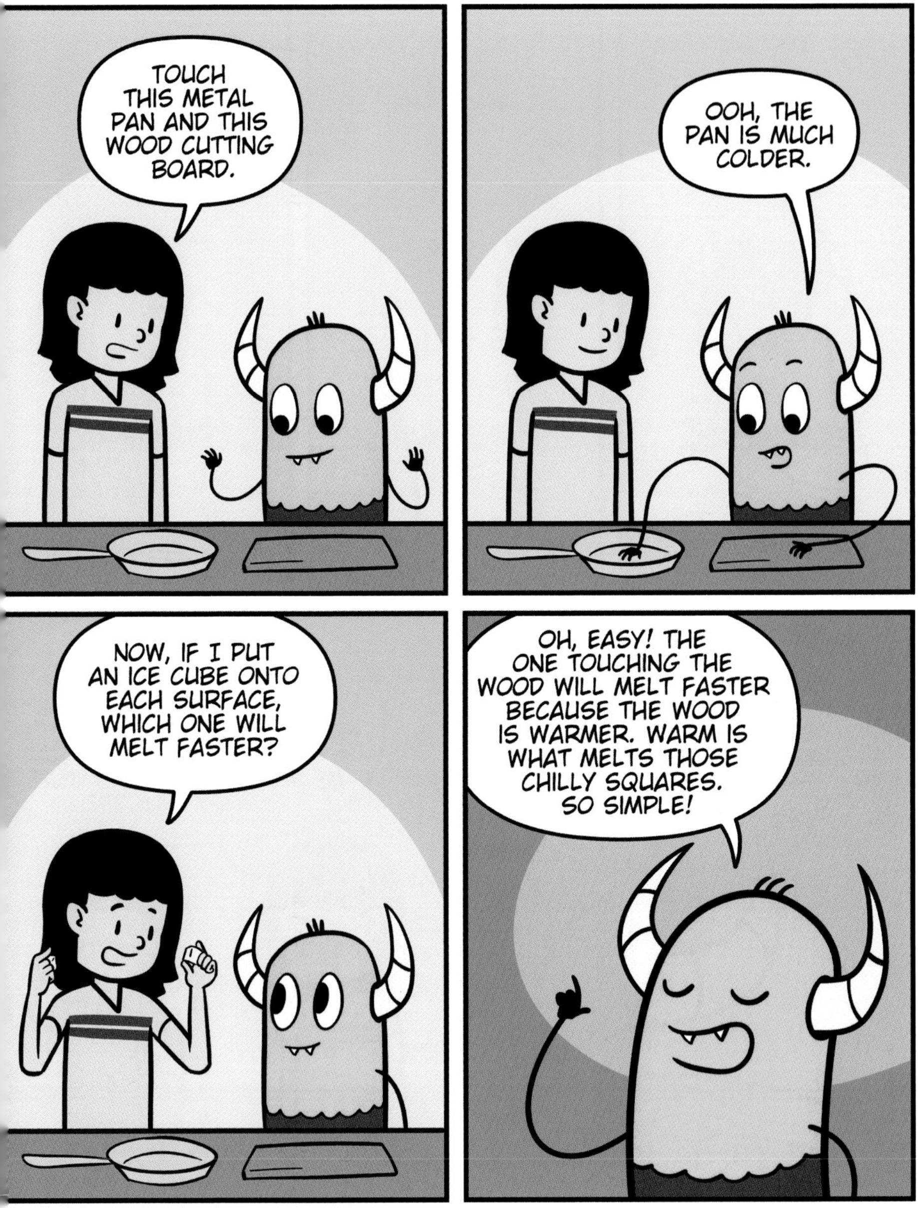
TOUCH THIS METAL PAN AND THIS WOOD CUTTING BOARD.
OOH, THE PAN IS MUCH COLDER.
NOW, IF I PUT AN ICE CUBE ONTO EACH SURFACE, WHICH ONE WILL MELT FASTER?
OH, EASY! THE ONE TOUCHING THE WOOD WILL MELT FASTER BECAUSE THE WOOD IS WARMER. WARM IS WHAT MELTS THOSE CHILLY SQUARES. SO SIMPLE!

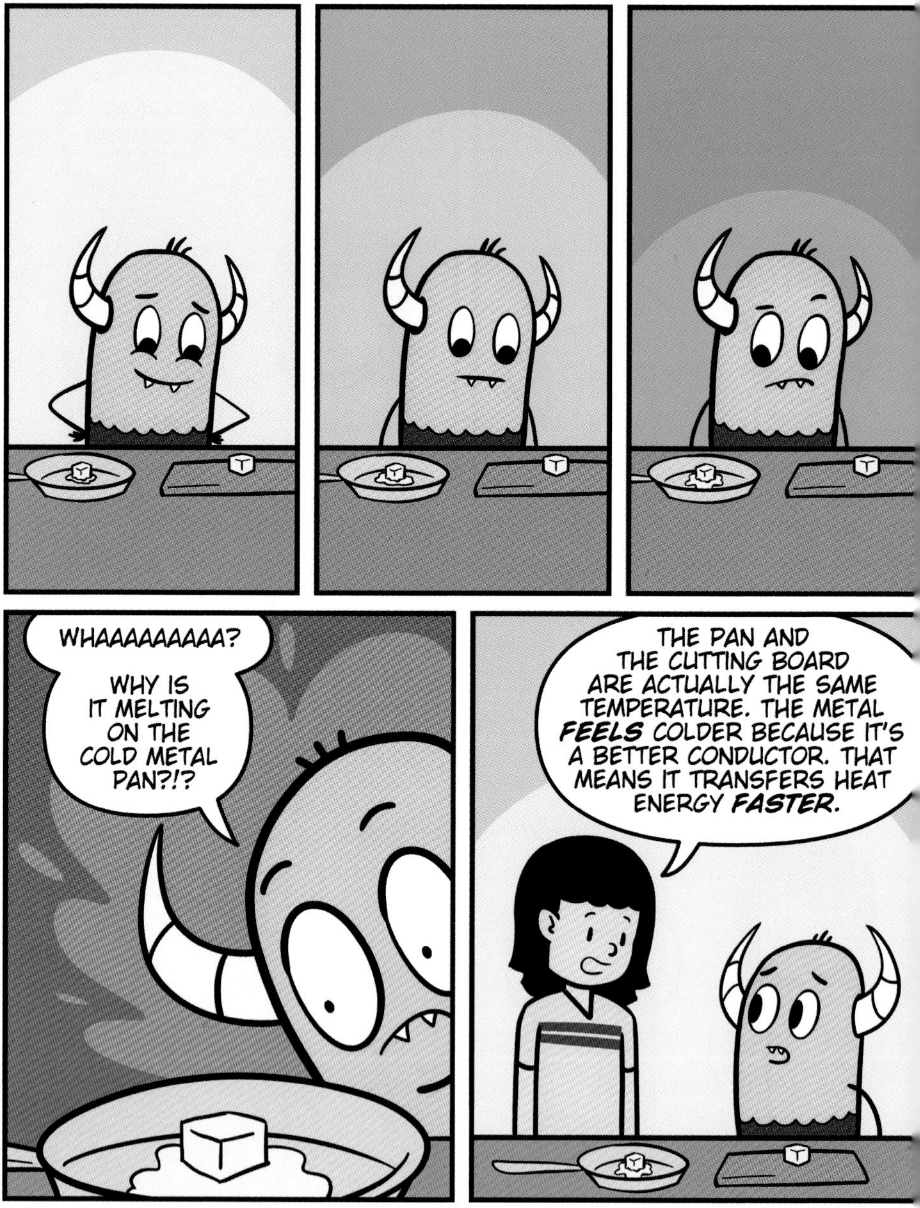
WHAAAAAAAAA?
WHY IS IT MELTING ON THE COLD METAL PAN?!?
THE PAN AND THE CUTTING BOARD ARE ACTUALLY THE SAME TEMPERATURE. THE METAL *FEELS* COLDER BECAUSE IT'S A BETTER CONDUCTOR. THAT MEANS IT TRANSFERS HEAT ENERGY ***FASTER***.

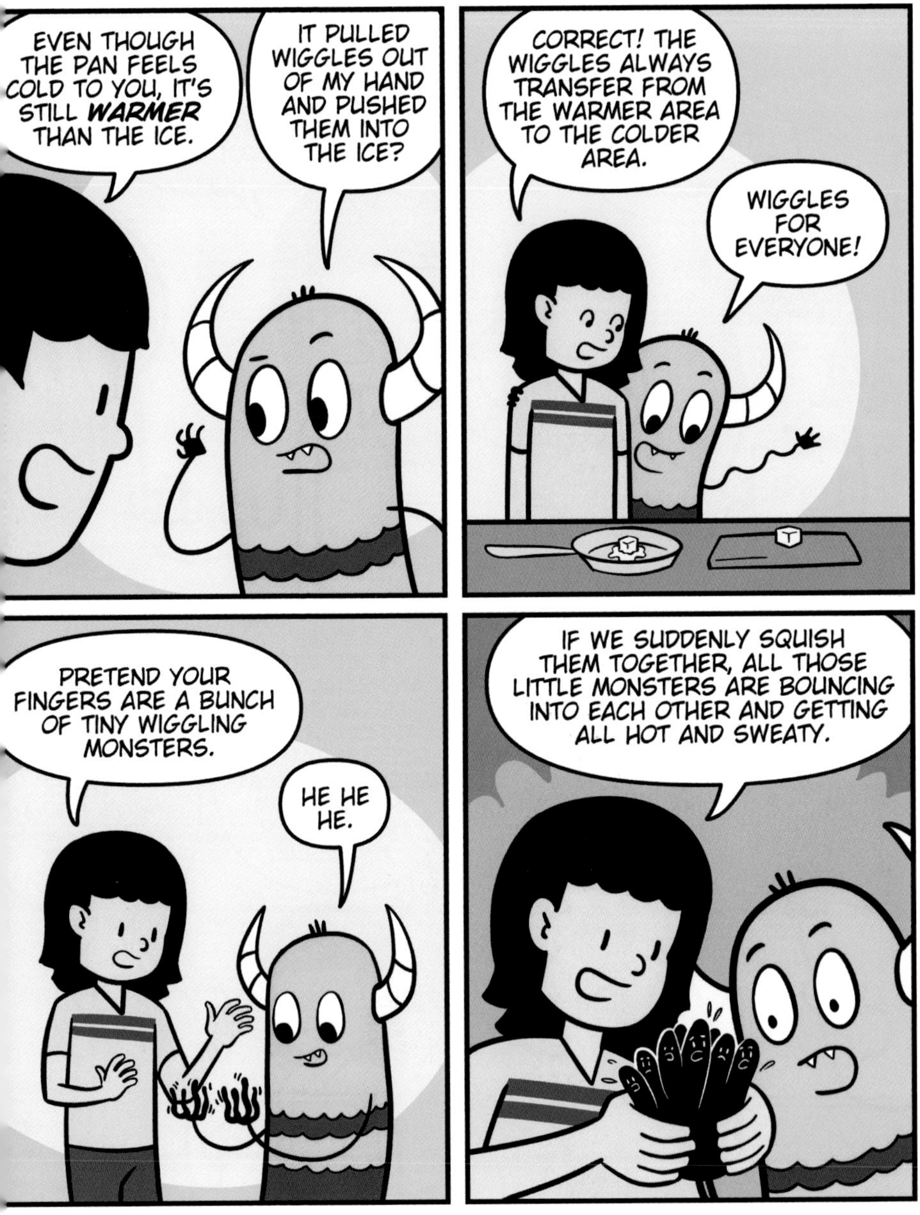
EVEN THOUGH THE PAN FEELS COLD TO YOU, IT'S STILL **WARMER** THAN THE ICE.
IT PULLED WIGGLES OUT OF MY HAND AND PUSHED THEM INTO THE ICE?
CORRECT! THE WIGGLES ALWAYS TRANSFER FROM THE WARMER AREA TO THE COLDER AREA.
WIGGLES FOR EVERYONE!
PRETEND YOUR FINGERS ARE A BUNCH OF TINY WIGGLING MONSTERS.
HE HE HE.
IF WE SUDDENLY SQUISH THEM TOGETHER, ALL THOSE LITTLE MONSTERS ARE BOUNCING INTO EACH OTHER AND GETTING ALL HOT AND SWEATY.

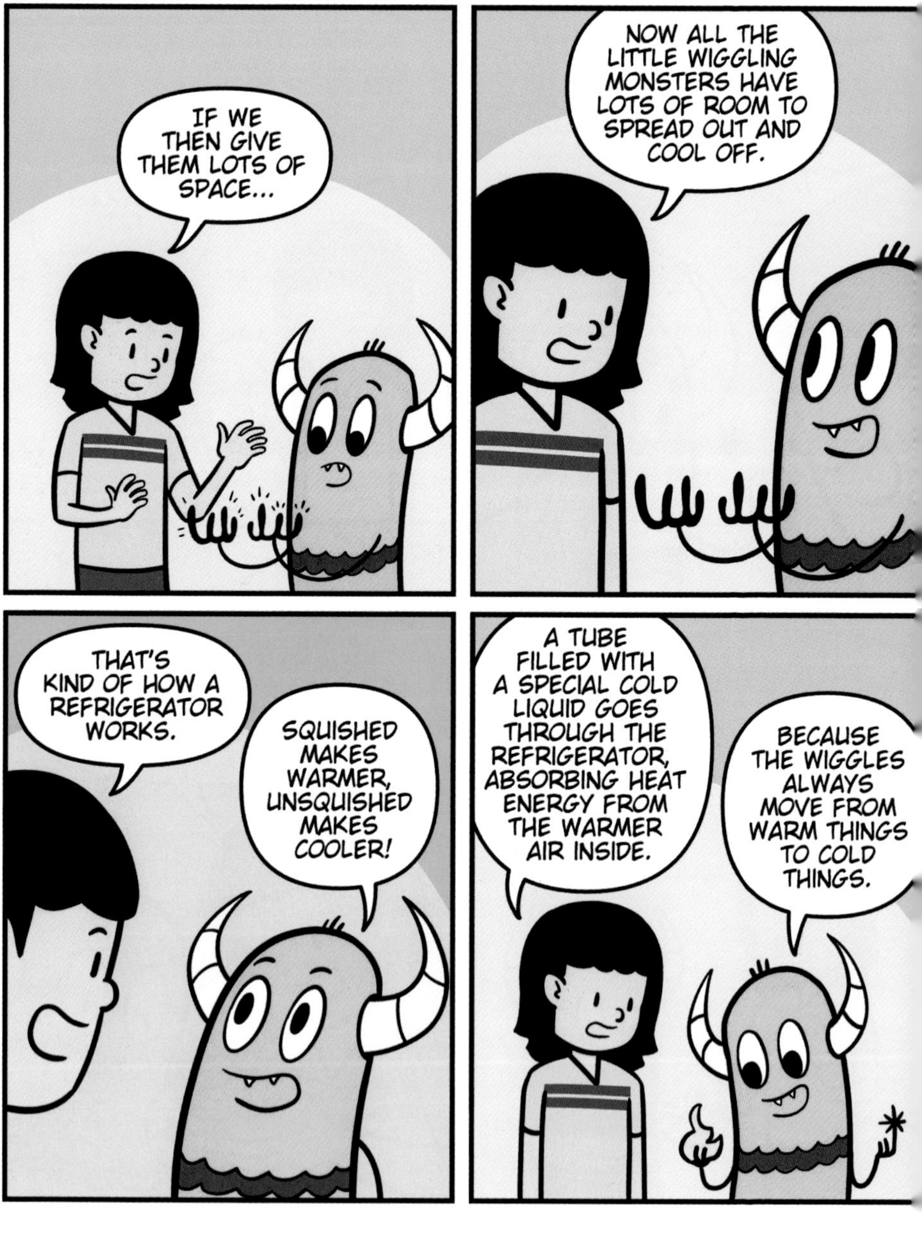
IF WE THEN GIVE THEM LOTS OF SPACE...
NOW ALL THE LITTLE WIGGLING MONSTERS HAVE LOTS OF ROOM TO SPREAD OUT AND COOL OFF.
THAT'S KIND OF HOW A REFRIGERATOR WORKS.
SQUISHED MAKES WARMER, UNSQUISHED MAKES COOLER!
A TUBE FILLED WITH A SPECIAL COLD LIQUID GOES THROUGH THE REFRIGERATOR, ABSORBING HEAT ENERGY FROM THE WARMER AIR INSIDE.
BECAUSE THE WIGGLES ALWAYS MOVE FROM WARM THINGS TO COLD THINGS.

CORRECT! THAT WARMER LIQUID GOES INTO THE COMPRESSOR. IT GETS SQUISHED INTO A SMALLER SPACE TO WARM IT UP EVEN MORE!

THE WIGGLES ARE GETTING SO HOT!

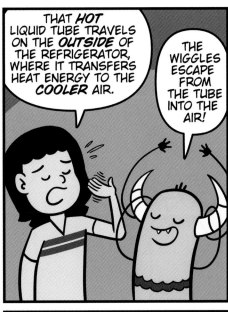

THAT *HOT* LIQUID TUBE TRAVELS ON THE *OUTSIDE* OF THE REFRIGERATOR, WHERE IT TRANSFERS HEAT ENERGY TO THE *COOLER* AIR.

THE WIGGLES ESCAPE FROM THE TUBE INTO THE AIR!

AFTER IT'S COOLED OFF, THE LIQUID IS UNSQUISHED, WHICH MAKES IT MUCH COLDER. THEN IT GOES BACK INTO THE REFRIGERATOR AND DOES THE LOOP AGAIN.

SQUISH TO MAKE IT *WARMER* THAN THE OUTSIDE AIR, AND UNSQUISH TO MAKE IT *COLDER* THAN THE INSIDE AIR.

THE REFRIGERATOR TAKES HEAT ENERGY FROM *INSIDE* THE BOX AND PUTS IT *OUTSIDE* THE BOX.

IT GETS THE WIGGLES OUT!

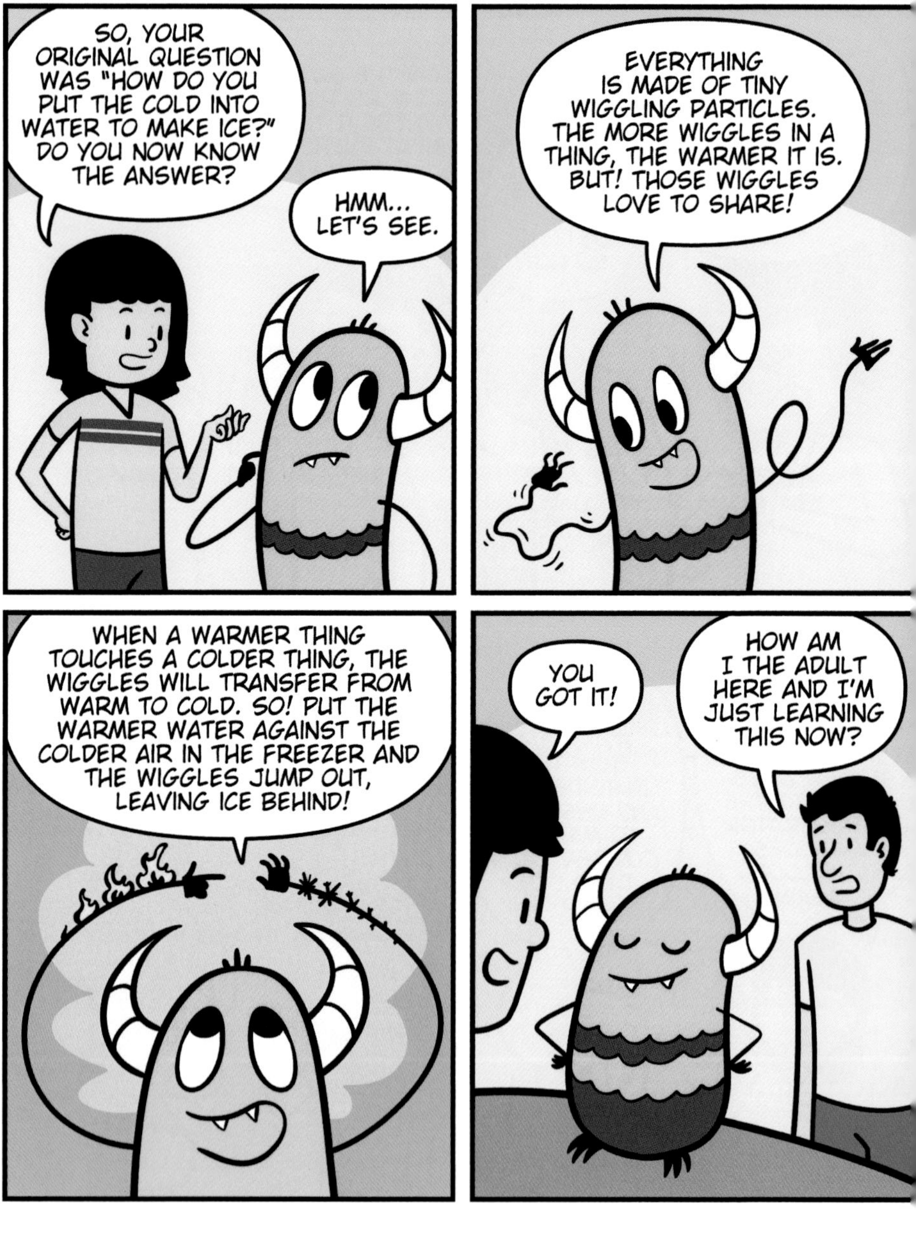
SO, YOUR ORIGINAL QUESTION WAS "HOW DO YOU PUT THE COLD INTO WATER TO MAKE ICE?" DO YOU NOW KNOW THE ANSWER?
HMM... LET'S SEE.
EVERYTHING IS MADE OF TINY WIGGLING PARTICLES. THE MORE WIGGLES IN A THING, THE WARMER IT IS. BUT! THOSE WIGGLES LOVE TO SHARE!
WHEN A WARMER THING TOUCHES A COLDER THING, THE WIGGLES WILL TRANSFER FROM WARM TO COLD. SO! PUT THE WARMER WATER AGAINST THE COLDER AIR IN THE FREEZER AND THE WIGGLES JUMP OUT, LEAVING ICE BEHIND!
YOU GOT IT!
HOW AM I THE ADULT HERE AND I'M JUST LEARNING THIS NOW?

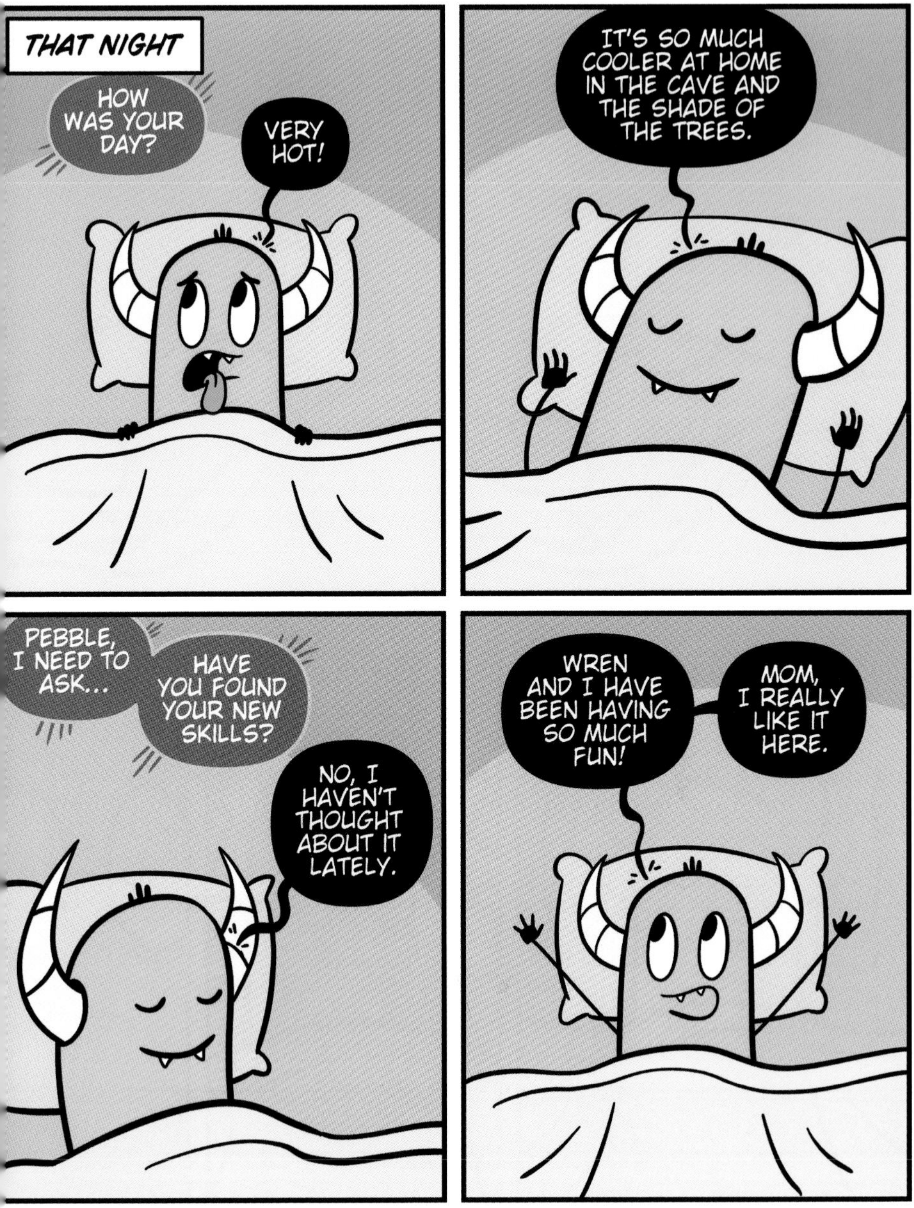
THAT NIGHT
HOW WAS YOUR DAY?
VERY HOT!
IT'S SO MUCH COOLER AT HOME IN THE CAVE AND THE SHADE OF THE TREES.
PEBBLE, I NEED TO ASK...
HAVE YOU FOUND YOUR NEW SKILLS?
NO, I HAVEN'T THOUGHT ABOUT IT LATELY.
WREN AND I HAVE BEEN HAVING SO MUCH FUN!
MOM, I REALLY LIKE IT HERE.

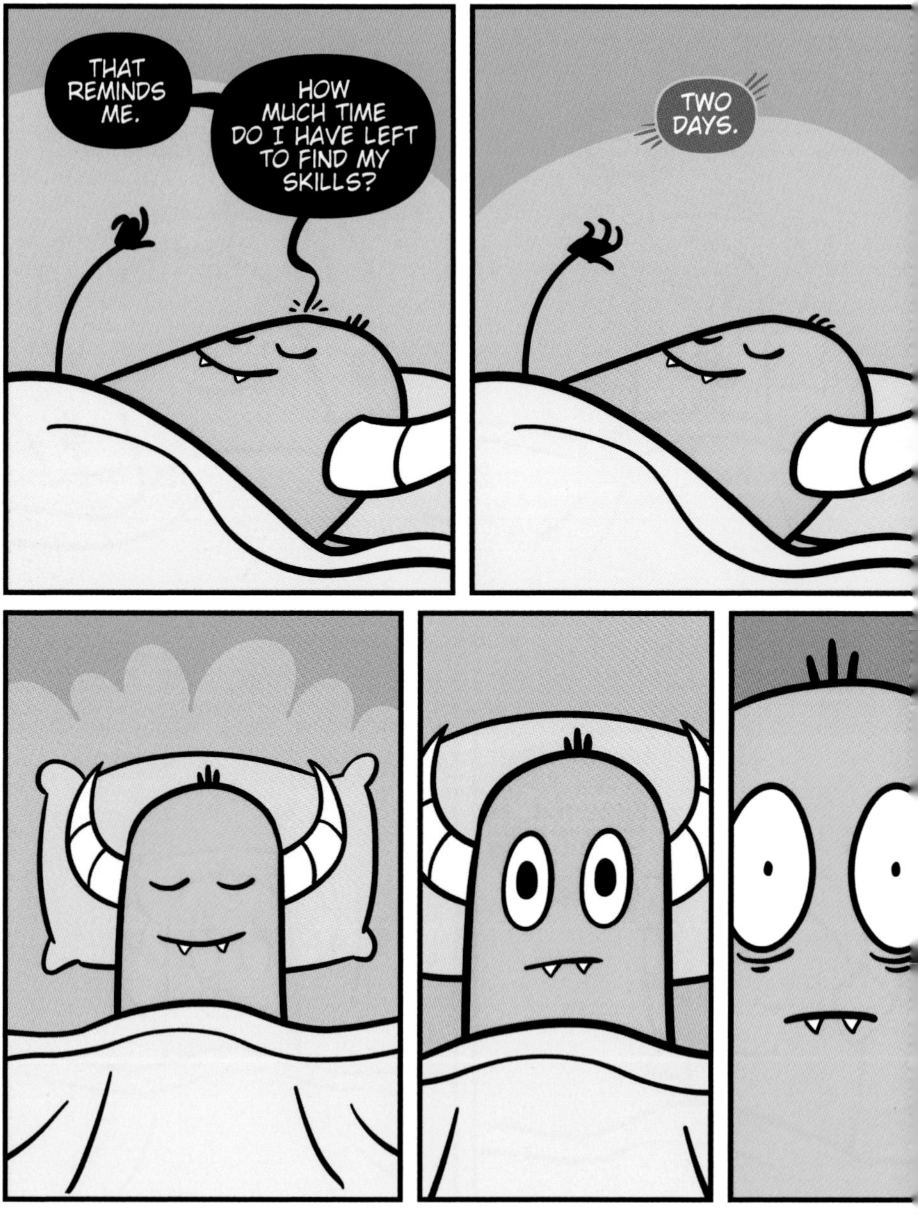
THAT REMINDS ME.
HOW MUCH TIME DO I HAVE LEFT TO FIND MY SKILLS?
TWO DAYS.

CHAPTER ELEVEN

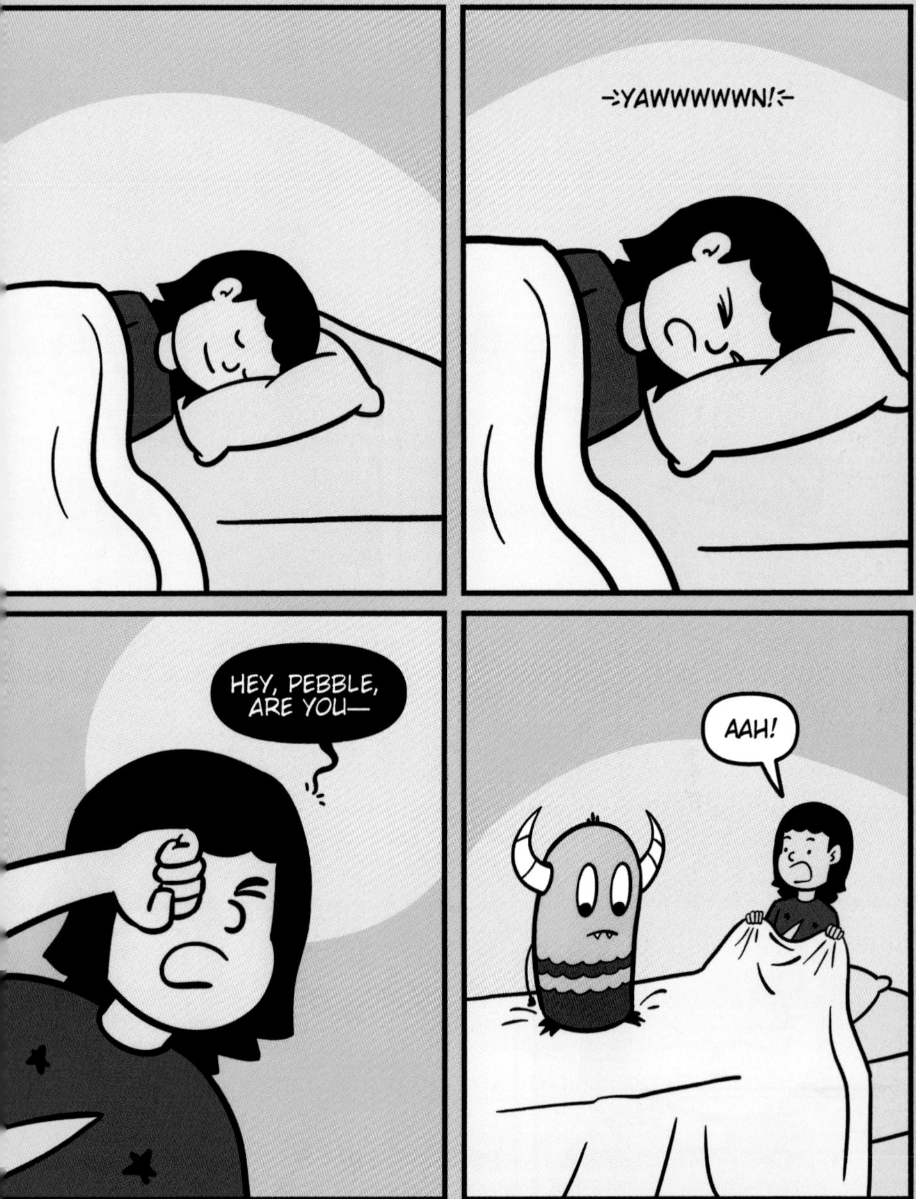

YAWWWWWN!
HEY, PEBBLE, ARE YOU—
AAH!

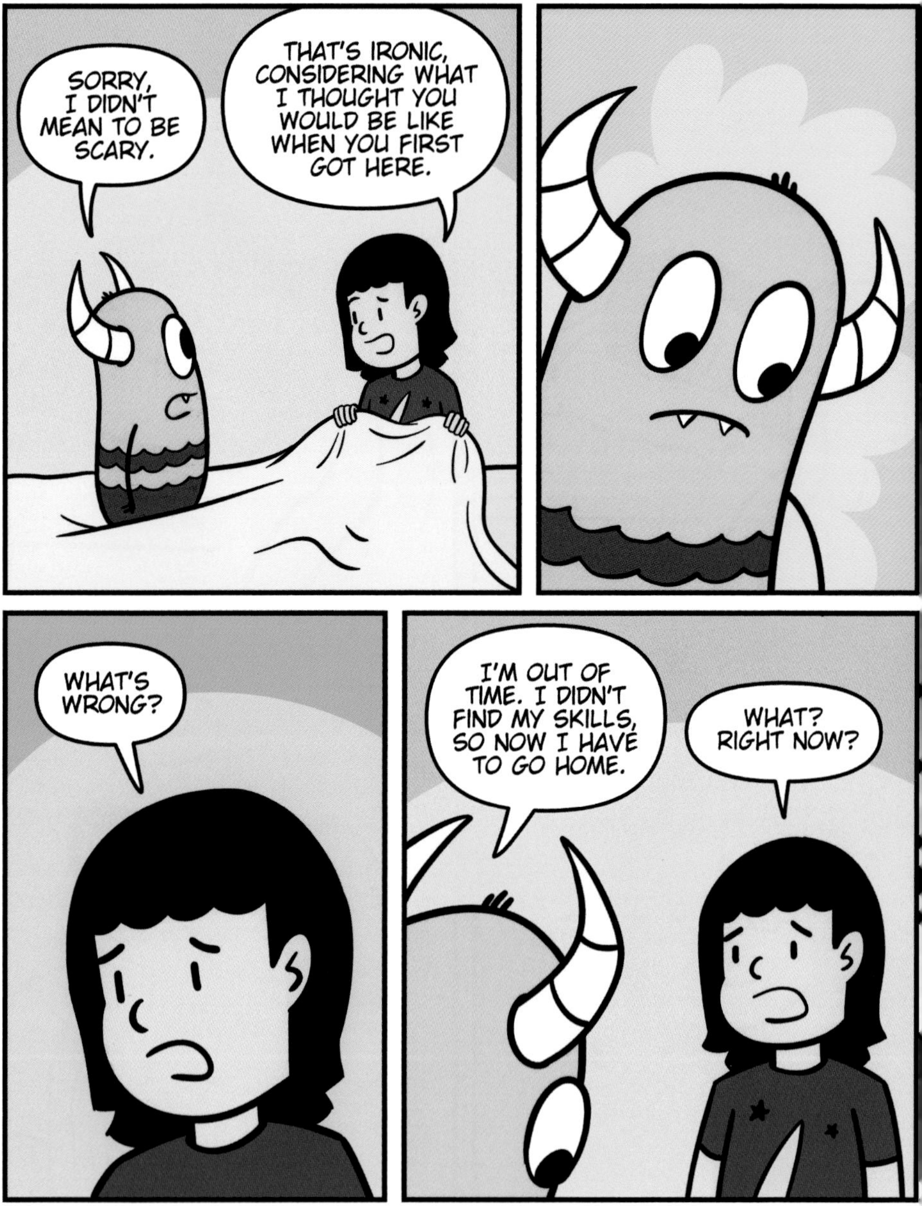
SORRY, I DIDN'T MEAN TO BE SCARY.
THAT'S IRONIC, CONSIDERING WHAT I THOUGHT YOU WOULD BE LIKE WHEN YOU FIRST GOT HERE.
WHAT'S WRONG?
I'M OUT OF TIME. I DIDN'T FIND MY SKILLS, SO NOW I HAVE TO GO HOME.
WHAT? RIGHT NOW?

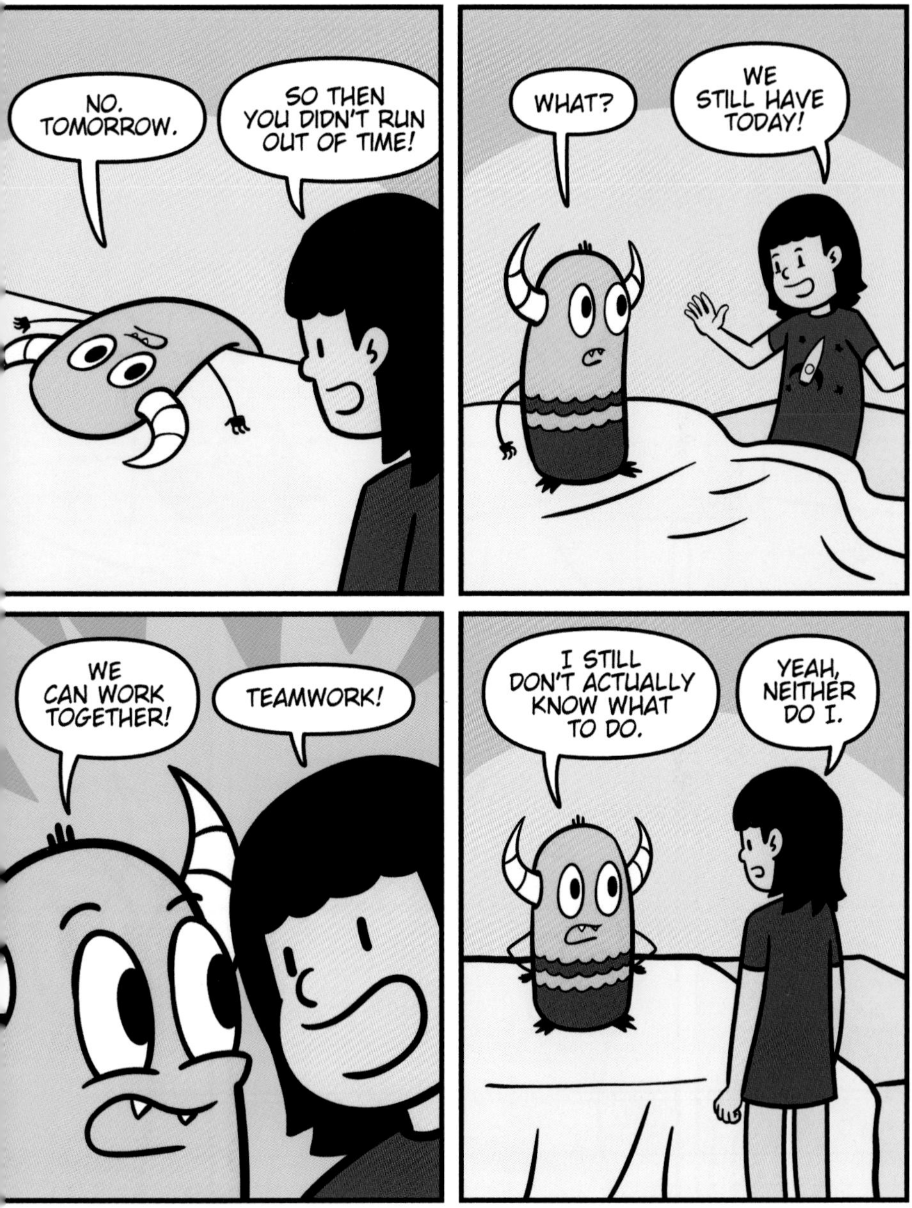
NO. TOMORROW.
SO THEN YOU DIDN'T RUN OUT OF TIME!
WHAT?
WE STILL HAVE TODAY!
WE CAN WORK TOGETHER!
TEAMWORK!
I STILL DON'T ACTUALLY KNOW WHAT TO DO.
YEAH, NEITHER DO I.

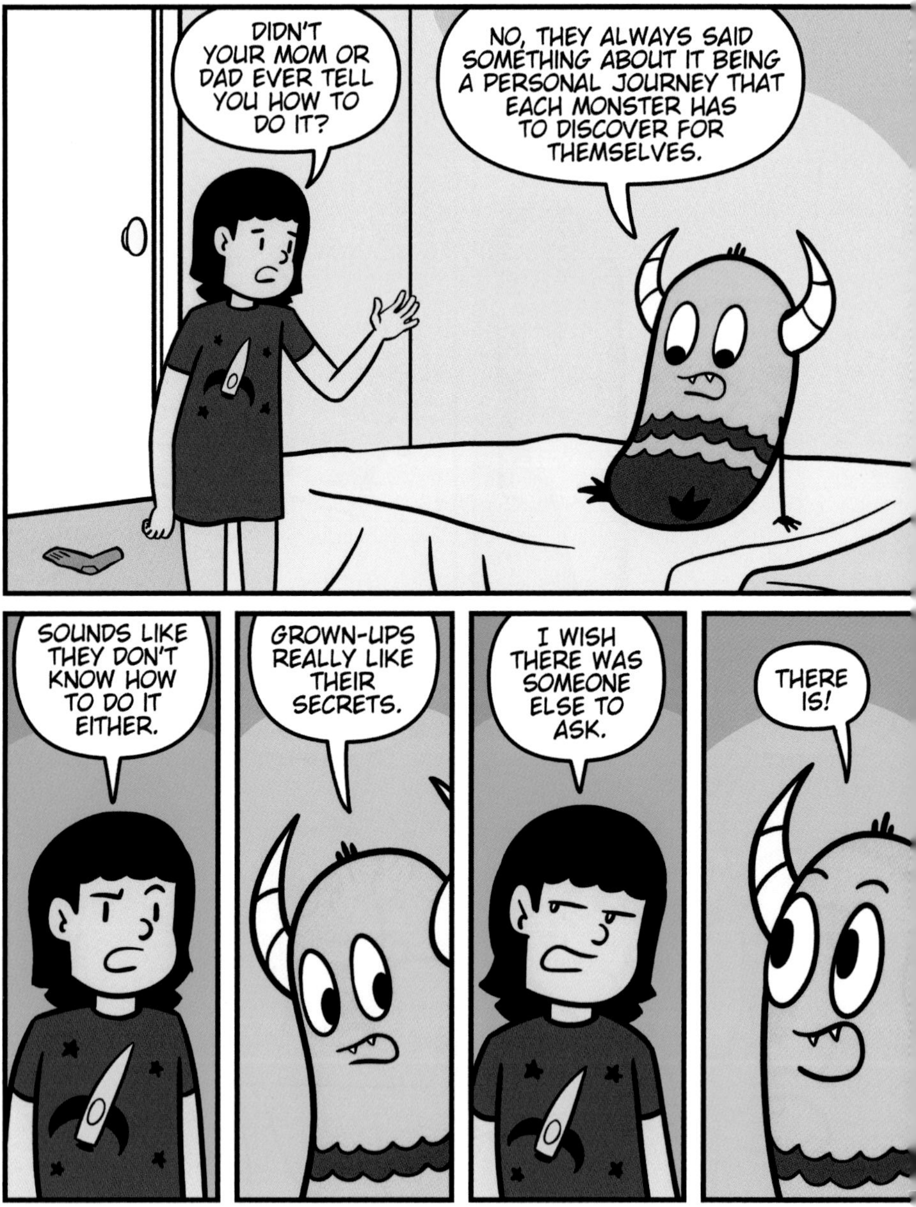
DIDN'T YOUR MOM OR DAD EVER TELL YOU HOW TO DO IT?
NO, THEY ALWAYS SAID SOMETHING ABOUT IT BEING A PERSONAL JOURNEY THAT EACH MONSTER HAS TO DISCOVER FOR THEMSELVES.
SOUNDS LIKE THEY DON'T KNOW HOW TO DO IT EITHER.
GROWN-UPS REALLY LIKE THEIR SECRETS.
I WISH THERE WAS SOMEONE ELSE TO ASK.
THERE IS!

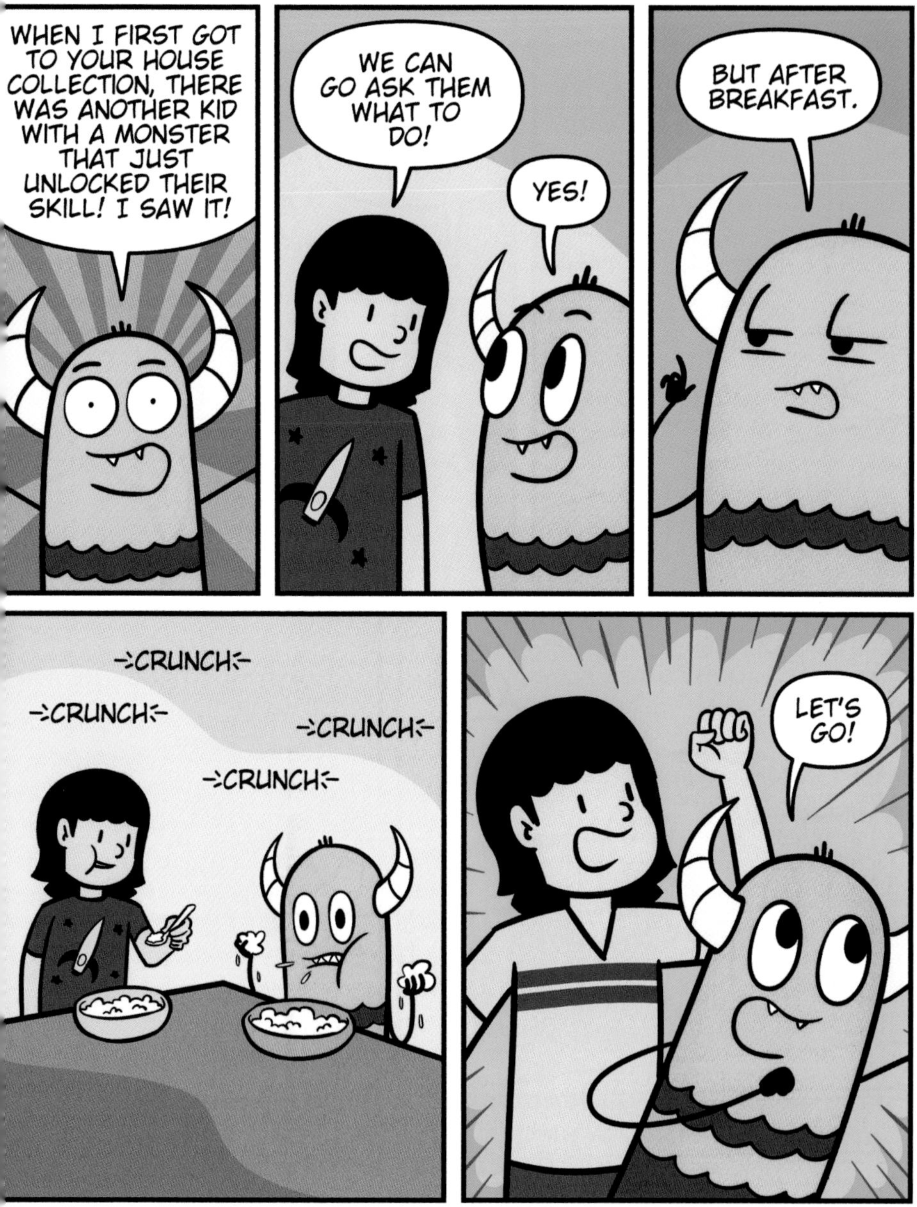
WHEN I FIRST GOT TO YOUR HOUSE COLLECTION, THERE WAS ANOTHER KID WITH A MONSTER THAT JUST UNLOCKED THEIR SKILL! I SAW IT!
WE CAN GO ASK THEM WHAT TO DO!
YES!
BUT AFTER BREAKFAST.
CRUNCH
CRUNCH
CRUNCH
CRUNCH
LET'S GO!

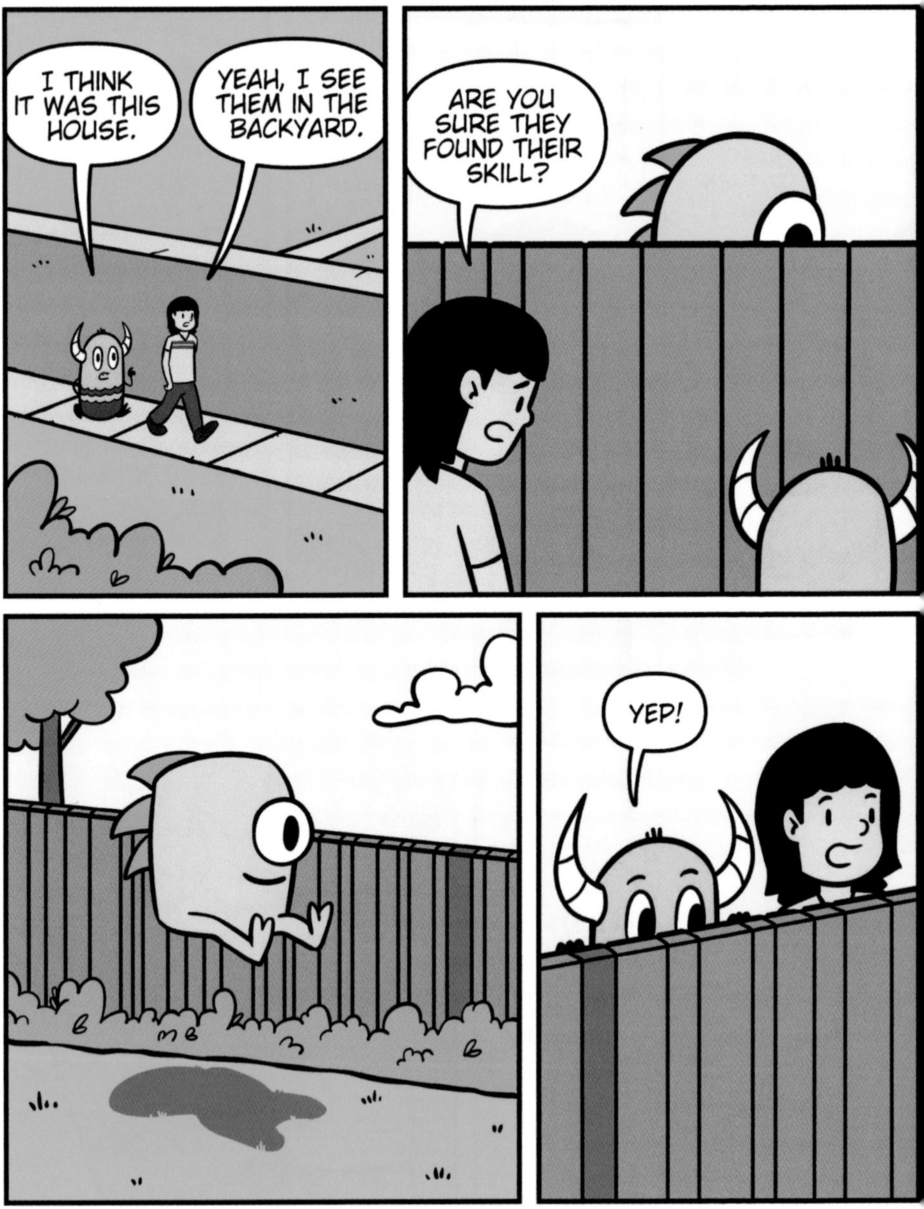
I THINK IT WAS THIS HOUSE.
YEAH, I SEE THEM IN THE BACKYARD.
ARE YOU SURE THEY FOUND THEIR SKILL?
YEP!

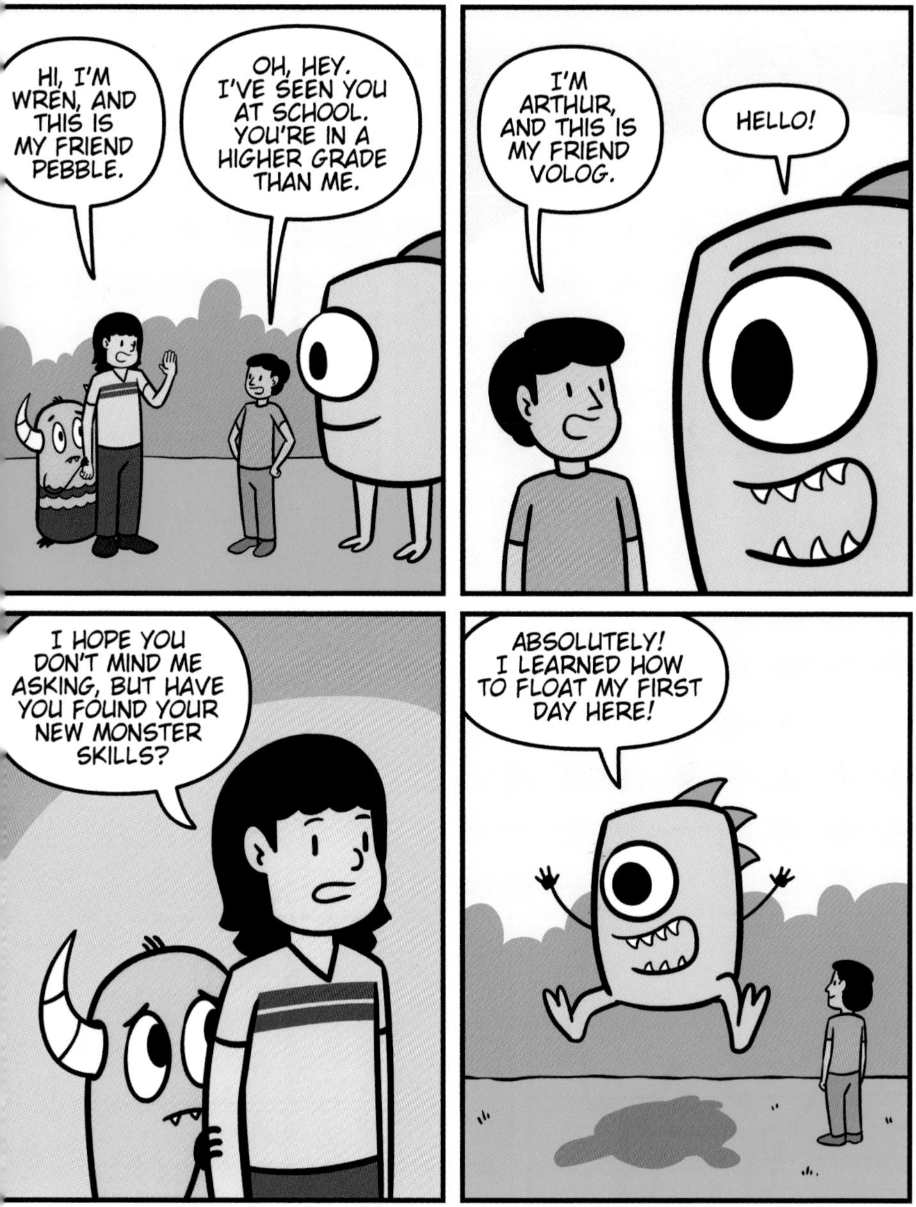
HI, I'M WREN, AND THIS IS MY FRIEND PEBBLE.
OH, HEY. I'VE SEEN YOU AT SCHOOL. YOU'RE IN A HIGHER GRADE THAN ME.
I'M ARTHUR, AND THIS IS MY FRIEND VOLOG.
HELLO!
I HOPE YOU DON'T MIND ME ASKING, BUT HAVE YOU FOUND YOUR NEW MONSTER SKILLS?
ABSOLUTELY! I LEARNED HOW TO FLOAT MY FIRST DAY HERE!

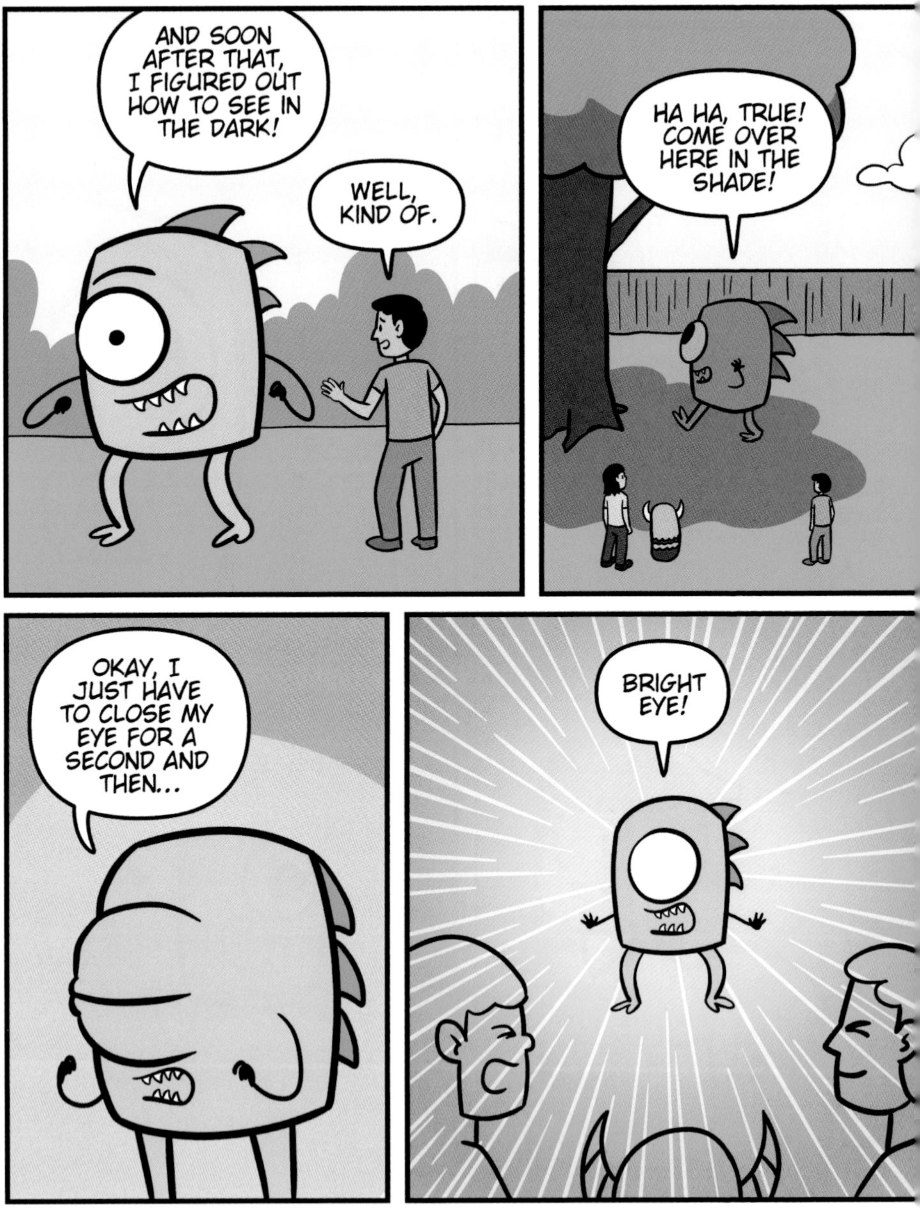
AND SOON AFTER THAT, I FIGURED OUT HOW TO SEE IN THE DARK!
WELL, KIND OF.
HA HA, TRUE! COME OVER HERE IN THE SHADE!
OKAY, I JUST HAVE TO CLOSE MY EYE FOR A SECOND AND THEN...
BRIGHT EYE!

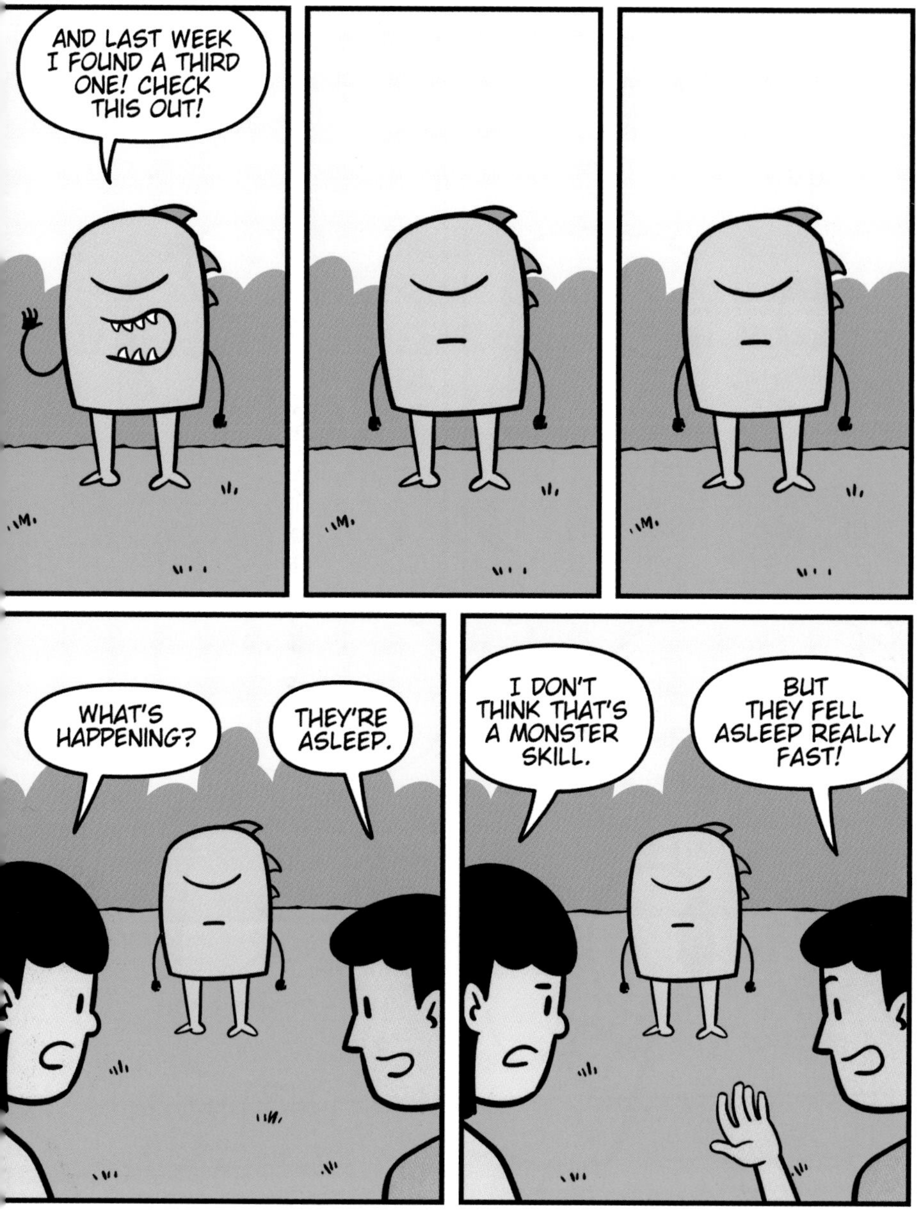
AND LAST WEEK I FOUND A THIRD ONE! CHECK THIS OUT!
WHAT'S HAPPENING?
THEY'RE ASLEEP.
I DON'T THINK THAT'S A MONSTER SKILL.
BUT THEY FELL ASLEEP REALLY FAST!

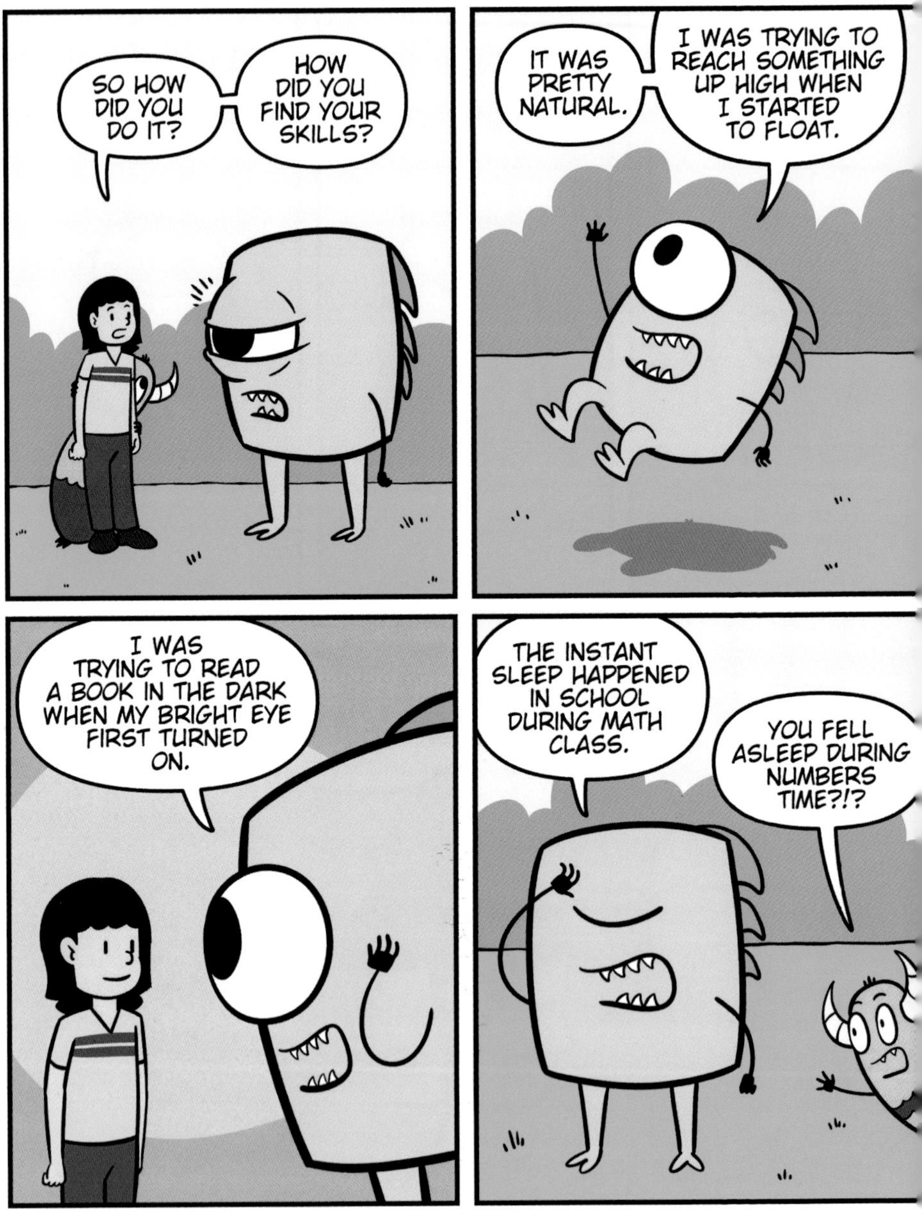
SO HOW DID YOU DO IT?
HOW DID YOU FIND YOUR SKILLS?
IT WAS PRETTY NATURAL.
I WAS TRYING TO REACH SOMETHING UP HIGH WHEN I STARTED TO FLOAT.
I WAS TRYING TO READ A BOOK IN THE DARK WHEN MY BRIGHT EYE FIRST TURNED ON.
THE INSTANT SLEEP HAPPENED IN SCHOOL DURING MATH CLASS.
YOU FELL ASLEEP DURING NUMBERS TIME?!?

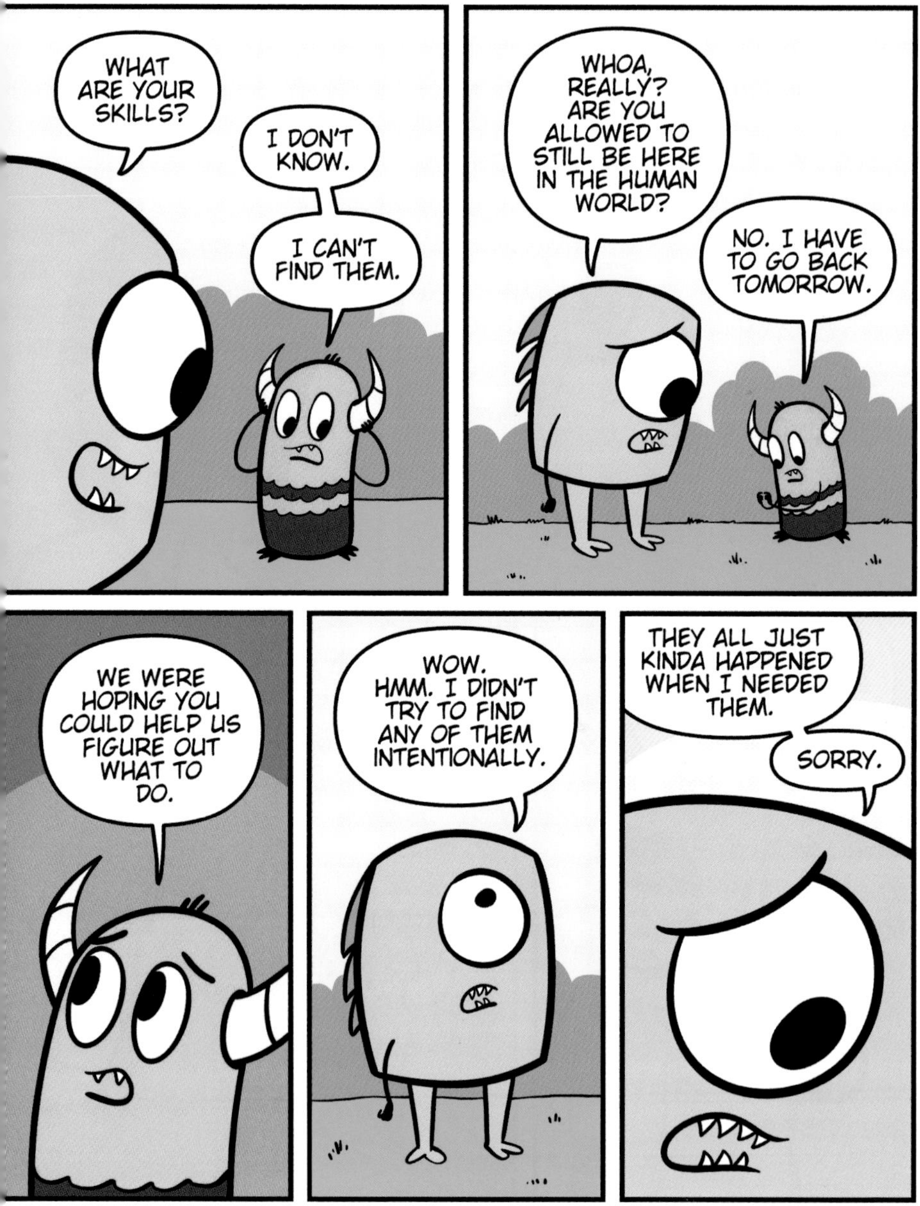
WHAT ARE YOUR SKILLS?
I DON'T KNOW.
I CAN'T FIND THEM.
WHOA, REALLY? ARE YOU ALLOWED TO STILL BE HERE IN THE HUMAN WORLD?
NO. I HAVE TO GO BACK TOMORROW.
WE WERE HOPING YOU COULD HELP US FIGURE OUT WHAT TO DO.
WOW. HMM. I DIDN'T TRY TO FIND ANY OF THEM INTENTIONALLY.
THEY ALL JUST KINDA HAPPENED WHEN I NEEDED THEM.
SORRY.

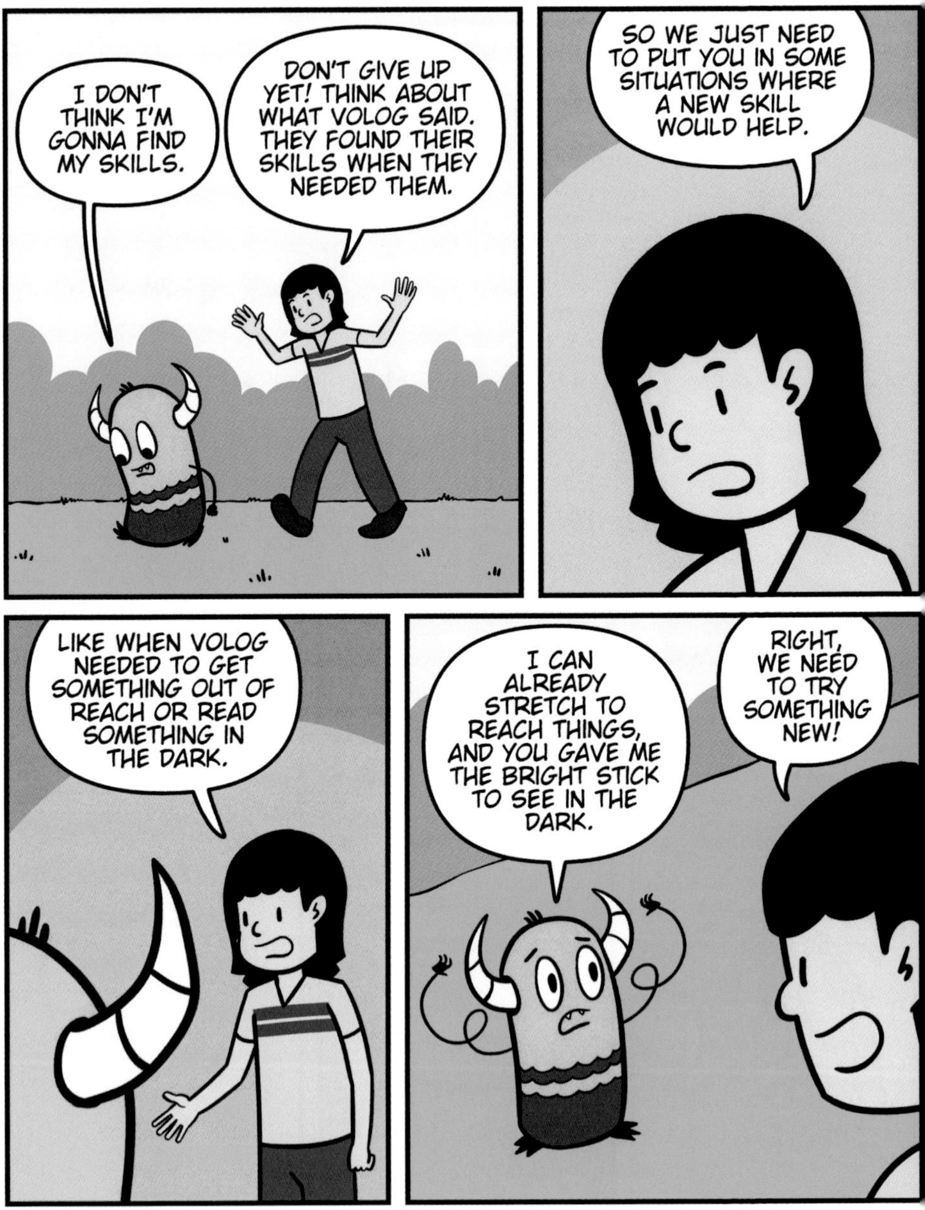
I DON'T THINK I'M GONNA FIND MY SKILLS.
DON'T GIVE UP YET! THINK ABOUT WHAT VOLOG SAID. THEY FOUND THEIR SKILLS WHEN THEY NEEDED THEM.
SO WE JUST NEED TO PUT YOU IN SOME SITUATIONS WHERE A NEW SKILL WOULD HELP.
LIKE WHEN VOLOG NEEDED TO GET SOMETHING OUT OF REACH OR READ SOMETHING IN THE DARK.
I CAN ALREADY STRETCH TO REACH THINGS, AND YOU GAVE ME THE BRIGHT STICK TO SEE IN THE DARK.
RIGHT, WE NEED TO TRY SOMETHING NEW!

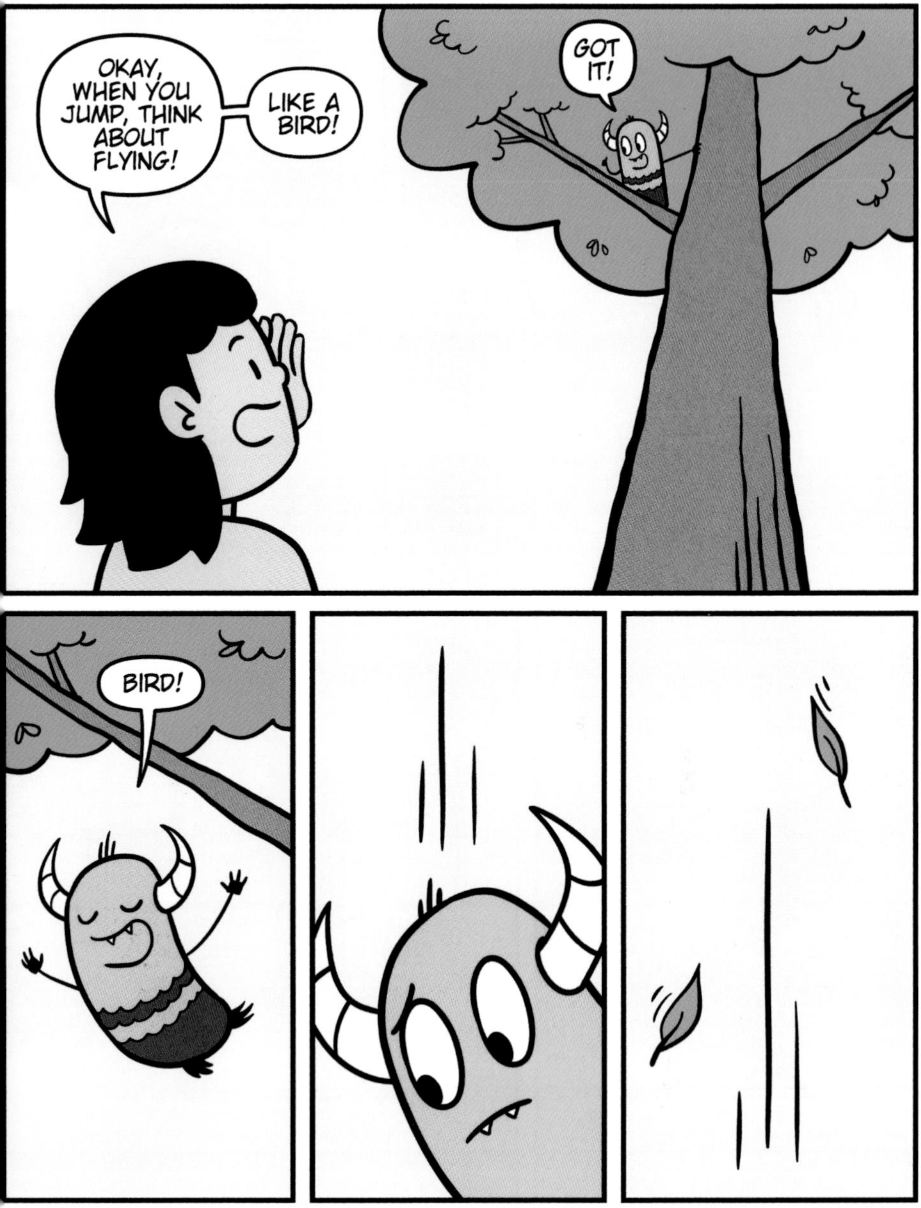
OKAY, WHEN YOU JUMP, THINK ABOUT FLYING!
LIKE A BIRD!
GOT IT!
BIRD!

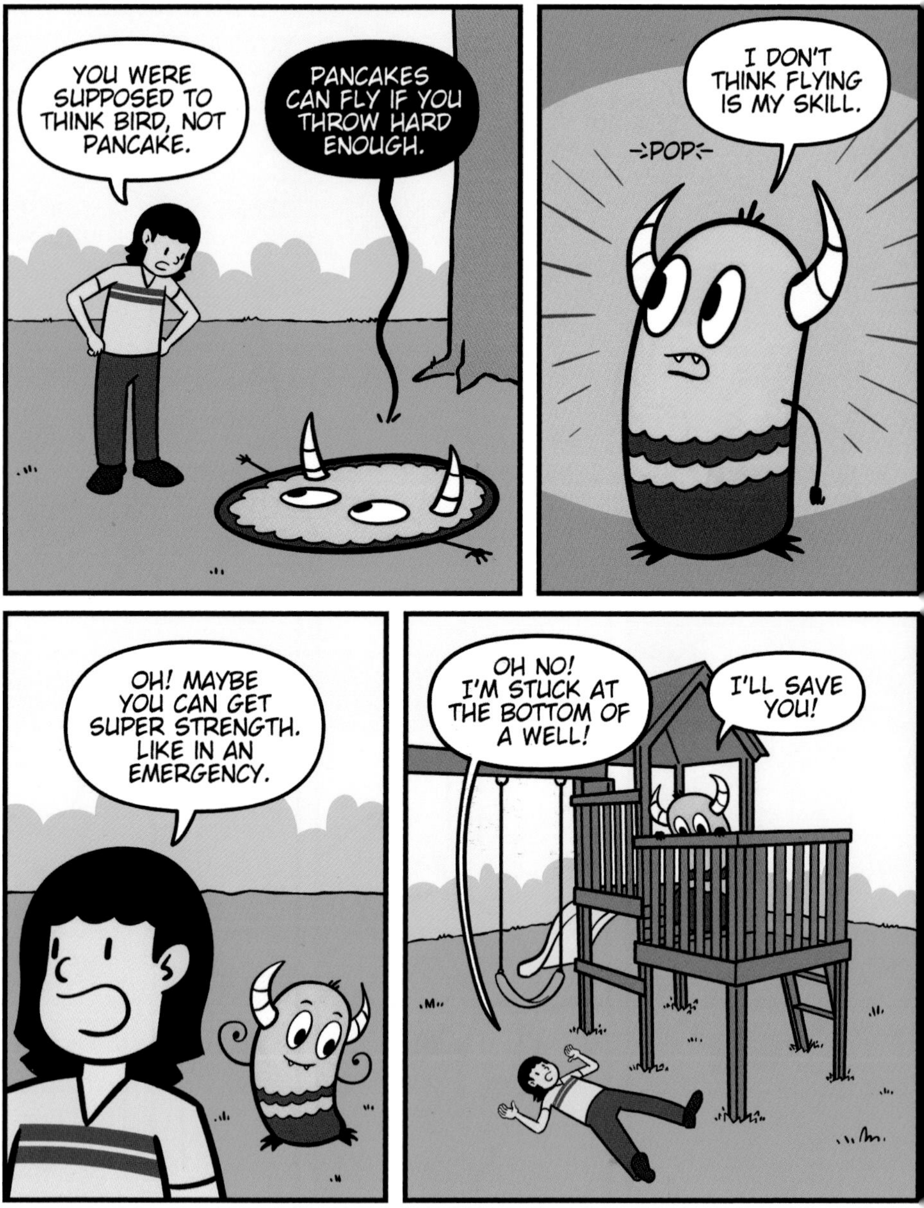
YOU WERE SUPPOSED TO THINK BIRD, NOT PANCAKE.
PANCAKES CAN FLY IF YOU THROW HARD ENOUGH.
I DON'T THINK FLYING IS MY SKILL.
POP
OH! MAYBE YOU CAN GET SUPER STRENGTH. LIKE IN AN EMERGENCY.
OH NO! I'M STUCK AT THE BOTTOM OF A WELL!
I'LL SAVE YOU!

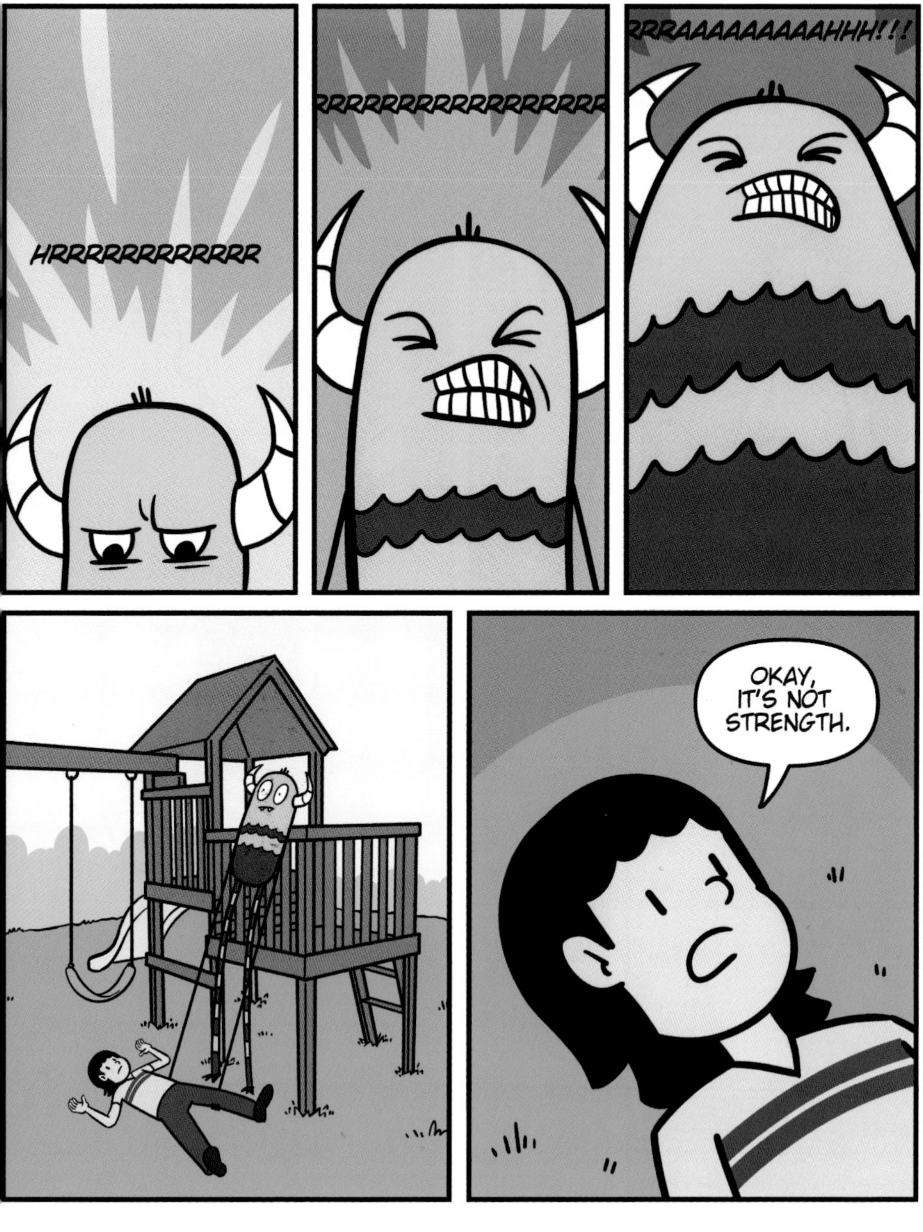
HRRRRRRRRRRRR
RRRRRRRRRRRRRRRRRRRR
RRRAAAAAAAAAAHHH!!!
OKAY, IT'S NOT STRENGTH.

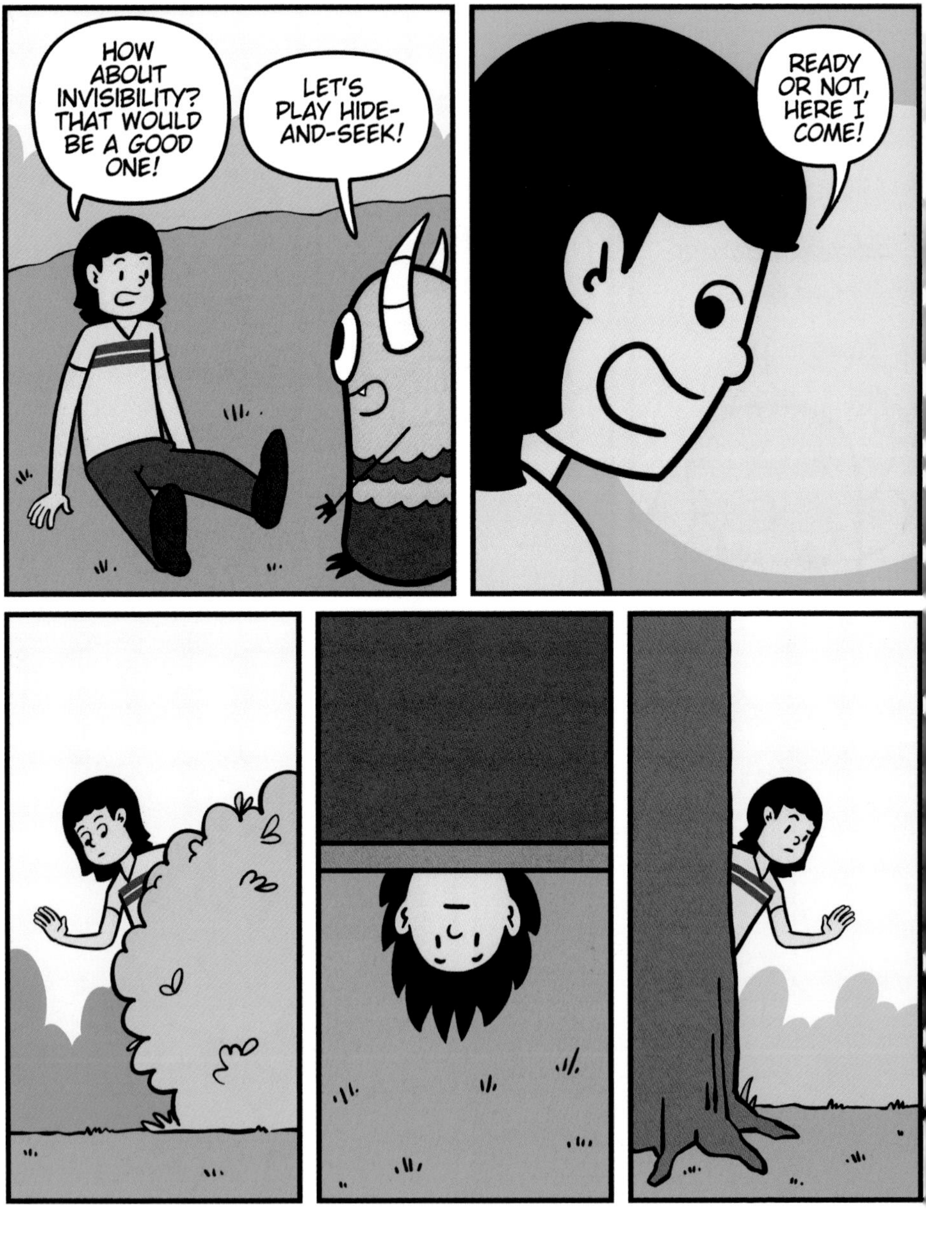
HOW ABOUT INVISIBILITY? THAT WOULD BE A GOOD ONE!
LET'S PLAY HIDE-AND-SEEK!
READY OR NOT, HERE I COME!

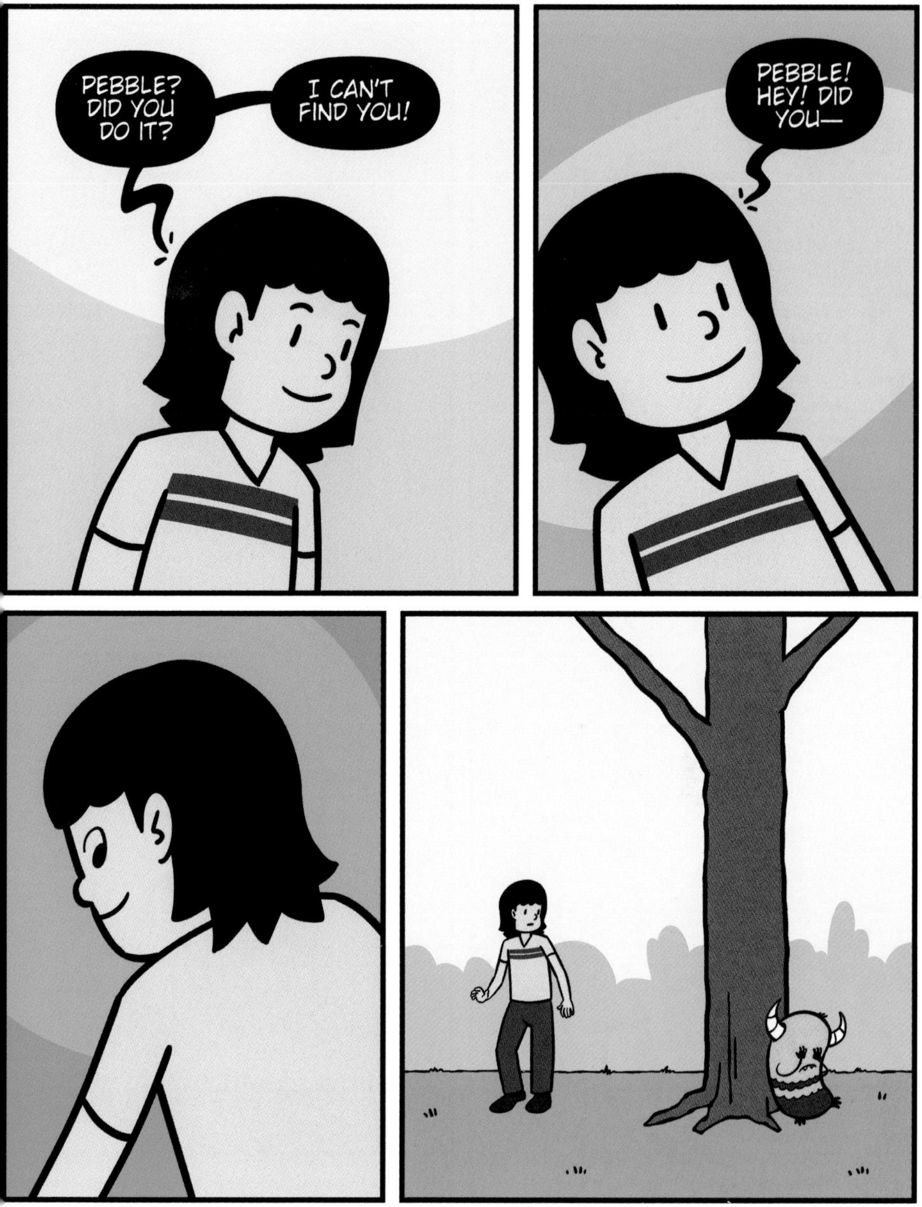
PEBBLE? DID YOU DO IT?
I CAN'T FIND YOU!
PEBBLE! HEY! DID YOU—

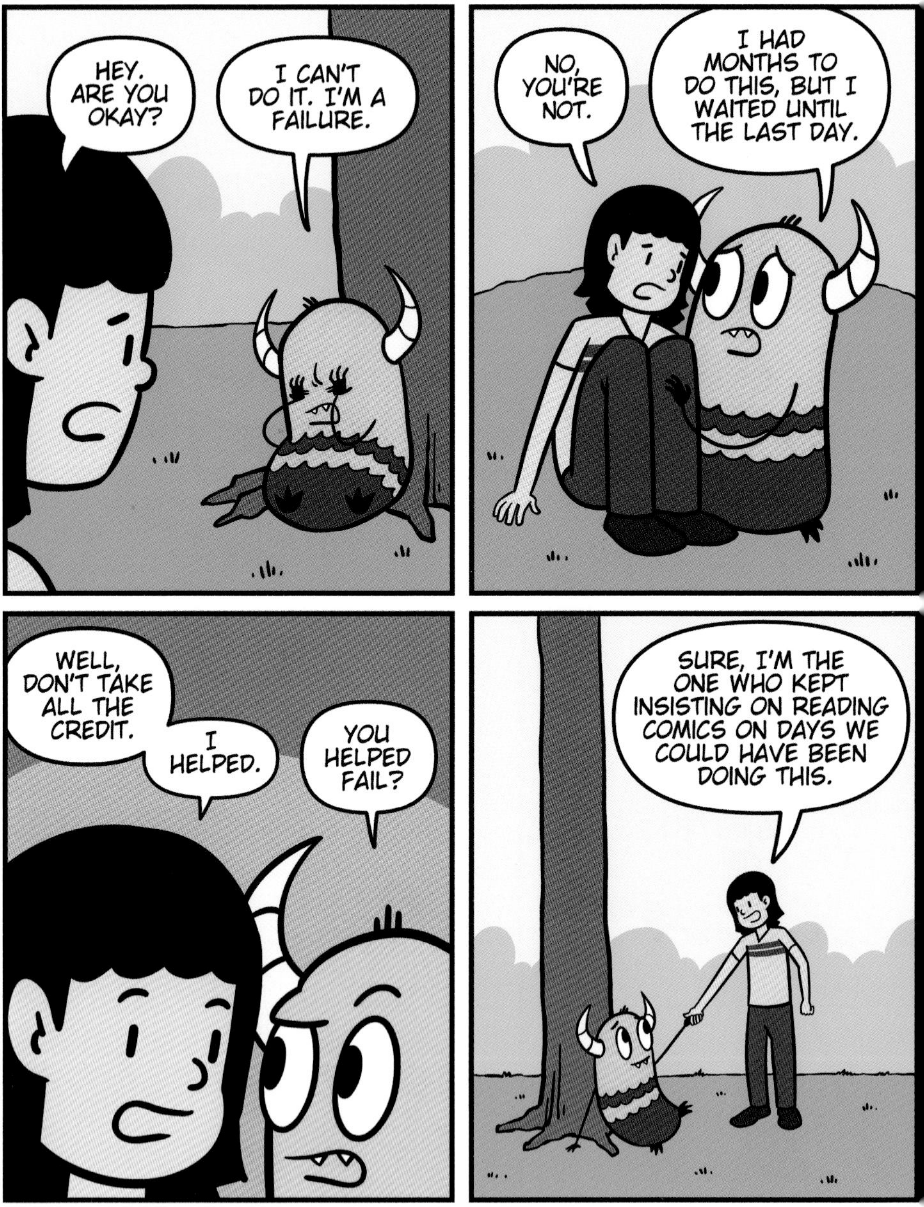
HEY. ARE YOU OKAY?
I CAN'T DO IT. I'M A FAILURE.
NO, YOU'RE NOT.
I HAD MONTHS TO DO THIS, BUT I WAITED UNTIL THE LAST DAY.
WELL, DON'T TAKE ALL THE CREDIT.
I HELPED.
YOU HELPED FAIL?
SURE, I'M THE ONE WHO KEPT INSISTING ON READING COMICS ON DAYS WE COULD HAVE BEEN DOING THIS.

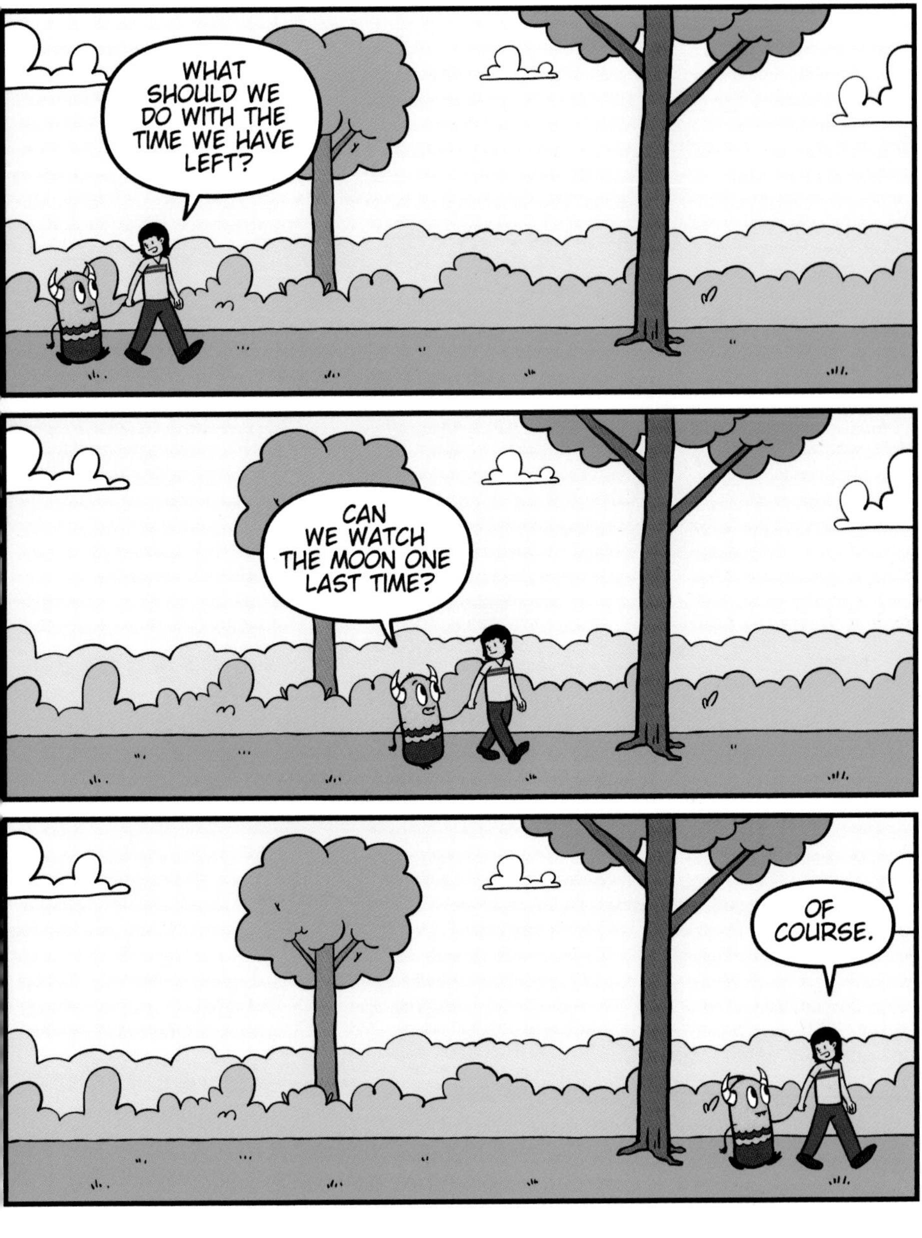
WHAT SHOULD WE DO WITH THE TIME WE HAVE LEFT?
CAN WE WATCH THE MOON ONE LAST TIME?
OF COURSE.

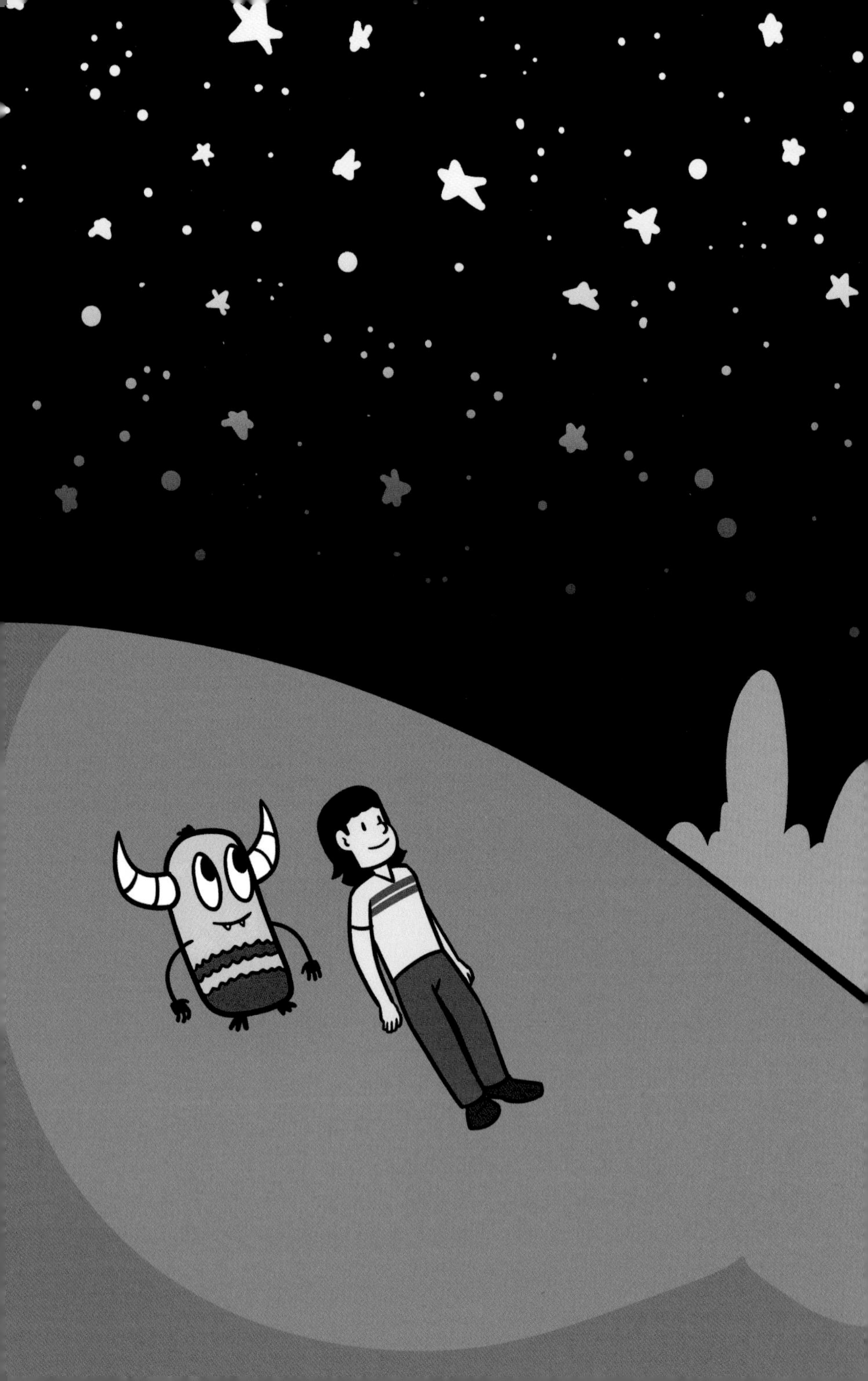

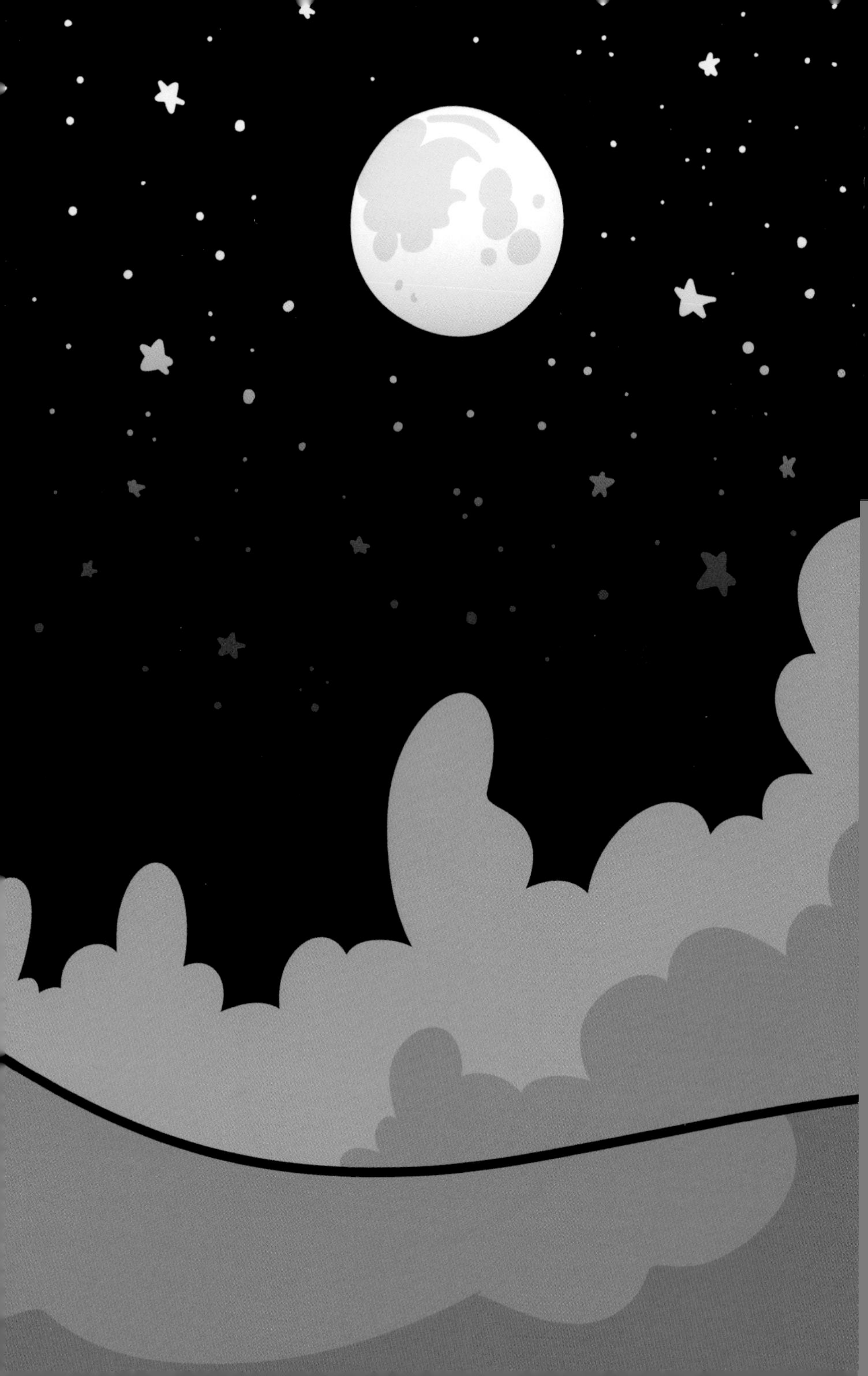

216

CHAPTER TWELVE

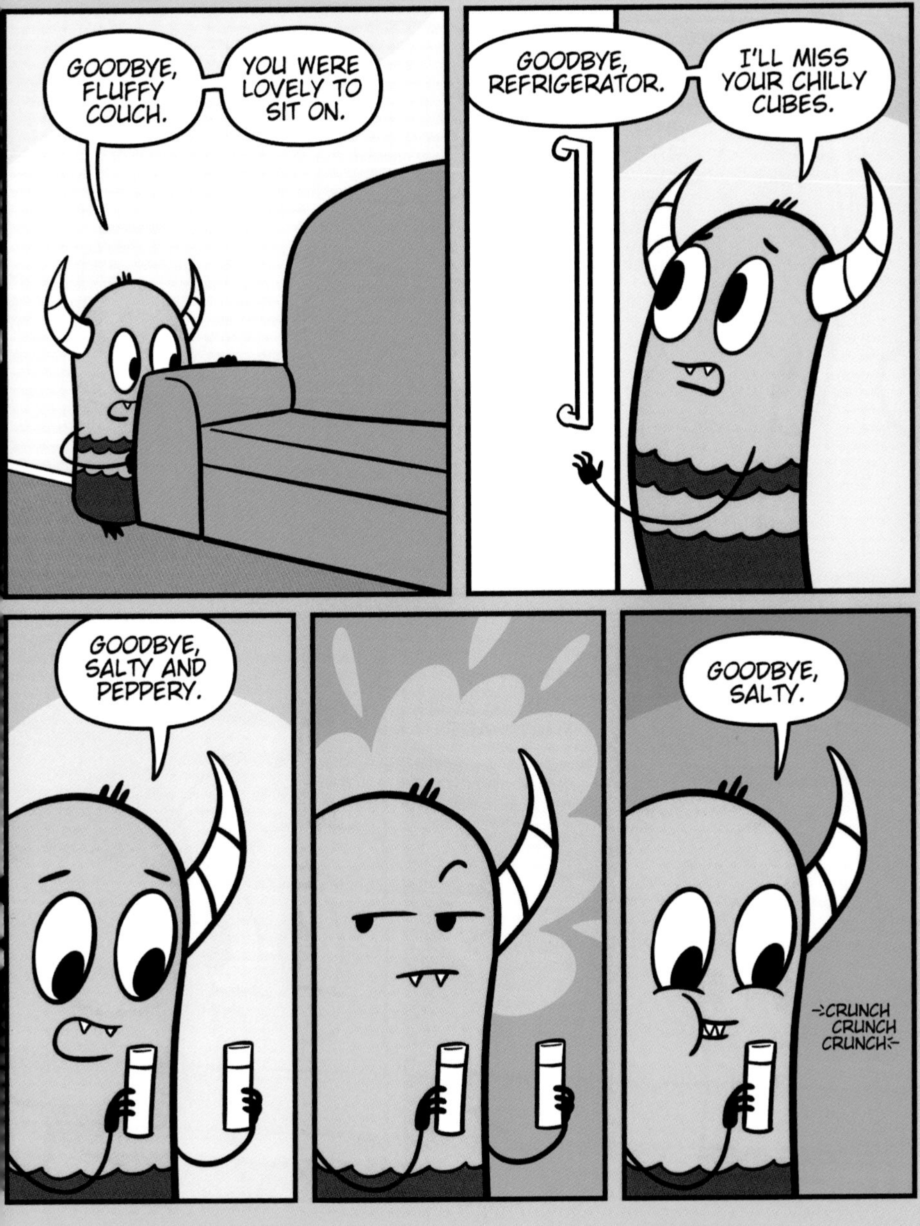
GOODBYE, FLUFFY COUCH.
YOU WERE LOVELY TO SIT ON.
GOODBYE, REFRIGERATOR.
I'LL MISS YOUR CHILLY CUBES.
GOODBYE, SALTY AND PEPPERY.
GOODBYE, SALTY.
CRUNCH CRUNCH CRUNCH

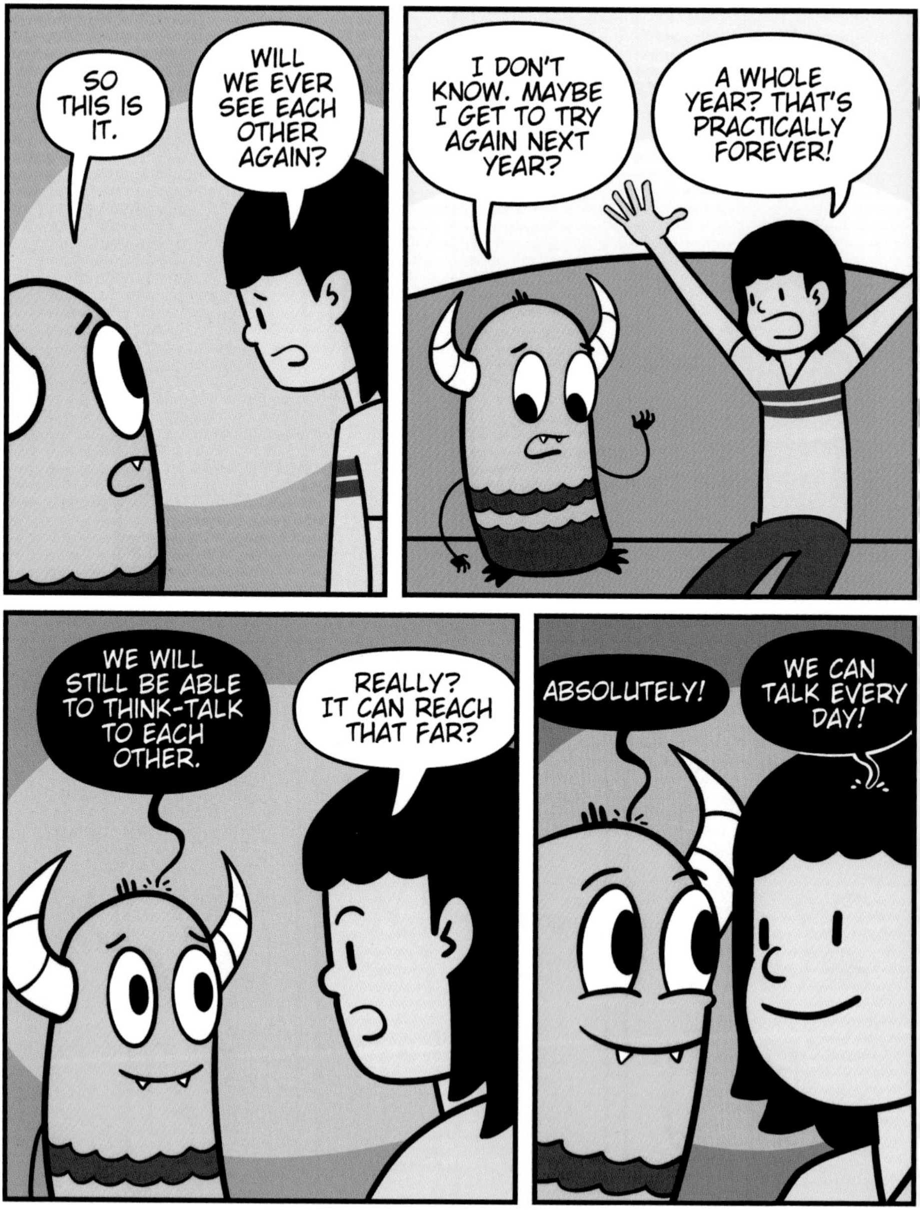
SO THIS IS IT.
WILL WE EVER SEE EACH OTHER AGAIN?
I DON'T KNOW. MAYBE I GET TO TRY AGAIN NEXT YEAR?
A WHOLE YEAR? THAT'S PRACTICALLY FOREVER!
WE WILL STILL BE ABLE TO THINK-TALK TO EACH OTHER.
REALLY? IT CAN REACH THAT FAR?
ABSOLUTELY!
WE CAN TALK EVERY DAY!

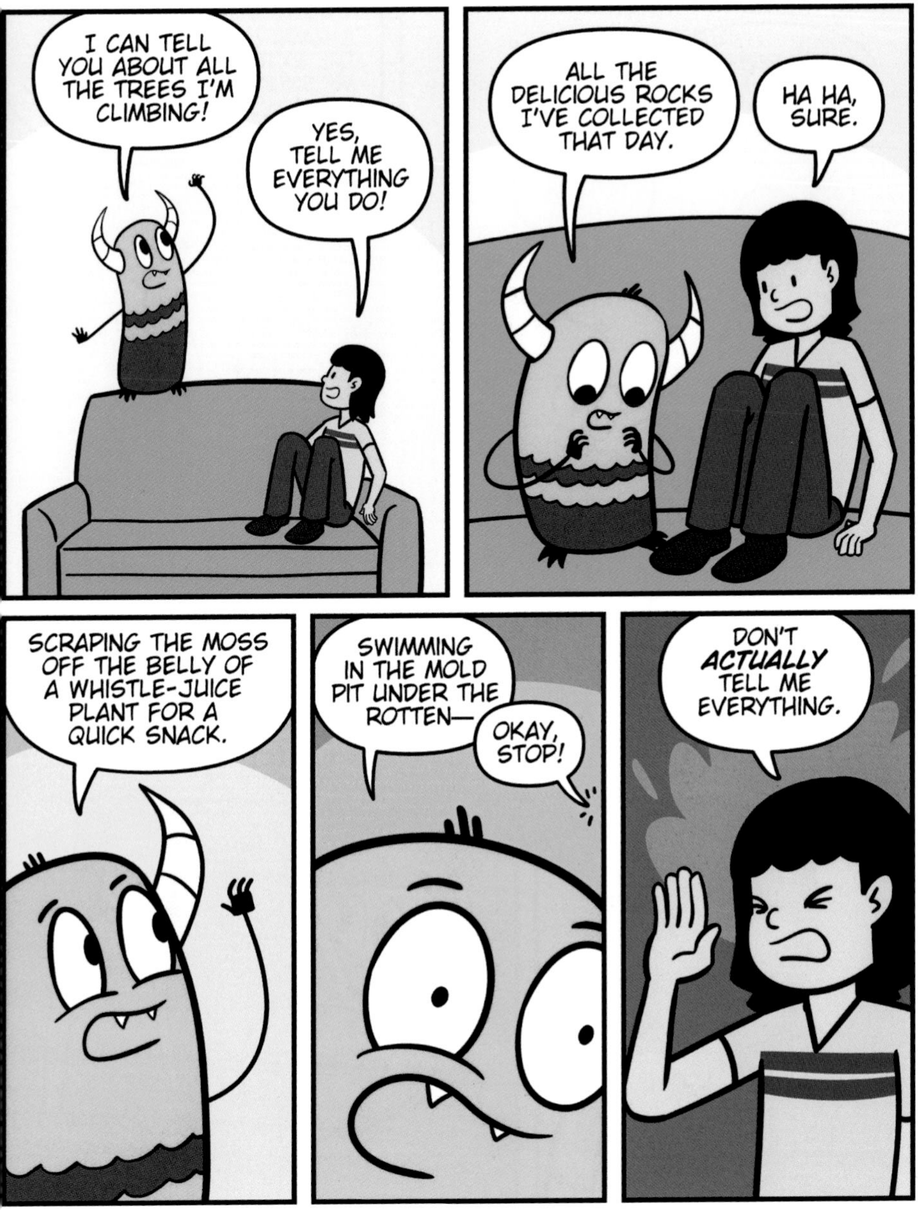
I CAN TELL YOU ABOUT ALL THE TREES I'M CLIMBING!
YES, TELL ME EVERYTHING YOU DO!
ALL THE DELICIOUS ROCKS I'VE COLLECTED THAT DAY.
HA HA, SURE.
SCRAPING THE MOSS OFF THE BELLY OF A WHISTLE-JUICE PLANT FOR A QUICK SNACK.
SWIMMING IN THE MOLD PIT UNDER THE ROTTEN—
OKAY, STOP!
DON'T ***ACTUALLY*** TELL ME EVERYTHING.

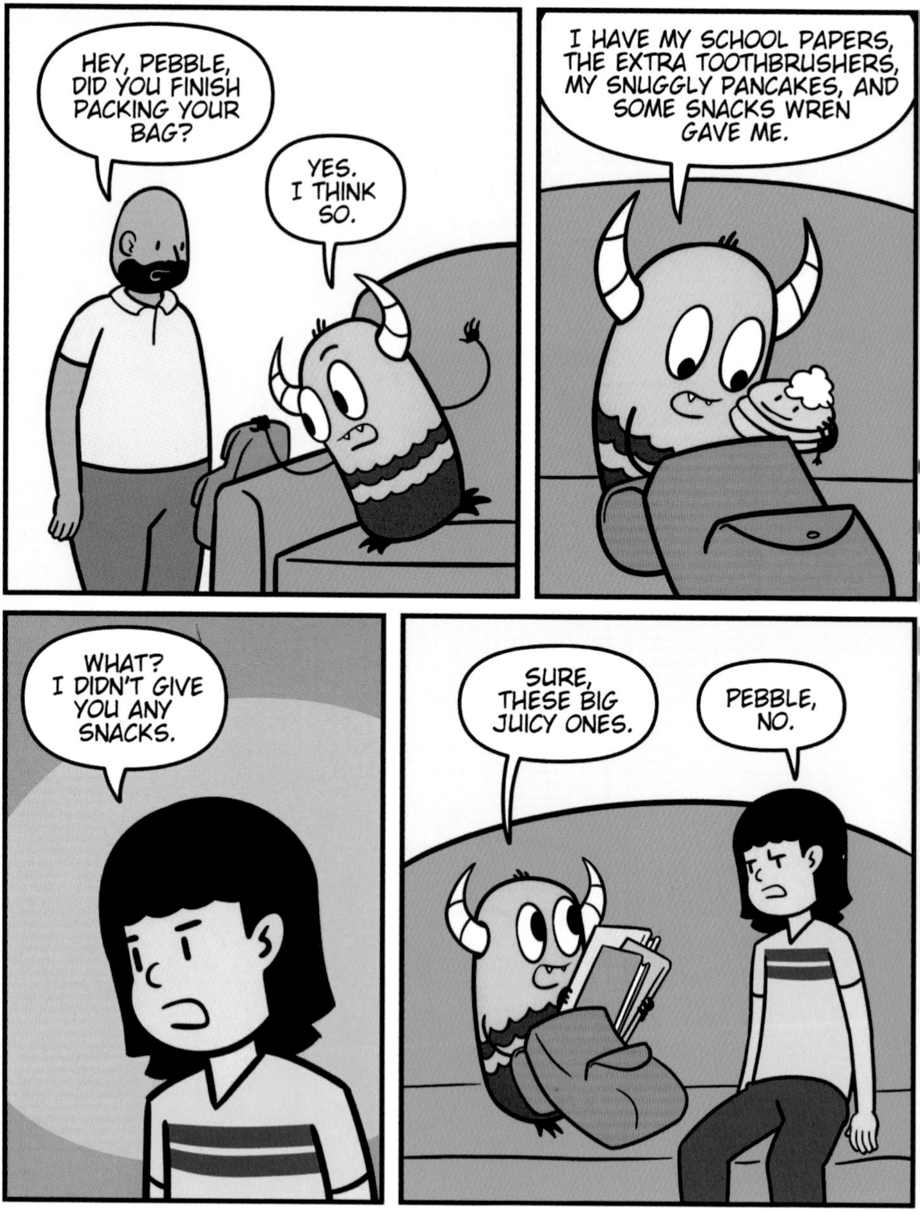
HEY, PEBBLE, DID YOU FINISH PACKING YOUR BAG?
YES. I THINK SO.
I HAVE MY SCHOOL PAPERS, THE EXTRA TOOTHBRUSHERS, MY SNUGGLY PANCAKES, AND SOME SNACKS WREN GAVE ME.
WHAT? I DIDN'T GIVE YOU ANY SNACKS.
SURE, THESE BIG JUICY ONES.
PEBBLE, NO.

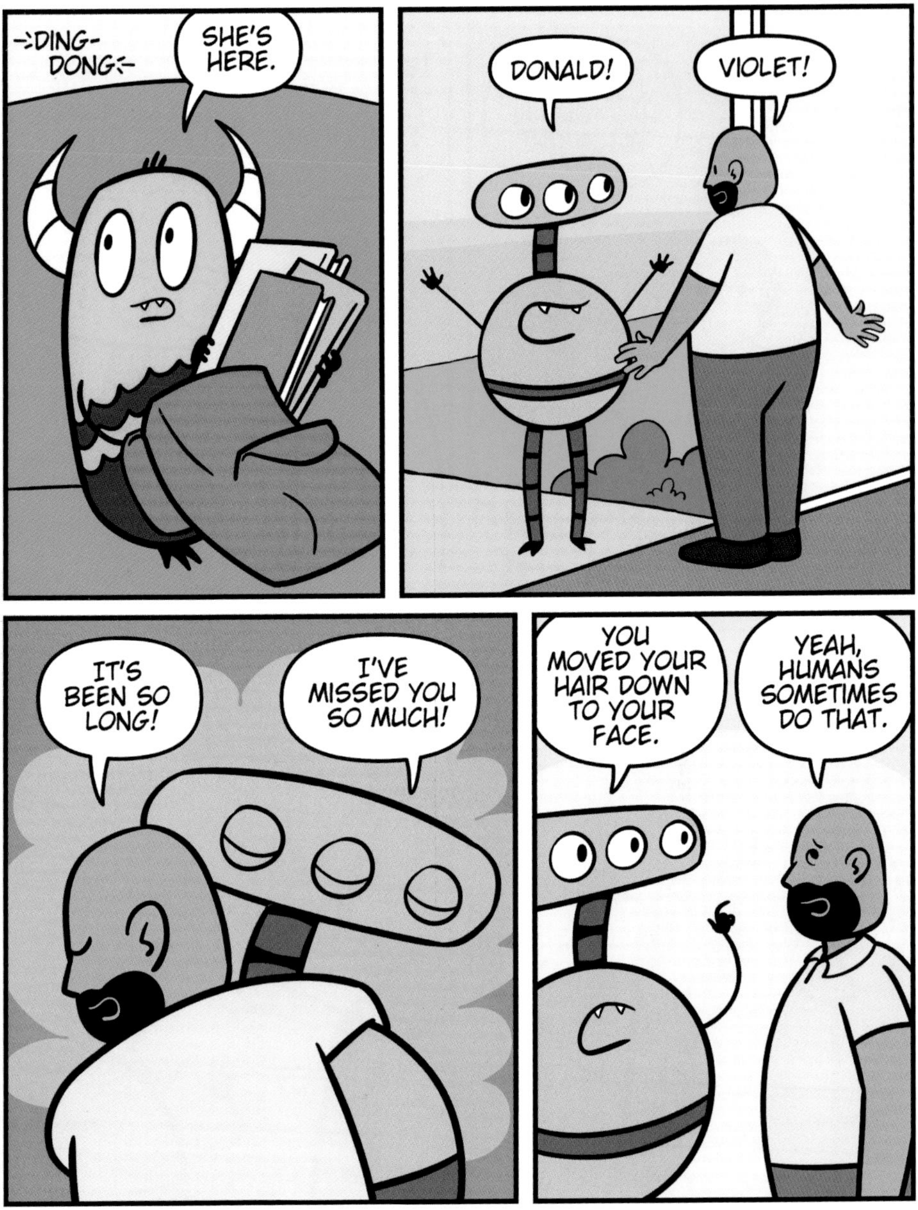
-DING-
DONG-
SHE'S HERE.
DONALD!
VIOLET!
IT'S BEEN SO LONG!
I'VE MISSED YOU SO MUCH!
YOU MOVED YOUR HAIR DOWN TO YOUR FACE.
YEAH, HUMANS SOMETIMES DO THAT.

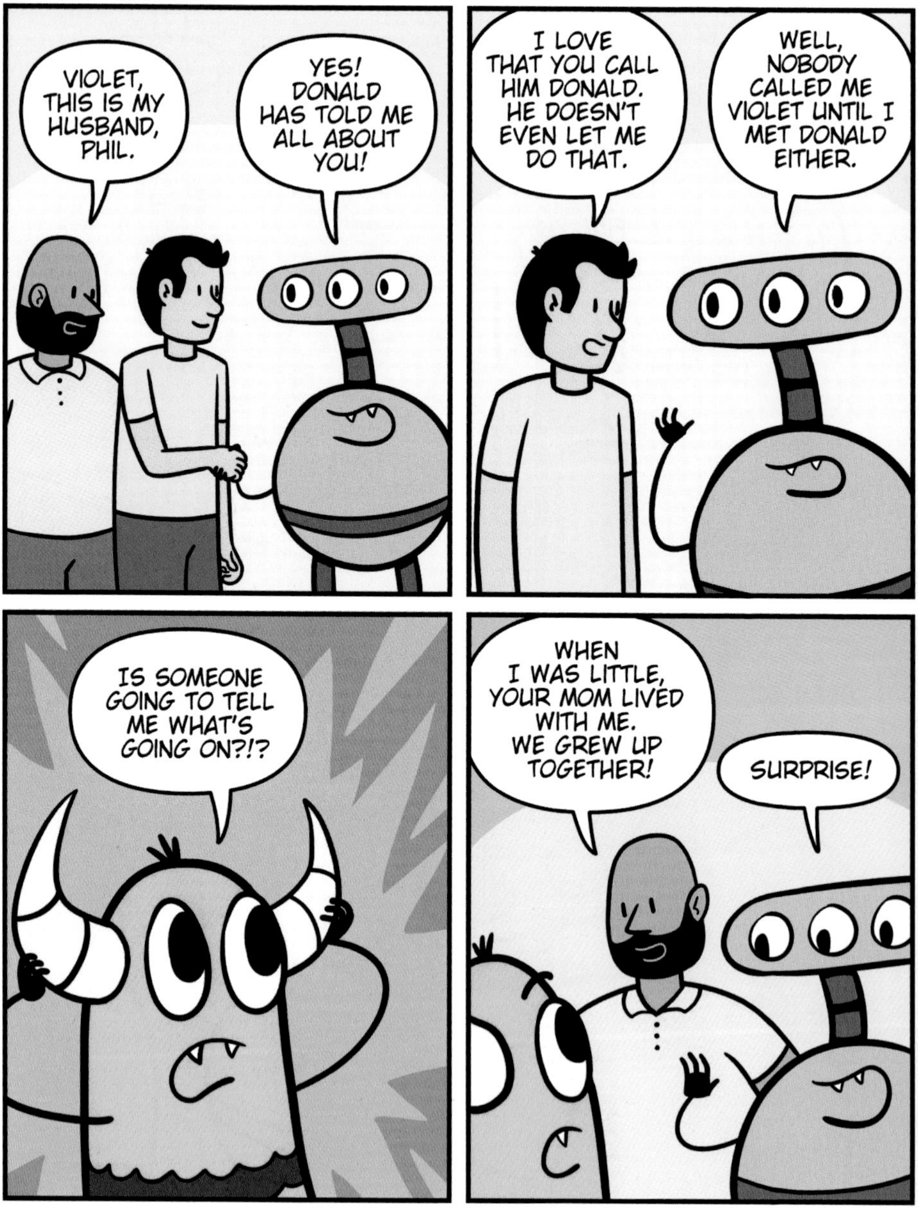
VIOLET, THIS IS MY HUSBAND, PHIL.
YES! DONALD HAS TOLD ME ALL ABOUT YOU!
I LOVE THAT YOU CALL HIM DONALD. HE DOESN'T EVEN LET ME DO THAT.
WELL, NOBODY CALLED ME VIOLET UNTIL I MET DONALD EITHER.
IS SOMEONE GOING TO TELL ME WHAT'S GOING ON?!?
WHEN I WAS LITTLE, YOUR MOM LIVED WITH ME. WE GREW UP TOGETHER!
SURPRISE!

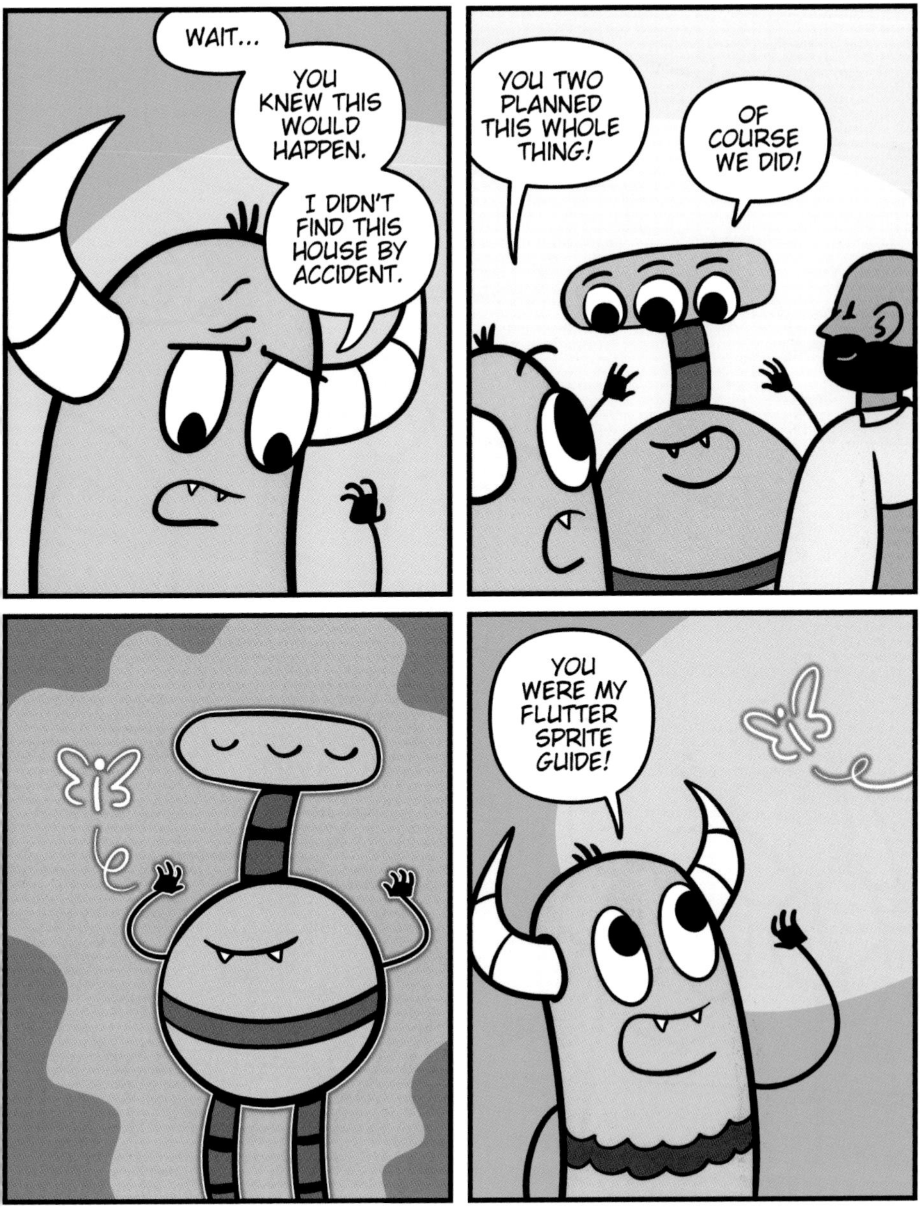
WAIT...
YOU KNEW THIS WOULD HAPPEN.
I DIDN'T FIND THIS HOUSE BY ACCIDENT.
YOU TWO PLANNED THIS WHOLE THING!
OF COURSE WE DID!
YOU WERE MY FLUTTER SPRITE GUIDE!

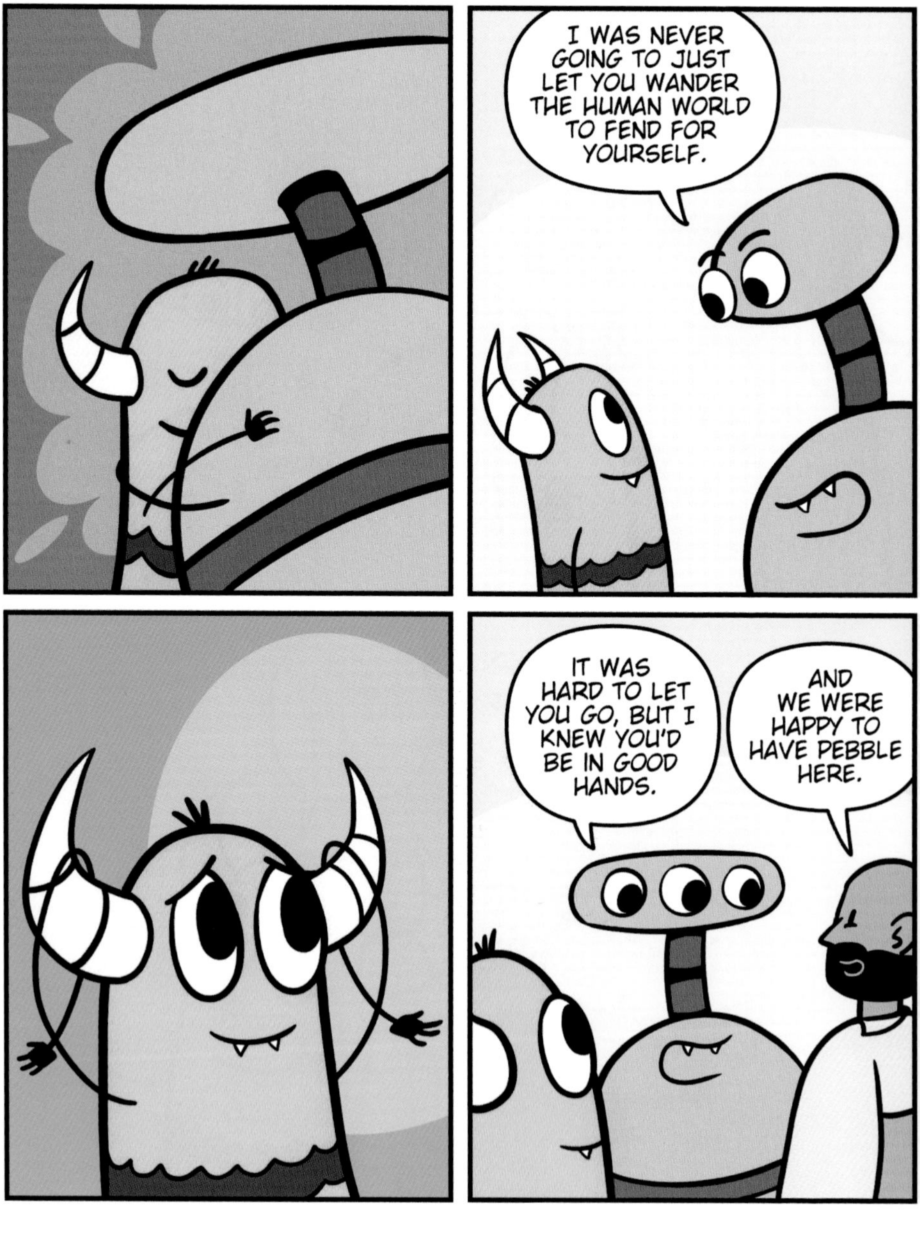
I WAS NEVER GOING TO JUST LET YOU WANDER THE HUMAN WORLD TO FEND FOR YOURSELF.
IT WAS HARD TO LET YOU GO, BUT I KNEW YOU'D BE IN GOOD HANDS.
AND WE WERE HAPPY TO HAVE PEBBLE HERE.

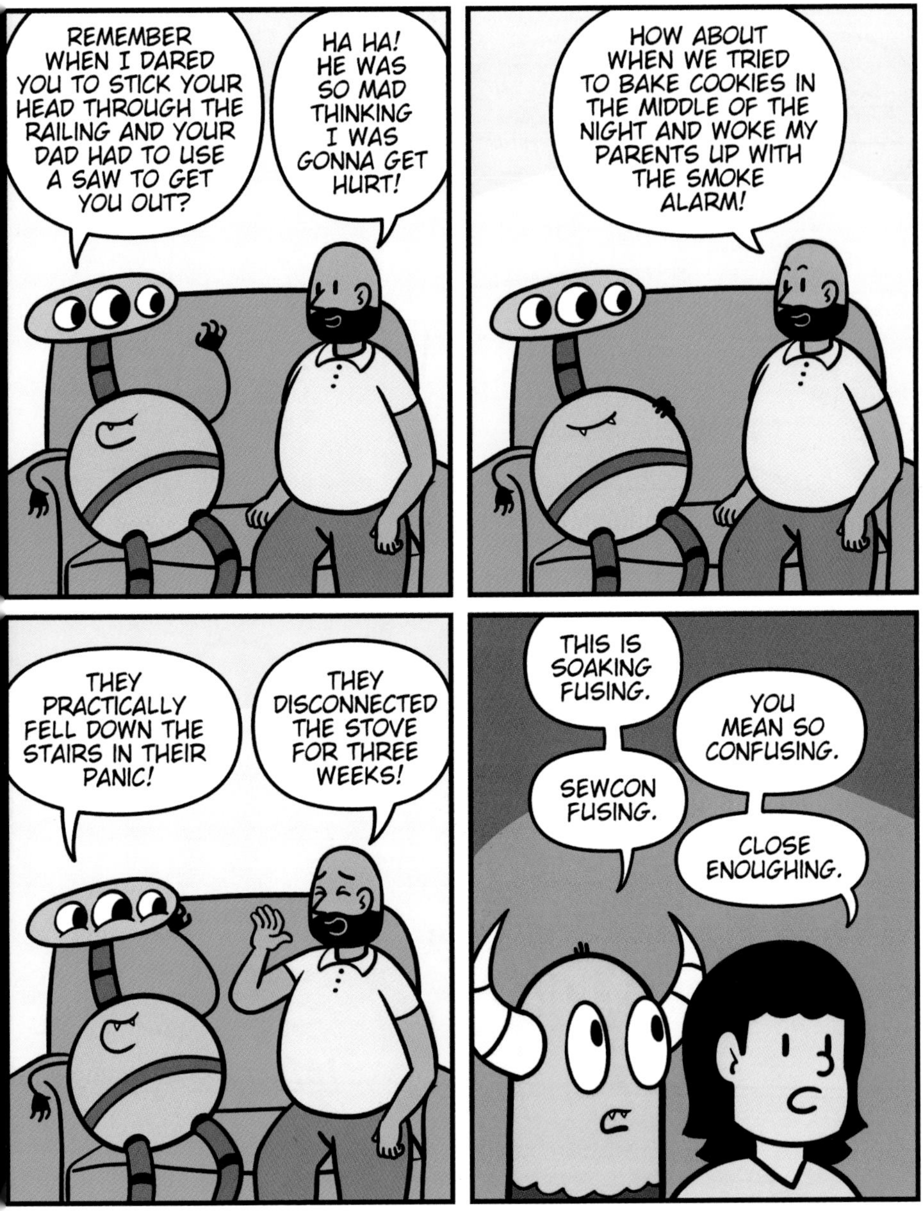
REMEMBER WHEN I DARED YOU TO STICK YOUR HEAD THROUGH THE RAILING AND YOUR DAD HAD TO USE A SAW TO GET YOU OUT?
HA HA! HE WAS SO MAD THINKING I WAS GONNA GET HURT!
HOW ABOUT WHEN WE TRIED TO BAKE COOKIES IN THE MIDDLE OF THE NIGHT AND WOKE MY PARENTS UP WITH THE SMOKE ALARM!
THEY PRACTICALLY FELL DOWN THE STAIRS IN THEIR PANIC!
THEY DISCONNECTED THE STOVE FOR THREE WEEKS!
THIS IS SOAKING FUSING.
SEWCON FUSING.
YOU MEAN SO CONFUSING.
CLOSE ENOUGHING.

WHAT ARE SOME OF YOUR FAVORITE THINGS ABOUT THE HUMAN WORLD?

I LOVE HOW DELICIOUS EVERYTHING IS!

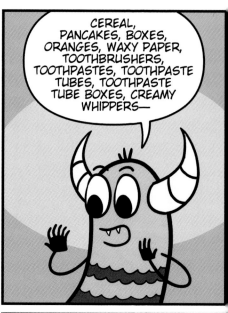

CEREAL, PANCAKES, BOXES, ORANGES, WAXY PAPER, TOOTHBRUSHERS, TOOTHPASTES, TOOTHPASTE TUBES, TOOTHPASTE TUBE BOXES, CREAMY WHIPPERS—

OH, I REMEMBER YOU THINKING ABOUT CREAMY WHIPPERS TO ME A FEW WEEKS AGO. I NEVER CAME ACROSS THAT ONE BEFORE.

DO YOU WANT TO TRY IT?

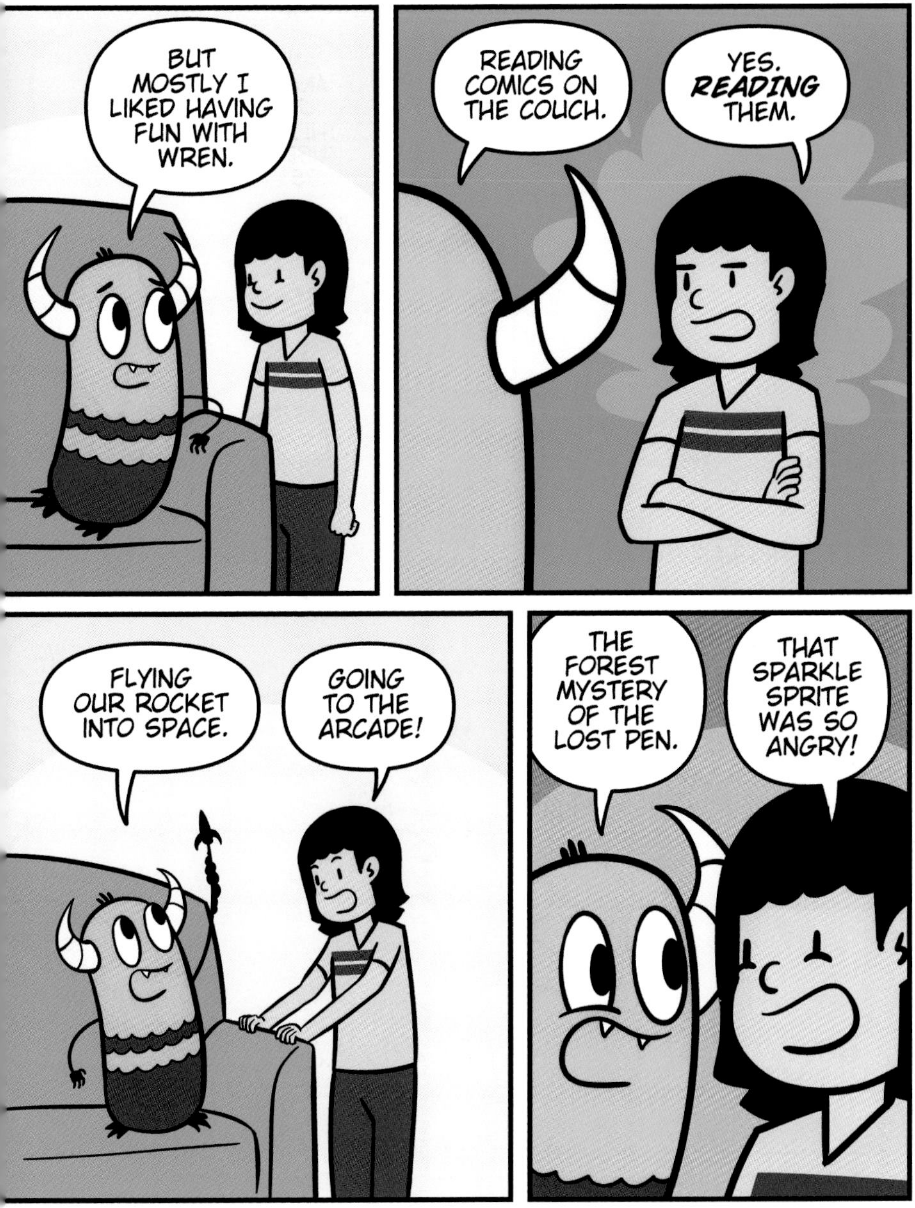
BUT MOSTLY I LIKED HAVING FUN WITH WREN.
READING COMICS ON THE COUCH.
YES. ***READING*** THEM.
FLYING OUR ROCKET INTO SPACE.
GOING TO THE ARCADE!
THE FOREST MYSTERY OF THE LOST PEN.
THAT SPARKLE SPRITE WAS SO ANGRY!

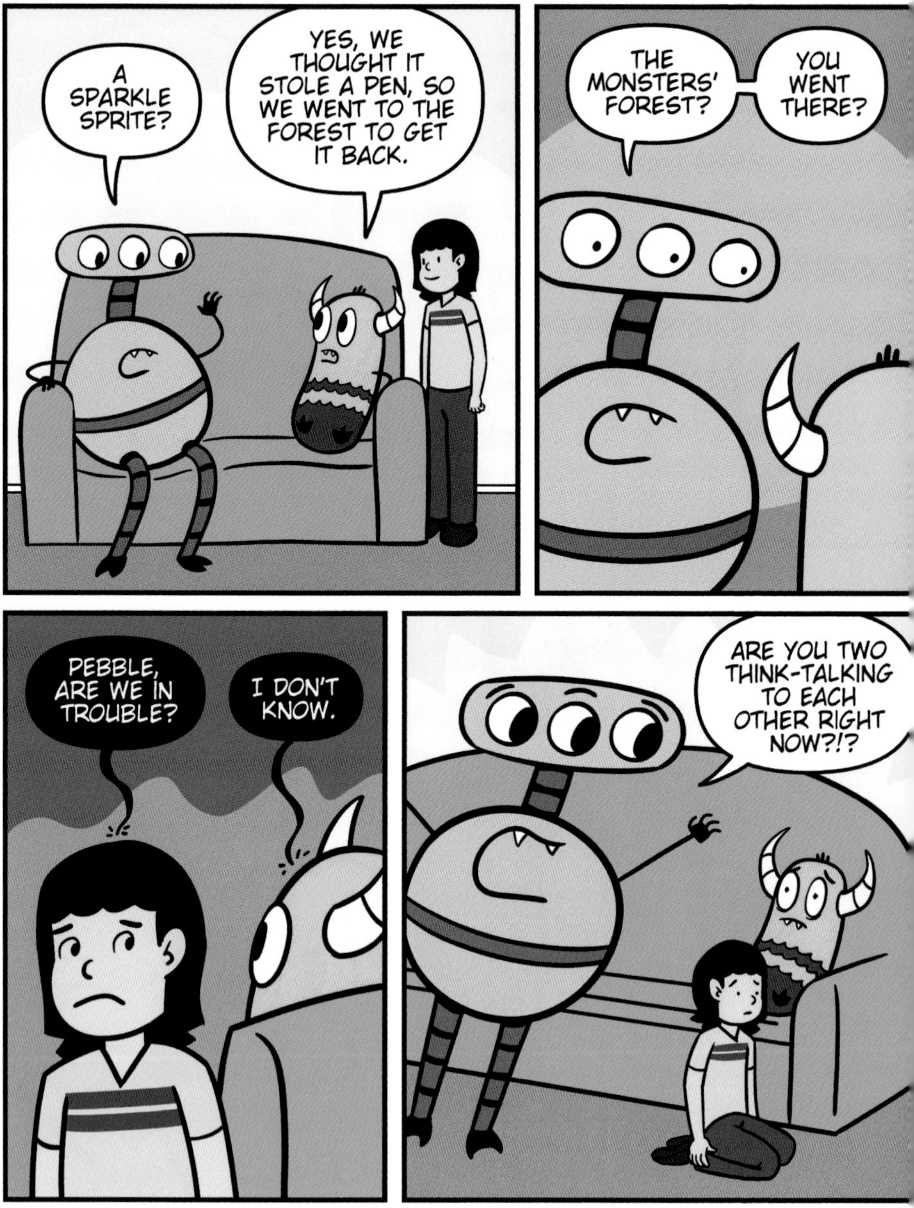
A SPARKLE SPRITE?
YES, WE THOUGHT IT STOLE A PEN, SO WE WENT TO THE FOREST TO GET IT BACK.
THE MONSTERS' FOREST?
YOU WENT THERE?
PEBBLE, ARE WE IN TROUBLE?
I DON'T KNOW.
ARE YOU TWO THINK-TALKING TO EACH OTHER RIGHT NOW?!?

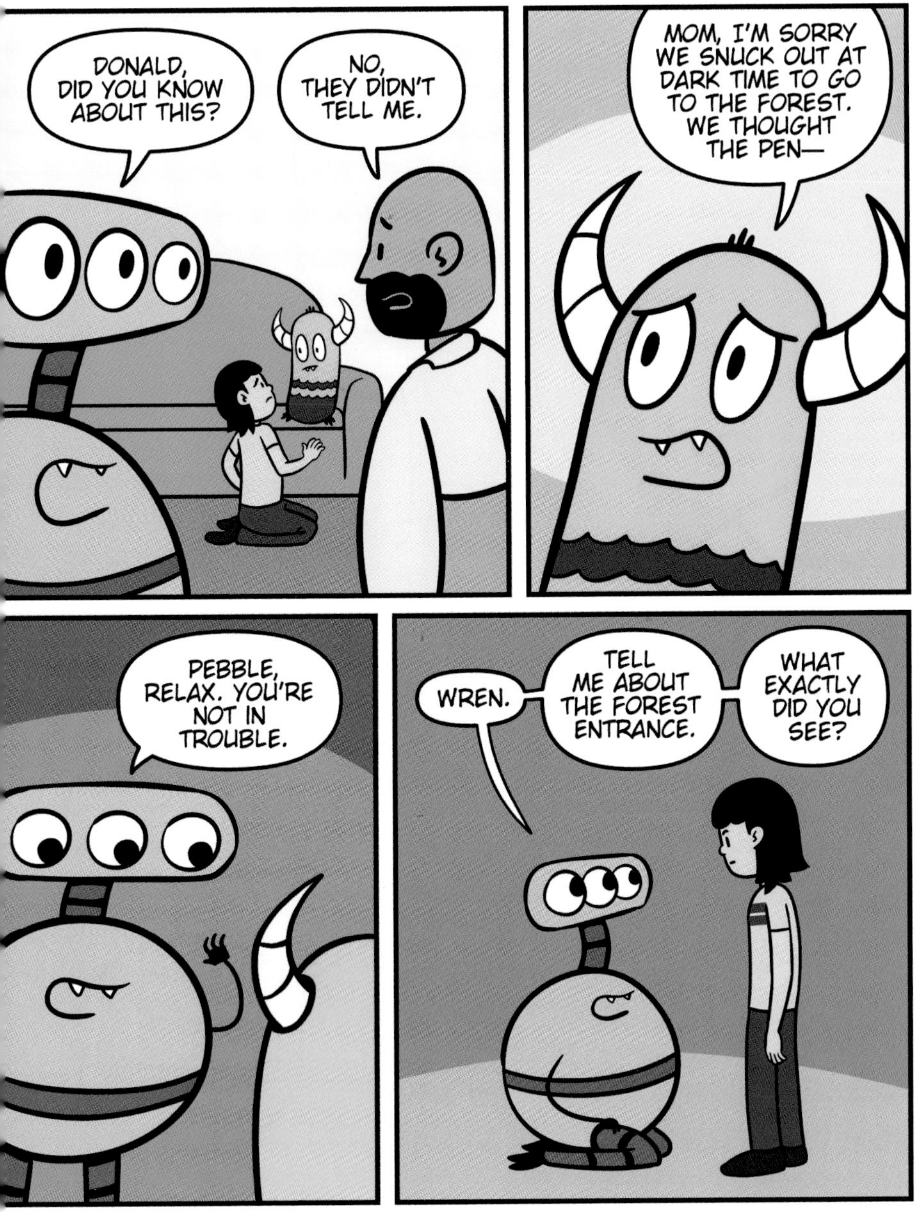
DONALD, DID YOU KNOW ABOUT THIS?
NO, THEY DIDN'T TELL ME.
MOM, I'M SORRY WE SNUCK OUT AT DARK TIME TO GO TO THE FOREST. WE THOUGHT THE PEN—
PEBBLE, RELAX. YOU'RE NOT IN TROUBLE.
WREN.
TELL ME ABOUT THE FOREST ENTRANCE.
WHAT EXACTLY DID YOU SEE?

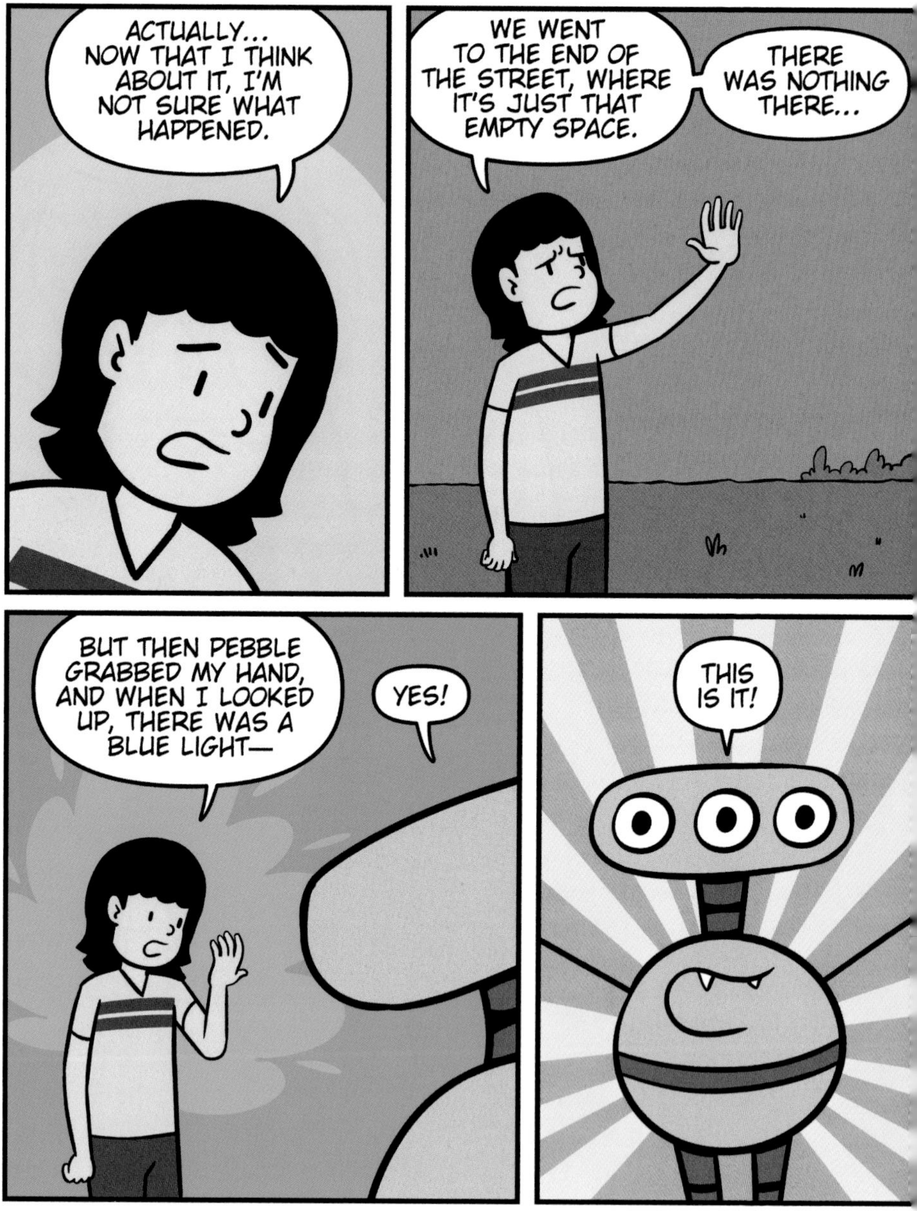
ACTUALLY... NOW THAT I THINK ABOUT IT, I'M NOT SURE WHAT HAPPENED.
WE WENT TO THE END OF THE STREET, WHERE IT'S JUST THAT EMPTY SPACE.
THERE WAS NOTHING THERE...
BUT THEN PEBBLE GRABBED MY HAND, AND WHEN I LOOKED UP, THERE WAS A BLUE LIGHT—
YES!
THIS IS IT!

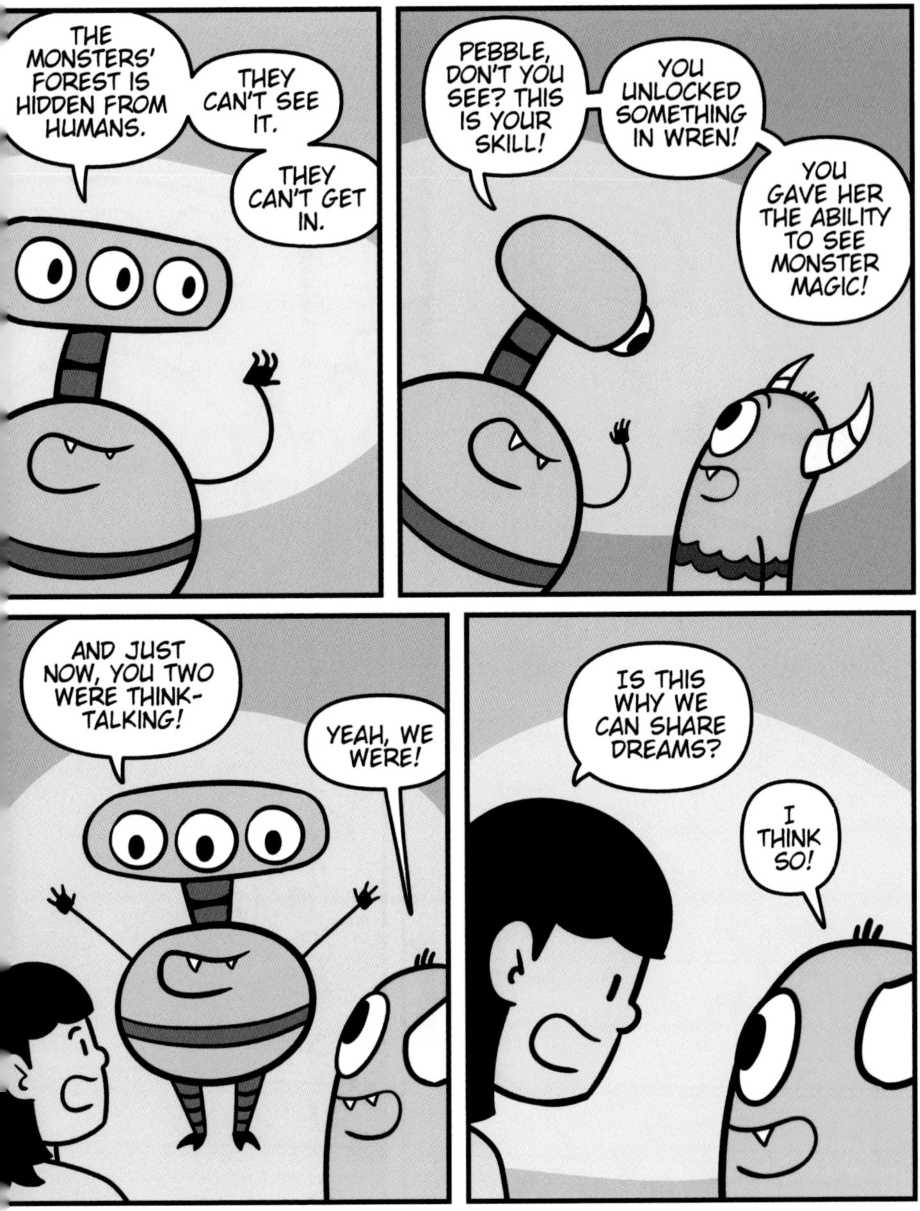
THE MONSTERS' FOREST IS HIDDEN FROM HUMANS.
THEY CAN'T SEE IT.
THEY CAN'T GET IN.
PEBBLE, DON'T YOU SEE? THIS IS YOUR SKILL!
YOU UNLOCKED SOMETHING IN WREN!
YOU GAVE HER THE ABILITY TO SEE MONSTER MAGIC!
AND JUST NOW, YOU TWO WERE THINK-TALKING!
YEAH, WE WERE!
IS THIS WHY WE CAN SHARE DREAMS?
I THINK SO!

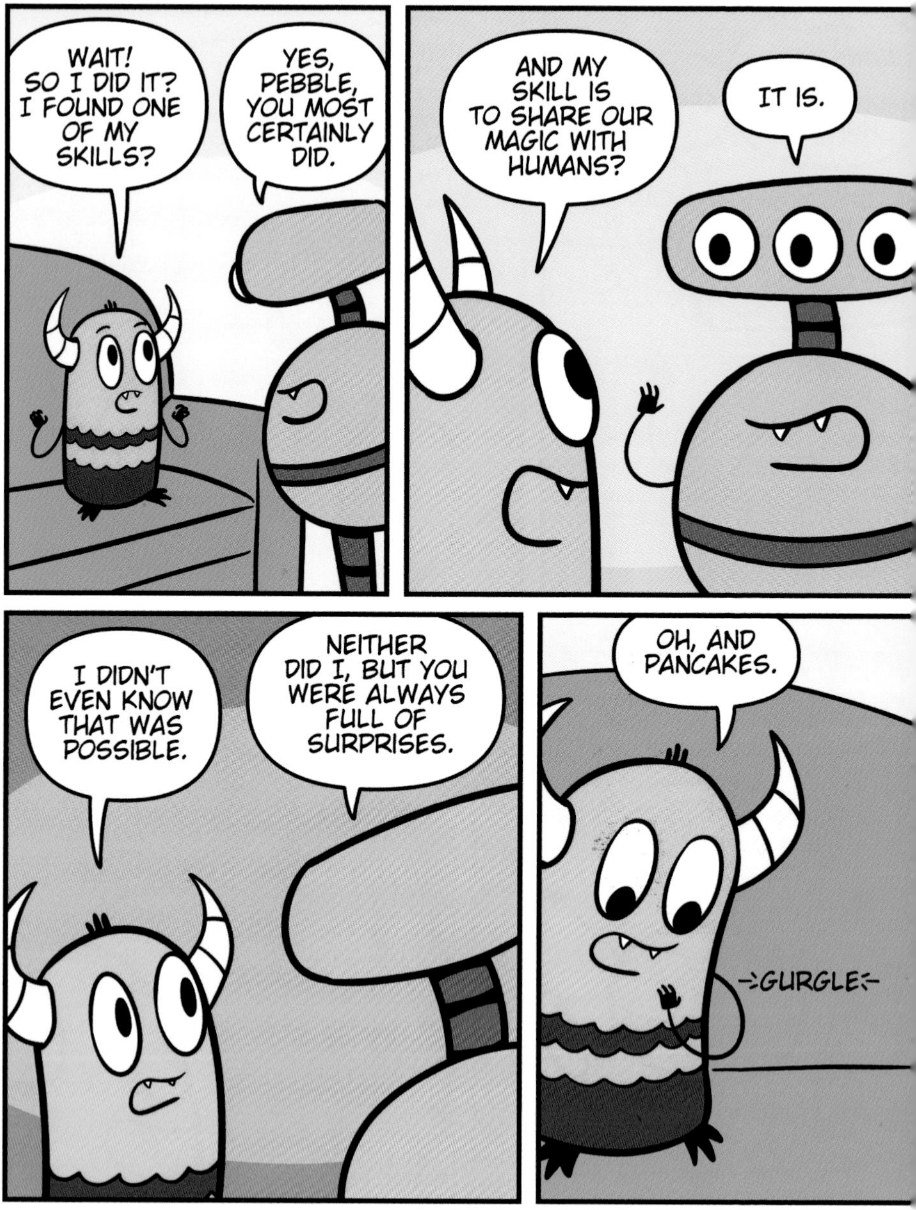
WAIT! SO I DID IT? I FOUND ONE OF MY SKILLS?
YES, PEBBLE, YOU MOST CERTAINLY DID.
AND MY SKILL IS TO SHARE OUR MAGIC WITH HUMANS?
IT IS.
I DIDN'T EVEN KNOW THAT WAS POSSIBLE.
NEITHER DID I, BUT YOU WERE ALWAYS FULL OF SURPRISES.
OH, AND PANCAKES.
GURGLE

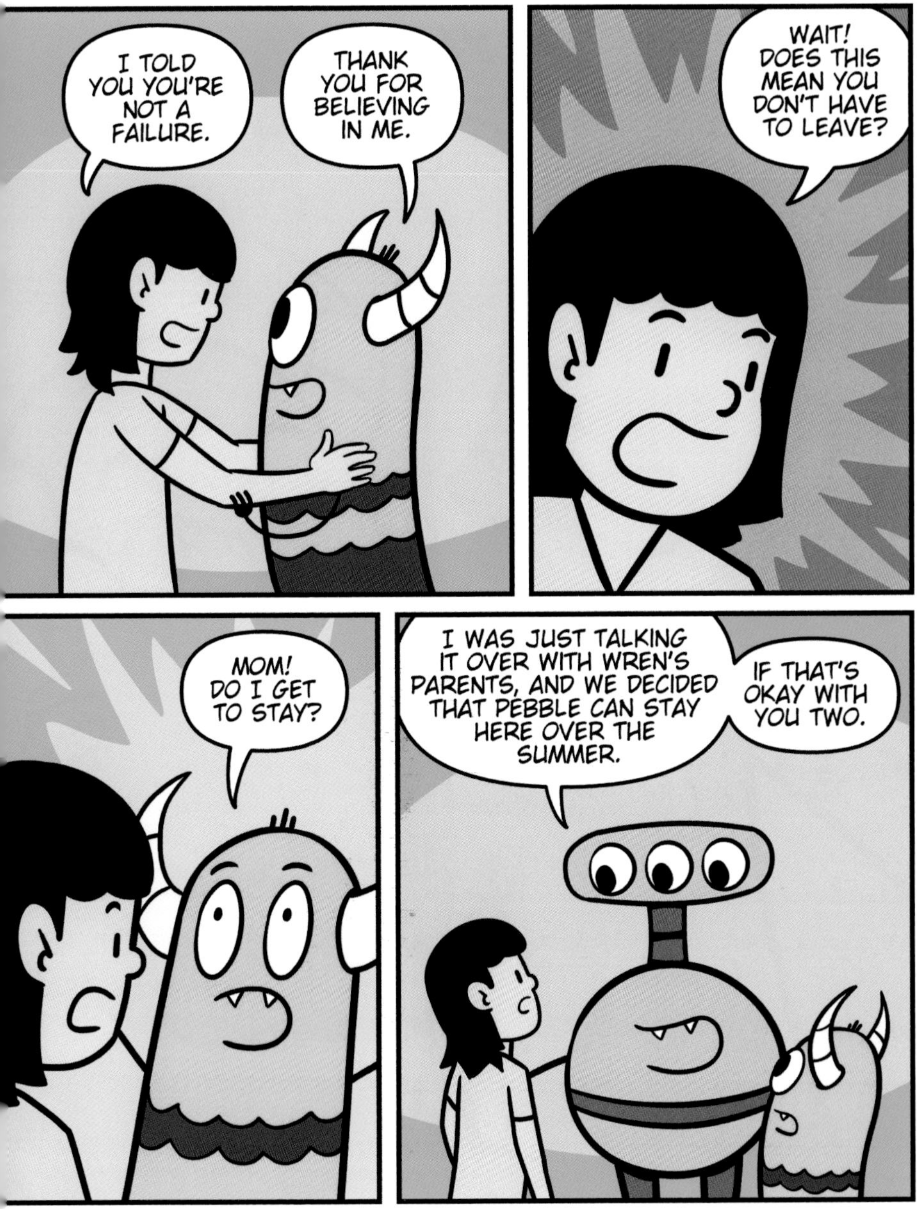
I TOLD YOU YOU'RE NOT A FAILURE.
THANK YOU FOR BELIEVING IN ME.
WAIT! DOES THIS MEAN YOU DON'T HAVE TO LEAVE?
MOM! DO I GET TO STAY?
I WAS JUST TALKING IT OVER WITH WREN'S PARENTS, AND WE DECIDED THAT PEBBLE CAN STAY HERE OVER THE SUMMER.
IF THAT'S OKAY WITH YOU TWO.

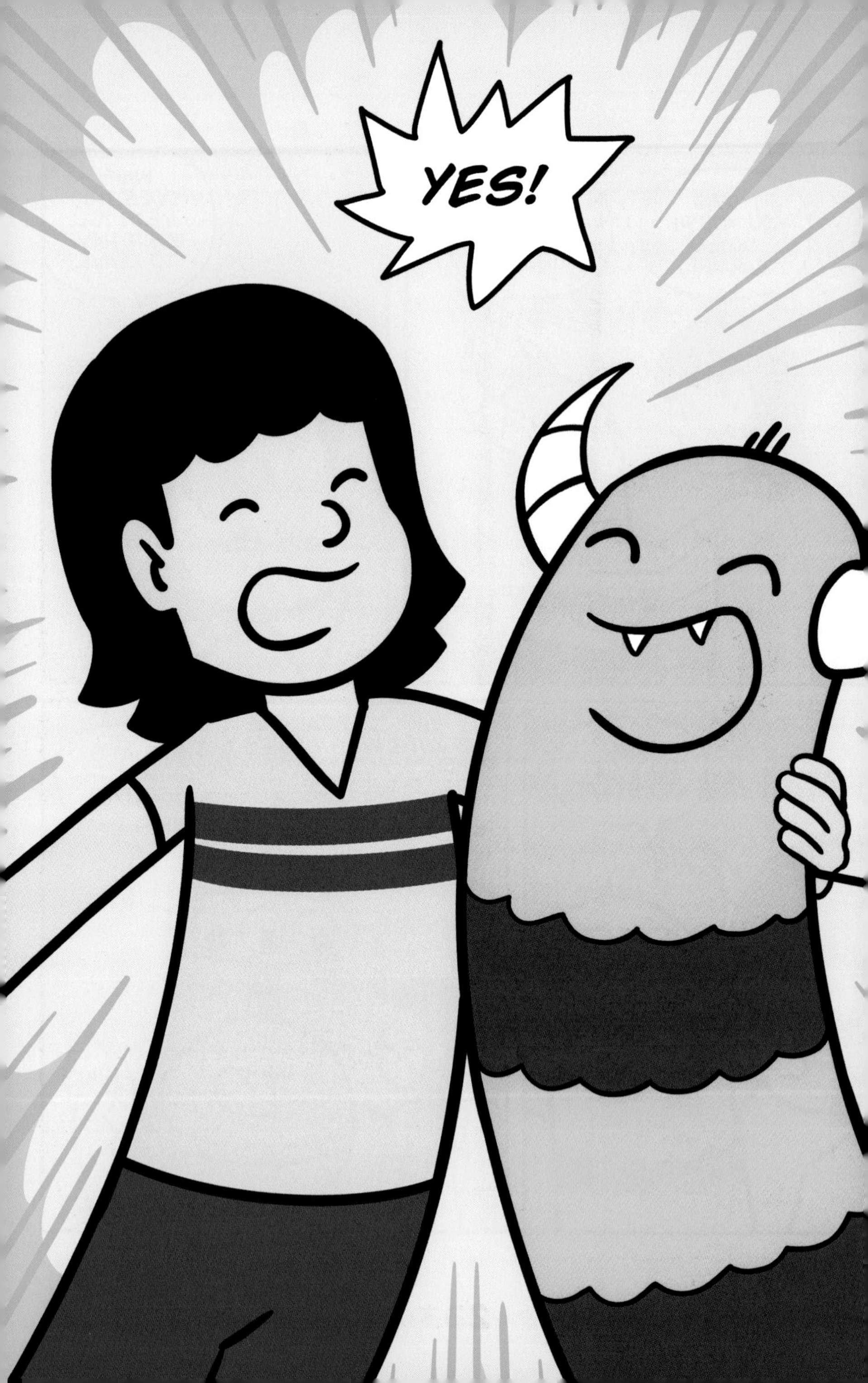
YES!

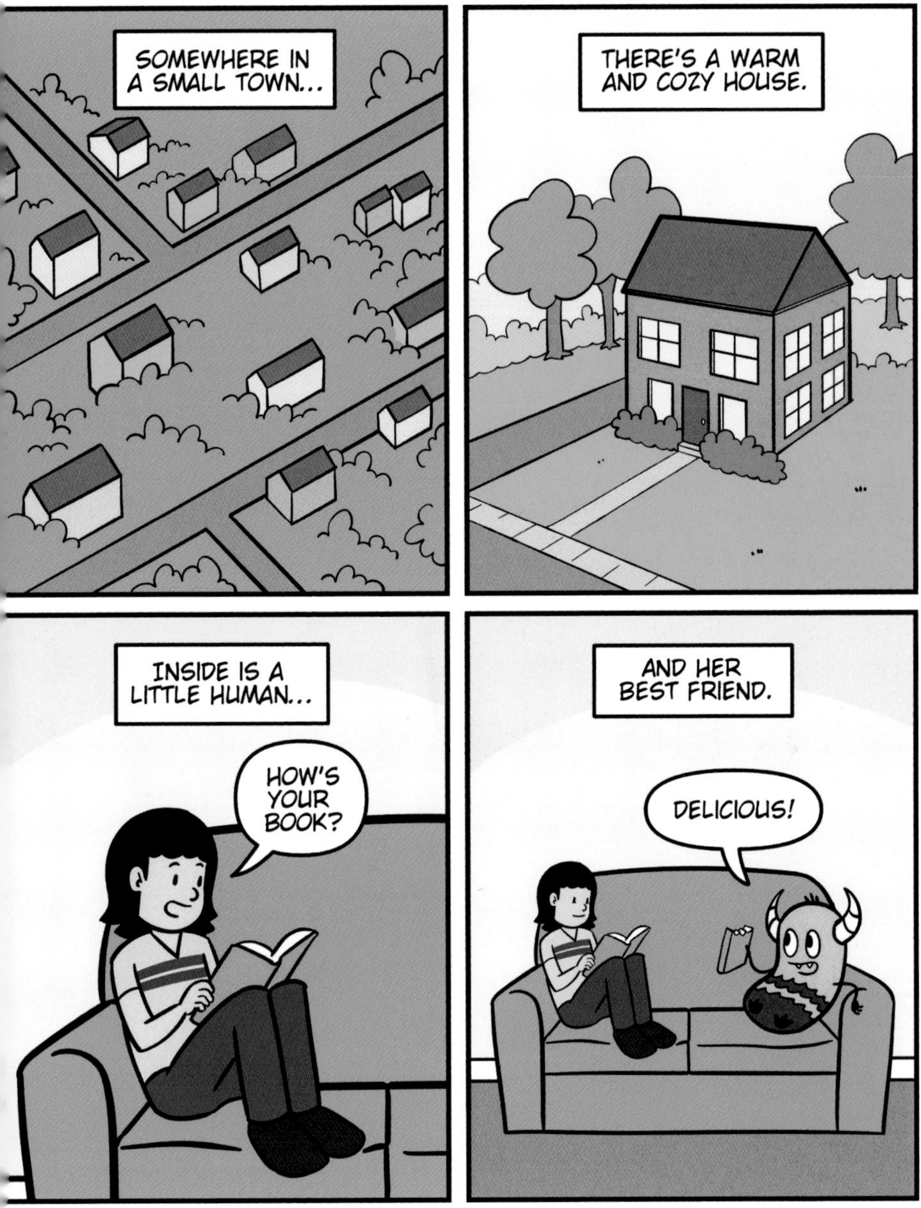
SOMEWHERE IN A SMALL TOWN...
THERE'S A WARM AND COZY HOUSE.
INSIDE IS A LITTLE HUMAN...
HOW'S YOUR BOOK?
AND HER BEST FRIEND.
DELICIOUS!

Clarion Books is an imprint of HarperCollins Publishers.
HarperAlley is an imprint of HarperCollins Publishers.

Pebble and Wren
Copyright © 2023 by Chris Hallbeck
All rights reserved. Manufactured in Bosnia and Herzegovina. No part of this
book may be used or reproduced in any manner whatsoever without written
permission except in the case of brief quotations embodied in critical articles
and reviews. For information address HarperCollins Children's Books, a
division of HarperCollins Publishers, 195 Broadway, New York, NY 10007.
www.harperalley.com

ISBN 978-0-35-854129-5 — ISBN 978-0-35-854128-8 (pbk.)

The artist used Clip Studio Paint on an iPad Pro with an Apple
Pencil to create the digital illustrations for this book.
Typography by Chris Hallbeck

23 24 25 26 27   GPS   10 9 8 7 6 5 4 3 2 1

First Edition

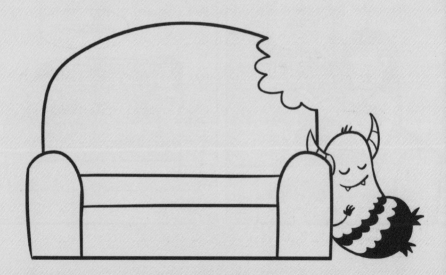